LUKE DELMEGE

BOOKS *by* CANON SHEEHAN

Glenanaar
Blindness of Dr. Gray
My New Curate
Geoffrey Austin: Student
The Graves at Kilmorna
The Triumph of Failure
The Queen's Fillet
Tristram Lloyd
Under the Cedars and the Stars
Lisheen
and others

LUKE DELMEGE

by

Canon P. A. Sheehan

Chicago · HENRY REGNERY COMPANY · *1955*

FOREWORD

IN THE present century, the priest and the priestly life have held a considerable fascination for novelists and playwrights. The significance of *Luke Delmege* is that this novel is *by* a priest about a priest, and is therefore filled with that inner light, that living grasp of the problem it presents, which only such a circumstance could guarantee. It is the second of a trilogy on the priestly life, its companions being *My New Curate* —the most popular of Canon Sheehan's works—and the *Blindness of Doctor Gray.*

Patrick Sheehan was born in Mallow (Diocese of Cloyne, Ireland) in 1852 and died as parish priest of Doneraile in the same diocese in 1913. He was born, therefore, into the weary years of post-Famine Ireland, and the greater part of his life was to be spent in the atmosphere of resurgence created by such great men as Michael Davitt and Parnell. All his work is instinct with a spirit of elevating patriotism and love of his people. Among the literati, he is remembered as the finest Catholic novelist Ireland has produced; but in his parish of Doneraile, where the prototypes of his novels still walk the picturesque streets, his memory lives on as that of a great priest.

Maynooth—the world's biggest seminary—figures largely in *Luke Delmege*. It was there that Patrick Sheehan studied for the priesthood, at a time when the revival of Scholasticism was having its impact and when the ideal of braininess—the mark of the "gun," to use the term of Maynooth slang—was dexterity in handling the rapier of syllogism. Yeats has distinguished two types of mentality: the *diagrammatic* and the *rhythmical,* and the second is that of the poet who finds the edge of the syllogism too keen and dry, and who thirsts for the sweep of humanity and the crisp crackle of the fine phrase swept to the rubbish-heap with three dry words: *Sic argumentaris, Domine.* Luke Delmege loved those words and became a "first of first" haloed with intellectual light: his creator,

v

Patrick Sheehan, distinguished him creditably, but had that spark of literary fire in him that tends to play havoc with dry syllogistic wisdom. Maynooth has always been suspicious of literary talent—a fact which may well explain why there is no other clerical name to put beside that of Canon Sheehan. "Far back in the 'sixties'," wrote Canon Sheehan, "literature had to be studied surreptitiously, and under the uncongenial but very effective shadow of Perrone or Receveur. It was a serious thing to be detected in such clandestine studies." Maynooth gave its blessing to what Sheehan called "the sawpits of logic" and frowned on "the moonlight and melody of Tennyson." There has been little change since then. It is not many years since an eminent member of that august College described literature as "sensuality," and since it was fashionable to feel superior to the only modern priest-writer that Maynooth has produced.

Canon Sheehan's first novel—*Geoffrey Austin*—was published anonymously in Dublin late in 1895, the year of his appointment to Doneraile. Two years later, the Rev. Dr. Herman J. Heuser, then editor of the *American Ecclesiastical Review,* read the novel, got in touch with the anonymous author, and commissioned a book from him. Canon Sheehan then wrote *My New Curate* and thus began an enormously successful literary career, the fruits of which were eleven novels, three volumes of essays, one book of poems and one volume of sermons. It is a magnificent achievement in some seventeen years, especially when it is remembered that he wrote in what hours of leisure he could allow himself from a busy task of pastoral care.

When *Luke Delmege* was first published in book form (1901), after having appeared as a serial in the *American Ecclesiastical Review,* there was a bitter and violent outcry against it, the tone being given by Monsignor Hogan of Maynooth who damned it outright as "stilted nonsense." There had been mutterings and mumblings previously, for the symbol of wisdom in Ireland is surely that pair of Sphinxes which incongruously adorn the entry to Maynooth College: there is virtue and wisdom in sitting like your grandsire cut in alabaster. Canon Sheehan made no answer to his critics; but perhaps we may catch something of his feelings through the words he wrote in *Luke Delmege* about Father Martin, that shy literary genius choked by the reaction to his first article: "But he was hooted from the literary stage . . . and he went back to his books and his dreams. He was, therefore, a cipher, a nonentity . . . in a loud-tongued, blatant land." The probability of a personal overtone in these words is strengthened by the fact that one of his own early articles—*The German and Gallic Muse*—is suggestively parallel to the subject he imagines as treated by the Father Martin of his own creation. There is a tradition of considerable authority that Canon Sheehan wrote an autobiography in which he dealt with all the pettiness that plagued his career as a writer, but that he burned it *propter caritatem* and on the advice of a priest whose sublime character is carried alive into *Luke Delmege* in the sweetness and grace of Father Tracey, the man through whom, above all others, Father Luke Delmege found the answer to those enigmas that were the very texture of his years. Canon Sheehan may indeed have performed an act of heroic charity in destroying this manuscript and leaving us only the picturesque but essentially unrevealing essay: *The Moonlight of Memory*. One cannot help a regret, however, that we are left with unsatisfying half-glimpses at second hand of the shadows that often peopled that moonlight.

The man who dismissed Luke Delmege as "stilted nonsense" had his soul smothered with what Sheehan himself called "the dust of the desks," and was pathetically blind to the fine poetry of its subject and its style, the richness of its vision, its humanity, its humor. There is the dominating figure of Luke himself, drawn with lines that quiver with sensitivity, an intellectual St. Sebastian pierced with the arrows of his own ceaseless self-questioning, losing himself among the dry and tinsel trappings of surface Catholicism and so-called "eclecticism," despising age-old wisdom in favor of new philosophies, presenting eloquently a Christ dressed in the robes of Plato, and finding himself through that Father Tracey—the priest with the broken boots, the green patched garments, and the soul of a seraph—who had once been described to him "as an awful example." . . . "You have come into the world worse equipped than if you had been born blind or lame," said Father Martin to Luke. "You have a hundred naked, quivering nerves, wide open on every square inch of your body." His stern advice to Luke was: "Harden your head in time"—a piece of wisdom that has always a drop of bitterness in its inception. There were no troubled depths in Father Pat, however, whose formula was "the grace of God and an honest face," to whom the children "sprang for affection" and "in whose hands the wildest collie or sheepdog was glad to lay his wet nozzle." Rivalling Luke for the limelight of the novel, is the Canon, a man who wears formality like a garment of ice, and who yet wins the affection of his people because they know the warmth under the formality. "Of priests we can offer a charmin' variety," wrote Graves in his famous song; and certainly that rich variety is superbly found in *Luke Delmege*.

No less compelling are what we may call the lay figures in the novel. It is in them that we find that racy humor of which Canon Sheehan became a connoisseur during those daily walks he took in his parish, talking to all and sundry. He loved this people, *his* people, whose symbol of courage and fidelity in utter desolation he saw in "the bare brown mud walls of an unroofed cabin, two holes, that once were windows and doors, staring like the sockets of a skull." He was not blind to their faults, but he was filled with a fine enthusiasm for the idealism in them that could produce a figure like Barbara Wilson, whose life story runs through *Luke Delmege* like a white filament of dazzling purity and sublime charity.

Luke Delmege is filled with the realism of Christianity, but also with its optimism. It is excellent that it should be re-issued as a "Thomas More Book to Live" at a time when novels inspired by Catholicism are almost apologetic to their readers for the optimism of divine grace which they allow to peep fitfully through the thick murk and the weary gloom. Grace sweeps like a wind through this novel; Light, Sweetness, Idealism live here unashamed. If the modern critic tends to feel alien to all this, it is because he has found his mental and spiritual home in a gray place where, in the words of Canon Sheehan, "the air is hot and thick with the breath of many mouths and the dust of many feet," and he has lost the key to the thwarted angel in every man.

MALACHY CARROLL

London, 1955

CONTENTS

BOOK I

CHAPTER I

Introductory

IT HAPPENED in this way. I was absorbed in a daydream—an academic discussion with myself as to whether demand created supply or supply elicited demand—a hoary question throughout all the debating societies of the world; and I was making but little progress toward its solution, when suddenly it solved itself in a remarkable manner. I thought I heard, above the rumbling and muffled thunder of the colossal printing press, far away in a certain street in New York, the word "Copy" shouted up through a telephone. The voice was the voice of that modern magician, the foreman printer. "Copy" echoed in the manager's room, where, amid piles of paper, damp, and moist, and redolent of printer's ink, the great potentate sat. "Copy," he shouted through his telephone, with something that sounded like a prayer—but it wasn't—to the editor, many miles away. "Copy," shouted the editor through his telephone—no! that hasn't come yet, but it will one of these days. But "Copy," he wrote three thousand miles across the bleak barren wastes of the turbulent Atlantic to one sitting on a rustic seat in a quiet garden in a country village beneath the shadows of the black mountains that separate Cork County from Limerick, and with Spenser's "gentle Mulla" almost washing his feet; and "Copy" settled the academic question forever. That mighty modern Minotaur, the press, must be glutted, not with fair youths of Arcady and fair maidens of Athens, but with thoughts that spring from the brains of mortals, and dreams that draw their beautiful, irregular forms across the twilight realms of Fancy.

This it is that makes literary men irreverant and unscrupulous. Was it not said of Balzac, that he dug and dragged every

3

one of his romances straight from the heart of some woman?
"Truth is stranger than fiction." No! my dear friend, for all
fiction is truth—truth torn up by the roots from bleeding
human hearts, and carefully bound with fillets of words to be
placed there in its vases of green and gold on your reading-
desk, on your breakfast-table. Horrid? So it is. Irreverent?
Well, a little. But you, my dear friend, and the rest of humanity will have nothing else. "Nihil humani a me alienum puto,"
said the Latin poet. We have gone a step further. We will have
nothing that is not human. The stage may be gorgeous; the
scenery painted by a master hand; the electric light soft, lambent, penetrating; the orchestra perfect from bass drum to first
fiddle; but the audience gapes and yawns, and is impatient.
There is something wanting. Ha! there it is, and we are all alive
again. Opera glasses are levelled, men and women hold their
breaths lest the least trifle should escape them; the mighty con-
ductor is nowhere; all eyes are strained on what?—a little child,
perhaps; a clown, an Italian shepherdess, a bandit, a fool,—
no matter, it is human, and it is for this figure that stage and
scenery, lights, flowers, and music become at once ancillary
and subservient. And so, when Copy! Copy!! Copy!! tinkled
like an impatient electric bell in my ears, I said: I must seek a
type somewhere. Look into your inner consciousness, said a
voice. No use! It is a *tabula rasa,* from which everything interesting has been long since sponged away. Call up experiences!
Alas! experiences are like ancient photographs. At one time,
I am quite sure, this elegant gentleman, dressed in the fashion
of the sixties, was attractive and interesting enough. Now, alas,
he is a guy. So with experiences. They thrill, and burn, and
pierce, then fade away into ghosts, only fit to haunt the garret
or the lumber room. No! get a living, breathing, human being,
and dissect him. Find out all his thoughts, dreams, sensations,
experiences. Watch him, waking and sleeping, as old Roger
Chillingworth watched Arthur Dimmesdale in that terrible
drama by Hawthorne. Then you have flesh and blood quivering and alive, and the world is satisfied.

Fate, or the Fates, who are always kind, threw some such
subject across my path in those days when imagination was
feeble and the electric bell was growing importunate. I knew
that he had a story. I guessed at it by intuition. Was it not

Cardinal Manning who said, when he was asked to imitate his
great compeers, Wiseman and Newman, by writing a novel,
"that every man carried the plot of at least one romance in his
head?" Now, this man was a mystic and a mystery. He was a
mystic, or was reputed one, because he had once—a young
man's folly—written something about Plato; he was called a
mystery, because he wore his hair brushed back from his forehead right down over his coat collar; and scarce one of the
brethren had ever seen his inner sanctum, or was ever able to
break through the crust of deportment which was always calm
and gentle and sweet, but which drew an invisible line somewhere between you and him—a line of mystic letters: "Thus
far shalt thou come, and no farther." Some thought that he
gave himself too many airs and was conceited; one or two
rough-spoken, hard-fisted colleagues dubbed him as Carlyle
dubbed Herbert Spencer: "an immeasurable——;" but there
he was, always calmly looking out on the tossing, turbulent
ocean of humanity from the quiet recesses of an unluxurious
hermitage, and the still deeper and more sequestered recesses
of a quiet and thoughtful mind.

Like all conscientious interviewers, I had made a few desperate attempts to get inside this mystery and unravel it, but
I had always been repelled. I could never get beyond the *ady-
tum* of the temple, though I coughed loudly, and put the shoes
off my feet with reverence. It was unapproachable and impenetrable. One day, however, it was borne to his ears that I
had done a kind thing to some one or other. He no longer said
with his eyes: You are a most impertinent fellow! The out-
works were taken. Then I wrote him a humble letter about
some old fossil, called Maximus Tyrius. To my surprise I received four pages of foolscap on the Fourth Dissertation:—

Quomodo ab adulatore amicus distingui possit.

Then, one winter's night, I was bowling home in the dark
from the railway station, and became suddenly aware that
voices were shouting warnings from afar off, and that the line
was blocked. So it was—badly. My mysterious friend was
vainly trying to cut the harness on his fallen mare, whilst his
trap, dismembered, was leaning in a maudlin way against the
ditch.

"A bad spill?" I cried.

"Yes!" he said laconically.

"Is the jar broke?" I asked.

"I beg pardon," he said stiffly. Then I knew he had not heard the famous story.

"Pardon me," he said. "I don't quite understand your allusions."

"Never mind," I said, with all the contempt of a professional for an amateur, as I saw him hacking with his left hand, and with a dainty mother-of-pearl-handled penknife, the beautiful new harness. "What do you want to be mutilating that harness for, when the trap has been kicked into space?"

"I thought 'twas the correct thing to do," he murmured. Then I said in my own mind: He *is* an immeasurable——.

"Here, Jem," I cried to my boy. He came over, and whilst I held up the mare's head, he gave her a fierce kick. She was on her feet in an instant.

"Where's your man?" I asked.

"I don't know," he said wonderingly.

We found the man, safe and sound, and fast asleep against the hedge.

"Come now," I said, for I had tacitly assumed the right to command by reason of my superior knowledge, *"montez!* You must come with me!"

"Impossible!" he said, "I must get home to-night."

"Very good. Now, do you think that you can get home more easily and expeditiously in that broken trap than in mine? Hallo! are you left-handed?"

"No, but my right arm is strained a little, just a little."

I took the liberty of lifting his hand, and a small, soft, white hand it was. It fell helpless. Then I saw that his face was very white. This showed he was a thorough brick.

"Is the jar,—I mean the arm,—broke?" he said, with a smile.

Then I knew he was human. That little flash of humor, whilst he was suffering excruciating pain, told volumes of biography. I helped him up to the seat, and, without a word, I drove him to his house.

The doctor called it a compound comminuted fracture of the ulna: we called it a broken wrist. But it was a bad business, and necessitated splints for at least six weeks. I volunteered to say his two Masses every Sunday, my own being supplied by a kind neighbor; and thus I broke down the barriers of chill pride or reserve, and saw the interior of his house and of his heart.

The former was plain almost to poverty; the latter was rich to exuberance. Four walls lined with books from floor to ceiling, a carefully waxed floor, one shred of Indian carpet, and a writing-desk and chair—this was his sitting-room. But the marble mantlepiece was decorated with a pair of costly brass Benares vases, flanked by a pair of snake candlesticks; and his writing-desk was of Shisham wood, and it perfumed with a strange, faint aroma the whole apartment. Over in one corner, and facing the northern light, was an easel; a painter's palette leaned against it, and on it was a half-finished oil-painting— one of those dreamy sea scenes, where the flush of the setting sun is deepening into purple, and the sleeping sea is curled into furrows of gold and lead. A large three-masted vessel, its naked spars drawn like the scaffolding of some airy mansion against the sky, was passing out into the unknown. It was the everlasting enigma of futurity and fate.

I had no notion of losing valuable time. I commenced business the first Sunday evening we dined together.

"I am a story-teller," I said, "and you have a story to tell me. Now, now," I warned, as I saw him make a feeble gesture of protest and denial with his left hand—"don't quote the Needy Knife-Grinder, an' you love me. You have seen a great deal of life, you have felt a great deal, you have resolved a great deal; and I must do you justice to say that you have nobly kept your resolution of retirement and seclusion from your species—that is, from brother-clerics. Here are all the elements of a first-class story—"

"But I've never written even a goody-goody story," he said. "I doubt if I have the faculty of narration."

"Leave that to me," I said. "Give me naked facts and experiences, and Worth never devised such fancy costumes as I shall invent for them."

"But," he protested, "why not seek more interesting matter? Here now, for example, is an admirable book, exemplifying the eternal adage: 'Human nature is the same the wide world

over.' I dare say, now, you thought that Anglican clergymen
are moulded into such perfection by university education, and
the better teaching of social life, that there is never room for
the least eccentricity amongst them."

"Let me be candid," I replied, "and say at once that such
has been my conviction—that at least so far as social virtues
are concerned, and the balancing and measuring of daily social
environments, they were beyond criticism. But have you discovered any freaks or prodigies there?"

"What would you think," he replied, "of this? A dear old
rector driven to resign his parish by his curate's wife, against
whom he had foolishly warned the aforesaid curate in the days
of his bachelorship. She affected to believe that he was an ante-
diluvian, spoke to him with the sweet simplicity of a child at
tennis parties and five o'clock teas; then discovered that once
he had preached a borrowed sermon, and ever afterwards remonstrated with him in public on the misdemeanor: 'Ah! you
dear old sly-boots, when you can preach *so* beautifully, why
do you give us that wretched Penny Pulpit so often?' "

"Look here!" I said, "that's a perfect mine. Have you any
more diamonds like that?"

"Well, not many. The mine is salted. But what do you think
of the good rector, who advertised for a curate, married, but
childless, to occupy the rectory, whilst the incumbent was off
to Nice on a holiday?"

"Well, did he get him?"

"Rather. But the lady was a dog-fancier, and brought with
her *fourteen brindled bulldogs*. That rectory and its grounds
were a desert for three months. No living being, postman,
butcher's boy, baker's boy, dared show his face within the gates.
Occasionally there was a big row in the menagerie. The mistress alone could quell it."

"How?"

"Can't you guess?"

"I give it up, like Mr. Johnston."

"Well, a red-hot iron, which she kept always in the kitchen
fire for the purpose."

"Rather drastic," I said. "Who could have thought it in staid
England? Verily, human nature is everywhere the same."

"Which proves?" he said questioningly.

I waited.

"Which proves," he continued, "that there is nothing half
so absurd as to deduce general sweeping propositions about
nations and races from very slender premises. The world is full
of strange faces and strange characters."

Then I knew he was coming around. And he did. Poor fellow! he had to take to bed a few days after, for the pain was
intense and the weather was moist. I had great doubts whether
our local physician was treating that dangerous wound scientifically, and I proposed a few times to call in some leading
surgeon from the city. The medical attendant indeed assented,
and I saw he looked alarmed. But my poor friend declined.

"It will be all right," he said, "and after all it is but a weary
world. Oh! to sleep and be at rest forever: to know nothing of
the weariness of getting up and lying down, and the necessities
of this poor body, its eating and drinking, and being clothed;
to be free from the eternal vexations of men, their vanity, and
folly, and pride. I shall dread to meet them even in Heaven.
'Look for me, my dear friend,' as a good poet has said, 'in the
nurseries of Heaven.' "

Then my heart went out to him, for I saw his had been a
troubled life, and day by day I sat by his bedside, whilst partly
as an anodyne to pain, partly to please me, he went over the
details of his life. Then, one day, I hinted that his life had been
a *carrière manquée,* and that he was a soured and disappointed
man. He raised himself on his left arm, and looked at me long
and wistfully. A slight discoloration had appeared above the
fractured wrist. He pointed to it.

"That is the black flag of death," he said. "You will find my
will in the lower locked drawer of my writing-desk. I have left
all to sick and poor children. But you are wrong. I am not
soured, or deceived, or disappointed. I have a grateful heart
to God and man. I have not had an unhappy life. Indeed, I
have had more than my share of its blessings. But, my friend,"
he said earnestly, "I am a puzzled man. The enigma of life has
been always too much for me. You will have guessed as much
from all that I have told you. I seek the solution in eternity of
the awful riddle of life."

He fell back in great pain, and I forgot my calling as interviewer in my sympathy as friend. Dear Lord! and the world
called this man proud.

"Now," I said, "you are despondent. Your accident and this

confinement have weighed on your nerves. You must let me send for Dr. S——. I'll telegraph to the bishop, and he'll put you under obedience."

He smiled faintly.

"No use," he said, "this is septicæmia. I have probably forty-eight hours to live. Then, Rest! Rest! Rest! It's a strange thing to be tired of life when I had everything that man could desire. This pretty rural parish; a fair competence; churches and schools perfect; and," he gave a little laugh, "no curate. Yet, I am tired, tired as a child after a hot summer day; and tired of a foolish whim to reconcile the irreconcilable."

"And why not give up this brain-racking," I said, "and live? Nothing solves riddles but work, and steadily ignoring them. Why, we'd all go mad if we were like you."

"True," he said feebly, "true, my friend. But you see, habits are tyrants, and I commenced badly. I was rather innocent, and I wanted to dovetail professions and actions, principle and interest (forgive the sorry pun), that which ought to be, and that which is. It was rather late in life when I discovered the utter impracticability of such a process. Life was a Chinese puzzle. Then, too late, I flung aside all the enigmas of life, and flung myself on the bosom of the great mystery of God, and there sought rest. But, behind the veil! Behind the veil! There only is the solution."

He remained a long time in a reverie, staring up at the ceiling. I noticed a faint odor in the air.

"You know," he said at length, "I was not loved by the brethren. Why? Did I dislike them? No! God forbid! I liked and loved everything that God created. But I was unhappy. Their ways puzzled me, and I was silent. There was nothing sincere or open in the world but the faces of little children. God bless them! They are a direct revelation from Heaven. Then, you will notice that there is not a single modern book in my library. Why? Because all modern literature is lies! lies! lies! And such painful lies! Why will novelists increase and aggravate the burdens of the race by such painful analyses of human character and action?"

"Now, now," I said, "you *are* morbid. Why, half the pleasures of life come from works of imagination and poetry."

"True. But, why are they always so painful and so untrue?

Do you think that any one would read a novel, if it were not about something painful?—and the more painful, the more entrancing. Men revel in creating and feeling pain. Here is another puzzle."

It was so sad, this gentle, pitiful life drawing to a close, and without a farewell word of hope to the world it was leaving, that I had neither comment nor consolation to offer. It was so unlike all my daily experiences that I was silent with pity and surprise. He interrupted me.

"Now for the great wind-up. To-morrow morning you will come over early and administer the last Sacraments. When I am dead, you will coffin my poor remains immediately, for I shall be discolored sadly and shall rapidly decompose. And you know we must not give our poor people the faintest shock. I wish to be buried in my little church, right under the statue of our Blessed Lady, and within sound of the Mass. There I spent my happiest hours on earth. And I shall not rest in peace anywhere but where I can hear the Mass-bell. You think I am wandering in my mind? No. I am quite collected. I often debated with myself whether I should not like to be buried outside, where I should hear the people walking over my grave. But no! I have decided to remain where the Divine Mother will look down with her pitying eyes on the place where this earthly tabernacle is melting into dust, and where the syllables of the mighty Mass will hover and echo when the church is silent betimes. And no foolish epitaph. 'Here lieth,' and 'pray for his soul.' That's all."

He was silent for a little while; but now and again a faint shudder showed me the agony he was suffering.

"I am tiring you," he said at length; "but sometimes I dream that in the long summer twilights, when my little village choir is practicing, some child may allow her thoughts, as she is singing, to pass down to where the pastor is lying; and perhaps some poor mother may come over to my grave, after she has said her Rosary, and point out to the wondering child in her arms the place where the man that loved little children is lying. We are not all forgotten, though we seem to be. Here, too, is another puzzle. I am very tired."

I stood up and left the room, vowing that I would leave that poor soul at rest forever.

I administered the last Sacraments the following day, after I had seen the doctor. He was much distressed at the fatal turn things had taken. "He had not anticipated; 'twas a case for hospital treatment; the weather was so sultry; he had dreaded amputation, etc. No hope? None." The patient was right.

And so two days later, exactly as he had anticipated, we were grouped around his bedside to watch and help his last struggle. But even in that supreme moment, his habitual equanimity did not desert him. Courteous to all around, apologizing for little troubles, solicitous about others, eagerly looking forward to the lifting of the veil, he passed his last moments in life. Then about six o'clock in the evening, just as the Angelus ceased tolling, he cried:—

" 'Tis the soul-bell, the passing-bell, is it not?"

" 'Tis the Angelus," I replied.

"Say it with me, or rather for me," he said. Then a few minutes later: " 'Tis growing very dark, and I am cold. What is it? I cannot understand—"

And so he passed to the revelation.

An unusually large number of the brethren gathered to his obsequies, which was again very strange and perplexing. He was buried as he had desired, and his memory is fast vanishing from amongst men; but the instincts of the novelist have overcome my tenderness for that memory, and I give his life-history and experiences. Am I justified in doing so? Time must tell.

I should, however, mention another circumstance. At the obsequies were two old priests, one bent low with years, the other carrying the white burden of his winters more defiantly. The former asked me:—

"Did Luke speak of me, or wish to see me?"

I had to say "No!"

He went away looking very despondent.

The other called me aside and said:—

"Did Luke express no wish to see me?"

Now, I was afraid of this man. He, too, was an oddity—a deep, profound scholar in subjects that are not interesting to the multitude. He was one of the few who knew Luke well.

"Yes," I said; "several times. But he always drew back, saying: 'Father Martin is old and feeble. I cannot bring him such a journey in such weather. Don't write! It will be nothing.' "

"Did you think that this accident was a trifle, and that there was no danger of fatal issues?"

I coughed a little and said something.

"And did you think it was right," he continued, "that the only friend he probably had in the world"—here his voice broke—"should have been excluded from his confidence at such a momentous time?"

"I really had no alternative," I replied. "I did all I could for him, poor fellow; but you know he was peculiar and you also know that he was supersensitive about giving trouble to others."

"Quite so. But when you saw danger, you should have summoned his friends. This is one of those things one finds it hard to condone. He has left a will and papers, I presume?"

"Yes," I said; "I have charge of all."

"Have you opened the will?"

"Not as yet."

"Please do so, and see who are the executors."

We opened the will then and there, and found that my troublesome interlocutor, the Reverend Martin Hughes was sole executor. He closed the will at once, and said, coldly:—

"Now, would you be pleased to hand over all other papers and confidential documents belonging to my deceased friend? You can have no further need of them—"

"I beg your pardon," I said; "the good priest just departed gave me a good deal of confidence. You know that I was in hourly attendance on him for six weeks. I asked him to allow me tell the story of his life, and he consented, and granted me full permission to examine and retain all his letters, papers, diaries, manuscripts, for that purpose."

"That puts a different complexion on things," said Father Hughes. "You fellows are regular resurrectionists. You cannot let the dead rest and bury their histories with them."

"But if a life has a lesson?" I ventured to say, humbly.

"For whom?"

"For the survivors and the world."

"And what are survivors and the world to the dead?" he asked.

I was silent. It would be a tactical mistake to irritate this quaint old man. He pondered deeply for a long time.

"I have the greatest reluctance," he said, "about consenting to such a thing. I know nothing more utterly detestable than the manner in which the secrets of the dead are purloined in our most prurient generation, and the poor relics of their thoughts and feelings scattered to the dust, or exposed on the public highways for the *ludibrium* of an irreverant public. And this would be bad enough, but we have to face the lamentable fact it is not the reality, but a hideous caricature of the reality that is presented to the public—"

"You can prevent that," I said meekly.

"How?"

"By simply taking the matter into your own hands. No man knew Luke Delmege half so well as you—"

"I'm too old and feeble for all that," he said.

"Well, let's strike a bargain," I replied. "Every page of this history I shall submit to you for revision, correction, or destruction, as seems fit, if you keep me on the right track by giving me as much light as you can."

"It is the only way to avert an evil," he replied. I told him I was complimented.

And so, with bits and scraps of frayed yellow paper, torn and tattered letters, sermons half-written, and diaries badly kept, I have clothed in living language the skeleton form of this human life. On the whole, I feel I have done it well, although now and again an angle of the skeleton—some irregularity—will push forward and declare itself. Sometimes it is an anachronism which I cannot account for, except on the score of great charity on the part of my deceased friend, who seemed to have preferred that his ignorance should be assumed rather than that charity should be wounded. Sometimes there is a curious dislocation of places, probably for the same reason. And sometimes I have found it difficult to draw the seams of some rent together, and to make times and circumstances correspond with the modern parts of our history. And if "the tear and smile" of Ireland alternate in those pages, it is withal a solemn history; and many, perhaps, will find in it deeper meanings than we have been able to interpret or convey.

CHAPTER II

The Illusions of Youth

HE WAS a young man, a very young man, otherwise he would not have been so elated when

Lucas Delmege, X——ensis,

was called out for the fourth time, and he had to request his diocesans to watch the huge pile of premiums he had already won, whilst he passed up the center aisle of the prayer-hall, and his bishop, smiling as he raised another sheaf of calf-bound volumes, handed them to him, with a whispered "Optime, Luca." And yet, if a little vanity—and it is a gentle vice—is ever permissible, it would have been in his case. To have led his class successfully in the halls of a great ecclesiastical seminary; to be watched enviously by five hundred and sixty fellow-students, as he moved along on his triumphant march; to have come out victorious from a great intellectual struggle, and to receive this praise from his bishop, who felt that himself and his diocese were honored by the praise reflected from his young subject—assuredly, these are things to stir sluggish pulses, and make the face pallid with pleasure. And if all this was but the forecast of a great career in the Church; if it pointed with the steady finger of an unerring fate to the long vista of life, strewn with roses, and with laurel crowns dropped by unseen hands from above, there would be all the better reason for that elastic step, and that gentle condescension which marked the manner of the successful student, when his admirers gathered around him, and even his defeated rivals candidly congratulated him upon his unprecedented success. Yet, withal, he was modest. Just a little spring in his gait; just a little silent reception of adulation, as a something due to his commanding position; and just a little moistening of his eyelids, as he dreamt of a certain

15

far home down by the sea, and the pride of his mother as he flung all his treasures into her lap, and his sisters' kisses of triumph for the beloved one—ah me! who would say nay to this? Let the sunshine, and the roses, and the love of thy loved ones play around thee, thou pale and gentle Levite, while they may. Soon the disillusion will come, the laurels will fade, and the sunshine turn to gray ashen shadow, and the tender and strong supports of home and love will be kicked aside by Time and Fate; but the arena of life will be ever before thee, and every fresh triumph will be a fresh conflict, and thou wilt be a friendless one and naked. But how didst thou come to believe that the quiet study hall was the world, and thou the cynosure of all eyes—the proverb in all mouths? Listen, dear child, for thou art but a child. The mighty world has never heard of thee, does not know thy name; the press is silent about thee; the very priests of thy diocese do not even know of thy existence. Thou art but a pin's point in the universe. He does not believe it. He has been a FIRST OF FIRST,[1] and the universe is at his feet.

His first shock was at the Broadstone Terminus of the Great Midland Railway. A young and unsophisticated porter was so rustic and ignorant as to raise his hat to the young priest as he leaped from the carriage.

"Why did ye do that?" said an older comrade. "Sure, thim's but collaygians. They won't be priested for another year or two."

The porter had not heard of Luke Delmege, and the First of First.

He ran his eyes rapidly over the newspapers in the restaurant, where he was taking a humble cup of coffee. There was news from all quarters of the globe—an earthquake in Japan, a revolution in the Argentine, a row in the French Chamber of Deputies, a few speeches in the House of Commons, a whole page and a half of sporting intelligence, a special column on a favorite greyhound named *Ben Bow,* an interview with a famous jockey, a paragraph about a great minister in Austria, gigantic lists of stocks and shares, a good deal of squalor and crime in the police courts, one line about a great philosopher who was dying—can it be possible? Not a line, not a word of yesterday's triumph in the academy! The name of Luke Delmege, First of First, was nowhere to be seen.

[1] First prizeman in his class.

Could he be, by any possible chance, in the photographer's windows? Alas, no! Here are smiling actresses, babies in all kinds of postures and with every variety of expression, favorite pugdogs, dirty beasts of every kind with tufts of hair on their tails, fashionable beauties, Portias, and Imogens, and Cordelias; but the great athlete of yesterday?

And the porters made no distinction between him and his fellow-students as he sped southwards to his home; a few school-girls stared at him and passed on; commercial men glanced at him and buried themselves in their papers; a few priests cheerily said:—

"Home for the holidays, boys?"

But Luke Delmege was but a unit among millions, and excited no more notice than the rest.

He could not understand it. He had always thought and believed that his college was the Hub of the Universe; and that its prizemen came out into the unlettered world horned and aureoled with light as from a Holy Mountain. Was not a prize in his college equivalent to a university degree; and was it not supposed to shed a lambent light athwart the future career of the winner, no matter how clouded that career might be? Did he not hear of men who folded their arms and leaned on their laurels for the rest of their lives, and were honored and respected for their boyish triumphs far into withered and useless age? And here, in the very dawn of success, he was but a student amongst students; and even these soon began to drop their hero-worship, when they found the great world so listless and indifferent. He is troubled and bewildered; he cannot understand.

Well, at last, here is home, and here is worship, and here is love. Ay, indeed! The news had gone on before him. The great athlete in the greatest college in the world was coming home; and he was their own, their beloved. It nearly compensated and consoled him for all the neglect and indifference, when, on entering beneath his own humble roof, where he had learned all the best lessons of life, he found the whole family prostrate on their knees before him. There was his aged father. He laid his newly consecrated hands on the gray head, and pronounced the blessing. He extended his hands to be kissed, and the rough lips almost bit them in the intensity of affection and love. The old man rose and went out, too full of joy to speak. The young priest blessed his mother; she kissed his hands—the hands, every line of which she knew with more than the skill of palmist. The young priest stooped and kissed her wrinkled forehead. He blessed his brothers, and laid his hands on the smooth brows of his sisters. Reverently they touched his palms with their gentle lips; and then, Margery, the youngest, forgetting everything but her great love, flung her arms around him, and kissed him passionately, crying and sobbing: "Oh! Luke! Luke!" Well, this at least was worth working for. Then the great trunk came in, and the vast treasures were unlocked, and taken out, and handled reverently, and placed on the few shelves that had been nailed by a rustic carpenter in the little alcove of his bedroom. There they winked and blinked in all their splendors of calf and gold; and Peggy refused to dust them, or touch them at all, at all, for how did she know what might be in them? They were the priest's books, and better have nothing to say to them. The priests are the Lord's anointed, you know. The less we have to say to them the better! But a few privileged ones amongst the neighbors were allowed to come in, and look at these trophies, and offer the incense of their praise before the shrine of this family idol, and think, in their own hearts, whether any of their little flaxen-haired gossoons would ever reach to these unapproachable altitudes.

The aged curate, who had given his Luke his First Communion, came in later.

"Well, Luke, old man, put on the Melchisedech at last? How are you, and how is every bit of you? You look washed out, man, and as 'tin as a lat,' as Moll Brien said when her son came out of jail. A few days' coursing on the mountains will put new life into you. The two dogs, *Robin* and *Raven,* are in prime condition, and the mountain has not been coursed since the great match in May. Ah! these books! these books! Luke's prizes, did you say, ma'am? They're vampires, ma'am, sucking the rich red blood from his veins. Thank God, I never bothered much about them! Here they are, of course: *Cambrensis Eversus!* By Jove! I thought that fellow was spun out long since. Why, in my time, thirty years ago, ma'am,—time flies,—that book was declared out of print; and here the fellow turns up as spruce as ever. A regular resurrectionist! Well, it's all the same. Nobody ever read him, or ever will. *O'Kane on the*

Rubrics! A good book. Poor Jimmy! The best soul that ever lived. Hurrah! *Murray on the Church!* Poor—old—Paddy! The tub of theology! *Crolly de Contractibus—*"

Here a dreadful shudder shot through his stalwart frame.

"Now, look here, Luke, you've had enough of these fellows. Come up to-morrow and dine with us. No one but Father Tim and one or two of the neighbors. What—"

"I've not called on the Canon yet," said Luke, timidly.

"Never mind! I won't ask *him.* You can call to-morrow. But not too early, mind! Between four and six. You may be in time for what he calls 'five o'clock tea.' Let me see! I'll say half-past four, so that you can have an excuse for getting away. Don't say you're dining with me, though. He'd never forgive you. Anything but that."

He fell into a fit of musing. There were some troublous memories called up.

"By the way, what about your first Mass?" he cried, waking up.

"I shall feel much obliged if you will kindly assist me, Father Pat," said Luke.

"Of course, of course, my boy," said the curate, "though, indeed, very little assistance you'll require, I'm thinking."

"If I could say my first Mass here under my father's roof," said the young priest, timidly.

"Of course, of course," said the curate. "Let me see, though. It's against the statutes of course, without the Bishop's permission; and I don't know—but we'll dispense with statutes on this occasion. Will you take long?"

"About half an hour, I think," said Luke.

"Ay, it will be many a day, your reverence, before Luke will be able to say Mass like you," said Mrs. Delmege. "Sure, 'tis you who don't keep us long waiting."

"No, indeed; why should I? Do I want ye to have camels' knees, like the poor old saints over there in Egypt?"

"Mike said there was no use trying to keep up with your reverence. Though you had the Latin, and I believe there are very hard words in the Latin, and we had the English, you bate us intirely."

"Look at that for you, now," said Father Pat, looking around admiringly.

"Thin, the last time he wint to Cork with the butter, he bought the weeshiest little prayer book you ever saw. 'Twas about half a finger long, and the print was mighty big. 'I have him now,' sez he; ' 'tis a quare story if I don't lave him behind.' Troth, and yer reverence, ye were at the *De Profundis* before he got to the *Pather Nosther*."

"Well, you see, ma'am, that's what comes from long practice. But I make it up in the preaching, you know," he said with a smile.

"Troth, an' ye do," said Mrs. Delmege, " 'tisn't much, but what ye says comes from the heart."

"There now, Luke, there's a critic for you. Look sharp, old man; but I forgot. You are going abroad. Happy fellow! 'Tis only in Ireland you come in for sharp hits. Well, don't forget to-morrow. Half-past four; not a moment later. I'm a model of punctuality. Good-day, ma'am; oh! by Jove! I was forgetting. Give us your blessing, my poor man. Isn't there some kind of indulgence attached?"

He bent his head reverently as he knelt and received the benediction.

"There, that will do me some good, whatever, and I want it."

"The best poor priest within the says of Ireland," said Mrs. Delmege, wiping her eyes, as the curate strode down the little footpath, and leaped lightly over the stile.

But though Luke echoed his mother's kind words, deep down in his heart there was a jarring note somewhere. What was it? That expression, "put on the Melchisedech"? Well, after all, it was a pretty usual colloquialism, and meant no irreverence. Then, saying Mass in a private house without episcopal sanction? How did that statute bind? Was it *sub gravi*? Luke shuddered at the thought of celebrating under such circumstances. He would write that evening to the curate, and put off his Mass till Sunday. There was something called *Epikeia,* of course, but—he was perplexed. Then, that awful rapidity in celebrating! The people noticed it and were shocked. But, after all, they liked it, and was there not something in the rubrics about the propriety of not keeping the people waiting? Who was he that he should judge his superior —a man of thirty years' standing on the mission? Then it dawned on his perplexed and puzzled mind that Father Casey had not even once alluded to the high places that had fallen

to the lot of the happy student in his college. He had spoken
to him as to an ordinary student, affectionately, but without a
note of admiration. Had he not heard it? Of course he had.
And yet, never an allusion to the FIRST OF FIRST, even in the
mother's presence! What was it! Forgetfulness? No. He had
seen the prizes and made little of them. Could it be that, after
all, he had been living in a fool's paradise, and that the great
world thought nothing of these academic triumphs that were
pursued and won at such tremendous cost? The thought was
too dreadful. The Canon will think differently. He is a highly
polished and cultured man. He will appreciate distinction and
academical success. And poor Luke felt irritated, annoyed,
distressed, perplexed. It was all so very unlike what he had
anticipated. He had not read: "For there shall be no remembrance of the wise no more than of the fool forever."

The next day Luke paid a formal visit to his pastor. He had
an old dread of that parochial house—a shrinking and tingling
of the nerves when he opened the gate and crossed the well-
trimmed lawn, and knocked nervously with that polished knob,
which sounded altogether too loud for his tastes. It was an old
feeling, implanted in childhood, and which intensified as the
years went by. Custom had not modified it nor habit soothed
it; and as Luke crossed the lawn at four o'clock this warm July
day, he wished heartily that this visit were over. He had often
striven in his leisure moments in college to analyze the feeling,
but without success. He had often, as he advanced in his col-
legiate course, and had begun to feel a certain self-reliance,
tried to gather his nerves together, and face with coolness this
annual ordeal. It was no use; and when the servant appeared
in answer to his knock, and announced that the Canon was in
his library, his heart sank down, and he paced the beautiful
drawing-room in a nervous and unhappy condition. Now, this
was unreasonable and unintelligible. Alas! it was one of the
many enigmas in his own soul, and in the vast universe outside,
that he was perpetually striving to solve.

Here was a man of advanced years, of most blameless life,
of calm, polished manner; a man who gave largely to public
charities, and who, as an ecclesiastic, was an ornament to the
Church; and yet men shrank from him; and like an iceberg
loosened by the Gulf Stream, he created around him, wherever
he went, an atmosphere of chilliness and frigidity that almost

isolated him from his fellow-men. What was it? He was a formalist that could not be laughed at; a perfected and symmetrical character where the curious and irreverent could place no flaw; the *arbiter elegantiarum* to his diocese; and the frigid censor of the least departure from the Persian laws of politeness and good deportment. If he had only had the good fortune to be laughed at, it would have saved him. If men could make a joke about him, they would have loved him. But no! Stately and dignified and chill, there was no such thing as presuming on such a lofty character; and there he was, his forehead in the clouds and his face above the line of perpetual snow.

Luke sat timidly in a dainty chair, with its wood-work inlaid with mother-of-pearl. He would have liked to sink into the easy depths of that voluptuous arm-chair; but he thought it would seem too familiar. How often, in later life, he thought of his nervousness and reverence, when a young student called on him, and flung himself carelessly on a sofa, and crossed his legs nonchalantly! Which was better—his own gentle awe and deep-seated reverence for authority and age and dignity, or the possible irreverence of after years? Well, this too, was a puzzle.

Luke lifted up his eyes. They fell on the portrait of a beautiful woman; a fair, oval face, with an expression of infinite sadness upon it. It attracted him, fascinated him. It was one of the numberless copies of the *Cenci* portrait that third-class artists turn out in Rome. It was believed by the Canon to be the original. When better informed in later years, Luke tried to undeceive the Canon, it was one of the many things that were not forgiven. But now he turned his eyes rapidly away from the beautiful face. He was in the first flush of his ordination. It was not right. It was sinful. His eyes rested on a glorious picture of the Divine Mother, that hung over the mantelpiece in the place of honor. Luke went into raptures over it, studied it, gazed on it, and every throb of pleasure was a prayer. Just then, a bevy of artificial birds, in a glass case beneath, began to flutter and chirp, and a deep gong tolled out musically the quarter. The door softly opened, and the Canon entered the room. He was a tall man, about sixty-five years of age, but remarkably well preserved. His hair was white, not silvery white, but flaxen-white, a curious and unpleasant shade of yellow running through it. He was clad in a soutane, such as canons wear, and which set off well his fine stately figure. His face, a strong, massive one, had an appearance of habitual equanimity that was rather acquired by strong self-discipline than natural. He spoke softly, and when he sat down he arranged his cassock so that the silver buckles on his shoes could be seen. A subtle, indefinable aroma exhaled from his garments. Luke remembered it well. It was one of those mnemonic associations from childhood that never fade.

"Sit down. I'm very happy to see you, Mr. Delmege," he said.

If he had only said "Luke" or "Father" Delmege, Luke would have worshipped him. The icy "Mista" froze him.

"Thank you, Canon," he said.

"I understand you have been ordained? Yes! That must be a great consolation to your—excellent parents."

"Yes. They are very happy," said Luke. "If I might presume to ask such a favor, it would make them doubly happier if I could say my first Mass in my own—in my—in their house."

"Impossible," replied the Canon, blandly, "quite impossible, I assure you, my—ah—dear Mr. Delmege. There is an—ah—episcopal regulation forbidding it; and the Bishop, unhappily —ah—and unadvisedly, I presume to think, has—ah—restricted permission to say such Masses to himself. I'm not—ah—at all sure that this is not a—canonical infringement on parochial—ah—privileges; but we must not discuss the subject. You are—ah—very young!"

The Canon seemed hurt, and Luke was silent.

"You have had—I hope," said the former, at length, "a fairly respectable career in College."

Infandum! this man had never heard of the FIRST OF FIRST! Luke was nettled.

"Fairly," he said laconically. The Canon noticed his mortification.

"Now that I remember, I heard some one—could it have been my curate?—say that you were doing fairly well. Indeed I think he said remarkably well."

"I took 'First of First' in Theology, Scripture, and Canon Law, and Second of First in Hebrew," said Luke, now thoroughly aroused by such indifference; "and I'd have swept the First of First in Hebrew also—"

"Dear me! how very interesting," said the Canon, "how *very* interesting! I hope it is the prelude to a—to a—very respectable career in the Church!"

"I hope so," said Luke, despondently. Alas! he had been taught that it was not the prelude, but the final and ultimate climax of all human distinction. The Canon continued:—

"If you continue your studies, as every young priest should, and try to acquire ease and a proper deportment of manner, and if your life is otherwise—ah—correct and—ah—respectable, you may, in the course of years, attain to the honors and—ah—emoluments of the ministry. You may even in your old age,—that is, supposing an irreproachable and respectable career,—you may even attain to—ah—the dignity of being incorporated into the—ah—Chapter of your native diocese."

"I could never think of reaching such an elevation," said Luke humbly.

"Oh! well," said the Canon reassuringly, "you may, you may. It means, of course, years and well-established respectability; but it will all come, it will all come."

Luke thought that time was no more, and that his purgatory had begun, when those blessed birds shook out their feathers and chirped, and the deep gong tolled out musically the half-hour.

The Canon rose and said:—

"Could you join us in a cup of tea, Mr. Delmege? We are—ah—rather early to-day, as we shall have a drive before dinner. No? Well, good-day! I'm most happy to have seen you. *Good*-day!"

Luke was stepping lightly down the gravelled walk, thankful for having got off so easily, when he was called back. His heart sank.

"Perhaps, Mr. Delmege," said the Canon, blandly, "you would do us the favor of dining with us at half-past six on Sunday? It's rather early, indeed; but it's only a family party."

Luke rapidly ran over in his mind every possible excuse for absenting himself, but in vain!

"I shall be most happy, sir," he said; "the hour will suit me admirably."

Ah, Luke, Luke!

CHAPTER III

The Sagacities of Age

AS THE young priest made his way hastily across the fields, already yellowing to the harvest, he became aware of a deep feeling of despondency glooming down upon him, although he was in the high zenith of youth, with all its prophetic promise, and the heavens were clear above his head. That engagement to dine was an ugly ordeal to be encountered; but, after all, what did he care? It was a couple of hours' agony, that was all. What then? Where did all this dismal anxiety and foreboding come from? He was fond, as has been said, of analyzing—a dangerous habit; and now, under the hot sun, he was striving to reconcile two or three things, the mystery of which the world has already declared to be insoluble. "A respectable career," "honors and emoluments," "a stall in the Cathedral;" these words jarred across the vibrant emotions of the young priest, and made him almost sick with their dismal and hollow sounds. Good heavens! was this the end of all—all the heaven-sent aspirations, all the noble determinations, all the conse-crated ideals that had peopled heart and mind only a week ago, when the oil was wet on his hands, and he trembled as he touched for the first time the chalice of the Blood of Christ? How paltry every human ambition seemed then; how ragged the tinsel of kings; how cheap and worthless the pinchbeck of earthly thrones! How his soul burned to emulate the heroism of saints—to go abroad and be forgotten by the world, and to be remembered only by Christ—to live and die amongst the lepers and the insane—to pass, with one swift stroke of the dull sword of the executioner in China or Japan, to his immortal crown! Why, it was only the prayers of his aged mother made him tear up that letter he had written to the Bishop of Natal,

25

asking as a favor to be deputed as chaplain in Robbin Island, where the outcasts and refuse of humanity were located, so that his life might be from start to finish one glorious holocaust in the sight of God! And now there remains, after all the glory, the gray ashes of a "respectable career,"—a comfortable home, honors and emoluments, and, as a crown of old age, a parish and a prebend! What an anticlimax! Luke groaned and took off his hat, and wiped the hot perspiration from his forehead.

But a sharper sting was behind. If all this was a shock and a surprise, what was he to think of all his ambitious labors for the last six years? Had he one single idea before his mind but self-advancement, glory, the praise of men, the applause of his fellow-students, except on that holy morning when the intoxication of divine dreams and hopes lifted him on the highest altitudes of the Holy Mount? And he said to his soul amidst its sobbing and tears: "*Unam petii a Domino: hanc requiram: ut inhabitem in domo Domini omnibus diebus vitae meae. Ut videam voluptatem Domini, et visitem templum ejus. Impinguasti in oleo caput meum: et calix meus inebrians quam praeclarus est!*"

Now, which was right—the tacit denial by men of the sublime doctrine of self-annihilation and love of lowly things and places, and, by consequence, their gospel of self-advancement preached from the house tops; or that sudden breath of the Holy Spirit—that afflatus spiced with sanctity and sorrow —that momentary intoxication, which has come but once or twice to saints and heroes, and in which they have spurned with holy contempt all that this earth holds dear? Which was right? It was the enigma of life, the antithesis of principle and practice. He saw, as in a vision, all the vast corollaries and scholia, that stretched away into the perspective of time, from one principle or another; he saw himself branded as a madman or a fanatic if he embraced the one, and scheduled in the markets of the world as a respectable and honored clergyman if he selected the other; here was pain, disease, dishonor; and here was peace, dignity, health, and wealth. He knew well whither the Divine Hand, palm-wounded, blood-stricken, pointed; but who am I, he said, to set my opinion before the whole world? I am a conceited fool to think that these diseased and morbid thoughts, that spring from an overstrained mind and irritable nerves, are to be assumed in preference to the calm and almost universal habitudes of mankind. I shall say to my soul: Sleep thee now, and rest. Let the future solve its own enigmas.

But then came back with trebled force the shame he felt when his old pastor put bluntly before him these dreams of advancement and ambition; and he just remembered that morning having read some strange things in his book of meditations. It was the articulate rendering of all the Spirit had been saying. Who now was right? This old man in the nineteenth century, or this strange, unnamed, unknown monk, who was calling to him across six centuries of time? The world was grown wise. Was it? Circumstances change principles. Do they? It was all very well in the Dark Ages, but this is the light-illuminated nineteenth century. Indeed? We are not to go back to mediævalism for our philosophy of life, when we have ever so many new systems of our own; and our *Illuminati* know a little more than your cowled monks with their sandals and bog-Latin.

"Not in vain the distant beacons, forward, forward let us range:
Let the great world spin forever down the ringing grooves of change."

Quite so. The "ringing grooves of change." Are we going back to manuscripts when we have print? Back to coaches when we have steam? Back to monasteries when we have hotels? Back to mortification, dishonor, forgetfulness, the *Innominati* of the cell and the tomb?

The hoarse wash of the Atlantic surges came mournfully to his ears, there in the brilliant sunshine; and as he turned away from his reverie and the sight of the restless but changeless ocean, he thought he heard the rebuke upborne—*Be ashamed, O Sidon, said the sea.*

"Begor, I thought you were petrified into a stone statue, Luke," said the voice of the good-natured curate. "I have been watching you, and whistling at you for the last half-hour; but I might as well be whistling to a milestone, and my breath is not now so strong either. 'The Canon has turned him into ice,' I said to myself, 'he's a regular patented refrigerator, even on

this awful day.' Phew! there's no living at all this weather.
Come along. The Murphies are waiting; and so are two of the
hungriest fellows you ever saw. But are you really alive? Let
me feel you."

So they passed into the humble parlor of the aged curate;
and, as Luke sank wearily into a horsehair arm-chair, very
much the worse for the wear, dinner was ordered by a few
robust knocks on the kitchen wall.

"Comin'," said a far-away voice, like that of a ventriloquist.

"You know Father Tim, Luke? And this is my old friend,
Martin Hughes, the greatest rascal from this to Cape Clear.
Come along now, boys, we're late, you know. Bless us, O Lord,
Amen. You'll take the liver wing, Luke. You've a good right to
it. They're your own. Ah! You've the good mother."

"And I venture to say," said Father Tim, digging the carver
with his left hand into the juicy recesses of the ham, "that
this fellow came from the same quarter. Ah! this *is* a parish
where men buy nothing but a scrap of butcher's meat."

"I suppose you've got your eye on it, Tim. You've no
chance, my dear fellow. Read up Valuy and Lord Chester-
field's *Letters* and the Manual of Etiquette. You unmannerly
fellow, what a chance you have of upsetting a polite young man
like me. Take the potatoes over there to Father Delmege,
Mary. I suppose now you're tired of the Queen's mutton? And
you tell me they don't give the students beer now? Well, that's
bad. What'll you take now? Try that sherry. No! A little
water?" he echoed in a tone of ineffable disgust.

"I think Father Delmege is right such a day as this," said
Martin Hughes, a kindly, soft-faced priest, who was generally
silent, except when he had a gentle or encouraging word to
say. "And, indeed," he added, "that beer was no great things.
It was a good day for Ireland when they did away with it."

"Well, of course, every one knows you're a queer fellow.
But Luke, old man, *are you really alive?*"

"Alive and doing fairly well," said Luke, laughing. *"Ab actu
ad esse valet consecutio.* And if this is not actuality I'd like to
know what it is."

"There now for you," said the host; "he has the dust of the
desks in his mouth yet. Begor, I suppose now I could hardly
remember to translate that."

"Don't try," said Father Tim; "nothing disturbs the digestion so much as serious thought."

"Faith, 'tis true for you. I'll let it alone. I'm better engaged. Mary, have that bit of mutton ready when I ring."

And so, amidst bantering, poking, story-telling, from the lips of these genial and kindly men, Luke soon forgot his introspection; and his nerves cooled down and were soothed by the totally informal and delightful conversation that shot, as if by web and woof, across the flowers and the viands. Then, when these contemptible dishes were removed, and they settled down to a quiet evening, Father Tim, crossing his legs comfortably, and squeezing with the dexterity begotten of habit the lemon into his glass, began to philosophize. He was slow of speech, unlike his dear friend, the host of the evening, and Spartan almost in his utterances, which he ground out slowly from the mills of thought.

"There's one advice I'd give you, Luke, my dear boy; and 'tisn't now, but in twenty years' time, ye'll thank me for the same. Harden your head in time."

"I beg pardon, Father," said Luke, wonderingly.

"For what, my boy?" said Father Tim.

"I didn't quite understand you," said Luke, timidly. "You said something—"

"I said," replied Father Tim, dropping in a tiny bit of sugar, "and I repeat it, harden your head in time."

"Let the boy alone," said Father Martin; "don't mind his nonsense, Luke."

"I said, and I repeat it," said Father Tim, "and 'tisn't now, but in thirty years' time, you'll value the advice; harden your head in time. You see 'tis this way," he continued methodically, "if you take one glass of wine, even that claret there, which is no more than so much water, and if it gets into your head, and your eyes are watery, and your knees weak, and you cannot say, three times running, the British Constitution, you are a drunkard and a profligate. But if you can drink a puncheon of the hard stuff, like this, and your head is cool, and your knees steady, and your tongue smooth and glib, you are a most temperate and abstemious man. 'Tis the hard head that does it. A civil tongue and a hard head will take any man through the world."

"But do you mean to say," said Luke, who was amazed at such a statement, "that that is the way the world judges of intemperance?"

"Of course it is," said Father Tim, "what else? The world judges what it sees—nothing else."

"But that's most shocking and unfair," said Luke. "Why, any poor fellow may make a mistake—"

"If he made such a mistake in Maynooth, how would he be judged?" said Father Tim.

"He would be promptly expelled, of course. But then, you know, men are on probation there, and it is natural—"

"Maynooth is the world," said Father Tim, laconically. "Men are always on probation till they pass their final, beyond the grave."

This was so good, so grand an inspiration that Father Tim gave up the next ten minutes to a delightful inward and inaudible chuckle of self-congratulation, intensified by Luke's frightened solemnity. Then he relented.

"Don't mind an old cynic, Luke," he said. "Diogenes must growl from his tub sometimes."

"By the way, Luke," said Father Martin, "you are mighty modest. You never told us of your triumphs at the last exam. He swept everything before him," he said, in an explanatory tone to Father Pat, the host. The latter was embarrassed for a moment, but only for a moment.

"Did you expect anything else from his mother's son?" he asked. "Why, that's the cleverest woman in the three parishes. Mike Delmege wouldn't be what he is but for her to-day. But Luke,—did you see all his prizes?" he suddenly asked. "Ah! my dear fellow, if Luke had six years more, he'd have a library like Trinity College."

"Did you top the class in everything, Luke?" said Father Martin.

"Everything but Hebrew," said Luke blushing. "You know that there—"

He was about to enter into elaborate explanations of his comparative failure there, and a good deal of Masoretic and Syro-Chaldaic philology was on his lips; but somehow, he thought of the whole thing now without elation, nay even with a certain well-defined feeling of disgust. That little reverie there above the sea, in which he saw, as in a mirror, the vanity and futility of these transitory and worthless triumphs, had well-nigh cured him of all his pride and elation; but he was wondering, between the vibrations of pleasure and disgust, at the eccentricities of men, now regarding his academical triumphs with contemptuous indifference, and again attaching to them an importance which his common sense told him was not altogether the vaporings of mere flattery. In fact, men and their ever-varying estimates of human excellence were becoming enigmatic; and, to his own mind, therefore, their instability proved the very worthlessness of the things they praised and applauded.

"You are all right now for life, my boy," said Father Martin, timidly. "You have made your name, and it is as indelible as a birthmark. All you have got to do now is to look down calmly on us poor fellows, who never got an *Atque*."[1]

"That's true," said the venerable host. "Why, when his time comes for a parish, we must build a town for him. There will be nothing in this diocese fit for him."

"They'll make him Vicar-Apostolic or Bishop, or something over there," said Father Martin. "He'll become a regular John Bull. If any fellow attempts to examine you for faculties, tell him you are a gold-medallist and he'll collapse."

"Or pitch *Cambrensis Eversus* at his head," said Father Pat.

"Well, I'm commencing well, whatever," said Luke, entering into the fun.

"So you are, my boy, so you are," said the host, encouragingly. "If you'd only take to the wine of the country, you'd infallibly rise in the profession."

"I'm dining with the Canon on Sunday," said Luke, demurely.

"What?" cried all in chorus.

"Had you the courage?"

"There's no end to the impudence of these young fellows!"

"My God!" said Father Tim, solemnly and slowly.

"The next thing will be your asking him down to dine at Lisnalee," said the host.

"And why not?" said Luke, flushing angrily. "What discredit is there in dining under the roof of an honest man?"

---

[1] The lowest college distinction.

"And why not?" said Father Pat, musingly.

"And why not?" said Father Tim, as from afar off.

"And why not?" said Father Martin, looking down mournfully on the young priest. Then the latter began to put a lot of turbulent and revolutionary questions to himself. Am I not a priest as well as he? Why should he not meet my mother and sisters, as well as I am expected to meet his relatives, if he has any? Who has placed this mighty chaos between us, as between Lazarus and Dives? It is all this infernal, insular, narrow-minded, fifteenth-century conservatism that is keeping us so many hundred years behind the rest of the world. Could this occur in any other country? And who will have the courage to come forward and pulverize forever this stiff, rigid formalism, built on vanity and ignorance, and buttressed by that most intolerable of human follies—the pride of caste?

"By Jove, I'll ask him," said Luke, aloud.

"No, my boy, you won't. Don't practice that most foolish of gymnastics—knocking your head against a stone wall."

"Then I won't dine with him," said Luke, determinedly.

"Oh, but you will," said Father Pat, admiringly. "Did ye ever see such an untrained young colt in all your lives? Now, you'll go on Sunday and dine with the Canon; and I think, if we can put our experiences together, you won't make any egregious mistakes. Where will we begin, Father Martin? Stand up and show Luke how to take the ladies in to dinner."

"Tell your experiences, Pat," said Father Martin, good-humoredly. "That will serve as a manual of etiquette—I mean your mistakes."

"I never made but one mistake," said Father Pat, with a show of pretended anger, "but that excluded me from the Kingdom of Heaven forever. It was all about one or two little beggarly peas. I had dined well—at least as well as could be expected when you have to have your eye on your plate and on your host at the same time. I was flattering myself that I had got through the miserable business with flying colors, when some evil spirit put it into my head to pick up a few little peas that lay upon my plate. Now, I didn't want them, but the old boy put them there. I put my fork gently upon one. It jumped away like a grasshopper. Then I tried Number Two.

Off he went like a ball of quicksilver. Then Number Three. The same followed, until they were gyrating around for all the world like cyclists on a cinder track. Then I got mad. My Guardian Angel whispered: 'Let them alone.' But my temper was up; and there I was chasing those little beggars around my plate, for all the world like the thimble-riggers at a fair. Now, I firmly believe there's something wrong and uncanny about peas; else, why does the conjurer always get a pea for his legerdemain; and that's the reason, you know, the pilgrims had to put peas in their shoes long ago as a penance, and to trample them under foot. Well, at last, I said: 'Conquer or die!' I looked up and saw the Canon engaged in an engrossing conversation with a grand lady. Now or never, I said to myself. I quietly slipped my knife under these green little demons and gobbled them up. I daren't look up for a few seconds. When I did, there was the Canon glowering on me like a regular Rhadamanthus. I knew then I was done for. He said nothing for a few days. Then came the thunder-clap. 'I could forgive,' he said, in his grandiose way, 'your solecisms—ha—of speech; your ungrammatical and—ha—unrecognized pronunciations; but to—eat—peas—with—a—knife! I didn't think that such a dread mortification could be in store for me!' He never asked me to dine from that day to this,—for which I say, with a full heart, *Deo Gratias*. But Luke, old man, look sharp. Let me see. Give him a few hints, Tim! Martin, try and brush up your etiquette."

"Tell me," said Father Tim, in his own philosophical way, "tell me, Luke, could you manage to hold a wineglass by the stem?"

"Certainly," said Luke.

"And hold it up to the light?"

"Of course," said Luke.

"Could you, could you, bring yourself to sniff the wine, and taste ever so little a drop, and say: Ha! that's something like wine! That *Château Yquem*, sir, is the vintage of '75. I know it, and I congratulate you, sir, upon your cellar!"

"I'm afraid not," said Luke, despondently.

"If you could, you were a made man for life," said Father Tim.

"Do you know anything about flowers?" he asked after a long pause.

"I think I know a daisy from a buttercup," said Luke, laughing.

"Could you bring yourself—you can if you like—to give a little start of surprise, somewhere about the middle of dinner, and gasp out in a tone of choking wonderment: Why, that's the *Amaranthus Durandi!* I was always persuaded that there was but one specimen of that rare exotic in Ireland, and that was in the Duke of Leinster's conservatory at Carton!"

Luke laughed and shook his head negatively.

"You lack the *esprit,* the courage of your race, me boy," said Father Tim. " 'Tis the dash that gains the day; or, shall I call it," he said, looking around, "impudence?"

After a long pause, he resumed:—

"Did ye ever hear of a chap called Botticelli?"

"Never!" said Luke, laughing.

"Why, my dear fellow, your education has been shockingly neglected. What were you doing for the last six or eight years that you never heard of Botticelli?"

"Somehow, I managed to get on without him," said Luke. "What was he—a cook?"

"No use," said Father Tim, shaking his head; "he'll be turned out ignominiously, and we'll all be disgraced."

"I'm afraid," said Father Martin, " 'tis too late now, Tim, to give him lectures on botany or the old masters; we must be satisfied with telling him what not to do."

"I suppose so. Go on, Martin," said Father Tim, resignedly.

"Don't eat out of the front of the spoon!" said Father Martin.

"Don't make any noise when eating; no more than would frighten a rabbit," said Father Pat.

"As you value your soul, don't put your hands on the table, between the dishes," said Father Tim.

"You're a teetotaller, aren't you?" said the host. "You're all right, tho' he thinks it vulgar; and so it is, horribly vulgar. But you won't be tempted to ask any one to drink wine with you. He'd never forget that."

"Don't say 'please' or 'thank you' to the servants for your life. He thinks that a sign of low birth and bad form," said Father Tim.

"Is there anything else?" said Father Martin, racking his memory. "Oh, yes! Look with some contempt at certain dishes, and say No! like a pistol-shot. He likes that."

"If he forgets to say 'Grace,' be sure to remind him of it," said Father Pat.

"Oh, yes! of course, and won't he be thankful?" said Father Tim.

"Well, many thanks, Fathers," said Luke, rising. "I must be off. Not much time now with the old folks at home!"

"Tell Margery we'll all be down for tea, and she must play all Carolan's airs—every one," said Father Pat.

"All right," said Luke, gaily.

He had gone half-way down the field before the curate's house when he was peremptorily called back. There had been a consultation evidently.

"We were near forgetting," said Father Tim, anxiously, "and 'twould be awful, wouldn't it?"

The other two nodded assent.

"If by any chance he should ask you to carve—"

"Especially a duck," chimed in Father Martin—

"Say at once that your mother is dead—that you know she is—and cut home for the bare life, and hide under the bed."

"All right, Father Tim, all right!" said Luke, laughing.

"But couldn't you manage about that wineglass—just to shut one eye, and say what I told you?" said Father Tim, in a pleading tone.

"No! No!" said Luke, "never!"

"By the way," said Father Martin, "do you know anything about poultry? Do you know a Dorking from a Wyandotte?"

But Luke had vanished.

"What are these professors doing in these colleges, at all, at all?" said Father Martin, when the trio returned mournfully to the table. "Why do they turn out such raw young fellows, at all, at all?"

"Why, indeed?" said Father Tim.

"Hard to say," said Father Pat.

CHAPTER IV

Dies Magna, Et—Amara

"FATHER LUKE, if you please, Miss," said Mrs. Delmege to her youngest daughter, Margery. I regret to say that that young lady was an incorrigible sinner in this respect; and this maternal correction was required at least ten times a day during the brief, happy days that Luke was now spending at home. It was "Luke," "Luke," "Luke," all day long with Margery; and the mother's beautiful pride in her newly ordained son was grievously shocked.

"You think he's no more than the rest of ye," said Mrs. Delmege, "but I tell you he is. He is the anointed minister of God; and the biggest man in the land isn't aiqual to him."

But how could Margery help the familiarity in her sisterly anxiety that Luke should make a glorious *debut,* first at last Mass the following Sunday; and secondly,—and I regret to say that I fear it was deemed more important,—at the Canon's dinner-table on Sunday evening?

"Sure I'd rather he was home with us on the last Sunday he'll spend in Ireland," said Mrs. Delmege. "And sure Father Pat could come up, and we could have a nice little dinner for 'em. But, after all, when the Canon asked him, it would never do to refuse. Sure it's just the same as the Bishop himself."

"I know that horrid Mrs. Wilson and her grand, proud daughter will be there, and that they'll be looking down on poor Luke—"

"*Father* Luke, Miss! How often must I be telling you?"

"Very well, mother. Be it so. But Luke and I were always playmates, and it sounds more familiar."

"But you must remember that Luke—ahem! Father Luke—is no longer a gossoon. He's a priest of God, and you must look on him as such."

36

"Of course, of course, mother, but I know they'll make him uncomfortable with all their airs and nonsense. To see that Barbara Wilson walk up the aisle on Sunday is enough to make any one forget what they're about. You'd think it was the Queen of England. I wonder she doesn't go into the pulpit and preach to us."

"Wisha, thin, her mother was poor and low enough at one time. I remember well when the Canon was only a poor curate, like Father Pat, God bless him! and when his sister was—well, we musn't be talking of these things, nor placing our neighbors. Perhaps, after all, there's a good heart under all their grandeur."

"I wouldn't mind," said Margery, stitching on a button on the grand new stock she was making for Luke, "but Father Martin said the other night that Luke—"

"There agin," said the mother.

"Could teach half the diocese theology. But what do these people care? I know they look down on him, and he's so sensitive. He won't stand it, I tell you, Mother."

So the sisterly anxieties ranged over every possible accident to her idol until Sunday morning came. Ah! that was a great day at Lisnalee. They were going to see their best-beloved at the altar of God. And Luke was going to celebrate, there on the predella, where he had knelt thirteen years ago, and raised, with fear and awe, the very vestments he was going to wear to-day. And there, at the same wooden rails, had he received for the first time his Holy Communion; the first of the many times, as child, student, minorist, subdeacon, deacon, he had knelt amongst the poor and lowly, Sunday after Sunday, during his happy vacations. It was all over now. Never more would he kneel there with the congregation. "Friend, go up higher." He had heard the words, and henceforth he was to stand on high as a mediator and teacher, where hitherto he had been the suppliant and the pupil. The little church was crowded to the door; and when Luke appeared, holding the chalice in his hands, a thousand eyes rested on his youthful face. He had just had a brief but animated debate in the sacristy.

"Was he to read the 'Acts'?"

"Certainly."

"And the 'Prayer before Mass'?"

"Of course."

"He never could do it."

"He must; and read the publications, too; and, Luke, if you could muster up courage to say a few words to the congregation, they'd all be delighted."

But Luke drew the line there. Trembling, half from joy, half from fear, rigid as a statue, he went slowly and reverently through the sacred ceremonies, with what raptures and ecstasies, God only knows! Once, and once only, had Father Pat ("a proud man this day," as he described himself) to interfere. It was just at that sublime moment called the "Little Elevation," when Luke held the Sacred Host over the chalice, and raised both to God and the Father, and murmured, "Omnis honor et gloria." Just then a tear rolled down the cheek of the young priest, and Father Pat had to say:—

"Hold up, man; 'tis nearly all over now."

But it took some minutes before he could compose his voice for the *Pater Noster;* and ever after, no matter what other distractions he might have had in celebration, he never repeated that "Per ipsum, et cum ipso, et in ipso" without remembering his emotions at his first Mass.

Father Pat had provided for the young priest a modest breakfast in the sacristy. It was a wise provision, for he had serious work before him—no less than to impart his priestly blessing to each and all of the vast congregation. It was a touching and impressive sight. There they knelt on the hard shingle—young and old, rich and poor, all reduced by their common faith to a dead level of meekness and humility; and the poor beggarwoman or *bodach,* who cringed and whined during the week at some farmer's house, now felt that here was neutral ground, where all had equal rights, and where no distinction was acknowledged. And so the brilliant sunshine gleamed through the whispering leaves, and fell on gray hairs, or the rich auburn tresses of some young girl, or the fair gold of some child; and through the green twilight the young priest passed, uncovered and full of emotion, as he laid his hands on some old playmate or schoolfellow, or some venerable village-teacher to whom he had been taught to look up with veneration from his childhood. And the little children doubled around trees, and shot down to the end of the *queue* to get a second

blessing, or even a third; and many were the boasts heard in
school that week of the many times some curly-headed youngsters had stolen the young priest's blessing. But was it all sunshine and music? Well, no! You see it never is. There must be
gray clouds to bring out the gold of the summer sun; and there
must be a discordant note to emphasize the melodies that sing
themselves to sleep in the human heart. And so, just a wee,
wee whisper blotted out for the moment all this glory, and
hushed the music that was kindling into a full-throated ora-
torio in the breast of the young priest. He was pushing his way
gently through the crowd that was jammed at the narrow gate
which led into the chapel yard, when he heard just in front of
him, and so near that he touched the rough frieze coat of the
speaker, these words:—

"But it is quare that he has to go on the furrin' mission. Sure,
'tis only thim that can't pay for theirselves in college that has to
go abroad."

"How do we know? Perhaps, after all, Mike Delmege is
not the shtrong man we tuk him to be."

"And I hard that Bryan Dwyer's son, over there at Alta-
mount, is goin' into the college to be a Dane, or somethin'
grate intirely."

"And sure they wint to college thegither. And if this young
man"—he threw his thumb over his shoulder—"is the great
scollard intirely they makes him out to be, why isn't he sint
into the college instid of goin' abroad?"

"Well, Father Pat, God bless him! says that Luke had no
aiqual at all, at all, in Manute."

"I suppose so. Mike Delmege has a warm corner; and sure
I see a fine flock of turkeys in the bawn field. Wan or two of
'em will be missin' soon, I'm thinkin'."

"I suppose so. Did ye notice how narvous the young priesht
was at the 'Acts'? Why, my little Terry could do it betther.
And what did he want bringing in the Queen for?"

"He's practicin'. He's goin' to England, I undershtand; and
he must pray for the Queen there."

"Begor, I thought the Church was the same all over the
wurruld. Wan Lord—wan Faith—wan Baptism—"

"Sh!" said his neighbor, nudging him; and Luke went home
with a very bitter sting in his chalice of honey.

It was not exactly the unkind allusions made by these ignorant cottiers, or the ill-concealed sarcasm about his own dearest ones, that nettled him. These things, indeed, were ugly, irritating facts; and to a proud spirit, they were doubly galling on such a day of triumph. But the Bishop had ignored him and his successes, and had kept at home and placed in a position of honor in his native diocese a student who had never distinguished himself in college, or even appeared amongst the successful *alumni* at the great day of distribution. What was all this? Had not the Bishop smiled on him, and congratulated him, and told him how he reflected honor on his diocese? And now he should go abroad for six or seven years, whilst his junior, a distinctly inferior man, was lifted over the heads of thirty or forty seniors, and placed at once in a responsible position in the Diocesan Seminary! Luke was choking with chagrin and annoyance. He put his hand to his forehead mechanically, and thought he found his laurel crown no longer the glossy, imperial wreath of distinction, whose perfume filled half the world, but a poor little corona of tinsel and tissue-paper, such as children wreathe for each other around the Maypole of youth.

He was very morose in consequence; and, when he entered the house, and found all gathered for the midday meal, he looked around without a word, and without a word passed the threshold again, and moved down toward the sea.

"Poor boy!" said the mother, affectionately; "that last Mass was too much for him, entirely. And sure I thought the people would ate him."

But Margery, with the affectionate instinct of a sister, saw deeper, but only said:—

" 'Tis this great dinner this evening that's troubling him. I wish he were left at home with us."

Luke crossed the fields rapidly, and then lightly jumping over a stile, found himself in one of those unfenced fields that slope down to the sea. A few sheep, nibbling the burnt grass lazily, scampered away; and Luke, jumping the rugged stones of a rough wall, found himself in a fisherman's cottage. The family were at dinner, and Luke, taking off his hat, said cheerily in the Irish fashion:—

"God bless the work! and the workmen too!"

"Wisha, thin, God bless you, Master Luke, and 'tis you're a

thousand times welcome! Mona, get a chair for the priesht."

"And this is my little Mona," said Luke, affectionately; "dear me, how she is grown!"

"And she got your reverence's blessing this morning, glory be to God! Wisha, thin, Master Luke, how my heart swelled whin I saw you at the althar."

"And wasn't Moira there?" said Luke. "Where is Moira?"

Moira was making her toilette, if you please, but now came forward blushing. Mona and Moira were twins, and it was Luke who insisted that they should be called Irish names.

"I have not much to boast of myself," he said, "but 'tis a shame that our little children should not be called by their beautiful Celtic names."

"This little fellow," said the father, pointing to a child, who was trying to choke himself with milk and potatoes, "was watching your reverence all the time. And sure, whin he come home, nothin' would do him but to get up on a chair, and say the 'Dominis wobiscum' like any priest. Wisha, who knows? Quarer things happen."

"I was thinking of taking a pull in the little boat," said Luke; "I see the oars and rowlocks in their old places. Is she staunch and sound as ever?"

"Staunch as ever, your reverence," the fisherman replied. "Will you want one of the byes?"

"No! I'll manage by myself. If you give me a hand to float her, I'll do the rest."

"And a good hand ye are at the oar, Father Luke," said one of the boys. "Begor, ye could turn her agin any of us."

"Now, now, now, no Blarney, Dermot! No, no, one will do! I'll keep her out for an hour or two."

"Just as long as your reverence plases," said the old man. "And, as the day is hot, we'll take down the sail, and make a yawnin' of it."

Luke pulled slowly out to sea; and the swift exercise, and the ever-changing aspects of the ocean, and the invigorating breeze, drew his thoughts away from the perplexing and irritating subjects that had lately been vexing him. There is something, after all, in what poets have sung about the soothing influences of Nature. Her mother's hand smooths down all the ruffled aspects and angry asperities of human feeling and thought; and her great silence swallows up in a kind of infinite peace, as of heaven, the buzzing and stinging of that hive of hornets, where

"Each one moves with his head in a cloud of poisonous flies."

No wonder that the best of the world's workers have sought peace in communion with the solitude of Nature, and strength from the great sublime lessons she teaches to those who sit at her feet. And it was with the greatest reluctance, and only by a tremendous effort, that Luke Delmege, this momentous day in his life, turned away from the sybaritic temptation of yielding himself up wholly to the calm and placid influences of sun, and sky, and sea; and, like so many other fools, sought peace, the peace that lay at his feet unsought, in a dread introspection of self, and a morbid and curious analysis of men's principles and thoughts about himself and his little place in the world. It was his first great plunge into the feverish and exciting pastime of analyzing human thought and action; and then trying to synthesize principles that shrank from each other, and became a torture and a pain from the impossibility of ever reconciling their mutual antagonism and repellence. It was the fatuous dream that Luke pursued through life with all the passion of a gambler around the green cloth; and it beckoned him away from work of solidity and permanence, and left him in middle-age a perplexed and disappointed man.

In another way, however, this was no novel experience. Very often, during his summer holidays, when his ambition had been stimulated by his academic successes to work more freely and largely for further distinctions, he had lain down in this same boat, and, looking up at the blue eye of Heaven, he had spent hours in revolving the terminology and meaning of some philosophical or theological puzzle, and had reviewed all the authors, and all the authors' opinions that had been arrayed for and against it. It was a practical and useful way of imprinting on memory all that books could tell; and very often, in the winter months that followed, he fell back gratefully on these *al fresco* studies, and the immense storehouse of matter he had accumulated with the sun as his lamp, and his desk the heaving sea. But this morning, as he rocked in the thwarts of his sea-cradle, and heard nothing but the chirp of a sea-lark, or the scream of a sea-gull, or the gentle lapping of the pure green water within six inches of where he lay, he had commenced the prœmium of the vaster studies, where no authors were to be trusted and experience alone could teach. But he was commencing his singular and irremediable mistake of supposing that the elusive and ever-changing moods of the human heart could be reduced by propositions to a level rule, and that human action was controllable always by those definite principles that he had been taught to regard as fixed and unchangeable truths.

Once and again, indeed, he raised himself a little, and allowed his eyes to wander over the beautiful, peaceful prospect that lay before him. Lap, lap, sang the tiny, sunny waves. He stretched out his burning hand, and they clasped it in their cool palms. He saw far away the green fields, as they sloped from the sea and were half dimmed in a golden haze. White specks, which he knew were the gentle sheep, dotted the verdure here and there; and great patches of purple heather stretched down and blended their rich colors with the deep red of the rocks, which again was darkened into cobalt, that the gentle waves were now fringing with white. Look long, and rest in the vision, O troubled soul! Why should the murmur of a few mites beyond that horizon of peace trouble thee? Altogether, thou art forgotten, there in thy Nautilus-boat on the bosom of the mighty deep. Cast from thee care, and forget the stings of the wasps who dare not come hither to fret thee! Alas! and is it not true of us, that we must have the bitter myrrh in our wine of life; and that we create cares for the luxury of fretfulness, where the world has left us in peace?

"There are two ways of looking at this question," said Luke in his soliloquy, as if he were addressing a class of students, "the subjective and the objective. Let us take the latter first as the more reasonable. Why should I be troubled because I am going to England and my class-fellow to the seminary? Which is the better prospect? Which would you select, if the matter were left to yourself? To see a new country, to get on to the gangway of the world, where all types of races are passing to and fro in endless variety, or to be shut up in a vulgar little place, teaching *Musa, Musae* to a lot of snivelling schoolboys, and decimal fractions to a crowd just freed from a country National school? To stand in the pulpits of cathedrals, and speak to an intelligent and well-read audience, those wonderful things you have been reading in Suarez or St. Thomas, or to blind yourself poring, night after night, over the *Georgics* of Virgil, or the *Anabasis?* To deal with inquiring, anxious minds, who listen to you breathlessly for the key to the mighty problems that are agitating them in their uncertainty and perplexities; to have the intense gratification of satisfying honest inquiry, and leading into the fold truthful but darkened souls, who will look up to you as their spiritual Father forevermore, or to lead successfully through a concursus a few brats, who are punning on your name, and drawing caricatures of your face on their greasy slates?"

"Ridiculous!" said Luke, aloud.

"But let us see the subjective side. You, Luke Delmege, First of First, that is Senior Wrangler in the first ecclesiastical college in the world, have been set aside coolly, but contemptuously, and the preference of a diocesan honor has been given to a student admittedly and distinctly your inferior! You have got a slap in the face from your bishop, not so gentle, though more metaphorical, than when he touched your cheek in Confirmation and said—(was it sarcasm? God forbid!)—*Pax tecum!* You are snubbed before the diocese; the stigma will cling to you during life, and be reflected on your family! Does not this arrangement imply that, in some respect, morally, of course—in character, in the power of ruling and governing, or teaching, you are distinctly inferior to your humble classmate? You know St. Thomas better; but *he* says his prayers better, my dear Luke! There is your distinct inferiority; and you see now how wise that old mediaeval monk was when he said:—

'Tunc videbitur sapiens in hoc mundo fuisse, qui pro Christo
   didicit stultus et despectus esse.'
'Tunc amplius exaltabitur simplex obedientia, quam omnis se-
   cularis astutia.'
'Tunc plus laetificabit pura et bona conscientia, quam docta
   philosophia.'
'Tunc plus valebunt sancta opera, quam multa pulchra verba.'

"Yes, yes," cried Luke, impatiently, as the boat rocked beneath him; "but that's all 'tunc!' 'tunc!' What about 'nunc!' 'nunc'? Can it be that men's judgments are like God's? Then why was so much stress laid upon our studies? Why were we applauded as brilliant and successful students? Why were we stimulated to study by every human incentive that could be held out to us? Why did the Bishop himself congratulate me if he had other ideas? Was there ever such a puzzle as the ways of men? The Sphinx and the Isis-Veil were nothing to them! Then I'll fall back on the realities—the objectiveness of things. There alone is truth. But is it truth?" said the puzzled young priest. He had never read:—

"Only this I have known, that God made man right, but he entangleth himself in an infinity of questions."

CHAPTER V

A Novel Thesis

"THERE is the Angelus, Luke," said Margery Delmege, anxiously, as Luke came in from the fields holding his Breviary open with one finger. "Hurry up, you'll hardly be in time; and it won't do to keep grand people waiting."

Luke did not reply. He had read somewhere of a saint who was reading the *Mirabilia* of None when a great monarch was announced, and he went on calmly reading. "He was in audience with the 'King of Kings.' " So Luke read on to the end, not noticing his sister's anxiety. Then he said the *Sacrosanctae,* and then:—

"Well, Margy, you were saying something?"

"I said you'll be late, and that won't do. There are your cuffs, and I put in your best sleeve-links; and let me see your collar. You must change that. Why, 'tis all damp. What have you been doing?"

Luke looked calmly down on the black tresses of his beloved sister, as she fussed and worried about his toilette.

"A regular Martha!" he whispered.

"Martha or no Martha, you *must* be turned out of this house decently. Mind, come home early—that is, as early as politeness will allow. And if that horrid Miss Wilson says anything offensive,—I'm sure she will,—treat her with silent contempt."

"All right, Margy. That's just in my way."

"And come home early, mind. Father Pat will be here to tea; and—what else?"

"Never mind, Margy. We'll resume the thread of our narrative in another chapter."

Margy watched his fine, tall figure as he swung down along the road, and then went back to get the tea things ready, but with misgivings and forebodings.

46

The irritation of the morning had one good effect. It had steeled Luke's nerves, so that it was quite in a self-confident, jaunty way he pulled the bell vigorously at the Canon's residence, and then gave a more timid knock. He was ushered into the drawing-room by the tidy little servant, and announced as "Father Delmege." Then he was frozen into ice. The two elderly ladies, dressed in black silk, with thin gold chains around their necks, looked at him for a moment, and then turned to each other.

"As I was saying, my dear, the report is that they are separated, or going to be. It couldn't end otherwise. All these naval fellows, you know, coming up there at all hours—well, well, we musn't be uncharitable."

The only other occupant of the room was a young man about six-and-twenty years of age, who, faultlessly dressed in evening costume, leaned languidly against the mantelpiece, and would have looked ineffably bored but that he appeared to derive untold gratification from the contemplation of his face in the looking-glass over the mantelpiece. Indeed, to further this ecstatic reveries, he had put aside carefully two bronze vases that held summer flowers, and had even pushed away the clock with the singing birds that had fascinated Luke a few days before. And let it be said at once that the reflected image was, without doubt, a beautiful one. A face, olive pale, was surmounted with a dark mass of hair that fringed and framed it to perfection, and through the tangled curls, a faultlessly white hand was just now running, and tossing them hither and thither with careful indifference. Two blue-black eyes looked steadily out from that white face, or rather would look steadily if they were allowed. But just now it seemed an effort to look at anything but that fair figure in the quicksilver. Languor, deep, somnolent languor, was the characteristic of this youthful face and figure; and a pained expression, as if the anticipation of the evening's pleasures was an unmitigated annoyance. He looked calmly at the young priest, and then resumed his studies. Luke, chilled and frozen, sank into a chair, and began to turn over the leaves of an album. Alas! he had not unloosed the clasp, when a very musical box chirped out: *"Within a mile of Edinboro' Town."* He closed the album hastily, but too late. On went that dreadful tinkling. He took up a book called *Celebri-*

ties of the Century. He was beginning to be interested, when the door shot open, and another guest, a solicitor, was announced. He was warmly welcomed by the ladies, got a languid nod and "Howda" from the Phidian Apollo, and took no notice whatever of Luke. He sank quietly into the sofa, and commenced the "clitter-clatter" of good society. Then the door opened again, this time to reveal unannounced a fair girlish form, and a face very like that of Apollo, but toned down by feminine taste into features that were singular in their beauty, but excluded all appearance of singularity. Luke was prepared for another cold douche of good society manners; but Barbara Wilson walked straight towards him, held out her hand, and said:—

"Father Delmege, you are ever so kind to come. Mother, this is Luke Delmege, of whom we have heard so often. This is my aunt, Father Delmege. Louis, have you met Father Delmege?"

The Phidian Apollo turned languidly around; and without removing his hand from his pocket, he nodded, and said:—

"Howda?"

"Mamma, you missed such a treat this morning. It was Father Delmege's first Mass; and oh! it was beautiful! And dear Father Pat was there, and the sun was resting on his beautiful white hair, like a nimbus. And we all got Father Delmege's blessing, and why didn't you preach? We were dying to hear you—"

"Well," said Luke, "you know, Miss Wilson, it is not customary to preach at one's first Mass—"

"Ah, of course, on ordinary occasions. But we wanted to hear you, you know. Where is the blue ribbon? Why don't you wear it?"

"The 'blue ribbon'?" said Luke, in amazement.

"Yes. Didn't you carry off the 'blue ribbon' in Maynooth? Father Martin said that there hadn't been so distinguished a course in Maynooth for over fifty years."

"Father Martin is too kind," murmured Luke, who had now thawed out from his icy loneliness, and felt grateful beyond measure to this gentle girl, who had, with the infinite and unerring tact of charity, broken down all the icy barriers of good society. Mrs. Wilson and her sister woke up, and manifested a little interest in the young athlete. The solicitor rubbed his hands, and murmured something about his old friend, Mike Delmege, "as good a man, sir, your respected father, as is to be found in the Petty Sessions District;" and even Apollo paused from his hair-teasing, and looked with a little concern and some jealousy at Luke.

Then the Canon entered with one or two other visitors, who had been transacting business with him, and dinner was announced.

"No, no," said Barbara to her uncle, in reply to an invitation; "I intend to sit near Father Delmege during dinner. I have lots to say to him."

Ah, Margy! Margy! thought Luke, what rash judgments you have been guilty of! Won't I surprise you with all the goodness and kindness of this contemptuous young lady?

The dinner was simple, but faultless. The conversation simmered along on the usual topics—sports, which occupied then a considerable share of public interest in Ireland. One young champion was especially applauded for having thrown a heavy weight some incomputable distance; and his muscles, and nerves, and weight, and training were all carefully debated. If ever we become a wealthy people, our national cry will be that of the ancient Romans—*Panem et Circenses!* Then came the Horse Show that was to be held in August. Here the ladies shone by their delightful anticipations of the great Dublin carnival. Then the Flower Show, just coming on in a neighboring town. Here the Canon was in his element, and said, with an air of modest depreciation, that he had been assured that:—

"My Marshal Niel—ha—shall certainly carry First Prize; but I know that my Gladiolus Cinquecentus will be beaten. A happy defeat! for Lady—ha—Descluse has assured me that this time at least I really must give her the—ha—victory."

"But, my dear Canon," said the solicitor, as if giving not a legal, but a paternal advice, and in a tone full of the gravest solicitude, "you ought not, you know. I assure you that a victory of this kind is not to be lightly sacrificed. Consider now the money value of the prizes—"

"Ha! Ha!" laughed the Canon, "the legal mind always runs into—ha—practical issues. The days of chivalry are gone."

"Well, now," said the solicitor, humbly, "of course, sir, you must have your little joke; but seriously now, consider the importance of gaining a prize in such a contest. After all, you know, horticulture is a branch of aesthetics; and you know, sir, with your vast experience, how important it is for the Church nowadays to be represented, and represented successfully, before our separated brethren, in such a delightful and elevating and refining pursuit as the culture of flowers."

"Ah, well, Mr. Griffiths; but chivalry—where is chivalry?"

"Chivalry is all very well," said Griffiths, driving home the argument, "but our first interest is—our one interest is—the Church. And consider your position—the leading representative of the Church in this district—I might say in this country. See what a dreadful injury to religion it would be if you were defeated, sir. Of course, 'tis only a flower; but it's defeat! and the Church, sir, mustn't be defeated in anything or it succumbs in all."

"There is something in what you say—ha—indeed," replied the Canon, "and I shall—ha—give the matter further consideration. But take a glass of wine."

"Ah, this *is* wine," said Griffiths, sniffing the glass and holding it up to the light. "Now, if I may be so impolite as to venture to guess, I should say that wine cost a *centum* at least."

"Add—a—twenty," said the host.

"I thought so. Very unlike the stuff we have to drink at our hotels, even on Circuit. Vinegar and water, and a little logwood to color it. This *is* wine."

"Mr. Sumner, you are taking nothing. Try that Madeira!"

Mr. Sumner was saying nothing, but he was steadily absorbing vast quantities of wine. He was one of those calm, beautiful drinkers, whose senses never relaxed for a moment whilst the new must was poured into the old bottle, and seemed to evaporate as speedily, as it was taken. Luke watched him wonderingly, and with a certain amount of admiration, and was stricken into silence partly by the surroundings, which to him were unique and awful, partly by the nature of the conversation, which tripped lightly from the muscles and calves of athletes to the fine points of a horse; and from the age of a certain brand of wine to the barometrical rise and fall of stocks and shares. He had been hoping in the beginning that the

course of conversation would turn on some of those subjects
that were of interest to himself—some great controverted point
in the literature or philosophy of the past, or some point of
heresy, or some historical fact that he could lay hold on, and
perhaps enchain the interest of his hearers. Wouldn't some one
say "Canossa," or "Occam," "Liberius," or even "Wegscheider"? Would they never turn the conversation into something
intellectual or elevating, and give him a chance? Once, indeed,
Barbara, in reply to an observation from her aunt that she was
killed from ennui in that country place, said laughingly:—

> "Lady Clara Vere de Vere,
> If time hangs heavy on your hands,
> Are there no beggars at your gate?
> Are there no poor about your lands?"

But alas! that was but a little puff of intellectual smoke
that speedily vanished in the clear atmosphere of utter inanity.
And Luke was bending over to say a complimentary word to
Barbara, when the silent signal was given and the ladies
arose. Luke was so absorbed in what he was saying that he
did not heed a gesture from the Canon. Then he awoke to the
thunder:—
"Father Delmege!"
and saw the Canon pointing angrily to the door. Poor Luke!
He had studied all his rubrics carefully, and knew them down
to every bend and genuflection; but he had never been told of
this rubric before. He blushed, stammered, kept his seat, and
said:—
"I beg your pardon. I do not understand—"
To add to his discomfiture, he found that Miss Wilson's
dress had got entangled around his chair. Blushing, humbled,
confused, he tried to disentangle the gray silk; but he only
made it worse. Then the Apollo arose with a calm smile,
raised the chair, gave the flounce a kick, and, opening the door
with a bow that would have made Count d'Orsay die with
envy, ushered the laughing ladies from the dining-room. The
Canon was so pleased with the achievement that he almost
forgave Luke; and Luke was questioning himself angrily:
Where now is all your learning and useless lumber? And why

the——do not the professors in our colleges teach us something about the practical issues of daily life?

"Anything new in your profession, Louis?" said the Canon, airily, as the gentlemen drew their chairs together and lighted their cigars.

"Oh, dear yes!" said Louis leisurely. "We are always forging ahead, you know; moving on with express speed, whilst you gentlemen of the Law and the Gospel are lumbering heavily along in the old ruts."

"Ha! Ha!" laughed the Canon. "Very good indeed! Lumbering along in the old ruts! And what might be the newest discoveries now in medical science? Some clever way of shortening human life?"

"Well, no! We are beginning to touch on your province, I think. Our sappers and miners are beginning to dig under your foundations."

"But you won't stir the grand old fabric, Louis?" said Griffiths. "You can't, you know. You'll find bones and skulls, of course; that's your province; but you'll never shake the foundations. Will he, Canon?"

"Oh, dear no! Oh, dear no!" said the Canon, feebly. "But those men of science are really—ha—very enterprising, and, indeed—ha—aggressive. But I cannot see, Louis, how your noble science can conflict with theology. The schools of medicine and the schools of theology are—ha—so very distinct."

"They merge in the psychological school, I should say," said Louis. "And psychology becomes physiology."

At last, at last, Luke, cometh your chance! Here is what you have been dreaming of the whole evening. Psychology! The very word he had rolled under his tongue a thousand times as a sweet morsel. The soul! the soul! Psyche, his goddess! whom he had watched and studied, analyzed, synthesized, worshipped with all the gods of science from the "master of those who know" downwards. No hound that had seen or scented his quarry was ever strung to such tension of muscle or nerve as Luke, when at last all the twilight vistas opened, and he saw the broad fields of knowledge and science before him, and Psyche, Psyche, like Atalanta in the fields at Calydon.

"How can psychology merge in physiology?" said Luke,

with dry lips, and in a nervous manner. "I always considered that physiology treated only of animal mechanism."

"And psychology treats of?" said Louis Wilson, blandly.

"Of—of—the soul, of course," said Luke.

"And is not the soul a part of the animal mechanism?" said his antagonist.

"Certainly not," said Luke. "It is conjoined with it and distinct from it."

"Conjoined with it! where?" said Louis. "I have made post-mortems again and again, and I assure you, gentlemen, I have discovered every other part of human anatomy; but that which you are pleased to call the soul, I have never found. Where is it? What is its location?"

"Now, now Louis," said the Canon, with feeble deprecation, "this is going far, you know. But, of course, this is only for the sake of —ha—ha—argument. This is only a—ha—post-prandial academic discussion. Proceed, Mr. Delmege."

Poor Luke was now getting a little excited. He had never been taught that first of accomplishments, self-control and reserve. Indeed, he had been so accustomed to success in the *theses* that had been arranged for students in his college, that he quite resented the very idea of being opposed or catechized by this young foppish doctor. When he folded his soutane in Maynooth and said, half-sarcastically, in the scholastic form:

"Sic argumentaris, doctissime Domine!"

his antagonist had gone down pell-mell before him. And the idea of this young freshman attacking the fortresses of Catholic philosophy was intolerable. In a word, Luke was losing temper.

"The veriest tyro in philosophy," he said (it was a favorite expression of his, when he wanted to overwhelm utterly an antagonist), "knows that the soul is a simple substance, residing, whole and indivisible, in every part of the human frame."

"This is part of the human frame," said Louis, pulling a long black hair from his forehead, "is my soul there? Then go, thou soul, into everlasting nothingness." He plucked the hair in pieces and let it fizzle away at the glowing end of his cigar.

"This is flippant, if not worse," said Luke. "No one holds that a separated member carries with it the soul."

"Do you not hold that there is a separate creation for each human soul?"

"Yes. That is of faith."

"Where's the necessity? If life springs from antecedent life (that is your strong point against biologists), and if the soul is existent in every part, when there is life, does not the soul pass on to the new life, and become the animating principle in its embryonic state?"

"That is heresy," said Luke. "That is the heresy of Tertullian. St. Thomas—"

"I thought," said his antagonist, blandly, "we were arguing as to facts, and not as to opinions."

"But I deny that opinions are opposed to facts," said Luke timidly.

"You may not be aware," said Wilson, "that the greater part of your treatises on Moral Theology are arranged with the most childish ignorance of physiological facts that are known to every school-boy who has passed his first medical."

"And are you aware," said Luke hotly, "that many of your profession who have passed their *last* medical are wise and humble enough to acknowledge that what you call facts are still the *arcana* and mysteries of Nature?"

"Perhaps so," said Wilson, airily. "But writers that lay down moral laws for the world, and base these laws on the operations of Natural Law, should try to understand these latter first. By the way, have you read anything of electro-biology?"

"No!" said Luke, humbly.

"Have you read anything about psychic forces through Animal Magnetism?"

"No," said Luke.

"Have you heard of Reichenbach and his theory of Odic Forces?"

Luke shook his head humbly. He was stunned by the noisy emptiness of words.

Wilson threw him aside as a worthless antagonist and addressed Sumner.

"Did you see the last by Maupassant, Sumner?"

"The last you lent me," said Sumner. "It is pretty tattered

now. But really, you know, Wilson, I think these French fellows go a little too far, you know. I'm not squeamish, you
know; but really, you know, that fellow makes your hair stand
on end."

Wilson laughed rudely and shrugged his shoulders.

"Men of the world musn't be squeamish about trifles—"

"Gentlemen," said the Canon, "I think we shall join the
ladies at tea."

"I shall give you a volume by Gabriele d'Annunzio, our
latest Italian writer," Luke heard Wilson saying to Sumner,
as he stood in the porch to finish his cigar. "Pity those young
clerical gentlemen don't read up with the requirements of the
day."

"I think you read too much, Wilson," said Sumner. "You
can't keep straight, you know, if you are too well acquainted
with these things, you know."

"Sumner, you have a hard head for liquor."

"It is not in the power of whiskey to make me drunk," said
Sumner, modestly.

"Well, I have a hard head in other matters," said Wilson.
"By the way, did you ever try laudanum?"

"No!" said Sumner. "I wouldn't venture beyond the bounds
of honest liquor."

"You ought. Nothing braces a man like it. You see there's
a total want of agility in these clergymen because they are
afraid of stimulants. I'm sure, now, my uncle would be almost
clever; but, you notice, he touches nothing. And that young
greenhorn—"

"Who?"

"That young clergyman—a mere farmer's son—do you
know that there is not on earth such a greenhorn as a clerical
student? Now, if he took a little opium, according to De Quincey's prescription, well boiled, and with plenty of lemonade or
orangeade, he would be passable—"

"Well, Louis, you bowled him over certainly."

"Yaas! I should say so. And good Lord! what an accent!
I wonder will he sing?"

CHAPTER VI

Adieux

◆

MORTIFIED AND irritated, vexed at himself for his short-comings, savage with others for their unkindness, Luke passed into the drawing-room. Somehow, his anger gave a tinge of pallor to his brown, healthy face, that made him look quite interesting; and it was with something like kindness that Mrs. Wilson beckoned him to a seat near herself on the sofa, and chatted affably with him for a few moments. She also engaged his services in helping around the tea from a dainty wicker-work table; and he was beginning to feel a little more comfort-able, though still determined to escape at the first opportunity, when the Canon asked him abruptly to turn over the leaves of the music on the piano, at which Barbara was now seated. Luke was about to excuse himself by saying with perfect truth that he knew nothing about music; but in a weak moment he rose, and whilst Miss Wilson's fingers wandered over the keys, he stood, statue-like and motionless, near her. In a few seconds she nodded, and he turned the leaf with the air of an expert; and then the full absurdity of the situation broke suddenly upon him, and dyed neck and face and up to the roots of hair in deep crimson of shame and confusion. For he remembered that at the last retreat a picture of a worldly priest was held up to their reprobation—a picture, not too highly colored, but grimly painted by a strong and merciless hand. There it was, lurid and ghastly, or pitifully ludicrous, as you choose or your mood may be—the limp, unmuscular, artificial cleric, who, with all the insignia of Christ and the Cross, is perpetually aping the manners and customs of the world, and in dress and manner and conversation is forever changing and shifting, like a mime on the stage. Ah! Luke! Luke! and hither hast thou

56

come, even on the day of thy first Mass. Burning with shame and self-scorn, he had sense enough left to whisper, "You will excuse me!" and retreated ignominiously to a corner, where, over the pages of an album, he thought unutterable things. He woke up, after what appeared to be an hour, by hearing the Canon say:—

"That duet from—ah—*Trovatore,* Barbara; or, perhaps, Louis would sing, 'Hear Me—ha—Gentel Maritana'!"

The two voices blended beautifully, and at another time Luke would have listened with pleasure, but not tonight. Oh, no! it has been a day of humiliation and suffering, and even the gentle spirit of Music for once fails to bring peace and healing on her wings.

There was a hushed and whispered colloquy between Barbara and her mother, and then the former, with some hesitation, approached to where Luke was sitting, and said timidly, holding her hands pleadingly before her:—

"Mother would like to hear you sing, Father. I'm sure you sing well—"

"I assure you, Miss Wilson, I'm quite unaccustomed to—"

"Now, I know you have a lovely baritone from the way you said the 'Prayers' to-day. Do, Father!"

What could he sing? "Believe Me, If All?" Hush! "Oh! Doth Not a Meeting Like This Make Amends?" Absurd! "There's a Bower of Roses by Bendameer's Stream?" Sickly and sentimental! Yes, he will, by Jove! He'll take a subtle revenge by ruffling the placidity of this smooth and aristocratic circle. Won't they laugh when they hear it at home? Won't Father Pat smite his leg like a Vulcan, and declare that it was the best thing he ever heard in his life? But it will be impolite and shocking! No matter! Here goes!

And drawing himself up to his full height, and leaning one arm on the mantelpiece, Luke sang out in the noble baritone, that had often echoed at Christmas plays around the gloomy halls of Maynooth—

"From Howth away to famed Dunboy,
   By Kerry's beetling coasts,
With lightning speed the summons flew
   To marshal Freedom's hosts.

> From Limerick's old historic walls
>   To Boyne's ill-omened tide
> The long-watched signal swelled their hearts } *bis.*
>   With Vengeance, Hope, and Pride."

The Canon was gasping and his face lengthening as in a spoon; the ladies smiled in horror; Apollo looked up, angry and contemptuous; Griffiths was about to say:—

"Now, you know, Father Delmege, that's rank treason, you know"—but on went Luke, his rich voice thundering out the song of rebellion in the ears of these excellent loyalists:—

> "They're mustering fast—see, Slievenamon
>   Its serried lines displays;
> Mark how their burnished weapons gleam
>   In morning's ruddy blaze;
> While proudly floats the flashing green
>   Where purl the Mague and Lee.
> Hurrah! my boys, we've lived, thank God, } *bis.*
>   To set the Old Land free!"

The Canon was shocked beyond expression; yet a tender old-time feeling seemed to film his eyes; for the Mague was rolling past his door, and the summit of Slievenamon could be seen from the window. Luke rapidly shook hands with the ladies, whilst Barbara, in her enthusiasm, asked:—

"Who wrote it? You *must* give me the words and the music, Father! 'Tis worth all the operas ever written."

He nodded to Griffiths, took no notice of the Apollo, shook hands with the Canon and thanked him for his hospitality, and dashed out into the cool air with a throbbing heart and a burning forehead.

He was pushing along in his swift striding way, and had reached the road, when he heard a flutter of silk behind him; and there was Barbara Wilson, a little out of breath and very white. He waited.

"Father," she said pleadingly, "I understand you are going on the English mission?"

"Yes," he said wonderingly.

"Might I ask where will you be?"

"I cannot say," he said, "but in one of the southeastern counties."

"Thank God," she said fervently. Then after some hesitation, and gulping down some emotion, "I want you to make a promise."

"If I may."

"You may meet my brother in England. He has been in Brighton, an assistant to a physician there. He is now in London attending St. Thomas' Hospital. If you meet him, will you be kind?"

"I'm not much attracted by your brother, Miss Wilson," Luke said bluntly.

"I know; but you are a priest, and his soul is at stake. You do not know, but I am afraid that he is—that he is—oh! my God! weak in his faith. You may be able to help him!"

"Of course, if I come across him in the course of my ministrations—"

"The Good Shepherd *sought out* the lost sheep," said Barbara.

"But, you know, one does not like a repulse," said Luke.

"It is a question of a soul," said Barbara, her eyes filling with tears.

"Say no more, Miss Wilson," said Luke, "you shame me. I heard your brother give expression to some shocking things this evening; and I confess I conceived a strong and violent aversion to him; but now that you have appealed—"

"Thank you, oh, so much! And there's something else about poor Louis—"

She put her fingers to her lip, musing. Then, after a pause, she said: "Never mind. You'll find it out for yourself; but you promise?"

"I promise," he said.

"And you won't allow his arrogance and pride to repel you?"

"I hope not," said Luke.

"God bless you!" she said fervently, clasping his hand.

"Hallo, old man! Alive and kicking?" was the cheery welcome of Father Pat, who, snugly ensconced in a capacious armchair in the parlor at Lisnalee, was stroking down the fair curls of a little lad, an orphan child of a younger brother, whom Mike Delmege had adopted. How calm, and simple, and homely the little parlor looked to Luke's eyes, dazzled and dimmed by the splendors of the Canon's house, and half-blinded from the emotions aroused during the evening. The image remained imprinted on the retentive retina of Luke's memory for many a day, and came up, amongst strange scenes and sights, to comfort him with its holy beauty. Often, in after years, when sitting at the tables of noblemen, who traced their blood back to the invaders, who bit the sands at Hastings, that cloud-dream of his seaside home rose soft and beautiful as a piece of enchantment raised to the witchery of soft music; and often, on the streets of Southwark at midnight, when the thunder of the mighty stream of humanity rolled turbid and stormy along the narrow streets, did he see, as in a far-off picture, narrowed in the perspective of memory, the white farmhouse above the breakers, and the calm, beautiful, twilight holiness that slept above it—a canopy of peace and rest. He saw the two windows that ventilated the parlor—the one looking northward over soft gray meadows and golden cornfields, that stretched away till they were lost in the purple and blue of the shadowy, mysterious mountains; the other looking southward over masses of purple heather, to where the everlasting sea shimmered in silver all day long, and put on its steel-blue armor against the stars of night. There was the teatable, with its cups and saucers and its pile of dainty griddlecakes, cut in squares, and fresh from the hands of Margery; and golden butter, the best that was made in the *Golden Vale;* and thick, rich cream; and fragrant strawberries, nestling in their grape-like leaves. And there was his good father, a stern old Irish Catholic of the Puritan type, silent and God-fearing and just, who never allowed a day to pass without an hour of silent communion with God, in his bedroom after the midday meal, and on whose lands the slightest whisper of indelicacy was punished by immediate expulsion. There sat the kindly mother, her beautiful white hair arranged under her snowy cap, and the eternal beads in her hands. There, gliding to and fro, was Margery—a perfect Martha of housewifely neatness and alertness; and Lizzie, the grave, thoughtful Mary of the household; and there was Father Pat, best and kindest and truest of friends, to whose arms children sprang for affection, and in whose hands the wildest collie or sheepdog was glad to lay his wet nozzle, after he had valorously defended his premises. Luke flung himself into the arm-chair by the southern window and asked Margery for a "decent cup of tea."

"Well, I suppose now you are fit to dine with the Duke of N——," said Father Pat. "You have passed your entrance examination into decent society tonight."

"It wasn't so severe an ordeal as I supposed," said Luke. "The Canon was kind; and Miss Wilson——"

Margery paused with the teapot high in air.

"Miss Wilson made everything easy."

Margery drew a long, deep breath of doubt, and shook her head.

"Do you know what I think, Father Pat?" said Luke.

"No. Go on," said Father Pat.

"That there's a lot of real kindness under all the Canon's formalism; and that he is at heart a good-natured man."

"Humph!" said Father Pat. "How did you come to that conclusion? For I have longer experience of him than you, and I have not reached it yet."

"Well, I don't know," replied Luke. "It is a little thing; but it is little things that tell. A straw, you know. I was singing——"

"You were singing?" said Father Pat.

"Did you really sing?" said Margery.

"What did you sing, Father Luke?" said Lizzie who was a more obedient pupil than her sister.

"I was just saying that when I was singing 'The Muster'——"

Father Pat jumped from his chair.

"You don't mean to say that you sang that red-hot rebel song in the Canon's presence?" he said.

"Every line of it," replied Luke, "and I have promised the words and the music to Barbara Wilson." He looked in a quizzical way at his sister.

"Well, I'm blessed," said Father Pat, resuming his seat, "but that beats Banagher. Wait till I tell Tim and Martin."

He looked at Luke with a certain feeling of awe during the rest of the evening.

"Well, I was saying," said Luke, coolly, "that I thought—

perhaps 'twas imagination—that the Canon's eyes softened, and that something like kindliness came into them, as from the memory of the past."

"Ay, indeed! and so well there might," said Mrs. Delmege. "I well remember when there wasn't a more tinder or more loving priest in the diocese than you, Father Maurice Murray. Sure 'twas well known that his sister had to lave him because he had not two shoes alike; and he used to stale the mate out of the pot to give it to the poor."

"I mind well the day," said old Mike Delmege, in a musing way, as if he was trying to call up a fast-vanishing picture, "when he wint in, and took up that poor girl, Bride Downey (she is now the mother of the finest childhre in the parish), out of her sick-bed, sheets, blankets, and all, and she reeking with the typhus, the Lord betune us and harm, and spotted all over like the measles, and took her over and put her in the van for the hospital, while all the people stood away in fright, and even the man from the workhouse wouldn't go near her. And it was you, Canon Murray, that arranged her bed in that workhouse van; and sure you took the faver, and went near dying yourself at the time."

"He's not the same man, Mike, since thin. They say the faver turned his head, and he got tetched," said Mrs. Delmege.

"No! but his grand sister, who ran away from the sickness, and wint up to Dublin, where she got into a castle or something, and married a big man, 'tis she that turned the poor man's head."

"I wish she had turned it the right way," said Father Pat, "for certainly 'tis screwed on the wrong way now."

"Father Martin says, too, that he is a rale good man under all his airs and nonsense—"

"Father Martin? No one minds him," said Father Pat; "he'd speak well of an informer or a landgrabber."

"Why, thin, now, Father Pat, no one knows as well as your reverence that there 'ud be many a poor family on the roadside today but for the same Canon. Sure they say that when they see his grand writing up in Dublin, with the turkey-cock on the top of the letther, and two swords crossed, that they'd give him all he ever asked for. And sure whin the Widow Gleeson was served last autumn, and there was nothing before her but

the workhouse, and the Canon wrote to the agent, but he had
only plain paper without the turkey-cock, they took no more
notice of him than if he was an ordinary poor counthry parish
priest. What did he do? He took the train up to Dublin, and
walked into the office. Phew! whin they saw his grand figure,
they ran into rat-holes before him. Believe you me, Father Pat,
there are very few priests in the country can make the Canon's
boast, that no little child will ever sleep in his parish without a
cover betune it and the stars."

"That's all right, Mike," said Father Pat; "but why doesn't
he keep his grand airs for grand people?—"

"Why," said Mike Delmege, "sure he must practice; and
where would he practice but on you and me?"

"Well, he might keep them for Sundays and holidays," said
Margery, who hated the whole lot, "or when his grand sister
and niece come down from Dublin, and speak plain to plain
people."

"True, Margery," said Father Pat; "we're a plain, simple
people, and we want plain, simple priests."

But somehow Margery didn't like that either.

"Luke," said Father Pat, buttoning up his coat, "do you
mean to say you're not joking, and that you sang 'The Muster'
tonight?"

"I was never so serious in my life," said Luke.

"You sang it all?"

"Every line!"

"Down to—

" 'No more as craven slaves we bend
    To despot, king, or queen;
    God shields the right,—strike sure and fast,
    'Tis for our native Green.' "

"Quite so!"

"And he didn't get a fit?"

"Not up to the time I was leaving."

"Well, he has got one now. I'll have a sick-call to him tonight. By Jove! what will Tim and Martin say? Well, let me
see! You're off on Friday. Tim will have you tomorrow;
Martin on Tuesday; you'll be with me on Wednesday. We'll

leave him to you, ma'am, on Thursday. Is that all right?"

"All right," said Luke.

"The best crachure that ever lived," said Mrs. Delmege, as Father Pat strolled down the moonlit field. Just at the stile he thought of something and came back. They were all kneeling, and Luke was reciting the Rosary. Father Pat heard the murmur of the voices, and paused. And there outside the window he took out his own Rosary beads and joined in that blessed prayer that echoes night after night from end to end of Ireland. Then he stole away quietly and mounted the stile.

"By Jove!" he said to himself, as he crossed shadow after shadow from the trees on the high hedges, "I believe he's in earnest. But who'd ever believe it? What will Tim and Martin say? We'll be talking about it till Christmas."

On Tuesday Luke called to see the Canon and make his adieux. He was not quite so nervous as on previous occasions, but he expected to receive a severe reprimand and a long lecture on his future conduct. Nor was he disappointed.

"I think it my duty," said the Canon, after they had exchanged preliminaries, "to say—ha—that there were a few things at our little—domestic meeting on Sunday which I—ha—could hardly approve of. Is it possible that you were never—ha—instructed by your professors to rise with the ladies after dinner, and hold the door open as they—ha—departed?"

"It is not only possible, but a fact," said Luke, with the old contentious spirit of logic-chopping coming back to him. "Besides, sir, I was engrossed at the time, and didn't hear you say 'Grace.'"

This was really good for Luke; but he didn't see how his rapier struck home.

"I can really hardly credit it," said the Canon. "It is painful to reflect that we alone should be supposed to learn, by—ha—some kind of intuition, the amenities of social intercourse."

The Canon was so pained that for a few moments there was dead silence, broken only by the ticking of the clocks.

"Then," he resumed, at length, " your *rencontre* with my—ha—clever nephew was hardly a happy one. I thought the interrelations between body and spirit were part of your—ha—philosophical curriculum."

"Your nephew was Christian enough to deny that there was

such a thing as soul at all," said Luke, flushing. The idea of being catechized on philosophy by this old man, who probably had never heard of a more recent writer than Tongiorgi or Liberatore! And all this to a "First of First"!

"Ha! that was only for a post-prandial argument," laughed the Canon. "But you lost temper and got confused. And you never heard of these—ha—Odic forces? Dear me! What are our professors doing? And with what singular equipments they furnish our young men for the battle of life!"

There was another spell of silence, during which Luke drew up to the bar of justice, and solemnly condemned his professors as a set of "effete old fossils."

"I should hardly," said the Canon, resuming, "care to allude to that—ah—ill-timed and rather vulgar—melody to which you treated us; but you are—ha—going to England, and your mission will be—ha—inoperative and ineffectual if you import into the ministrations of your daily ministry such treasonable principles as those contained in that—ha—street-ballad. You were never taught operatic music in Maynooth?"

"No, sir," said Luke; "it was sternly interdicted."

"Dear me! how reactionary! And it is so—ha—refining. Did you notice that pretty duet, 'Ai nostri monti'?" The Canon placed the tips of his fingers together.

"Yes, it was pretty," murmured Luke.

"And my nephew's rendering of 'Hear Me, Gen—tel Mari-tana'?"

"I did not follow that," said Luke.

"And then to compare that fiery *Marseillaise,* which you so unwisely, but, indeed, rather melodiously rendered! Do you think now really—ha—that 'Hurrah, me boys,' is an expression suited to a drawing-room audience, or do you not see that it would be more fitting in a street-corner ballad or the heavy atmosphere of a—ha—tap-room?"

Luke was silent and angry.

"It is quite possible," continued the Canon, "that you will be thrown a good deal into—ha—English society. You may be invited to dine with the—ha—aristocracy, or even the—ha—nobility. I hope, my dear young friend, that you will never forget yourself so far as to introduce into such lofty and refined circles such dithyrambic and—ha—revolutionary ballads as that under discussion."

Luke said nothing, but continued tracing the pattern of the carpet.

"You must sink your extreme national sensibilities," said the Canon, "in the superior ambitions of the Church, and take care not to offend the prejudices of our dear English brethren by too-pronounced references to those—ha—political issues on which we—ha—differ."

There was truth in all that the Canon was saying, though put rather brutally, and Luke had only to listen. Then there was a surprising change of front.

"I have written to the Bishop and obtained the requisite permission for you to celebrate three Masses in your father's house, not only now, but on all subsequent occasions when you may—ha—be resident in your paternal home—"

"Oh, thank you so much, Canon," said Luke, most gratefully; "that's a great favor."

The Canon went on, not noticing the ebullition.

"As I was saying—ha—I think this arrogation of rights that are parochial seems hardly consistent with Canon Law; but I have not insisted too warmly on my privileges as parish priest, lest I should seem wanting in the respect due to the lofty dignity of the episcopal bench. But I took—ha—the opportunity of remonstrating with His Lordship for having set aside one of my parishioners, and selected one of rather mediocre abilities, if I am rightly informed, for a position in the diocesan seminary which demands both talent and character."

Luke was at first bewildered. Then he saw through the Canon's kindness beneath his coat of buckram.

"I'm sure I'm greatly obliged to you, sir, for such trouble. I confess I did feel some annoyance at first, but now I should prefer to go to England."

"And I quite approve of your decision," said the Canon, suavely; "indeed, it is one of the chief regrets of my life that I was unable to graduate on the English mission. Nevertheless, the slight to my parishioner remains, and I shall not forget it."

Here the Canon sank into a reverie, as if meditating a subtle revenge against the Bishop.

"Do you know," he said, waking up suddenly, "anything of the science of heraldry?"

"No," said Luke, promptly.

"That's a very serious loss to you," replied the Canon;

"what *did* you learn, or how did you employ your time?"

"To tell the truth, I'm beginning to think," said Luke, "that whatever I learned is so much useless lumber, and that I must get rid of it somehow and commence all over again."

"A very proper resolution," said the Canon. "Now, let me see!—Delmege! That must be a French or Norman name. Could your family have been Huguenots?"

"They were Palatines," said Luke. "They lived over there at Ballyorgan in the valleys, and became Catholics several generations back."

"How very interesting!" said the Canon. "Our family, as you are aware, are Scotch—Murray, Moray. It was one of my ancestors who held the painter of the boat for Mary Queen of Scots when she was escaping from that castle, you know; and it was the great queen who, extending her gloved hand to my —ha—ancestor, gave our family its motto. 'Murray,' she said, 'Murray, *sans tache.*' I hope," continued the Canon, after a pause, "that I and my family will never bring a blot upon the fair escutcheon of our noble house."

Luke did not know exactly what to reply, but he was saved the trouble; for the Canon rose, and saying, in his most grandiose manner, "that he understood it was customary to demand —ha—a young priest's blessing," to Luke's consternation, the old man knelt humbly on the carpet. Luke repeated the words, but dared not, from old veneration, touch the white hair. And the Canon, rising, placed an envelope in his hands, and said:—

"When you have said your three Masses, kindly say ten Masses for me! Good-bye! I shall hope—ha—sometimes to hear of you from your excellent father. Good-bye!"

The astonished and bewildered young priest opened the envelope when he had passed out of sight of the presbytery, and took out, with mingled feelings of surprise and gratitude, a note for five pounds.

" 'Tis a queer world," said Luke. "I wonder when shall I understand it." If you value your peace of mind, Luke, let the mighty problem alone! It has vexed humanity from the beginning, and shall remain insoluble to the end. Find your work and do it. But who was ever content with this? Or what greatest sage was ever satisfied to look at the Sphinx of life without asking the meaning in her eternal eyes?

CHAPTER VII

En Route

THE NEXT few days passed pleasantly and cheerfully for Luke. The inestimable privilege of being able to say Mass in his father's house blessed and hallowed the entire day; and if occasionally he allowed himself to be tormented by the accidents and circumstances of life, or by grave questionings about men and their ways, all these vexatious troubles evaporated the moment he sat with his three clerical friends; and all jarring and dissonant sounds were merged and disappeared in the glorious dithyramb of friendship.

The three friends were known in the diocese as the "Inseparables." They formed a narrow and exclusive circle of themselves, and all candidates for admission were sternly blackballed. They dined together and supped together on all festive occasions. They took their summer holidays together at Lisdoonvarna; and there they insisted that their rooms should be on the same corridor and adjacent, and that their chairs should be placed together at the same table. At Kilkee, which is popularly supposed to be the hygienic supplement of Lisdoonvarna, just as the cold douche is supposed to wind up a Turkish bath, they bathed in the same pool or pollock hole, went together to Loop Head, or the Natural Bridges of Ross, fooled around during the hot day together; and if they ventured on a game of billiards after dinner, two played and the other marked. If any one else came in or interfered, the three walked away together. At home, they were equally exclusive. Every Sunday evening, winter and summer, they met, to "celebrate the Eleusinian mysteries," said jealous outsiders, but in reality to dine; and the dinner on each occasion, and at each table, never varied—chickens and ham, followed by a tiny piece of roast mutton;

68

one dish, generally of apples, as second course, and that was all. The only occasion when there was a shadow of a cloud between them was when Father Martin got a new housekeeper, and she treated her guests to what she was pleased to call a chancellor-pudding. The guests looked at it suspiciously, but declined to partake. Father Martin, always gentle and polite, made profuse apologies. "Give me the old horse for the long road," said Father Tim. So, too, the "Inseparables" held the same opinions on politics, the only difference being that Father Martin looked upon such things from a theoretical and academic standpoint, whereas Father Tim held himself passive, and Father Pat was disposed to be fiercely and relentlessly aggressive. Some said it was genuine, downright patriotism; some thought it was opposition to his pastor. No matter. There it was; and the great newspapers spoke of him as a "true soggarth, who was upholding, under difficult and trying circumstances, the noblest traditions of the Irish Church." These laudatory lines Father Pat had cut out, and pasted into the cover of the *Pars Aestiva* of his breviary, where they formed occasionally the subject of an *impromptu* meditation. And as these three excellent men were obliged to make their wills in conformity with the statutes of the diocese, it was understood (though this of course was a secret) that the two executors of him who should predecease the others were to be the survivors. What the last survivor was to do history does not tell.

And yet, with all the unbroken intimacy extending over many years, no three men could be more unlike in character, disposition, and education than the "Inseparables." Father Pat was an open-air priest, who lived in the saddle, and was the familiar and intimate of every man, woman, and child in the parish. We might say, indeed, in the three parishes; for his brother clerics often good-humoredly complained that he forgot the rectification of the frontiers, and poached rather extensively on their preserves. He had a genuine, undisguised horror of books. His modest library consisted of St. Liguori in two volumes, Perrone in four, Alzog in two, and Receveur in ten. There were, also, about fifty volumes of the Delphin classics, which had come down to him from a scholarly uncle; and in the midst of these was a single volume of De Quincey, with an account, amongst other essays, of the last days of Kant. This volume was the occasion of perpetual inquiry and interrogation.

"Where in the world did I pick it up? Who the mischief was this Kant? What a name for a Christian! Martin, I am sure I must have stolen it from you in a fit of abstraction."

But he would not part with it—not for its weight in gold. It had served him well a few times. It was always lying on the parlor table, except during meals, when it went back to the bookshelf; and once a high-born English lady, who had called to inquire about some poor people in the neighborhood, took it up, and said:—

"I'm glad to see you interested in my favorite author, Father."

And once, when the Bishop paid an *impromptu* visit, he found Father Pat deeply immersed in abstruse studies.

"Reading, Father Casey?" said the Bishop, as if he were surprised.

"Yes, my Lord," said Father Pat, demurely.

The Bishop took up the volume, turned over the leaves with a slight uplifting of the eyebrows, looked at Father Pat questioningly, looked at the book, and sighed.

There were a few prints of sacred subjects around the walls, one or two engravings signed Kaufmann, which Father Pat was told were of priceless value. But the masterpiece was over the mantel; it represented three or four horses, bay and black, their skins shining like mirrors. One was hurt, and a groom was chafing the fore foot. It was by one of the old masters, and it was called "Elliman's Embrocation."

"Take down that vulgar thing," said his parish priest, on one of the few occasions when he visited his curate. Father Pat obeyed, but put it back again. It was the source of innocent and ineffable pleasure to him.

Father Pat didn't preach. He only spoke to the people. Hence, after thirty years of zealous ministration, he remained a curate; and there seemed no likelihood that he would ever be asked, in his own words, "to change his condition."

Father Tim Hurley was pastor of a neighboring parish—a one-horse parish. He had no curate—a fact in which he took great pride when speaking to his fellow pastors, but which he deplored, almost with tears in his eyes, when in the company of curates. Once, in his early days, he had had the supreme misfortune of making an excellent *bon mot,* and an unwise admirer had called him "Thou son of Sirach." From that day forward he assumed the aphoristic mode of speaking; and sometimes it was a torture to his friends to see him, in much agony, laboring to twist and extort from his inner consciousness some pithy phrase that would help him to conserve or extend his reputation. Under the unwise advice of his friend Father Martin, he had laid in a stock of writers who had been remarkable for their wit and powers of repartee; but it was mighty hard to bring around Rochefoucauld in a conversation about the diocese, or Epictetus when they were talking about the harvest. And so Father Tim was driven, by the stress of circumstances, to fall back upon his own originality; and if, sometimes, he failed, he found, on the whole that in his flights of fancy his own gray feathers were better than borrowed plumage.

Father Martin, again, was almost a direct antithesis to his friends; and as it was from him Luke's future life took some of its color, I must give him a little more space just here.

Father Martin Hughes was not originally intended for the Church, but for the Bar. For this purpose he had spent two years in Germany, passing from university to university, lodging in humble cottages by the banks of legendary rivers, or in the solitudes of black mountain forests; and here he had learned to prize the simple, cleanly lives, gray and drab in their monotony, but gilded by the music and the mystery that seems to hang like a golden cloud above the Fatherland. In after life he often recurred, with all the gratefulness of memory, to the kindliness and unaffected politeness of these simple peasants and wood-cutters; and the little marks of sympathetic friendship, such as the placing of a bunch of violets with silent courtesy on his dressing-table, or the little presents on his birthday, when his portrait was decorated by some Gretchen or Ottilie, were graved indelibly on a memory almost too retentive. Then the pathos of the German hymns, sung by a whole family around the supper table, and to the accompaniment of a single table-piano, such as you see in every German household, haunted him like a dream; and when, by degrees, he began to realize that this country, which but a few years back had been cursed by a foreign tongue, had now, by a supreme magnificent effort, created its own language, and a literature unsurpassed for richness and sweetness, he saturated himself with the poetry and philosophy of the country, which gave a new color and embellishment to life. Not that he troubled himself much about the cloudy metaphysics of this school or that, or the fine hair-splitting of philosophical mountebanks who ridiculed the scholastics for logic-chopping, yet imitated in untruth the worst features of systems they condemned; but he allowed the fine mists and mountain dews of Schiller, Richter, and Novalis to wrap him around and saturate his spirit, and thanked God that He had given poets to the world. The last months of his pilgrimage he had spent above the Necker, in the grand old town of Heidelberg, and he never saw it after but in such a sunset dream of coloring, and such an overhanging heaven of azure, as arches the golden landscapes on the canvases of Turner. But it was there and in the lonely recesses of the Hartz mountains, where village after village clustered around the church spire and the white tombs of the dead, that the gentle afflatus was breathed on him that turned his thoughts from the forum to the pulpit and from the world to God. But he never abandoned his German studies during all his after life. He had conceived the original and apparently extravagent idea of engrafting German ideas, German habits and manners on the peasantry at home, and he had written one thoughtful article on the affinity between German and Irish thought and tradition. He thought to show that German idealism and Celtic mysticism were the same, and that the issue of an alliance between the thoughts and sympathies of these nations should necessarily be a healthy one. But he was hooted from the literary stage. France, and France alone, was to be our wet-nurse and duenna—and Father Martin went back to his books and his dreams. He was, therefore, a cipher, a nonentity, for a silenced voice is supposed to denote and symbolize emptiness in a loud-tongued, blatant land. Then, again, his accomplishments and learning were merged and forgotten in the fact that he was the gentlest, the most imperturbable of men. And partly by native disposition, partly by habit and cultivation, he had come to that pass when he did not think it worth while to differ with any one about anything. He answered, "Quite so!" to the most absurd and extravagant statement. Hence, after conferences and such like he was generally reputed dull, because he did not choose to take part in discussions, which had no interest for him. But there was a tradition amongst the "Inseparables" that after these occasions strange sounds of laughter used to be heard from the recesses of his library. But this was a mistake. It was only a musical box that used to play twelve airs, and which always required winding on these particular occasions. So said the "Inseparables" to the gentiles; but they had a Freemason secret amongst themselves that Father Martin did verily and indeed enjoy a joke. And in one of the secret recesses of his library, which no one was allowed to penetrate but the "Inseparables," he had a large ring or rosary of photographic portraits—Kant, Fichte, Schelling, Hegel, Goethe, Wieland, Richter, Novalis, and Herder. The center panel was for a long time vacant. Then one day it was filled—filled with a cabinet portrait of a man who, at his own dinner table, used to say by gestures, if not articulately to his worshipers and sycophants: "Behold, am I not your lord and master?" and they answered him and said: "Yea, verily, thou art our lord and king." And the horrible story went abroad that Father Martin, the demure monk and eremite, used to sit in his arm-chair for hours together, contemplating this circle of genius with the center of conceited emptiness, and laugh loud and long at the dismal contrast.

Luke was privileged to spend his last three days in Ireland in the company of these kindly men. Why he was admitted within the magic circle was a great puzzle to him, the only answer to which he found in his prospective exile. The profit he derived from this intercourse was probably not an appreciable quantity; but his nerves got smoothed out and calmed. It is true, indeed, that Father Tim gave labored utterance to one or two of his oracular sayings, which, not being quite consistent in their moral bearing with what Luke had been taught, occasioned him not a little anxiety and scruple. For example, Father Tim strongly inculcated on Luke the paramount necessity of "not selling himself cheap."

"The world takes you, my boy, at your own valuation. Hold your head high, and put a big price on yourself."

"But surely, Father," remonstrated Luke, "that would be quite inconsistent with Christian humility."

"Humility? God bless me, my boy, you'll be pulled and

dragged through the mud; you'll be trampled into compost by the hoofs of men if you attempt to make little of yourself."

Luke was silent.

"An eel has a better chance than a salmon," said Father Tim, on another occasion, "of making his way in the narrow and twisted and shallow channels of Irish life." After a long pause of pleasure, he added: "But an eel is not a salmon for all that."

The brethren nodded assent.

"You have a good name to go to England with, my boy," he said, at his own dinner-table on Monday evening. "Who was the fool that said: 'What's in a name? A rose by any other name would smell as sweet.'"

"A great fellow called Will Shakespeare," said Father Martin.

"I thought so. One of those birds who hatch the eggs of others. Now, will any one tell me that Delmege—and if you pronounce it in the French fashion so much the better—is not a wholesomer name for an exile than O'Shaughnessy or O'-Deluchery? You'll find that this fellow will come back to us with an accent like a duchess, and that he'll find out that his ancestors fought at Poictiers, and that he is a first cousin, in the collateral line, to Joan of Arc."

"It is a curious form of insanity," said Father Martin, "and every one is more or less affected."

"Except myself and Father Pat. I could never trace the Hurleys or the Caseys beyond the three-year-old and four-year-old factions. But I believe they were very conspicuous in these crusades." He added, in his tone of quiet sarcasm: "When I get a little money together, which is a rather problematical issue at present, I'm going to get my notepaper crested, like the Canon—two shillelaghs rampant—very rampant—on a background of red—very red, with the motto, *Nemo me impune lacessit,* or its Irish translation, *Don't tread on the tail of my coat;* and I'll also pay for Father Pat's, for he'll never have a penny to bless himself with."

"And wouldn't you kindly suggest an heraldic crest and motto for Father Pat?" said Father Martin.

"Certainly. A death's-head and crossbones couchant, on a black ground, with the motto of Napoleon: *Frappez-vite—*

frappez-fort, or in the vernacular: *Wherever you see a head, hit it!"*

"No! no!" said Father Martin; "that would not be appropriate. Give him the surgeon's knife and the motto, *Rescissa vegetius resurget."*

To explain which parable we should add here that Father Pat was an amateur surgeon, principally in the veterinary department. He had a little surgery, a room about eight feet square, off the hall; and here he performed operations on animals that would have made Lister die of envy. Here he had put into splints the broken leg of a blackbird, who, in exchange for the gratuitous service, then and there abdicated his freedom, and became the melodious companion of the priest. Here, too, dogs of all shapes and breeds were brought to him, and whilst he treated them with infinite gentleness, and they licked his hand in gratitude, and the wistful, swimming look gathered into their eyes, as indeed into all eyes, human and other, in crises of their lives, some thought that he dropped a tear into the embrocation, and moistened the ointment in this old human way. In spiritual matters, too, he was an able and tender physician. I am not sure that he was a distinguished theologian, or that he could weigh opinions in the balance, like that sensitive plate in the Bank of England, that flings good coins to the right, and light, spurious ones to the left, and quivers, as if in doubt, when a dubious coin is submitted, and reasons in its own mechanical way, and finally drops it. But Father Pat had a sovereign remedy, a pure anæsthetic, an antiseptic salve for all the wounds of humanity, and that was *Epikeia.* It was never known to fail him, and the consequence was that patients flocked to him from town and country and went away rejoicing.

"I can't make it out," he said. "I'm not much of a theologian, and the Lord knows I'm not a saint. I suppose 'tis the grace of God and an honest face."

"No matter," said Father Tim, in reply; "he'll never come to decent notepaper. Ah, me! if Pat had only held his head high, how different he would be today! Luke, my boy, hold your head high, and let every year increase your valuation."

"Tell him about Tracey," said Father Pat; "it might frighten him."

"About Tracey, that poor *angashore* in the city? Well, he's an awful example. He had a good parish—as good a parish as there is in the diocese. It is my own native parish—"

"It is the Siberia of the diocese," hinted Father Martin.

"It's my own native parish," said Father Tim, "and though I shouldn't say it, there's as good a living there—well, no matter. What did our friend Tracey do? Instead of thanking God and his Bishop, he flew into the face of God, he insulted the Bishop, he insulted the people, and he insulted me." The memory of the insult was so vivid and painful that Father Tim could not speak for several seconds.

"He began to make meditations, if you please, with the result, of course, that he went clean off his head. His delusion was that he was too elevated as a parish priest. God bless the mark! and that his salvation would be more secure on a lower rung of the ladder. He resigned his parish and became chaplain to a city hospital. He is low enough now. He may be seen wandering around the streets of the city with a coat on him as green as a leek, and he looks like an anatomy. Of course, he is off his head; and the fun is, he likes to be told it. And if you'd politely hint that he has been, and must have been, suspended for an occult crime, he'd shake your hand like a hungry friend whom you had unexpectedly asked to dinner."

"By Jove!" said Luke, forgetting himself, and striking the table, "the first vacation I get, I'll make a pilgrimage to the city and kiss that man's feet."

"That's easy enough," said Father Tim, "because his shoes are usually well ventilated, and he's not shy about showing his toes. Meanwhile, Luke, spare these few glasses of mine. They are all I have, and this is a hungry parish."

"Tell me, Father Martin," said Luke, as the two went home together, "is that true what Father Tim told about that priest in Limerick? Because one never knows when he is serious and when jesting."

"Literally true," said Father Martin, with that tone of seriousness which was natural to him, and which he only suppressed in moments of relaxation.

"And are cases like this very rare?" asked Luke.

"Not so rare as you may imagine," replied Father Martin, "but not so remarkable."

"I suppose the man is worshiped," said Luke, gauging the popular estimate by his own.

"Quite the contrary. He is regarded by all as an imbecile. The people only think of him as one 'tetched in his mind.' "

But the brethren—his own—who understand his heroism?"

"Oh!" said Father Martin, with a long breath. "Well," he said deliberately, "here too, there is compassion, but no great admiration. He is not called a fool, but he is treated as such. I remember a few months ago a magnificent sermon, preached by a great pulpit orator, on 'Humility.' It was really beautiful, and the picture he drew of St. Francis, hooted by the people of his native town, and called 'a fool,' was photographic in its perfect details. But when he met Father Tracey, with his old green coat at the dinner table afterwards, it was delightful to see his condescension. He shook hands with him, apparently with some reluctance, but said immediately after to one of a group of his admirers, 'Poor fellow! poor fellow!' But the cream of the joke was that an excellent man, immediately after, spoke of the distinguished orator as the exact and happy antithesis of wretched failures like Father Tracey."

"It's a dreadful enigma," said Luke, wearily mopping his forehead. "I don't know where I am."

"You see Father Tim's advice was not so far absurd as you seem to think. We are all like frogs in a swamp, each trying to croak louder than his fellows, and to lift his stupid head somewhat above them out of this dreary Slough of Despond. And for what, think you? That he might have a better opportunity than his fellows to see the fens and quagmires of this dreary existence, and inhale the more deeply the marsh-miasms of this fever-stricken and pestilential planet."

"But, surely, you do not agree with what Father Tim said?" said Luke, in an accent of despair.

"I fully agree with his conclusion that, if you are humble and lowly and self-effaced, you will certainly be crushed into compost under the hoofs of wild asses. But—" He stopped, and Luke watched him.

"I believe, also, that the highest Christian teaching is true; and that no real work is done in the world except by humble and lowly men. Did you notice the two photos on my mantelpiece?"

"Yes; your idols?"

"According to mood. When I am disposed to be contemptuous or scornful or too zealous, I turn to Savonarola; he was my
deity for half my life. When I am in a gentle and charitable
mood, I light a taper before the Curé of Ars."

" 'Tis all a mighty puzzle," said Luke.

"Ay, 'tis a mad world, my merry masters," answered the
priest. Then, after a long pause, he said:—

"I dare say you're pretty tired of the advice and wisdom of
your seniors. But you have had a great misfortune. You have
come into the world worse equipped than if you had been born
blind or lame. You have a hundred naked, quivering nerves,
wide open on every square inch of your body. Happy you if
you had been born with the hide of a rhinoceros. As this is not
so, I say to you, first, with the Grecian philosopher—

"*Habita tecum.* Dwell as much as you can with your own
thoughts. Secondly,—

"Make God your companion, not men. Thirdly,—

"Feed not on ephemeral literature, but on the marrow of
giants. Good-bye! till tomorrow."

On Friday afternoon, Luke was launched on the high seas
in the London steamer, and into the mighty world at the same
time. The enigma of life was going to be shown him for solution on larger canvas and in deeper colors in the strange and
unfamiliar environments of English life.

BOOK II

CHAPTER VIII

Albion

NOT THE WHITE CLIFFS of Dover, but the red loam of Devonshire downs, where the sandstone was capped by the rich teeming soil, saluted our young exile the following morning. He had risen early, and, shaking off the mephitis of a stuffy cabin, had rushed above, just as the sailors were swabbing the decks. Here he drew in long, deep breaths of the crisp, cool sea air, as he watched the furrows cut by the coulter of the sea-plough, or studied the white towns that lay so picturesquely under the ruddy cliffs. "And this is England," Luke thought. "England, the far-reaching, the imperial, whose power is reverenced by white, and black, and bronzed races; and whose sovereignty stretches from the peaks of the Himalayas to the Alps of the southern Archipelagoes." Luke couldn't understand it. She lay so quiet there in the morning sun, her landscapes stretched so peaceful and calm, that symbol of power, or of might far-reaching, there was none.

"I thought," said Luke, aloud, "that every notch in her cliffs was an embrasure, and that the mouths of her cannon were like nests in her rocks."

" 'Tis the lion *couchant et dormant,*" said a voice.

Luke turned and saw standing close by an officer of the ship, a clean-cut, trim, well-defined figure, clad in the blue cloth and gold lace of the service. His face, instead of the red and bronze of the sailor, had an olive tinge, through which burned two glowing, gleaming brown eyes, which just then were sweeping the coast, as if in search of a signal.

"I have often had the same thoughts as you, sir," he said, as if anxious to continue the conversation, "as we swept along here under more troublous skies and over more turbulent seas than now. It is the silent and sheathed strength of England that is terrible. I have seen other powers put forth all their might by land and sea: I have not been moved. But I never approach the English coast without a feeling of awe."

"I dare say it is something to be proud of," said Luke, who was appreciative of this enthusiasm, but did not share it.

"Perhaps not," the officer replied; "it is destiny."

"You see the Cornish coast," he continued, pointing to a dim haze far behind them, in which the outlines of the land were faintly pencilled. "Would you believe that up to the dawn of our century, fifty years ago, that entire peninsula was Catholic? They had retained the Catholic faith from the times of the Reformation. Then there were no priests to be had; Wesley went down, and today they are the most bigoted Dissenters in England; and Cornwall will be the last county that will come back to the Church."

"Horrible!" said Luke, sadly.

"And yet so thin is the veneering of Protestantism that their children are still called by the names of Catholic saints, Angela, and Ursula, and Teresa; and they have as many holy wells as you have in Ireland."

"It must be a heart-break to the priests," said Luke, "who have to minister amid such surroundings."

"I only speak of it as a matter of Fate," said the officer, dreamily. "It is the terrific power of assimilation which Protestant England possesses."

"You must be proud of your great country," said Luke.

"No, sir," said the officer, "I am not."

Luke looked at him with surprise.

"Ireland is my country," the officer said in reply, "and these are our countrymen." He pointed down into the lower deck, where, lying prostrate in various degrees of intoxication, were four or five cattle-dealers. They had sought out the warmth of the boiler during the night; and there they lay, unwashed and unkempt, in rather uninviting conditions. Their magnificent cattle, fed on Irish pastures, were going to feed the mouths of Ireland's masters, and tramped and lowed and moaned in hideous discord for food, and clashed their horns together as the vessel rolled on the waves. It was altogether an unpleasant exhibition, and Luke turned away with a sigh.

In the early afternoon, the boat, after sheering close under

the Eddystone lighthouse, swept around the beautiful wood-
lands and shrublands of Mount Edgcumbe, and the splendid
panorama of Plymouth harbor burst on the view. Here again
Luke was disappointed. Everything looked so calm, and peaceful, and prosperous, that he found it difficult to understand
that there to the left was one of the greatest dockyards and
marine emporiums and store-houses in the world; and his eye
ranged along until, hidden under the bosky covers and the
abundant foliage of Mount Edgcumbe, he saw a long, low wall
of concrete, and there were the bulldog mouths of England's
cannon.

"Going ashore, sir?" said the chief mate, the officer who had
previously accosted him.

"No," said Luke, dubiously.

"Let me introduce my wife and little girl, sir," he said politely. "We are running in, as I am leaving Marguerite with the
Notre Dame nuns here."

"You are going further, Father?" said the lady, with frankly
polite Irish manner.

"Yes," said Luke, "I'm going to London. I have a sister
Margaret also," he said, tenderly watching the child's eyes,
"but we call her Margery."

"We shall be lonely after our little woman," said the officer;
"but she will be in safe hands."

"Do you know what *Marguerite* means, little one?" said
Luke.

"No, Father," said the child.

'It means a pearl. Be thou," he said, assuming a tone of
unwonted solemnity, "a pearl of great price."

"Bless her, Father," said the Catholic mother.

And Luke blessed the child.

All that day, whenever he had a spare moment from his
Office and a few necessary studies, he was absorbed in two
reflections. The awful spectacle of those drunken men in the
morning haunted him like a nightmare. They had risen half
drunk from their hot, hard bed, and stupidly had passed him
near the gangway with a maudlin: "Fi' morn'n, Fazzer!" And
he was studying all day the mighty problem, that has occupied
more attention than half the more serious problems of the

world. What is it? What is it?—the fatal bias towards intoxication that seems to distinguish the race? Indolence, vacuity of thought, the fatal altruism of the race? What is it? Or is it only a political calumny?

And side by side, alternating rapidly with the bitter reflection, came the question: Why will not Irish mothers educate their children at home? Have we not convents, etc? Why, it is Irish nuns who are teaching here in Plymouth and throughout England. What is in the English air that the same teachers can teach better here than at home? Or is it the everlasting serfdom of the race, always crouching at the feet of the conqueror, always lessening and depreciating its own large possibilities? Let it alone, Luke, let it alone! Except, indeed, as an exercise, to while away a long afternoon under sleepy awnings, and to soothe your nerves with the dull mechanic interplay of questions that are forever seeking and never finding an answer, let it alone, let it alone! But Luke was not made thus. He had a great taste for the insoluble.

Late in the evening he heard the same officer chatting freely in French, and with the absolute ease of a native, with a young governess who was returning to her home from Ireland. He listened, not with curiosity, but just to see if he could distinguish one word. Not a word! And he had got a prize in French in his logic year. "Hang Wegscheider and the Monophysites," thought Luke.

Now, I should like to know where is the connection between Wegscheider, a fairly modern German, and people that lived fifteen centuries ago? But that is the way the lobes of the brain work and interchange ideas, not always sympathetic, or even relevant, especially when the schoolmaster is in a passion, and demands too much work at once from his willing pupils.

Next day the vessel had swung into the gangway of the world—that mighty sea-avenue that stretches from the Downs and the Forelands right up to London Bridge. The vessel's engines were slowed down, for this was a pathway where the passengers had to pick their steps; for all along the banks at intervals, where the plastic hand of man had built wharves and quays, there was a plantation of bare masts and yards that cut the sky; and now and again a stately steamer loomed up out of the eternal haze, and grew and swelled into colossal blackness; then passed and subsided into the dimensions of a waterfowl that troubles the tranquil waters with swift alarm. Bound for the Orient, and laden with freights of merchandise —from the mechanism of a locomotive to the Brummagem-made idol for far Cathay; bound for the Occident, and laden to the water's edge, and stuffed chock-full with rolls and bales from the looms of Manchester; bound for the roaring Cape and the sleepy isles of the Pacific; bound for the West Indies and the Bermudas, whence Nature has tried in vain to frighten them with her explosive earthquakes or the dread artillery of her typhoons; or homeward from far climates, and with the rusty marks of the storm on their hulls, and their sailors staring at the old familiar sights on land and water—like fairy shuttles, moving to and fro across the woof of many waters— the fleets of the empire came and went, and Luke fancied he saw the far round world as in a magic mirror, and that he smelt the spices of Sultans and the musk of gardens of Persia, as the stately argosies swept by. It was a magnificent panorama, and recalled the times when the *Mare Magnum* was swept by the oars of the Roman triremes, and dusky Ethiopians sweated at the galleys of their Roman masters. Then the vision faded, and in the raw cold of an exceptionally sharp morning, Luke stepped across the gangway and looked down at the mighty sewer of a river, and came face to face with all the squalor and fætor of London life.

He was calmly but courteously received at the presbytery attached to the cathedral; and it surprised him not a little to perceive that his arrival was regarded as an event of as ordinary importance as the closing of a door or the ticking of a clock. He took his seat at the dinner-table; and he might have been dining there for the last twenty years, so little notice was taken of him.

He was a little surprised when he was told:—

"Delmege, if you want bread, you can get it at the sideboard; but cut the loaf even, please."

He was a little amused when some one asked:—

"I say, Delmege, is it a fact that the curates in Ireland give dinners at a guinea a head?"

He replied: "I have dined with curates and even with parish priests lately, and the dinner did not cost a cent per head."

"Tell that to the marines," was the reply.

And he was almost edified, yet partly nonplussed, when his former interrogator took him out promptly after dinner to show him the slums, and coolly told him on returning that he was to preach to a confraternity that evening.

But what struck him most forcibly was, the calm independence with which each individual expressed his opinion, and the easy toleration with which they differed from each other, and even contradicted, without the slightest shade of asperity or resentment. This was a perpetual wonder to Luke during his whole career in England.

The following Friday he was submitted to a brief examination for faculties. His examiners were the Vicar-General and the Diocesan Inspector, a convert from Anglicanism.

"In the case of a convert," said the Vicar, without preliminaries, "whom you ascertained to have never been baptized, but who was married, and had a grown-up family, what would you do?"

"I should proceed with great caution," said Luke, to whom the question seemed rather impertinent and far-fetched. He had been expecting to be asked how many grave professors were on this side, and how many excellent writers were on that side, of some abstruse theological problem.

"Very good," said the Vicar, "and then?"

"I think I should let it alone," said Luke.

"Very good. But these good people are not married. Could you allow them to remain so?"

"It depends on whether they are *bona fide,* or *mala fide,*" said Luke, reddening.

"Of course they are *bona fide,*" said the Vicar. "Look it up, Delmege, at your convenience."

"How would you refute the arguments for continuity amongst the Anglican divines?" said the Inspector.

"How would you prove to a lunatic that black is not white, and that yesterday is not today?" said Luke. Ah, Luke! Luke! where are all your resolutions about interior recollection and self-restraint? You are far from the illuminative state, as yet!

"That will hardly do," said the Inspector, smiling courteously; "remember you have to face Laud and the Elizabethans, and Pusey and the host of Victorian divines, now."

"We never thought of such things," said Luke; "we thought that the old doctrines of Transubstantiation, Purgatory, Confession, etc., were the subjects of controversy today. No one in Ireland even dreams of denying that the Reformation was a distinct secession."

"Very good, very good," said the Inspector. "One more word. In case you had a sick-call to St. Thomas's Hospital here; and when you arrived, you found the surgeons engaged in an operation on a Catholic patient, which operation would probably prove fatal, what would you do?"

"I would politely ask them to suspend the operation for a few minutes—"

"And do you think they would remove the knives at your request, and probably let the patient collapse?"

"I'd give the patient conditional absolution," said Luke faintly.

"Very good. You wouldn't—a—knock down two or three of the surgeons and clear the room?" said the Vicar, with a smile.

"N-no," said Luke. He was very angry. Dear me! no one appears to have heard of Wegscheider at all.

"That's all right," said the examiners. "You'll get the printed form of faculties this afternoon. Confessions tomorrow from two to six, and from seven to ten. Good-day."

Luke went to his room. He was never so angry in his life before. He expected a lengthened ordeal, in which deep and recondite questions would be introduced, and in which he would have some chance at last of showing what he had learned in the famous halls of his college. And lo! not a particle of dust was touched or flicked away from dusty, dead folios; but here, spick and span, were trotted out airy nothings about ephemeral and transient everyday existencies; and he had not got one chance of saying—*"Sic argumentaris Domine!"* Evidently, these men had never heard of a syllogism in their lives. And then, everything was so curt and short as to be almost contemptuous. Clearly, these men had something to do in the workaday world besides splitting hairs with a young Hibernian. Luke was angry with himself, with his college, with that smiling ex-parson, who had probably read about two years' philosophy and theology before his ordination; and with that grim, sardonic old Vicar, who had never opened a treatise since he graduated at Douai or Rheims. Hence it happened that at dinner, when a strange priest asked simply what percentage of illiterates were in the diocese, and the old Vicar grimly answered:—

"About fifty per cent—mostly Irish and Italian"—Luke flared up and said:—

"We weren't illiterate when we brought the Faith of old to your ancestors, who were eating acorns with the boars in your forests, and painting their dirty bodies with woad; and when your kings were glad to fly to our monastaries for an education, nowhere else obtainable on this planet."

The stranger patted Luke on the back, and said "Bravo!" The Vicar pushed over the jug of beer. But they were friends from that moment. A gnarled, knotty, not in any sense of the word euphonious old Beresark was this same old Vicar—his steel-blue eyes staring ever steadily and with anxious inquiry in them from the jagged penthouse of gray eyebrows; and his clear, metallic voice, never toned down to politeness and amenity, but dashed in a spray of sarcasm on bishop, and canon, and curate indiscriminately. He would blow you sky high at a moment's notice; the next minute he would kneel down and tie the latchets of your shoes. A wonderful taste and talent, too, he had for economics; not ungenerous by any means, or parsimonious; but he objected very strongly to any abstraction of jam on the sleeve of your soutane, or any too generous distribution of brown gravy on the thirsty tablecloth.

Saturday came, and Luke braced himself for the second great act of his ministry—his first confession. He had scampered over the treatise on Penance the night before; and just at two o'clock he passed, with fear and trembling, to his confessional. He had said a short, tremulous prayer before the Blessed Sacrament; had cast a look of piteous appeal towards the Lady Altar, and with a thrill of fear and joy commingled, he slipped quietly past the row of penitents, and put on his surplice and stole. Then he reflected for a moment, and drew the slide. A voice from the dark recess, quavering with emotion, commenced the *Confiteor* in Irish. Luke started at the well-known words, and whispered *Deo gratias*. It was an

ancient mariner, and the work was brief. But Luke recollected
all the terrible things he had heard about dumb and statuesque
confessors; and that poor Irishman got a longer lecture than
he had heard for many a day.

"I must be a more outrageous sinner than I thought," he
said. "I never got such a ballyragging in my life before!"

Luke drew the slide at his left; and a voice, this time of a
young girl, whispered hoarsely:—

"I ain't goin' to confession, Feyther; but I 'eard as you wos
from Hireland, and I kem to arsk assistance to tek me out of
'ell!"

"By all means, my child," said Luke, shivering, "if I can
assist you in any way; but why do you say that you are not
going to confession?"

"I ain't prepared, Feyther. I ain't been to confession since
I left the convent school, five years are gone."

"And you've been in London all this time?"

"Yaas, Feyther; I've been doin' bad altogether. It's 'ell,
Feyther, and I want to git out o' 'ell!"

"Well, but how can I assist you?"

"Ev you gi' me my passage, Feyther, to Waterford, I'll beg
the rest of the way to my huncle in the County Kilkenny. And
so 'elp me God, Feyther—"

"Sh—h—h!" said Luke. A cold perspiration had broken out
all over his body. It was the first time he was brought face to
face with the dread embodiment of vice.

His next penitent was a tiny dot, with a calm, English face,
and yellow ringlets running down almost to her feet. Her
mother, dressed in black, took the child to the confessional
door, bade her enter, and left her. Here even the mother, in all
other things inseparable from her child, must not accompany.
The threshold of the confessional and the threshold of death
are sacred to the soul and God. Unlike the Irish children, who
jump up like jacks-in-the-box, and toss back the black hair
from their eyes, and smile patronizingly on their friend, the
confessor, as much as to say, "Of course you know me?" this
child slowly and distinctly said the prayers, made her confession, and waited. Here Luke was in his element, and he lifted
that soul up, up into the empyrean, by coaxing, gentle, burn-

ing words about our Lord, and His love, and all that was due to Him. The child passed out with the smile of an angel on her face.

"Wisha, yer reverence, how my heart warmed to you the moment I see you. Sure he's from the ould counthry, I sez to meself. There's the red of Ireland in his cheeks, and the scint of the ould sod hanging around him. Wisha, thin, yer reverence, may I be bould to ask you what part of the ould land did ye come from?"

Luke mentioned his natal place.

"I thought so. I knew ye weren't from the North or West. Wisha, now thin, yer reverence, I wondher did ye ever hear tell of a Mick Mulcahy, of Slievereene, in the County of Kerry, who wint North about thirty years ago?"

Luke regretted to say he had never heard of that distinguished rover.

"Because he was my third cousin by the mother's side, and I thought yer reverence might have heard of him—"

"I am hardly twenty-three yet," said Luke, gently, although he thought he was losing valuable time.

"Wisha, God bless you; sure I ought to have seen it. I suppose I ought not to mintion it here, yer reverence, but this is an awful place. Betune furriners, and Frinchmen, and I-talians, and Jews, and haythens, who never hard the name of God or His Blessed Mother, 'tis as much as we can do to save our poor sowls—"

"You ought to go back to Ireland," said Luke.

"Ah! wisha, thin, 'tis I'd fly in the mornin' across the say to that blessed and holy land; but sure, yer reverence, me little girl is married here, and I have to mind the childhre for her, whin she goes out to work, shoreing and washing to keep the bit in their mouths—'In the name av the Father, and av the Son, and av the Holy Ghost. Amin—' "

"Father," said a gentle voice, as Luke drew the other slide, "I am ever so grateful to you for your kindness to my little one. She's gone up to the Lady Altar; and I never saw her look half so happy before. You must have been very gentle with my dear child."

Luke's heart was swelling with all kinds of sweet emotions. Ah, yes! here, above all places, does the priest receive his reward. True, the glorious Mass has its own consolations, sweet and unutterable. So, too, has the Office, with its majestic poetry, lifting the soul above the vulgar trivialities of life, and introducing it to the company of the blessed. So, too, has the daily, hourly battle with vice the exhilaration of a noble conflict; but nowhere are human emotions stirred into such sweet and happy delight as when soul speaks to soul, and the bliss of forgiveness is almost merged in the ecstasy of emancipation, and the thrill of determination to be true to promise and grateful to God. Here is the one thing that Protestantism—the system of individualism and pride—never can, and never will, fathom.

With something akin to rapture, Luke Delmege put off his surplice and stole, after a hard afternoon's work, and knelt and blessed God for having made him a priest.

CHAPTER IX

The Realms of Dis

AND NOW commenced a strange life for our young Levite—a life whose circumstances clearly obliterated every lingering trace of desire for far, heroic deeds, which, like martyrdom, would mean one short spasm of pain, and then—the eternal laurels. He began to feel that there was something even higher and nobler than all this—the daily, hourly martyrdom of conflict with Satan and sin—the struggle with evil in its Protean shapes—evil preached from house tops in strong, Satanic accents—or more mildly through the press and literature, from the boards of theatres, and the millions of pamphlets and leaflets, that fell, like the flakes of fire in the *Inferno,* on the raw and festering souls of men. Sometimes he walked, for study's sake, through crowded streets, or watched the hideous mass of humanity from the roof of an omnibus. Sometimes he would stand for a dizzy moment at a chemist's window in London Road, and stare at the swirling, heaving, tossing tide of humanity that poured through the narrow aqueduct. Never a look or word of recognition amongst these atoms, who stared steadily before them into space, each intent on coming uppermost by some natural principle of selection. Luke began to have bad dreams. Sometimes he dreamt of the city as a huge dead carcass, swarming with clotted masses of maggots, that squirmed and rolled in its dread putrescence. Sometimes he saw Britannia, as pictured on coins, with her helmet and trident; but there hung a huge *gôitre* on her neck, and that was London. But most often he saw the city as a tenth circle in the *città dolente.* Pale ghosts wandered through dark and narrow streets, or herded in fetid alleys. They appeared to be absorbed in a silent, but dread and exorbitant quest. What it was, Luke could not see. Some found the desirable thing, and tried to walk along unconcernedly for fear of being robbed; but there were dark sentinels posted along the avenues, who glided from their lairs and stole the prize even from the most wary passengers. And over all was the smoke of Hell and the brown twilight of the realms of Dis.

After this dread dream, which he was unable to shake off for many days, he never saw London but as a shadowy picture of somber and lurid lights. Whether the early sunsettings of September lighted the blind streets; or the tender grays of October threw a haze around the dying splendors of parks and terraces—he saw only the London of his dream—*terram desertam, et tenebrosam, et opertam mortis caligine*. He began to be alarmed for his health, and he visited a certain physician. A long statement of symptoms, etc., under the keen eyes of Æsculapius. Prompt reply: "Late suppers. Irish stomach not yet habituated to English roast beef and potted salmon. All will come right soon. WORK!"

Luke took the prescription, and faithfully followed it. He worked in schools and slums, in confessional and pulpit, in hospital and asylum, till his fine face and figure began to be known; and threw a sunbeam into the tenebrous and sordid places where he had to go. And some one said—it was a holy Irish nun—"God sent you!" Ah! These wonderful nuns! The glorious *vivandières* in the march of the army of Christ! No stars bedeck them, or crosses; no poet sings them; no trumpets blare around their rough and toilsome march and struggle; but some day the bede-roll will be called, and the King's right hand will pin on their breasts the cross of His Legion of Honor. And often and often, as Luke's heart failed him, and he felt he was powerless against the awful iniquity that surged around him, the sight of these Sisters, moving quietly through hideous slums, and accepting insults as calmly as their worldly sisters receive compliments; or their white lips blanched by the foul air of their schools, and the reeking *sordes* that exhaled from the clothes of these poor waifs, whom they were rescuing from Stygian horrors, smote him with shame, and nerved him by the tonic of noble example for far higher and greater work. And over all the fætor, and the smoke, and horror played lambent flashes of Celtic wit and humor, as brave men jest when

shells are crashing and bullets are singing around them.
"Come, see our recreation garden," said one, who seemed to
want recreation badly, so pale and hollow-cheeked she looked.
She led him up five flights of stairs, then bade him go out on
the leads and look. He did and stood. There was a square patch
of blue overhead. All around were brick walls. It was the
recreation ground of a prison. He passed around the parapet,
and touched with his hand the grimy ledges where the London
smoke was festering. And such little pathetic stories as of the
child who shouted: "D—n you, don't drown me!" when the
baptismal waters were poured upon her head; or the pretty
ancient legend of the mariner convert, who could never get
beyond "Father, Son, and Holy—Water;" or the apology of
the old Irish apple-woman for not being able to recognize the
Figure of the Crucified, "because, ma'am, I haven't my spectacles wid me, and my sight is wake." Ah me! These are the
little tragic amusements of mighty martyrs in the crowded
amphitheatre of London life. Sometimes, too, when Luke felt
as an airy, gauze-winged butterfly, beating vain wings against
the granite walls of ignorance or vice, and his heart sank down
in despair, the feeble courtesy and "God bless you!" of a poor
woman, or the smile of a London flower-girl, with her pretty
little bow, and, "Do, please, Father,"—would inspirit him. Or
when striding along some populous street, with all the gaudy
'Arrys and flippant 'Arriets around, he would dream of Ireland, and what she might have been, suddenly a band, with a
green flag, and golden harp, and a rush of green-and-gold uni-
forms, would burst upon him with music and color, and every
man would give the military salute, there as they tramped the
London pavement in military order, to their young beloved
officer. And he would say to himself: "A race to work for and
die for, with all their faults." And above all would float the
far-off dream of the white, thatched cottage above the cliffs,
and the murmur of the sea, and the purity and simplicity that
o'er-canopied with clouds of gold the azure vault that bent
above his Irish home at Lisnalee.

Luke preached his first sermon very much to his own satisfaction. He had heard ever so many times that what was required in England was a series of controversial and argumentative sermons that might be convincing rather than stimu-

lating. Then one day he read in a Church newspaper that a certain Anglican divine had declared that Calvinism was the bane and curse of the Church of England. Here then was the enemy—to be exorcised by a course of vigorous lectures on Grace. Here Luke was master. The subject had formed part of the fourth year's curriculum in college, and Luke had explored it to its deepest depth. He read up his "Notes," drafted fifteen pages of a discourse, committed it to memory, and delivered it faultlessly, with just a delicious flavor of a Southern brogue, which was captivating to the greater part of his audience, and delightful from its very quaintness and originality to the lesser and more select. Now, Luke was a Molinist, and he told his congregation so. He demolished Calvin and Knox first, and when he had stowed away all that was left of them, he told his wondering and admiring audience that the Thomist and Scotist positions had been carried by assault, and that the Molinist flag was now waving above the conquered garrisons. Many more things he told them, as their wonder grew; and when Luke stepped down from the pulpit, he felt that the conversion of England had now in reality begun. Not that he was very vain; but it was hard to get rid of the ideas that six years of success and flattery had imprinted on a very plastic and susceptible character. And Luke felt much in the same position he had so often occupied in Maynooth, when he spun syllogisms as a spider spins his webs, and drew unwary flies into their viscous and deadly clutches.

The opinion of the congregation varied. That very large section in every congregation to whom the delivery of a sermon is a gymnastic exercise, which has no reference to the audience other than as spectators, considered that it was unique, original, but pedantic. One or two young ladies declared that he had lovely eyes, and that when he got over the *brusquerie* of his Irish education, he would be positively charming. One old apple-woman challenged another:—

"What was it all about, Mary?"

"Yerra, how could I know? Sure it was all Latin. But I caught the 'grace of God' sometimes."

"Well, the grace o' God and a big loaf—sure that's all we want in this world."

A rough workman, in his factory dress, asked:—

"Who is this young man?"

"A new hand they've taken on at the works here," said his mate.

The opinions of the clergy were not audibly expressed. Luke, indeed, heard one young man hint broadly at the "wind-mill," by which he understood his own gestures were meant. And another said something about a "pump-handle." A young Irish confrère stole to Luke's room late that night, and on being bidden to "come in," he threw his arms around Luke, thumped him on the back, ran up and down the room several times, and went through sundry Celtic gyrations; then:—

"Luke, old man, I'll tell you, you've knocked them all into a cocked hat."

The Vicar-General said nothing for a few days; then:—

"Delmege, have you got any more of these sermons?"

"Yes, sir; I have the series in 'Notes.' "

"Burn them!"

"Take the *Dublin Review* to your room, volume by volume," he added, "and study it. You've got quite on the wrong tack."

Luke had his first sick-call. It was urgent. A marine was dying down at the Naval Hospital near Stokeport. With all the alacrity of a young missioner, Luke passed rapidly through the streets, entered the huge archway of the hospital, inquired the way hastily from a passer-by, was directed to a hall-door, knocked, and was ushered by a trim servant-maid into a hand-somely furnished drawing-room.

"Very unlike a hospital ward," thought Luke. "Perhaps the parlor of one of the nurses or the matron."

He was left here for a long time, wondering at the pictures and books, the dainty accumulations of years by some soul that evidently had taste and wherewith to satisfy it. Then the door softly opened, and a clergyman, clad in library costume, short coat, etc., entered, gravely saluted him, bade him be seated, and commenced a calm, serious conversation. Luke's bewilderment was increasing, and with it an ever-deepening anxiety about his poor patient, who then and now might be struggling in his death agony. He never saw his mistake, until at last he rose, and the clergyman escorted him to the door, and thanked him for his friendly visit. He had sense enough left to ask the way to the hospital, which was kindly pointed out, and where he found his patient in the death-agony and unconscious.

The dying man lay in a little cot at the right-hand side of the long, empty ward. There was no other patient there. An attendant, clad in brown cloth, decorated with brass buttons, sat on the bed, coolly reading a newspaper. The hand of death was on the face of the poor consumptive. His eyes were glazed, and the gray shadow flitted up and down at each convulsive breath.

"Is this the Catholic patient?" asked Luke, anxiously.

"Yaas, he be a Cawtholic, I understan'," said the man.

"He is dying," said Luke, who had never seen death before.

"Dead in hexactly twenty minutes," said the man, taking out his watch and measuring the time. He restored the watch to his pocket and continued reading the paper.

This awful indifference smote Luke to the heart. He knelt down, put his stole around his neck, tried to elicit an act indicative of conscious sorrow from the dying, failed, gave conditional absolution, administered Extreme Unction, and read the prayers for the dying. The attendant continued absorbed in his paper. Then Luke sat down by the bedside, watched the flitting changes on the face of the dying whilst murmuring a prayer. Exactly at the twenty minutes specified the man rose up, folded his paper, stretched himself, and looked. A last spasm flashed across the gray, ashen face of the dying; the breathing stopped, fluttered, stopped again, came slowly and with painful effort, stopped again, then a long, deep breath, the eyes turned in their sockets. That soul had fled. A mucous foam instantly gathered on the blue lips and filled the entire mouth.

"Did I tell 'ee? Twenty minutes to the second," said the man, as he wiped the foam from the dead man's lips, and lifted the coverlet, flinging it lightly over the face of the dead man.

It was this cool indifference that smote the senses of Luke most keenly. For a long time he could not frame a word to express it, as it appeared to him. Then he stumbled on what he afterwards regarded as the strongest characteristic of this English people—their surprising "individualism." For while the unit was nothing in this seething turmoil of millions, the individual was everything to himself. Society might ignore him, despise him, calculate him; but he, understanding all this, went his own way, unheeding and indifferent—a solitary in the awful desert of teeming human life. Everywhere it was the same. Whilst all around the splendid materialism of England asserted and showed itself; whilst shops were packed full of every kind of luxury and necessary, and the victuallers and pork-butchers vied with the fruit-sellers in exhibiting every form of human food; whilst public baths were springing up in all directions, and everything ministering to human wants was exhibited in superabundance; whilst a perfect system of police and detective supervision guarded human life and safety, each solitary individual walked his way alone. You might live in a street for twenty years and not know the name of your next-door neighbor; and you seemed to be labelled and ticketed for State purposes, without the slightest reference to your own well-being, except so far as you were a component unit of the State. It was a huge piece of perfect and polished mechanism —cold, clean, shining, smooth, and regular; but with no more of a soul than a steam-engine. Often when the dread rattle and roar of the huge mechanism tortured the overworked nerves of Luke Delmege, and he felt as if he had been condemned for life to be imprisoned in some huge, infernal Tartarus of cranks and wheels, and the everlasting roar of steam and machinery, he would steal into some quiet street, where, hidden and un-seen, as God in the mighty mechanism of the universe, crouched some humble church; and sitting on the rude benches he would watch for an hour or two the red lamp swinging before the tabernacle, and break out into a soliloquy to ease his overburdened heart:—

"Lord, Lord! how lonely and silent, how hidden and neg-lected Thou art! Of all the millions who swarm in this hideous city, how many, how few, are aware of Thy awful Presence! There they pass and repass, Thy creatures, made by Thy hands, and yet to return to Thee! They are bent on business, on pleasure, on sin; but Thou art silent and they do not know that Thou art near! Thy name is cried in the street; but Thou, the dread reality, art but an abstraction and chimera! They think of Thee, as afar off on Sinai or Calvary; they do not know that Thou art here within touch of their hand and sound of their voice. Weary statesmen, burdened and overladen with thought, are yonder in that pile. They want wisdom, but know not where to seek it—world-wisdom, for they rule the world, and have assumed Thy prerogatives and responsibilities without the knowledge that could enlighten, or the judgment that can discern! And there close by is the mighty temple where once Thy praises were sung and Thy Sacred Presence rested; but 'Ichabod' is now written over its porches. Not Thy Presence, but the dust of many who have done Thee dishonor, is there. And here around are souls perishing from hunger and feeding on husks; and they have forgotten to cry to their Father for bread. Verily, Thou art a hidden God, and the world does not know Thee!"

This loneliness of our Lord in His London tabernacles invariably led Luke to the cognate reflection of the loneliness of God and His hiddenness in His universe. He was rather drawn to this reflection by the habit he had acquired of meditating on the ineffable attributes of God, since the day when his venerable professor told an admiring class that he had remained up half the night before, absorbed in a reverie, after having read Lessius on the ministry and prerogatives of the angels. But whereas, in the lonely fields and on the silent seas and lakes of Ireland, he had been penetrated only by the majesty and immensity of the Creator, here in seething, riotous, tumultuous London, the loneliness of God affected him even to tears.

"Tonight," he said, "in all England, but two or three small communities will watch with God. Tonight, whilst all England with its thirty millions are asleep, one or two tiny communities, there in Devonshire, here in Parkminster, there in Leicester, will startle the solemnity of the night with psalms of praise and canticles of adoration. 'Praise the Lord, all ye nations; praise Him, all ye people.' Alas! no. All the nations and all the peoples are busy with other things, and the Lord of the universe, bending down to hear the voices of the darkness, of the earth, must turn back with disappointment to the tumultuous worship of His Heaven."

And then the thought startled him—could it be that God is as forgotten in the vast Heavens as on earth? Are all the mighty spirits that people the universe, hover over infant planets, guide colossal suns, revel in the crimson and golden belts

of far fairer worlds than ours, and are endowed with higher
and more perfect faculties and senses—are all these immortals
as forgetful of God as we? And is God as lonely in His universe
as here amongst the five millions of London? It was a dreadful thought but impossible! It is only on earth that the mighty
Maker is ignored. More shame for those who know Him—to
whom He hath revealed Himself!

And then Luke's thoughts would turn to Ireland of the
saints.

"It ought to be a vast monastery," he said; "one grand, everlasting choir of psalm and hymn, where the praises of God
would never cease—never know pause or suspension day or
night."

Alas! he did not know until after many years how far the
splendid materialism of England had infected and attenuated
the spiritualism of Ireland; and how hearts were throbbing, and
eyes looking far forward and eagerly, and ears were straining
for the rumble of machinery and the mechanism of Mammon,
rather than for the thunder of mighty organs and the raptures
of exultant choirs.

Nor did he know how the spirit of the supernatural in his
own breast was already pluming its wings for flight, and how
new ideas—the spirit of the age—were supplanting it. He only
felt dimly that he was carried on, on, on in the whirl and tumult
of some mighty mechanism; that the whir of revolving wheels,
the vibration of belts, the thunder of engines, the hiss of steam,
were everywhere. And that from all this tremendous energy
were woven fair English tapestries—stately palaces and an-
cestral forests, trim villas and gardens like Eastern carpets—
and that the huge machinery also tossed aside its refuse and
slime—the hundreds of thousands that festered and perished
in the squalor of the midnight cities. For over all England,
even in midsummer, hangs a blue haze, and over its cities the
aer bruno, in which the eye of the poet saw floating the spirits
of the lost.

He stepped from the silences of God and the roar of London
was in his ears.

CHAPTER X

"The Strayed Reveller"

DOCTOR WILSON was in his study. He was engaged with a patient. So the faithful servitor told the few jaundiced patients who were waiting below and striving under a rather sickly gas-jet to read *The Graphic* and *The Jester;* or mutually comparing each other's liver symptoms, and talking of the latest pharmaceutical wonder. Dr. Wilson's patient, or patients, were of a peculiar type; and he was searching diligently for one whom he failed to find. There they were—all yet discovered,—invisible to you or me; but plainly visible there in that dark chamber, under the tiny moon of light cast from a reflector. Unseen themselves, but agents of unseen powers for the destruction of human tissue, and therefore of human life, they swarmed under the microscope; and Wilson felt about as comfortable as in a powder magazine, or with a charge of dynamite beneath his feet. But he *would* find it—that—microbe of hydrophobia, which no man had yet discovered; he would find it and write a treatise on it, and then—*Sir* Athelstan Wilson!

"Come in!"

"Mrs. Wilson would like to know, sir, whether you intend going to the theatre tonight."

"No!" sharp and laconic. Then—

"Send up those patients; let me see—Mr. Carnegie."

Louis Wilson heard his father's decision, heard and rejoiced.

"I shall accompany you, mother."

"No, dear. I shall not go."

Louis Wilson regretted the decision deeply, but smiled.

Mrs. Wilson idolized her son. Louis Wilson despised his mother. Her worship disgusted and amazed him. His contempt intensified her idolatry. He played on her wretched feelings as

101

on a shattered and shrieking instrument,—petted her, laughed at her, coaxed her, contemned her, made her furious with passion or maudlin with love, repelled her, as at a dinner party a few evenings before, when he hissed at her behind his cards: "Hold your tongue, and don't make a fool of yourself;" won her back by a lurid description of London revels, in which he played no inconsiderable a part. Of his father he was somewhat afraid, probably because he had to look to him for ways and means. There had been one or two scenes by reason of certain debts that Louis had contracted; and the father, to relieve his feelings, used language somewhat stronger than is sanctioned by conventional usage. Louis regarded him coolly, told him such expressions were ungentlemanly, that he had never heard the like amongst the high elemental society in which he moved—in a word, made his father thoroughly ashamed of himself. But there are certain limits even to a doctor's finances; and Louis, once or twice, had to look elsewhere. This did not increase his filial affection, which now was blended with dread and hate, disgust and aversion.

"I think I shall have a cigar, then," said Louis to his mother. "I shall hardly return to supper."

"The Doctor won't like to see you absent, Louis," said his mother.

" 'Tis his night at the Lodge," said Louis. "He won't miss me."

The last patient (all but the hydrophobic microbe, who positively refused to be diagnosed or to pay a fee) was dismissed; the last guinea pocketed; the last entry made; and the Doctor, a wearied man, with a weight of care showing in gray hairs and puckered eyes, entered the drawing-room.

"Where's Louis?" he demanded peremptorily.

"Gone out for a cigar," said his wife.

"Confound that cub," said the father. "I believe he hates his home and despises us all."

"Now, really, Athelstan, you are unjust to the boy. You repel him, and, domesticated as he is, you drive him where he is better appreciated."

"Better appreciated?" echoed the Doctor, lifting his eyebrows.

"Yes, better appreciated," said the good mother. "You ig-

nore the poor boy, and he is frightened of you. Yet I heard
Lady Alfroth say the other day at the levée that that boy was a
perfect Adonis. What's Adonis, Athelstan?"

"Adonis," said the Doctor, "was an infamous puppy, who
did not reflect much credit on his admirer, nor she on him.
Does *she* make herself the Venus of Euploea or the Venus of
Apelles, Bessie?"

"I don't know anything about them," said poor mamma.
"But I do know that my boy is admired by the highest ladies
of the land, and that you'll drive him to destruction."

"Humph! He is pretty far on the road already. Where's Barbara?"

"I don't know. Probably in some of the slums, with a basket
on her arm and a poke bonnet, like those bold Salvation Army
people."

"Barbara should be at home. Can it be possible that, with
her domesticated tastes, you may be driving her to destruction?"

"I'm sure I do all in my power to bring her into decent society. I have had every kind of invitation for her—to balls and
tennis parties; but the girl has low tastes, I regret to say—"

"Inherited from whom?"

"Not from me certainly. You are constantly taunting me
with being too fond of society."

"H'm! Look here, Bessie, let us compromise. Bring up your
brother, the Canon, and I'll give a dinner. Who knows—we
may meet an 'eligible' for Barbara."

"She'd rather be kneeling at the feet of a friar," said Mrs.
Wilson; but her heart jumped at the suggestion.

"Well, that is low enough," said the Doctor; and he laughed
at his little pun.

"Whom shall we ask?" said Mrs. Wilson.

"Oh! it makes no matter. The Canon will obliterate everybody. By the way, isn't there a big English preacher coming
over here soon?"

"Yes," said Mrs. Wilson. Her plans were ripening to perfection. "He's a near relative to the Duke of B——."

"Bessie, the gods are smiling on thee. If ever you care for
Heaven after you have the Duke's relative at your shoulder,
I'm an apothecary. But, by Jove, won't there be fun? We'll pit

the Canon against the celebrity; 'twill be worth a prize-fight in Arizona."

"What day shall we say?" asked Mrs. Wilson, who bore her husband's bantering by reason of her triumph.

"Any day you please, but immediately after the Horse Show. Calthrop is coming over, and I want to show him something worth remembering."

"That horrid fellow from Cambridge, who wrote about germs and things?"

"Exactly. He is the leading germinologist of the day, except Weismann."

"Will he wear his apron—and—things? 'Twould be hardly right, you know, in the presence of the clergy."

"He will, then, and you'll see streaks of hell-fire, red and yellow, across his breast. Here goes for a cigar! If the cub enjoys a cigarette, why shouldn't the old bear enjoy a cigar?"

Mrs. Wilson was alone with her own thoughts and plans for a few minutes. Then a gentle step was heard on the stairs, and Barbara, looking pale and wearied, came in. She flung her hat on the sofa, tidied up her hair, and asked her mother might she have a cup of tea there in the drawing-room.

"I suppose you may," said her mother, peevishly. "Although I must say, Barbara, you would consult better for our respectability if you would conform more closely to the requirements of elegant society."

There spoke the Canon's sister. Barbara said nothing. After tea she drew over a chair, and, taking up a magazine, asked anxiously:—

"Where is Louis, mother?"

"You care little about Louis or any of your family," answered Mrs. Wilson; "if you did, you would not avoid meeting those who might be of service to us, and affect the society of the low and disreputable city slums."

Barbara was rather accustomed to these monologues, and answered not at all. Mother should speak or go mad.

"Your father at last is meeting my wishes, and is about to entertain. Can you help me to form a list?"

"Certainly, mother," said Barbara. "Is it—I hope not—a ball?"

"No. That's some relief for you. He is about to invite some distinguished people to dinner to meet the Canon."

"Uncle?"

"Yes. You seem surprised."

"And what persons—what class are going to meet uncle?"

"Do you think father would ask any one that was not respectable?"

"Oh, no! But if I am to help you, I must know is it a medical, a clerical, or a legal dinner?"

"You are becoming sarcastic, Barbara,—a dangerous accomplishment for a young lady."

"Now, mother, let us not bandy words. Whom are you going to ask?"

"That is what I want to know. Mr. Calthrop is coming over."

Barbara laid down her pen, and looked in pained surprise at her mother.

"Then you can't ask any priest to meet *him*," said she.

"I would have you know," said Mrs. Wilson, angrily, "that my brother shall be the guest of the occasion. If he should be present, no other clergyman can object."

Barbara was silent.

"We shall ask Monsignor Dalton and Monsignor Williams. Can you think of any one else?"

"There is Father Elton, of——Street. He is a very distinguished man—"

"I am afraid it would hardly do to ask any one beneath his own dignity to meet my brother. There's a certain etiquette in these cases."

"But Father Elton is a Fellow of the Royal Society, and has frequently lunched at the Castle."

"Oh!" said Mrs. Wilson, with a gasp of surprise, "indeed! By all means put down Father Elton. I didn't know he was so distinguished. Then put down Sir Archibald Thompson, of the College of Science, and Algy Redvers, who admired you so much at the Denison's party, and—"

"Mother?"

"Well?"

"Will they come? It will be awkward if you get refusals."

"Barbara!" said Mrs. Wilson, in a faltering tone, "how

dare you say such things! Will they come? I should say so."

"Mother, must this be?"

"It must, child," said mother, weeping silently, "but I wish it were over."

Dr. Wilson attended the meeting of Lodge No. 8, Moulton Street, and was made happy thereby. He had long since learned that it was only by diligent and servile attention to the plenipotentiaries who ruled the Lodges, and, indeed, every other department in his country, that he could hope for advancement in his profession. True, he had an excellent and growing reputation, an excellent and growing and paying *clientèle;* for, after all, when you have a "liver," it makes very little difference even if it is Catholic boluses, ordered by Catholic doctors, that relieve you. This is sometimes controverted at the Lodges; and it is maintained that even bottles and pills should have the compass and square written or indented. But a certain residuum of desirable patients did trickle into the study of Dr. Wilson, and that residuum created an appetite for more. Then there were certain honors and emoluments that were absolutely in the gift of the Lodges; and these are desirable things, except to a certain class of fanatics, who, like Oriental fakirs, prefer poverty and retirement. Sometimes, indeed, a "sop to Cerberus" is flung to Catholics, when the tables are too redundant and there are no Protestant mouths to feed; and it is Christian and consoling to witness the intense and maudlin gratitude with which the morsels are received and wept over. But how did Dr. Wilson know that he would be there when the crumbs fell, or that some more audacious and hungry Papist might not snatch the coveted morsel? This is a matter admitting of no uncertainty. Brother Wilson, Lodge No. 8, cannot be overlooked.

The meeting was over, the night was moonlit, and Dr. Wilson strolled home leisurely. He was accosted at the corner of Denton Street:—

"Friend, I owe thee something, and I should wish to repay thee!"

"Oh! some other time, Mr. Pyne," said the Doctor, recognizing a city magnate, one of the last remnants of the Quaker community, who are fast losing their characteristics and merging into mere Protestants.

"It is not money I owe thee, friend," said the Quaker; "I have paid thee all that was due; but I owe thee gratitude."

"A rare and unintelligible debt," thought the Doctor.

"I had a liver," continued the Quaker, "and I felt like the saintly man of old, who, when threatened by the Pagan magistrate—'I shall drag the liver out of thee,' answered with Christian gentleness, 'I wish to God you would.' Now, thou hast holpen me to bring that rebellious and ungodly member into better dispositions, and I am grateful to thee, and I should wish to repay thee."

There was a pause, the Doctor smiling at the Quaker's drollery.

"Thou hast a son?" said the latter, at length. The smile died from the Doctor's face.

"He is young and inexperienced, and he hath a fatal gift," continued the Quaker. "And there be a foolish woman, and clamorous, who sitteth on a seat in the high place of the city, and she saith, 'Whoso is simple, let him turn in hither.' But he knoweth not that the dead are there, and that her guests are in the depths of hell."

"This is all pedantic and ambiguous, Pyne," said the Doctor, testily. "You mean something grave. Would it not be better to explain it fully?"

"Seeing is better than hearing," continued the Quaker, in his solemn way, "better even than faith. Come."

He called a cab, and the two drove in silence along winding streets and open thoroughfares, until they came to a fashionable suburb. Here the cab stopped, and the two gentlemen alighted. They moved rapidly along the smooth pavement and stood before a large mansion, whose hall and windows were unlighted, and over which hung the stillness of death.

"Whatever thou seest here," said the Quaker, "wilt thou promise to make neither sign nor sound of recognition? It is important."

"Yes, I promise," said the Doctor, strangely perturbed.

They mounted the steps slowly. The bell tinkled, and a footman appeared.

"Are the guests assembled?" said the Quaker.

"Yes, sir," said the man, deferentially.

"And the banquet ready?"

"Yes, sir," replied the man.

"That will do. I shall find my own way."

He passed rapidly up the broad staircase, dimly lighted here and there by a colored lamp. The Doctor followed. Their footsteps fell softly on the thick stair-carpet, and did not disturb the solemn silence. A few steps led off the main stairs. Here a door was opened; but a thick heavy *portière* hung down. The Quaker drew it gently aside, and they found themselves in a large dining-room, now fitted as a theatre; but all the lights burned low until but a faint twilight filled the room, save at the end, where a narrow stage was brilliantly lighted with electric lamps. Hence they stood and then sat unseen by the audience—a crowd of ladies and gentlemen, all in evening costume, and who besides were so interested by the stage tableau that they could not hear the almost noiseless entrance of the visitors. Nor did the visitors heed them; for their eyes were riveted on that same stage, where, clad in fawnskins, with a thyrsus in one hand and a winecup in the other, and apparently in an advanced state of intoxication, was Louis Wilson, in the capacity of the "Strayed Reveller." He sat, or rather reclined, on a couch, softened by mosses and ferns; the fawnskin had slipped from his shoulder, which gleamed like marble; the dark curls hung low on his neck as he raised his face upward towards the enchantress of Cyprus—Circe. She was clothed in Greek costume, her hair filleted and knotted by circlets of gold and precious stones, and her feet quite bare. Near her stood Ulysses, grim and weather-beaten, his mariner's clothes rather tattered and seaworn, and on his face was a look of gladness as of one who had escaped shipwreck, and yet as of one who had determined not to be taken in the toils of the enchantress. Circe was just repeating the words:

> Foolish boy! why tremblest thou?
> Thou lovest it, then, my wine?
> Wouldst more of it? See, how it glows
> Through the delicate flushed marble,
> The red creaming liquor,

Strown with dark seeds!
Drink, then! I chide thee not,
Deny thee not the bowl.
Come, stretch forth thy hand—then—so,
Drink, drink again!

and Louis repeated:—

Thanks, gracious One!
Ah, the sweet fumes again!
More soft, ah me!
More subtle-winding
Than Pan's flute-music.
Faint—faint! Ah, me!
Again the sweet sleep.

"I wish to God he'd never wake out of it," hissed the Doctor. "I'd rather see him dead a million times than thus."

"Hush! hush!" said the Quaker. "Come out!"

"No, I'll see the damnable thing to the end," hissed the Doctor. And they did. Then, with a sigh, the Doctor went out, followed by his friend.

"What's all this infernal business about?" said the Doctor. "What do they call this Devil's Drama?"

"Now, now, friend, thou art unreasonably excited," said the Quaker. "This is a harmless poem enough; written by a very excellent good man; and now more or less degraded into what they call *Tableaux Classiques*. If thou wert to see thy excellent son as Perseus, rescuing that fair lady, Andromeda—"

"And who is that harridan?" said the Doctor.

"A most excellent wife and mother. Didst thou never hear of the beautiful Mrs. Wenham, wife of one of the *aides-de-camp* to Lord ——?"

"Certainly," said his companion. The Doctor softened a little under the magic of the name, though he felt his son's degradation keenly.

"And that old Silenus—who is he?"

"The reputable and pious Crawford, whose name stands behind six figures at the Exchange."

"The old ranting hypocrite! I thought he did nothing but

cheat on the Exchange, and sing psalms with old toothless cats, and slander over their tea-tables!"

"Now, friend, thou art irritated, and therefore unjust. Even the godly and the pious must have legitimate recreation; and thou knowest the object is charitable."

"Indeed! I should be much surprised if my young cub ever did a charitable thing in his life."

"Oh, yes!" said the Quaker. "Thou shouldst not object. Is it not one of the tenets of thy own Church—the end justifies the means? And what can be more laudable than to wean away young baby Papists from their darkness and superstition and bring them into the sunlight of the Gospel freedom? Good-night, dear friend!"

And the kindly sarcastic Quaker went his way. Next morning the microbe patients had a little rest. There was a scene, a violent scene, in the Doctor's study, in which, for once, the Doctor's honest anger overwhelmed and subdued the keen sarcasm of his son, whilst Barbara and her mother, with white faces, were trembling in the drawing-room. That evening the mail boat from Kingstown had on its deck a very distinguished passenger, with a good deal of the manner and airs of a foreign prince. And then Louis Wilson had to face the humiliation and misery of his London lodgings during the long vacation, when all the world was abroad, except the vulgar. He would have fretted a good deal but for two resources—the care of his face and figure, and a certain tiny flask which he carried with him everywhere, and a few drops of whose magic elixir wafted him to a Mahometan paradise.

CHAPTER XI

Circe

"I'LL INSIST on cook taking an action for libel against that fellow," said Dr. Wilson, the morning after the great dinner. "Why, he touched nothing but a biscuit and an apple. Did he think we were going to poison him?"

No! Not exactly. But the "great man," besides being extremely and habitually abstemious, as all great thinkers ought to be, had really some uncharitable suspicions about the cookery of the outer barbarians. He stirred the soup as carefully as if he had expected every moment to turn up a baby's finger, for he had heard that a great archbishop had once had that delicacy offered him by a Maori chief; and really, you don't know, you know! And he passed by dish after dish as if he were playing "Nap" and held a decidedly bad hand. But withal, he was very nice and brilliant; and, though pang after pang of mortification and shame shot through the anxious breast of the hostess, and she feared that it was all a *fiasco,* after her days of work and nights of worry, nevertheless the afterthought: "But he is an Englishman, and near cousin to the Duke of B——" acted as a soothing and mollifying unguent on hurt and bruised feelings. Then, too, the quick sword-play of words between the "great preacher" and Mrs. Wenham—!!! What, you ask, with a line full of notes of exclamations, do you mean to say Mrs. Wenham—Circe!—was there? Yes, indeed, and very much in evidence. There had been an angry intermarital debate as to the propriety of asking her, on that same night when Louis was peremptorily ordered from his father's house; but the name had already been inserted on Mrs. Wilson's list, and how could they think of offending one of the greatest potentates at the Castle? The Doctor bit his lip. It wasn't a case for explanations. And

111

he was obliged to admit that Mrs. Wenham was charming. With the splendid individualism of her race, she came to the banquet in a simple dress. Whilst some of the other guests had as many rings on each finger as the poles of a curtain, she had but one. But in a moment she coolly monopolized the conversation, or rather dualized it with her distinguished fellow-countryman. The imperial and dominant race assumed proprietorship here, as in all other departments. The Scythians were silent.

It is quite true, in the beginning, Circe gave a little start of surprise on beholding so many representatives of the Church Militant around her. But this quickly subsided. After all— that is, after she had, by a vigorous process of reasoning, conquered that instinctive and reverential dread of the priesthood which is common to Mrs. Wenham and the world, and argued, rather vainly, that they were no more than those Ritualistic clergymen whom she had met so often, and so often despised, she concluded that they were, after all, only humans, and, as such, legitimate and easy prey. And, to save time, she thought she would conquer the *generalissimo,* and all the subalterns would then capitulate.

"You find the country interesting?"

"Yes," he replied, feeling his way. "So far, I am, indeed, highly interested."

"Your first visit?"

"My first visit," he replied, "and one to which I have eagerly looked forward."

"I hope, then, you will turn the pleasure into a study. You will find a good many things to interest you."

"I have found a great many interesting things; and even a larger number of interesting persons so far," he said, with a bow and smile.

"If you had had the good fortune and the better taste of being at the Horse Show these last days, you'd have seen still more interesting studies. There was an immense number of clergymen there—more, indeed, than I have ever seen at hippodromes elsewhere. I should say it was a curious ethnological study—that almost universal taste of Irishmen for horseflesh."

"You speak as if you had not the honor of being an Irishwoman," said the great one.

"I am English—or rather Scoto-English," said Circe.

"It is quite a disappointment," said the great one; but they shook hands metaphorically across the table, as Stanley and Livingstone, when they stepped out of the shade of the palms and bamboos, and recognized the pith helmets and revolvers. It was the only trace and visible sign of civilization that had been left them.

"That passion for horses and dogs has been always a characteristic of our people," said a Monsignor. "We must have been a nomadic race at one time."

"I have been reading somewhat like it in one of Matthew Arnold's poems," said a lady. "I think it was 'Sohrab and Rustum.'"

"Is he not the author of the 'Strayed Reveller'?" said Dr. Wilson directly to Mrs. Wenham.

She looked at her interrogator blankly for a moment, then colored a little, then frowned, then answered:—

"I never read modern poetry." It was a bad hit, but she had passed through many campaigns.

"By the way, Mrs. Wilson," she said blandly, "I understood that your boy was in Dublin. I did hear some ladies enthuse rather too markedly about him a few days hence. But how can the boy help being so handsome?"

"Jezebel!" said the Doctor, between his teeth.

"And it is quite a series of conquests," said the woman of the world, turning to Barbara; "you, little witch, mesmerized that young fool, Kendal, at the Denison's the other day. By the way, Doctor, look out for the list of Jubilee honors. Great complaints that the medical profession has never yet been sufficiently represented or acknowledged there."

"*Wer kann die Weiberchen dressiren,*" said Father Elton, breaking in upon the conversation from a quiet chat he had been carrying on with the younger of the two Monsignori. He did not understand the sword-play between the Doctor and Mrs. Wenham; but he saw that there was some veiled antagonism there, and it interested him.

"You are well read in ancient legend and poetry?" he said, turning towards Mrs. Wenham.

"Not quite as well read as you *savants,*" she said, bridling under the interrogation; "but quite well enough acquainted with them to know that they used up all human thought, and that all the pallid and sickly growths of modern times are ideas transplanted into uncongenial climates and soils."

"There, now, Dr. Calthrop," said Father Elton, "there's what your clever countrywomen think of all your miraculous discoveries in science—pallid and sickly transplantings."

" I didn't include science," said Mrs. Wenham; "but as *you* have said it, I adhere to it," which was generous of Mrs. Wenham, and seemed to imply a new interest in this Roman priest.

"I would give a good deal to be assured of that," said Calthrop with slow emphasis, for he was a heavy man; "I assure you I am quite tired of the deification of my masters, and I have long suspected that they have but feet of clay."

"It is only a simple and familiar fact in all human history. I cannot speak much for your department, Doctor, for I am extremely sorry to say I do not know what it is, but there is one general and unmistakable fact or principle in nature—flux and reflux; and there must be, as George Eliot puts it, an equivalent systole and diastole in all human inquiry."

"Carlyle is the author of that expression, I think," said Father Elton.

"No! George Eliot," said Mrs. Wenham, looking steadily at him. "I won't permit my favorite to be robbed by a Scotch parrot, that screams in broken German."

"Oh! oh!" said Father Elton, "and you said you were half Scotch. Is there a general propensity among the Celts to turn the spit?"

"Your remark, Mrs. Wenham," said Dr. Calthrop, after a good deal of thought, "has impressed me. I shall look up the ancients. And you say there's nothing new under the sun?"

"Nothing," said Mrs. Wenham; "even human nature is unchanged. Even your Christianity," she said, looking calmly around on all the clerics, from her great fellow-countryman down to the Canon, and up again to Father Elton, "is but a repetition of the ancient philosophies, Greek, Egyptian, and Hindoo."

"Except that?" said Father Elton, insinuatingly.

"I except nothing," she said, fixing her glowing eyes upon him.

"Except that?" Father Elton repeated, smiling.

"Except that the ancient philosophies made their professors humble; and—" she stopped, fearing to proceed.

"And that Christianity is the culmination and perfection of all. Dear me, think of a nineteenth-century lady actually quoting St. Augustine!"

"Oh! the days of miracles are not yet departed," she laughed.

"No, indeed," said Father Elton, drawing himself together. "I remember," he continued, "a rather curious incident that occurred to myself only a few months ago. You've all heard of Knock, of course. Well, I was really anxious to see for myself all that could be authenticated about these marvelous apparitions. So I went down, put up for a few days in an improvised hotel, and looked around. I saw nothing but the miracle of the people's faith and piety, and the miracle of suffering ever patiently borne. We are the most incredulous of mortals, except when facts swim into the sunlit domain of Faith. Well, one evening at dinner, I sat near a young gentleman from Dublin, who also had been prosecuting inquiries. He asked me bluntly what I thought—that is, what the Church thought about miracles. I explained the doctrine as simply as I could. When I had finished, he said in a simple way:—

" 'I am an unbeliever. I was brought up a Protestant, but I have lost all faith. But I am of a rather curious turn of mind; and I have so much natural religion left that I am interested in other people's beliefs. This brought me here. I shall test every case, I said, and ascertain where delusion ends and miracles begin. I know the tremendous power exercised by the mind over the body and how nervous maladies can be cured by mere mental concentration. But let me see one clear case of consumption or hip disease or cancer healed, and I shall think it necessary to retrace my steps and reconsider my position. Now just watch this! A few evenings ago, just at the dusk, I went up to the church accompanied by my mother and sister. We stood opposite the gable where the figures were supposed to have appeared. There was an immense crowd, staring with dilated eyes to see what was about to come out from the invisible silences. Probably I was the only cool and exacting and incredulous spirit there. My mother and sister were Protestants, but sympathetic. I stood between them, leaning one hand on the shoulder of each. The Litanies—is that what you call them?—commenced. I had no sympathy with all these meta-phorical expressions: "Ark of the Covenant," "Morning Star," "Tower of David"; but I admitted they were beautiful. The innumerable candles were lighting; and I was looking around, coolly scrutinizing the faces of the believers, when to my utter amazement I saw the statue of the Virgin slowly expand to life-size; I saw the flesh-color come into the cheeks and neck; I saw the eyes open widely and look down with infinite pity at me. I was entranced, fascinated, mesmerized. I pressed my hands heavily on the shoulders of my mother and sister, and cried in a passionate whisper: Look! look! It was not a momen-tary phasis; it lasted all through to the end of the Litany; and there I stared and stared at the phenomenon; and all the time the eyes of the Virgin were fixed on me with that peculiar ex-pression of sadness. "Don't you see it?" I cried passionately to my friends. "See what?" they exclaimed. "Why, the apparition! Look! look! before it disappears!" "You are bewitched!" my sister cried; "there is absolutely nothing but the statue and the lights!" I said no more, but continued to gaze. Once and again I shut my eyes and then rubbed them vigorously. But there was the apparition unchanged, until at the last strophe of the Litanies a mist seemed to swim before it, and then slowly the figure dwindled down to the size of the statue, the flesh-tints disappeared, and in a few moments I saw nothing but the clay image and the lifeless eyes. But were I put on oath then, I should have said that there was an apparition. The hallucina-tion lasted only a little while. When I had got back to my hotel I was convinced it was an optical delusion. And so it is with all your miracles—the action of a disordered stomach upon the optic nerve.'

" 'And your mother and sister?' I said.

" 'They were more impressionable,' he replied. 'But it is all evaporated in the swing and swirl of life.'

"I had quite forgotten the incident," continued Father Elton, "and even the name, until it all came back as you were speak-ing, Mrs. Wenham. I think,—but I am not quite positive,—that the gentleman's name was Menteith."

All through the little narrative Mrs. Wenham's large eyes

were fixed on the speaker, wondering, speculating, angry, frightened. When Father Elton had finished, she looked down modestly at her folded hands, and said meekly:—

"That is also my name. And your acquaintance was my brother. I remember the circumstance well."

"Oh! indeed," said Father Elton, "how curiously I have stumbled on such an interesting circumstance. And now, Mrs. Wenham, did the experience of your excellent brother really impress you?"

Mrs. Wenham looked as innocent as a Child of Mary on the day of her profession.

"I have never failed to say the Rosary of the Virgin every day since then," she said.

Father Elton looked long and steadily at her. She calmly returned the gaze. Then Father Elton turned aside to the nearest Monsignor; and he must have heard some excellent stories during the next twenty minutes, for he laughed and laughed until the tears ran from his eyes.

There was a silence of embarrassment for the next few minutes, broken only by a gallant attempt on the part of the Canon to collect the scattered forces.

"Might I ask—ha—" he said, addressing the preacher, "do you—ha—use the same heraldic crest and motto as the Duke of ——?"

"No!" came uncompromisingly from the great preacher.

"How very interesting!" said the Canon.

"We have no time to think of such things in England," said the preacher.

"Dear me!" said the Canon. "I thought you had no responsibilities—ha—except an occasional sermon."

"The sermon is only a recreation, particularly when I have had to preach to such an intelligent audience and to meet such interesting company as I have been favored with this evening," said the preacher.

"Then we—ha—hope to have the honor of a repetition of your visit?" said the Canon.

The preacher shrugged his shoulders.

As the ladies filed out, Father Elton held the door open. Circe was last.

"It was not a matter to be spoken of at a public dinner table," she whispered; "but you must really take me up, and bring a poor lost sheep into the true fold."

"With great pleasure," he replied.

Ah, Circe! Circe! A great enchantress you may be with budding Apollos and young Adonises, who have not yet put on the calm of the eternal gods; but "your sweet eyes, your low replies" will never turn these steeled and passionless priests into porkers, Circe!

She tried her wiles on more yielding material, and ascertained in twenty minutes from Barbara, (1) that her father was really anxious for a title; (2) that her brother had left Dublin rather unexpectedly, why and wherefore Barbara did not know; (3) that Barbara was thoroughly ashamed of this evening dress she was wearing, and had striven successfully to cover it with all kinds of webs and woofs of lace; (4) that she had a great dread of Father Elton, who was so clever, and a great reverence for the purple, and a great love for certain uncouth, barefooted mediævalists down there in a street that was generally festooned with all manner of human integuments, and that was only held together by the Caryatides, who, with arms akimbo, sustained from morning to night its creaking and rotten postels and architraves; (5) that Barbara's little soul had no other ambition or craving for pleasure except a quiet hour after a hard day's work, down there in the dimly lighted church, where the great lamp swung to and fro, and there was silence, but for the rattle of old Norry's beads.

And the woman of the world, calling up her own history, and the many secret histories that were locked up and sealed in the cabinets of memory, looked this young girl over, and looked through her eyes and the lines of her mouth, and satisfied herself that there were no secret corridors and avenues there. Then the woman of the world, wondering at this curiosity, put a few other leading questions, which glanced harmlessly off the armor of a pure ingenuous soul. Then the woman of the world fell into a deep reverie, and woke up to hear herself whispering: "The days of miracles are not passed. It is a child, and a miracle."

Later on, when the gentlemen had entered the drawing-room, it was noticed that Mrs. Wenham was rather silent and thoughtful.

"A clever woman, playing a clever part!" thought Father Elton.

"A little bored by the Scythians," thought the preacher, "as indeed, I confess myself to be."

"Jezebel is repenting," said Dr. Wilson. "Has she a fore-shadowing of the dogs?"

Not at all, for the prophets were all dead. She took an early leave. Barbara would accompany her to her carriage. Dr. Wilson said a frigid goodnight. Barbara whispered:—

"You may be able to do something for papa, Mrs. Wenham."

"You may be assured I will, for your sweet sake," said Mrs. Wenham.

"And—and—if ever—that is, you may meet Louis in London, will you—won't you—oh! dear Mrs. Wenham!—"

"There, go in from the night-air, you little saint, décolletée," said the woman of the world, as she said "good-bye!"

"There are a few innocents still left in the world," she said to the mute who accompanied her. " 'Tis a pity; for Rachel will yet have to shed tears. And there should be no tears! none!" she cried almost viciously. "But steeled nerves and stony hearts and minds that won't turn back on the inevitable. What dreadful fate is before that child? For she cannot be spared. The soldiers of Herod are abroad, and the air is full of the sound of weeping. I should like to see her God, though. Let me see—ten—'tis early, is it not?"

She pulled the cord and gave a direction to her coachman. He said nothing, but turned the horses' heads, though he went near falling off his perch.

Then the woman of the world found herself in the dark porch of a church, whither she had picked her way, but with dreadful misgivings as to the condition of her silks and shoes. Dark figures flitted by her in the dim light, dipped their hands somewhere, muttered their charms, and disappeared. She entered, but saw nothing but a few yellow jets that darkened the gloom. She moved up the center aisle, and saw the red lamp swinging. She watched it eagerly. It had some curious fascination about it. She had seen similar lamps burning before *eikons* in Russia once, when her husband was military attaché to the Court; and she had often seen the same lamps at the corners of the Italian streets before images of the Madonna. But they weren't like this altogether. What was it? Then she discerned slowly that she was not alone, but that the church was crowded. For faces paled from out the darkness, and whispers and a cough broke on her startled senses. She saw long rows of men and women, mute as statues in the halls of the dead. What were they doing? And that red lamp? She was seized with a sudden panic and fled.

"May the sweet Mother of God protect you, and may God give you a happy death and a favorable judgment," said a voice from the darkness of the porch.

"It was a plunge in the *Inferno*," she said. "What madness came over me?"

Death—Judgment! Death—Judgment! Death—Judgment! Death—Judgment! So sang the merry wheels, as "low on the sands, loud on the stones" her carriage whirled away.

CHAPTER XII

Critical and Expository

"YOU REALLY surprise me, Father Elton," said Dr. Calthrop, when the gentlemen had sat down with an air of unspeakable freedom and lighted their cigars, "and you interest
me, because I really must admit that we are disposed sometimes to suffer from swelled heads in our generation. But now,"
he said coaxingly, "do you not really dread us? We have
pushed you back behind the ramparts, and are just forming
en echelon for the last attack."

"To vary the simile," said Father Elton, smiling, "tell me,
did you, a city man, ever chance to see the rooks following
the sower in a ploughed field?"

"Yes, yes, to be sure," said the Doctor.

"Well, you know, we are the rooks. Every French *gamin*
is taught to say: *Quoi! quoi!* after us in the streets. But, as you
are well aware, the careful and thrifty rooks follow the track
of the sower to pick up the seeds he has dropped, and assimilate them. They are not afraid of the sower. And they laugh,
actually laugh, at the hat on the pole and the streaming rags,
which are supposed to frighten them."

"I cannot well follow you," said the slow Doctor.

"Well, my dear sir," said Father Elton, "we are the rooks.
You are the sowers. Every fact you drop from the bag of
science, we assimilate it for our own use. You may label it
'Poison' if you like. We laugh and pick it up. Your scarecrow
—the end and final judgment on all religion and revelation,—
we look at it boldly, cackle at it contemptuously and fly away."

"I see," said the Doctor, laughing. "But some day the sower
will get mad and string up one or two of you."

"That would be unscientific," said the priest. "And, above
121

all other things, the rooks have faith in the philosophy and imperturbability of the seed-sower. To string up one or two of us would be a retrograde proceeding; and science is essentially progressive."

"But the whole tone of you gentlemen in matters of controversy appears to me to be distinctly apologetic. There is a rubbing of the hands and an action of deprecation observable in all your literature that seems to say: 'For God's sake, don't annihilate us altogether!' "

"I cannot speak of Irish controversies," said the preacher, breaking in suddenly, "but for us in England let me say that we hold our heads as high as any philosophers or unbelievers. Perhaps, Doctor, you mistake courtesy for want of courage."

"Well, no," said the Doctor, in his slow, heavy way; "but I confess you solicit aggressiveness on our part by your delightful humility, and your rather pronounced and deferential obsequiousness to men of science. Things weren't so, you know; and your new attitude makes us suspicious."

"We *are* 'umble, very 'umble, Doctor," said Father Elton, who now put on his war-paint over his drawing-room manner. "You are quite right. We are most literal in our Christianity. We turn the one cheek when the other is smitten; and when you take our coats, we fling our cloaks after you. We are dreadfully deferential and apologetic. In fact, the science of apologetics is our only science at present. Amongst our learned brethren, a new discovery in science, or a pretended one, is hailed as if a new star had swum into our horizon; and when you discover a new germ, or find out something new about cells, they take off their hats and genuflect, and say: *Venite, adoremus!*"

"Now, now, Father Elton, really now, this is an exaggeration," said the preacher.

"If I—ha—understand the reverend gentleman aright," said the Canon, grandly, "he—ha—means an act of worship to the Creator, for the—ha—unexpected development in the—ha—what-you-call-'ems."

"Canon," said Father Elton, bitterly, "I mean nothing of the kind. I mean that a certain class of our co-religionists are so infatuated by their enthusiasm, or paralyzed by their fear, that they worship every new development of physical science; and that, in the worship of the animalcula, they forget what is due to the Creator and His authority on earth, instead of saying: 'Go on, go on, ye delvers in darkness. Every jet of flame you cast on the secrets of Nature lights a lamp for us before the shrine of the Eternal.' And the whole thing is ludicrous. As that excellent lady said, a few minutes ago, it is but the systole and diastole in all human inquiry. The ghost of Democritus has appeared in the nineteenth century; and he rattles his chains, like every decent ghost—'atoms,' 'germs,' 'cells,' we hear it all *da capo,* only Weismann differs from Eimer, and Siciliani differs from Binet. And now, at last, whilst they have been delving away in the subterranean vaults of Nature, the very soul of Nature has flown upwards, and escaped the vision of the dwellers in darkness. But at the mouth of the pit, lo, the watchers behold it, and shout down to the blackened pitmen, with their tallow candles and smoking lamps: 'Come up! come up! there are colossal potentialities in the psychic capacities of matter. It is easier to explain the soul than the phenomena of inheritance, and the psychic capacities are developing themselves. Come up, come up quickly, or you may stumble upon God!' "

"I admit there's a defect somewhere," said Dr. Calthrop.

"There is," said Father Elton, who intended to silence the enemy's guns forever, "there is. And that is, you men of science have been a little premature in discounting the science of metaphysics. We Catholics pursue the two together. You have abandoned the mind-science forever. Hence, you see Nature through a telescope; we through a binocular. And we get the better view. And we are satisfied not to see too far or too much. 'I am all that has been, that shall be; and none, amongst mortals, has hitherto lifted my veil.' Or, as one of your few thoughtful poets has put it:—

> " 'Shall any gazer see with mortal eyes?
>   Or any searcher know by mortal mind?
>   Veil after veil must lift—but there must be
>   Veil after veil behind.'

The star—the cell—the soul—these be impenetrable enigmas."

"Well, of course, we make all allowance for you Irishmen,"

said the preacher; "but you are not placed in our difficult position, and, therefore, you cannot understand our mode of action. We are dealing with a powerful and prejudiced antagonism, which, with singular disingenuousness and want of candor, is forever repeating the cat-calls of past prejudices against us. You know, of course, that there is a congenital belief in the Protestant mind that we are opposed to the natural sciences, and that we dread them."

"Yes, and you encourage that belief by your artificial enthusiasm. 'You do protest too much, gentlemen.' What you want is a Christian Pascal, just as we want another Swift, to heap scorn upon all anti-Christian philosophy in every shape and form."

"But we shall be called 'aggressive.' "

"And why not? After nineteen centuries of a career, marked in every cycle and century by miracle, surely our time has come to hold up to the eyes of the thoughtful the ragged vesture and the pasteboard idols of the world. Believe me, my dear Father, that our want of aggression and determination is the main cause of our want of larger success. Give back blow for blow, and scorn for scorn. Vinegar cut through the Alps for Hannibal; milk and honey would not have done it."

"Tertullian was not canonized," said the preacher.

"No; and he was justly refused canonization. But will any man contend that Tertullian did not do more, by his fierce invective, to undermine the strength of Pagan and Imperial Rome, than any of his meeker brother-apologists?"

"Well, but you must admit, Father Elton, that our Church enjoys far greater liberties under the English flag than under any foreign power, even though nominally Catholic."

"Certainly. But what then?"

"Well, then, it behoves us to be patient and circumspect."

"Yes. Obey the higher powers. That is our teaching. But I am not speaking of the higher powers. I am speaking of the lower, infernal powers, who, through science, literature, and a vulgar and venal press, use every opportunity to defame us, and hold us and our teachings up to ridicule, and who are the secret conspirators that hold the strings of governments, and move their puppets at their will. Look at your literature, how

defiled it is with anti-Catholic scurrility! Did you ever hear of
a Catholic writer who held up an Anglican parson or Non-
conformist minister to scorn? Never. But your whole literature
reeks with infamous calumnies on our priesthood. Why, half
your novels deal with Jesuits and the Inquisition. And your
'seer and prophet,' when he is not shrieking 'Oh! heavens,' or
'*Ay de mi*,' is ridiculing the 'simulacrum' of a Pope, or screaming about an imaginary 'dirty muddy-minded, semi-felonious,
proselytizing Irish priest,' who is supposed to have disturbed
the by no means normal equanimity of 'his goody.' What is the
result? Voters become smitten with the virus and madness of
bigotry; then statesmen are influenced, and Acts of Parliament
passed, and the whole thing is liberty and progress. Why, witness all Catholic France today, passing meekly under the yoke
at the dictation of a few anti-Catholics! But the pitiful thing
is that we sit down and tamely submit to all this. If we want
a clear proof of the continuity of our Church with that of the
Catacombs, it is found in our serfdom. The Angel of the
Apocalypse may mark our foreheads with the mystical sign of
Tau; but, by Jove, the Angel of Destiny has branded the *Sigma*
of slavery on our backs."

"I am afraid, Father Elton," said the preacher, "your desire
to emphasize your contentions has led into the national tendency towards exaggeration. I assure you we get on very well
over there in 'darkest England,' and that we are not so sensible
of persecution, perhaps because not so sensitive about trifles,
as you imagine. Besides, our people are really not so much
influenced by literature as you seem to imagine. It would
surprise you to find how little my countrymen care about their
prophets. They think more of their purveyors and their bread
and ale."

"We had but one 'man' in our century," said Father Elton,
pursuing his own train of thought, "and that was he who
armed his Irish subjects in New York, and then told its mayor
that the first contingent of savage bigots that made its appearance in the city would find that city in flames!"

"I am—ha—afraid, gentlemen," said the Canon, who was
very much disturbed, "that we are approaching—ha—rather
questionable and—ha—dangerous subjects, that may—ha—
introduce in their train some—ha—slight acerbity that would

mar the harmony of this pleasant meeting. Suppose we adjourn
to the—ha—more equable and—ha—temperate atmosphere
of the drawing-room."

Father Elton and the preacher walked out together.

"The good Canon," said the latter, "did not quite seem to
understand his uncomplimentary allusion. He implies that we
have been indulging a little freely."

Father Elton laughed, but looked annoyed.

There was a family conclave late that evening.

"Why don't they do something for that Father Elton?" said
Mrs. Wilson. "Why don't they make him a Monsignor or
something? Why, he's not even a Doctor of Laws!"

"Why do they make boobies of baronets, and judges of
jugglers? Why are they always putting round men into square
holes, and *vice versa?*" said her husband.

"I am—ha—more convinced than ever of the—ha—wisdom of the Church," said the Canon, "in not having advanced
to—a—ha—position of respectability and honor one who
holds such extreme views. That clergyman is—ha—positively
revolutionary, and—even—ha—anarchial in his ideas."

"Are there many like him in Ireland?" asked Dr. Calthrop.

"Most happily, no!" said the Canon. "The vast number of
our clergy are amiable, industrious, respectable members of
society; strictly observant of the laws of their—ha—Church;
and obedient and—ha—respectful to constituted forms of
government."

"Because if you had a few thousand, or even hundred, of
that species with his intelligence and vivacity, you need not
have been whining for your Catholic University so long," said
the Doctor.

"I can't see for the life of me what these clergymen dabble
in science for. It is bad enough to have 'priests in politics,' but
'priests in science,' monopolizing our every department, and
possibly anticipating our discoveries, would be intolerable,"
said Dr. Wilson. "That man, now, seems to have been reading
up all our scientific authorities. Did he quote Shaler and Eimer,
Calthrop?"

"Ay, and seemed to know them well. After all, it touches
their own department; and I must say that I brought that unpleasant discussion on myself. But I confess your good clergy-

man is to me a greater surprise than anything I have seen on this memorable visit. How little we know of each other!"

"Mrs. Wenham thinks very highly of him," put in Mrs. Wilson, diffidently. "I heard her say to Barbara: 'That is a man to hold souls in leash.' "

"That's women's ways," said her husband. "They like a master. They are ambitious to rule; but they love being ruled. No woman can be an autocrat. She must have a higher power to worship."

"Did you say, Bessie," asked the Canon, "that that—ha—excellent clergyman visits at the—ha—Vice-regal Lodge and lunches at the Castle?"

"There is no doubt about it, Canon," she replied. "He is even a favorite with Lady——, who consults him on many points."

"Then I presume he suppresses—ha—his rather advanced and—ha—subversive principles; and probably presents the teachings of the Church in an—ha—attractive guise."

"Depend upon it, he does nothing of the kind," said Dr. Calthrop; "he is not a man to water down his principles, and if he did, he would lose all his piquancy."

"But the recognized authorities, sir, the—ha—representatives of the Queen, how can they listen without—ha—emphatic protest to such disloyal principles?" asked the Canon.

"Oh, these eccentricities are quite tolerable, and even amusing," said the Doctor, "to Englishmen. It is only when we see such principles reduced to practice by silent and steady organization that we bring down the whip."

"But the language, sir!—" said the Canon.

"We never mind *talk;*" said the Doctor; "it is the silence we dread." And the Canon thenceforward was dumb.

"There's a letter from Louis by the evening mail," said Mrs. Wilson, addressing her husband.

"A modest request for twenty pounds?" asked the Doctor, lifting his black eyebrows.

"No, indeed. You can read it. There's nothing of that kind in it." And the filial letter ran thus:—

"DEAREST MOTHER:—Arrived here quite safely on the 11th and looked up my old diggings. Things were pretty rough and disorganized, as I was not expected so soon by the housekeeper. None of my chums has returned, and London is yet a desert. The natives are just now swarming on the cool hillsides or in the deep valleys of the Alps, or leaning over the gunwales of their yachts in the Mediterranean, or fishing in the Norway rivers. But there is a pretty large crowd of country cousins in the streets, very open as to their mouths, but very close as to their pockets. They move in squads, and seem to be in a condition of chronic panic. You can imagine how dull all this is! Nothing to do. Hot streets, blazing skies, no society. Well, a little. We had a meeting of the pre-Raphaelites on Monday evening, in which, before parting for the long holidays, several arrangements were made. I am booked for a lecture on 'Turner' some time in January. We had also a garden party up the river at Uskholme. A select few of the rabble of artists, poets, musicians, etc., met at the house of Lady L——, whom you already know as a patroness of the arts. She asked me to come. I pleaded headache, sunstroke, several engagements. No use. I had to go. It was delightful. Slightly barbaric, but rather novel and quite fit for *blasé* people. But these things don't suit me. I am working hard. I have got permission from the Resident Surgeon to attend St. Thomas's every day. I go through every ward and every case in succession. It is weary work. But I have an axe to grind. By the way, tell Barby I am *not* neglecting the 'one thing necessary.' I was at Vespers at the Cathedral on Sunday evening. The music was gorgeous; the ceremonial superb. But the sermon!!! Alas! who was the preacher, think you? Our young peasant friend, who sang that rebel song that so shocked uncle. It was awful. Just a *potpourri* of mediæval absurdities—free-will, grace, pre-determination, prescience. And such an accent! Great heavens! You could cut it with a knife and hang your hat on the splinters thereof. What *are* they doing in those Irish colleges? I have heard an acquaintance say that a young priest is the greatest greenhorn in existence. But our Church is deeply concerned in these things. No Protestant could take away with him anything but contempt after hearing this scholastic rhodomontade. Far different was another experience of mine. I went over lately to hear Dr. Vaughan, Master of the Temple, preach. Don't be alarmed, dear mother! You know Catholics can go where they like here, without prohibition. Such calm, majestic, well-reasoned, well-delivered language I had never heard before; and such self-reliance without affectation, and self-restraint without coldness.

"I wish I were a theological student, and could sit under his chair."

"Is that all?" said Dr. Wilson.

"That's all," said the proud mother, "except a few trifling personal remarks at the end."

"The young cub!" said the father.

"I think," said the Canon, "that that is—ha—an admirable letter. It manifests distinctly four or five—ha—features that are very consoling. It is clear that our dear boy is moving in—ha—excellent society. That distinguished lady who—ha—had the goodness to invite him to her garden party must have seen something more than usually attractive in Louis. Then, his devotion to—ha—study—clinical, is it not, Doctor? What zeal and perseverance it needs to remain whole days in the—ha—dreadful wards, in momentary—ha—danger of contracting disease! Then, his attention to his—ha—religious duties. Vespers are not—ha—obligatory in our Church, Dr. Calthrop; but you see how early—ha—impressions and careful Christian training mold the—ha—entire future career of our boys. What is that, Bessie? The music was—ha—"

"Gorgeous!" said Mrs. Wilson, consulting the letter.

"I am sure that is—ha—excellent criticism," continued the Canon. "And then his witty, indeed, rather too free—ha—remarks on preaching! But, then, young men, young men! And his solicitude for the Church—the appearance she—ha—makes before the public! How lamentable that they will not turn out—ha—better types from our colleges! Mark the—ha—distinction between this—ha—rude young Celt and that refined and polished clergyman—named, Bessie?"

"Dr. Vaughan, Master of the Temple!" said Mrs. Wilson, again consulting the letter.

"Dr. Vaughan, Master of the Temple," echoed the Canon. "And how does Louis—ha—describe this clergyman's eloquence?"

"Calm, majestic, well-reasoned, well-delivered," said Mrs. Wilson, reading.

"Calm, majestic, well-reasoned, well-delivered," echoed the Canon, leaning on each word with emphasis. "I should say that such a—ha—discourse was most creditable and—ha—respectable."

"What would you think of Louis becoming a theological student?" said Dr. Wilson.

The Canon saw the sarcasm, and winced.

"I should say, indeed," he replied, "that at this period of his career it would be—ha—inadvisable to change. But I am—ha—quite sure that whatever profession Louis adopts, he will maintain the honor—ha—of our family, *sans tache*."

"Come, Calthrop, and have a final cigar," said the Doctor.

"I say, Wilson," said Dr. Calthrop, as he pinched off the end of his cigar, "you'll forgive the comparison; but your good brother-in-law reminds me strongly of the 'Father of the Marshalsea,' or Casby."

"He is neither," said Dr. Wilson, "but quite an ingenuous, good man, who has put on a little mannerism with age. Some think it the result of disease, for it is certain he was a red-hot rebel in his youth. There is a curious story told of him. When he took possession of his first parish, he had scarcely arrived when he got a message from the local magnate to have his church cleared of pews, benches, and seats early on Monday morning, for that the landlord's corn should be threshed there."

"What?" cried Dr. Calthrop, removing his cigar.

"I am speaking of facts," said Dr. Wilson. "The priest took no notice of the order, but summoned some few sturdy parishioners; and when the landlord's men had arrived, they were confronted with quite a regiment of rapparees. They were unprepared, for this had never occurred before. They had always been allowed to thresh their corn on the chapel floor. They had to retreat, and inform at headquarters that there was an insurrection; and then—"

"And then?" said Dr. Calthrop, deeply interested.

"And then the landlord asked the priest to dine; and ever afterwards there was a cover laid for the priest in the mansion; and he actually got permission to hang up a bell in an extemporized turret."

"It seems to me," said Dr. Calthrop, "that we English will begin to understand you somewhere about the day of general judgment."

"I'm afraid we'll hardly be disposed to continue the acquaintance then," said Dr. Wilson. "We'll have to part company that day, if not before." Dr. Calthrop laughed.

"But the little affectations of the Canon date from that event," said Dr. Wilson. "He became a man of peace, and is one of five or six of his profession in Ireland who believe in landlords—and the Utopia, where the lion lies down with the lamb. Hitherto he has been justified. His parish is a paradise. He has a considerable private income, and it all goes to improving the condition of his people. The cabins have become cottages. The old manure heaps are swept away. Flowers, vegetables, new breeds of poultry—everything novel and progressive he has introduced. No one dares oppose him. He is an autocrat, or rather a patriarch. His very mannerism affects the people strangely. When he stands at the altar on Sunday morning and says 'Ha!' you would think Moses had come down from the mountain, so reverential and awed are the people. He doesn't boast; but what the Jesuits did in Paraguay, he is doing in his own parish."

"I'm so glad you told me. I'm really proud to meet such a man," said the guest. "O si sic omnes!"

"But like all his class, who are not entirely absorbed in their sacred duties, he must twine his tendrils around something. And he has chosen Louis and Barbara instead of a dog or a horse."

"I am not surprised at his affection for his niece," said Dr. Calthrop; "she is the gentlest and sweetest girl I have ever seen. I have never seen a hawk and a dove in close company till tonight, when I saw that woman sitting near her at the dinner table."

"Ay!" said Dr. Wilson, and his voice would have broken sadly but for that blessed cigar; "but like all things else, she will leave me. Now, I could spare Louis easily, but I can't spare her. She'll go and he'll stay; and I am not certain which will be the more bitter trial."

"Go where? Where will she go?" said Dr. Calthrop.

"Look here, Calthrop! You cannot understand. It is all the d—d literalness of this religion of ours. 'Go sell all thou hast and give to the poor;'—'Consider the lilies of the field;'—'What doth it profit a man?'—'Deny thyself, take up thy cross, and follow me.' This is what we are ever hearing; and these young featherheads believe it all and take it letter by letter."

"It sounds very like the Gospel, though," said Dr. Calthrop.

"Of course. But this is the nineteenth century. 'Consider the lilies of the field!' What chance would any unfortunate man have, with such a belief as that, amongst the army of rabid and unscrupulous Orangemen here in Dublin? He would be in the workhouse in a month."

"I suppose so," said Dr. Calthrop, smoking leisurely.

"Now, there's the beauty of your religion," said Dr. Wilson. "It fits you like a dressing-gown—ease, beauty, elasticity. You can sit, stand, or lie. You can be anything you like—Turk, Jew, or atheist, Freemason, agnostic, Socinian,—but no one minds. You can rob, steal, swindle, and sit down calmly the following Sunday and hear that such have no place in the Kingdom of Heaven. I call that delightful. But let one of our musty, barefooted friars say, with certain emphasis next Sunday: 'Come, rise up, and follow the footsteps of blood,' why, every little girl is dying to start at once for China or Japan, and get her little neck chopped off by some pig-tailed savage. And this will be the way with Barbara. Instead of a few balls and parties, and then a decent marriage, she will become a 'servant of the poor,' or kitchen-maid to a parcel of lunatics."

"And your son—has he similar notions?"

"Will sow his wild oats, I suppose."

"And then?"

"And then depend on his uncle for a dispensary."

CHAPTER XIII

Racial Characteristics

LUKE DELMEGE had passed through the stages of primary education at a national school, of secondary education at college; he was now enrolled as graduate in the great University of the World. Books were his professors, and men were his books. The former were fairly consistent in their teaching; the latter were forever puzzling and troubling him with their strange inconsistencies. The fragments of the best human literature that have escaped the corrosion of centuries could be pieced together and made a harmonious whole; but not even charity itself, the best and most cunning of artists, was able to reconcile with themselves, or with any standard of truth or principle, the ever-varying eccentricities of men. Hence came Luke's final temptation, to which he succumbed, as we shall see—namely, to live in ideas, not in action; and hence, here in the Babylon of the world, he yearned from time to time for more liberty of thought, free from action; for a little solitude to soothe weary nerves and a perplexed mind.

One of the many weary things that puzzled Luke in these, his novitiate days, was the tremendous waste of power, moral and intellectual—the output of energy and zeal in every parish in England, and the infinitesimal results. He could not understand why all England should not be gathered into the fold, as sheep would flock to a mountain refuge at the approach of a storm. Here was Truth; here was Peace; here was Grace! Why dwell ye in the valleys of darkness when the mountain of light is so near? Why perish in the storm when the shepherd beckons to the safety of His fold? He took up the weekly papers. Yes! Life, vitality, energy everywhere. Sermons, exhortations, organizations—sermons, convincing and appeal-

133

ing; exhortations, pathetic and luminous; organizations, perfect and vital; but it was ploughing the sea and casting seed on the desert. The claims of the Church were irrefragable and invincible. So Luke thought and felt. He took up an Anglican paper. His eye caught the lines:—

"And whilst thus we can contemplate with pride and satisfaction the history of our Church from the days of Augustine until now; its purity of doctrine, untouched by superstition; its consistency and comprehensiveness; its beautiful ritual, that never degenerates into mummery; and the vast number of heroic souls it has given to the world and the world's most sacred causes, we are speechless with astonishment at the insolence of this Italian mission, that has unhappily got a foothold in our midst. It is as if a colony of hinds was sent to colonize and civilize a university."

Luke read it over twice with blazing eyes. Then he rolled the paper into a knot; and played Rugby football around his room for the next half an hour, accompanying the amusement with the following soliloquy: "The English truthful? They are the greatest liars and hypocrites on the face of the earth. They are too contemptuous to stoop to lying in private life. They care too little about you to condescend to lie. But in politics, commerce, religion—whenever a point has to be gained, they will lie like Satan." He raised the subject at dinner that day. His confrères laughed. It was only Celtic effervescence.

"But you know, Delmege," said Arthur, a bright young priest, "if you want to practice a *pas seul* or an Irish jig in future, please try the Chapter-room, and don't throw down my ceiling."

A few days later he crossed Westminster Bridge, and doubling hither and thither through narrow streets, he stood before a mediæval church. It looked like a piece of Pompeii dug from the dust of centuries. He entered. The beautiful stained glass almost blinded him with its colors; but he only cast one curious look around, said a short prayer, and went out. It was not art, but a man he was in quest of. He knocked at the presbytery door and was ushered into a small, gloomy parlor. Its furniture consisted of a round mahogany table, two chairs, and a dilapidated sofa. The day was dark, and the gloom so great that

Luke could not read Compline. In a few minutes the door opened and a priest entered. He was a tall, handsome man, very dark with thick black hair, just turning to gray, and great glowing eyes, that gave one at once the idea of great penetration and strength. The first quick view said unreservedly: "This is a giant amongst men—one who will leave his mark on the age." But alas! it was as if a lay figure had its props suddenly loosed; for after the first brief salutation, the world-weary priest flung himself on the sofa with a gesture and an aspect of infinite weakness or pain.

Luke timidly put a few questions on some theological subject, which were courteously answered; and then, passing his hand across his forehead, this great convert said:—

"I know you will excuse me, Father, when I tell you that I am not at all well, and even conversation is painful and wearying. I am threatened with *neurasthenia* from overwork, and I must go abroad. Allow me to say good-evening."

Luke stammered an apology as he took the proffered hand. He looked up onto the finely cut, worn face; and as he thought "this man sacrificed a thousand a year, and broke every family tie for the sake of truth, and is now a martyr to work for Christ," his heart repented of his rash judgments on the race; and with Celtic impulsiveness, he stooped and kissed the white hand that lay in his own, and departed with strange sensations.

"Neurasthenia! Thank God, we never heard of that in Ireland. But is it a subject to thank God for? Is it not better to wear out than rust out? And is there not something in that singular philosophy of St. Paul about 'spending and being spent for Christ?' And 'omnia detrimentum feci, et arbitror, ut stercora?' Which of the two would you choose, Luke? To pass on, in smooth and placid respectability to the canon's stall foreshadowed for you by the Canon, or to be utterly wrecked in middle age like this martyr-priest, who has now to go abroad and be supported by charity for the remainder of his life?"

There is no doubt whatever that this latter is the more heroic. But is it prudent? Is it consistent with common sense?

And Luke was confronted with another puzzle. And if he felt that the sublime philosophy of Christianity was altogether in favor of self-sacrifice and suffering, on the other hand the "common sense of all mankind" was just as emphatically against it. And which is right? Dear me! dear me! what an enigma is life! But that weary figure and furrowed face haunted Luke for many a long day.

It was evening now. The lamps were lighted, and he turned back into the church. The seats were being gradually filled, and Luke determined to wait for Benediction. He sat under one of the gas jets and took out his diurnal to finish Compline. Then, just as the sacristy clock tolled seven, the same wearied, broken priest, preceded by a few acolytes, emerged from the sacristy and knelt before the high altar. He looked stooped and shaken, and his voice was almost inaudible as he recited the Rosary. There was a short, sweet hymn to our Blessed Lady; and then the tired priest ascended with difficulty the steps of the pulpit.

"Surely he's not going to preach?" said Luke.

Ah! yes, he was. No relaxation or intermission here, until the poor frame sinks to rise no more. It was a voice from the grave. It sounded so gentle, so mournful; and the preacher seemed to experience such tremendous difficulty in seizing and arranging his fugitive thoughts, that Luke every moment expected a bad break-down. It was quite clear that the faculties of the mind were refusing to work. They had been driven too hard, and were in revolt. And so there were repetitions and very inconsequential arguments, and a very few words were mumbled and mouthed as if from a semi-paralyzed tongue; and a few verbs were misplaced and mispronounced, and there was an agonized look on the preacher's face, as if he were face to face with a trial whose issue might be fearful and sudden. Luke couldn't bear it. He looked away and thought: Only a few years ago this man had won the Ireland Scholarship and the Newdigate Prize at Oxford, and was in a fair way towards a Fellowship and a Mitre. What a sacrifice! What a change! Then the concluding words came clear and solemn: "You shall know the truth, and the truth shall make you free." These were the last public words of the speaker, and Luke was perplexed to hear them. During the solemn rite of Benediction that succeeded, Luke saw only bowed heads, nor was there even a whispered prayer; but at that most touching prayer which is said just as the monstrance is replaced upon the throne, that prayer for the conversion of England and that takes one back insensibly to Roman catacombs and pagan imperialism, Luke thought he heard the sound of sobbing.

"It cannot be," he said; "these English are too stolid."

But a few moments later he saw faces of well-dressed ladies wet and glistening with tears, which immediately were wiped away; for, you know, we are English, and, above all things else, we must not yield to sentiment or demonstrative piety, and Luke thought—racial characteristics are humbug. The human heart is the same everywhere.

He passed rapidly along the streets on his way homewards. He was brought to a sudden standstill on the sideway of the Strand by a long *queue* of men, two and two, who, ranged on the outer edge of the pavement, waited in calm, stolid silence for something that was slow in coming. There was quite room enough on the inside path for pedestrians. What is it? A funeral? No, not at such an hour. It was only fifty or sixty men, waiting for a place in the theatre close by. They were as silent as mutes. "What a laughing, rollicking, joking crowd that would have been in Ireland!" thought Luke. "Verily, they take their pleasures sadly! After all, they *are* a stolid, unfeeling race! And what mercurial beings are we!"

Just then, an arm was locked in his, and a very marked Hibernian voice exclaimed:—

"Well, Luke Delmege, who'd ever think of seeing you here, waiting to get into the Gaiety? The world is topsy-turvy enough; but I never thought you could turn such a somersault."

Luke laughed at the absurdity, as he recognized an old college acquaintance, who had "cut" in his physic year, had then become a successful journalist, and was now one of that famous band of *matadores* who were fretting the flanks of John Bull.

"Come along," said the "Mimber," "we'll have a cup of tea here at the 'Marguerite,' and then you must come to see a field night at the House. No! no! no excuses! there's electricity in the atmosphere, and sure to be a thunderclap tonight."

"Then why are you not at your post?" said Luke; "isn't the House open since four?"

"Quite so, old man, if you allow me to use such a familiarity with an old chum, but we allow the animals to feed from seven to half-past eight. Then, when well gorged with meat and wine, they're an easy prey."

"And do you keep your heads cool?" said Luke. His friend lifted up a cup of tea, and nodded significantly.

"Tell me," said Luke, "and you can tell me, for you have experience, do you believe in 'racial characteristics'? The problem is puzzling me dreadfully." The Member laid down his cup, took out a cigarette, lighted it, looked long at Luke, and spoke:—

"Racial characteristics? I do, firmly. I believe, for example, that we, Irish, are the coolest, most judicious, most calculating, far-seeing race on the face of the earth. Our cunning is Ulyssean; our wisdom is Promethean, and, as for tenacity, nothing in all creation can beat us—but an oyster! Come!"

They walked rapidly down by Trafalgar Square, past the great Whitehall buildings, and, just as they approached the Westminster Palace Yard, on a sudden the vast rush through the crowded thoroughfare stopped as if by magic. Stately carriages, gaily dressed pedestrians, cabs, horses—all stood still, as if petrified. The Member looked calmly at the imperial demonstration in his honor for a moment, then moved across swiftly, and, unlocking his arm from that of the astonished Luke, he said:—

"You go around by the public entrance. I shall meet you in the lobby in a moment."

Luke had not long to wait in the famous lobby, just long enough to see that, if there be on the face of the earth a levelling, democratic spot, where all distinctions are fused down, and all human hopes concentered and unified in one desire, it is here. That desire is to see your own Member. Luke had not long to wait. Gaily and happily at ease, dispensing smiles all round, yet maintaining a certain unperturbed dignity, his friend appeared. The policeman saluted and shouted: "The Reverend Luke Midge." Luke admitted the impeachment, and was led into the inner sanctuary through rows of marble busts and stately pictures of long-buried statesmen, whilst the disappointed mob howled in their hearts outside. Into the inner lobby, sacred to statesmen, mixing amongst notabilities, rubbing his shoulder against Cabinet ministers, the wondering

Luke passed with his guide, who accosted a gorgeous official and demanded a ticket for his friend.

"You can have a seat in the gallery, sir," said the official with awful deference, "but I regret to say that all the seats are taken under the gallery."

"I beg your pardon. There's one vacant," said the Member. "I insist on having that seat."

"That seat, sir, belongs to Lord Vavasour. He's just dining with the Secretary for Home Affairs, and has kept it engaged till his return."

"You should know the rules of the House, sir," said the Member. "No stranger can retain a seat, except he is in actual possession."

"Quite true, sir," said the official. "You must not consider me discourteous; I was trying to smooth matters. Name, please?"

"Delmege!" said the Member, as the official handed the ticket to Luke, who, half ashamed and almost terrified, passed wondering up the narrow stairs, and in a moment was in the "House." It was a wonder, a surprise, a disappointment; but we needn't repeat the old story here. Luke sat still on his narrow bench, and gaped.

"Take off your hat, please!"

Luke had forgotten his politeness and his loyalty. The official said quietly and politely: "It's like a school, sir; and, by-and-bye, you'll see some rough horseplay."

"Does this—this—assembly control the destinies of 300,-000,000 people?" asked Luke.

"It thinks so!" said the man.

Just then the supporters of the Government began to drop in. Luke was on the Government side of the House. There was a low balustrade between him and them. In they came, flushed as to face, and very white as to capacious shirt front. They congregated in groups of three or four, and began to exchange remarks. There was a pleasant odor of whiskey and patchouli in the air. "I thought the English never drank spirits," said Luke. "The racial characteristics are a puzzle."

Yes, the air was electric. You couldn't tell why. There were no indications. There was no great debate on. Members lounged and chatted and laughed. There were no drawing up and marshalling of forces, no organizing of battalions, no arrangement of reserves. But the air was electric. You felt it tingling in your fingers, and running up along your spine. The servant felt it.

"There's something on tonight, sir!" he said.

Three feet away from where Luke sat, close to one of the pillarets that sustained the gallery, a very little man, with a very long coat, a bald head, and a heavy mustache that curled up to his ears, was engaged in earnest consultation with a colleague. "The leader of the House, sir," whispered the servant.

At last, the hours stole on to eleven, and Luke began to think it was time to go home. His friend, the Member, came over, sat on the balustrade, and began to chat gaily. Not a word between him and the full-dressed mob around. They'd have torn him limb from limb if they dared.

"Going home?" he cried to Luke. "You'll do nothing of the kind. The Lord has given you a chance that will never occur again."

Just here, an old officer, gray-headed and gray-bearded, spoke to the Member. He was a suppliant—a humble, abject, beseeching client. He begged and entreated the Member to bring on some wretched thing about pensions, or to promise to speak if the bill were introduced.

"I shall do nothing of the kind," said the Member, haughtily. "We have other work before us tonight." The officer slunk away, cowed and discomfited. Luke's opinion of his country was rising steadily.

"Now I must be off," said the Member. "There is big-wig in the chair. Now, sit fast, old man. And look here! Don't let your feelings overcome you! If you cheer, or toss up your hat, they'll turn you out, and you won't see a bull-baiting again."

And so Luke waited patiently, now watching the confused, anxious crowd at the ministerial side of the House, and again fixing his eyes on that silent, serried mass that thronged the lowest benches on the left of the Speaker's chair. And here, the object of all vision, of all thought, of all anxiety, sat the Man of Mystery, silent, immovable, whilst anxious ministers looked to him for a sign or some articulate utterance of what he was brooding over and plotting there in the corner seat just below the gangway. At last, one of his lieutenants rose, and moved the adjournment of the House. The proposal was met with a shout of indignant scorn. A division was demanded, and Luke, with the rest, was relegated to the lobby. In a few minutes it was over, and they returned. The Government had a sweeping majority. There was a cheer of exultant triumph. The first lines of the enemy had been repulsed. The debate went on. Then quietly, a second lieutenant rose in his place, and moved the adjournment of the House. This time a yell broke from the ministerial benches. The adjournment was fiercely and angrily refused. A division was demanded, and another Pyrrhic victory gained. There was a mighty shout from the ministerial lists. Calm and immovable sat the Irish *guerrilleros,* whilst their opponents, wild with passion, appeared to be lashing themselves into frenzied madness. The debate went on; and just as the hands of the clock pointed to twelve, a division was again demanded. With suppressed, but badly suppressed passion, the leader of the House leaned forward on the despatch-boxes and hissed:—

"If we have to remain in session for forty-eight hours the Government is determined that this measure shall pass; nor will the House adjourn until that is accomplished."

The captain of the *guerrilleros* sat silent and grim. And then a peal of electric bells; and then the solemn march through the turnstiles; another Governmental victory, and the House settled down to business again. Then arose another of the lawless but disciplined phalanx, and moved the adjournment of the House. There was another angry yell; and again Agamemnon spoke:—

"I assure the honorable gentlemen at the other side of the House that the Government has no intention of yielding on that point, and that the House must remain in session until this measure is carried."

Then the Silent One arose, and eight hundred beings, the flower of English intellect, hung breathless on his words. They were few. Passing his hand behind his coat-collar, and then running it down through his thick hair, he spoke in the echo of a whisper; but it was heard in every cranny in the building:—

"The Right Hon. gentleman refuses to adjourn the House. I tell him the House will adjourn, and the sooner the better."

It was a plain challenge to the omnipotence of England, and as such was accepted. This time there was no shouting. The division bell rang. The members trooped through the turnstile. Another victory for the Government; but the leader of the House again came forward, and leaning his arms again on the despatch-boxes, he said, almost humbly:—

"There's no use of prolonging the useless debate in the face of such obstruction. The House stands adjourned." The officials laughed. The ministerial following was bewildered. Then, as they recognized their defeat, they muttered curses on their leaders; and angry, shamed, disappointed, they trooped from the House. The victors did not even cheer. Luke thought: "I'll never believe in racial characteristics again. I knew they were always humbug!" His friend, the Member, came over.

"Wasn't that pretty? Crumpled up, like a piece of tissue-paper!"

"Can you keep it up?" queried Luke. His friend looked long and earnestly at him.

"Yes, till victory, which we, the descendants of kings, shall then most royally throw away. 'Did I really hurt you, poor old Bull? I'm awfully sorry. Get up, old man, and come have a drink.' That's the finale to the comedy you have witnessed. Good-night!"

The great clock of St. Stephen's was chiming "one" as Luke crossed Westminster Bridge.

"Glad I have a latch-key," he murmured; "the old Vicar wouldn't like it, and he sleeps with one eye open."

A party of revellers was coming towards him. They tried to jostle him off the footpath. At another time he would have yielded; but the spell of conquest was upon him. He resisted, and came into personal contact with one, who was almost intoxicated. It was Louis Wilson. He, too, recognized Luke; and turning away, he said to his companions:—

" 'Tis only a peasant priest from Ireland. I know a little of the fellow. He hath a pretty sister."

The next moment Luke's strong hand was on his collar, and he swung him around.

"Now, gentlemen," said one of the revellers, "this is Westminster and not Donnybrook. Keep quiet, or bedad, and begorra, you will find yourselves in the lock-up."

"Your names, gentlemen, please," said an officer, moving up.

Luke heard as in a dream: "11 Albemarle Buildings, Victoria Street."

Wilson passed on.

"Never mind, sir," said the officer, as Luke fumbled for a card; "it will rest here unless he prosecutes. But take no notice of these fellows in future."

There was no real sleep that night for Luke. Amidst the agony and shame and remorse that kept the wheels of his brain burning and revolving, he thought of country and home. He saw the calm peace of Ireland resting as in a cloud above and beyond this hateful Tartarus. He would give worlds to be at home—at home at Lisnalee, pencilled in shadows above the misty, beloved sea. He would sacrifice a few years of life to be in the midst of the kindliest people on earth, away from these horrible automatons; and he saw with tears the little parlor, and the "Inseparables," and Father Tim dropping aphorisms at leisure, and at leisure dropping slices of lemon into his glass. And then the burning shame came back again, and, as he dropped into an uneasy slumber, he muttered: "I believe there are racial characteristics after all."

When he woke from unhappy dreams next morning the specters had vanished. London, life, ambition, a great future were all before him. Lisnalee was a gray, blurred shadow of the past.

CHAPTER XIV

Weighing Anchor

IT WAS inevitable that an airy, impetuous, variable spirit like this should, under pressing circumstances, weigh anchor and drift with the tide. Gradually, as his fine genius asserted itself, he rose above all his confrères, both in the excellence and the efficacy of his work and in his unquestionable superiority of intellect. The Rev. Luke Delmege was beginning to be noticed. His Bishop, who had returned from Rome, and then from a long round of visitations, appeared not to remark him particularly, which Luke, in his rising pride, set down to national prejudice. Once the Bishop said:—

"Delmege, you are not quite so mercurial as the generality of your countrymen. Don't you like your surroundings?"

Then Luke protested that he was happy, very happy, and did not seek a change.

Once, too, the old Vicar said in his rough, kindly way:—

"Here you are again, Delmege! It is a bad thing for a young man when the papers notice him. You'll have as much space soon as Madame Seigel's Syrup."

But the younger men were more explicit and generous. His name had gone across the river, and he had been invited to preach at the Commercial-Road, and to lecture to working-men at the Mechanics' Hall in Holborn. He had pushed on his schools until the Inspector wondered at his own report, and the Diocesan Inspector had asked for him as an assistant.

Meanwhile, and, of course, imperceptibly, all this externa-tion was affecting his character deeply. His soul was starved. All his energies went off in enthusiastic work. He never per-ceived that it was sheer materialism, when the soul was absent. In the beginning he consecrated his work and put a soul into it.

144

Then, as vanity assumed control and men's praises echoed around him, he pushed forward wildly. Work, work, work—here was his cry! The gentle personal love for his Divine Master hallowed and sanctified his earlier efforts; but by degrees this evaporated in favor of a Cause. But the Cause was an Impersonality, though he called it "the Church." If he had identified the Church with its Divine Spouse, all would have been well. But no! The honor of the Church, the advancement of the Church, the glory of the Church—words always on his lips, and of such awful and hallowed significance,—conveyed no meaning, no life to his actions. He would have been deeply offended, if any one had hinted that he had degenerated into a form of worship that is generally veiled under a sacred guise —and only labelled by the truthful malice of the world, or the still more truthful revelations of humility—egotheism. Did not the ancient monks say, *Laborare est orare?* And here just now is not the sage of Chelsea preaching the same divinity of work? And is not Stanley in Christ Church, and Jowett in Balliol, stimulating the flagging energies of Oxford undergraduates by the same? Work, work, work, for it is the law of the universe,—the laws of birth and death, of stars and flowers! Work, because thereby you are identified with Nature by obeying its sacred laws, and thereby alone is true happiness attainable! If any one had whispered to Luke in these days, when he thought he was soaring on the highest altitudes of inspiration: "Come apart and rest a little while!" he would have scorned the suggestion as a temptation to abuse of the highest instincts and betrayal of the most sacred interests.

It was rather fortunate for Luke that, amidst the inevitable jealousies aroused by all this publicity, he had just strength of mind enough to move steadily onward, though not unbiased or undisturbed. He had not yet had experience enough to write on the tablets of his mind the Pauline summing up of existence —*intus timores;* but his life was not lacking in those external modifications which the Apostle styles—the *foris pugnæ.* Unfair and unfavorable criticisms, little hints of possible imprudences in public utterances, vague suggestions of subdued heresy, the complete suppression of some fine public lecture—these were the drawbacks in a buoyant and most hopeful career. In the moments of doubt and depression that followed,—and

they were many,—a memory of past times, of the frugal ban-
quets of the "Inseparables," of Father Tim's drolleries and of
Father Pat's kindness, would recur to him; and sometimes there
would float across the *unda irremeabilis* a tiny letter from the
cottage above the sea at Lisnalee, or from the library of Father
Martin—hopeful, cheerful, amusing, as a butterfly would float
in from spring meadows and lose itself in the horrors of some
Lancashire factory, or as a child would place a flower in the
fingers of a bronze and unfeeling statue. Then Luke had a
friend. And it needs not the sacred endorsement of Holy
Scripture, or the expansive comments of that great interpreter,
Shakespeare, to be assured that the best gift of the gods to man
is a true and truthful friend. And Luke's friend was not afraid
to tell the truth. Witness this. They were walking on the banks
of the Serpentine.

"I always choose this place for quiet meditation," said the
friend, in an explanatory tone to Luke, who was rather surprised to be suddenly introduced into the mighty gangway of
Life-Guards, servant-maids, and babies; "here you are alone,
as much alone as Werther and his stars. You meet no one that
will trouble the rim of your hat; babies—God bless them!—
are happily unconscious. The other elements of civilization
here in the heart of the world are too much engrossed with
each other to heed you. I am alone with the stars. Now, Delmege, old man, can you bear an operation? For I am going
to do what my judgment calls the rashest and maddest and most
ungrateful thing—I am going to pull a friend's tooth. It is
quite true that tooth is aching. Nevertheless, man is an ungrateful animal. I know you won't bite; but promise not to say a
cuss-word. I can't bear that."

"All right," said Luke, "go ahead! I'm used to it. There
never before was such a target for the small shot of gratuitous
advice. I am as bad as if I had the influenza. Every old woman
at home made herself a Minerva, and every old duffer a Men-
tor. And here it is worse. It is quite clear the world regards me
as a complete and unmitigated fool!" Which little speech
shows how far Luke had gone in the way of the "galled jade."

"Now, look here," said the candid friend, "all that's quite
true—"

"I beg your pardon," said Luke, stiffly.

"Ahem! I mean that—you know—it may be quite true, you know—that advice, very well meant—you know—does not always comprehend the entire surroundings—look at that impudent slut with that soldier!"

"Oh! I thought you were alone with the stars," said Luke; which at once restored his friend's equilibrium.

"Well, now, look here, Delmege, it seems to me that you have two careers before you. On the one hand a life of usefulness and labor, hidden, unsuspected, no storms, no triumphs, but a reward exceeding great; and on the other a life of blare and brilliancy, thunder and lightning, honors and crosses, and then—"

"I understand," said Luke. "You'd have me choose the humbler and safer path?"

"Well," said his friend, dubiously, "perhaps!"

"Let me tell you," said Luke, "once and forever, that I have deliberately chosen the other; not because of its honor and emoluments—I despise them! but the Church requires it. Ours is not the Church of the Catacombs, but of Constantine!"

"It's a truth and a fallacy," said the candid friend. "Meanwhile, allowing all that, and presupposing that you are right in your decision, I don't admit it, you know—"

"Don't admit what?" said Luke.

"That the Church requires very brilliant men, or that the world is much in need of them."

"The world regards the Church as a molehill," said Luke; "a subterranean, cryptic, concealed system, burrowing under all the states and governments of the world,—its conspirators blinking and purblind in the light of day, and with vision enough only to plot, and delve, and undermine all the institutions of civilization."

"Out of which of the infidel reviews did you pick that rhodomontade?" said the friend.

"There now," said Luke, "you are losing temper, and the tooth is not yet drawn."

"Quite true. But now for the operation. I think you are going too fast and will get derailed. All this newspaper notoriety, 'able controversialist,' 'brilliant lecturer,' etc., is quite enough to turn any head not well screwed on; and yours, you know, ah—"

"Go on," said Luke, "go on."

"I'm hurting you," said the candid friend.

"Oh! not at all," said Luke. "I rather like it. It is so ingenuous, you know. You were saying something about my head."

"I see I'm hurting you," said the friend. "Now, I'll put it in a better way. Did you ever feel an impulse to go down on your knees and kiss the hem of the garment of some poor, half-witted, illiterate old duffer, who knew just enough of Latin to spell through his breviary, but who was doing, with sublime unconsciousness, the work of his Master?"

Luke was struck dumb. These were almost his own words, expressed with enthusiasm not quite two years ago.

"Once," he said faintly; "but I had no experience."

"And did you ever," said the friend, not noticing, "did you ever feel an irresistible inclination to get behind some great, intellectual prodigy, who was sweeping the whole world before him apparently, and with one glorious *coup-de-main* block his hat before all his admirers?"

"Never," said Luke, emphatically. "I think that is narrow-minded and illiberal."

"Well, I did," said his friend, dryly.

"Look here, now, Sheldon," said Luke, "once and forever let me say that I feel, and am sure, that the unnatural delay in the conversion of England is primarily due to this cause. You, English, are so narrow and conservative and petty in your views that you'll never appeal successfully to the broad human spirit of the age. You don't understand the *Zeitgeist*. The whole trend of human thought is to reconcile revelation with intellect; and out of the harmony to evolve a new and hopeful instauration of human blessedness. Now, we must take our rightful place in this renascence. It won't do to be silent. Or, rather, we must speak out boldly and confidentially, with large, free interpretations of natural and supernatural revelations, or hold our tongues altogether. *Falls er nicht schweigt!*"

"Good heavens!" said Father Sheldon, "where did you pick up that horrible jargon? What in the name of common sense, man, are you reading?"

"There now, there now," said Luke, "you don't read, my dear fellow. There's the great drawback. There's no use in arguing further. We move on different planes of thought. By the way, are you coming over to Bermondsey to dine tomorrow?"

Father Sheldon said nothing. He had failed to pull that tooth; and of all botches in creation, an unsuccessful dentist is the worst.

"Poor fellow," he said in his own *sanctum* afterwards, "he's on the down grade, though he appears to be sky-flying. That rush for Mass in the morning, and the substitution of the Rosary for the Office are bad signs. German snatches won't make up for it. Well, the retreat is at hand, thank God! Who knows?"

The retreat came, and the retreat was over; and Luke was the same—only worse. The preacher was a distinguished man, and, therefore, a failure in that line. Luke was delighted—and was lost. "He had never heard such command of language before;" "he did not know, till then, how religion could be lifted so beautifully into the regions of transcendentalism;" "how philosophy, in the hands of a master, can be made the handmaiden of religion;" "and how both together can be clothed in iridescence by the mastery of our mother tongue;" "yes, of course, he was apologetic, and why not? He was speaking to his equals, and was quite right in assuming that they knew all that he knew;" "he said 'sheol' for 'hell'; well, why not? It's the correct word, if you go so far;" "and he always spoke of 'eschatology' in place of 'eternity'; very well, isn't that the scientific term?" etc., etc.

"Ah!" he said to Father Sheldon, "these are the men we want. I'd give half a year's salary to see him invited over to Ireland to give a series of retreats. Wouldn't he wake them up from their lethargy? Wouldn't he show them what culture and education can do?"

"I thought your country used to be called the 'Island of Saints'?" said Father Sheldon.

"Certainly; so it was. You tried to rob us of that as of everything else. But you can't!"

"But the preacher said that the saints and their lives were never intended for imitation, but for admiration."

"And quite right. Do you mean to say that Simon Stylites would be allowed to remain twenty years or twenty days on the obelisk in these times?"

"Perhaps not. But what then becomes of your countrymen and their distinguished title? If there's no room for one saint, what do we want with a whole island full of them?"

"Look here, Sheldon, you are a horrible reactionary—a mediævalist—an Inquisitionist! How in the world will men like you ever convert England?"

"I'm not sure that it's worth converting," said Father Sheldon, lazily; "but I'm sure of one thing—that the modern idea that we are to hold up our saints, our beautiful saints, Francis and Ignatius and Alphonsus, Clare and Rose and Scholastica, as so many dime-museum freaks, to be looked at and wondered at as Divine Curiosities and no more—is the most horrible conclusion which our Catholic neologists have ever reached."

"I give you up, Sheldon," said Luke. "I'll write tonight to a confidential friend in Ireland to get over Father Azarias as soon as possible. He has a big field there."

"I suppose so. May the Lord grant you, Irish, a good conceit o' yersel's."

They were sitting at coffee in the library. It was Sunday, and dinner was at four P.M., instead of the usual hour, one o'clock. The Bishop had said a few pretty things about the distinguished preacher the day before at dinner. But the Bishop was inquisitive. He liked to gather opinions—an excellent thing. You need never adopt them, like the good Irish prelate who declared with emphasis that he never took an important step without consulting his canons. "But do you always follow their counsels, my Lord?" The Bishop, emphatically: "Never!"

But they were at coffee.

"How did you like the retreat?"

Luke was effusive and enthusiastic. The Vicar said: "So far as I am concerned, he might as well have been playing a flute the whole time. It was certainly very pretty."

"Father Sheldon, what are you poring over there?" said the Bishop. Father Sheldon was a great favorite. In a solemn, but half-careless manner, as if he had stumbled on a chance passage, Father Sheldon read from the big, brass-bound Bible:—

"Michæas said to Achab, King of Israel: 'Hear thou the word of the Lord. I saw the Lord sitting on His throne, and all the army

of heaven standing by Him, on the right hand, and on the left.'
And the Lord said: 'Who shall deceive Achab, King of Israel, that
he may go up and fall at Ramoth-Galaad?' And one spake words
in this manner, and another otherwise. And then came forth a
Spirit, and stood before the Lord, and said: 'I will deceive him.'
And the Lord said: 'By what means?' And he answered: 'I will go
forth, and be a lying spirit in the mouth of all his prophets.' And
the Lord said: 'Thou shalt deceive him, and shalt prevail: go forth
and do so.' "

The Bishop was silent, and serious. The Vicar shook all
over, and snorted once or twice, which was his way of laughing boisterously. A young priest said: "You haven't brought
much charity out of the retreat, Father Sheldon!"

Luke said: "There is no use in talking here; Father Sheldon
is a bronze statue, with his face turned to the past!"

"That's all right, Delmege. But when a man comes to dress
and drill one hundred priests, so as to refit them for better
work amongst a few hundred thousand souls, and when, perhaps, one of these captains is himself trembling in the balance,
we expect something else besides 'Sing a song of sixpence,'
and 'Isn't that a dainty dish to lay before the king?' "

You'd like to see a portrait of Luke Delmege just at this
time. Well, here it is:—

"11 ALBEMARLE BUILDINGS, VICTORIA ST., W. C.

"DEAREST MOTHER:—I went up for my first-half a week ago,
but got plucked. The questions were beastly. MacKenzie, an old
Scotchman, who lived on oatmeal till he came to London, and now
doesn't know himself, was my chief examiner. He asked the most
absurd questions,—the percentage of fibrin in the blood, the specific difference between enteric and adynamic fever, the effect of
hydrocyanic acid, etc. I was thoroughly made up in surgery, for
which I have a peculiar taste, yet he never asked a question, except
something ridiculous about the treatment of embolisms, and I
could have given him lights in psychological and mental science,
where I am A 1, but he never asked a question. Then, he's not a
gentleman. 'Young mon,' said this red-headed Highland savage,
'I'd recommend you to qualify as a hairdresser. It is a branch of
surgery, ye ken.' I have reported him to the trustees, and demanded
a second examination. Dr. Calthrop is down here, examining in

bacteriology, and, pardon the pun, he's backing me up. By the way, tell Barby that her clerical friend is coming out. He now parts his hair in the center, and has assumed an Ionic-Doric accent. But I must say he preaches well and effectively. In fact, he's becoming a crack lecturer on this side. I cannot compare him, of course, with the Master of the Temple, for there will be always wanting that *esprit* and those little *nuances* of thought and expression that denote the university man. But he is strong and versatile, and I think, when he gets into the Attic accent, he will do fairly well. Just tell Pap that there was a blunder in the examination programme, and I am going up again. Perhaps he may write to Calthrop, who is a power here. I'll let him know later on about MacKenzie, and he'll probably give him a wigging. Evidently, the uncouth fellow didn't know who I was.

"Ever affectionately,

"Louis J. Wilson, B.A."

One of the effects of which epistle was this:—

"Dublin, Sept. 8, 187—.

"Rev. Dear Father:—I must write to tell you how proud and pleased we all are at seeing your name so frequently in the *Catholic Times* and *Tablet,* and in so honored a way. And now comes a letter from Louis, enthusiastically sounding your praises. I should give extracts, but I am afraid I should hurt you. But he is a great admirer of yours, and I cannot help thinking that our dear Lord has created this reverence and admiration in order that you may exercise a holy controlling influence over poor Louis in the midst of London temptations. I am supposing that you have not met him as yet in London; but his address is: 11 Albemarle Buildings, Victoria Street, London, W.C., and I am sure, if you could spare time to call on him, he would be highly pleased and flattered by your condescension. Do, dear Father! *It is a question of a soul and its future,* and your reward will be exceeding great. Sophy Kennedy, an old schoolmate of mine, now in Kensington, has also written to say she has been to hear you; and when I told her you were a friend of mine (this was presumptuous, of course) she actually sent me congratulations, and doubted if I'd acknowledge 'small people' any more.

"I am taking up too much of your valuable time with my nonsense; but our next letter from Louis will be a breath from Paradise.

"I am, dear Rev. Father, respectfully yours,

"Barbara Wilson."

"A pan of hot coals on my head!" said Luke. "I must really look up the lad. I dare say he has forgotten our little *recontre*. Of course, he felt he deserved richly what he got."

And, accordingly, some days later, he again crossed Westminster Bridge, and found his way to Albemarle Buildings. The Buildings were laid out in flats, on the French system. A respectable, middle-aged woman kept the keys.

"No, Mr. Wilson was not a home—had gone to the 'ospital," she supposed, "and would not return till late. He rarely dined at 'ome."

Luke was turning away, not too disappointed, for he dreaded the interview, although prepared to be very conciliatory and condescending, when the woman said:—

"I perceive you're a clergyman, sir, and perhaps a friend of this young gentleman."

"Well, we are acqaintances at least," said Luke, straining at the truth, "and I am much interested in him."

"Well, then, sir," she said, "if some one would take him in 'ands. I fear he's not doing well. Would you walk upstairs, sir?"

They went upstairs, although Luke felt that he was intruding somewhat unwarrantably on the privacy of another. The woman unlocked a door and ushered him into an apartment filled with some strange, pungent, aromatic odor, such as hangs around a druggist's or perfumer's shop. There was chaos everywhere. Pipes of all shapes and forms, pots of unguents, masks and wigs, photographs, some quite fresh, some faded, of actresses and beauties. There were two side by side in a frame. One was subscribed "Circe"; the other, which Luke recognized as Barbara's, was simply marked by one red spot, which Luke soon discovered was a heart on fire. Over the mantelpiece hung a splendid enlarged photograph of the Canon, and in the frame was inserted a shield with the arms of the Murray family, and their motto, *Sans tache*.

"It would cost me my situation, sir," she said, "if it were ever known that I brought you here; but I am a mother, and I know wot it is to see the young go astray. Has this young gentleman a father or mother? I know he has a sister, for every post brings 'im a letter from 'er. He never mentions his parents."

"Yes. I understand his parents are living. I know little of them; but I know his sister and their uncle." He pointed to the photograph.

"Well, sir, the poor young gentleman is doing badly. He often comes 'ome hintoxicated, has picked up with a dangerous lot—"

"Does he read?" queried Luke, looking around in vain for thick folios and bones.

"A good deal of these," she said, pointing to a heap of tattered novels. "But these are the real dangers,"—she pointed to the photographs, and took down a phial from the mantelpiece.

"He can take all that in a day," she said, pointing to the label, "enough to kill ten men. And he won't stand much longer, sir; mark my words, he won't stand much longer, unless some one steps in to save him.

"You won't see him sometimes for days together," she continued. "I knocks and knocks, and, thinks I, we'll have a crowner's inquest here soon. And then he comes out a-shaking all over like a haspen, an' his face a-shining like the hangels. But it ain't hangels, but devils, he has seen."

"I'm much obliged to you for your confidence," said Luke, coming downstairs. "I must see to it at once."

"And you won't mention to no one what I have showed you?" said the woman.

"Never fear," said Luke.

"A pretty bad case!" he thought, as he wended his way homewards; "a pretty bad case. I must write to his sister or uncle. And this is the fellow I was half-afraid of a couple of years ago in that drawing-room. It needs travel and experience to know the world after all, and to know that there are few in it that are not beneath you."

Which shows that Luke had now fully adopted the philosophy of one of his Mentors, and was holding his head—very high.

BOOK III

CHAPTER XV

Aylesburgh

"I HAVE been thinking of making some changes in the Cathedral staff," said the Bishop to the Vicar in the library. "I'm not too well satisfied with the seminary, and should like to see more life and progress there. Would not Father Sheldon, with his very high ideas about the priesthood, be an admirable guide for young students?"

"Certainly," said the Vicar, "except that, like myself, he speaks too plainly sometimes."

"Very true," said the Bishop. "There would be some danger there. And I must remove Delmege—"

"Delmege?" said the Vicar, quite alarmed.

"Yes, for his own sake. I see clearly he is rather too interested in the platform—too little in the pulpit."

"He speaks well, and is doing excellent work," said the Vicar.

"True; but is all that he says either useful or edifying, do you think?"

"Well, he does rub the wrong way sometimes," said the Vicar, reluctantly.

"I had been thinking of speaking to him seriously about some of his utterances," said the Bishop. "That perpetual harping on the English schism and on Irish fidelity does not exactly please our English audience. '*We* kept the Faith in Ireland when, at the dictation of a savage king, *you* flung aside the glorious heritage,' does not soothe the British mind."

"I should say not," said the Vicar, laughing. "But it is the truth, not its utterance, that is painful."

"Then," said the Bishop, resuming, "I turned over a file of

157

newspapers the other day, and came across this singular passage in one of his lectures:—

"The English mind is by nature antagonistic to Catholic truth. It was not Luther, it was the legend of 'Faust' that prepared the way for the Reformation. The world was tired of asceticism and saints. So were the English. They wanted the gods, their liberty, their sensuality. They found their gods in such satyrs as Luther and Henry; they found their liberty in the assertion of individual freedom; sensuality followed. And if all England were Catholic again, and the Pope presumed to order an additional fast-day, you would call out the Reserves and mobilize the fleet at Spithead."

"Yes, I remember," said the Vicar, laughing. "The fellow has the knack of putting the truth unpleasantly. I remonstrated with him. 'Is it true or false?' he said. 'Perhaps true,' I replied. 'Then why not tell it?' he said. He can't understand that it is not always desirable to advance unnecessary truths."

"He wants experience," said the Bishop. "I was going to say 'correction.' But, you know, these fire-eating Irishmen won't take correction. Then I thought of sending him to Whitstable. But that is too great a responsibility—"

"I shall miss him greatly," said the Vicar. "He is a fine, manly young priest; hits straight from the shoulder, and is undoubtedly a clever fellow. What a pity these high-blooded natives won't bear the bit!"

"Then I thought of Aylesburgh," said the Bishop. "I could bring up old Collins here. But would Drysdale be able to control this young enthusiast?"

"I think so. Delmege, the moment he recognizes the sanctity of his pastor, will be as wax in his hands."

"Be it so, then," said the Bishop.

"I shall miss him sadly," said the Vicar, with something that seemed like a sob. "No doubt, we are a leaden lot."

The following Sunday evening there was an important function in the Cathedral. The Bishop was to assist in *Cappa magna*. Luke was to preach.

All were assembled in the inner sacristy just before the ceremony commenced. Luke was slightly nervous. It was the first time he had to preach in the Bishop's presence, and, say what you please, it is an ordeal to speak before an accomplished preacher, who also holds the keys of life and death.

"Would you assist the Bishop?" said Arthur, who was master of ceremonies, "whilst I look after the altar."

Luke moved forward and took up the *Cappa magna*. Now, the *Cappa magna* is the most beautiful of all the beautiful vestments with which Mother Church, in her great love, clothes her children. I cannot conceive how any lesser genius than that of Michelangelo could have devised it. A judge's ermine is nowhere in comparison, and even the coronation robes of royalty pale into insignificance before it. But, like all beautiful things in Nature and art, it must be handled with science and skill and delicacy. You succeeded by a hair's breadth, and it is a success. You fail by a most trifling misdirection, and it is a consummate and irremediable failure. Now Luke had neither science—because he knew nothing about this airy, fluffy, delicate thing; nor skill—because he had never touched it before; nor delicacy—for his strong, muscular fingers had not yet tapered into sensitive, nervous points. But he had all the confidence of inexperience. He took up the beautiful silk and ermine in his arms, and tossed it lightly over the Bishop's head. The Bishop shouted: "Take care!" But it was too late. The Bishop found that the long, shining masses of crimson silk hung like a curtain before him.

"You have put it on wrongly," he said angrily.

Luke tried to remedy the blunder by shifting the ermine around. It refused to be shifted. Luke was as crimson as the silk. He pulled and shifted and tugged.

"Take it off," said the Bishop.

More easily said than done. Luke lifted it, and then found the Bishop's head hopelessly entangled in the mighty mazes of the silken net. Then came a series of objurgations and apologies accompanying the tremendous conflict, whilst every moment seemed to involve the Bishop more hopelessly in the silken intricacy. The brethren moved not. There was a faint sound as of a titter; but no! British equanimity and self-poise were proof against the temptation, and no one stirred from his statuesque position to help the struggling agonistæ. It was too good to terminate or interrupt. They enjoyed it in British fashion by looking at one another. Just then the master of ceremonies came in. He ran his hands into the pockets of his soutane, looked around calmly, and said aloud: "Well, I'm blessed!" Then, moving forward, he pushed Luke gently aside with "Allow me!" and, putting his arms under the tangled silk and ermine, he gently lifted it, turned it around, kicked back the long, shining train, and it was done. Then he ordered all forward, and Luke, with burning face and tingling nerves, took his place in the procession. He found it difficult to compose himself during Vespers, and forgot all about his sermon in the painful retrospect, until Arthur bowed to him, and took him over to receive the episcopal blessing. The Bishop saw his embarrassment, and showed, as only a Bishop can, some invisible and intangible kindness. Then Luke was in the pulpit. He stammered through his text; then recovered himself, and spoke the first four sentences of his sermon well. His clear, metallic voice tolled slowly through the great overcrowded building, searching into every corner, as he leaned on every syllable and accented every final consonant. Then, in an unhappy moment, his memory reverted to his little *gaucheries* in the sacristy, and, as the shame came back, he forgot the trend of his discourse and began to flounder through some dreary platitudes. But pride came to his relief, and his heart began to pump blood into his brain, until all the faculties fortified took up their work again, and the paralysis ceased, and the faithful and pliant instrument obeyed the soul; and without blunder or flaw, the beautiful discourse flowed on to the end, and men drew breath and said "It was good!" After Benediction, and before divesting himself even of his biretta, the Bishop came over, shook Luke warmly by the hand, and said:—

"I have rarely heard anything so beautiful and practical!" which, from a Briton, meant a good deal.

Next day Luke was in his library. The spirit of work had now seized him and possessed him, until he felt work, work, work, was the elixir of life. He had now determined to plunge deeper than ever into his slums, and to drag out of their horrors the souls that were festering there. For this purpose he had drawn up a large map, showing every street, lane, alley, and court in his district, and was just giving the finishing touches to an aristocratic and classical spot, called

Granby Court, Granby Lane, off Spittal Alley,

when the door opened and the Bishop entered.

"At work, Delmege?"

"Yes, my Lord!"

"What would you think of going to Aylesburgh?"

"Ay—ay—Aylesburgh?" stammered Luke.

"Yes; I am sending you on to Drysdale. He is a brusque Briton, but a good fellow. You'll like him. When could you be ready?"

"Oh! at any time your Lordship pleases," said Luke, somewhat nettled, and thinking this might mean a fortnight's notice.

"Well, it's just now three. There's a train at half-past four. Could you meet it?"

Then the whole thing burst on Luke's mind, and he said, stiffly, as he rose: "If your Lordship pleases!"—and passed out of the room.

Whilst he was engaged in packing his few books and clothes, a timid knock was heard, and Father Sheldon came in.

"What's up?" he cried in amazement.

Luke turned away.

"What's the matter, Delmege? Where are you going?" said Father Sheldon, quite alarmed.

"Never mind," said Luke, turning around. "Look here, Sheldon, you are all the same—a pack of hypocrites. I tried to believe otherwise; but now my turn has come."

"I don't understand you," said Father Sheldon. "Are you going back to Ireland?"

"I wish I were," said Luke, bitterly. "Only that I have engaged myself for seven years, I should go back by the first train."

"But, for heaven's sake, man, what is it all about?"

"It's all about this—that I'm ordered off to Aylesburgh at an hour's notice, as if I had the plague. Of course I should have expected it. The moment a young Irishman makes him-

self useful, or—or—a—remarkable, that moment he's shifted
to some obscure place."

"There may be some reason," said Father Sheldon, diffidently.

"Of course there is. The universal reason of jealousy. I
shouldn't mind so much, but the good Bishop was kind and—
hypocritical enough to pay a marked compliment last night,
and then—"

"I'm extremely sorry," said Father Sheldon, moodily.

"There's more Saxon duplicity," said Luke, bitterly. "I'm
quite sure there's not one in the house who is half so glad as
you are—"

"Be it so," said Father Sheldon, going out.

As Luke passed down the corridor, he stopped for a moment
at the Vicar's door and timidly knocked.

"Come in!" said the gruff, well-known voice.

"I'm going," said Luke, briefly.

"I know it," said the old man. "There's a quarter due."

"I'm sorry for leaving you, sir," said Luke, with a gulp; "you
have been very kind, and I couldn't go away without saying
good-bye!"

The Vicar was writing. He folded the paper in an envelope,
and handed it to Luke.

"Good-bye, Delmege," he said. That was all.

"All alike," thought Luke. "Made out of putty and then
frozen."

It was a week before he opened the envelope. Instead of
£7 10s., the quarter's salary, the check was written for £15.

A two hours' run brought the sad and disappointed Luke
to his new home. He drove rapidly to the presbytery. The
rector was not at home. The housekeeper left his luggage in
the hall, and did not even show him his room. He went out
to see the church, muttering "brusque and British enough!"
The little church was very dark, and the air was redolent with
incense. He said a little prayer, and looked around, trying to
imagine his congregation.

"Somewhat different from the Cathedral," he thought. "I
shall not have to raise my voice here." He went behind the
choir screen, and examined the music. He then studied the

brass tablets on the benches, with the names of the pew-proprietors. There was no "Lord," not even a "Sir."

"The Canon would be disappointed," he whispered. He meant himself, though he did not know it. He started at some names. They were connected with art and literature. "I must mind my P's and Q's here," he whispered. "Let me see." He went up to the predella of the altar, and looked around, casting his voice in imagination up to the stained Crucifixion that lighted the front gallery. " 'Twill do," he said. He meant "I'll do." He examined the cards in the pews again. " 'The Misses Pardoe!' " he said. "I wonder who are these. 'Fräulein von Essler;' 'Mademoiselle Deshayes;' rather cosmopolitan. 'Jeremiah O'Connor.' Hallo, Jeremiah!

'Quae regio in terris, nostri non plena laboris?'

'Arthur Henry Halleck!' Can this be the *Nineteenth Century* reviewer? After all, I shall have some one to speak to."

Just then a visitor arrived in the shape of a great brown shaggy retriever, ringed all over with bronze curls. Gravely and sedately he moved up the aisle, until he reached to where Luke was standing watching him. He then as gravely lifted his right paw, which Luke instantly grasped.

"Good-day, old fellow," he said; "you're the first to welcome me. I'd swear you are an Irishman." So they passed into the presbytery again. This time the rector was at home. He rushed out, a fussy little man, his gray hairs all tossed awry, fussily shook hands with Luke. "You, Delmege?"—took up the hat-box, bade Luke take the portmanteau—"Come along to your room; you'll have to rough it here, you know. There! A place for your books, bed, chair, table. You'll have some tea?"

"At the usual time," said Luke, coldly. He thought there was hardly sufficient recognition of his dignity. Then he sat down and looked around sadly. It was not a prepossessing kind of room. It was very large, with a very low ceiling, worm-eaten boards, pretty large rat-holes in the corner, cupboards where ghosts might hide—altogether a rambling, antique, haunted, mysterious kind of room, such as you might see in ancient castles, long since disused. One thing redeemed its darkness and general mustiness. There was a noble window, opening on a tiny plot of grass, and commanding an extensive view of a high, brown, bare wall, which Luke soon found was the northern gable of a hideous Wesleyan conventicle. For hence in the long summer twilights, and the long winter nights, did Luke often hear the dismal wailings of Calvinistic hymns, droned out by raucous male voices or the shrill trebles of women, and the eternal burden was:—

> Oh! let us be joyful, joyful, joyful,
> When we meet to part no more!

But there was one hymn, redolent of Calvinism and discord, which was sung morning, noon, and night in this dreary conventicle. It haunted Luke like a specter, and he confessed that, to the very end of his life, it sent his heart into his boots. It was all about being saved! saved!! saved!!!

"If these be the pæans of the elect," thought Luke, "I wonder on what unimaginable minor key are pitched the wailings of the lost!"

It was his first introduction to the gloom and desolation of the English religion.

"And these are the people who, through their writers, through Dickens and Arnold and the host of globe-trotting cynics, try to turn into ridicule the sweet, sunny religion of Italy and Spain! But they produced a Faber, Luke. Well, that saves them somewhat."

There was a short service and Benediction on Thursday evening, at which, to Luke's surprise, there was a very large attendance. And here he noticed that almost invisible but terrible line of demarcation, that in all English churches separates the imperialists from the helots. The front benches were sparsely filled with well-dressed, stately English; the last two benches were well filled with poorly dressed Irish, whose very attitude was an apology. And back in the gloom of the porch, hidden in the shadows of the confessionals, the exiles thronged, and swayed to and fro, and flung out their arms in adoration, and shook their beads, as long ago on the mud floors and whitewashed cabins in the Irish hills. Luke couldn't stand it.

"Stand up, and go on to those vacant seats," he said per-emptorily.

"God bless your reverence; but we'd rather be here." And there they remained.

It was his first little *rencontre* with his pastor. He referred, in not very measured terms, to this heretical exclusiveness in the House of the Great Father.

"There should be no distinction of class here, as there shall be none on the Day of Judgment. And, from my experience of England, Doctor, I tell you that the one secret of the Church is this: Preserve what you have got and develop it; don't waste your energies in fishing in barren waters."

"*Your* experience?" said Dr. Drysdale, mildly and apologetically. "You've been a good many years in the country?"

"Two years and six months," stammered Luke, blushing at his own conceit.

"Oh! I nearly agree with you, my young friend," continued the rector; "but there are practical difficulties, which, perhaps, at some future time, you, too, may be invited to solve. For example, did it occur to you that there is a heretical gas company that insists on being paid every quarter; and a heretical corporation that demands rates; and an organist who, though not a heretic, wants bread and butter; and a sacristan who, though an excellent Catholic, must be fed as becomes a Briton; and last, not least, a most estimable young Irish confrère who, perhaps, too—but, perhaps, I'm wrong?—Can it be that our idealistic brethren across the Channel live, in a balloon-like way, on fresh air?"

"Ye have left them precious little else to live on," said Luke, who was half angry, half amused.

Nevertheless, his training had already habituated him to common sense, and he rather admired the rector.

Luke preached on Sunday evening after Compline. Luke preached well. He did not anticipate a very distinguished or appreciative audience, and his nerves were calm under the in-difference. But when his practiced eye detected quite an aristo-cratic and educated audience, he pulled himself together, and directed his train of thought in the channels that might suit them.

"I dare say they have heard me," the dear little idol whispered, "and expect something. I must not disappoint them."

And here let it be said that in these two years and a half Luke had picked out of reviews and pamphlets more theological information than he had acquired in his four years' divinity course. And now he had to study more closely, and address his studies to special subjects, because he found, in a few weeks, that he was now addressing not only a congregation of converts, but that, every Sunday evening, his audience was largely composed of Protestants of every shape and hue, from the eager solicitor, or doctor, or banker, down to the dragoon from the cavalry barracks, who, during the discourse, sliced oranges for his best girl. This latter episode, indeed, rather disturbed Luke's equanimity at first, and his Celtic temper brought him perilously near an explosion; but he became accustomed to the unintentional irreverence, and, after a few Sundays, ceased to notice it.

Then he found that, on Monday morning or Tuesday, a Baptist, or Socinian, or Unitarian would claim an interview with the object of controverting some statement in the sermon of the previous evening; and Luke became suddenly aware that there was a good deal to be studied and considered before he could break through the crust of self-opinion that gathers round the right of private judgment.

But we are anticipating. On the first Sunday evening, when Luke entered the presbytery, expecting to receive the congratulations of his rector, he was surprised to find the little parlor full of parishioners. Three or four families were represented, from father, grave and solemn, and mother, smiling and happy, down to grown maidens and youths with great black eyes and pale faces, and even little children, who looked up boldly and inquiringly at the new assistant. There was a little amicable rivalry amongst them, and the question was— who was to secure this clever, handsome, young Irishman as guest for the evening.

"Now, Mr. Godfrey, you are always monopolizing our priests. There was no such thing as getting Father Collins to come to us."

"Oh! dear, dear! and we used to say that Father Collins lived at the Hermitage."

"Now, Mr. Godfrey, we really must make a rule that will not be infringed upon. We must have Mr. Del—Del—"

"Delmege," said Luke, smiling happily at this battle in his honor.

"We must have Mr. Delmege *every* Sunday evening, and on alternate Thursdays."

"Really, Mrs. Bluett, you are most grasping and intolerant. I appeal to the Doctor."

The Doctor was tossing up the long ringlets of a little maiden of five summers, and here looked up.

"I'm sure," he said, shrugging his shoulders, "I shan't interfere. If you could manage to divide him, as Solomon intended with the baby, it would be all the better."

Mr. Godfrey, however, bore away the prize triumphantly. Luke had sense enough to whisper to his rector: "Shall I go?"

"By all means. But don't stay later than ten. They'll like you all the better."

And this was Luke's first introduction to a good pastor, whom ever after he regarded as the greatest and the dearest of the "dii majores" who were enshrined in the secret temple of honored friendship, and to the circle of the gentlest and sweetest people that he had yet or ever known. It is quite true, indeed, that he had some academic discussions from time to time with his pastor, generally on political topics, but these, too, were tacitly avoided after a while. And for a time he was embarrassed and puzzled at the idiosyncrasies of English life. He couldn't manage cold roast beef and cheese and ale at eight o'clock at night; and old John Godfrey was considerate enough always, when placing his hand on the cover of the Stilton, to shout: "Look out, Father Delmege!" So, too, he found it hard to understand how grave men of forty or fifty could spend hours over a stupid game of dominoes, with nothing but counters in the pool; and he thought whist insufferable. Sometimes, too, he fidgeted in his chair as he sat around a winter's fire, and a calm, Carthusian silence pervaded the whole family circle.

"Isn't this enjoyable, Father Delmege?" John Godfrey would say, taking the long clay from his mouth and exhaling a mighty cloud.

"Very," Luke would answer, adding in his own mind, "not quite as bad as a jail, but a great deal worse than a college."

But he got used to it, and his nerves were gradually toned down into the silky smoothness that reigned everywhere around him. And he began to see great deeps of affection and love far down beneath the icy surface; and every day he was made aware of genuine kindness, gentle, undemonstrative, unobtrusive, until he grew to love these grave, pleasant people, and they loved him in turn.

"Bah!" he used to say angrily to himself sometimes, "there's only a sheet of tissue-paper between the two races, but politicians and journalists have daubed it all over with the visions of demoniacs. When will the great man arise to drive his fist through the obstruction and let the two peoples see each other as they are?"

And the great, white-haired Canon at home began to rise steadily in his esteem, and Lisnalee became more shadowy and cloudy than ever.

Luke would not sing "The Muster" now.

"I really must write to Sheldon," he said. "I treated him badly. I am almost tempted to write the Bishop and thank him. But I'll express it later on."

CHAPTER XVI

Enchantment

THE CANON sat in his favorite arm-chair in his rectory at home. The morning sun streamed in, and made a glory of his white hair, as of an Alp in the sunlight. The Canon was happy. And he was happy because he had not yet attained everything he could desire. For, you know, the unhappy man is he who, like poor Herder, has got everything that even Shakespeare offers to old age, and has nothing to look forward to this side the grave. There were some things yet to be desired, to be reached unto, to be seized,—to be enjoyed? No! The enjoyment is the pursuit; it ceases when the hand closes down on the prize. And yet, with every consolation around him, and that most sublime of consolations, the growing happiness of his people, forever under his eyes, there were some misgivings— the rift in the lute, the fly in the amber, which are inseparable from all kinds of human felicity. A letter lay open on the table. It was a pathetic letter, and more pathetic still, it contained a poem. This the Canon read over and over, and the tears were in his eyes. Yet the Canon was happy, for he was a good man, and he had the power of relieving misery always within his reach. Indeed, it would be difficult to say which was the happier—the benevolent Canon, who presented some poor woman with a brace of Orpingtons, with the assurance that she would have a glorious "cluck" in the springtime, or the poor woman who was just about to enjoy the pleasures of proprietorship. And when he had got thirty per cent knocked off the rents of his tenantry, he walked on air for several days afterwards. So the Canon was happy, for he was writing a check for ten pounds this morning, and the check was made payable to Louis Wilson. The old fool! says some one.

Not at all! You'd do the same yourself, my indignant friend,
if you had a little account at your banker's, and if you chanced
to have these lines addressed to you:—

> He stood afar, as one without a God,
> Waiting in darkness for the deeper night,
> When sleep would come—the long and soulless sleep,
> That seemed to him more peaceful than the hope
> Of future immortality.
>
> In the silence of that solemn midnight hour,
> While calmly slept the world, and stars kept watch,
> And the land was flooded with the moon's weird light,
> And the heavens and the earth were steeped in beauty,
> He laid him down thus wretchedly.
>
> And a ray of moonlight glittered on the blade,
> That leaped with deathly swiftness to his heart;
> And the stars looked down in pity as he sank
> With closed eyes, among the sleeping flowers,
> To rest forever peacefully.

The Canon was not a critic; nor had he an ear for music,
or a finical respect for accents and syllables. He had only an
imagination. And he saw the moonlight, and the sleeping
flowers, and the crushed grass, and the blade with the dark
stain—ugh! and the Canon wept with pity, and debated with
himself long and earnestly whether he would not change that
check and write fifty. But the check was posted to No. 11
Albemarle Buildings; and the good housekeeper, whose rent
had fallen into sad arrears, chuckled as she guessed: "A check
from his huncle!" But the Canon went around these days in an
anxious and happy mood, fearful that every post would bring
him an account of a coroner's inquest. But to all outward appearance he was the same grand, majestic Canon, and the
people said: "How great and how happy!"

During these happy months, Luke Delmege was floated
along in a current of calm peaceful work, broken only by the
innocent pleasures of refined and beautiful social surroundings.
He had time to think at last, though he never ceased to work.

And one of his thoughts was this: This fever and fret of work, work, work—What is it all for? What is the object of it? The answer was: Work needs no object but itself, because work is its own reward. There was something in it, but it was not quite satisfactory; for, in that case, an immortal being had no higher object in life than a steam-engine. He proposed the question often to himself; and he proposed it at a happy gathering at a certain house, which had gradually become his salon and academy. Here invariably once a week, sometimes twice or thrice a week, Luke had the inestimable privilege of meeting a small, select coterie of esoterics, representative of every branch of literature, science, and art, and even divinity. For here came many soft-mannered, polite, well-read Anglican clergymen, who stepped over from their snug, if dingy, houses in the Cathedral close, and brought with the man atmosphere of learning and refinement and gentle courtesy, which had a perceptible effect on the character and manner of this young Hibernian. And here, mostly on Wednesday evenings, were gathered celebrities, who slipped down from London by an afternoon train and went back at midnight; and Luke began to learn that there were in the world a few who might be masters and teachers forever to a *First-of-First*. And Luke grew humble, and began to sit at the feet of some Gamaliel, and his quarter salary was spent long before he had received it in buying books, the very names of which he had never heard before. And with his plastic Irish nature, he had begun to fit in and adapt himself to these new environments, and even his dress bespoke a change. And he studied, as carefully as a novice in a monastery, to subdue the riotous and impassioned elements of his nature, and to become as silky and soft and smooth as those with whom he associated.

But he proposed the question to Amiel Lefevril, one of the three maiden sisters who presided over the salon, and who had heard a good deal from Catholic friends about this new light, which had suddenly dawned from Ireland on the gray monotony of a dull English cathedral town. And it came around in this way. The lady had got a letter from the great Master of Balliol, who had just finished his work on the *Republic* of Plato, and one sentence ran thus:—

"You have endless work to do in your own sphere; and you must finish that, and not fancy that life is receding from you. I always mean to cherish the illusion, which is not an illusion, that the last years of life are the most valuable and important, and every year I shall try in some way or other to do more than in the year before."

"You see," continued Amiel, "these are the words of an old man,—a great old man; and how applicable to you, before whom the years are spreading in a long, sunlit vista."

"But—but," said Luke, with the old *sic-argumentaris* style, but now, oh! so modified, "life must have an object. There must be an ideal—an object to attain."

"*Distinguo!*" said the lady, and Luke almost jumped from his chair at the old familiar word. "If you are selfish and self-centered you need no other object than the tonic of daily work to strengthen and purify every mental and moral faculty. But there is a higher plane to which you will reach, and where you become divinely altruistic. That is, when you acknowledge and understand that the crown of life is self-surrender, and when the interest of the individual is absorbed in the interests of the race."

It sounded sweetly, and wrapped Luke's senses around as with an atmosphere of music and perfume; but his judgment was not convinced.

"I thought I heard some one enlarge a few nights ago— yes, indeed, it was Canon Mellish—on the world-weariness of all our great writers and workers—on the dread despair of Arnold of Rugby and Matthew Arnold—on the justification of suicide by George Eliot, and the wish that it could be justified by Carlyle."

"Quite so," answered Amiel. "The necessary result of too great enthusiasm—the reaction from the *Schwärmerei* towards ashes and weeping. But, brother, you were unhappy in your illustrations. Those bright lights whom you mention burned for themselves only, leaving smoke and darkness behind them. You and we must seek better things."

"I cannot quite grasp it," said Luke, vainly stretching towards the insoluble. "I see some great idea underlying your thesis, but I cannot seize it."

"Then I must take you by the hand, and lead you into the inner circle of the mystics. You know, of course, that all great thinkers now understand the nature of Life's symbolism— that the whole world of experience is but the appearance or vesture of the divine idea or life, and that he alone has true life who is willing to resign his own personality in the service of humanity, and who tries unceasingly to work out this ideal that gives the only nobility and grandeur to human action— that is:—

Seek God in Man!

not

Man in God,

which latter has been the great human heresy from the beginning."

It sounded nice, and it gave Luke a good deal of food for reflection. This self-surrender, this absorption in the race, the *Ego* lost in the All, and immortal in the eternity of Being— this is the very thing he sought for; and was it not the thing the martyrs sought for—the high-water mark of Catholicism? He ventured to hint vaguely at the matter to his rector, who rubbed his chin and seemed to smile, and said:—

"I think, Father Delmege, you had better keep to John Godfrey and his pipe, and leave these Anglo-French blue-stockings alone."

Luke pronounced the old man reactionary.

"However," said Dr. Drysdale, "you want work for humanity. All right. I'll hand you over the county jail. You will meet some pretty specimens of humanity there."

" 'Tis all this horrible mechanism," said Luke; "these English cannot get over it. Man is only a tiny crank in the huge machine—that's all they can conceive. How different this teaching—Man, a Symbol of the Divine!"

Yet the beautiful, smooth mechanism was affecting Luke unconsciously. He no longer heard the whir and jar of machinery, or saw the mighty monster flinging out its refuse of slime and filth in the alleys and courts of southwest London; but the same smooth regularity, the same quiet, invincible energy, was manifest even here in the sleepy cathedral town. Here was the beautiful tapestry, pushed out from the horrid jaws of the great mill; beautiful, perfect, with all fair colors of cultured men and stately women, and woven through with gold and crimson threads of art and science and literature. And Luke felt the glamour wrapping him around with an atmosphere of song and light, and he felt it a duty to fit himself to his environments. He was helped a good deal.

"Quick, quick, quick, Father Delmege; you're two minutes late this morning. These people won't wait, you know."

Luke felt his pastor was right; but he could not help thinking: God be with Old Ireland, where the neighbors meet leisurely for a *seanachus* on Sunday morning, and sit on the tombstones and talk of old times! And no one minds the priest being half an hour late; nor does he, for he salutes them all affably as he passes into the sacristy, and they say "God bless your reverence!"

Or: "Look here, look here, look here, Father Delmege; now look at that corporal! There you have not observed the folds, and it must be all made up again."

Or: "Could you manage, Father Delmege, to modulate your voice a little? This is not the Cathedral, and some of those ladies are nervous. I saw Mrs. S—— start and look pained whilst you were preaching yesterday. It was like an electric shock."

"God be with Old Ireland," thought Luke, "where the people's nerves are all right, and where they measure your preaching powers by the volume of sound you can emit."

But he did tone down his voice, until it became a clear, metallic tingling, as of sled-bells on a frosty night.

They had long, amiable discussions on theology during the winter evenings after dinner. In the beginning, indeed, Luke would break out occasionally into a kind of wild hysterics, when the grave, polite old man would venture a contradiction on some theological question. Luke did not like to be contradicted. Had he not studied under——at college? And had he not experienced that the right way to discomfit an antagonist is to laugh at him, or tell him he is quite absurd? But the gravity of this dear old man, his quiet, gentle persistence, began to have an effect on Luke's vanity, and gradually he came to understand that there are a good many ways of looking at the same thing in this queer world, and that it were well indeed to be a little humble and tolerant of others' opinions. For the truth forced itself on Luke's mind that this old man, although he never studied in the hallowed halls of his own college, was in very deed, a profound theologian, and when Luke, later on, discovered quite accidentally that this gentle man was actually the author of certain very remarkable philosophical papers in the *Dublin Review,* and that his opinions were quoted in the leading Continental reviews, he was surprised, and thought—who could ever believe it?

This idea of toleration Luke was slow in grasping. He had such a clear, logical faculty that he could see but one side of a question, and was quite impatient because others could not see it in the same manner. There is reason to fear that at his first conference he was positively rude. He had a good deal of contempt for English conferences. It was fencing with painted laths instead of the mighty sword-play that goes on in Ireland. One brief case about Bertha and Sylvester, who had got into some hopeless entanglement about property, etc., and that was all. Now, all the other priests calmly gave their opinions; but Luke should blurt out impatiently:—

"That's not what *we* were taught, and no theologian of eminence holds that."

Canon Drysdale rubbed his chin, and said:—

"I had some correspondence with Palmieri on the matter. Would my young friend do us the favor of reading his reply?"

And Luke, angry and blushing, read his own refutation.

But the beautiful lessons of toleration and mildness and self-restraint were telling insensibly on his character.

One evening at the salon he ventured even to ask questions. A grave, elderly man had been saying that he had just visited Bunsen in Germany, and that Bunsen was a grand, colossal heathen.

"Did you," said Luke, shyly, "did you ever come across Wegscheider in Germany?"

"Weg—Weg—no, I cannot remember. Let me see—Weimar, Wieland, Wein, Weib, Weg—could he be anything to old Silas?" said the traveller, gravely.

"No!" said Luke, a little nettled. "He was only a theologian; but he was heterodox, and I thought you might have met him." This was really good for Luke. He was getting into the ways of polite society.

"I think," he whispered to an Anglican parson, who was always extremely kind, "that Wegscheider was a Sabellian."

"What's that?" said the parson.

"Oh! I thought you knew all about heretics," replied Luke.

"A pretty compliment," said the Anglican. "No, I never heard the word, except flung occasionally at a Bishop as a nickname by one of our papers."

Later on in the evening Luke startled a little circle who were gravely enlarging on the evolution of the race, and conjecturing the tremendous possibilities that lay before it.

"Considering what has been done," said Olivette Lefevril, "and how we have grown from very humble origins into what we are today,"—she looked around and into a large mirror and arranged a stray curl,—"there is no, absolutely no, limit to the developments of humanity. Something higher, and something even approaching to the anthropomorphic conceptions of the Deity is even realizable."

"There is not much hope for it," said a belligerent journalist, "so long as the nations are at one another's throat for a trifle; and so long as gentlemen in morning dress in their comfortable cabinets can get the unhappy proletariat to blow each other to atoms for their amusement."

"Ah! but war," said Clotilde, "war, dreadful as it is, is but the sifting and selection of the strongest and the best. Nations emerge from war and renew their strength as the eagle's."

"And see," said a blue-spectacled lady, "how we have eliminated mendicancy from our midst. A mendicant is as extinct as a dodo."

"I should give all the world to see a beggar!" broke in Luke, rashly.

"A beggar! a real, live beggar, with rags and things?" broke in the chorus of the startled multitude.

"Yes," said Luke, confidently, "a real, live, leprous beggar

—a very Lazarus of sores, if only to help us to recall some things we read of in Scripture."

"Ah! but my dear Mr. Delmege, you quite forget that all this took place in Syria and in the close of the ancient cycle. This is England, and the nineteenth century."

"Quite so," said Luke, appealing to a Canon, "but what says the Scripture—'The poor you shall always have with you'!"

"What, then, becomes of the evolution of religion?" shrieked a lady. "If there is to be no progress, where comes in your Christianity?"

"I think," said the senior Canon, "that Mr. Delmege is right and wrong,—right in his interpretation; wrong in his application. The text he has quoted means: 'Blessed are the poor in spirit, for theirs is the Kingdom of Heaven.' "

"Of course. And that embraces us all," said Olivette. "I'm sure, now, that sometimes I feel quite embarrassed by these accessories of civilization. Can we not do, I say sometimes to myself, with less? Are not these ornaments of life unnecessary and a burden? I sometimes feel, that, like dear St. Francis, I should like to go abroad and—and—see the world."

"How could you get on without your easel and brushes and palettes?" said Clotilde. Olivette was the artist of the family.

"Oh! I should hire a little Italian boy to take them for me, and we could spend days on the Umbrian Mountains, and paint, oh! such delicious bits of scenery, and eat nothing but olives and grapes, and drink only water—snow-water from the fountain-peaks of the Apennines, and—and—a little Falernian."

"And then, dear," said Clotilde, "you could go down into the convents, and copy those dear crucifixions of Angelico, and the sweet 'Ecce Homo's'; and oh! Olive, if you could bring me back one—only one copy of that divine 'Scourging,' by Corti!"

Olivette shuddered, and said coldly:—

"No! no! our Heine has stopped all that. No more painful realism, like the visions of Emmerich; but sweet-faced Agneses, and Cecilias, and perhaps, now and again, a divine Juno, or the flower-face of an Oread."

So Luke's little observation drew down this admirable discussion on Scripture, political economy, art, etc., and Luke felt not a little elated as the giver of inspiration and the originator of ideas. Dear me! to think that he, the child of an Irish farmer, should be not only a member, but even a leader, in this select coterie in the center of British civilization! And Carlyle took years to make the British public forget that he was the son of a Scotch mason! Luke was floating on the enchanted river.

He was accompanied to the door by the sisters.

"I really think I shall paint your picturesque beggar," said Olivette.

"No, no, dear, don't spoil your art-fancies," said Clotilde. "What would the 'Master' say?"

Luke felt half-jealous of that "Master."

"If you could spare time," he said, "I should like much to have a picture of that ship in the 'Ancient Mariner'—the sea smooth as glass, the sun setting, and her skeleton spars making a scaffolding against the daffodil sky!"

"You shall have it," said Olivette.

"Good-night, brother! Don't forget the *Atta Troll!*"

"Good-night, brother!"

"Brother, good-night! The *Laches* for Thursday!"

"Bah," said Luke; "there's only a sheet of tissue-paper between the races; but politicians and pamphleteers have daubed it all over with ghouls and demons on both sides. When will the valiant knight come and drive his lance through it, and let the races see each other as they are?"

It was close on midnight when Luke reached the presbytery. A light was burning in Dr. Drysdale's room. Luke went softly upstairs. The old man was at the door of his bedroom.

"I must say, Father Delmege, that you are keeping of late most unseasonable hours—"

"I was detained by some gentlemen from London," stammered Luke. "It appears that midnight is considered quite early in London."

"This is not London. This is Aylesburgh. There is a parcel and some letters in the dining-room."

Luke went downstairs. He was chilled and depressed at this

reproof. He eagerly opened the parcel. He had ordered from a bookseller on the Strand a pretty fair collection—Goethe's *Wilhelm Meister,* Comte's *Catechism of Positivism,* Mill on *Liberty,* Herbert Spencer on *Progress and Education,* etc. Instead of the bright, spruce volumes he had expected, he found four dingy, clammy duodecimos. Turning to the gas-jet, he read the almost obliterated words on the back:—

"BREVIARIUM ROMANUM: PARS AESTIVA."

"Who has offered me this insult?" he said. "I suppose Sheldon, who is so much concerned about my eternal salvation."

He tore open the first letter. It was from Father Sheldon, and ran thus:—

"MY DEAR DELMEGE:—A Miss Wilson, from Ireland, called here today to inquire for you. She said you were deeply interested in her brother, Louis, a young medical student, at St. Thomas's. She had not heard of your removal to Aylesburgh, and seemed disappointed. She has come over to act as housekeeper and guardian angel to her brother. From our brief conversation I could gather that she is eminently qualified for both offices. I don't despair of the Island of Saints yet. I think there's one left. She wished that I should enclose to you their address."

　　*　　　　　*　　　　　*　　　　　*

The second letter ran:—

"MY DEAR LUKE:—We expect you over without fail for your sister's wedding. Your protracted exile is causing some anxiety here. It is probable, as you have already heard, that Margery will enter in Limerick. You know that poor Father Tim has gone to meet his brother, Ecclesiastes, in Heaven. He left you his Breviaries and a parting word—to hold your head high!
　　　　　　　"Yours affectionately,
　　　　　　　　　"MARTIN HUGHES, P.P.
"Seaview Cottage, Knockmany."

Luke took up the Breviaries rather gingerly. The cover had

been originally of red morocco; but the years had wrought havoc with red and gold. They were black, grimy, clammy, from constant use; for then, as now, the Breviary is the poetical anthology, the manual of philosophy, the compendium of theology and patrology to the Irish priest. Luke put down the volumes with a shudder, and then washed his hands.

CHAPTER XVII

A Last Aphorism

'TWAS TRUE, indeed. Father Tim was dead. He had carried his little stock of wisdom, and merged it in the great supernal Wisdom that guides, oh! so unerringly, yet imperceptibly, the little currents of our lives. There never was a man so proud of his philosophy as Father Tim; never a man who knew so little of the world. His happy consciousness of the former faculty, his happy unconsciousness of the latter defect, or blessing, made him a most lovable man.

During this spring the influenza, then quite an unpleasant novelty, was raging in his parish; and night and day he swept the mountains from cabin to cabin on his little cob. Then when the epidemic had ceased and the flock was saved, the pastor was struck down, and fatally.

Father Martin was beside himself with grief. Father Pat was too scientific to be oversolicitous about his friend. But he did all that a scientist could do; and wonderful were the pharmaceutical remedies that he prescribed. Alas! Father Tim was a fatalist.

"When a man's time comes, where's the use in putting back the hands on the clock?" he said. There was no possible reply to this.

And so, one evening in March of this sad year, Father Martin made up his mind to discharge conscientiously his duty as a friend and brother priest, and warn his good neighbor that the sands were running fast, and it was high time to prepare for the last great journey.

"Of course, Martin," said the poor patient, feebly, "it is a long road, and there's no turning back when you start. But there are no cross-roads either, Martin, where a man could lose his way."

181

"That's true," said Father Martin. "Now we'll see about the spirituals first, and then the temporals."

The ceremony did not take long, and then he made his profession of faith.

"It isn't faith, Martil," he sobbed, "with me, but bision, thalk God."

"That's true, Tim," said Martin, deeply affected. "I'm sure the Blessed Virgin herself will come for you."

"Ha! ha!" said the dying man, "no wonder she should— no wonder she should! She'll be very ungrateful, and that's not her way, you know, if she doesn't be standing there at the foot of the bed when the light is going out."

"And you're quite sure you're not afraid to die?"

"Afraid? Afraid of what, man? No! 'Better soon than sudden,' said I; and it is something to go before God with your senses about you."

"That's true," said Martin, gravely. "Now, about your will. Where is it?"

"There in the cupboard, such as it is," said the patient.

Father Martin went over, and after some careful searching amongst old receipts and rubbish, he found the will. It was written on a sheet of notepaper, and ran thus:—

"In the name of God, Amen.

"I, Timothy Hurley, make this my last will and testament. I leave my dear friends, Father Martin Hughes and Father Pat Casey, fifty pounds each for Masses for my soul, to be said at once. *Bis dat qui cito dat.* I leave my successor fifty pounds for the poor of the parish. *Dispersit, dedit pauperibus.* I leave the Reverend Mother of the Presentation Convent, Limerick, one hundred pounds for the children of the convent schools. *Sinite parvulos ad me venire.* I leave the Superioress of the Good Shepherd, Limerick, one hundred pounds for her poor penitents. *Erravi sicut ovis quæ periit.* I leave my parish, with the Bishop's consent, to Father Pat Casey, because he's a silent man, and knows how to consume his own smoke. And my Breviary I leave to Father Luke Delmege, with the parting advice: Hold your head high, and always put a good valuation on yourself! My soul I leave to Almighty God and His Blessed Mother, for they have the best right to it.

Signed: "TIMOTHY HURLEY,
"Parish Priest of Gortnagoshel."

Father Martin read the document without a smile. Then—

"There are a good many legacies here, Tim. Now, where's all the wealth lodged?"

"Wealth? What for? I haven't a penny, except you find some lose silver on the mantelpiece."

"But you have bequeathed in this will nearly, let me see, over £350. Why did you make such a will if you have nothing, as I suspected?"

"But didn't the Bishop order us, under pain of suspension, to make our wills in three months from the retreat?" said Father Tim, struggling with the fading breath.

"Of course. But that supposed you had something to leave. You have been very generous with nothing, Tim."

"Well, I thought sure that a full measure is better than an empty sack. And sure, if there's nothing there, they can get nothing."

"Pat and I will take care of the Masses, whatever," said Father Martin.

"God bless you, Martin. I knew you would."

"I'm afraid, Tim, the Bishop will hardly admit that you have the right of presentation to your parish."

"Well, to tell you the truth, Martin, I never thought he would. But he's fond of a joke; and I said to myself: 'Well, now, Tim, when his Lordship hears this, he'll clap his hands and say, that's a good joke, and I won't balk him.' "

"Ah! but that preaching," said Martin.

"Look here, now, Martin, there's too much preaching altogether. If there's anything I'm sorry for, it is that I talked too much. Sure, 'tisn't the water that runs down the river that turns the mill, but the water that's caught in the mill-race."

"That's true, Tim," said Martin; "but bishops want men to preach; and if you remember your Selva, you know that it is laid down as the first duty of a parish priest."

"And you think the Bishop won't heed the joke?" said Father Tim, faintly.

"I fear not," said Father Martin. "He has been very hard on poor Pat for that same thing."

There was a long pause, during which the breath of the dying priest came only in gasps and sobs. Then for a moment it became easier.

"Martin."

"Yes, Tim."

"Martil, I'b goib to leave you somethib," said the poor priest, with a sob.

"I wouldn't doubt you, Tim," said Father Martin.

"Martil, we were always goob friends."

"Always, Tim."

"Martil."

"Yes, Tim."

"I'b goib to leab you Tiny."

Here Martin became quite as affected as his friend.

"I won't take her, but on one condition," he said.

"What is it, Martil?"

"That you throw Tony into the bargain."

"Gob bless you, Martil! I knew I coulb depenb ob you."

Here it may be remarked that Tiny and Tony had been baptized in a Christian manner and with Christian names. They were the children of a young medical doctor who had come down to Gortnagoshel, and after a desperate fight had secured a dispensary worth £100 a year. When he had secured this prize, almost at the cost of his life, he won himself another prize, this time a real one, in the shape of a young wife, brought up in a Dublin hot-house of luxury and ease, and suddenly transferred to this Libya by the seashore. But they were happy together, and very much happier when Christina was baptized on Christmas Day; and a year later when Antony was placed under the direct patronage of his mother's favorite saint. For she had a great devotion to St. Antony, and always sealed her dainty letters with the mysterious *S. A. G.* Then one day the cloud came down. The young doctor took typhus fever in a mountain cabin and died. And the young mother could not be kept back from him even by the exceeding love she bore her children; but she, too, sickened and died. And on that lonely evening, when her soul was straining between God and her bairns, it was Father Tim that let loose that sweet spirit for God by taking on himself the duty of father and protector of the motherless ones.

"Sure 'tis as easy to fill two mouths as one," he said; and they came home with him and grew into his soft and affectionate heart.

"I'll tell you what it is, Martin," said the faint voice; "you're doing too much; but God will bless you."

"I tell you what it is, Tim," said Martin. "I'll take the children home now, and come to see you again."

"Gob bless you, Martil," said the grateful heart in its sobbing.

Easier said than done, though, to borrow an aphorism. Tiny and Tony were done up by the housekeeper and brought in in solemn state. Tiny was gorgeous in pink and white. Tony was almost supercilious. He had assumed the *toga virilis,* and, by natural instinct, had his hands plunged deep in his pockets. He looked curiously from Martin to his guardian, and almost shouted with joy when he was told to say good-bye, for he was henceforth to live and lodge at Seaview Cottage. Not so Tiny. When she was placed high up on the pillow to kiss good-bye to her guardian, she sobbed and wept and pleaded.

"Come now, Tiny," said Father Martin, "and we'll go home together."

"Noa, noa, noa, noa, noa," sobbed Tiny, with her arms around her guardian's neck. Who said *"La donna e mobile"?*

"Martil," said Father Tim, sobbing with the child.

"Yes, Tim," said Martin.

"I dilk I'll keeb Tiny until—until 'tis all ober," said Father Tim.

"All right, old man," said Martin. "I'll be back in a few minutes. Come, Tony, old boy!"

A few minutes drew on to a few hours, and when Father Martin returned it was clear that the end was at hand.

"Martin," said the dying man, feebly.

"Yes, Tim."

"Do you think will that *omadhaun,* Daly, be at my Requiem?"

"Very probably, Tim. Every man in the diocese will be there."

"Could you keep him out of the choir?" said Father Tim. "He's an awful roarer."

"I'm afraid not. He generally leads, you know."

"If I hear him yelling, Martin, and if I see him twisting his head around to see are the people admiring him, 'twill make me turn in my coffin."

"Never mind him, Tim. He won't trouble you, I'll promise you."

"Martin."

"Yes, Tim."

"Would you read one of the Psalms for me?"

"Which, Tim?"

"The *Benedic*—, Martin. 'Twas you introduced me to it."

Father Martin took up the time-stained Breviary, and read that glorious Psalm. He was murmuring along verse after verse, until he came to "Quomodo miseretur pater filiorum, misertus est Dominus timentibus se; quoniam ipse cognovit figmentum nostrum. Recordatus est quoniam pulvis sumus; homo, sicut foenum, dies ejus; tanquam flos agri, sic efflorebit."

"Martin."

"Yes, Tim."

"My mind was wandering when I spoke about Daly. Give me another absolution."

Martin imparted the Sacrament again. Then, after a pause, Father Tim said:—

"Martin."

"Yes, Tim."

"Are you there?"

"Yes, Tim."

"My sight—is—leaving me. But—didn't—I—tell—you, Martin?"

"What?"

"That the—Blessed Virgin—would—come for—me?"

"You did, Tim."

"There—she—is, Martin!"

"Where?" said Father Martin, staring wildly.

"Look—there—over her—picture. Yes," he said, speaking to the invisible, "I'm ready. Never—refuse—a—good—off—"

And Martin was alone in the room.

There was a vast gathering at the obsequies. Father Daly did chant the Antiphons, and the most magnificent music of the Catholic burial service; and I am afraid he did twist his head around sometimes to see the effect on his audience, but the silent slumberer made no sign. These things were of no concern to him now or forevermore.

When the white ring of the assembled priests was broken
up around the grave after the wailing of the *Benedictus,* and
of all assembled only the dead priest and Father Martin remained, the people closed around the coffin. And then

> "In all arose a great wailing."

The men stood silently weeping; the women were demonstrative in their outburst of sorrow. Some knelt and beat the coffin
with their open palms; some lifted hands to heaven; all cried:
"God be with him that is gone!" And you could hear strange
stories narrated of his goodness and self-sacrifice; and his wisdom had passed into a proverb amongst a proverb-loving
people.

"Many's the time he said to me: 'God is good; and He said
He would.' "

"Ay, indeed, 'A stout heart for a long road,' he used to say.
And sure we wanted the pleasant word to keep our sperits up."

" 'Darby,' he used to say, 'Darby, never let a fox get on your
shoulder to pluck the grapes. If you do, Darby, believe me
very few will drop into *your* mouth.' "

"Wisha, what'll become of thim little orphans, I wonder?
Sure, they have no one now but the grate God!"

"Whisht, 'uman, they're down at Father Martin's."

"God bless him! Sure he has the kind heart. But poor Father
Tim! poor Father Tim! The heavens be his bed tonight!"

There is no harm in feeling a sense of justifiable pride when
one makes a great discovery. Hence, we congratulate ourselves on the unique distinction of having found that the dis-
tinctive term of popular canonization in Ireland is that word
"poor." The man who is spoken of as poor is an admired and
loved man. "Poor Father Tim!" "Poor St. Joseph!" "The poor
Pope!" Is it not significant that an impoverished race, to whom
poverty, often accentuated into famine, has been the portion
of their inheritance and their cup for nigh on seven hundred
years, should take that word as the expression of their affection? Happy is the priest to whom it is applied; he has a deep
root in the people's hearts.

It was never applied to the great Canon. He was so lofty, and

great, and dignified, that every one felt it would be a mis-
nomer. But we retain a lingering affection for him, for he was
a most worthy man; and this time we shall oppose the popular
verdict, or rather supply the popular omission.

The poor Canon was convalescent. He, too, had been attacked by that most irreverent and undiscriminating invader,
the influenza. But he had a curate, and Father Tim hadn't.
That made all the difference in the world. Father Tim went
to heaven; the Canon remained in the valley of tears. And he
was weak, and languid, and depressed. He had heard of his
neighbor's demise.

"A good poor fellow," he said, "but somewhat unformed.
Quaint and almost—ha—mediæval, he could hardly be styled
—ha—a man of the world. But he was a simple, unadorned
priest."

This was said to Barbara, who had come down from Dublin
to nurse her uncle.

"I understood," said Barbara, in reply, her kind heart
always anxious to say the kind word, "that he was guardian
to Anna Bedford's little children. Oh! it was so sad!"

"Imprudent, my dear child!" said the Canon. "Or, rather
a series of—ha—imprudences. Think of that young lady,
leaving the—ha—luxuries of her Dublin home to live in such
a remote and—ha—uncivilized place. And this on one hundred pounds a year! And then the imprudence of that—ha—
excellent clergyman in taking the grave and serious obligation
of their—ha—maintenance and education. We shall never
learn ordinary—ha—prudence in Ireland."

"You have had a letter from Louis, uncle?" said Barbara,
anxious to change the subject.

"Yes!" said the uncle, whose many imprudences there now
flashed on his mind. He thought Barbara was personal in her
remarks.

"I want you, Barbara, for the—ha—future to remain here.
I shall give you up the keys of this—ha—establishment—"

"I'm afraid, uncle, much as I should like to be your companion, and the quiet country life would have many attractions for me, I am called elsewhere."

"Mother can manage without you now, my dear child,"
he said. "And suppose you were to form a respectable—ha—

alliance by marriage, she would have to dispense with your services."

"It is not mother that needs me, uncle," she said, weeping softly, "but poor Louis."

"Then you have heard something to cause grave apprehension?" said the Canon. "I thought that Louis was promising to have a most respectable—" He did not finish the diplomatic phrase. It hurt his conscience.

"I don't know," said Barbara; "but I have presentiments, and I am anxious."

"You don't think he has any tendency now towards—ha—well, evil companionship?"

"I don't know," she murmured. "London is a dangerous place."

"You would not suspect that he had any leaning towards—ha—I can hardly express myself," said the Canon, blandly, "towards—well—intoxicating drinks?"

"I hardly dare think on the subject," she said.

"And, of course," said the Canon, with that consummate diplomacy in which he considered himself past master, "it never entered into your mind that—that—ha—he might have —it is only a—supposititious case, you know,—ha—contemplated self-destruction?"

"Oh! uncle! uncle!" cried Barbara, in a paroxysm of grief, "why did you not tell me sooner? Oh! Louis, Louis! I shall never forgive myself."

The Canon was greatly troubled. He hated scenes. They disturbed his equanimity, and left his nerves tingling for hours after. And he felt now how unreasonable it was of Barbara not to have accepted his diplomatic suggestions in a diplomatic manner. Women are so unreasonable; their intuitions and instincts rush so far ahead of reason.

"Now, Barbara, this is unreasonable, and not at all—ha— what I expected from you. A young lady brought up as you have been should have acquired—ha—more composure of manner."

"But, uncle dear, if what you have hinted at were only remotely possible it would be dreadful beyond endurance. Poor Louis! we have not treated him well!"

"Now, now, Barbara, please let us not continue the painful

subject. I am not well. I am depressed, and—ha—these harrowing subjects are really—well—embarrassing."

"I'm sure I'm so sorry, uncle; but when could I go?"

"Well, dear," the Canon said, his natural benevolence conquering, "I think you are right. Indeed, I must say now that I suggested to your—ha—excellent mother months ago that Louis—ha—needed a protecting hand—"

"Mother never told me—Oh! dear!—Oh! dear!" sobbed Barbara, in her agony.

"Well! never mind, child; there is no harm done. You can make your preparations at once; and leave for London as soon as—ha—you are able."

"Oh! thanks, dear uncle," said Barbara; "I shall leave tonight, with your permission. And you mustn't think me cruel or ungrateful, dear uncle, to leave you until you are quite beyond convalescence. But, you know—"

"Quite enough, Barbara," he said. "I understand you, my child. I shall give you money for your journey; and there is a most estimable young—friend—or—rather parishioner of mine in London—a young priest—I think, by the way, you met him here at one time."

"You mean Father Delmege, uncle," she exclaimed. "Oh, yes! he has been very kind to Louis—that is, I mean, I think he has been—"

"Well, I shall give you a letter to that estimable young clergyman, and ask him to help you in the—ha—exceedingly arduous task you have undertaken."

There was silence for a few minutes.

"And, Barbara!" exclaimed the Canon.

"Yes, uncle dear."

"If you thought well of it, perhaps you might deem it—ha—prudent to bring Louis back to Ireland—"

"Father and Louis do not seem to understand each other," she said sadly.

The Canon paused, debating the prudence of what he was going to say. For the Canon in his youth had been a most unselfish, imprudent creature, given to all kinds of generous, mad impulses (witness that girl in typhus whom he had placed in the ambulance waggon, as he would now call it), and therefore it behoved him to be on his guard.

"I meant," he said, "that perhaps,—it is only a suggestion,
—that perhaps Louis and you might take up your residence
here until such a period as would insure his thorough reform—
I mean convalescence."

"Oh! uncle, you are too good; you are too good! I *will* bring
Louis back; and oh! we shall be so happy."

And Barbara, rash, daring little girl, actually took the soft
hand of her unresisting uncle and kissed it. He did not with-
draw his hand, nor was he offended.

And so a few days afterwards Louis Wilson stared with wide,
colorless eyes, in which the pupils were but a pin-point, and
out of a very glassy face at an apparition that framed itself in
the doorway of his room. And some one, he dreamt, took up
his shaking hand, from which the finger-nails were mouldering,
and kissed him. And the good old housekeeper announced to
the other lodgers a few days later that "a hangel had come
hall the way from Hireland to the puir young gentleman;" and
that her honest conscience was at rest. And Barbara was very
happy, for things were not altogether so bad as she had
dreaded; and she knew that she had one great friend in London—the Rev. Luke Delmege.

And the Canon had a letter from his Bishop to the effect
that his Lordship was promoting his curate, the Rev. Patrick
Casey, to a parish in a far part of the diocese; and that he was
sending him another curate. Who will say that a Bishop cannot enjoy a joke? Well, half-way! For Father Pat did *not*
succeed to Gortnagoshel, as his good friend wished; yet he
got his incumbency at last, and he owes his benefice to that
stray joke that found its way into the most absurd and informal
will that even a Lord Chancellor could devise.

CHAPTER XVIII

Disenchantment

LUKE DELMEGE crossed over from Holyhead by the night boat. He had called for a moment at his old presbytery and seen the dear old Vicar and Father Sheldon.

"More civilized," thought the Vicar, "but not quite so attractive."

"Of course you'll run over to see the Wilsons," said Father Sheldon. "They are now—"

"I should like to do so very much indeed," said Luke, "but really I have no time. The mail goes about five or six o'clock, I think, and I have a few purchases to make."

"Miss Wilson will be disappointed," said Father Sheldon.

Luke shrugged his shoulders.

Next morning, sleepy and discontented, he wandered around Dublin waiting for the down mail. If he had had time, he would have run down to see his own *Alma Mater;* but there was no time. He thought Dublin—the Dublin that had appeared to him in his student days, now so long, so very long ago, a fairy city of splendor—dingy and mean. He shrank into himself as he saw coatless, grimy men actually treading the pavements of Grafton Street. The pyramid of humanity, that poverty piles around the O'Connell Statue and Nelson's Pillar, seemed a revolting picture. He passed into Shephen's Green. He rather liked the ponds, and cascades, and the flowers; but the people seemed so shabbily dressed. And then he nearly stumbled over a few corpses—no! they were only tramps sleeping on the grass of the Green. "How horrible!" said Luke.

And this is the University College Chapel! It sounds well. The very words have glamour and a meaning all their own. He went in to say his Office and make a short visit. He was enraptured. The architecture, the marble of walls and pillars, the dusk in which the altar was hid, the pulpit where Newman had preached, all appealed to his newly formed fancies. He went into the dim twilight of the side chapel, and remembered having read that there on that altar, with that same small circular window letting in sunlight, and moonlight, and darkness, the great Oratorian used to say Mass. He called up the scene, and behind that scene, and above and around it, he saw what might have been; and the ghosts rose up under the spell of imagination, the specters of magnificent possibilities that never had passed beyond ideas. He thought he heard the bell ringing for Vespers—a sweet, soft, mournful bell, that tolled out of the mists and shadows of dreamland. There was a murmur of voices suddenly hushed, and the shuffling of feet, and one by one a vast concourse of men filed into the church. They were dressed in academic fashion, their long gowns or togas falling loosely around the ordinary dress, and they carried the well-known square caps in their hands. A few had blue hoods, falling down gracefully over their shoulders; and one or two, quite distinguished from their fellows, wore red. But there was a gravity, a composure, a sense of personal dignity and reverence about all, that made Luke think he had seen nothing like it since the day of his ordination at Maynooth. When all were seated, a priest, clad in cope and accompanied by many acolytes, came to the altar and intoned the *Deus in adjutorium meum intende*. The choir took up the chant; the organ pealed out, and then there was a glorious burst of masculine voices, that echoed from side to side, as strophe and antistrophe in a great Christian chorus, and seemed to beat around the walls and to be caught up to the ceiling; and the pause at the antiphons became painful, until they swelled out again into the rhythmic thunder of a thousand voices. But all the sweet, beautiful memories of his college came back to Luke when the *Magnificat* was intoned, and the great prophetic voice of the young Queen Mother swelled out into the deep thrilling accents of her followers and clients. Then again a painful pause; and Luke heard a voice, at first plaintive and feeble, and then firm and resonant, and piercing like shafts of light into every corner of the chapel and every recess of the human hearts that were throbbing under the magic of mighty words, and the strange overwhelming influence of a great and exalted character. And there was no eloquence such as Luke then understood it; no beautiful, rounded periods, emphasized by action; but simple, plain truths, and put in such a way as to admit of no contradiction or question, for they carried conviction even to the critical or sceptical, if such had found their way into such a sympathetic circle. And it was all about life and its issues; its worthlessness *in se;* its tremendous importance relatively, and the sacred responsibilities that are intrusted to a race, feeble and impotent and transient, but endowed with infinite possibilities; and powers for evil and good, that cannot be measured in time, for time has only the transparent tissue of a cloud, but must be thrown upon the background of eternities for the revelation of their nature and importance. But Luke drew all his faculties, now expanded into admiration and enthusiasm, together when the preacher went on to say that every one understood how utterly insignificant was this world and man's life, unless a light was thrown on both from eternity. No man would care to work or suffer for a paltry and perishable race. All the vast cycles of human history are merely a point in time, just as our earth and the visible universe are but grains of sand in infinity. All the dreams of mortals, therefore, all the aspirations of great idealists, all the music of poetry, all the high and lofty conjectures after human perfection, are tales without meaning or moral, until you suppose man's immortality. Religion, therefore, is an absolute necessity if life is to have a meaning; and hence, in every scheme of liberal study, metaphysics must enter and become a constituent, nay, the principal constituent, if it were only to show the mere materialist that, even outside and beyond religion, there are mysteries upon mysteries ever waiting to be solved. And then the preacher passed on to Ireland, its history, its martyrdom, its mission; and told these young souls that the last chapter was not yet written, would not be written for centuries to come; for that a race with a priceless history and a present unencumbered with material problems, must have of necessity a rich and glorious future. What that future was to be Luke could not hear, for already his mind was busy with many problems evoked by the preacher's words, and for the hundredth time Luke was face to face with enigmas. Then the vision vanished, and Luke was alone. He shook the dream from him to see two young girls staring at him curiously. He took up his hat and passed down the aisle. Under the gallery he paused to look around and wonder where his beautiful dream had vanished. He saw only the sacristan testing the brass locks on the money boxes and looking suspiciously toward him.

At the very best, indeed, and under the most favorable circumstances of climate, the railway trip on the Great Southern line is decidedly uninteresting. Ireland's beauty spots lie around her high coast-line, like jewels around the lips of an enchased goblet. But the gray shadow of an April sky also hung down around brown bog and scraggy field, and, though the promise of May was in the air, bud and flower wrapped themselves cosily in their cradles and would not venture into the light. They "did not like this weeping nurse; they wanted their laughing mother."

And so Luke thought he had never seen anything so melancholy and sad. There was a look of age and decay about everything. Here and there they swept by the skeleton of some old ruined abbey and castle, that was just kept from falling by the tender support of the kind ivy. That was history. And here and there, more frequently, he saw standing the bare brown mud walls of an unroofed cabin, the holes, that once were windows and doors, staring like the sockets of a skull. There was the mark of the fire on the chimney-wall. Where were they now, who had wept and laughed, and sung and mourned, as they sat around that sacred hearth? Perhaps it is an etching on the memory of some great capitalist in Omaha or Chicago; perhaps for him that ragged hawthorn before the door is the life-tree Igdrasil, waving its mighty branches and intoning in the night wind, though its roots are deep down among the dead.

It was evening, cold and raw, when Luke stepped from the railway carriage, and saw the quaint old sidecar and the rough, shaggy horse, that were to carry him some miles to his home. He did not see the old servant at first, until a voice as from far-off spaces, said close by:—

"Yerra, thin, Masther Luke, and sure it is I'm proud to see you."

"Ho, Larry," said Luke, with an effort, and with an effort

shaking the rough hand of the old man, "and how is Nancy? But you're looking very old, Larry."

"The years are tellin', Masther Luke," said the old man, who was somewhat chilled by the appearance and grand manner of him whom he had known from his childhood; " 'tisn't young we're gettin', Masther Luke!"

"And the side-car looks so old and shabby," said Luke; "why don't they get it upholstered?"

"Well, thin," said Larry, somewhat offended, as it seemed to imply a censure on himself, " 'twas only last summer we got it done up; but the winther and the rain took a lot out of it, your reverence."

"And the poor old mare! Why, when was she clipped, Larry? She doesn't reflect much credit on your grooming."

"She was at the plough all the spring, your reverence," said Larry, "and the weather was too cowld to clip her."

He thought his old "Masther Luke" was changed a good deal. He dropped the familiar title.

As they drove along, the aspect of the landscape seemed intolerably melancholy and dull. The gray fields, that had not yet sprung into green, the thatched cottages, the ruined walls, the broken hedges, the ragged bushes, all seemed to Luke, fresh from the prim civilization of Aylesburgh, unspeakably old and wretched. Ruin and dilapidation were everywhere.

"It's a land of tombs and desolation," he thought. As he drove up the long, hawthorn-shaded avenue that led to his father's house, the gloom deepened. During his college course, when "home for the holidays," how his heart used to beat, until he shouted with glee, as he passed up along the quick and thorn hedges! How he used to jump on the car to gather a leafy branch to be waved in his triumphal march towards home; and how his cheery hallo! would bring out all the collies and retrievers with their glad oratorios of yelping and barking; and there in the background was the aged, stooped figure of his good father, and the sweet face of his mother under the crown of her beautiful snowy cap, and Lizzie and Margery— well, but 'tis just the same scene now! Alas, no! the disenchantment has come! The dogs are barking, indeed, and there are the dear old figures, and there is Lizzie alone, for Margery is pacing the garden walks far away amongst the Good Shepherds of Limerick. But it is not the same. Oh, no! nor ever shall be again. He hath eaten of the tree of knowledge, and the Eden of his childhood has vanished. They all noticed the great change. Lizzie almost cried. The father said nothing. A reticent, silent race, these old Irish fathers were. The mother, ever faithful, could only feel pride in her glorious boy.

"He was so grand and grave. Ah! wisha! what a pity poor Father Pat wasn't here! What a proud man he'd be this day!" she thought.

But the rest felt that a stranger had come to visit them, and there was restraint and a little affected formalism.

"Has the priest come?" said Peggy, when Larry was putting up the mare.

"He has," said Larry, crossly.

"How is he lookin'?" said Peggy.

"Oh! grand intirely," said Larry. "But we must borry the Canon's coach for him. Begor, he'll be wantin' me to put on brass buttons and a high cockade."

Peggy looked at him suspiciously.

"Keep yer jokes for some one else," she said.

"And so, Lizzie," said Luke at the tea-table (dear me! how plain this white-and-gold china looked after the tea equipages at the salon), "you are going to be married?"

"Yes," said Lizzie, blushing, and with a little toss of her head.

"Well, I'm sure I hope you have made a good selection," said Luke.

"Well, thin, indeed he is," said the mother; "as dacent a boy as there is from here to Cork, and that's a big word. He hasn't all the money we expected; but, sure, he's a kind, graceful boy, and he comes of a dacent family."

"And Margery has run away from you?" said Luke. "I didn't think her thoughts took that direction."

"Thim gay youngsters," said the mother, "are the first to inter the convents. They pretind nothing but coortin' and larkin'; and thin, all of a suddint, off they go and laugh at us all. But you're not atin', Father Luke."

"Oh! yes, thank you, I'm doing very well," said Luke. "And Father Casey has gone?"

"He has; and God be wid him, and may his journey thry

with him! Sure, manny's the wan will miss him; and the place is lonesome widout him."

"And the Canon, how is he?" said Luke.

"Grand intirely; but this sickness—the hinfluenzy they call it—took a shake out of him. He hasn't the ould spring in his walk, and he's stooped a little. But God will spare him to his people manny a day yet!"

"And who has succeeded Father Pat?" asked Luke.

"Oh! thin, a man that will make us mind our P's and Q's, I tell you. Glory be to God! he'd rise the roof off your head if you hard him on Sunday morning—"

"He's a black, determined man," said Mike Delmege. "He appears to mane what he says."

"I'm doubtful if he and the Canon will pull together," said Mrs. Delmege. But this was heresy to Mike Delmege, who could not perceive anything of his priests less than absolute perfection.

"Lave 'em alone! lave 'em alone!" he said. "They understan' theirselves better than we do."

"Well, sure, I'm only sayin' what everybody says," apologized Mrs. Delmege. "But, Father Luke, what about yerself? Sure, we saw your name on the paper; and didn't me heart swell when Father Pat brought it up and pointed to it. 'There,' he said,—God be wid him, my poor, dear man!—'there's your son for you! He'll never come back to this misfortunate counthry again! They'll make him a bishop over there!' Poor Father Pat! Poor Father Pat!"

"Well," Luke said, "we're getting on pretty well. A good deal of work; and work must be done over there, I tell you! It isn't like the old country!" It was Luke's first criticism, but by no means his last, on his native land.

"But, father," he said, "why don't you touch up the old place? I'm sure it looks very shabby and—old."

"We were thinkin' of that same, indeed," said his father; "but we were puttin' it off from day to day; and, indeed, we could do it aisily," he continued, "for we have made by the butther this year alone the rint and over it. Since the Canon, God bless him, showed us what to do, and how to make a pinny of money with the eggs, and the butther, and the chickens, we were never better off, thank God! and every family in the parish can say the same."

"The new curate doesn't like it," said Mrs. Delmege. "He says 'twill all come toppling down some day like a house of cards. He believes in the Lague!"

"The League?" said Luke, half angrily. "It seems to me that you'll never be done fighting in this unhappy country. It's always agitation, agitation! Now, it seems to me that the Canon is not only superior in station and ability to any of your priests, but he alone appears to have struck the one thing that was necessary to make the country a happy Arcadia."

"Ah, yes! He's the good man, God spare him long to rule over his parish!"

"And when is Lizzie to be married?" said Luke. He was already impatient of home, and anxious to be back in Aylesburgh.

"On Thursday, wid God's blessin'!" said the mother.

"And I hope now," said Luke, "that there shall be no scenes of rioting and revelling, but that everything shall be conducted in a Christian civilized manner."

"Oh! of course," said the mother. "We'll only have a few of the neighbors; and, I suppose, the little boy will be bringin' a handful of friends wid him. We'll have a bit of dinner in the barn; and, perhaps, the boys and girls would want a little dance—that's all."

It was the portrait in miniature of what was really before the good mother's mind; but she was afraid that the dignity and grandeur of her distinguished son would be ruffled at the reality.

Next day Luke called on the Canon. It was evening, and it was deepening into twilight, as he walked up the well-known gravelled path, and knocked, no longer timidly, but with an air of assurance, almost of contempt. He was shown into the drawing-room, as of old. There everything was the same as he had ever known it; but there was a vast change somewhere. Where? In himself. He looked now with critical disdain on the *Cenci* portrait, and he thought the Madonna commonplace. And that glass case of artificial birds! Olivette Lefevril would have given it away to a tramp. And here, not quite three years ago, he had sat, a timid, nervous, frightened young priest, and there had leaned against the mantelpiece that wretched young *roué,* who actually had the effrontery to argue with him. Yes, indeed, there *was* a change. The gentle, timid young Levite had departed; and here, in his stead, has come the self-reliant, collected, independent man of experience and—of the world. The birds shook their wings, as of old, and chirped. The gong tolled musically, and here is the Canon.

"How do you do, Mr. Delmege?" as of old.

"Well, thank you," said Luke, with a pronounced accent. The Canon collapsed. Luke was merciful.

"I hope I see you well, sir," said Luke. "I was rather sorry to hear from my father that you were still suffering from the effects of this most unhappy epidemic."

"Yes, indeed!" said the Canon. "I cannot say that I have—ha—yet quite recovered from the effects of the disease." The Canon was watching Luke narrowly. He hoped to see some faltering, some weakness. No! Cool, calm, self-possessed, Luke sat bolt upright in his chair, and held his hat and gloves without nervous awkwardness. Those three years in England had made a change.

"And you have lost your curate?" said Luke.

"Yes!" said the Canon, blandly; "at last! at last! the Bishop took compassion on his gray hairs, and—ha—as the vulgar saying is, he threw a parish at him."

"And Father Tim gone also?"

"Yes, poor fellow! Kind and good, but inexperienced. Really," said the Canon, looking at his visitor keenly, "our clergymen seem to want a good deal of that—ha— mannerism and —ha—polish, and—ha—knowledge of life which—ha—intercourse with other nations seems to create or develop."

"I'm hardly prepared," said Luke, who swallowed the compliment as a morsel of sweet savor, "to offer an opinion; but I certainly do think that there are a good many customs and habits at home that probably would be permitted to fall into desuetude if we had larger experience. I have already said to my good people at home, and you will permit me to say to you, sir, that nowhere have I seen such rational efforts to promote the welfare of the people as in your parish, and at your suggestion, and under your supervision."

"I thank you, sir," said the Canon; "and yet there are some who not only do not share that opinion, but who actually strive to—ha—embarrass me in my efforts at—ha—ameliorating the conditions of my people. But let us dismiss the subject. You are—ha—thrown a good deal in contact with the better classes—the aristocracy in England?"

"The better classes? yes! The aristocracy of talent? yes! The aristocracy of birth? no! My mission is in a cathedral town, and there is a good deal of select society, both amongst Anglicans and Catholics."

"And I should—say, a total absence of distinction, not to say bigotry?"

"Such a distinction is utterly unknown," said Luke. "There is even more deference paid to a Catholic priest than to an Anglican. In fact, I have said more than once that between the races, Irish and English, and between the different forms of religion, there is but a sheet of semi-transparent paper; but demagogues have daubed it all over with hideous caricatures on one side and the other."

"I most cordially agree with you, my—ha—dear young friend," said the Canon, quite delighted. "I'm very pleased, indeed, to see that your—ha—experience of our brethren coincides absolutely with the—ha—convictions I had formed, purely, indeed, I may say, by calm reasoning on a vexed question.

"By the way," said the Canon, after a pause, "have you met my nephew, Louis, in London?"

For the first time Luke showed signs of embarrassment. He shifted uneasily on the chair, and stammered.

"I have met him," he said, "but under circumstances rather unfavorable to—to—a—to our further intimacy. But you know I no longer live in London. I have been transferred for some months to Aylesburgh."

"Oh! indeed!" said the Canon. "My niece has gone over to act as—ha—superintendent of Louis' little ménage; I am sure that, if I am to judge from his letters, he is mixing in excellent society, and is quite—well, respectable."

"I did pay him a formal visit," said Luke, "but unfortunately, he was absent, probably at the hospital."

"Very probably," said the Canon. "Indeed, I might say

certainly. He is rather too devoted to his profession."

There was a pause. Luke found it hard to continue the conversation and maintain his respect for truth.

"You have come over for your—ha—sister's marriage?" said the Canon at length.

"Yes," said Luke. "She wishes that I should marry them."

"By all means! my dear young friend," said the Canon. "By all means. I understand that this—young—*fiancé* is an extremely respectable young fellow."

"I have heard so," said Luke, rising. "I should like that my father and mother should be made comfortable in their old age."

"Of course, you will dine with me on Sunday," said the Canon. "Shall we say five o'clock?"

"Many thanks, sir," said Luke, thinking, as he passed down the gravelled walk: There are changes here too; the Canon has grown to be very, very old—everything is old! And he no longer dines at seven, but at five! What a change backwards! Retrogression everywhere! I would have preferred a seven o'clock dinner! I hope Father Pat and Father Tim won't ask me. What am I thinking of? They are gone!

Was Luke sorry for his dear old friends? He ought to have been, and he knew it. But then, what can a man do who has been obliged to adopt new ideas of life? You must adapt yourself to your environments—that is a cardinal principle. You must go with the tide—that's another. Yet he was not quite sure. He looked out over the mysterious sea. It was cold, chill, irresponsive. There was no voice. Or was it that the inner sense of the man was stifled, and that Nature, failing the human sympathy, refused to send back its echo?

CHAPTER XIX

The Stranger and His Gods

LUKE DELMEGE was disgusted, utterly and painfully disgusted. He was able, by an effort, to reconcile himself to the solemnities of the marriage service, especially as the great Canon was only in a subordinate place; but the after-events chafed his nerves and did violence to his conceptions of the proprieties. For at an Irish wedding all the barriers of caste, wealth, and position are taken down and there is a delightful open-heartedness, which sometimes, it must be confessed, has a tendency to become riotous and orgic. Hence the loud, clamorous benedictions of the blind, the halt, and the lame, gathered in from all the neighboring parishes, hurt the nerves of Luke Delmege, and offended his sense of sight and hearing, and did violence to his theological principles. It was hardly a month since he had declared amongst the esoterics his passionate desire to see a real, live, Scriptural beggar—a very Lazarus of sores and rags; and lo! here they are, qualified every one to sit by the pool of Bethesda, or wash in the pool of Siloe. And now he heard, for the first time, of the "seventeen" angels who hould up the pillars of heaven," and the "special blessing of Michael, the Archangel," and the "sowls in Purgatory who would be relieved that day," and many other strange and mystic sayings, too sacred even to be written. And yet Luke was not enthusiastic. Then there was the glorious musical duet, that Crashaw might have immortalized, between the famous blind fiddler from Aughadown and the equally famous piper from Monavourleigh. Nothing in the Homeric ballads could equal it.

"Now, your sowl, Thade, give it to him."

"Gi' me that rosin, Kate." And Kate would hand the rosin to her blind husband, a splendid, stalwart Tipperary man, but "wisdom at one entrance quite shut out." And then, as the fine fury rose, and the spirit of the music of rivalry possessed him, the sightless orbs would roll in their sockets, as if demanding light! light! and his face would whiten and his feet tremble under the divine intoxication. And such music! Weird, and tragic, and melancholy, till the merry audience were hushed into solemnity and tears; and the divine chords would wail out into an attenuated echo, and the musician would lean down and hearken, as if he were not quite sure whether he held the strings or was only dreaming that the soul of his violin was throbbing itself away into sleep and silence. For this big Tipperary man was a horrible bigamist! He had two wives: the one at his side, who ministered to his temporal wants, and the other, the sweet spirit who woke to music from his instrument. And there was jealousy; but what could the poor woman do, when it was that detestable rival that earned the daily bread? So now she affected pride, pride in her husband's power, as she gazed on the entranced audience. But hark! here are all the fairies in Munster, with Cleena at their head! Such a mad revel of musical sounds, crowding on one another, and jostling one another aside, and running along in mad, tumultuous riot, until the spirit seized the multitude, and every pair of feet was going pit-a-pat to the contagious and imperious merriment.

"Begor, Den, you'll never bate that. That's the grandest chune wos ever hard. Hould up, man! Here, have a sup to rouse you!"

No! Den, the piper, could not disturb the fine harmonies of his brain with that dangerous liquor. The occasion was too critical. His honor depended on his interpretation of his thoughts on the magic keys. Bate? No, no! Wait till ye see!

"Will ye have the 'Modhereen-na-Sidhe,' or the 'Fox-Hunt,' byes?" he said, with an affectation of forced calmness.

"The 'Fox-Hunt,' the 'Fox-Hunt,' " shouted all. Well they knew it was his masterpiece, the ultimate of perfection on reeds and stops. Then, if you shut your eyes, you heard the soft patter of the horses' hoofs at the meet, and the move toward the covert, and the occasional crack of a whip, and the faint bugle-call. Then the awful silence as the hounds are put

in, and then the deep, solemn bay and the mighty chorus of a
hundred dogs as the quarry was found, and the harkaway!
shouted by the huntsman. And you needed no interpreter.
Every man in the audience made himself one.

"Good, Den, yer sowl to glory! Give it to 'em, man!"

"They've found him! they've found him!"

"There they are aff! Tally-ho!"

"Whisht, ye divil, there they are, acrass the ploughed field!"

"Gor, wouldn't you think you saw 'em!"

"There! he's run down at last. Listen! listen! how the dogs
yelp!"

And the bellows and the chanter went puffing along, as the
music interpreted the minds and moods of men, until, at last,
it died away into a soft moan or echo of pain.

"He's dead, begor! Listen to him crying! Who's got the
brush?"

Dear me! and people talk about "Parsifal" and "Lohengrin,"
I believe, in some far-away places yet. Some day they'll find
that the germ and soul of all art and music is still haunting the
enchanted shores of Ireland.

But Luke was disgusted; and still more so when the sounds
of merriment arose, and jokes and laughter passed around the
mighty table in the barn, and all the rude chivalry of one sex,
and all the primitive coquetry of the other, accompanied the
loud laugh and the scraps of song that rippled around the
mighty gathering.

"Mother, how long is this going to last?" whispered Luke.
Mother was wiping her eyes with delight and pride. That
wedding at Lisnalee would be the talk of the country for the
next twenty years.

"The fun is only beginnin'," she said; "God bless the good
neighbors; sure we never thought we'd have sich a crowd.
Many a good match will be made today. God be wid the time
when Mike and me—"

"I think I shall slip away," he said; "they won't mind, I
suppose?"

"Wisha! no, indeed. Plase yerself. And there's the Canon
risin'."

There was a hush of respect and attention, and the whole
assembly rose as the Canon said good-bye. Where in the world

is there such tender, reverential courtesy to the priest as is
shown by their loving flocks in Ireland?

Luke had said good-day to the Canon, and did not know
what to do. He was engaged to dine at Father Martin's at five,
and it was yet but midday. He strolled down the fields to the
sea, and entered the fisherman's cottage. There was no one
there but Mona. The child had grown, and was passing over
the borderland into self-consciousness. He said:—

"How de do?"

The frightened child courtesied and blushed; he got a little
ashamed of himself, and said kindly:—

"Is this my little Mona? Dear me, how tall you are grown!
Where are they all?"

"Up at the wedding, sir," she said demurely; "but I'll call
father." She was glad to go.

She went to the door, and gave a view-hallo, which was
answered far down the beach. Meanwhile, Luke, not knowing
what to say, began to examine the rocks and shingle, and tried
to recall old times. But the old times were shy of the stranger
and refused to come back. At last, the fisherman came, struggling and panting; and, after a few salutations, the old pet
boat was again on the deep. There was a faded sunshine, like
dull gold, on sea and land, and Luke pulled through the sunlit waves without seeing them. Then, a mile or so from land, he
shipped the oars in the old way, and lay back in the stern. No
use, Luke, no use! Land and sea are the same; but not the
same. There is the same inextinguishable loveliness on sky
and wave. There are the brown cliffs and the purple heather;
there are the sheep and the young lambs of spring; but oh, how
desolate, how lonely!

"What has come over the country?" asked Luke. "I could
not believe in such a change in such a short time. It is a land
of desolation and death."

Ay, indeed, for Nature, jealous mother, has turned a cold,
icy stare on her recreant son! He has abandoned her, and, like
a woman as she is, she must have her revenge. And here it is!
She has disrobed and dislimned herself. She has taken all the
color out of her face, out of her seas and clouds, and she shows
the blank, white visage and the irresponsive stare of a corpse.

She can never be the same again to him. He has abandoned her for other loves—for the trim and painted and artificial beauty of England, and she hates him. He put down his hand into the sea with the old gesture, but drew it back in pain. He thought the cold wave had bit him. He pulled back dreamily to the shore. The old fisherman met him to take up the boat.

"Where is Mona?" he said.

But Mona, the sunny-haired child, was nowhere to be seen.

Only four sat down to dinner in the neat, tasteful parlor at Seaview Cottage. Father Martin introduced Luke to Father Meade, the successor at Gortnagoshel to dead Father Tim. Father Cussen, the Canon's new curate, he had met at the wedding. A cloud hung over the party. The "Inseparables" were separated. Death and the Bishop had done it, and Father Martin was sad.

"A change since you were here, Luke," he said. "Dear me! do you remember how we coached you for the Canon's dinner?"

"Yes," said Luke; "there's nothing but change here, and for the worse. The country appears to me to have sunk into a condition of hopeless mendicancy."

"Do you perceive so great a change in three years?" said Father Cussen.

"Yes," said Luke. "I cannot tell you how the piteous whining of those beggars shocked me this morning. This indiscriminate charity, which means universal mendicancy, appears to be unreasonable and uneconomic."

"You did not say 'unchristian'?" gasped Father Meade.

"N-no!" said Luke.

"Because it isn't," said Father Meade. "There now for you, my young man! Because it isn't!"

"Perhaps not," said Luke, who was not in his argumentative mood; and, indeed, he thought the poor old man quite an unworthy antagonist.

"Because it isn't!" said Father Meade again, aggressively. "Whatever you say about your political economy, which I suppose, you have picked up in England, where every poor man is a criminal, we love the poor in Ireland, and will always keep 'em with us!"

"Pretty safe prophecy, Father," said Luke, who rather disdained arguing on such a subject. "Nevertheless, I totally object to indiscriminate alms-giving as calculated to miss its
object, and degenerate into culpable sanction of the vicious
and dishonest."

"Fine language, fine language, me young friend; but suppose you turned away a saint from your door, or, say, our
Divine Lord Himself, how would you feel?"

"Uncomfortable," said Luke; "but I never heard of such a
thing as possible."

"Well, I did, and what is more, I was the guilty one meself,
may God forgive me!"

This was delightful. Luke hardly expected such a pleasure
as to meet the supernatural so closely, face to face. He flicked
away the crumbs from his coat and settled himself to listen.

"You'd like to hear it?"

"Certainly," said Luke, smiling.

"Well," said the old man, his face kindling, and his whole
manner assuming a tone of deep reverence, "it happened to me
twice; the third time, if I am forgetful of God's warning, will
be my last. A few years ago I was sitting at dinner, when the
door-bell was rung violently. I had had a busy day and I was
fairly bothered from beggars. I resolved that, come what
would, nothing should tempt me to give another penny that
day. I watched the tongue of the bell wagging, and I said to
meself: 'That'll do, me boy!' Just then came a second pull,
and I thought the bell was down. I jumped up angrily and went
to the door. It was almost dusk. There was a tall, gray figure
in the porch. He had no head-covering, but he had a red
muffler around his neck and a kind of belt or cord around his
waist. He handed me a letter. I didn't look at it, but handed
it back without a word. Without a word the figure bowed and
passed down the walk into the road. I went back to my dinner.
No! I couldn't touch a bit. The figure haunted me. I put on
my hat and rushed out. There wasn't a sign of him to be seen.
I could see the road from my wicket for a mile or so in each
direction. I looked up and down. There was no one visible. I
strolled up to the police barrack. They are always on the look-
out. No; no one of that description had passed. I went in the
opposite direction to the forge. No; the boys had seen no one. I
came back, uneasy enough in my mind, I can tell ye!"

"Whom do you suppose it to have been?" asked Luke.

"St. Francis himself," said the old man. "Within a week I was down with the worst fit of sickness I ever had."

"And the—a—second apparition?" said Luke, humoring the old man.

"The second was in Dublin," said the old man, solemnly. "I was returning from the summer holidays, and had little money left. I was strolling along the quay from the Four Courts to the Bridge, and, with a young lay friend, had been examining the pile of books outside a second-hand bookshop. Just before we came to where a side-lane opened on the quay, a tall, dark man accosted me. He was white as death, and had a look of untold suffering in his face. Again, like my former visitor, he said nothing, but mutely held out his hand. I shook my head and passed on; but in a moment I recollected myself, and wheeled round. There was the long quay, stretching as far as the eye could reach. Not a trace of him! I hurried back and spoke to the book-dealer, whom I had left standing at his stall. He had not seen him. I said no more; but at dinner I interrogated my young friend.

" 'Did you notice a man that stopped us on the quay?'

" 'Yes,' he said; 'I did.'

" 'Did you think now that he appeared to be in pain?'

" 'I never saw such a face of suffering before,' he said.

" 'Did he—now,' I tried to say, unconsciously, 'did he remind you of any one in particular?' 'Well,' the young man replied, 'if I may say it, he reminded me awfully of our Lord!' In three days I was on the flat of my back again, and no one thought I could ever recover. The third time—"

"Well, the third time?" queried Luke, smiling incredulously at the old priest.

"The third time won't come if the Lord leaves me my senses," said the old man.

It was really delightful to Luke to be brought into such immediate contact with mediævalism. What a splendid story for the salon! He would make the "Master's" hair stand on end. And perhaps Olivette would make her Franciscan pilgrimage to Ireland instead of Assisi. Who knows?

There was no further discussion. The two guests went away early. Luke and Father Martin were alone.

"I make," said the former, "the most frantic resolutions not to be tempted into discussion in Ireland; because, although I have subdued our national tendency to hysterics, I cannot be always sure that my opponent has acquired the same self-command."

"You did very well," said Father Martin, dryly.

"Yes, indeed! but I was afraid the old gentleman might prove aggressive, he took such a tone at first."

"It was fortunate that we did not stray into further discussion, particularly on the relativity of races. We should have had a most magnificent blow-up from Father Cussen, who declares that everything evil comes from England."

"Of course; he hasn't been yet out of his country," said Luke. "You must see England close at hand and Ireland in perspective to understand the vast and radical difference."

"He has only just returned from England," said Father Martin.

"A flying visit?"

"No; a holiday lasting over seven years."

"It is incomprehensible," said Luke. "Why, his accent—"

"He has retained his native Doric, and it sits well on as eloquent a tongue as ever you heard."

"Then he cannot have had experience of the better side of English life," said Luke. "I'm sure it is only since my pro—removal to Aylesburgh that I have come to see the many and very beautiful traits of the English character. It seems to me we have such a lot to learn."

"For example?" said Father Martin, mildly.

"Well, take Church matters. You, here, have no public services worth naming—no great celebrations, no processions, no benedictions, no great ceremonial to enliven the faith by striking the fancy of the people—"

"You mean, we don't put every benediction in the newspaper, and every presentation of a gold watch or a purse of money?"

"Well, no; perhaps that's overdone. But now I've learned so much from contact with Anglicans. I have learned, first of all, to esteem my college career as so much wasted time—"

"I thought you were *First of First?*" interposed Father Martin, wickedly.

"Quite so," said Luke, wincing; "but my dear Father, who

cares over there for our insular distinctions? Then I have
learned that our theological course is about as wise as a course
in theosophy and occultism; nay, less wise, because *these*
subjects are discussed sometimes; theology, as we understand
it, *never!* No one ever dreams today in England of making a
frontal attack on our recognized positions. They *simply* ignore
us. Look at all the trouble we had in those two treatises on
the Trinity and the Incarnation! It was labor wasted; water
flung on the sands—"

"I have read somewhere lately," interrupted Father Martin,
"that five or six Anglican bishops, and a very large percentage
of the clergy, are Unitarians."

"Well?"

"I should say your Trinity and Incarnation would come in
well there."

"You don't quite understand," said Luke, loftily. "These—
well—painful subjects are never alluded to in polite society.
They are gently tabooed. Conversation turns on the higher
levels of humanitarianism and positivism, instead of raging in
endless vortices of controversy."

"And the sum total of this new dogma is?"

"Seek the God in man; not man in God!" said Luke, grandly. "Work, toil, suffer in the great cause—the elevation and
perfection of the race."

"You saw that cloud, passing there across the black hill?"
said Father Martin.

"Yes," said Luke.

"That is your humanity, its history and its importance."

"But the Divine immanence in man—the spirit of genius,
the elation of duty, the rapture of righteousness—all the signs
of what the Jewish prophet called 'the Lord's controversy'—
are these nothing in the eternities?"

"That's all foolish jargon," said Father Martin. "I have been
there, and I know it all. But if you want to make your gods
out of a few wretched bipeds, who eat carrion, and drink
Oriental drugs to keep the wretched life in them, and clothe
themselves in unlovely garments by night and snore unto the
stars, I'm not with you. I'd prefer the gods of Greece."

"But you don't see," said Luke impatiently. "The race is
evolving through possibly the last cycle of human evolution

towards the Divine. Shall we not lend a hand here? Is it not clearly England's destiny to bring all humanity, even the most degraded, into the happy circle of civilization, and evoke from Afghan and Ashantee the glory of the slumbering godhead?"

"Good heavens! why didn't you say all that an hour ago? I'd give up my next holiday at Lisdoonvarna to hear you say that before Cussen."

"I shouldn't mind," said Luke, grandly.

"And you really think England has got a Divine mission? I never think of England but as in that dream of Piranesi—vast Gothic halls, machinery, pulleys, and all moving the mighty, rolling mechanism that is crushing into a dead monotony all the beauty and picturesqueness of the world."

"That is, bringing it up to a level of civilization and culture," said Luke.

"And why did the Almighty create the Afghan and the Ashantee, to be turned, in course of time, into a breeched and bloated Briton? If England's civilization was that of Catholicism, I can understand you. But even if it conserved, raised up, illuminated fallen races, as the Spaniards did, and the Portuguese, it might be yet doubtful if there was a Divine mission to break up noble traditions for the sake of a little more refinement, where England's mission is to destroy and corrupt everything she touches—"

"Now, now, Father Martin, this is all congenital and educational prejudice. Look at your own country and see how backward it is."

"What you call congenital prejudice," said Father Martin, gravely, "I call faith. It is our faith that makes us hate and revolt from English methods. To the mind of every true Irishman, England is simply a Frankenstein monster, that for over seven hundred years has been coveting an immortal soul. He has had his way everywhere but in Ireland; therefore he hates us."

"No use," said Luke, who had hoped for sympathy at least from the grave and learned man. "No use! Did you ever read the *Atta Troll?*"

"Never!"

"Nor any of Heine's?"

"One or two trifles," said Father Martin indifferently. "Very little light or music came out of the *Matratzengruft.*"

"Did you read the *Laches?* We have had it for discussion lately. The 'Master of Balliol' was down, and threw extraordinary light on the philosophy of Plato. Why isn't Plato read in our colleges?"

"There is no time for such amusement amongst more serious matters. Plato is a huge bundle of sophisms, without a grain or scintilla of solid wisdom."

"Dear me! Father Martin, I really didn't expect all this from you. I thought that you, at least, would sympathize with every effort towards the higher light."

"The higher light? My poor boy, you are dazzled with a little display of green and yellow fireworks. You don't see the calm, patient, eternal stars beyond."

Luke went home moody and perplexed. He had been positively certain that he was on the right track; that the world was to be conquered by the world's weapons—learning, knowledge, light, science, literature, seized by the Church, and used with deadly effect against the world. This he had been taught everywhere—by the Catholic press, by men of "light and leading" in the Church, by his own convictions. But clearly, opinion on the subject was not quite unanimous. But then this is Ireland—quaint, archaic, conservative, mediæval.

"I wish I were home," said Luke. *Home* was Aylesburgh.

"My young friend has just taken his first false step," said Father Martin to his books; and, strange to say, it was before a huge thirteen-volume Bekker's Plato he soliloquized. "Yes!" he said, as if in defiance to the mighty ghost, "yes! the first false step—the πρῶτον ψεῦδος, my most learned friend. And he has taken Father Tim's advice with a vengeance. He holds his head very high."

Luke entered the farmyard. The sounds of mighty revelling came from the lighted barn; the swift music of the violin, the pattering of many feet, the loud laugh. Over in a corner, two farmers, a little balmy, were professing unbounded and everlasting friendship, whilst debating about a few shillings of the marriage money in a prospective match. Here and there a few couples strayed around, enjoying the beautiful night, and possibly speculating about their own futures. From a neighboring hedge sang Philomel!—no, that's not it! From a neighboring haystack came a mighty chorus sacred to the groves and Bacchus:—

Ohe! Ohe!
Evoë! Evoë!
Iacche! Iacche!

Luke knew it well, and its accompaniment:—

"Poetic for Bacchus, ye d—d young numskulls. Believe it on the authority of a Trinity College man, banished for his sins to Bœotia."

It was the bugle-call from play, uttered by the old Kerry hedge schoolmaster. Luke almost felt the swish of the rattan. It was also the vesper song of the same, after he had worshipped his god and his steps were unsteady.

"There is no use, mother, in my thinking of sleeping here tonight," said Luke.

"Indeed!" said the mother; "there is a little music in the barn—"

"There are two fellows stupidly drunk there in the yard," he said, "and I suppose, several more around the grounds."

"Wisha! I suppose they took a little taste too much, and it overcome them; but there was never such a weddin' in the barony before—"

"I'll go down to the Canon and ask a bed."

"Do, alanna! do. Indeed you wouldn't get much sleep tonight here."

And mother leaned over on the settle to finish her Rosary.

Luke and the Canon—or should it be the Canon and Luke? —dined in solitary state on Sunday. It was a little lonely, but dignified. Luke and his host had now many ideas in common about things in general, and especially about the very vexed question of which seven centuries of the united wisdom of statesmen, legislators, political economists, etc., have failed to find a solution. The Canon had found it. He had turned his parish into a happy Arcady. *His* houses were neat and trim; *his* people comfortable; no poverty, no distress. "All these unhappy mendicants at your—ha—sister's wedding were imported. There's not even one—ha—professional mendicant in *my* parish."

"I hope," said Luke, "that, now that you have established this happy condition of things, the intellectual progress of the people will keep pace with their material prosperity."

"I hope so," said the Canon, blandly; "in fact, I have only to suggest it—and—"

Tum! tum!! tum!!! Tum! tum!! tum!!! crashed out the big drum beneath the windows, the shrill fifes squeaked, and the scaffold song of the Manchester martyrs, attuned to the marching song of American battalions, broke on the ear, whilst a vast multitude surged and thronged along the road that swept by the Canon's grounds. The windows rattled under the reverberation, and continued rattling, for the band had stopped opposite the rectory to serenade its occupant, and charitably infuse a little patriotism into him. He was stricken dumb with surprise and indignation. For ten minutes the thunderous music went on, punctuated now and again with cheering, and then the crowd moved away. Not far, however. They had taken possession of the national school-house, and were holding a Sunday meeting.

It took some time for the Canon to recover his equanimity. He was quite pale with annoyance. He tapped the mahogany gently with his polished nails, and said in a pitiful way to Luke:—

"Isn't that very sad? Isn't it pitiable? What an—ha—object-lesson for you, my dear young friend, about the condition of this distracted country!"

Luke could say nothing but stare at the fire, where the logs were blazing, for the winter lingered yet. There they sat silent, while now and again a burst of cheering came up from the school-room, where Father Cussen was haranguing the mighty audience.

"Just think of the grave impropriety involved in this," said the Canon. "There is the—ha—desecration of the peaceful Sabbath evening; the exciting of—ha—dangerous passions, and that young clergyman has been so forgetful of the duties of his sacred office as to usurp my—ha—legitimate authority, and take possession of *my* schools without the least reference to me."

"Whatever he thought of the political aspect of the question," said Luke, "I think he should have had your permission about the schools. I dare say there's some explanation. But are these people the beneficiaries of your kindly exertions in their behalf?"

"Some. Not all. This young clergyman's theory is that the condition of the people is insecure, notwithstanding my exertions, and, I am privileged to say, my influence with the landlords. Why, no landlord or agent would *dare* interfere with *my* people. I need only lift my hand and they would retire."

"The whole thing is very sad," said Luke; "I wish I were back in England."

Next day, his good mother showed him with pride and gratification the numberless presents that had been showered upon Lizzie. Lizzie helped. For a quiet young lady, as she was, no one would have expected a deep and dreadful cut.

"This is from Father Pat," she said.

"God bless him," said her mother.

"And this from the Canon."

"I wouldn't doubt him," said Mike Delmege.

"And Father Martin sent this beautiful set of breakfast ware; and Father Meade, whom we hardly know, this biscuit-aire; and the nuns of the Good Shepherd these lovely books; and our new curate, Father Cussen, this History of Ireland—"

Very true, Lizzie; very true; Father Luke Delmege's valuable present to his sister is conspicuous by its absence.

"You'll be able to tell Margery all about the weddin'," said the good mother.

"I'm afraid I shall have hardly time to call," said Luke; "I've overstayed my leave of absence already."

CHAPTER XX

Eclectic Catholicism

IT IS quite certain that Luke Delmege regarded these four years at Aylesburgh as by far the happiest of his life. Here he had everything that a fine intellect and rather refined taste could require. He had leisure for thought in the intervals of almost unintermitting work; or, rather, this ceaseless work supplied material for thought, which again interacted and created its own outcome in ceaseless work. He gave himself a day's recreation every Monday, after the great Sunday sermon. At least, he took out Pio, the great brown retriever, and spent the day in the country. One of the relics of this time is before the writer in the shape of a bamboo cane, notched and indented by Pio's teeth, where he dragged it from the river. But on these excursions by the lonely river, the ever active mind was at work—now on the subject of the next sermon, now on the conversation the last night at the salon; again, on the many, very many societies for the general amelioration of the race, of which he was either an active or an honorary member. These included a society for the rescue of discharged prisoners, a society for the suppression of public vice, a society for the housing of the poor, a society for the purification of the stage, etc., etc.

"I don't see your name, Father Delmege," said the dry old rector, "on the committee for making statesmen truthful, and introducing the Seventh Commandment on the Stock Exchange."

Luke concluded that the old man was jealous. The old man had a good deal of temptation to become so. He was nobody. Luke overshadowed him utterly.

217

"You'll preach at Vespers on Sunday evening, of course, Father Delmege?"

"I should be most happy indeed; but it is Dr. Drysdale's turn on Sunday evening."

"Oh! how unfortunate! And the Lefevrils are coming. Could you not effect an exchange?"

"I should most gladly do so; but, you know, the rector would hardly like the suggestion."

"Do try, Father. It's really more important than you imagine or I can explain. I'm sure, if you knew how *very* important it is—"

"I fear it is quite impossible, Mrs. Bluett—"

"Oh dear! The doctor is such a dear old soul, but he *is* dry. There, I've made a horrible pun; but, dear me, he is so tedious, and I shouldn't care, but of all evenings—"

No wonder Luke worked at his sermons! He sat at his desk at ten o'clock on Tuesday morning, and worked steadily to midday. By Friday evening he had written fifteen pages of a sermon. On Saturday he committed it to memory, and, without the omission or alteration of a word, he delivered it on Sunday morning, at the Gospel of the *Missa Cantata* or at Vespers in the evening. And during these four years he never ventured to speak publicly without having made this careful and elaborate preparation. In after years he often wondered at himself, but admitted that he dared not do otherwise. He never knew who might be listening to him in this strange land, where every one is so interested in religion, because every man is his own pope; and so uninterested, because he cares so little what all the other popes, even the Archbishop of Canterbury, may hold or teach. But the discipline was good for Luke. It gave him a facility in speaking which lasted through life.

Now, Dr. Drysdale was not jealous. He was too old, or wise, or holy, to be aught but amused, ay, indeed, and anxious, about his young confrère. Amused he was, and very much amused, at the Celtic impetuosity with which Luke flung himself into every kind of work. His strenuous manner, generous, self-sacrificing, was such a contrast to his own placidity that it was quite interesting in the beginning. Then it became a matter of grave concern to the gentle old priest.

"This is a valuable and interesting book," he would say, pushing over a volume by some great Catholic author to Luke, for he was a member of St. Anselm's Society, and this was one of the societies of which Luke was not a member. "Take it to your room and read it at your leisure."

Luke would take it; but Mill and Heine and Emerson had got hold of him just now, and he would bring it back uncut after a few days, with a remark that was meant to be pregnant and suggestive:—

"All the poetry of the world is in the Catholic Church; and all the literature of the world outside it."

Or: "It seems to me that the whole of our philosophy consists of junks of indigestible propositions, garnished with syllogisms of froth."

The rector would rub his chin and say, "Humph!" which is eloquent, too.

On Sunday afternoon the rector would say, "Spare me half an hour, Father Delmege, and help me at the altar!"

The "Altar" was a privileged one in this sense, that no one, not even the president of the Altar Society, was allowed to touch it for any purpose whatsoever. The arrangements of the cloths, the vases and their flowers—all were the rector's exclusive province, where no one dared interfere. But he took especial pride in the decoration of the high-altar for Sunday evening Benediction. It was a labor of love that extended over three hours of the Sunday afternoon. There were sometimes from one hundred and twenty to a hundred and fifty candles to be placed ready for lighting; and the vicar had a fancy that there should be a special design for each Benediction. Then, as a final touch, he tipped the wick of each candle with a preparation of melted wax and paraffin—a chemical compound in which he took great pride, and he had serious thoughts of patenting it. That chemical and its jam-pot was a perpetual source of wonder to Luke. I fear the wonder was slightly contemptuous. To see this excellent old man, Doctor of Divinity, Dublin Reviewer, correspondent with French and Italian philosophers, studiously mixing that oil and wax, and then standing on a ladder, as he put up, and took down, and rearranged candles and flowers, was a something far beyond Luke's comprehension. In after years, when his eyes were widely opened, Luke dropped some bitter tears over that jam-pot and—himself.

"Impossible, sir!" he would explain, in reply to his vicar's invitation. "I really have something serious to do. Can't you let the ladies or the sacristan attend to these things?"

The old man would not reply, except to his unseen Master.

But Luke was happy, and his great happiness was in his dealings with converts. Here he had a broad field for learning, tact, and sympathy. To lift these trembling souls over the quagmires and shaking bogs of unbelief; to enlighten, cheer, support under all the awful intellectual and spiritual trials of incipient doubt, until he had planted them safely at his feet on the firm ground of Catholic faith and practice; to witness their almost exultant happiness, when, the final step being taken, with closed eyes and gasping breath, they at length found themselves in the home of serene security; to open to their wondering vision all the splendors and beauties that they had hitherto seen under distorting and bewildering lights; to share in their happiness and gratitude,—ah me! this is ecstasy, and Luke felt: Yes! here is my vocation; here I have found my life-work! And if ever a doubt crossed his mind about his studies at this time, he hushed the complaining voice with the dogmatic assurance:—

"The first step towards conquering the enemy is to enter the enemy's arsenals and handle his weapons."

There were some drawbacks, indeed. Now and again some giddy girl, or some conceited Scripture-reader, would go through the form of conversion, and then "revert." One day a lady wished to see him. She was closely veiled. She insisted on being received into the Church then and there. Luke demurred. He took her down to the Convent of the Faithful Companions, and placed her for instruction under Reverend Mother's care. He felt quite proud. This was evidently a lady of distinction. A few days later he strolled down leisurely to ask after his convert. Reverend Mother met him with a smile.

"No; the lady had not returned. She was a lunatic, who had slipped from her mother's carriage whilst her mother was shopping; and the bellman had been ringing the city for her since."

Luke got into a newspaper controversy. There was a very, very High-Church rector in the neighborhood. He had far more candles than the mere Romans, and his vestments cost twice as much as theirs. He reserved the Precious Blood (so he thought, poor man!), and had a special lunette made for the phial at Benediction. He gave awful penances, in imitation of the primitive Church, and always, once or twice a year, he refreshed his superlative orthodoxy by a furious attack on the unoffending Romanists. Some of his congregation were edified and strengthened by these violent philippics, especially a few whose relatives had passed over to Catholicity and made them "suspect"; a good many were disgusted, for, even in Ritualism, the Englishman asserts his individual freedom of thought; but most of the congregation were amused.

"He doth protest too much," they averred. "It is all on account of that dog, Pio, who has the good taste to come to our Church on Sundays."

Yes; but not to worship. Pio had the amiable habit, acquired in some mysterious manner, of trotting down to the Ritualistic church every Sunday morning, and there, posted at the gate, of scrutinizing carefully every face and figure that passed in to service.

"The Roman priests sent him," said the vicar, "to see if any of their stray sheep had wandered into the true fold."

But the vicar was mad. And the *Aylesburgh Post* was just the vehicle for his insanity. Such scorn, such hatred, such cool, undiluted contempt for "his" parishioners, "these Romish priests," were only equalled by the mighty organs of the sect elsewhere; and the fierce philippic was generally followed by an angry demand for dues or tithes from "his parishioners." The rector read the paper with a smile and put the letter in the fire. Not so Luke. Luke wore a good, broad seam of white along the fine red carpet in his room, and a good, broad path along the tiny square of grass in front. Luke was deep in thought, and Luke's thoughts found issue in words. The excellent editor of the *Aylesburgh Post* had never received such a document before, even from the High-church vicar. Deep, cutting sarcasm, quotations from Anglican divines that would make a statue blush, refutations that were irrefutable, and logical sequences that were undeniable—and all couched in language that seemed to set the paper in a blaze! The editor read with a smile, and dropped the paper into the wastebasket, then looked to see if there were danger of conflagration.

Luke went around with his burning secret for twenty-four hours. He expected to cause a sensation in the city, probably a large secession from Ritualism,—at least, a long, fierce, angry controversy, in which he, calling on all his vast resources, would infallibly come out as victor. The second day was a day of fever and unrest. The third morning came. There was a second sarcastic letter from the High-Churchman, and just a little editorial note:—

"We have also received a communication from L. D. on this interesting subject. The gentleman knows well how to use his pen.
ED. *A. P.*"

As on a former occasion, Luke played Rugby football around his room, much to the amusement of his rector, who read that footnote with intelligent and comprehensive pleasure, and Luke broke forth into a hysterical soliloquy:—

"Fair play! British fair play! They're the greatest humbugs and hypocrites on the face of the earth! Here is an open attack, uncalled for, without pretense of reasoning or exciting cause. Here is a reply, fair, temperate, judicious, and lo! it is suppressed. It is the old, old story. They talk of truth when they lie! They talk of religion when they blaspheme! They talk of humanity when they rob, and plunder, and kill! They talk of fair play when they are tying your hands to smite you!" Which shows that Luke's exuberant admiration of everything English did sometimes suffer a pretty severe frost-nipping. He never spoke to his good rector on the matter. He disburdened his conscience elsewhere.

"Nothing reminds me so much of what we read about the calm constancy and fortitude of the early Christians," said the great "Master" one of these evenings, "as the peace that seems to come down and hover over the souls of recent converts to Catholicism."

"Ah, yes, to be sure," said Amiel Lefevril; "the whole motive and genesis of Catholicism seems to be found in seeking pleasure in pain. I consider our religion higher and deeper, for that we seek pain in pleasure."

The Master smiled. His pupils were advancing in Platonism.

"This is one reason," she continued, "why I cannot embrace Roman Catholicism, attractive as it otherwise is. It seems to be founded on selfishness. Its charity is forever seeking a guerdon, either in the esteem of others or in the exquisite sense of self-exaltation, or in the final reward of a heaven. Is it not higher and nobler and loftier to act and think for the abstract *Idea* of benefiting humanity? So with prayer. I can understand prayer as an ecstasy of thought of the Infinite; an unlifting of soul to the spheres; a conscious merging of the *Ego* in the *All*. But your everlasting whinings for mercy, your prayers against the laws of Nature, are unintelligible. And as for penance, what is it but the delight of pain—the subtle, emotional suffering that bathes the self-conscious flagellant in an ecstasy of bliss?"

"You seem, Miss Lefevril," said Luke, timidly, "to overlook what lies at the bottom of all ascetic practices and prayers— the essential dogmas or truths of religion."

"Oh," said Miss Amiel, "truth? There is no such thing, except as an abstraction. Hence I always hold that we are all— that is, all good people are—practically the same. And each soul is at liberty to select its own beliefs and form an aggregate for itself."

Luke looked wonderingly at the Master, who appeared to be highly pleased with his pupil. He ventured however to protest.

"I cannot really follow you, Miss Lefevril," he said; "it seems to me a logical sequence from no truth to no principle."

"I spoke of beliefs," said Miss Amiel. "There is a natural and logical sequence between belief and principle."

"And how can there be faith without an object—and that object, Truth?" said Luke.

"Dear me! how shall I explain?" said Miss Amiel. "You know, of course,—indeed, I think I have heard you say so,— that mathematical proofs are the most perfect?"

Luke assented.

"That there is nothing so certain as that two straight lines cannot enclose a space?"

Luke nodded.

"And that every point in the circumference of a circle is equidistant from the center?"

"Quite so!"

"But these things do not and cannot exist, except as abstractions of the mind. There is no objective truth there, because there is no object at all. The same with all truth, for all truth is immaterial and purely subjective."

"Then you don't believe in God?" said Luke, bluntly.

"Oh dear, yes. I believe in my own concept of God, as do you!"

"Or in hell, or in a future life?" gasped Luke.

"Dear me! yes, yes, I believe in hell—the hell we create for ourselves by misdoing; and the immortality of myself, my soul, passing down through the endless ages in the immortality of my race!"

"I regret to say, Miss Lefevril, you can never become a Catholic with such ideas!"

"But I *am* a Catholic. We are all Catholics. We all have the same spirit. Mr. Halleck is a Catholic, yet not the same as you—"

"I beg pardon. Mr. Halleck is a communicant at our church and has made profession of our faith."

"Of course he has. But Mr. Halleck's subjectivity is not yours, or Mr. Drysdale's, or Mrs. Bluett's, or mine. Each soul dips into the sea and takes what it can contain. Surely, you cannot say that these poor people, who live in Primrose Lane and frequent your church, and the learned Mr. Halleck, hold the same subjective beliefs?"

"So much the worse for my friend Halleck, if that be true!" Luke had enough nerve to say.

"Not at all! He simply is an eclectic Catholic, as we all are—the Master, the Dean, Canon Merritt, even Mr. ——," mentioning the name of his High-Church friend.

Luke started back in horror.

"How can you associate the names of Mr. Halleck, the Dean, Mr. Merritt, with that—that vulgar man?"

"But, my dear Mr. Delmege, we are not now speaking of vulgarity and refinement, but opinions—thoughts—beliefs—"

"And the whole of your beliefs is pure scepticism," said Luke.

"Not at all," smiled Miss Amiel; "you do not understand. You really must read Plato on Ideas, until you grasp the meaning of Subjective Idealism, or what I have called eclectic Catholicism."

Luke began to feel that his rector was right, and that he would be more at home with old John Godfrey and his pipe. But the toils were around him, and, whilst his faith was perfect, the grace of illumination was as yet far away. He was groping in the dark vaults of what he was pleased to call "the enemy's arsenals."

Hence, too, issued a wonderful sermon which Luke preached one Sunday evening about this time. He was hardly to blame; for an idea had sprung up about this time in England that heresy was to be conquered by affecting not only a knowledge of its mysteries, but even its extravagances of language. And there was a scarcely concealed desire to attenuate the doctrines of the Church so as to fit them nicely to the irregularities of error. The idea, of course, was the exclusive property of neologists, and was regarded, not only with suspicion, but with condemnation, by older and wiser heads, who preached in season and out of season that it is not to mind and intellect that the Church looks, but to conduct and character, that is, the soul. But it is hard to convince young heads of this. So Luke had been for some time introducing into his sermons strange quotations, very like the Holy Scriptures, yet most unlike, and they were a grievous puzzle to his good rector. This evening, for the special illumination of a very large section of his audience, a number of commercial young men, who were in the habit of flocking to the Catholic church on Sunday evenings to hear this brilliant young orator, he chose for his subject the "Sacred Books." An excellent subject, excellently illustrated. But unfortunately, in the inexperienced hands of Luke, who was at this time probably penetrated by his growing love for Plato and his schools, the side scenes became more attractive than the great central picture, until at last the sermon began to descend into a mere defence of naturalism. It was all very nice and flattering to human nature, and

Luke narrowly escaped an ovation when he wound up a brilliant sermon, after several quotations from the *Book of Thoth,* with this from another:—

> With ease he maketh strong, with equal ease
> The strong abaseth; the illustrious
> He minisheth, and him that is obscure
> He raiseth up; yea more, even He, who wields
> High thunders, and in mansions dwells above,
> With ease makes straight the crookt, and blasts the proud.
> Hear, and behold, and heed, and righteously
> Make straight the way of oracles of God.

Clotilde declared the sermon magnificent.

Mary O'Reilly said to Mrs. Mulcahy:—

"Did ye ever hear the like o' that? 'Tis like a sthrame of honey comin' from his mout'. It takes the ould counthry, after all, to projuce the prachers. Sure, the poor Canon, God be good to him! with his hummin' and hawin', isn't a patch on him. I suppose they won't lave him to us!"

The Canon took a different stand. He prayed earnestly, during Benediction, for light. Then, after tea, with slight nervousness, and most careful to select his words judiciously, he opened up the subject:—

"Was that sermon, Father Delmege, might I ask, prepared, or was it *ex tempore?"*

Luke, who was expecting a compliment, said promptly:—

"Prepared, of course. I never speak in that pulpit without committing every word of a manuscript to memory."

"I am sorry to hear it," said the old man, with some hesitation. "I was hoping that, perhaps, its indiscretions were attributable to haste and nervousness. I cannot conceive how a Catholic priest could sit down calmly and write such irrelevant and injudicious things."

Jealousy again! thought Luke. He said:—

"Perhaps, sir, you would kindly explain. I am quite unconscious of having said anything indiscreet or liable to disedify."

"It is quite possible that you have not disedified," said the rector; "I'm sure I hope so. Because our own people are pretty indifferent to these very learned subjects. But do you consider the fatal effect your words might have in retarding or altogether destroying the incipient operations of grace in the souls of others?"

"You may not be aware, sir," said Luke, playing his trump card, "that these lectures are the main attraction to a rather important section of our separated brethren, who come to our church on certain evenings to hear and be instructed."

"How long have you been here, Father Delmege?" said the rector.

"Very close upon four years," said Luke.

"How many converts have you had under instruction?"

"I cannot count them," said Luke.

"How many have you received into the Church?" asked the Rector.

Luke found he could easily count them on his fingers. He was abashed.

"And of these, how many have persevered?" said the old man, driving his investigations home.

Luke had to admit that nearly half had 'verted again.

"Yes!" said the old man; "and if you ask the cause, you will find it to be your too great liberalism, which to me seems to be—pardon the expression—a half apology for heathenism."

Luke was hurt.

"I'm sure," he said, "I do not know exactly where I'm standing. Our leading men glorify the learning, the research, the fairmindedness of these very men I have quoted tonight; and the very books I drew from have been favorably reviewed and warmly recommended by our leading journals. Do you want me to go back to the Catechism and to explain 'Who made the world'?"

"You might do worse," said the rector. "But, to be very serious, Father Delmege, I think the sooner you give up the company of these liberals and free-thinkers the better. I have often blamed myself for not speaking to you plainly on the matter."

"It was Mrs. Bluett introduced me to that circle," apologized Luke; "and Catholics frequent it. Halleck is always there."

"Halleck is a good fellow," said the rector; "but he has brought into the Church a little of the Englishman's indefeasible right of private judgment. If I were you, I'd give up these literary seances and look more closely after your own poor people."

"Very well, sir," said Luke. He said to his looking-glass, very soon after:—

"The old story. These Englishmen want the aristocracy all to themselves."

CHAPTER XXI

The Submerged Tenth

WE MUST not do Luke Delmege the injustice of supposing, even from his good rector's allusion, that he was altogether careless about the primary obligation of a Catholic priest— the care of the poor. Indeed, he rather prided himself on being able to pass, with equal zeal, from the drawing-room to the kitchen, and from the castle to the cabin. His figure was a familiar one to the denizens of Primrose Lane. For here congregated a small colony of exiles from Ireland and Italy; and here, into the dread monotony of English life, were introduced the picturesqueness and dramatic variety which appear to be the heritage of the Catholic races. Sometimes, indeed, Luke, with his admiration of English habits and ways, was not a little shocked at irregularities which are anathematized by the English religion. The great pagan virtues of cleanliness and thrift were steadily ignored. In their place came faith and piety, enthusiasm and idealism, that were utterly unintelligible to the prosaic neighbors around.

"A family of Hirish peddlers, sa, and a family of Hitalian horgan-grinders," was the answer of a portly dame to one of Luke's inquiries. "They are very huntidy, sa, in their 'abits."

"Thim English, yer reverence, they're haythens. They don't go to church, Mass, or meeting. They think of nothing but what they ate and drink."

Which sums up neatly the controversies between the races, with which economists have filled not only volumes, but libraries.

Luke at this time was quite flattered at being considered an Englishman; and when his country was decried, instead of flaring up in the old passionate way, he politely assented. And

229

yet, he really loved his own people, would take a pinch of snuff from Mrs. Mulcahy, and say the *Banacht Dia*—the beautiful prayer for the Holy Souls, that is never omitted on such an occasion in Ireland. And he loved his little Italians— their strange, grotesque gestures, their beautiful liquid tongue; and he went so far as to nurse and fondle the bambinos, and to be interested even in intricacies of the "horgan." And he did shudder a little occasionally when he had to pass through a crowd of English girls with their white, pale faces, and when he had to undergo a bold scrutiny from the irreverant gaze of some English laborers. In the beginning, too, he had to submit to an occasional sneer—"I confess," or "Hour Father," as a gang of young Britishers passed by; but by degrees he became known, and these insults ceased. But it was in the county prison that he became most closely acquainted with the "submerged tenth," and here he had some novel experiences.

A quick pull at the jangling bell, a courteous salute from the officer, a jingling of keys, the monastic silence of the vast hall, laced with the intricacies of iron fret-work in the staircases that led to the galleries, from which again opened up and shut the gates of the tombs of the living—nerves shrink at the thought until nerves become accustomed to the ordeal. Then, an unceremonious unlocking of cells and a drawing of bolts— an equally unceremonious slapping to of the heavy iron door, and Luke is alone with a prisoner. He is clad in brown serge, with just a loose linen muffler around his neck. His name?

"Casabianca. Is as innocent as ze babe unborned. Was in ze French navee. Quartur-mastere. Yes. Saw some foreign serveece. Has a vife. (Weeps sadly.) And leetle childrens. (Weeps loudly.) Ees a Catolique. Knows his releegion vhell. Ees starved. Eferyting is so tirty. Did noting. Vhas arresteed, he know not vhy; but he has six monz to serve."

Later on Luke found he was not quite so innocent. He gave Luke several lessons in prison life; showed him how to take out the stopcock when the water was shut off in the pipes, and through the empty pipes to establish telephonic communication with his neighbors; showed him a new telegraphic system by knocking with the knuckles on the wall; showed him divers ways of hiding away forbidden material.

Allons! The bell rings and he is ushered into another cell.

Here is a stalwart Irishman, awaiting trial for having, in a fit of drunkenness, abstracted a pair of boots that were hanging outside a draper's shop.

"You'll get three months!" said Luke.

"I hope so, sir. I may get seven years' penal servitude. It's my second offence; and if they find I'm an Irishman, I shall be certainly sent to penal servitude."

"Impossible! nonsense!" said Luke.

The prisoner got seven years. His little wife from Kerry fainted.

Here, too, were sailors from Glasgow, and Paisley, and Liverpool, in for refusing to go to sea in water-logged vessels, and who purchased their lives with three months' starvation.

Luke was very indignant. The perfect mechanism of English methods was beginning to pall on him. It was so silent, so smooth, so deadly, so indifferent. He had a row with his rector over the matter. And at the Lefevrils he said:—

"I know it is civilization; but there's something wanting. What is it?"

He expressed in emphatic language his difficulties to John Godfrey. John, usually so phlegmatic, flared up.

"The people must be protected, and what is to protect the people but the law?"

"But seven years' penal servitude for a freak in a fit of drink! Do you understand it? Can you imagine the horror, the desolation, the misery, the despair, of these seven years of hell?"

"That's all right. But the law—the law!"

The law was the fetich. You dare not whisper a syllable against it. Not the law of God, but of man.

"You, Irish," said the rector, "are by nature opposed to law and order. You sympathize with crime—"

"I beg pardon," said Luke. "We convict criminals, we condemn crime."

"Then why commit crime?" said the rector.

"Commit crime? Ireland is the most crimeless country in the world," said Luke.

"Tell that to the marines!" said the rector. Luke didn't. He knew that on certain subjects the British mind has one of the symptoms of incurable insanity—the *idée fixée* of Charcot.

He thought it would be a nice subject for the salon. Such

social problems were often debated there, and there was as much theorizing as in Parliament. He broached the matter delicately—the dreadful inequality of punishments under the English law. They gnashed their teeth. He had blasphemed their god.

"Your countrymen are curiously sympathetic with crime."

"There is more crime committed in one day, one hour, in England than would be committed in Ireland in a century," said Luke, repeating the usual formula.

"Ah! yes, perhaps so; but they are a lawless race."

"They don't break God's laws," said Luke.

"God," said Amiel, "is another name for order—*Kosmos*, as Satan is disorder—*Chaos*. It is the universal order of Nature that any deflection from its rules must inexorably meet its punishment. The English law is the interpreter of Nature, that is —God!"

Luke bowed; but he thought he heard the snarl of a wild beast somewhere. He said diffidently:—

"It seems to me that Carlyle, not Christ, is the prophet of the English people."

"Christ interpreted by Carlyle," said Amiel.

"I never met His Name in Carlyle's twenty-two volumes," said Luke.

But ever after, as he watched curiously the little, shy, half-suppressed indications of affection in the families to which he was welcomed, and which revealed their inner secrets to him, he could not shake aside the thought that had fastened on his fancy of the lioness and her cubs—

Mouthing her young in her first fierce kiss.

But this awful, unbending, retributive justice—this appeal to the brutality of nature—made him shudder, whilst it fascinated him. It was the dread grinding of the blind mechanism that was always haunting him—the voice of a soulless creation.

Luke was asked, the following Sunday, to officiate at Sea-thorpe, a fashionable watering-place, just then springing into eminence on the south coast. He had to travel forty miles by train, and he reached the village at dusk. He was directed to a lonely house down by a sheltered quay, and called Aboukir Mansion. Here he was met by the ubiquitous Irishman and his wife, and it was a warm greeting from hands that had dug in the silver mines at Nevada, and had held a musket in the trenches before Sebastopol. And he needed it, for it was a large, roomy mansion, bare of furniture, except such as was absolutely necessary—just the kind of place where Dickens would locate a mysterious murder and make the walls tell of it. Next morning, at ten o'clock, he faced his congregation. It consisted of six servants, the lord of the manor, and a magnificent St. Bernard dog. The two latter were located within the sanctuary, as became their dignity. The others were without. The chapel was the old dining-room; but the altar had been once in the place of honor in a famous Capuchin convent on the Adriatic coast. Luke was about to commence Mass, when a certain figure, clothed in clerical costume, arrested his arm and said aloud, with a strong nasal accent:—

"Come, let us adore!"

Luke was about to resent the interruption when the figure knelt and gravely intoned:—

"Come, let us exult in the Lord, let us rejoice in God our Helper; let us come before His presence with thanksgiving, and make a joyful noise to Him with psalms."

And the congregation muttered:—

"The King to whom all things live; come, let us adore."

So the superb psalm went on to the end. But Luke was nowhere. He inquired afterwards who the interloper was. A village tailor, who had been received into the Church a few weeks before.

Then came the *Missa Cantata,* sung by the choir; and at the Gospel Luke preached for thirty minutes. The old man slept; but he congratulated Luke warmly afterwards. The Irishman was in ecstasies.

"Why, you are akchally an orator, yer reverence!"

Luke admitted the impeachment.

He was to dine at the manor at eight o'clock. He held an afternoon service at five. This time there was a crowd, a curious, gaping crowd of villagers, who gathered in fear and trembling to see what the Papists were doing. Amongst them Luke noticed two ladies in black.

"They have been attending the church for ten years," said the sacristan.

"Then they are Catholics?" asked Luke.

"No! nor ever will be," was the answer.

Luke was received in the drawing-room with frigid politeness. The old man sat in his arm-chair, his dog beside him. There was a clergyman in the room and his four daughters. He was the old man's nephew and expectant heir. For the old man had married his Irish cook, who had converted him. Then she went to heaven to receive her reward. The estate was entailed.

Dinner was announced. The old man looked at Luke. Luke returned the gaze calmly. The old man was disappointed. It was the duty of the chaplain to wheel him in to dinner. Luke had failed to understand, and the nephew dutifully took his place, wheeled the old man out of the drawing-room, into the corridor, right to the head of the table, the huge mastiff walking gravely by his side. Luke was allowed to say grace. In the course of the dinner the nephew touched the decanter and looked at his uncle. He was a clergyman, and in his fiftieth year.

"Might I have one, sir?"

"Yes, *one*," said the old man.

It was a beautiful act of reverence to old age, or was it— mammon?

When the ladies had retired, the three gentlemen sat around the fire. There was solemn silence. Luke was uneasy. His nervous temperament was not yet wholly subdued, although he had acquired the art of being silent for ten minutes; but a quarter of an hour was too great a strain. He addressed the old man:—

"I dare say a good many yachts run in here in the summer and autumn months?"

The old man was asleep.

"Did you see Stanley's latest?" Luke said to the nephew.

"Stanley? Stanley?" coughed the clergyman. "Never heard of him."

"He has just returned from his tour through Egypt and the Holy Land. He accompanied the Prince of Wales."

"He must have had a jolly time. Franked all the way, I suppose?"

Luke saw the trend of his thoughts, poor fellow!

"I like Stanley," he said, "although he's as hard on celibate clergy as Kingsley —"

"The awful fool!" muttered the clergyman.

"But then he had his five or six thousand a year, and no children."

The poor man groaned.

"Now," continued Luke, "I always pray for two persons— the Pope that invented celibacy, and the Chinaman that invented tea."

"So do I! So do I!" said his neighbor. "That is, I don't know about that Chinaman; but I like that Pope. God bless him!"

Luke watched the fire.

"Look here," the other whispered, " 'tis all rot!"

"I beg your pardon," said Luke.

"I say 'tis all rot," repeated his companion. " 'Tis all L.S.D."

"I can't quite catch the subject," said Luke, "though I understand the predicate."

"All this rubbish about religion. Why, any man can be religious on a thousand a year. Any man can be holy on two thousand a year. Any man can be a saint on five thousand a year. It's all this way. To be a saint you must be at peace with the world. Very good. But with five thousand a year, where's the trouble? Why, man, you can't have an enemy. Who'd say boo to a fellow with five thousand a year, a palace, and a carriage? Phew!"

"I hope your excellent uncle has twice five thousand a year!" said Luke, consolingly.

But there came such a look of terror on the poor fellow's face that Luke changed the subject immediately.

"That's a magnificent St. Bernard!"

"A true blood! The monks gave him to my uncle!"

"That was kind."

"I suppose they thought St. Bernard would like it. He liked the English, you know!"

"I did not know. I'm deeply interested."

"I don't know much about these things; but I heard a clever

fellow of ours say that St. Bernard gave the Pope of his day a
rap over the knuckles, and that he opposed the doctrine of the
Immaculate Conception."

"Indeed! That must be a clever fellow," said Luke sarcastically.

"Oh, yes! And, therefore, St. Bernard must be one of us,
you know."

"I see. Any one that protests?"

"Exactly. Any man that makes a row against things as they
are—"

"Eh? eh?" said the old man, opening his eyes.

The nephew was paralyzed. But the old man dropped
asleep again.

"You were saying?—" said Luke.

"Sh! No, sir, I was not saying."

"Well, you implied that you gather everything clean and
unclean into the capacious sheets of heresy. I have noticed
that. I remarked the other day to one of your canons that it
was a singular fact in the Revised Version of the New Testament, whereas every rationalist and free-thinker is quoted,
there's not a single Catholic writer even mentioned."

"Of course not; of course not," said the nephew, who was
watching his uncle anxiously.

" 'Tis the tradition of your Church," said Luke, "and when
the old men die—"

"Eh? eh? Who said I was dying?" exclaimed the old man,
and dropped asleep again.

"For God's sake stop and look at the fire," said the alarmed
nephew. "If he hears anything again 'tis all up."

"All right," said Luke.

So they watched the fire until the old man became restless
again.

"What's his weak point?" whispered Luke.

"The view," whispered the nephew, in an alarmed way.

Luke got up and went to the window. It was a something
to be proud of. As one looked down from the almost dizzy
height, over the roofs of detached villas, each nestling in its
own dark-green foliage, and out across the quiet village to
where the sea slept, stretching its vast peacefulness to the horizon, the words leaped to the lips:—

Charmed magic casements, opening on the foam
Of perilous seas, in faery lands forlorn.

But it was the peace, the Sabbath peace of a Sabbath evening
in England, that stole on the senses, and wrapped them out
of the bare, bald present into the music and magic of the past.
And, irresistibly, Lisnalee and all its loveliness rose up before
the mind of Luke. It was now an infrequent and faint picture.
Luke had blotted it from his everyday memory. He had said
good-bye to his own land forever. After his last visit, when
everything looked so old and melancholy, and every white
cottage was a sepulchre, he had tacitly made up his mind that
his vocation was unquestionably to remain in England, work
there and die there, and he only awaited the expiration of his
seven years' apprenticeship to demand an *exeat* from his own
Bishop and affiliation to his adopted diocese.

"Yes," he said to himself, "everything points that way. I
have found my *métier*. I must not throw it aside. I have no
business in Ireland. I should be lost there, we must not bury
our talents in a napkin."

But somehow, standing in this broad bay-window, this long,
summer twilight, Lisnalee would project its bareness and sadness across the calm beauty and the snug prosperity of this
English village. He tried to blot it out. No; there it was, floating
above the real landscape, as a mist floats its transparency over
a sleeping lake. And he remembered that fierce argument he
had with his own conscience, as he rocked on the boat the
afternoon of the great day when he said his first Mass.

"I was right," he said; "if I had remained at home, what
should I be now? A poor, half-distracted professor in a seminary, or a poor, ill-dressed, ill-housed curate on the mountain,
and see what I am!"

And Luke lifted his watch-chain and thought of his greatness.

"Eh? eh?" said the old man, waking up finally. "What did
you say?"

"I say," said Luke, promptly, "that there is not in the world,
except perhaps at Sorrento or Sebenico, a view to equal that."

"Ha! did ye hear that, George?" chuckled the old man;
"did ye hear that?"

"Yes, sir," said George; "Mr. Delmege has been raving about it the whole evening."

"Mr. Delmege has excellent taste," said the old man; "here, George, the ladies await tea."

He took occasion to whisper to Luke:—

"I wish the Bishop would send you here. I have endowed the mission—a hundred a year. And you should dine with me every day. Eh?"

"It would be delightful," said Luke. And as he walked slowly, step by step with the yawning mastiff after the arm-chair of the host, he pictured to himself a home in this delight-ful village, with books and pen and paper, crowds of converts, a quarterly article in the *Dublin,* select society, an occasional run to the city or to Aylesburgh to preach a great sermon, correspondence with the world's *literati,* then ecclestiastical honors, and beautiful, dignified age. Alas! and his Master's mind was weaving far other destinies for him; and swiftly and suddenly this vision of the priestly Sybarite vanished.

Next day the old man broached the subject again. He had set his heart on having a resident priest at Seathorpe. Luke referred him to the Bishop; but he more than hinted that the project would be exceedingly agreeable to himself.

"Dear me!" he said, as he returned to Aylesburgh by the morning train, "how swiftly we pass to extremes. It's a seesaw between the 'upper ten' and the 'lower five.' Which do I pre-fer? Hardly a fair question. But if I had not the prospect of that horrid prison before the mental landscape, and Primrose Lane, would life be the brighter? Who knows?"

He drew the subject around deftly that evening after tea. The good Canon was anxious to enter into, and guide rightly, the strange, emotional nature that was thrown into his hands. But he confessed himself at fault. He had studied every phase of Luke's character, watched every mood, and reluctantly had come to the conclusion that the fine spirit would never go far wrong, yet never reach any great height. The very instinct that forbade the former would debar the latter. And the Canon thought the time had come for a change. Luke had made some vigorous efforts to escape the thraldom of too intellectual soci-ety; but the toils were around him, and an evening at home or at one of the quiet Catholic houses was intolerably dull. Where would all this end? The Canon often asked himself the question; and asked the same question of the flowers he placed and replaced around his Master's throne; and asked it of the white flames that sprang up around the altar; and sometimes paused in his walk, and held his Breviary open without reading it, and stumbled at certain verses:—

"Homo, cum in honore esset, non intellexit."

"Does that apply to my young friend?"

"Decident a cogitationibus suis; secundum multitudinem impietatum eorum, expelle eos; quoniam irritaverunt te, Domine."

"Dear me! dear me! God forbid!"

"How did you like Seathorpe?" he said to Luke at supper.

"Very much indeed! What a quaint old place the mansion is; and what a quaint old fellow the proprietor!"

"Yes! the Church is not making much headway there," said the old Canon.

"It needs a resident priest," said Luke, "one who would give all time and attention to the possibilities of the place."

"Yes! It would be a nice mission for a young man of energy who could keep his head."

"I don't think there's much to tempt a man to insane things there," said Luke.

"Except the worst danger—loneliness and the *taedium vitae.*"

"Yes; but if a man has his books, and his pen, and his work cut out for him—"

"Quite so, if he is a strong man. But if he be a weak man, it is certain danger."

"Solitude has always been the mother-country of the strong and the elect."

"Just what I have been saying," said the Canon. "A mother-country to the strong; a howling and dangerous desert to the weak."

Luke thought that there was an undercurrent of meaning in the Canon's words; but there was nothing to catch hold of or resent.

"I shouldn't object to a mission there," he said bluntly.

"Ah! I see you're tired of us here. Well, who knows? Meanwhile, you would do well to visit the prison tomorrow. Tuesday is your day, I believe."

"Yes," said Luke. "Nothing has turned up there?"

"Nothing unusual," said the Canon, quietly. "There is a soldier, a countryman of yours, up for shooting his officer through the heart on the barrack-square at Dover."

Luke studied the gas-jet for a long time when the Canon had gone to his room.

CHAPTER XXII

Euthanasia

SIR ATHELSTAN Wilson had got all he coveted in this life, and all he desired in eternity, which he regarded as a vague, ill-defined, and unscientific quantity. He had snatched out of the melée of life and from under the teeth of Orange mastiffs a dainty morsel. They gnashed their teeth in rage; and he—well, he was not satisfied. Who is? Well, where's the use in tearing a moral to tatters? But there were two things that spoiled his pleasure. That agile and most modest microbe still declined his solicitations, and there was a blank in his life besides. For he missed, in the morning and the evening, the face and figure of his child; the little caresses that smoothed out, at least in fancy, the furrows and fissures of Time and Care. And then he did not understand why she should be sacrificed. He always thought Antigone a fool to trouble so much about a corpse.

"Why don't these clergymen mind their own business?" he said to his good wife. "They are forever intermeddling in family matters. Barbara would be here at home but for that excellent brother of yours."

"I'm sure the Canon is not to blame," she whispered; "Louis could not be left alone, and you know this house would be no asylum for him."

"I never intended it should," said the doctor. "That young gentleman must reap his wild oats where he sowed them. But if your charitable brother is so devoted to Louis, has he not a room at his presbytery to give him?"

"He has already offered his hospitality to Louis and Barbara," said the mother, with a little of the old spirit. "When they return from this brief trip they will stay with their uncle until Louis' health is completely restored."

" 'Twill be a protracted visit," said the doctor.

"It will be a pleasant one," retorted Lady Wilson. "Thank

God, *my* children have found in their priests their best and kindest friends."

Which shows that Lady Wilson had a little both of mother love and mother wit.

Luke Delmege did not visit the prison on Tuesday. He came up to town to make definite and final arrangements with the Bishop to affiliate to his adopted diocese. He had already written home to demand his *exeat* from his native diocese; and, as Seathorpe had blotted out Lisnalee from the map of his future, he thought he might as well make assurance doubly sure by taking out his affiliation at once. The Bishop was from home, and Luke asked Father Sheldon for a walk, in which he might unbosom himself to his friend. The latter did persuade him to call on the Wilsons; but they were out for a short visit, said the old housekeeper.

So the two good friends, Celt and Saxon as they were, once more found themselves amongst soldiers and babies on the well-trodden banks of the Serpentine, where Father Sheldon some years back had tried to extract that ailing tooth, and had failed egregiously.

"I need hardly tell you, Sheldon," said Luke bluntly, "that I have come to town with a purpose. My seven years' probation is up, and I am about to affiliate, once and forever, to this diocese."

Father Sheldon walked along slowly and in silence.

"I've made up my mind," said Luke, continuing, "that my work lies here in England. Everything points to it. So far, I have been fairly successful; and I have no doubt but that a still wider and more—well, useful career lies before me."

"You have given the matter a good deal of consideration?" said Father Sheldon.

"Yes. In fact, I have made up my mind on the subject since my last visit home."

"H'm. I'd advise you to return to Ireland!"

"What?" said Luke, stopping and looking angrily at his friend.

"I'd advise you to return home as soon as you are free to do so," said Father Sheldon, quietly. "You will do better there than here."

"I don't understand you, Sheldon," said Luke. "Do you mean that I've been a failure here?"

"N-no," said Father Sheldon, languidly. "But I think that eventually you would make better strides with your feet upon your native heather."

"You speak as one not knowing," said Luke. "Why, man, if I were to return now, I should have to commence all over again."

"How is that?" asked his friend.

"You see, everything in Ireland is fixed in a cast-iron mold. They don't understand change, which is progress. Everything is judged by age. You buy a bottle of wine—the first question is: How old is it? You buy a horse: How old? Everything is old, and feeble, and decrepit; and no matter how distinguished a man may be in England or in America, you sink down to a cipher the moment you touch the Irish shore; and a Newman or a Lacordaire takes his place at the end of the queue. No one asks: What can you do? or, What have you done? But, How old are you? How long have you been on the mission? Result: After a few spasmodic efforts, which become convulsive, you sink into a lethargy, from which there is no awakening. You become aged, not by years, but by despair."

"That is sad. But you have work, nevertheless, have you not?"

"Of course, but uncongenial. Every round man is in a square hole, and every square man in a round hole. There's a great friend of mine (you must come over to see him)—"

"No, thank you," said Father Sheldon. "I don't value life too highly, but I don't care to throw it away in curiosity."

"You're joking. They'll pray for you in the Cathedral while you're in the proximate danger of death; but I was saying that distinguished man, a graduate of Heidelberg, a good German scholar, is banished to a strip of sand down by the sea, which he calls a parish. I assure you he would do honor to any diocese or church in England."

"Pretty bad. Have you approached the Bishop here?"

"No, not yet. But that's all right. I don't want much. I'm not ambitious. But there's a little place down here in Sussex, where a resident priest is badly wanting. I shall propose to the Bishop to allow me to open a mission there. Of course, the income is miserable, but I can eke out a subsistence with my pen."

"Have you tried as yet that expeditious way of making ends meet?"

"Well, no. But I know that Dr. Drysdale manages to make a clean hundred a year with his pen."

"Oh! Well," said Father Sheldon, shrugging his shoulders, "I suppose you must only await the Bishop's decision. By the way, do you know Halleck?"

"Yes, well. A clever fellow. Indeed, the only one in my congregation that I fear on Sundays."

"Indeed? You needn't fear him much longer, I think."

"How? Is he going abroad?"

"No. But he has started a religion of his own, like all good Englishmen. He calls himself an 'eclectic.' "

"By Jove! I didn't hear that. Now that I remember, Drysdale was speculating lately what he would do with certain people who were what he called latitudinarian."

"Well. And what did he decide?"

"He would not admit them to Sacraments. Rather hard, I thought. I didn't know he meant Halleck. Where did Halleck split?"

"Nowhere in particular. Slipped his anchors and went a-ground."

"That's horrible. I must look him up, poor fellow, and bring him back. I always told Drysdale that these frigid sermons of his would do mischief. He couldn't understand that we must keep pace with the age and read up all that it has to say. You couldn't expect a man like Halleck to sit still under first, secondly, thirdly, fourthly, fifthly, sixthly of the old-fashioned *prônes*. But it is so hard to convince old fossils of these things that seem axiomatic."

"Quite so. But Halleck went further. It was an article in the *Athenæum* that revealed him. Something about the *Book of Thoth*."

Luke turned white and crimson alternately. It was a dread shock to a soul that, if anything, was faithful beyond measure to his old principles and beliefs. The thought that he, Luke Delmege, through false notions of culture, sprung from human vanity, should actually be instrumental in wrecking the faith of an able and distinguished convert, was too horrible. He could conceive no more dire calamity. He knew well what Father Sheldon meant; and the old text about "the lying prophets" smote on his memory. He foresaw the consequences to himself. But he was too generous to heed them. He only thought that he had been instrumental in imperilling, if not altogether ruining, the salvation of a soul. The two friends walked up and down in silence for a time. Then Luke moaned aloud; but, choking down his emotion, he said humbly:—

"Let us return. I must catch the evening train to Aylesburgh."

It was a very gentle, conscience-stricken man that entered the county prison next morning. In cell 21, on the first corridor, he found his prisoner.

"Pretty bad business, sir," said the warder. It was the old, old story. The proud and effeminate imperialist, fresh from the voluptuousness of the capital, and the strong-thewed gladiator from Scythia, grimed from the soot of battle, and hardened from the baptisms of fire. And it was all for England, and England did not know it. How could she? And how could that imbecile understand the awful death he was summoning from a smitten soul, when he walked around that clean, brave man, and called him, "a dirty Irish pig."

"Wance more," said the pig, "and he's in hell."

"Keep quiet, ye ruffian," said his comrade, "and let the divil and his piper pass."

Too late. For the piper piped:—

"One step to the rear, you, sir, till I examine your kit."

Then the cartridge was slipped quietly into its deadly cradle.

"And thin," said the prisoner, "he kem in front av me, and laughed. An' somethin' snapped in me head, and my finger tetched the thrigger; an' he was lying in a heap on the ground. That's all!"

"There's no defence possible here," thought Luke.

None. And in a few weeks the sentence went forth. Death for death.

"I've wan request to make, my Lord," said the prisoner. "Gi' me the priest, and let me be hanged in half an hour."

Monstrous! That would be contrary to all precedent. It would be abominable cruelty. Four weeks at least should intervene. Four weeks of fiendish torture—the torture of seeing a cruel and inevitable horror creeping hour by hour and minute by minute before one's eyes, without a hope of escape or mitigation. Four weeks of slow death, to which the brutalities of the Sioux and the Comanche were mercy. For there, whilst the knives quivered in the victim's flesh, and the tomahawks sang over his head, his blood was on fire with anger and pride; and, as in the heat of battle men will not feel the sting and smart of wounds, so under physical torture men heed neither pain nor death. But lo! that awakening in the morning from dreams of childhood—from daisied meadows and laughing streams and brilliant sunshine to the whitewash of the condemned cell, and the dread specter of the fatal morning one day nearer; and Oh! the long hours of consciousness, unbroken by one single moment's distraction from the tense horror that haunts him; and Oh! the presence of these silent warders, watching, watching, lest the wretched victim should escape the vengeance of the law; and the very luxury of the food that is proffered and sent away uneaten, as if food could quench the burning wheels of a brain on fire with dread foreboding; and the cold, calculated sympathy, whilst the meshes are tightening around the doomed one; and finally, the hideous drama on the fatal morning, to which the horrors of the Roman arena were but stage representations, so cold, and callous, and inexorable does the hand of man choke out the immortal soul; and then the unspeakable mockery of calling this hideous and hidden tragedy a "painless death"; Oh! 'tis all too dreadful even for this polished and cultured generation, that knows nothing and cares less for the charity of Christ.

It was a happy distraction for Luke that his sympathies were engaged in soothing the last days of this unhappy man; for his own supreme folly would otherwise have driven him half-mad. Yes! Halleck had apostatized; and the fine eclecticism of Amiel Lefevril could not mitigate the shame or the horror. The positive, divine truth of the Catholic truth never struck Luke Delmege so forcibly as when he realized that playing with the ineffable mysteries of faith was a dangerous game. Doctrines to be proved; objections to be met; principles to be defended—all this sounded commonplace to a dialectician, and scarcely affected his sense of responsibility. But "a soul lost by your misdirection!" The thought was too dreadful. The sad work of preparing a criminal for death came as a relief. But how Luke was tortured during that month of gloom his diary testifies.

"*August* 18.—Said Mass for Halleck. Poor fellow gone abroad. No trace. Visited Donnelly. Bearing up well, he says, but in the morning when he wakes and the dread horror strikes him! Is very repentant, poor fellow. Discussion with Canon about capital punishment, on theological principles. Where and when was society invested with the supreme attribute of taking human life? He could only say, in the old formula, 'Commencez, Messieurs les assassins!'

"*August* 20.—Letter from Sheldon. Wilsons going abroad. Letter from Father Martin. Great annoyance at home at the thought of my leaving my native diocese. Saw poor Donnelly. The good nuns spent two hours with him today. Very much consoled. 'Father, if I could get my blood up, 'twould be all right. Would it be any harm to pick a quarrel with these poor fellows and have a friendly fight? If they'd take me out wanst a day and scourge me, 'twould make me mad, an' I'd have somethin' to think about besides the drop.' Paid a short visit to the Lefevrils. Rarely go there now. They cannot understand my awful trouble about Halleck. 'He's made no change,' they say; 'he's as he always was.' The devil himself cannot knock this notion of private judgment out of the minds of these people. Why should he, indeed? 'Tis his trump card.

"*August* 21.—Sunday. Mass at convent. Preached at *Missa Cantata*. The Canon very kind about Halleck's affair. He actually, for the first time, said a kind word about my sermon, which I considered commonplace. Why are the old so economical about kind words to the young? They are cheap; and God only knows what a splendid tonic is a kind word. I cannot get poor Donnelly out of my head. His face haunts me. The drawn look on the cheeks, the staring eyes, the cold, clammy perspiration on his forehead and in his hands. What a mercy if they had hanged him a fortnight ago! Yet another fortnight—twenty thousand minutes of anguish, and each minute a hell! I cannot sleep these nights. Donnelly and Halleck haunt me. Which is worse—the dead soul or the strangled body?

"*August* 22.—The Canon and I have a bad falling-out about this poor fellow. I put it bluntly to him last night after tea: what right has society, if it has the right to destroy human life at all, which I emphatically deny, to heap up torture of this kind on a condemned man, and then plunge him into a fearful and appalling death? Why does not she—I suppose it is *she*—use the more merciful form, the Socratic hemlock or chloroform? Who gave society the right to torture as well as to kill?

"Letter from Bishop. Rather ambiguous. A great many if's and

but's. Who knows? Perhaps, after all, I shall return to Ireland.
Infandum!

"*August* 24.—Reading up St. Thomas today. Ugh! It's like
eating sawdust after Mill and Stewart. Why—well, there I am
again, always questioning, always puzzled. A letter from the old
gentleman at Seathorpe, asking whether I had considered his proposal. Certainly, my dear old friend, but others have to consider
too. Wrote today to Donnelly's P.P. in Ireland. 'Av I had took his
advice I wouldn't be here the day.' *Sic damnatus!*

"*August* 25.—Letter from Olivette Lefevril, inclosing one from
Halleck and detailing his future plans. Evidently uneasy in his
horrible apostasy and flinging all the blame on me!!! 'Quite clear,'
he says, 'that a good many Roman Catholic clergymen are of my
way of thinking. Indeed, it was the sermons of our good friend,
Mr. Delmege, that gave this fresh bias to my thoughts!' What a
beastly lie! The fellow was always a free-thinker and hardly concealed it. I defy any one to quote a single passage from my sermons
that is not orthodox!

"*August* 27.—Looked up all my sermons yesterday again.
There's not a word that could be construed, even by the foulest
imagination, into an apology, or the faintest shadow of excuse for
heresy in any shape or form. Why, 'tis the very thing I have always
hated and loathed. But these hypocrites are forever seeking to fling
over the blame of their apostasies on others. Even the good Cardinal: 'England did not abandon the faith; she was robbed of it.'
Bosh! Poor Donnelly calmer, except in the morning. Yes; one
gets used to everything in this world!

"*August* 29.—Nothing would do this old gentleman but to drag
up this infernal question again. He seems to gloat over the horrible
approaching death of poor Donnelly. I wonder was Christianity
ever preached in this country? 'Coming near the end, sir!' said the
old governor today, rubbing his hands, as if he were after playing
a game of whist. 'Bearing up well, poor chap!' Casabianca complaining and whining that his nerves are disturbed by the sounds of
the carpenters at the scaffold! Ugh! Isn't it horrible? I suppose I'll
never sleep again. I was alone, after Benediction tonight in the
church, trying to say a prayer for poor Donnelly. Alone with HIM!
Then a sudden horror seized me, and I fled.

"*August* 30.—'A couple of days more, yer reverence, and 'twill
be all over. Yer reverence, wouldn't ye say a little word to rouse
me and make me forget meself? Whin the nuns come here I'm all
right for hours after.' I wonder what does the poor fellow mean?
The Canon opened up the matter again tonight. Society has to use
the law as a deterrent and a punishment, as well as a protection.
This I denied *in toto.* Society has a right to protect itself—no more.

Can it be protected by locking up criminals? If so, then it has no right to murder. If it has a right to take life, then that should be done in the easiest and decentest manner. 'But this is a painless death!' No use in talking. The English have no imagination. A painless death! A death into which all the horrors of hell are concentrated; a death to which all the alleged tortures of the Middle Ages were the sweetest ecstasies. I wonder will I keep my reason the fatal morning? I have been thinking of asking Drysdale to take my place. But poor Donnelly won't have it. Oh! if I could but sleep. And Halleck attending Mass and going to Communion in Chalons, so the papers say.

"*September* 1.—The Canon hints broadly that I'm not wanted in the diocese. *He bien!* The world is all before me, where to choose. But have I cut the ground from under my feet at home? Let me suppose that the Bishop sent over my *exeat,* as I requested, where am I? Nobody's child. Donnelly, I fear, will lose his reason, and so shall I. There's a look as of a maniac in his eye. The nuns soothe him wonderfully with the story of the Passion of our Lord. 'Spake to me of that,' he says, 'an' I'm all right.' I try to console him with the assurance that we are all moving in the same direction as himself. 'Spake to me of *that,*' he says. Poor fellow! And he looked into the black mouth of the cannon without fear, in the mutiny, when the Sepoys had actually touched the powder with the fuse.

"*September* 2.—Said Mass for poor Donnelly. Looked up all my past sermons again. I offered to submit them to the Canon last night, and let him say was there anything objectionable in them. 'No thank you!' was his reply. Letter from my clerical friend at Seathorpe, asking me to use my great influence with his uncle to secure an advance of a few pounds; or, if I preferred, to advance the money myself. Donnelly in a bad state. Eyes staring; hands trembling; no food. Something will snap in his head again, I fear. He told me this morning he had a sunstroke in India. This accounts for a good deal.

"*September* 3.—Visited Donnelly. Strange to say, he's cooler and quieter than he has been since his sentence. Poor fellow! He made me sole legatee. Medals, Lucknow, Oude, a cane wreathed with serpents, an idol stolen from a Burmese pagoda, and a stone —topaz, I think—which, he says, seen under a peculiar light, breaks into flames, etc. What a strange history! The history of a vagrant and ubiquitous race, that hate their country when they are in it, and yearn for it when they are absent. I wonder shall I sleep tonight. . . . Broke down in resolution this afternoon, and asked the Canon to accompany poor Donnelly to death. I can never face it. 'No thank you!' was his reply. I wonder what strange chemical did the Lord mix with the clay from which He fashioned these good English?"

Here the diary breaks off and is not resumed for many a day. It would appear that Luke, after a sleepless night, woke, sick and weary, to the dread dawn. The excellent Canon was to say the convent Mass, and Luke was to come straight from the prison, after the execution, to celebrate the Holy Sacrifice for the poor dead soldier. That program had to be altered. Luke did brace himself for the frightful ordeal; did go to the prison, where a strange thing took place. For the strange grace was given to the poor condemned of a moment's distraction from his awful fate; he saw the horror in Luke's face worse than his own. He noticed his trembling hands, his white, drawn face; and, with the sympathy of his race, he forgot himself in his anxiety for his poor priest. "Bear up, yer reverence!" he said, as they pinioned his hands; " 'twill be all over in a minit; don't let thim Prodestans," he whispered, "say ye broke down." In vain. With horror, shuddering through every limb, Luke stepped along, the poor, condemned man reciting the Litanies, and, at the same time, trying to console the priest. Stupefied and only semi-conscious, he stood on the scaffold, shuddered at the cool, calculated arrangements for destruction; watched, as in a dream, the stare of the warders, and the doctor, with his watch in his hand, and the cruel machinery. The priest dare not look on the face of the doomed man, which at this supreme moment was tightened, every nerve and muscle tense with agony. Then there was a frightful crash, a stifled moan of human pain, and the swish of the body, as it plunged into the gloom of the pit. Luke felt the rope tightening, as it dragged the shrieking soul from the body; then easily vibrating, as a beast that holds its prey, it swung to and fro within a foot from where he stood. Then, like a drunken man, he staggered from the scaffold and made his way to the corridor. He heard some one say, "Not a hitch!"

The Governor followed hastily to proffer hospitality. That must never be forgotten.

"It passed off well, sir! Quite a painless death! You look pale! Have a glass—"

But Luke had fainted and fallen heavily on the tiled pavement.

CHAPTER XXIII

The Rhine Falls

"YOUR YOUNG men shall see visions, and your old men shall dream dreams." And Father Meade, successor to Father Tim in the parish of Gortnagoshel, had a dream. And although he had been teaching for forty years that it was sinful to give credit to dreams, fortune-telling, or to attach any importance to omens and accidents, it is regrettable to have a record that Father Meade believed in that dream. He thought he was down by the sea, near Father Martin's, and it was a wild, tempestuous night; dark as Erebus, but for the white flecks in the tumult of waves and the white sheets that floated to his feet. He did not know what brought him there; but as he gazed out on the midnight desolation he heard a cry afar off; and out from the swirl of waters, and conquering the screams of the storm, came clearly and distinctly to his ears the words: Allua! Allua!! Allua!!! Then he thought Luke Delmege rushed down from the cliffs and plunged into the boiling waters, and— Father Meade awoke, and when he had gathered together his scattered senses, he asked himself angrily: What did I eat? For he prided himself on his constitutional habits, and had arranged with his stomach and the Fates that he would see a century at least. Then he decided it was "corned beef," a dish rather dangerous from its attractiveness.

"I should have taken a second tumbler," he murmured, and dropped to sleep again.

But when morning dawned, and he sat meditatively by his fire, for the frosts had come early this year, his dream recurred to him again and again; and Allua! Allua! rang in his ears and floated across the lines of the psalms in his Breviary. And somehow the syllables were familiar, although memory refused

251

to unlock the secret for a long time. Then, very suddenly, as is the wont of memory, a scene flashed out upon his mind. It was a convent school, there in the heart of the city; and there was an "exhibition." That is, the children were all in their Sunday dresses, and there were great piles of currant-cake on the side tables, and very beautiful singing of grand old Irish melodies, and an address to himself. And then a dear little child stepped to the front and, with inimitable self-possession, commenced to recite Callanan's famous poem:—

There is a green island in lone Gougaune Barra.

But she tripped at the next line, for the Easter hymns were in her ears, and she blundered into—

Where Alleluia of song rushes forth like an arrow.

And Allua became her nickname from that day forward.

Now, Father Meade, then a dashing young curate, was enthusiastic; and, in his delight and ecstasy, he made a speech, and the speech contained a promise. It was a rash one, as may be supposed.

"Wherever," he said, "you, my little children, may be scattered in after life—North, South, East, West, America, England, Australia, New Zealand—you must count upon me as your father and your friend, and appeal to me, nay, command me, to come to your assistance should you ever require it."

He often thought of that promise in after life, although he was seldom called upon to redeem it. For somehow, there, in their humble homes and by lonely firesides, the hearts of these Irish priests are forever stretching out and yearning after their exiled childen, and wondering what has become of the lads who served their Masses in the mountain cabins, or held their horses' heads during a sick call; or the little maids, who peeped from their humble snoods, and wondered at the awful might and dignity of the priest, or blushed at the faintest praise in the dingy school. But now, after a lapse of thirty years, "Allua of song" has called to him to keep his promise, and Allua is in trouble and wants him. He was puzzled, and thought of consulting his housekeeper. Then he dreaded her sarcasm. She was always trying to make him practical, to keep him from giving good shoes, "that 'ud bear to be soled agin," to a tramp whose toes were in evidence; or stealing some of her fine, home-cured bacon, that she was reserving for a grand party. Then he tried to shake off that dream and that memory. No use! There it was, and the voice of the dream in his ears. Then he thought of consulting his neighbor, Father Cussen. The worst thing a parish priest could do is to consult a curate about anything. He'll tell the world about it and crow over you ever after. Father Meade finally decided to go down and see the scene of the midnight horror, and judge how far it was real and how far imaginary. It was a good, brisk walk; but Father Meade intended to be a centenarian, and that was a long way off as yet. So he took his stand on the shelf of rock, just where he had stood in his dream, and looked out over the mighty waste. All along, over to where a faint dim line of haze marked the eagle beak of Loop Head, the sea stretched in almost provoking calmness. Not a ripple, on this calm September day, fretted the polished surface, save where, right in the center of the vast estuary, a very faint ruffling marked where the great leap of the mighty river was challenged by the insweeping tide. But there was neither wind nor wave; and yet, as the old priest looked, he found it not difficult to imagine that Allua! Allua! was borne to his ears across the waste of waters. He turned homewards, puzzled and anxious; but as his road ran down by the shrubbery that fringed the outer wall of Father Martin's garden, he thought he might give a call. The result was that a few days later, when Luke had recovered from the shock he had received and was able to open his correspondence, he read:—

"My dear Father Delmege:—If you should come across, in your travels through London or elsewhere, a little girl (but now, I suppose, a young woman), answering to the name of Allua, tell her I have got her message, and will befriend her, if she is in trouble, as I suspect.   Faithfully yours,
                    "William Meade, P.P."

"That's an exact counterpart to the letter addressed: 'My son in America,'" said Luke; and he thought no more of it.

Especially as the same mail had brought him a letter from his Bishop, very kind and sympathetic, warning him of the seriousness of the step he was meditating, and assuring him of a mission at home if he could only make up his mind to return.

"I think," his Lordship wrote, "as you were educated for your own diocese, you ought to serve in your own diocese. But I shall not recall you against your own wishes."

"Then the ground is not quite cut from under my feet," said Luke; and he wrote promptly to say that he would return for the 1st of October, after a brief trip on the Continent, whither he had been ordered by his physician.

He ran up to the city to explain his intentions. He remained for dinner. He was seated next a mighty traveller—a kind of latter-day Abbé Huc, who was infinitely polite and condescending, asked Luke many questions, and gave him valuable information as to his route to Switzerland. Luke was very happy in thinking that his own amiability promptly secured friends in all directions. There was not a word about Halleck, or the slightest allusion to Canon Drysdale or Aylesburgh. His seven years' apprenticeship was unnoticed. Nor was there a syllable of regret that he was no longer to labor and live amongst them.

Two nights after, Luke stood on the platform of the station at the frontier town of Herbesthal. His train was shunted to make way for the great continental express. Luke walked up and down, having given his valise to a porter, and he saw representatives of every nation under heaven. At twelve o'clock the great express rolled in, lighted from stem to stern; and the long corridor that ran from end to end of the train was thronged with passengers, whose very presence indicated that their lines had been cast in pleasant places in this life, and that they were determined to make the most of the opportunity. Luke was half afraid of these elect of society; for, although he had learned a good deal during his apprenticeship, he was fortunate enough as yet to have retained a little of his idealism. He had not yet reached that dread stage in life where everything has become mean and commonplace under the gray aspects of experience. But he ventured to look at all these grand personages, and one figure and face arrested him. The gentleman was dressed in a gray travelling suit, and had a

Scotch plaid shawl rolled round his shoulders; but it is—no—
it must be the face of the Abbé Huc. The face was looking
down with calm indifference at Luke, with the unmistakable
expression: "I know you well, but I don't want to improve the
acquaintance." But Luke's Celtic impetuosity refused to accept
the hint; and half sure of himself, and yet afraid to commit a
stupid blunder, he approached, lifted his hat, and said:—

"Pardon, Monsieur: je suis un prêtre Catholique—"

The traveller drew himself up proudly, and said stiffly:—

"Et moi, je suis aussi un prêtre Catholique."

Luke was dumbstricken. This was the man by whose side
he had sat two nights ago, and who had been as polite and
solicitous as if he had known Luke for a lifetime. Luke drew
back now, stung with the cold refusal of acquaintanceship;
and the train moved on. But the Abbé Huc watched him,
watched him to the end. Luke was learning a little of the
world, and the knowledge was creating a strange yearning for
home.

There was a pretty little episode just as his own train was
about to start. Like all good travellers, Luke was determined
to guard against imposition, but to be generous. And so when a
gorgeous official approached him and said something in German, of which Luke understood but the one word, *commissionaire,* Luke shook his head sadly. But when the porter came up
with his valise, Luke was generous and even royal. He handed
the porter a coin, which he thought amply rewarded him for
his labor. The porter smiled, lifted his hat, bowed, and departed, but returned in a moment furious. He leaped into the
carriage, and gesticulated wildly, holding the wretched coin
in his hand, and muttering *pfennig; pfennig!* It would be difficult to say by what process of reasoning Luke had persuaded
himself that a pfennig was the German equivalent of a franc;
but so it was; and this accounted for his royal gesture. But
there was a difference of opinion clearly; and it emphasized
itself in sundry gestures and objurgations, the magnificent
commissionaire looking on approvingly.

"Un pfennig! oui, oui! c'est un franc!" said Luke.

The porter stamped about the carriage and tore his hair.

"Cela suffit pour vous!" said Luke, calmly, and determined
not to be swindled.

The German appealed to the stars and angels. These failing, he appealed to the commissionaire. The latter rolled out a string of decasyllables. Luke was convinced it was a conspiracy. He talked wonderful French. They talked wonderful German. At last the train moved out slowly. The porter clung to the carriage door to the last. Then, breathing a parting malediction, he leaped down, panting and perspiring. Luke leaned back in the carriage, as they plunged into the night, and congratulated himself on his firmness.

And then through all the wonders of Cologne and the Rhine; and up, up, through the Black Mountains of the Hartz, through the thirty-eight tunnels that gaped out of the corkscrew railway, swallowed the train and disgorged it; up, up, through pine forests and along the crest of hills, in whose bosom nestled the loveliest valleys, each with its church and spire and cemetery, until at last they rested at Bingen. Then a plunge downwards and they were at Schaffhausen, where the mighty legendary river curvets and ricochets in childish humor before assuming the majesty of its seaward course.

Here Luke sojourned for two days—golden days that ever shone pale but resplendent from the mists of memory. That Sunday at the Schweizer-Hof was a dream for a lifetime. He went down to early Mass at the village, heard the beautiful Gregorian for the first time since he left Maynooth; heard, without understanding, the sermon in German that stretched through three-quarters of an hour; breakfasted at 11:30, and lounged through the day under golden sunshine, the great river fretting itself at his feet, and the horizon serrated with the yellow crests of the mighty Alps. In the afternoon he sauntered out for a walk and climbed Hohen Flüh. After the narrow and limited and choking surroundings of the past seven years, the superb panorama that opened to his eyes from the high summit of the hill fairly took away his breath. "Lord," he said, lifting his hat, "it is good for us to be here." He felt free again. The clear air, the almost boundless horizon, the vast infinity of the mountain barriers, closing the vista, yet opening the imagination to undreamed sublimities, the long ribbon of the Rhine flowing amidst its vineyards and orchards, the villages clustering under red roofs here and there across the landscape, a hill, crested with crumbling castle, as if Nature were trying

her 'prentice hand before she attempted her eternal master-
pieces, and moving here and there, little groups of peaceful
Germans, enjoying the sweet Sabbath air—Luke thought for
a moment, as he sat and listened to three German children,
singing a Sunday hymn, there amongst the pines, of the squalor
and fœtor, the smoke and sin, of the mighty mill called England. The noise and the jar and the cold, deadly, soulless
mechanism were far away. "Ugh!" said Luke. "Thank God I
am done with it and the ugly dream forever." He turned round
to descend the declivity and came face to face with Halleck.

Had they been two Celts they would have passed each other
with a scowl. One was a Briton, and he said:—

"How do you do, Mr. Delmege? This is a rare pleasure."

"How do you do?" said Luke, too surprised to say more.

"I did not know that you had come abroad," continued Halleck. "Let me hope that you intend a long sojourn in this delightful country."

"A long sojourn of twenty-four hours," replied Luke.

"I'm very sorry. I know no place that appeals so strongly
to one's sense of freedom. When you plunge into those tunnels
of the Alps, you feel choked, as if the air were compressed into
a solid mass by the weight of snow and granite. Here you are
free, with a boundless horizon and unlimited loveliness."

"Yes," said Luke, carried on by the stream; "I often heard
that, to see the Alps to advantage, one must approach them
from Italy."

"Quite so," said Halleck. "And you must return? I was
hoping for the pleasure of your society and cooperation here.
I am reading in the library at St. Gall's for a work I expect
to issue soon from the press, and you could be of much assistance."

"I regret that my assistance heretofore has been to give your
thoughts a wrong bias," said Luke, seizing the opportunity.

"Indeed! A wrong bias. Pray, how?"

"I regretted to hear that it was some sermons of mine drove
you from the Church."

"But I have not been driven from the Church. That is quite
a mistake. Nay, more, I cannot be driven."

"But pardon me for the harsh expression, the Church has
repudiated you, and you cannot approach the Sacraments."

"Cannot? Why, I do. I have been to Communion this morning down there at Schaffhausen."

"We regard such conduct as sacrilegious and dishonorable," said Luke, exasperated by Halleck's coolness.

"Oh! and who cares what you regard? Your opinion is of no consequence to me whatsoever."

"I have not sought this interview, Mr. Halleck," said Luke, "and with your permission I shall terminate it. But you have no right to utter a calumny; and, as a gentleman, you should promptly retract what you wrote to Miss Lefevril concerning my misdirection."

"But if it is true? Your theology may allow it; but I, as an English gentleman, cannot tell a falsehood."

"But your statement that our priests were—well—liberal, and, indeed, rather free in their opinions; and that I especially shared that liberalism, is incorrect and, pardon me—a lie. We hold firmly and unreservedly the dogmatic teachings of the Church."

"Then you must take the alternative—that your knowledge of the English language, which, indeed, like everything English, does not lend itself to the restrictions of dogma, is extremely limited. You don't seem to understand the vast responsibilities of words in solemn places."

"It may be so," said Luke, humbly.

They were silent for a few minutes. The three little Swiss girls were still singing beneath them on a rustic seat, under a clump of firs. At last Halleck spoke:—

"Let us not part in anger, Mr. Delmege. I am sorry I have hurt you. But—the faithful Israelites would do well, during their captivity, not to look too curiously on the gods of Babylon."

Halleck raised his hat as he passed down the steep steps to the road.

Had this taken place in London it would have given Luke a fit of depression for several days. Here, in the bright sunshine and crystal atmosphere, he flung the moment's chagrin instantly aside. So, too, in the afternoon, the discovery that a pfennig, instead of being equivalent to a franc, was equivalent to the hundredth part of a franc, sent the blood mounting to Luke's forehead, but only for a moment.

"That porter should have assassinated me," he said, and thought no more of it. Only there was a craving in his heart, growing every minute, for the peace and serenity, the security and happiness, of home.

"The crust of bread and the cruse of water are better than the fleshpots of the Egyptians," he thought.

He left the vast dining-hall early that evening. The splendors of society were beginning to pall on him. He craved rest for thought from the glitter and sparkle of fashion; and long before the last dishes were brought around, he had ensconced himself in the gas-lit veranda at the farthest window. Here, with a small round table by his side, and some coffee and rusks, he hid behind a heavy curtain, and awaited the illumination of the falls.

At half-past nine the entire body of visitors had assembled in the veranda, and the lights were lowered until the place had become quite dark. Darkness, too, hung over the valley, and no one could dream that man was there. But a pearly glimmer, as of twilight, shone where the eye was drawn by hearing, as the fall fretted in the shallows, or was torn into streamlets by the granite rocks beneath. Then, as at light's first dawning, a faint pink, roseate in its heart, and fading into purple, streamed across the valley, and the falls blushed under the revelation, and seemed to answer louder to the call of light. And so the pink dawn hovered o'er the valley, until it paused, hesitated, faded, and there was darkness again, but for the voice that pierced it—the voice of many waters in the night.

Luke turned around, and saw standing, quite close to his chair,—for every seat was occupied,—a feeble old man and his daughter. He leaned heavily on her arm, and his white hair made a light in the darkened room. Instantly Luke arose and proffered his chair. The young lady thanked him, as the old man sank wearily into the arm-chair. She took her place near him, and Luke went back into the shadows and sat on a rough bench that ran around the wall. The falls were lighted again with green and then with blue lights, and the waiters came and raised the gas-jets. Man's little play with mighty nature was over.

As Luke rose to pass from the veranda, a voice said to him:—

"I didn't know in the darkness that it was Father Delmege we had to thank for his courtesy."

It was Barbara Wilson. Luke flushed with pleasure. After all his neglect, it was comforting to know that he had unconsciously done a small favor. And then through her lips his country and home spoke to him.

"Miss Wilson!" he said. "It is an unexpected pleasure to meet you. I didn't know you were travelling with your father."

"It is not father," she said, her lips trembling; "it is Louis. You will scarce recognize him."

She led him over to where Louis was still sitting. His face was turned outward towards the night, and it was the face of death. His sad eyes saw but darkness, and his trembling hands clutched at the air, as the hands of a half-perished outcast spread for warmth before a fire. And his hair streamed down on his shoulders, and it was white in the dreary gas-light, not with the venerable silver of honored age, but with the ghastly luster of blanched and bloodless youth. He turned at his sister's voice and tried to rise, but fell back helplessly.

"Yes, of course, Father Delmege," he said, not looking upwards, but out into the night, his weak memory trying to grip the slippery and evanescent shadows of the past. "Yes, of course, Father—I beg pardon—how do you do, sir? I hope you are well."

"Don't you remember, Louis dearest, don't you remember Lisnalee and uncle, and all our pleasant days? This is Father Delmege, who is always so kind."

"To be sure, to be sure. How do you do, sir? I hope I see you very well," said the poor invalid.

"Now, Louis dear, do rouse yourself. Tomorrow we shall go on to Lucerne, and you must pick up strength for the journey. Were not the illuminations beautiful? It was Father Delmege who kindly gave us his place."

"To be sure, to be sure. How much do I owe you, sir? I always pay promptly. But, Barbara, why did you let them throw that horrid limelight on the stage? No artist would have done it. If Elfrida was to throw herself from that bridge it would be in the darkness. I saw her; 'twas well done, I tell you. Madame Lerida *is* an artist. Did you hear that scream? Oh! Oh!"

Barbara raised her head and looked pitifully at Luke.

"There," said Louis, still wandering, "there she goes adown the stream, her long hair floating behind her, and she tossed from side to side of the rapids. Hark! there 'tis again! Elfrida! Elfrida!"

This he shrieked aloud, so that the waiters paused as they arranged the breakfast tables, and one or two timid visitors hurriedly fled the veranda.

"This won't do," said Luke, kindly; "we must get him away."

"Come, dearest," said Barbara, her hand around Louis' neck. "Come, 'tis bedtime."

He rose wearily, seemingly anxious to follow his dream through the night and adown the river.

"It was a clever impersonation," he continued. "That leap from the bridge was perfect. But to throw that vile calcium on such an *artiste* at such a moment was an outrage, sir, an outrage!"

"This is Father Delmege, Louis dear," said Barbara, as Luke helped the poor invalid forward. "You remember, don't you?"

"Of course, of course. How do you do, sir? I hope I see you well."

Luke helped along the corridor, and then stood still, at the foot of the staircase, watching the two figures, the white-haired imbecile, and the tall, lithe form of the fair sister, toiling wearily step by step up to the second corridor. Then he went out into the piazza. The full moon was now rising, and just casting her beams down the valley and across the chasm to the old castle that held watch and ward over the turbulent youth of the river. How paltry and mean are the feeble attempts of men, contrasted with the enterprises of the Almighty! The wretched illumination of an hour ago—what a sacrilege on the majesty of nature, now that nature itself was triumphant! Luke gazed down the valley; but he saw—the two weary figures toiling up the long stairs—strong, tender womanhood supporting a broken and disjointed manhood. He saw a sister's love covering a brother's shame. He saw the old Greek sacrifice again—the sister imperilling her life and honor to pay due, solemn rites to the dead. How paltry his learned and æsthetic friends seem now! How contemptible their dreary platitudes! How empty

and hollow their fine theorizing about humanity and the race!
"Seek the God in man!" Was there ever such blasphemy? And
himself—what had been his life for seven years? Compared
with the noble self-surrender of this young girl, how hollow
and empty and pitiful had been his fine sermons, his dignified
platitudes, his straining after effect, his misdirection. Conscience for the first time whispered "Idiota," but too faintly to
be heeded.

A hand was laid on his arm, and Halleck, removing a cigar
from his mouth, said:—

"I would recommend you, Mr. Delmege, to get that young
friend of yours home as soon as possible. It will be hardly
pleasant for her to travel with a coffin."

He went to his room—a very beautiful room, with its par-
quetted floor, polished and spotless—but he could not sleep.
He did not desire it. He coveted a few hours of the luxury of
thought. He had so much to think about, and so many thoughts
and memories fraught with the pain of pleasure, and so many
with the delight of pain. He opened his window, through which
the full moon was streaming, and stood on the balcony that
overhung the garden. The night view was limited, for the
garden sloped upwards to a little wood, where, laced against
the moonlight, the iron-work of a summer-house was traced.
He leaned over the balustrade and gave himself up to thought.
It was a turning-point in his life. Just then the deep tones of
the church-bell tolling the midnight hour floated up the valley,
and Luke thought he heard voices in the garden beneath.

"Here come Lorenzo and Jessica," he said. " 'How sweet the
moonlight' etc. I must go."

Ah, no! Not moonlight lovers, with all the glamor of affection and the poetry of life streaming around them, but the
wrecked life and the guardian angel again. Slowly they came
from the shadows into the moonlight, and Luke was not
ashamed to observe them. The poor gray head lay heavily
against the sister's shoulder, or rather on her breast, as she
twined her arm around his neck and supported his failing
steps. Clearly there was no sleep for that fretted and irritated
brain, or such sleep only as makes the awakening, heaven.
Slowly they passed under the balcony, and here Luke heard
the prayers that Barbara whispered in her brother's ears—
whispered, because her gentle spirit feared for the sleepers

overhead. But Luke could hear the rattle of the beads as they slipped through her fingers, and could see the flashing of the silver cross in the moonlight. On, on they went slowly, as the gravel groaned beneath the heavy steps of the invalid. And as they passed, Luke saw the beautiful uplifted face and the rich, black hair caught back from the pure white forehead. And as he closed the window of his bedroom softly and brushed his eyes, he said:—

"She is not mortal. She is a spirit and a symbol. It is my country's heroism and sorrow."

Next morning, without a moment's hesitation, he came over to the table where Barbara and Louis sat, and said:—

"Miss Wilson, *we* must return immediately. I am *en route* for Ireland, and you and Louis must come."

She gave a little glad cry of surprise and said:—

"Oh, thank God! We have got our orders. The landlord has demanded our rooms."

"Very good. Now, get ready."

"But, Father, we must not take you out of your way."

"Never mind," said Luke. "Our whole study now must be to get Louis back to London."

"And Ireland. Oh, how happy we shall be with dear uncle! You know he has asked us to come to him until Louis is quite restored."

"I am glad to hear it. Yes, your uncle is a good man. Cheer up, there are glad days in store for us all."

And so Luke Delmege, the optimist, argued, encouraged, cheered the lonely girl on that weary journey to Lucerne, Geneva, Paris, London, and set them down at No. 11 Albemarle Buildings, and felt that he had never been happier under the sublime elation of a little self-sacrifice.

It was late at night when he arrived from Switzerland, and, after he had left Barbara and her brother at their lodgings, he made his way across the city and the bridge to the Cathedral. He was thinking of many things—Halleck, Dr. Drysdale, Barbara, Louis, Seathorpe, Lisnalee, England, Ireland, the past, and his future. He had cut through the city by a short passage through the slums, but he had no fear. He knew the places well. The wretched pavements were silent of the noise of human traffic, for midnight had not come. He had just emerged into a square well known to him, for it had been in his district

formerly, when he saw a crowd gathering around a cab a little
ahead of him, and the portly English driver gesticulating violently. As he passed he heard the latter saying, in a tone of
anger and impatience, to the crowd:—

"A rum hold Hirish passon. Wants to get down 'ere somewhere; but I'm blessed if the hold bloke knows where. But
I'll make 'im pay; I will, I tell you."

Compassion for a countryman in distress, even though he
were a heretic, made Luke pause and approach. As he did, he
heard a deep voice from the dark recess:—

"Did the Lord ever make a stupid lot as these English? They
don't know their own country. Come here, honest woman, and
direct me. Glory be to God, and isn't that Luke Delmege?
Luke! Luke! come here! There's me dream out!"

Luke came nearer, and recognized, with an effort, the Rev.
Father Meade, incumbent of Gortnagoshel.

"What in the world?"—he was about to say, when Father
Meade interrupted.

"You got my letter? Of course you did. I knew ye'd be looking out for me. But, I couldn't rest easy, night or day, till I
come. But, Lord, what a pack of savages! They don't know
their own names. Tell that ruffian on the box to drive us to
Denham Court."

"You're in Denham Court, Father Meade," said Luke, "but
what wild goose chase are you on now?"

"Wild-goose chase? Faith, it isn't, me boy! Now, find out
No. 25 S—whatever S is!"

"I see," said Luke; "drive 25 South, my good man, just over
there."

"Now, so far, so good. Allua is here," the old priest whispered to Luke, "and I'm come for her."

He showed Luke a wretched slip of paper, in a still more
wretched envelope, sealed with soap, stampless, ink-stained,
and yellow; and surely enough—"Denham Court, 25 S., London, S.W." was marked there.

"What next?" thought Luke. But he said:—

"You may not know, Father Meade, the character of this
place and its neighborhood. This is a place where a person
must be careful—"

"I neither know nor care," said the old priest; "all I know is that Allua is here, that she is in trouble, and has called for me; and here I am. Stay here, my good man," he said to the driver. "If you stir from that spot, I'll take the law of you."

"All right, sir," said the driver; "but you'll have to pay for it."

"Come, Luke," said Father Meade, cavalierly, as he walked coolly into the wretched hall and up the broken stairs. "Ah, if I had that bosthoon in Ireland!"

On the first landing he knocked at four doors in succession. There was some shuffling and pulling of chairs, but no answer. Up the creaking stairs again, and again he knocked, and no reply.

"They're all asleep, or dead," he said.

Higher still and higher, till they came to an attic. Here was the sound of voices. They entered a wretched room. A feeble light was burning in a tin sconce. And by the faint illumination they saw a wretched pallet, on which lay an invalid in the last stages of consumption. She was gray and old, but her eyes were young as they challenged the priest.

"You got my letter," she said faintly in an English accent.

Father Meade hesitated. No one but the Father who is in heaven could recognize in that poor wreck, the child—the convent child of so many years ago. And the accent entirely bothered Father Meade.

"Are you Allua?" he said doubtingly.

"I am," she said faintly. "You're changed too, Father; but the Blessed Mother sent you. Take me from this."

Father Meade hesitated. He always boasted that he was "a man of the world"; and whenever, at a visitation dinner, he had to propose his Bishop's health, he always wound up the litany of praises by declaring that his Lordship was, above all things else, "a man of the world." So he was not going to be taken in by a girl with an English accent.

"I came for you," he said, "but I want to make sure. Say the lines again."

The poor patient smiled at the absurdity. But she gathered her strength and repeated:—

There is a green island in lone Gougaune Barra,
Where Allua of song rushes forth like an arrow.

"Good," said Father Meade. "And you said?" he cocked his ear.

"I said—'Alleluia of song,' because the priests were saying Alleluia all that week."

"Good," said Father Meade. "And I said?"

"You said—'My little children, wherever you are, North, South, East, West, remember I am always your father and your friend; and whenever you are in trouble call on me and I'll come to you.' "

"Never say another word," cried Father Meade. "Come here, you whipsters, dress her at once, and be quick about it," he cried to the two girls, who sank back from the awful presence of the priests.

The two priests went downstairs, Luke bewildered, Father Meade exultant.

"No use in talking," he said, "God beats us all. Just when we think we are doing something of ourselves, He steps in and shows His hand."

"Where are you going to take that poor girl?" said the practical Luke.

"Oh, I never thought of that," said Father Meade. "I'll take her to some hotel, and off to Limerick in the morning. Of course, she thinks I don't know anything; but I know all." And he winked at Luke.

In a few minutes the girls came downstairs, bearing the invalid between them. The hope and its realization had braced her up, and she looked almost vigorous as she stepped from the dreadful place.

"You ain't agoin' to take that there gal in the cab?" said the driver.

"Aren't I? Mind yer own business, me man, or I'll make you."

"Then you'll pay for it, I tell you," said the man in his bewilderment.

Gently and reverently they got the poor girl into the cab, Luke standing by motionless. He was wondering what Amiel Lefevril would say to such divine altruism as this. The two girls stood at the door. They had said good-bye to their companion. Sorrow, hopelessness, despair were on their faces. And just as the driver flicked his horse, and they were moving off,

they flung out their hands in a sudden gesture and sobbed:—
"Father, Father, don't leave us!"

"Eh? Eh? What's that? What's that? Stop, you ruffian, or I'll
knock you down. Come here, me poor girls. What do ye want?"

"We want to go with you, Father, anywhere, anywhere. Oh!
for God's sake, Father, don't leave us!"

What could he do? It was most imprudent; but he had too
much faith in God to hesitate.

"Come!" he said, whilst the cabman growled furiously, and
Luke gazed in stupid amazement. "Come, and let God do the
rest!"

Luke called to see the Wilsons next morning. He found
Louis actually revived. There had been a reaction after the
journey. Luke told them, with laughter and horror, of the
Quixotic drollery of Father Meade.

"He's taking them to Limerick," he said, "to the Magdalen
Asylum there. I have a sister in that convent, you know, Miss
Wilson. Some day I hope to have the pleasure of making you
acquainted with her. We shall call some day when we shall
have leisure."

He was surprised to see her start and put her hand over her
heart with a gesture of pain. The very suggestion of fallen
womanhood was such a shock and surprise to such a pure
soul. Magdalen! Magdalen! the dearest of all the saints outside the charmed circle of the Incarnation—how does it happen that there is a sting of pain in all the honeyed sweetness
of that dear name?

"She must have been told of Margery's unkind remarks,"
thought Luke.

"Now it is all settled," he said. "I shall be at Euston to meet
the 8:30 down mail on this day week. And you shall both
meet me there. Is that all settled?"

Of course. Quite understood. Everything now was moving
smoothly.

CHAPTER XXIV

The Hall of Eblis

FATHER SHELDON was sorry, downright sorry, for his friend and confrère, Luke Delmege. As a good Briton, he was bound not to manifest this regret in any way. But he had pleaded with the Bishop, again and again, not to allow this bright young genius to leave the diocese, and be flung away on the tame and easy work of an Irish mission. The old Vicar warmly seconded his efforts, although neither knew of the other's sympathetic coöperation. But the Bishop judged otherwise; and if he ever mistrusted his own judgment, the opinion of Dr. Drysdale tended to confirm his belief that the conversion of England must be accomplished without the assistance of the Rev. Luke Delmege.

"I don't agree with Drysdale," said the Vicar, when the Bishop had explained the many letters of the former. "He belongs to the old school—timid, fearsome, conservative. We want the young, who despise consequences, so long as the great object is attained."

No use. It was decided to let Luke go, and Father Sheldon was very sad. It was one of the reasons why he leaned his head heavily on his hands, one of these dark September evenings, just after Luke had returned from his trip. He didn't care to light the gas. He sat in the twilight and was sad. The hour was wearing on to supper-time, when one of the housemaids knocked, and told him a lady wished to see him.

He rose promptly, and went down to find Barbara Wilson waiting for him. The gas-jet was burning; and he saw that she was crying and in terror.

"Father," she said, "I'm in great trouble. Louis is gone!"

"Dead?" said Father Sheldon, slightly shocked.

268

"No, not dead; but he has escaped; gone I know not where. I left him for a moment this evening to see an old school friend, who had called; and he has vanished, and Oh! Father, I fear such dreadful things."

"Have you no trace? He was of remarkable appearance."

"Not the least. I have spoken to all the police on the beat; but there's not a trace. Oh, dear! it is the river, the river, I dread."

The supper gong was ringing, but Father Sheldon did not hear it.

"I must go with you," he said. He rushed into the church and said a hasty prayer; then, taking his hat and cane, he went out on the wild chase. Whither? North, south, east, west, the wilderness of streets stretched before him; and, as he hesitated, the wild tumult of the sweeping multitude almost took him off his feet.

"Nothing but God can guide us!" he said. "Let us move on and pray. Have you the least suspicion?"

"Only that he might have gone to a theatre, or Mrs. Wenham's, or an opium-den. Oh! dear, dear, and his soul was just saved!"

"It is not lost," said Father Sheldon, hurrying along; "and you alone can save it yet."

They took a cab, down to the Criterion, the Alhambra, the Gaiety, places that Louis used to frequent in his heyday. In all these the people were pouring in a deep, wide stream. The police on guard saw no one answering their description of Louis. The officials were too busy to give more than a laconic No! Back again throughout the crowded streets on their hopeless quest for soul and body, Barbara weeping and softly praying, her companion staring under gas-lamps to catch a glimpse of a skull and a mass of whitened hair. Was there ever such a hopeless effort, ever such a weary and despairful attempt? Up and down, up and down the dreadful streets of the City of Dreadful Night.

"I fear it is hopeless," said Father Sheldon. "Miss Wilson, let me see you home, and I shall place the matter in the hands of a detective."

No, no. That will not do for a sister's love for a brother's soul. She gratefully thanked the good priest, but insisted that he should now return. The night quest and the night sorrow should be her own.

"One more attempt," he said; "and then I shall leave you to God. What is the name and address of that—woman?"

Back again through the dreary streets, in and out, until they plunged into the quietness and solitude of a fashionable square, drove past massive railings and marble flights of steps now in the glare from some lighted drawing-room, now in the gloom of the shadow of an unoccupied mansion. Yes, here it is, brilliantly illuminated; and Barbara, seeking a lost soul, stands under the heavy gasalier in the vast hall. Servants in scarlet livery swept by her, stared at her, passed away. Doors opened and shut, and revealed the magnificence of splendidly decorated rooms. There was a buzz of conversation somewhere in the vicinity. And the pale, beautiful girl stood like a statue in the hall—stood and despaired. What could a stooped, and shattered, and broken invalid be doing in a place like this? She was asked into a small parlor behind the drawing-room, and in a few moments Mrs. Wenham entered, stared angrily, advanced, and said, in a tone of icy contempt:—

"Well?"

She was dressed for a ball, dressed with all the luxury and taste and even splendor society demands from her elect. She was quite as tall as Barbara, and wished she was quite as beautiful. But no! There was a grace and sweetness in this young girl that threw all the meretricious splendors of the other woman in the shade. And the woman of the world saw it, and it did not please her.

"You remember me, Mrs. Wenham," said Barbara, faltering. "We met in Dublin some years ago, and you were so kind."

The cold face stared blankly at her. Barbara felt there is no hope here.

"I understood that my brother Louis used sometimes—sometimes—"

How could she put, poor child, in the world's language her wild thoughts?

"Your brother Louis used—sometimes—?" repeated Mrs. Wenham, slowly.

"Sometimes," wept Barbara, "used visit here, owing to your

great kindness. And he's lost—he's lost—Oh! dear Mrs. Wenham, he's lost! He has gone out tonight, and we know not
whither. But Oh! if you could tell me—he's so unwell, so near
death; and Oh! his soul, his soul! He's not fit for the judgment."

The woman of the world turned pale. She had intended to
dismiss this girl haughtily, angrily, contemptuously. But these
words staggered her resolution. Once before, and only once,
and that was just after leaving the company of this same young
girl, she had heard similar words. Not since or before. These
hideous things were shielded from her carefully as midnight
draughts, or reeking drains, or the chance pollution of fetid
air. What had she to do with such things—this spoiled and
petted child? They were for the poor and the vulgar—the
housemaid and the butler—not for her. They were for the
proletariat—the toilers, the laborers, as a just retribution for
their misdeeds, and a proper perquisite for criminal poverty;
but not for the scented and curled darlings of fortune. And
here this young girl, with the clear-cut pallid face, the round,
calm forehead, and the gracious eyes, presumes to introduce
the horrid specters. She dismissed her.

"I know nothing of your brother, my good girl, and I must
bid you good-night!"

And she touched the bell. Barbara vanished in the darkness,
but the specters remained. And, as the stately lady swept
around the ballroom, that most detestable orchestra, particularly that deep, solemn 'cello, would keep wailing, Death!
Judgment! Death! Judgment! It was a new waltz, just imported
from the halls of eternity.

"No use, Father, no use! I must seek Louis alone now."

"I shall not leave you here on the London streets," said
Father Sheldon, decisively.

But she persisted. The cab rolled away, and left Barbara
standing transfixed on the pavement. She looked around the
dreary square—all the more dreary because so brilliantly
illuminated. All the splendor, and comfort, and light, and
beauty chilled her by the contrast. Then she looked up to
the stars, and—

"Whither now, O my God?"

It was horrible. It was a night-walk through Hell. Black
figures leaped out of the darkness, stared at her, muttered

some cabalistic words, and vanished. Rude men whistled into her face, and said some things that would be dreadful, but they were happily unintelligible. Once and again a policeman flashed a lantern in her face, and muttered something. And on, on she stumbled, for she was now growing weak, and she had to lean against a gas-lamp for help from time to time. Then on again, on through the darkness, into the circle of light thrown by a side-lamp, and into the darkness again. A few times she stopped to accost a stranger, and ask did he see Louis; but she was rudely answered with an oath, and thenceforward desisted from asking questions. And on, on, with a vague hope that Louis was somewhere near, and that she would find him. But nature was steadily conquering, and, at last, she had to sit on the curbstone and rest. She was falling into a fitful slumber when her name was called from out the night. She listened and looked. She heard a mighty river fretting its way into the darkness beneath her, and on the lap of the river a dark form was tossed. It tossed out its hand helplessly into the turbid waters, and a great nimbus of white hair floated back upon the wave. Once more she heard her name called from out the night, and she woke, chill and stiff. She stood up and stumbled forward. Her hands sought help. She clutched the iron bars that ran around some large building, and groped her way onward from bar to bar. They led her to a gate. It was open. And high against the star-lit sky, the peaked gables of a church cut upwards. She stumbled against a door and pushed it. It opened inwards, and she was in the church. A faint smell of incense half revived her. She groped along from bench to bench, until she stood beneath the red lamp. Then she sat down and rested. Oh! but not the rest that she had known for so many years in that unspeakable Presence; not the calm, sweet languor that steeped her innocent soul in such a bliss of peace there in the old church in the far city, after a day amongst the leprous and the poor. No; this was a mighty crisis in her life; and the voice was pealing from out the night. She rose up and went to the Lady Altar, and prayed for her brother's soul as she had never prayed before. And as she prayed, a light struck her—an idea so terrible, so appalling, that she shrank from the dread inspiration. She was called upon by the Unseen to make a sacrifice for the beloved soul. And such a sacrifice, great God! It was too dreadful. She shrank from it in terror. But the voice was calling from out the night. A soul, the soul of the beloved, was at stake! Again she prayed. And again the Unseen spoke. And again the poor soul protested. Anything else, anything else, but *that!* But the voice was calling importunately from the night. There was no time for hesitation. She rose up and dressed for the sacrifice; then stood before the High Altar and its Tabernacle. Once, twice, she tried to speak her vow, and failed. Once, twice, weak nature protested against a divine inspiration and decree. But now every moment was precious. And on a sudden impulse of divine self-surrender, she flung out her arms, like the limbs of a cross, and uttered the mighty words that spoke her doom and the redemption of her brother. The mighty Thrones, that swung round and round the altar, stopped in their adoring flight, poised themselves on their wings, stared at each other, stared at the silent Tabernacle, and looked down on the white, tearless face of the victim. But no sound broke the stillness of the sanctuary. Yet the Heart of Christ throbbed quicker beneath the accidents of His great Sacrament—throbbed quicker as at the grave of Lazarus, and at the voice of Magdalen, and surely no such tremendous sacrificial vow had ever passed human lips before.

Then a new, strange strength possessed her. She drew on her gloves calmly, and without a tremor calmly picked up her beads and umbrella, calmly genuflected, with just a whisper of silent protest against the dread exorbitance of God, and passed into the night again. She stumbled against some person in the darkness and begged pardon humbly.

"Yerra, ye needn't," said an unmistakable Hibernian voice, "ye didn't hurt me much."

"Thanks be to God!" said Barbara; "surely you are an Irishman."

"I ought to be, for me father and mother afore me were," said the voice. "But, begor, I'm beginning to think that I'm a *mixtum-gatherum* of all the quare people in the world; and that's a big worrd."

" 'Twas God and the Blessed Virgin sent you," said Barbara, realizing that this was the agent of the Most High in the fulfilment of His part.

" 'Tis many a long day since I hard the worrd," said the policeman, taking off his helmet. "What may be yer throuble?"

Simply and directly Barbara told her story, there in the darkness outside the church.

It was so wonderful, so incredible, that his suspicions became aroused. He had very large ambitions in the detective line, and it would never do to be caught so easily.

"Come over here to the lamplight," he said, gently but firmly holding her by the arm. "Now, young 'uman, do you see a feather bed in me oi?" he said, lifting up his eyelids in a comical way.

But something in the gentle face smote him with sorrow, and, dropping Barbara's arm hastily, he doffed his helmet, and said humbly:—

"I beg your pardon, Miss, a thousand times. I didn't know ye were a lady."

"Never mind," said Barbara. "But come, help me. There is no time to lose. God has sent you."

He drew his whistle, and at the shrill summons another constable instantly appeared. He whispered a few words to his comrade, and then, turning to Barbara, said:—

"Come!"

He led her from the main thoroughfare down a side street that led to the river, for a cold draught of wind swept up the street, and cooled gratefully the burning forehead of Barbara. Then another turn, and they passed into a police office. The inspector sat mutely at a desk, poring over a pile of papers. One gas-jct shaded by an opal globe, flickered over his head. He looked at the constable and said nothing. The latter told his story as circumstantially as he could, and wound up in a whisper, so that Barbara could not hear:—

"Begor, 'tis like hunting for a needle in a bundle of sthraw."

"Broderick, you're a fool," said the inspector to his fellow-countryman, for he, too, was of that desperately lawless race, who are the guardians of the law in all the cities of the world. "Go into the kitchen and get the lady some tea, and be quick about it."

When Barbara came out from the day-room, refreshed and strengthened, for now she felt sure that God was doing His part faithfully, although He had demanded such a fearful price from her, the inspector was standing, gloved and hatted, and a cab was at the door. He lifted Barbara in gently and followed.

"Where are we going?" asked Barbara.

"To the third of the three places your brother haunted," said the officer. "Did you tell that fool it was an opium-den?"

"Yes, indeed," said Barbara, wondering that she had not thought of the place before.

"And Albemarle Buildings, Victoria Street, was your brother's address?"

"Yes, yes," said Barbara, eagerly.

"Then he's not far from Albemarle Buildings," said the officer. He said no more. Barbara took out her beads, and prayed softly to herself.

They sped swiftly to the Victoria-Road Station, passed down some narrow streets, and stopped. The officer alighted, and went into a large building, from which he presently emerged with another officer. They were consulting together. Barbara watched them eagerly. Then there was a hasty order to the driver, and the cab sped forward again. Then, after one or two sharp turns, they stopped before a long, low shed.

"Your brother is probably here," said the inspector; "but how shall I know him?"

"I shall go with you," said Barbara.

"No, no; this is no place for a lady," said the officer. "Let me know his appearance, and some distinguishing signs, and if he is there I shall certainly find him."

But fearing some violence from one cause or another to her beloved one, Barbara insisted. The officer offered his arm to the door, a small, low, shabby door, that seemed to open nowhere. He pushed it, and it yielded. They groped through the darkness to a heavy curtain, that screened the light, and pushed it aside. They were in the Hall of Eblis. Readers of Beckford's wonderful vision will remember the ghastly sight that met the eyes of Vathek and Nouronihar, when their curiosity was gratified, and they entered the fortress of Aherman and the halls of Argenk. Even such was the dread spectacle that smote on the senses of Barbara and the officer in this abode of the living-dead. A heavy cloud, charged with the dread vapors of opium, hung thick and opaque on the ceiling; and its folds, too heavy for the atmosphere, curled down and curtained the floor.

Bleared lamps shone through it, and lighted its thick volumes, and scarcely threw a dim shadow on the floor, where, piled against the walls, and stretched in every hateful and abominable posture on filthy mattresses, lay the stupefied victims of the deadly drug. Some lay like dead logs; some had sense enough left to lift their weary eyes and stare, like senseless images, on the intruders. Some were yet in the beginning of the dread trance and were smoking leisurely. It was a mass, a squirming yet senseless mass of degraded humanity, and Barbara clung close to the officer, as they passed down the hall, sometimes stepping over a prostrate form, and the eyes of the devoted girl almost starting in fear and curiosity and the dread hope that here at last her quest was ended.

They had come to the end of the hall and had turned back to examine the dreamers on the other side, when a figure, almost buried under the superincumbent forms of others, turned lazily and helplessly and muttered something. Barbara stopped, clutched the arm of the officer, and pointed. The inspector pulled aside one or two helpless figures; and there, curled up in a state of abject impotence, was Louis Wilson. Barbara was on her knees in a moment beside her brother, fondling him, caressing him, with one dread fear and hope—would he live?

"This is he," she said. "Now for the last mercy. How shall we get him hence?"

They raised the senseless form between them, and, by a mighty struggle, drew it down the floor and to the curtain. Here a figure stopped them.

"Hallo, I say, what's this?"

But the officer flung the fellow aside; then followed him, and, after a few words, the fellow came over and relieved Barbara of her burden. They huddled the senseless figure into the cab, and sped homewards.

In the gray dawn of the morning, two anxious figures stood by Louis Wilson's bed, watching, watching, for a sign of returning consciousness. The doctor had administered some powerful restorative, which, if it took effect, would bring back the vacant mind once more to partial self-knowledge. But the heart was hopelessly diseased, and there was no chance of recovery. Barbara was quite easy in her mind. She knew that the

Eternal should keep His contract. Not so Father Sheldon. He knew nothing of the tremendous interchange that had taken place that night between the young girl and her God. He only saw with human eyes, and judged by human reason. But he was a priest, and this was a soul in peril. And so he knelt and prayed, sat and walked, always watching, watching, for the one faint ray of light that would herald the return of reason in that helpless form. He had done all that the Church allowed to be done under such awful circumstances; but, partly for the sake of that immortal soul, partly for the consolation it would impart to this devoted girl, he prayed and wished that, at least, one act of sorrow or charity might be breathed by the conscious intelligence before it was summoned to final judgment. The dawn grew to day; sounds of renewed traffic, suspended only for a couple of hours, began to echo in the streets again; now and again a street-call was heard, as boys rushed here and there with morning merchandise; a company of soldiers swept by to catch a morning train. Barbara had left the room for a moment, when the patient woke—woke, feebly and faintly, and stared at the window and at the face bending over him.

"Barbara!" he moaned in pain.

"Barbara is here," said Father Sheldon, "and will be delighted to see you so revived."

"Why are you here?" Louis asked.

"Because you are in danger, and I am a priest."

"Oh! I remember. I had a dream. I thought I was away in Switzerland or somewhere; and there was a stage, and illuminations, and a tragedy. And we came home, and you were so kind."

"Tell me, Dr. Wilson," said Father Sheldon, "have you any objection to make your peace with God and to receive the Sacraments of the Church?"

"Not the slightest. But Barbara must be here. I should like to make my confession to Barbara. I could tell her everything."

That wasn't to be, however. He did the next best thing. He confessed and was absolved. And when Barbara returned, and saw the candles lighting, and the purple stole around the priest's neck, and the light of reason dawning in eyes that had, heretofore, stared into abysses of ghastly phantoms, she flung herself on her knees in mute thanksgiving to God for the mighty grace.

And then her woman's heart sank sadly as she thought: Yes, clearly He demands the sacrifice, as He has clearly wrought His miracle of love. Yea, Lord, be it so! Who am I to contravene the purpose of the Most High?"

And so the Rev. Luke Delmege was grievously disappointed on arriving, with all his heavy luggage of books, etc., at Euston Station, and quite punctually, to meet the 8:30 down mail, when he found himself alone. He paced the platform impatiently and looked eagerly at every one that alighted from cab or hansom. The last bell rang. He had to take his place alone. For, alas! one of his expected fellow-travellers was sleeping peacefully in Highgate Cemetery, and the other he was to meet only after many years.

"There's no use," said Luke, "in trying to teach our countrymen anything. Even the best fail hopelessly to appreciate the necessity of punctuality."

BOOK IV

CHAPTER XXV

Altruism

DR. WILSON was in his study the following morning when a visitor was announced.

"A priest?"

Dr. Wilson shrugged his shoulders. "Show him up."

When Luke entered the room in a calm, independent way, the following interrogatories were jerked at him. He was not asked to take a seat.

"Name, please?"

Luke gave it slowly and distinctly.

"Parish priest, or curate?"

"Neither."

"Secular, or regular?"

"I have not come to consult you professionally," said Luke. "I have just come from England. If I needed your services, I would pay for them, and decline to be catechized."

"Oh, I beg your pardon," said the Doctor, shuffling around. "I really didn't mean—won't you please take a seat?"

"I had some slight knowledge of Mr. Wilson and his sister in England," said Luke. "We travelled from Switzerland together; and we had arranged to leave Euston yesterday together. They failed to keep the appointment, and I just called to express a hope that nothing of serious importance could have prevented them."

"Then you know nothing further?" said the doctor, eyeing Luke closely.

"Absolutely nothing," said Luke.

"I now remember that your name was frequently mentioned in Barbara's letters, especially the latest. Then, you do not know that my son is dead?"

281

Luke was horrified, though he might have expected it.

"Yes," continued the Doctor, "he is dead. And his sister has written to say that she too is dead to us and the world—she has entered some convent."

"You surprise me very much," said Luke. "I understood that they were to return and remain with their uncle, Canon Murray. And I presumed that, at least, Miss Wilson would return—"

"Of course, sir. And, in the ordinary and proper course of things, she should have returned. And I tell you, sir, it is this unnatural and improper severance of family ties that is prejudicing so many people against the Church."

"I am not the custodian of Miss Wilson's conscience," said Luke. "I presume she has excellent reasons for her course of conduct. At least, she struck me as one of the most gentle and self-sacrificing beings I ever saw."

"Quite so, sir. There's the sting of it. If she were worthless, or likely to be troublesome, your convents would have nothing to say to her."

"I cannot enter into that question," said Luke. "There are many circumstances that tend to guide young people in the direction of the religious life. But, at what convent or in what Order has Miss Wilson entered?"

"That I don't know. They won't allow her to tell even her father. She simply writes to say, she is dead to the world, and desires to be forgotten. That is all."

"That means she has joined the Poor Clares, or the Carmelites. They are austere orders, and observe strict seclusion from the world."

"I don't know. I dare say they have told her to write thus. They dreaded my parental authority, lest I should remove her. And, by heavens!" cried the Doctor, smiting the desk before him, "I will!"

Then the strong man broke down.

"I didn't care what might happen to that young—well, he's dead—but my heart was in that girl. And to think she should have turned her back upon me in my old age—"

"It is the usual lot of families to be separated," said Luke, kindly. "Miss Wilson might have married, and gone to India; and you might never see her again."

"True! true! let us dismiss the subject. Will you see Lady Wilson? She will be anxious to hear all about that last journey from Switzerland."

Luke remained a long time in Lady Wilson's drawing-room going over detail after detail to soothe the mother's feelings. But, ever and again, when he passed into a eulogium of the sister's virtues, the impatient mother would bring him back from the digression. Louis! Louis! it was of him she wanted to hear.

The delightful altruism of the Irish character broke suddenly upon him at luncheon in the coffee-room of the Montrouge Hotel. As he washed his hands in an adjoining room he was accosted by a great, tall, bushy-whiskered man, who, in his shirt-sleeves, was making his ablutions rather demonstratively.

"Nice day, sir?"

"Yes. Rather cold for October."

"Oh! I perceive you're from across the Channel. I have the greatest esteem for the English character, sir! I always say we have a great deal to learn from our neighbors. Coming to see Ireland, sir? You'll be delighted and disappointed. Going south to Killarney, of course?"

"Yes. I am going south," said Luke, on whom the familiarity grated. "I am an Irish priest."

"Oh! I beg your reverence's pardon," said the other, dropping at once into the familiar brogue. "Begor, now, we don't know our priests from the parsons. They dress all alike."

"An Irishman always distinguishes," said Luke.

"To be sure! to be sure! Now, whenever I'm in England, I always go to Sandringham. I have a standing invitation from the Prince of Wales to stay with him whenever I'm in England. 'Wire me, Fitzgerald,' he said, 'and I shall have my carriage waiting for you. No ceremony. One good turn deserves another.' Are you lunching here, your reverence? As good as you can get in the city. But ask for the under cut of the sirloin. Say Fitzgerald recommended it."

Luke had vanished. He was afraid the standing invitation might be expected of himself.

"What can I have for luncheon?" he asked the waiter.

The waiter jerked the napkin over his left shoulder, placed his two hands on the table, and asked confidentially:—

"Well, now, and what would yer reverence like? I suppose ye're thravelling for the good of yer health, and ye want somethin' good?"

"Quite so. Then let me have a cut of roast beef—the under cut, you know!"

"Begor, we're just out o' that. There was a party of gintlemin come in a few minits ago; and the divil a bit but the bone they left."

"Well, let me see. Have you roast mutton, or a fowl?"

"Bedad, we had yesterday. But this is the day for the roast beef."

"I see. Well, look here, I'm in a hurry to catch a train. Let me have a chop."

"The very thing. While ye'd be sayin' thrapsticks. Wan or two?"

"Two. And some vegetables."

"And what will ye dhrink?"

"Water!"

The waiter straightened himself, rubbed his chin, and stared at Luke meditatively. Then he went to the kitchen.

"Can I have some second course?" said Luke.

"To be sure, yer reverence. Anything ye like."

"Any stewed fruit?"

"Any amount of it, yer reverence. But won't ye take anything to dhrink? It's a cowld day, and ye have a long journey afore ye?"

"I'll have a tiny cup of coffee after dinner. Is this the fruit?"

" 'Tis, yer reverence. Just tossed out of the tin."

"What are they?"

"Well, begor, yer reverence, I'm not quite sure meself. I'll ask the cook."

"Oh, never mind. It's all right."

But the good waiter insisted, and came back in a few minutes with a mighty pile of rice pudding.

"There, yer reverence," he cried; "take that. Sure I kem round the cook wid a bit of blarney. That's good for ye. Let them things alone."

And he removed the stewed fruit contemptuously. Luke

handed him a sovereign. He almost fainted. When he had recovered, he went over to the window, Luke calmly watching
him, and held the sovereign up to the light. Then he glanced
at Luke suspiciously. A second time examined the coin, and
then rang it on the table. Then he bit it, and rang it again.
Finally he vanished into the kitchen.

"You seemed to have doubts about that sovereign?" said
Luke, when he emerged with the change.

"Is it me, yer reverence? Divil a doubt. Doubt a priest, indeed! No, yer reverence, I'm a poor man, but I knows me
religion!"

"Then why did you ring it, and bite it, and examine it?"

"Is it me, yer reverence? Oh no, God forbid that I should
forget meself in the presence of a priest."

"But I saw you do it," said Luke, who was fully determined
to let no such insincerity pass unreproved.

"Ah! sure that's a way I have," said the waiter. "They thry
to break me av it, but they can't. I got it from me poor father,
—may the Lord have mercy on his sowl!"

"Amen! Go, get me a cab."

Luke was hardly seated in a second-class carriage, when a
commercial traveller entered, fussed about, arranged vast piles
of luggage everywhere, sat down, coiled a rug around him,
and took out a newspaper. In a few minutes he was staring
over the edge of the paper at Luke. The latter was busy with
his own thoughts—regrets after Aylesburgh, memories of
little kindnesses received, the regretful partings, the little farewell presents. He lifted up the soft rug. It was a present from
the school children. Then he looked out on the somber landscape, and thought of his future. Well! At least the new life
would have the interest of novelty. And, then, he was not
welcome in English clerical circles.

"A fine evening, sir. Going south?"

The poor fellow couldn't help it. He had tried to attract
Luke's attention in sundry little ways, but in vain. He had to
make a bold attempt. Nothing could have annoyed Luke Delmege so surely. He wanted time for thought about a hundred
things; he had been used to silence. The brusquerie of that
Dublin doctor had irritated him; so, too, had the waiter's
prevarication. He had met nothing like it in England, where

everything was so smooth, polished, mechanical; and there was no room for sudden and abrupt departures from recognized rules.

He answered coldly. The traveller was offended, drew his rug more tightly around him, and anathematized priests in general.

But, just then, that beautiful side of Irish altruism, which is not vanity and curiosity, was revealed. A lady placed two children in the carriage; and left them, on their long journey to the farthest extremes of Kerry, to the care of the guard and the benevolence of the public. The little girl, a child of five years, hugged her doll, and beamed on her fellow-passengers. Her brother curled himself up on the cushions and fell asleep.

"You don't mean to say," said Luke to the guard, "that these children's mother has left them thus unprotected for such a journey?"

"Oh! yes, your reverence. They're as safe as in their cradles. They're Prodestans," he whispered, as a caution.

And Luke thought of "the lady with the bright gold ring on the wand she bore," and her dazzling beauty, lighted safely around the island of purity and chivalry.

And it was delightful—the little interludes at the stations where the train stopped for a moment on its rapid course southwards. At every stop the guard thrust in his peaked cap and bearded face to look after his pretty charge.

"Well, an' how're ye gettin' on?"

"Very well, thank you," the child would lisp with such a pretty accent, and such a winning smile.

"An', how'se the doll?"

"Very well, thank you."

"What's that her name is? I'm always forgettin'."

"Bessie Louisa. This is my youngest doll, you know."

"Of course, of course! And ye're all right?"

"All right, thank you."

"Good! Tay at the Lim'rick Junction.'

Twenty minutes later, the same colloquy would take place.

"Well, and how're ye gettin' on?"

"Very well, thank you."

"And how'se the doll?"

"Very well, thank you."

"Mary Jane, isn't it?"

"No, no! this is Bessie Louisa."

"Of course—Bessie Louisa! Where are me brains goin' to? And did she sleep?"

"Yes. She slept the whole way."

"Good. An' ye're all right?"

"All right, thank you."

"Good again. We'll have tay at the Lim'rick Junction."

But the benevolence was not limited to the guard. Oh! no. Every one in the carriage, now well filled, became the self-constituted guardian of the children. That boy must have been sick for a fortnight, after his return home, so well filled he was with cake and fruit. Even Luke thawed out from his frozen English habits, and sat near the little girl. She told him wonderful things about that little doll, showed him all her trousseau, including a lace skirt, which she said papa wore in his baby-days; told him the names of flowers by the wayside, and gave strange names to the ponies that scampered away from the onrushing train. He was half jealous when the hirsute guard appeared, and the child smiled at her friend. And then *da capo:*—

"An' how're ye gettin' on?"

"Very well, thank you."

"And how'se the doll?"

"Very well, thank you."

"Mary Anne Kate, isn't it?"

"No, no, no, no! Bessie Louisa."

"Of course, of course! An' ye're all right?"

"All right, thank you."

"Good! We ordhered tay at the Junction."

That "tay at the Junction," was a wonderful ceremony. Every one—guard, porters, passengers—was interested. And when the young waiter, in tight brown uniform, and with a ribbon of bright brass buttons running from collar to boot, came bearing aloft the tray and its steaming contents, there was almost a cheer. There never was such a number of improvised, amateur, and volunteer waiters in the chambers of the great. A landlord, who had a piece of flint in the place of a heart, a military swashbuckler who had stabbed and sabred a hundred Paythans in the Himalayas—even an attorney, volunteered their services. Luke was selected by the young empress; but he shared the honors nobly, by allowing the landlord to butter the bread and the attorney to pour out the tea. He gave Bessie Louisa to the bold *sabreur*. And on went the train merrily, the child eating, laughing, smiling at these worshippers of her unconscious attractions, until they came to the next junction, where she dismissed them with royal bounty.

Luke had to go further. His young charge almost crowed with delight when he told her. And then, she fell fast asleep. Half dreaming, half conscious, always waking up to smile, she lay wrapped in the warm rug that Luke had drawn around her, pillowing her head on his arm, and watching in the growing twilight the shadows deepening on the smiling face. Once or twice he tried to read his Office; but in vain. He laid it aside.

"God won't blame me," he said. "It is the shadow of His mighty wings that envelops us; and He hath given His angels charge over us to keep us in all our ways."

And Luke, too, fell asleep, the child resting on his arm. He reached home at night, and had an effusive welcome. The following day he called on the Canon. The good old man looked stooped and aged.

"Have you any news—of—ha—Barbara, Miss Wilson?" he said.

"None," said Luke, "but what her father told me—that she had entered some convent."

"Quite so. I am quite sure that she will—ha—rise to something responsible and—ha—respectable."

"I hope Miss Wilson wrote to you, sir, explaining her intentions," said Luke.

"Ahem! yes. But she has not entered into details. I dare say she will write again."

The Canon, too, was nettled. He could see no cause for such great secrecy and such haste.

"I understand that—ha—in England a young lady, well connected and talented, might rise to—a—very dignified position?"

"Yes, indeed. Amongst the Carmelites at the old convent at Lanherne, the Reverend Mother has the dignity of a mitred Abbess. At least," said Luke, hastily correcting himself, "she has the privilege of a crosier, which ought to be equivalent to a mitre."

"Then believe me, sir," said the Canon, "the day Barbara's virtues and talents are recognized, the—ah—community will raise her to the most dignified and respectable position in their power."

There was a few moments' silence.

"And you have returned to—ah—resume work in your own diocese?" said the Canon.

"Yes, sir. I was hoping, indeed, to be able to give my services to the cause of religion in England; but it was decided otherwise. I am just going to see the Bishop about my future arrangements."

"Quite so. You will kindly take a letter from me to his Lordship. I wish very much that I could detain you—ah—here; but you know it might establish a dangerous precedent—"

"I'm sure I'm extremely obliged to you, sir," said Luke. "But I hope that I shall be placed, sooner or later, somewhere near, that I might be able to see you sometimes."

The Bishop was very kind, and would have wished to place Luke in some leading position; but all things in Ireland, especially ecclesiastical, are governed by iron rules, the hardest and most inexorable of which is custom. Luke got his appointment to a country mission.

"You will find the parish priest somewhat quaint," his Lordship said, "but a saint."

Luke called on Margery, now Sister Eulalie. She looked to her brother's eyes lovelier than ever in that most beautiful habit, specially designed by our Lord for his favorite Order of the Good Shepherd. Margery was enthusiastic about her dear brother.

"But, Luke, you're horribly changed. Where did you get that grand accent? And you are so stiff and solemn and grave. I'm half afraid of you."

Yes. Luke was very solemn and grave, partly from natural impulse, partly from his English training. Margery said she didn't like it. But she did, deep down in her heart. And when one of the Sisters whispered to her, "You ought to be proud of your brother"—Margery was proud, very proud. And a little indignant, too. What did the Bishop mean by sending her glorious brother to a wretched country parish, all moor and mountain; whilst here, in the city, so much energy and eloquence and personal magnetism were wanting?

"I don't know what's come over the Bishop," she thought. "And he always spoke so highly of Luke."

"Luke dear," she said, "you mustn't mind. You are sent there just for a time to save appearances, and to prevent jealousy. Before twelve months, you'll be here at the Cathedral. Now, say you don't mind, do you?"

"Oh, not at all," said Luke, airily. "I have had no reason to expect anything better. I made my bed, and I must lie in it."

"Now, that's a note of discontent," said Margery, with her quick intuition; "never mind! I suppose this old parish priest is like dear old Father Meade!"

"Oh! by the way, has that visionary called?" said Luke.

"Yes," said Margery. "He called. We were full. But he would take no denial. 'God sent them,' he said, 'and take care you are not found fighting against God.' "

"It was the wildest expedition a priest ever entered on," said Luke. "Such utter contempt for prudence, and even for the proprieties, was never seen before."

"Those are the men that move mountains," said Margery. And Luke didn't like it.

Then Margery drew out of her little treasury sundry little gifts—a pyx-case, a little bundle of corporals and purificators, an oil-stock cover, a number of Agnus Deis for the poor, etc.; and Luke took them with half a sigh, thinking of the new life before him; then he kissed his little sister, and departed for his mission.

"We cannot stand you now, Eulalie," said one of the Sisters. "A brother like that would turn any one's head."

But Sister Eulalie felt a little sinking of the heart somehow. There was something wanting in that grand, stately character.

"I wonder will the poor like him," she said.

Luke passed an uneasy night. Whether that quilt was too heavy, so very unlike the soft down quilt at Aylesburgh, or this feather bed was too soft, or these blankets were too coarse or hard, or whether it was that heavy odor around the room, as if the windows had not been raised for a long time,—at any rate, he was restless and troubled. And when in the gray dawn of the October morning, he heard a sound of moaning in the next room, occupied by his pastor, he rose up, and fearing that the old man was ill, he knocked gently at his door. In answer to "Come in!" he entered. The old man, fully dressed, was leaning over a chair, on which was a large black crucifix, and there he was pouring out his soul to God with sighs and tears.

"I was afraid, sir," stammered Luke, "that you had been taken ill—"

"Go back to bed, boy, and stay there till I call you," said the old man.

Luke returned, wondering, and looked at his watch. It was just five o'clock. Luke shivered. But when, after breakfast, he strolled out to see the surroundings of his future life, he groaned aloud:—

"Good heavens! It *is* Siberia, and I am an exile and a prisoner."

The morning was fine, and a gray mist hung down over field and valley, and wet the withering leaves, and made the red haws, that splashed the whole landscape, as if with blood, glisten and shine. But the mist could not conceal the gray, lonely fields, the cocks of hay, half rotten, left out by some careless farmer to rain and frost; the brown, black mountains, seamed and torn in yellow stripes by the everlasting torrents. Here and there, across the desolation, were green nests, where some comfortable farmer resided; and here alone a few scraggy trees broke the monotony of the landscape.

"It's a land of death and ruin," said Luke. He returned. The old man was reading a paper.

"Have I anything to do, sir?" said Luke.

"Oh, to be sure, to be sure," said the old man. "You might look at the stables, and see how is that little mare. That ruffian spares the elbow-grease, I promise you. And see if he has got in them mangolds; and if the thatch is keeping right on that hay. And, in the afternoon, you might drive over to see the school at Dorrha. I'm afraid that teacher is pulling a cord with the assistant, and the children are neglected."

"At what hour is luncheon?" asked Luke.

"Wha-at?" said the pastor, in alarm.

"Luncheon, sir? At what time is luncheon on the table?"

"There's no such thing here, young man," said the pastor. "You'll get your dinner at three o'clock, and your tea at eight, if you like. I never take it. That's all."

"Oh! very good, sir," said Luke, reddening. "I didn't know. I only wanted to be quite sure, and punctual about the time."

"That needn't trouble you much," said the old man. "If there's anything in this country we've enough of, 'tis time, and water."

Luke strolled out, and looked. It was a dreary sight. The stone wall that surrounded the presbytery grounds had fallen in several places, and the moss-grown stones lay piled in hopeless confusion. A few scraggy hawthorn trees, now loaded with red berries, sprang up here and there. The yard was littered with dirty straw; geese, hens, and turkeys waddled around, picking the fallen grain, and occasionally quarrelling; the mare was stamping in the stable; and the boy was nowhere. Oh, yes! he was. Leaning luxuriously against a hedge, the dripping of whose bushes he did not heed, and smoking leisurely a short clay pipe, was the boy. He did not see Luke. He was in a reverie. It must have been a pleasant one, for occasionally he removed the pipe from his mouth, and gave vent to a long, low chuckle. Sometimes he grew serious, and even angry, as he held the pipe poised in one hand, and the other came down on the unresisting air, hot and heavy. Then he resumed his pipe with philosophical placidity. It was a pity to disturb such dreams, but Luke was inexorable. He had a mission, and that was to wean away the Irish character from its picturesque irregularity, and to establish in its stead the mechanical monotony of England. He did not say so, because the grinding of machinery was still hateful to him. But he had a firm, deeprooted conviction that the one thing wanting in Ireland was the implanting of English ideas, English habits—thrift, punctuality, forethought, industry; and that he was the apostle of the new dispensation. Hence he broke the dream of this hedge-side visionary; and the pipe, at the same time, fell from the mouth of the dreamer, and was shattered.

"You have nothing to do, I suppose, this morning?"

"I have, your reverence," the boy answered sullenly.

"Then, why not do it?" said Luke.

"I was waitin' for the min to turn up about thim mangels," said the boy.

"And, whilst waiting, could you not get that grease for the priest's horse?"

"What grase, your reverence?"

"The parish priest says the mare is ruined for want of elbow-grease," said Luke.

The man looked at his interrogator keenly, looked him all over, laughed deep down in his heart, as he had never laughed before; but said, with a face of preternatural solemnity:—

"Very well, your reverence; I'll see to it."

The parish priest was very much surprised for several days at the very unusual hilarity that prevailed in the kitchen; and sometimes Ellie, the under servant, found it difficult to avoid tittering, when she brought the dishes to table.

Luke visited the school at Dorrha. It was a poor, little mountain school, with about seventy pupils. A few tattered maps, from which the sharp pointers had long since worn away the political divisions of countries, hung around the walls; a clock stared silently at the ceiling; and on a blackboard were certain hieroglyphics supposed to be geometrical. The teacher made a profound bow to Luke. Luke responded.

"Would his reverence take a class?"

"With pleasure."

"Which would his reverence please to examine?"

"It made no difference. Say the sixth."

"They'll be afraid of your reverence," whispered the teacher. "They have been reading all about you in the paper; and they know all about Maynooth."

Here was the *First of First,* buried in silence for seven long years, trotted out again in dear, magnanimous Ireland.

The children did look frightened enough, especially when Luke ordered them to keep their heels together and hold up their heads. Alas! that is not so easy. The weight of seven centuries of serfdom is upon them. How can they stand straight, or look you in the face?

Then, Luke was too precise.

"If you want to read well," he explained, "you must give full expression to every vowel and lean on every consonant.

There, now, what crime did that final *g* commit that you elide it? I don't see *h* in water. Hold up your heads. Look me straight in the face," etc., etc.

Luke thought the lesson quite absurd. It was about political economy, and was very dismal and abstruse. He flung the book aside. He would commence the education of these children on new lines.

"Do you know anything of hygiene, children?"

No. They had never heard of the goddess Hygeia.

"I notice that your teeth are, for the most part, decayed or in the process of decay. Do you know what that proceeds from, or how it may be arrested?"

"Atin' sweets," they said in a chorus.

"Perhaps that is the remote or secondary cause. The immediate cause is want of phosphates in the blood. Do you know what phosphates are?"

"We do."

"Well. What are phosphates?"

"Guano—manoor."

"Not quite. You're confounding two things." And Luke went on to explain the arterial supplies to the teeth, and the reflex nervous action on the brain; the absolute necessity, therefore, of eschewing tea, and living on phosphates, like oatmeal. He was a confirmed tea-drinker himself.

Before the Angelus bell tolled that evening, it was reported through the parish that a Protestant parson from England had visited the school, and had recommended the children to go back to the diet of the famine years.

CHAPTER XXVI

The Secret of the King

FATHER TRACEY, ex-parish priest, chaplain to the City Hospital, was rejoiced, humbled, elated, stupefied, one of these days in early October. His conduct, indeed, gave rise to not a little comment. When a man stands still in the midst of a crowded street and stares at the ground, and then drives his stick into it fiercely, and walks away with his head in the air, people are apt to be unkind in their conjectures. But, to have seen him read his Office these days was a rare and portentous experience. For he kissed the ground, and abased himself a hundred times before his Maker; and, then, at the *Laudate's* flung out his arms, like a cross, and sang them into the ears of heaven. It was all about something that had happened at the death of Allua. For Father Tracey was also chaplain to the penitents at the Good Shepherd Convent. He had been offered the chaplaincy to the nuns, but declined it with a shiver.

"Who am I," said he, "to take these saints up the steep ladder of perfection? But, if your Lordship would let me look after these poor penitents—"

He had his wish; but never after spoke of his charge as "penitents"; that implied some harshness. They were "his little children," or "his saints." Now he had seen wonderful miracles wrought amongst his saints—miracles of grace and mercy unimaginable—souls, visibly snatched from hell; souls, lifted to the highest empyrean of sanctity, and the holy old man wondered, exulted, and was glad.

"There isn't in the world," he said, "a happier old man than I. What did I do, that God should be so good to me?" And he plunged his stick into the ground.

Well, Allua, little child of the convent-school, had passed through the hell of London life, and had been snatched from the deeper Hell by the mercy of her Lord. And Allua was about to die. The poor child had passed through terrific temptation, since she had been safely housed beneath the sheltering arms of the Good Shepherd—temptations from circumstances in her former life, temptations from the unseen—lastly, temptations to despair. Margery, who was privileged to be near her, described these temptations as fearful in the extreme.

"You can see everything that the Saints have told," she said; "everything but the faces of the evil spirits."

Father Tracey was troubled during these eventful days. He asked for redoubled prayers, for daily communion. Then, in his great anxiety and humility, he sent for Father Meade. And so, when the end had come, the poor dying penitent saw bending over her the two familiar faces of the priests who had saved her, and then came a moment of supreme tranquillity.

"'Tis all over now, Father. But oh! it was terrible whilst it lasted."

And then in profound peace and ecstasy the poor trembling soul passed into the arms of the Good Shepherd. It was early morning and Father Tracey went straight to the altar and celebrated Mass. Margery was privileged to bring him his humble breakfast; for Margery was a great favorite. It was very amusing to see the young Sister putting little dainties into the old priest's plate, and the old man as carefully putting them aside. Sometimes Margery succeeded by clever little stratagems.

"Most people don't eat that, Father. They say it isn't nice. *I* wouldn't eat it."

"Indeed?" the good old man would reply, as he gobbled up the dainty. And then he would gravely shake his head.

"Why don't you brush your hat, Father? There, I've done it now. Can't you send up that old coat, and we'll have it dyed here? There now, you're horrid this morning. You came out unshaved."

And Father Tracey would blush, like a girl, and apologize for his negligence.

"You want to make me like that grand brother of yours, who'll be our Bishop some day, I suppose. Ah me! Those clever young men! Those clever young men!"

And Margery, with her hands folded beneath her scapulary, would silently pray that her grand brother might some day be even as this poor, despised old priest.

But this morning there was great colloguing. They had heard or seen something supernatural, there in that Infirmary; and Father Tracey was crying with joy and ecstasy, and Margery was crying to keep him company.

"I can't believe it," said Father Tracey, trying to gulp down his tea. "It's too grand—or, God forgive me, why should I say, 'anything too grand' for the Father of all miracles and mercies?"

"It's quite true, then," said Margery. "I didn't notice it myself, until you called for prayers for poor Allua in her agony. Then, I went straight to Mother Provincial, and told her. She warned me that I was not to speak of it to any one but you. And, I suppose, you'll never keep the secret. Men never can, you know."

"I wish," said the old man in his ecstasy, "that I could shout it from the house tops and the mountains, and call all men to pray and glorify God. But, my dear, to tell the truth, I was surprised that our prayers were heard so soon. God does not give way so easily, always. I see it all now."

He paused for a moment.

"And you positively tell me—?"

"Positively. Do you doubt me, again?"

"No. But—"

"I tell you 'tis true. And our good Mother knew it all the time; but not a word. She is very prudent. And I saw her once or twice, when she thought no one was looking, going down on her knees, and kissing the ground!"

"God bless her!" said the old priest. He went back to the Infirmary. The frail, shattered form lay, oh! so peaceful and calm, in the glorious transfiguration of death. She still wore the penitent's habit; her beads were wreathed around her fingers, which clasped a crucifix; and a few flowers were pinned here and there to her dress. But the face—once more the face of a little child, had been sculptured into unearthly beauty by the chisel of Death, who stood by and waited for he worked only in solitude, and seemed to say: "Mark! how I can beautify before I destroy. So too shall the reincarnation come after destruction."

Father Meade came up, too, after Mass and breakfast. He knew nothing of the great secret.

"It's a beautiful sight, William," said Father Tracey, "God

will bless you for this beautiful soul, redeemed to Him."

But Father Meade only stooped down, and blessed the fore-head of his little child, and whispered:—

"Good-bye, Allua!"

And when Margery accompanied the old chaplain to the gate, and had made sundry comments, on his green coat, and brown hat, and frayed and fringed habiliments, he seemed not to mind, but now and again would stop and plunge his stick into the ground, and ask, as if he had never heard it before:—

"God bless me! you don't tell me?"

"But I do; Father dear, what an unbeliever you are!"

"And I mustn't pretend, you know, to know anything, I suppose?"

"No. You're to go on, as if you saw nothing, and shut your eyes, and mouth!"

"God bless me! that will be hard. And, you really tell me? And Reverend Mother knew it all the time?"

"There, now! Good-bye! If you show by sign or token that you know anything, you'll be expelled; and then, what will your saints do?"

"God bless me! you don't say so? Very well, you won't see me as much as wink one eye."

But he was hardly an adept at deception. Every one of his many acquaintances knew that something was up. And some wise people, watching his ecstatic features, said amongst themselves:—

"He has seen *something*. Could it be the Blessed Virgin?"

Margery walked back from the gate very thoughtfully, and reached her cell. Not the following Sunday, but some Sundays later, she penned a letter to her great brother. He, too, was passing through strange and novel experiences.

"I can see the quaintness, but I cannot see the sanctity of this old gentleman," thought Luke, as they sat after dinner and chatted. The old man, following a time-honored custom of thirty years, had made two tumblers of punch, and pushed one towards his curate.

"You'll only get one, young man," he remarked, "but 'tis a decent one."

"I never touch the like," said Luke, with a contemptuous sniff.

"Oh!" said the old man; and it was a rather prolonged exclamation.

"Here, Jer," said the housekeeper, when the glasses were removed. Jer was the meditative boy who was always found in the vicinity of the kitchen about dinner time. " 'Tis your luck; though faith, you don't desarve it."

"Ellie, will you have a little sup?" said Jerry, generously. But Ellie gave him a look of withering contempt.

"Here's your health, ma'am," said Jerry, adding in his heart: "May the Lord help our young priesht to keep his pledge faithfully all the days of his life."

This went on for three evenings. The fourth evening a strange thing happened. The prodigy caused much perturbation in the kitchen, and afforded Jerry abundant food for anxious reflection as he sat under his favorite hawthorn. What was the explanation? Had the young priest forsworn his pledge and gone the way of his fathers? Impossible. Had the parish priest swallowed both? Equally impossible. Then, the following evening, but one tumbler came out of the parlor; and henceforth, but one—and the vast perspective of tumblers, reeking hot, and extending to eternity, vanished, like a pleasant dream.

What had happened was this. The good old pastor, a slave to habit, not heeding Luke's refusal the first evening, continued concocting the second tumbler on the succeeding nights.

"May I have a cup of coffee, sir?" said Luke.

"Coffee? No, young man, you may not. There is no such thing ever made in this house. You can have tea for breakfast, and tea for tea, and a glass of good punch at your dinner. That's all!"

"Thank you!" said Luke curtly.

The fourth evening the old man brewed the two tumblers as he had done for thirty years; and pushed one towards Luke. Luke thought it was intended as an insult. He took up the steaming tumbler, and going over, he raised the window, and flung the liquid into the grass. Then he put down the window, and bringing back the empty glass, resumed his seat. The old man said not a word.

Each of these lonely winter evenings, precisely at eight o'clock, the household assembled for the Rosary; then, all lights were put out. Luke used retire to his bedroom, with what thoughts and memories may be conjectured. The remembrance of the past with all its intellectual pleasures haunted him; the future with all its dread possibilities frightened him. Was this to be his life? Dreary days, spent in idleness and unprofitable attempts to raise a helpless and dispirited people; and dreadful evenings, when he could not escape from himself, but had to face the companionship of thoughts that verged on despair. Yet, he made gallant attempts. Youth and hope were on his side; and there was no retreat. He had burned his ships. And, after all, why could he not do what the Canon had done in and around Lisnalee? That was Arcadia; this Siberia! Well, the brave soul is that which bends undauntedly to the hopeless task. He would try.

"Now, I don't want to hurt your feelings, Conor," he would say to a parishioner; "but don't you know that that festering heap of compost is a nest of typhus and diphtheria? The horrible miasma pollutes the entire atmosphere, and fills the house with disease?"

"I suppose so, your reverence; but, begor, no one died in this house for the past three ginerations, except of ould age."

"That is exceptional," Luke would reply; "but, apart from the question of sanitation, don't you think that a few flower beds would look better than that dismal swamp?"

"Of course, yer reverence, but we'd have to pay dear for them."

"Not at all. A few wallflowers in spring, and a few tufts of primroses—there are thousands of them in the springtime in the hedgerows,—and a few simple geraniums in the summer, would not cost you one half-crown. Now, Lizzie, don't you agree with me?"

"I do, Father," Lizzie would say.

"So do I, yer reverence; but it isn't the cost of the flowers I'm thinkin' of, but the risin' of the rint. Every primrose would cost me a shillin'; and—"

"I thought that was all past and gone forever?" said Luke.

The poor man would shake his head.

"I daren't, yer reverence. Next year, I'm goin' into the Land Court agin; and, begor, the valuators and commissioners would put it on, hot and heavy, if they saw a sign of improvement about the place."

"Good heavens!" Luke would say. "Then 'tis your interest to drag everything back to prairie conditions instead of improving house and land and gardens?"

"You've said it, yer reverence," said Conor.

This horror oppressed Luke keenly. In the beginning he used flare up in anger when a poor peasant would come to him on a sick-call or other business.

"Put on your hat. Don't you see 'tis raining?"

"Yes, yer 'anner."

"Stop that infernal word. Call your priest 'Father.'"

"Yes, yer 'anner."

"Look here, my poor man. Hold up your head, look me straight in the face, and call me 'Father.'"

"Yes, yer 'anner."

Then Luke would fume and foam, and preach lessons on independence and manliness, and that God should be feared, not men; and he quoted the example of our Lord, and His firm, respectful, dignified bearing before Herod and Pilate. Then, after a while he desisted. It was no use. And in the cold, raw winter, as he rolled along on his side-car, and saw the poor farmers with down-bent heads, and faces burnt by the bitter wind, driving the heavy ploughs into the hard, unyielding earth, he thought with intense bitterness that that poor toiler was laboring, not for his own little family over there in that wretched cabin—that meant only bread and potatoes,—but for the agent, that he might have his brandy and cigars; and for two old ladies in a Dublin Square, that they might give steaks to their lap-dogs; and for a solicitor again above them, that he might pay for his son in Trinity; and, on the highest pinnacle of the infamous system, for the lord, that he might have a racer at the Derby and St. Cloud, and a set of brilliants for Sadie at the *Opéra Comique*. And he thought with a shudder, that he heard, here in the peaceful Irish valley, the grinding and jarring of the dread engine of English law. Can it be, he said, that the horrid thing has stretched out its tentacles and grinds and grasps with its inexorable unconsciousness, even here? But he put the dread thought aside. Had not the great Canon risen buoyantly over all these difficulties, and created his little paradise? How was it done? And Luke was puzzled.

He was also puzzled by another circumstance. It was the

quaint, strange language of this mysterious people. It was quite clear that they regarded this earth and this life as of but little moment.

"Wisha, yer reverence, 'tis good enough for the short time we're here. Sure 'tis here today and away tomorrow!"

"Yer reverence, why should we throuble about this dirty body? Sure, 'tis good enough for the worms."

"I'm goin' to me long home, yer reverence; and 'tis time. If we hadn't much here, sure we'll have plenty hereafter."

Luke didn't like all this. It sounded indeed dreadfully like the Scriptures: "Take ye no thought for the morrow;" "Which of ye can add to your stature;" "Consider the lilies of the field;" "Seek ye first the kingdom of God," etc., etc. The whole thing was horribly reactionary. But, these quaint Irish peasants were dreadfully like those fishermen of old; and their philosophy of life was suspiciously a reflection of that which was preached by the Sea of Galilee; and which all men have agreed to pronounce Divine. But where then was the philosophy of the salon, and the delicious humanitarianism of Amiel Lefevril? Seek ye the God in man? Evidently these poor people didn't believe it possible—that strange quest of the *Illuminati*.

It was on one of these wintry days that Luke received his sister's letter. It ran thus:—

"DEAR LUKE:—I cannot help writing to ask your prayers, and if not too much, a remembrance in the Holy Sacrifice (perhaps, if you have time, you may give a whole Mass), for one of these poor penitents whom dear Father Meade brought from England. Oh, Luke! such a death! It was horror after horror in the beginning. Then, such serenity and peace. It was a miracle; and we couldn't understand it. But I saw something that explained all. Still it is a great secret; and I must not tell. Father Tracey (but you don't know Father Tracey, the dearest old priest that ever lived) knows it too, and is in ecstasies. But we must not tell. But God is so wonderful. Some day, perhaps.

"Will you be going home soon? Do, dear Luke, they're dying to see you. I hope you like your mission. Try to like it, dear Luke. You know it is only temporary, and you will make it very happy if you take up and foster the poor. That makes life all rosy and sunshiny. There! I suppose now you will say: That's not English. I don't mind. But, Luke, dear, be humble; be very humble. We all need be. I wish I could tell you the great secret. But some day, perhaps.

"I suppose Reverend Mother will never allow this scrawl to pass.
"Your loving sister,
"EULALIE."

"Conventual, not conventional!" said Luke. "There is one grain of common sense. I must run home, if only to see Father Martin, and ask his advice about getting away from this unhallowed place forever."

Father Martin was not at all sympathetic.

"There is no reason why you should not do what all the excellent priests of the diocese have done before you," said Father Martin. "They all have had to commence in the same way, and most seemed to find pleasure where you experience despair. Do you think that the life of a priest should be one long holiday of social and intellectual pleasures?"

"N-no," said Luke. "That's not it. If I had work, work, work, from dawn to dark, I shouldn't mind. But, this enforced idleness—and the daily contact with all that is sordid and—hopeless—is enough to give any man the blues."

"Well, tastes differ. Father Cussen says he is supremely happy, except when he thinks of England; and then he is disposed to be profane. He is forever thanking God that his lot is cast in holy Ireland, among such a loving people."

"I cannot see it," said Luke, in despair. "It is England, England everywhere, when we have to blame ourselves."

"Do you think so?" said Father Martin, looking him straight in the face.

"Well," said Luke, "there are faults on both sides, I suppose. I admit, indeed, this system of land-tenure is abominable—"

"We won't discuss it," said Father Martin. "Are you reading?"

"No. Why should I? All my books are in their cases in the stables. I dare not unpack them."

"Why?"

"Why? Because, first, I shall not remain here. Secondly, there is no room to put them in. Thirdly, those women would ruin them. Fourthly, where is the use of continuing one's studies in such a country?"

"Phew," said Father Martin. "You have a lot to learn, and unlearn yet, which is not found in books."

"I have learned that life is very miserable, whatever," said Luke.

"A priest shouldn't complain," said Father Martin. "He is a soldier. The outpost duty is not pleasant; but it *is* duty. The Church was not created for priests; but the priesthood for the Church."

"I have been hearing that, *usque ad nauseam,*" said Luke. "And yet, every one is anxious to get the pillows under his elbows."

"Not every one," said Father Martin, gravely. "There are numbers of priests, young and old, in this diocese, and elsewhere, who are happy in serving God under worse circumstances than yours—silent men, whose life is one great sacrifice."

"And not one gleam of intellectual pleasure?" said Luke, doubtingly.

"Except the elation of duties well discharged; and such companionship as they can afford each other."

"Pretty doubtful!" said Luke, shrugging his shoulders. "Better solitude than that fellow!"

He pointed to the photograph of the poor priest, around whom Father Martin had grouped his demi-gods.

Then, noticing a look of pain and displeasure on the face of his friend, he said:—

"I admit, indeed, there are a few compensations. There is a vague sense of home, and freedom from anxiety about money matters that one never experiences in England. Then, somehow, the landscape is gaining on me. I have seen coloring across the moors and the breasts of mountains that would make an artist's fortune, could he fix it on canvas. And, then, certainly the little children are very attractive. The one thing that strikes every English visitor to Ireland are the children's eyes—*das Vergissmeinnicht blauste Auge!*—"

"For heaven's sake, Luke, don't talk that way before the brethren. You'd never hear the end of it."

"I shall go my own way, Father Martin," said Luke. "If there be one thing I despise before another it is the eternal deference to human opinion."

"You may be right," said Father Martin. "But, life needs its little adjustments; I was going to say its little stratagems."

That evening Father Martin sat long and anxiously near his little stove in the library—thinking, thinking of his young friend. Very few would have spoken to Luke as he had done; but he loved Luke, and would not spare his feelings. "The Bishop must take him to the city," he said. "This violent change in his circumstances is too much for him."

Then his eye caught the photographs.

"I never thought it was so easy to scandalize the young," he said. "I wonder in what fit of diabolical uncharitableness did I put that photograph there?" He took down the frame and unscrewed it from behind. He then removed the picture that represented "conceited emptiness," and put it carefully in an album. He balanced the remaining photographs for a long time in his hand. At last, he dropped them, one by one, into the stove.

"Satan, or self, which is the same, is looking through their eyes," he said. "The crucifix is enough for an old man."

And Luke went back to his lonely room, and sat on the rude deal chair these long, weary, winter nights, watching the rough iron bedstead, and the thick red quilt, and the painted washstand and the broken jug; hearkening to the heavy breathing of his good pastor in the next room; and thinking, thinking of the beautiful past, that had vanished so swiftly, and wondering through what narrow loophole would he escape the unendurable present and the unpromising future.

And there in the city, in a room far worse furnished, knelt an aged priest, who thanked God for his supreme and unalloyed felicity, and who cried in loving wonder to the pale face on his crucifix: "Lord, Lord, what have I done to deserve it all? Stop, stop this flood of delight, or I'll die."

And when routed from his wretched pallet at midnight, he drew on his dingy clothes, and murmured, "What poor soul wants me now?" And when lighted by the night-nurse along the gloomy wards, where tossed poor diseased humanity, and some sleepless patient caught the light of his holy face, and murmured, "God bless you!" and when he came to the couch of the dying, and saw the happy look creep into the wistful, eager face, that now turned to Death tranquilly, for here was the man who could transform the King of Terrors into an Angel of Light,—he murmured as he uncovered the pyx, and knelt before the Divine Healer of Humanity:—

"Lord! Lord! how wonderful art Thou! and how generous! And what a dread purgatory I shall have for the heaven Thou hast given me here!"

CHAPTER XXVII

A Great Treasure

LUKE DID not remain long with the quaint pastor, who was also a saint. This latter fact Luke took a long time to realize, although he had the Bishop's word for it. He could not quite understand how the aureole of sanctity hung around that old man, who apparently did nothing but examine his hay and turnips; and varied his visits to the barn and haggart by strolling down to the front gate to get a chance conversation with a passing parishioner. Then the strange blending of rare old Irish melodies with fervent prayer almost shocked Luke. He often listened at his bedroom window to his pastor, moving leisurely about the little garden beneath, and humming, alternately with the psalms of his office, that loveliest of all Irish songs, that always reminds one of the wind wailing over the misty, wet mountains—*Savoureen dheelish, Eileen Oge!* But it sounded very sweet, and sad, and lonely—there in that lonely place, with nothing to break the silences but the querulous cries of fowls, or the swift exultant chant of a bird, or the wind, that always, even in summer, wailed, like a ghost seeking rest. But gradually Luke felt himself in a kind of sanctuary, the very atmosphere of which was prayer. The old priest moving about the room, the old housekeeper in her kitchen. Ellie in the yard—all seemed to be holding an eternal unbroken communing with the Unseen. So too with the people. The old women, bending beneath the *brosna* of twigs and branches for the scanty fire, the young mothers rocking their children's cradles, the old men bent over the ashes in the open hearth, the young men in the fields,—all, all appeared to think and live in prayer, which was only suspended to attend reluctantly

306

to the meaner business of life. And if the old priest broke through the psalter, in a moment of regretful unconsciousness, to murmur *Savourneen dheelish,* the young mother would sometimes break in upon her lullaby, *Cusheen Loo,* to whisper a prayer to the ever present Mother and Divine Babe for her own sleeping child. And the sweet salutations: "God save you!" "God save you kindly, agra!" spoken in the honeyed Gaelic—all bewildered Luke. The visible and tangible were in close communion with the unseen but not less real world behind the veils of time and space.

It was this want of touch with the supernatural that was the immediate cause of Luke's removal. The remote cause was the kindly letter that Father Martin wrote to the Bishop about the young, and so far, unhappy priest. Surrounded in spirit with the grosser atmosphere which he had brought from abroad with him, he failed to enter into the traditions and beliefs of the people—not, of course, in essential dogmas, but in the minor matters that go to make up the life and character of a people. In trying to modify these for better and more modern practices, he was right and wrong. He could never understand why the people should not fit in their ideas with his; or the necessity of proceeding slowly in uprooting ancient traditions, and conserving whatever was useful in them. Hence he was often in conflict with the people's ideas. They were puzzled at what they deemed an almost sacrilegious interference with their habits; he was annoyed at their unwillingness to adopt his ideals. But they had too deep and reverential a fear and respect for his sacred character to say anything but what was deferential. But the old men shook their heads. At last, he touched a delicate nerve in the Irish mind, and there was a protest, deep, angry, and determined. He had touched their dead.

He had protested often and preached against Irish funerals and Irish wakes. He could not understand the sacred instinct that led people, at enormous expense and great waste of time, to bury their dead far away from home, sometimes on the side of a steep hill, sometimes in a well-covered inclosure in the midst of a meadow. It was with a certain feeling of impatience and disgust he headed these lonely processions of cars and horses and horsemen across the muddy and dusty roads, winding in and out in slow solemnity for fifteen or twenty miles,

until at last they stopped; and the coffin was borne on men's
shoulders across the wet field to where a ruined, moss-grown
gable was almost covered with a forest of hemlocks or nettles.
Then there was a long dreary search for the grave; and at last
the poor remains were deposited under the shadow of the
crumbling ruin, ivy-covered and yielding to the slow corrosion of time, whilst the mourners departed, and thought no
more of the silent slumberer beneath. Luke could not understand it. He preached against the waste of time involved, the
numbers of farmers brought away from their daily work, the
absurdity of separating husband from wife, in compliance
with an absurd custom. He had never heard of the tradition
that had come down unbroken for a thousand years—that
there in that lonely abbey was the dust of a saint; and that he
had promised on his deathbed that every one buried with him
there should rise with him to a glorious resurrection. And
these strange people looked askance at the new trim cemetery,
laid out by the Board of Guardians, with its two chapels and
its marble monuments erected over one or two of the Protestant dead. They preferred the crumbling walls, the nettles and
hemlock, and the saint, and the abbey, and the resurrection.

Luke was called to see an old parishioner who was dying.
The old man lay, a figure of perfect manhood even in age, on
a low bed, under a chintz canopy, to which were pinned various pictures of the saints. The priest discharged his duties with
precision, and turned to depart.

"Your reverence?"

"Yes," said Luke. "Can I do anything for you?"

"I want you to say a word to rise me heart for me long
journey, your reverence."

"To be sure," said Luke, who then and there gave a long
dissertation on immortality, chiefly culled from the *Phaedo*.

"Your reverence, I don't understand wan worrd of what
you're sayin'; but I suppose you mane well. Will the *Man above*
have anything agin me in His books?"

This dread simile, prompted by sad experiences of the
agent's office, shocked Luke.

"I'm sure," he said, "Almighty God has pardoned you. You
have made a good confession; and your life has been a holy
and pure one."

"And did your reverence give me a clare resate?" asked the old man.

Here was the agent's office again.

"I've given you absolution, my poor man," said Luke. "You must know that God has pardoned you all."

"Thanks, your reverence," said the old man, relapsing into silence.

Luke said Mass reluctantly in the house when the old man had died. He hated the thought of saying Mass under the poor and even sordid circumstances of these country houses. The funeral was fixed to leave at eleven o'clock.

"Eleven o'clock *is* eleven o'clock," said Luke, with emphasis. "It is not five minutes to eleven, or five minutes after eleven; but eleven, you understand?"

"Av coorse, yer reverence. 'Tis a long journey to the abbey and we must start airly."

"I can't see why you wouldn't bury your father over there in the new cemetery," said Luke.

"He wished to go with his own," was the reply.

Luke was at the house of mourning at five minutes to eleven. There was no sign of a funeral. He protested.

"The hearse and the coffin have not come, yer reverence," was the reply.

"But why not? Were they ordered?"

"They were orhered to be here on the sthroke of tin," was the answer.

At about half-past eleven the hearse was driven up leisurely.

"Why weren't you here at the time appointed?" said Luke, angrily.

"The toime appinted?" said the driver, coolly. "Yerra, what hurry is ther? Isn't the day long?"

Luke gave up the riddle. Half-past eleven came, twelve, half-past twelve; and then the neighbors began to gather. Luke's temper was rising with every minute that was thus lost. And then he began to notice the young girls of the house rushing out frantically, and dragging in the drivers and jarvies to the house of mourning, from which these soon emerged, suspiciously wiping their mouths with the back of the hand. Luke seized on one.

"You've had drink there?" he said.

"A little taste agin the road, yer reverence," the man said.

"That's enough," said Luke. He tore off the cypresslawn, which the priests in Ireland wear in the form of a deacon's stole, and flung it on the ground. Then he turned the horse's head homeward. There was a cry of consternation, and a shout. But Luke was determined. He peremptorily ordered the man to drive forward. One or two farmers begged and besought him to remain, and even caught his horse's head. Luke took the whip and drove his horse into a gallop; and never drew rein till he entered the yard.

"You're home early," said the old man.

"Yes," said Luke, laconically.

"You didn't go the whole way? Anything wrong with the mare?"

"I didn't attend the funeral," said Luke. "I saw them dispensing drink; and the statutes forbade me to attend further."

"The wha-at?" said the old priest.

"The statutes—the statutes of the diocese," said Luke, impatiently.

"Phew-ew-ew-ew!" whistled the old man. And after a pause: "You'll have a nice row over this, young man. They may forgive all your abuse of the country, and your comparisons with England; but they'll never forgive you for turning your back on the dead. And Myles McLoughlin was the decentest man in the parish."

"But are not the statutes clear and determinate on the point?" said Luke. "And where is the use of legislation, if it is not carried out?"

"You're not long in this country?" said the old man.

"No—no!" said Luke.

"I thought so," said the good pastor, rising in a pre-occupied manner. He went over to the window and looked out. He then began to hum *Savourneen dheelish,* and Luke knew there was an end to the dialogue.

The following Sunday, after last Mass, at which Luke had explained and justified his action very much to his own satisfaction, a deputation called on the parish priest. They demanded the instant removal of this Englishman. The old man tried to "soother them down," as he said. He might as well have tried to extinguish a volcano. They left in silence. One said:—

"You wouldn't have done it, yer reverence; nor any of our ould, dacent prieshts, who felt for the people."

Luke thought it was all over. His arguments were crushing and invincible. There was no answer possible. He thought men were led by logic—one of his many mistakes. The following Sunday, when he turned around to say the Acts, there was no congregation. Mounted scouts had been out all the morning to turn the people away from Mass. No one dared come. The following Sunday the same thing occurred. Then Luke felt it was serious. He wrote a long letter in self-justification to the Bishop, and then demanded his removal. The Bishop would have supported him and fought with him for the maintenance of a great principle, but the old quiet pastor implored him with tears to remove this wild curate, and restore peace. And Luke was removed in promotion.

Father Martin heard the whole story, and wrote a long, kind, firm letter, which made a deep impression on his young friend. The closing sentence was a strong recommendation to be "all things to all men," like St. Paul, and to remember "that life required its adjustments, and even its stratagems," from time to time.

It was a happy change in more senses than one. The moment the people had won the victory, they relented. They were really sorry for their young priest. Several assured him that it was "only a parcel of blagards, who weren't good for king or country," that had caused all the row. Luke said nothing; but left, a mortified, humbled man. He knew well that although he had maintained a great principle, it had left a stain on his character forever.

He was promoted, however, and this time to a pretty village, hidden away in a wilderness of forest,—a clean, pretty little hamlet, with roses and woodbine trailed around the trellised windows, and dainty gardens full of begonias and geraniums before each door.

"It's a piece of Kent or Sussex, which some good angel has wafted hither," said Luke.

Everything was in uniformity with this external aspect.

There was a fine church at one end of the village, a neat presbytery, and the dearest, gentlest old pastor that ever lived, even in holy Ireland. He was an old man, and stooped from an affection in the neck, like St. Alphonsus; his face was marble-white, and his long hair snow-white. And he spoke so softly, so sweetly, that it was an education to listen to him. Like so many of his class in Ireland, experience and love had taught him to show the toleration of Providence and the gentleness of Christ towards every aspect of wayward humanity.

"You will find," said Father Martin, in his letter to Luke, "your America here. If Rossmore and Father Keatinge do not suit you, nothing will. Try and relax your horrible stiffness, that freezes the people's hearts towards you, and be 'all things to all men,' like that great lover of Christ, St. Paul."

So Luke made frantic resolutions, as he settled down in a neat two-story cottage in the village, and unpacked his books, and arranged his furniture, that this should be a happy resting-place, at least for a time, and that he would adapt himself to his surroundings, and be very cordial and friendly with the people.

"All things to all men!" Dear St. Paul, did you know what elasticity and plasmatism, what a spirit of bonhommie and compromise, what vast, divine toleration of human eccentricity you demanded when you laid down that noble, far-reaching, but not too realizable principle? Noble and sacred it is; but in what environments soever, how difficult! This fitting in of human practice, indurated into the granite of habit, with all the hollows and crevices of our brothers' ways, ah! it needs a saint, and even such a saint as thou, tent-maker of Tarsus, and seer and sage unto all generations!

Luke found it hard. Cast into new environments, how could he fit in suddenly with them? Suave, gentle, polished, cultivated, through secret reflection, large reading, and daily intercourse with all that had been filed down into tranquil and composed mannerism, how was he to adapt himself to circumstances, where a boisterous and turbulent manner would be interpreted as an indication of a strong, free, generous mind, and where his gentle urbanity would be equally interpreted as the outer and visible sign of a weak, timid disposition, with too great a bias towards gentility. Yet he must try.

"Well, Mary, how are all the bairns?" he said cheerfully to a young buxom mother, who carried one chubby youngster in her arms, and was convoyed by two or three more.

"Wisha, begor, your reverence, we have but one barn; and 'tis nearly always imphty."

"I meant the children," said Luke, flushing.

"Oh, the childre! All well, your reverence. Spake to the new priest, Katie; there now, ducky, spake to the priest, alanna!"

But Katie was shy and put her finger in her mouth, and looked up in a frightened way at his reverence.

"Shake hands, little woman," said Luke, cheerily, "and we'll be good friends. Shake hands!"

But Katie declined. Probably she had heard that it was not considered polite for a lady to offer her hand to a gentleman on a first introduction. Now, if Luke had been wise he would have closed the conference there. But he was determined to win that child.

"What have I done to you, little woman?" he said. "Let us be friends. Come now, shake hands." Katie still declined.

"Shake hands, miss, with the priest," said the mother, shaking her angrily.

"Let her alone," said Luke. "She'll come round immediately." But Katie was not coming round.

"Shake hands, miss, I tell you," said the mother, now fast losing control of her temper. Katie wept the tears of childhood.

"Begor, we'll see," said the mother, "who'll be mistress here. Hould him," she cried to a servant girl, transferring the baby to her arms. Then Katie was spanked, notwithstanding the piteous appeals of Luke, who was horrified at the results of his intended kindness. He put his fingers in his ears to keep out the screams of the child, at which ceremony the servant-maid laughed rudely; and Luke rushed from the cabin.

"Wisha, 'twasn't the poor child's fault," said the mother in subsequent explanations to a neighbor, "but his gran' accint. 'Twas enough to frighten the child into a fit."

One would have thought that this was a lesson. But to Luke's mind babies were irresistible. The cold, calm way in which their wide round eyes, so frank and honest, stared at him until he winked; the unfathomable depths in these same eyes,

as if they were wondering, wondering, wondering, "Where
did I meet you before?" made Luke half a heretic. He was
beginning to believe in the *anamnesis* of the human mind, and
the faculty of recalling a previous existence. This was confirmed by the free and active interpretation of the nurses or
mothers.

"Sure, she knows you, yer reverence. Look at the way she
looks at you. You know the priest, ducky, don't you? What's
his name, darlin'?"

"Gluck! gluck," says baby.

"Luke! Luke!" echoes mother. "Glory be to you, sweet and
Holy Mother, did ye iver hear the likes before? And sure she's
as like your reverence as two pins."

"She's an uncommonly pretty child," said Luke, in unconscious self-flattery. "I never saw such eyes before."

"And she's as cute as a fox," echoes mother. "Wisha, thin,
yer reverence, though I shouldn't say it, I had priests in my
family, too. We have come down low in the world enough;
but there was thim that wance held their heads high. Did ye
ever hear of wan Father Clifford, yer reverence, who lived over
at Caragh? 'Twas he built that gran' chapel, the likes of which
isn't in the country. Well, sure he was my mother's gossip. And
I had more of them, too. But let bygones be bygones. Sure,
when you're down, you're down!"

During this modest assertion of high respectability (for "to
have a priest in the family," is, thank God, the patent of honor
in Ireland), Luke and the babe stared wonderingly at each
other. Now, he had read somewhere, how on one occasion, a
party of rough miners out West, who had been banished from
civilization for years, on coming down from the gold-pitted
Sierras, with their wallets stuffed with nuggets and their very
clothes saturated with gold dust, had met a nurse and a child.
They stared and stared at the apparition. And one huge giant,
who had not been washed since his baptism, and who was a
walking armory of revolvers and bowie knives, stepped before
his fellows, and offered the girl two handfuls of gold dust if
she would allow him to kiss the child. The young lady herself
was not consulted. But, as the big miner stooped down and
touched the pure lips of the child, a cold sweat broke out on

his face and forehead, and he trembled under the fever of a sweet emotion.

Luke thought and was tempted. He said good-bye to the mother, and stooping down touched with his lips the wet, sweet mouth of the child. He walked away, leaving serious wonderment in the child's mind, but infinite gratitude in the mother's; but he had to steady himself against a tree for a few moments, whilst the current of strange, unwonted feelings surged through his veins.

"That's a good man," said a rough and ready farmer, who had begun the process of "edjication," and was supposed to be critical, and even anti-clerical in his sympathies. He had watched the whole proceeding from behind a hawthorn hedge.

"He has a soft corner in his heart, however," said the happy mother.

But it was a fatal kiss! Luke had examined his conscience rather too scrupulously that night, and decided that these little amenities were rather enervating, and were not for him. And there was a deep disappointment and even resentment in the parish, when it was found that the superior attractions of other babies were overlooked, and that there was but one who was highly favored.

All this was a fair attempt for one who was working by the rules of art, as well as by the inspirations of nature. But he was a foreigner, and awkward in his approaches towards an impressionable and sensitive people.

His really serious troubles commenced when he had to get a "boy." We say "serious," for in this quaint, old-fashioned country it is the "minor humanities," not great cataclysms, social and political, that constitute the factors of daily existence. Luke had been assured that a "boy" was a necessary and indispensable evil. "You must get him, but he'll break your heart." It might be imagined that, reared in a country house, and with a young Irishman's innate love and knowledge of horses, Luke would have understood perfectly how to deal with a servant. But no! He had been so completely enervated and washed out by his intercourse with the soft refinement of his English home, that he was almost helpless. Then his tastes were of the library, not of the stables; of the kings' gardens of books, not of mangolds and potatoes; and he looked around helplessly for a qualified man to see after his horse and cultivate his garden. He had not far to seek. Dowered with the highest recommendations from the archdeacon of the diocese, a young man, neatly dressed, and with a decidedly military appearance, proffered his services.

"Did he understand horses?" Horses? Everything, except that he was not born amongst them. He then and there told Luke awful things about spavins, ring-bones, and staggers, that Luke had never heard of, or had completely forgotten.

"But if her feet are right, and she takes her oats, she's all right. Lave her to me!"

"She has a white star on her forehead," said Luke, anxious to show the mare's high breeding.

"What?" said the boy, as his face lengthened.

"She has a white star on her forehead," stammered Luke.

"That's bad," said the boy, solemnly. "No matter," he said, in a professional tone, "I'll make up for it."

"Do you know anything about flowers?" asked Luke, timidly. The fellow saw the timidity, for he was studying Luke closely.

"Flowers? Ax Lord Cardoyne's gardener, who took first prize at the 'Articultural Show in Dublin last summer, what he knew. Yes! Ax him, who reared the Mary Antinetty Rose, that—"

There was a long discussion about wages. A king's ransom was demanded; and it was asked, as a *sine qua non* that he should be "ate" in the house. Luke demurred, but no use. Luke cut down the wages to the lowest common multiple; and then John Glavin played his trump card. Taking out a dirty roll of yellow papers, tobacco-stained and scented, he proffered one with the cool air of having thereby victoriously settled the question. From this it appeared that John Glavin was an honest, industrious young man, with a good knowledge of the management of horses, and some ideas of horti- and floriculture. He was recommended, his wages having been paid in full.

"The archdeacon does not mention sobriety?" said Luke.

"What?" said John, indignantly. "Who says I'm not sober? The archdayken knew better than to insult me!"

"It would be more satisfactory, however," said Luke.

"I wouldn't lave him," said John. "He says to me, 'John,' he says, 'it is usual to put in *timperate* in a discharge; but John,' says he, 'I've too much respec' for your feelings, an' I won't. But if iver anny one hints,' sez he, 'that you are not a sober man, remimber you've an action agin him for libel, or even,' sez he, sez the archdayken, 'even for shlander'—"

"I see," said Luke. "Now, what wages were you getting?"

"I'd be afeared to tell yer reverence," said John in a soothing and merciful tone.

"Oh, never mind!" said Luke. "I can bear a good deal."

"Well, thin," said the rascal, putting his hand rapidly across his lips, "as yer reverence forces me to tell ye, I suppose I must—thirty pounds a year. Not a pinny less!"

"I shall give you twelve," said Luke, decisively.

John walked away. His feelings were hurt. He came back.

"Your reverence wouldn't insult a poor boy. But come now, let us say twinty, an' be done."

"That'll do," said Luke. "Be off."

To Luke's intense surprise John was cracking jokes with the housemaid, and enjoying an excellent dinner, at one o'clock in the kitchen. He then took possession of the place. But on many an evening, in the local public house, he uttered his jeremiads over his downfall. From having been "archdayken's man" to be reduced to a "curate's boy," what a fall!

It need not be difficult to ascertain the precise cause of John Glavin's dethronement. Perhaps he had exhausted too many "tail-ends" on the kitchen stairs; perhaps he had been caught with his ear to the keyhole on some official occasion; perhaps some important letters looked as if other than the master's eyes had seen them. But, he was dismissed; and the archdeacon had to undergo a severe cross-examination as to the cause. Because a great archbishop, from foreign parts, being on a visit to the archdeacon, had taken a violent fancy to the fellow and expressed a desire to secure him for his own service at a handsome salary. He had taken a violent fancy to John, for at dinner John, whose speech was approaching the inarticulate, and whose eyes had a faraway look in them and were decidedly aqueous, invariably addressed the archbishop as: "Me Grace!" Oh! yes. John had been to school in his younger days, and had

been subjected for several hours that day to a most careful
tuition on the housekeeper's part as to the use of possessive
pronouns in addressing dignitaries.

" '*My* Lord,' and '*your* Grace,' " said the housekeeper. "Do
you understand, you fool?"

John said he did, and he went around all day muttering the
talismanic words. But, alas! what can a poor fellow do, when
his nerves fail under the eyes of the "farseers," and especially,
when the wheels of thought are inclined to stand still.

"John, a potato, please."

"Yes, me Grace!"

"John, would you get me the salt?"

"To be shu', me Grace!"

"John, pass that wine."

"The sherry, me Grace?"

"No. The claret."

John's watery gaze floated over the table, where things had
become horribly confused and exaggerated; but he failed to
see the claret decanter.

"John!"

"Yes, me Grace!"

"Where's that claret?"

"Cummin', me Grace."

"John!" thundered the archdeacon.

"Yes, me Grace!"

"Go downstairs and stay there!"

"More likely to stop half-way," said the archbishop. "He's
sitting now on the top step, weeping. Archdeacon, that fellow
is a treasure. Will you give him to me?"

The archdeacon was annoyed at the exhibition. Besides,
the archdeacon was nowhere. John worshipped the star of the
first magnitude, particularly as it had developed into a constel-
lation. When he noticed the bishop, he called him by way of
compensation, "Your Lord!" The archbishop maintained that
it was "Oh Lord!" he said; but that was a mistake. Then and
there, however, the archbishop saw a prize, and coveted it.
Alas! for John, and all human attachments. The master clung
to him, and then—dismissed him. It happened thus. The archdeacon had been absent from home for a few days. His carriage was waiting for him at the railway station; but to his

surprise, John, instead of alighting with his usual alacrity, clung with statuesque tenacity to the seat. A porter proffered his services and opened the carriage door. When they reached home, John was still statuesque. The archdeacon suspected a great deal, but said nothing. A few hours later, just as the archdeacon was sitting at dinner, he heard the rumble of carriage wheels in the yard and the heavy tramp of the horse's feet. "What's up now?" said the archdeacon. He went to the front door just as John was leading the horse and carriage from the yard, and looked on for a few moments in silence. John, too, was silent and abstracted, and preoccupied with deep thought. At last the archdeacon said:—

"Where are you going?"

"Where 'ud I be goin', is it, me Grashe?"

"Yes! that's what I asked. Where—are—you—going?"

"Where 'ud I be goin' but down to th—train?"

"For what?"

"For whash? To meet your Grashe, to be shu!"

"I see. Going to the train to meet me?"

"Yesh, m'Grashe. D'ye think I'd lave you yere all ni', mi Grashe?" John was looking far away over the archdeacon's head.

"Take back that horse at once," said the archdeacon.

"An'm I no' gon' to meet your Grashe?"

"Take back that horse at once, I say."

"Bush you'll ketch yer det o' cowld, me Grashe!"

"Take back that horse, I say."

"If you diesh, what'll become o' me? Boo-hoo!" wept John.

The next day he was dismissed, and the archdeacon was left to his fate. But he had to stand a terrific cross-examination at a subsequent visit from his guest, the archbishop, who could only by the greatest difficulty be restrained from making an effort to secure "the treasure."

"I'd have taken the fellow at any cost," said the archbishop, as he related the episode to a friend in after years, "but the doctor told me I should take my choice between apoplexy and asphyxia, if ever I brought him to table."

Luke drew the prize, and secured the treasure.

CHAPTER XXVIII

Mary of Magdala

IN THE home of the Good Shepherd the religion of our Lord reaches its culmination. No wonder that the favorite representation of Christ in catacombs and elsewhere for three hundred years was this of the yearning and merciful Saviour. How well those early Christians knew His spirit, when they placed a kid, and not a lamb, on His shoulders! "I came not to call the just, but sinners." Yes! charity first and then the Crucifixion—the mystery of suffering. And here in the city of the Violated Treaty, under its crumbling, historic walls, and just outside its ruins, nestled such a home. You might pass through the city a hundred times and not know that such an institution was there. You might visit the historic bridge, and the Treaty Stone, and never know that here also was a place where the might of the Lord was visibly triumphant. You might hear elsewhere of the miracles of Christianity—here you could see them. You might read of battles, fought, won, or lost, around the Two Standards: but here you can see the bleeding and wounded *vivandières* in Satan's army snatched from the battlefield, and sheltered in the camp of Christ. And here, if you had faith, that is, if you opened your eyes, and brushed aside the film of habit, you might see miracles, and saints, and prodigies, such as you read of in the Gospel, or in mediæval times, when perhaps you wished you had been born then. So, at least, thought Father Tracey, who was never harsh in his judgments, except when he deplored that crass stupidity of men, that will not see what is under their eyes.

"Nonsense, child," he would say to Margery, "to talk about the age of miracles as past. Here are miracles; and saints, as great as ever were canonized."

320

Then he would repent of such rashness, and correct himself.

"Of course, I don't mean—that is, my dear—I don't mean to say that the Church should canonize all my little saints that die. But you know—I mean that our Lord will—that is, I suppose, you know—my dear—"

"Of course, Father. That is, we, poor nuns, have no chance with your saints."

"No, no. I don't mean that. But, you know, you are all very good; but there are different degrees of sanctity—some Apostles, some Doctors—"

"Yes. But Mary Magdalen is the next to the Sacred Heart, just a little outside the Blessed Virgin, and she is dragging up all her little saints with her? Isn't that what you mean?"

"I'm not sure, my dear. The Imitation says, that we must not make comparisons, you know."

"Yes. But tell me now, suppose you had your choice of a place in Heaven amongst the band that 'follow the Lamb, whithersoever He goeth,' and sing that incommunicable canticle; or of a place with Magdalen and her wounded following, which would you take?"

"That's a hard question, my dear. But, to tell the truth, my dear, I'd be far more comfortable with the latter."

"I knew it," said Margery, exultantly. "I've won ten rosaries from Mechthildes."

But whatever be said of the different beatitudes of Heaven, it is quite certain that living amongst the rescued sheep was not all beatitude on earth. Sometimes a poor soul would struggle in the arms of the Shepherd to get back to the horrors of the battlefield; would dream of gas lamps, and the midnight, and the fierce, exultant madness of sin. And, sometimes, there would be depression and even despair, as the awful visions of the past arose before some poor soul; and the dreadful suggestion would paralyze every effort at reparation: How can I ever enjoy heaven, when so many souls, lost by my illdoing, are tortured in hell? These were hard trials for Father Tracey.

"No use, Father, I *must* go!"

"Have we been unkind, my dear? Or, is there something else you could wish for?"

"Oh, no, no, Father dear; but I *must* go!"

"Well, dear, don't act hastily. This, you know, is a temptation from the Evil One. Go in, and say a little prayer to the Sacred Heart; and I'll send Sister Mary to you."

"No! no! don't! I won't see *her*. She'd *make* me stay. And I must go!"

"Well, sure, there's time enough. Go in, child, and pray."

He, dear saint, had great faith in prayer. But he believed the prayers of Sister Mary to be invincible. Was it not Sister Mary's prayers that had saved so many souls from perdition? Was it not Sister Mary's prayers that drove the evil spirits, howling in dismay, from the deathbed of Allua? Was she not the custodian of the King's secret, who could do as she pleased with the King's treasurers? And never yet did a poor penitent, eager to fly unto the dread attraction of the world, hear the voice of Sister Mary, but her eyes were opened and she saw beneath her feet the yellow flames curling up from the abyss.

And who was Sister Mary, or to give her her full title, who was Sister Mary of Magdala? Well, a poor penitent, too, who had sought refuge here from the world. The report was that she had been a great sinner. Even hardened women spoke of her past life with a vague hint at horrors; and, sometimes, when Sister Mary pressed too hard on a relapsing sinner, and spoke of hell, it was broadly suggested that she had sent a good deal of fuel to the fire.

"That handsome face of yours, if all were known, drew many to drink and hell."

And Sister Mary did not contradict, but only bowed her head meekly, and prayed and argued ever so strongly for the wayward and the tempted.

It would appear, too, that she had been a lady of very high rank, and had toppled down from circle to circle of the Inferno, until God took pity on her and brought her here. And here she developed such sanctity that the community and her sister penitents were bewildered; but all agreed that there was a saint—a real, downright, heroic saint—amongst them. But by far the most surprised and bewildered amongst this sacred community of nuns and penitents was the confessor, Father Tracey. He did not know what to make of it. He was confused, humbled, nervous, ashamed. The first time he saw this young penitent was at a "play." For this glorious Sisterhood used up every human means that talent or the divine ingenuity of charity could suggest to wean away these poor souls from the fierce attractions of sin and the world. And so there were plays, and concerts and dramatic entertainments, and *tableaux vivants,* and all kinds of innocence dissipation for the "penitents." And these harmless amusements were very successful in cheating the poor souls of the more deadly draughts of sin, until grace and habit finally triumphed. Well, at one of these entertainments, Sister Mary of Magdala was chief actor. She personated a fine lady of the world, suffering from nerves, and in consultation with a lady specialist. It was very amusing, and the audience were in convulsions. Venerable old penitents, who had done their fifty years of purgatory in this asylum; young penitents, fresh from the pollution of the city and with the remnants of rural innocence still clinging to them; dark, gloomy souls, the special prey of the tempter; and the gentle Sisterhood, presiding over all,—all yielded to the irresistible merriment. Sister Mary had doffed the penitent's dress and was clad in the finery of the well-dressed woman of the world. It became her well. She was every inch a lady, and all the sweetness and delicacy of her early training shone through the absurdity of the part she was playing.

"Ladies from the city, my dear?" whispered Father Tracey to Margery. "How good of them to come in and amuse these poor girls!"

"No; they're our own children," whispered Margery.

"But that grand young lady, my dear? why, she's fit for a palace."

"That's Mary of Magdala," said Margery, smiling. "She's now a great saint; but they say she was awful."

But, oh! the pity of it, when the performers disappeared amidst the plaudits of the audience and the rough criticisms of some poor creatures, and immediately reappeared in the penitents' costume—blue dress and mantilla, and high, white Norman cap—and took their places amongst the inmates again. Father Tracey was choking with emotion, as he watched that young girl, disrobed of her natural dress and clad in the strange livery that hid, and yet hinted at, unspeakable shame. And she so calm, so unconcerned, without a blush at the frightful transformation, and accepting so gratefully the rough congratulations from her sister penitents, as she sat on the lowest bench and lifted up the beads of old Sister Paul and toyed with them like a child.

"I tell you, my dear," said Father Tracey, "that if Heaven is the place for those who become little children, that poor child will be at home there."

And the good old priest became frightened at Sister Mary of Magdala. He almost began to think he had been mistaken in not taking charge of the nuns instead. And when he recognized her voice in the confessional he got a violent fit of coughing and turned away his head and pulled up his old cassock over his knees, and, instead of the long, fervent exhortation he usually addressed to his saints, with such emotion that he set the most hardened aflame with the love of God, he only muttered, with averted head:—

"Yes, yes, to be sure, my dear, to be sure."

Margery and he used to have long spiritual conferences on this subject.

"I'm sure I don't know what to do, my dear," he would say. "Can you help me? Isn't there a book written by a good, holy man, called Scaramelli, or something like it, for the direction of these holy souls?"

"There is, indeed, Father. But, sure you have knowledge and inspiration enough for these poor penitents."

"Me? I don't know anything, my dear. I was, you know, what they call *minus habens* in Maynooth."

"What's that, Father?"

"Well, it's the very opposite of what your great, clever brother was."

Margery shuddered.

"He was at the head of his class; I, at the foot of mine. Why I was 'doctored' twice."

"Doctored? O, I am so glad!"

"Yes, my dear,—'doctored.' That is, I was compelled twice to read the same treatises for a second year."

"And wasn't that good, Father?"

"Yes, my dear; but it meant awful stupidity. Somehow I could not understand things. I used to look at those books and papers; but my head would swim round and round, and I used to see the words without understanding what they meant. Why, it was the wonder of the whole college that they ordained me at all."

"I suppose so, Father," said Margery, trying to keep back her tears.

"It was, my dear. And I suppose I'd be digging potatoes today, which would be my proper vocation, but for old Dr. Whitehead. They all agreed that I should go. They said I'd disgrace the Church, which was quite true. And the senior professor of theology said that I knew no more about theology than a cow about a holiday. But poor Dr. Whitehead asked, could I manage to get up the ceremonies of the Mass? and they shook their heads. 'Well, I'll teach him,' he said; 'and he must be a priest.' May the Lord be kind to him—and—forgive him."

"Well," said Margery, "did you learn them?"

"In a kind of way, my dear. Sometimes I do be puzzled; and I look up, when I should look down; and, at the Conference, the Bishop never asks me anything, lest I should make a fool of myself."

"I'm afraid you want Scaramelli badly, Father. It was well for you you didn't get charge of us."

"Ah, that was out of the question, my dear. And the Bishop saw it the moment I hinted at the thing. I'd have the all of ye half-cracked by this time."

"And so you think Mary of Magdala is a saint?"

"Think? I know it. And suppose now, I should misdirect that grand soul, or fail to lift it upwards, what a frightful responsibility! I'm thinking of asking the Bishop to remove me, and—"

"You'll do nothing of the kind," said Margery, thoroughly frightened. "You'll just stay where you are."

"Perhaps so, my dear. But I'll tell you now what you could do for me. You could read up all about St. Catherine of Siena, and Blessed Angela of Foligno, and Mary Magdalen de Pazzi, and let me know what their confessors used do. Or, I'll tell you. If you'd be so good as to write to your brother (he's a very distinguished theologian, you know), and pretend nothing, but ask a few questions, which I will put to you from time to time, perhaps—"

"The very thing," said Margery. Adding in her own mind, " 'Tis a direct inspiration."

"Then, you know, I could feel sure that I was supported by sound Catholic theology; and I couldn't go very far astray."

"I will," said Margery. "And so they were going to turn you out of Maynooth?"

"So they were, my dear, but for Dr. Whitehead."

"And you would be now digging potatoes?"

"Yes, my dear, in a flannel waistcoat and hobnailed boots."

"H'm. A decided improvement, I should say, on your present wardrobe. At least they'd keep out the rain."

And Sister Mary of Magdala was quite unconscious that she was exciting such interest; but went around in her penitent's garb, and washed and scrubbed, and ironed, and did all kinds of menial offices for the aged and sick, and took gratefully their awkward gratitude.

"God bless you, alanna!" or, "God bless you, Mary, and forgive you, and forgive us all, for all we ever done against His Holy and Blessed Name!"

And they wondered, poor souls, in their own dull way, at the wonderful skill of the Divine Artist, who could raise this spirit of sweetness, this lily of light, out of the sordid and reeking refuse of the regretful past.

Meanwhile, Dr. Wilson had advertised all over England for the missing Barbara; and had even employed private detectives to find out the convent in which she was hidden. A foolish thing, for if Barbara had done God's will in entering religion, as she had said, there was little use in fighting against God; and, if it were not God's will, then Barbara would very soon find her way home. But the Doctor was not well acquainted with such things. So he spent quite a little fortune in the vain quest. He was helped a good deal in his resolution by a remark dropped by that excellent lady, Mrs. Wenham, who, having returned to Dublin, had called for a double purpose—to visit the Wilsons formally, and to consult the Doctor professionally. For, alas! that we should have to relate it, the beautiful and accomplished Mrs. Wenham, Circe and Siren, was but mortal; and the dread forerunners of death were playing suspiciously around that frail complexity of charms which had sent more than one fool to destruction.

Her visit to the drawing-room was short. The eternal plaint of the mother's heart was wearisome. It was all Louis! Louis! and the woman of the world, with all her contempt for the pretty little puppet, would just prefer that he should be allowed to sleep in peace. It was monstrous that these ghosts of memories, and memories of ghosts, should be summoned up by the heart of a foolish mother at a pleasant morning call.

"It is quite a seance of spiritualists," she complained to her muff. "She'll ask me to summon this little idiot from Hades."

"I beg pardon," she said sweetly to the sorrowing mother, "does not your religion afford you some consolation in your bereavement?"

"It does, of course," said the weeper. "But it cannot bring Louis back."

"But you can pray, can you not, for—what's this the expression is—for the eternal repose of his soul?"

"Of course," said the mother. "And I have prayed. Indeed, I have. But death is death, and judgment."

Mrs. Wenham rose hastily. Here were those dreadful words again—always connected with these people. Death! Judgment! and at a morning call!

She entered the Doctor's study. Here it was Barbara! Barbara! Had she seen her? Did she know her? Was there ever the faintest clew to her whereabouts? And the father's eyes pleaded piteously with the strange woman.

"Yes," she said, "Miss Wilson had called on her at a very unseasonable hour, and had appeared rather excited and disturbed in her mind. She spoke in a rather rambling manner; and appeared hardly able to control herself. She would not like to say that Miss Wilson was quite demented—but—"

It was quite clear that Miss Wilson had not entered a convent, or that she would be soon sent home.

"I thought," said Mrs. Wenham, "that it was the highest ambition of Roman Catholics to see their children in religion? Now, I assure you, I have often thought that I should so like to be a nun. I have seen such pretty pictures of them,—at the hospital, kneeling to the cross, singing their hymns; and they

looked so pretty—such lovely faces, turned upwards to the
skies—such peace, such happiness, to which we, poor women
of the world, are strangers!"

"Let us change the subject," said the Doctor. "You wished
to consult me?"

Yes. And the consultation went on. And lo! as a result, the
pretty nun faces vanished, and a grim death's head appeared,
floating through the eyes and in the words of that horrid
Doctor. And she besought him, imploring him to reconsider
his verdict. So young, and the world so bright!

"I regret to say, Mrs. Wenham, that everything you tell
me seems to confirm my judgment."

And Mrs. Wenham wept. Death and Judgment seemed to
follow this family as footmen.

The Canon, too, was deeply interested. He had written
piteous letters to great ecclesiastics in England. He had always
written on his crested notepaper with the family arms and
motto, *Sans tache!* and he signed himself "Maurice Canon
Murray." He would have given a good deal to be able to
add Archdeacon, or Dean, of X——. But that was not to be,
yet a while. He received, after some delay, very courteous
replies; but there was no news of Barbara. If she had entered
an English convent it could hardly have escaped the notice of
the authorities. At last, one day a letter came from the south
of England, stating that a young lady, answering in all respects
his description of Barbara, had entered a branch of a foreign
institution, lately domiciled in England owing to the persecu-
tions in Germany, but hinting a doubt that there must be a
mistake, for this Order admitted as postulants only the children of noble or, at least, aristocratic families. The Canon was
indignant, and wrote back a dignified letter to his correspondent, asking, somewhat sarcastically, whether he was aware that
her father was a Dublin baronet, and her uncle Canon of
X——. The next post brought an apologetic reply; and it
assured the Canon that all doubts were cleared up; and that
it must have been his niece who had entered the novitiate of
the *Dames de Saint Esprit*. She had been sent to Austria to
complete her two years' novitiate.

"I thought so," said the Canon, grandly. "And I shall be

very much surprised if she does not reach the highest—ha—
distinction in her Order!"

And fancy—an old man's loving fancy, swept him even
farther; and he would dilate at length on the present and
future prospects of his niece. And when the poor old people,
who had been recipients of Barbara's charity, when she visited
her uncle, asked him, with the tender and tenacious gratitude
of the poor: "Wisha, yer reverence, may I make bould to ask
you where Miss Wilson is, God bless her?" the Canon would
answer: "Yes, my poor woman, I am happy to inform you that
my niece, your benefactress, has—ha—entered religion—
become a nun, you know, in a community exclusively reserved
for the highest continental families." And when the poor would
express their joy and surprise: "Wisha, we knew God would
always have a hand in her, the sweet young lady—" the Canon
would say: "Yes, indeed. Some day Miss Wilson will reach the
highest dignities in her Order, and probably become its mitred
Abbess."

And "mitred Abbess" became the standing puzzle and
enigma to the parish for many months. When the word
"mitred" came to be understood, it caused grave head-shaking
and heart-trouble.

"The notion of a bishop's hat on a little girl like that," was
almost a scandal. Father Cussen was consulted.

"Psha!" he said. "Mitred, indeed! 'Tis the mitre he wants
himself. And it should be a pretty high one, for his head is
always in the clouds!"

Nevertheless, the Canon was gratified; and the people conceived a larger idea of his power and might, and the greatness
of the family.

And even Dr. Wilson was reconciled to the idea, when he
discovered that his beloved child was enrolled amongst the
nobility of France and Austria.

"After all," he said, "the Church is a beneficent mother,
and happily provides shelter for her children in every grade of
life."

CHAPTER XXIX

A Parliamentary Dinner

IT WAS part of the programme that Luke should invite his brother priests to dine. He was one of the few curates who enjoyed the privilege of "separate maintenance"; and the privilege entailed some responsibilities, and amongst them, the initial one of giving a "house-warming." He had some nervous qualms and difficulties about it. His prim, cold, English manner had not made him a favorite with the brethren, whose quick, breezy, volatile ways he disliked, and whose attempts at easy familiarity he rather resented. But, he felt he should come down from the stilts, if he were to get on at all in this strange country, where every one seemed to live in a kind of indolent and easy undress.

"I hope, my dear young friend," said the gentle and kind old pastor, in that tone of urbane and deferential friendship which characterized him, "that you will not go to any extremes in this little entertainment. Your revenue here will be extremely limited; and, in any case, it is always well not to be singular."

"O, no, sir!" said Luke. "I shall attempt nothing beyond what is usual on these occasions. To be very candid, indeed, I should just as soon not be obliged to hold these entertainments. I don't care much for them; and I have a lively horror of a dining-room and all its appliances."

"You know you must command everything you require here," said the old man. "If you would kindly send up your servant, my housekeeper will be most happy to send you any glass, or table-linen, or cutlery you require."

"I am sure I'm most grateful, sir," said Luke. "We shall say five o'clock on Thursday."

The dinner passed off well. Even the stiff formality of the

330

host could not subdue the vitality of his younger guests, which effervesced and bubbled over in jest, and anecdote, and swift, subtle repartee. Nowhere on earth is there such wit and merriment as at a clerical dinner in Ireland. May it be always so, in this land of faith and frolic!

John was waiter; and John was gorgeous in white front and swallow-tailed coat. This idea of a waiter was rather an innovation, which some were disposed to resent; and it palled a little on their spirits, until there was a stumble, and a crash of broken glass in the hall, and the spell was broken. Luke flushed angrily. John was imperturbable. He explained afterwards:—

"Where's the use in talkin'? Sure, things *must* be broke."

It was the calm philosophy of Celtic fatalism.

Now, Luke, as he had once explained before, had made the most determined, cast-iron resolution never, under any circumstances, to be inveigled into a discussion on any subject, because, as he explained, it is impossible to conduct a debate on strictly parliamentary lines in Ireland. This, of course, was very chilling and unfriendly; but he thought it wiser and safer. Alas! for human resolutions! What can a man do, in Charybdis, but fling out his arms for succor?

"That reminds me," said a young curate, who had been classmate with Luke in Maynooth, "of a legend of our college days, of a student, who was strictly forbidden to enter the rooms of a professor, his uncle. He tried several stratagems, but in vain; for Jack was as 'cute as a fox. Then, he struck on the plan of dragging up the coal-scuttle, and tumbling over it, just at Jack's door. And Jack should come out to see and help the poor servant in his emergency. And then—the warm fire, and the glass of wine."

"I don't see the application of your anecdote," said Luke, who was very much put about by the accident in the hall.

"Let me see," said the other. "I don't think I intended any application. But let me see! Oh, yes! I really would not have noticed that clever Ganymede were it not for that crash in the hall. Accidents are required to develop genius."

"It is really interesting," said the old pastor, "to behold how easily our people fit into their surroundings. You can turn an Irishman into anything. A skilful alchemist, that is, an able statesman, could take up all the waste material in Ireland, and turn it into all beautiful forms of utility and loveliness. I knew that poor fellow," said the old man, in his kind way, "when he nearly broke the heart of the archdeacon by his insobriety and untruthfulness. I never thought that you could transform him so rapidly."

The little compliment made Luke proud, and broke his cast-iron resolution into smithereens. He called for more hot water and coffee, and settled down to a pleasant academical discussion.

"Yes," he said, folding his napkin over his knees, "the Irish are a plastic race; but the mould in which they are newly cast should never be allowed to run cold. If it is so suffered, they are stereotyped forever. It is a land of cast-iron conservatism. You cannot break away in originality without becoming a monster. It is the land of the Pyramids and the Sphinxes, with all the newer races staring at it, and giving it up as a puzzle."

"It would no longer be a puzzle," said the young priest above mentioned, "if we were allowed to solve it in our own way. But, it has ever been our misfortune that a blind man is always called upon to solve the riddle."

"I'm not quite so sure of that," said Luke, tossing his soutane over his knees, with the old *sic-argumentaris* gesture; "our ecclesiastical department is not so much meddled with; and behold where we are!"

"And where are we?" said the other.

"I should say somewhere in mediæval times," said Luke. "Compare our ideas of man's fitness or unfitness for a certain position, with those which obtain the wide world over. In every other department of life you ask, Is this man fit? In our department, you ask, How long is he on the mission? So, too, you never judge a man's actuality by the net amount of work he has done, or is capable of doing, but by, What did he get? The meaning of which enigma is, what prizes did he take in the days of his small clothes and his seminary?"

"You shouldn't complain, Father Delmege," said an old priest; "Maynooth has left its hall-mark upon you, and you cannot rub it off."

"Thank you, Father," said Luke; "but it is just as absurd to speak of a man as a great theologian, because he gained a prize in theology thirty or forty years ago, as to speak of a man as a great warrior, because he was captain in a successful snowball sortie at Eton; or as a great artist in black and white, because he drew a caricature of his teacher on the blackboard of a country school."

"I often heard that Eton won Waterloo," said the other.

"One of the world's, or history's, falsehoods," said Luke. "It was the starved commissariat of the French, and the treachery of Grouchy, that lost Waterloo, and the well-filled kettles of the British, and the help of Blücher, that won it. It was the victory of stupidity and roast beef over genius and starvation."

"Now, nonsense, Delmege; every one admits that in the career of every great man his early triumphs are recorded as indications of his future."

"I have not noticed it," said Luke, "because all the great men of *my* acquaintance never cast their heroic shadows in the halls of a university; but this is Ireland all out. You attempt to nail the shadows on the grass, and then believe them realities."

Luke had scored. It was a Pyrrhic victory, and a dangerous one, for it flushed him. His cast-iron resolution was now flung to the winds.

"But to return," he said. "We are just passing through another transition stage, where the new moulding of our people's character is about to take place. Let us be careful that the new ideals are right, before the genius of the race is fixed forever."

"There are so many artists at the work now," said the young priest, "that they can hardly blunder."

"I'm not so sure of that," said Luke. "In a 'multitude of counsellors there is much wisdom,' but that supposes that the counsellors can agree upon something. I see nothing before us but to accept the spirit of the century, and conform to the Anglo-Saxon ideal."

This was known to be Luke's pet hobby; but he had never formulated it before. The whole table flared up in an angry flame of protest.

"The Anglo-Saxon ideal? A civilization where Mammon is god, and every man sits with one eye on his ledger—the other on his liver!"

"The Anglo-Saxon ideal? A nation of dead souls, and crumbling bodies!"

"The Anglo-Saxon ideal?" The young priest before mentioned was on his feet, gesticulating furiously, his hoarse rasping voice drowning the angry protests of the brethren. Luke drew quite pale under the commotion he had excited.

"Yes," he said, "you have to face civilization for good or ill, or create a civilization of your own. The people are losing the poetry of the past—their belief in Celtic superstitions and creations. Can you create a new poetry for them? and can you fight, and beat back your invaders, except with their own weapons?"

"Better the whole race were swept into the Atlantic," said the young priest, "than that they should compromise all their traditions and their honor by accepting the devil's code of morals. One race after another has been annihilated in this Isle of Destiny for four thousand years. But they passed away with honor untarnished. So shall we!"

"Oh, my dear Father!" said Luke deprecatingly, "if you are prepared to sit down and accept the inevitable, all right! There is no need for further argument. Let us fold our togas around us as we fall. But if the struggle is still to continue, there is not much use in kite-flying, in the hope that we are going to call down the lightnings of heaven on our opponents."

"I suppose 'tis Destiny," said the young fire-eater, resuming his seat. "But, better be exterminated a hundred times than turned into money-grubbers and beef-eaters."

"It's only the cyclical movement in all history, noticed by all great thinkers, and formulated by Vico and Campanella," said Luke, now victorious and exultant, and *forgetful,* "the *corsi* and *ricorsi* of all human progress; and there is one great luminous truth running through it all—that he who cannot govern himself must allow himself to be governed by another; and that the world will always be governed by those who are superior in nature."

It is a little thing that turns the Irish mind from anger or despair to laughter.

"Would you please pass down the *corsi* and *ricorsi* of that coffee and hot water?" said a young wit; and lo! the discussion ended in a roar of merriment.

Just then a sweet, clear, girlish voice, just outside the window, which was raised this warm, summer evening, sang softly,

and with great feeling, the first lines of Lady Dufferin's pathetic
ballad:—

I'm sitting on the stile, Mary, where we sat, side by side.

It was so sweet and mournful, there in that Irish village, with
the golden sun streaming over the landscape, and the air
warmed and perfumed with the sweet odor of the honeysuckle
that clambered around the window; and it seemed so appropriate, that the priests were hushed into silence. It wrapped
in music the whole discussion, which had just terminated. It
was the *caoine* of the Banshee over the fated race.

I'm biddin' you a long farewell, my Mary, kind and true!
But I'll not forget you, darlin', in the land I'm goin' to;
They say there's bread and work for all, and the sun shines always
    there.
But I'll not forget old Ireland, were it fifty times as fair.

Not a word was spoken at the dinner table till the singer concluded. It was the infinite pathos of Ireland!

The girl came to the open window, and pleaded. She was a
tall, slim girl, dark as an Italian, the hood of her light, black
shawl scarcely concealing the black curls that hung down on
her forehead. The plate went round; and she held more silver
that evening in her hands than she had ever seen in her life
before.

"If Father Meade were here," said Dr. Keatinge with a
smile, "he would say it was the ghost of Erin—the wraith of a
departed people."

"I'll not forget you, darlin'," soliloquized the young priest;
"but they *do* forget you, darlin'; and what is more, they despise
you. And there isn't on earth, or in the nether hell," he said
vehemently, bringing his hand down heavily on the table, "a
more contemptible being than he, who, seduced by the glitter
and glare of foreign civilizations, has come to despise his
motherland."

"Now, now, now, that song has excited you, Cole," said his
neighbor.

"I'm not excited," he protested; "but I tell you, 'tisn't English steel, but foreign gold, we fear."

"Never mind, Cole," said another, "the *corsi* and *ricorsi* will swing around again in their cycles, and Ireland will come uppermost!"

"Yes!" he hissed, "if she does not forget her destiny."

"And what might that be, Cole?" shouted one or two, laughing at his vehemence.

"What might that be? *What would have been the destiny of the Jewish race if they had not rejected Christ?*"

"Delmege, compose this fellow's nerves, and sing 'The Muster.'"

But no! Luke had forgotten "The Muster"—he couldn't recall the words—it was many years since he sang it, etc. He sang:—

Oh! doth not a meeting like this make amends?

"I wouldn't doubt him," said the fire-eater. "He's the Canon's pupil, and an apt one."

The guests dispersed early; and Luke was alone—and unhappy. What was the reason that he always felt miserable after much contact with men? And especially, when he returned to himself after a temporary dissipation of thought, why was he always angry with himself and dissatisfied? Every touch of the external world made this sensitive nature shrink more closely into itself, except when he had something to look up to and to worship. With all his professions of practical wisdom, he was forever craving after an ideal that was shy and unrevealed.

As he passed from the heated atmosphere of the dining-room into the cool garden that was behind the house, he heard the soft patter of feet in the kitchen, and a low whistling sound. Both were faint and muffled, as if with an effort of concealment; and then the whistling broke out into articulate language:—

(Forte) "Welt the flure, Biddy McClure!"
(Andante) "Show them the right step, Mary McCarthy!"
(Fortissimo) "Yerra dance to the music, ye divils!"
(Adagio) "At—the—widow—McLau—au—au—ghlin's pa—a—a—a—rty!"

Then the dancing ceased.

"I'm too warrum," said Mary, "and I'm tired afther all the cookin' and slushin'."

"An ye did it well, Mary," said John, the musician; "I never saw a betther dinner at the Archdayken's."

"Wisha! for the luv of God, stop the 'Archdayken's,' " said Mary, who despised flattery; "it's nothin' but 'Archdayken' here, and 'Archdayken' there. Why didn't you sthop wid him, whin you were there?"

"Take that, John," said one of the boys, who had dropped in, with that easy familiarity which is common to the country.

"I didn't mane any harrum," said John humbly. "But it was a grand dinner, out an' out; I heard the priests say so."

"You'll have a nice pinny to pay for all the glass you broke," said Mary. "The masther looked like a jedge wid his black cap."

" 'Twasn't that made him mad," said John, "but that little red priesht from Lorrhabeg. Begor, he pitched into the masther like mad."

"He met his match, thin," said Mary. "I'd like to see wan of 'em excep' the parish priesht, who could hould a candle to him."

"What was it all about?" said one of the neighbors, unable to restrain his curiosity.

"No saycrets out o' school. If you tell this 'purty boy,' he'll have it in all the public-houses in the parish before Sunday," said Mary, the loyal.

"Wisha, 'twasn't much," said John. " 'Twas all the ould story of England and Ireland. The masther said we must all be English, or be swept into the say. The little wan pitched the English to the divil, and said we're Irish or nothin'."

"And who got the best of it?" said the "purty boy."

"Hard to say," said John. "They were all talkin' thegither, and jumpin' up, like Jack-in-the-Box excep' the quite ould parish priests. And thin that girl came, and you'd think they wor all in their cradles."

"Begor, they're a quare lot," said the purty boy. "They're as like childre as two pays. Get wan of 'em into a tearin' rampage about the dhrink, or a dance, or a bit of coortin'; and thin say a word about the Blessed Vargin, or the ould land, and you have him quite as a lamb in a minit."

"The English and the landlords would have aisy times but for 'em," said Mary.

"Thry that jig agin, Mary," said John. "I'll get the concertina."

"No," said Mary; " 'tis too warrum."

"I'm thinkin', John," said the purty boy, "of gettin' me taylor to make a shuit for me, like that. What 'ud it cost?"

"More than iver you see in your life," said John, angrily.

"But we could get it secon'-hand, like yoursel'," said the other.

"Stop that," said Mary, peremptorily. She objected to a duel. "Remimber where ye are. Get the concertina, John. The masther won't mind."

"Fun, fighting, and praying," thought Luke. "The Lord never intended the Irish to work."

He strolled along the village street, the quiet, calm beauty of the evening stealing into his soul, and stilling the irritation and annoyance of that dinner table. The purple mountains in the distance seemed to contract and expand, as the shadow or the sunlight fell upon them. The air was heavy with the odors of roses and woodbine, and yet cooled with the breezes that floated down from the hills, over whose sharp ridges were pencilled darker lines, as you see in the horizon lines of the sea. The old men sat smoking their clay pipes leisurely. The old women pondered and meditated, with that air of resigned peace so peculiar to the Irish. A crowd of children were laughing and playing in the main street, gambolling in circles, and singing that folksong, that is common to the children of half the globe:—

> London bridge is broken down,
> Grand, said the little dear:
> London bridge is broken down:
> Faire Ladye!

> Build it up with lime and sand!
> Grand, said the little dear:
> Build it up with lime and sand,
> Faire Ladye!

On the bridge were perched twenty or thirty young men, resting after the day's toil; and listening to the soft wailing of a flute, played by one of their number.

Luke passed swiftly through all. The old people arose, and courtesied, the men taking their pipes from their mouths. Luke said: "How d'ye do?" They did not understand. They were accustomed to something different from their kind old priests. "How are you, Maurya? How are the pains?" "Cauth, when did you hear from the little girl in Boston?" "The murphies are gettin' dry, Pat." "To be sure, man; send over for the saddle in the morning, and keep it as long as you like." "That's the finest clutch of chickens I saw this year," etc., etc.

"He's a fine man, God bless him," said the women, as they resumed their seats. "But he's mighty proud."

The children ceased from play, as he approached, and ran to their mothers. The boys leaped from the bridge, and saluted. The player hid his flute. They all could tell where the curate lived; but oh! he was a thousand miles away from their hearts. He passed out into the country under the thick twilight of the beeches. The privet hedges threw out their white blossoms, heavy with the odors which the bees loved; the sweet woodbine twined in and out of the hawthorn and brier; and the white clover, stamped by the feet of the voluptuous kine, wafted its sweetness to the passer-by. Far away some girls were singing an old Irish air; and, as Luke stopped to listen, and watched the blue smoke curling upwards in a straight line from the cottages, he heard the flute again wailing out another Irish threnody, *The Coulin*. Then, the voices of the children rose, clear and shrill again:—

> London bridge is broken down,
> Grand, said the little dear:
> London bridge is broken down:
> Faire Ladye!

The problem of the inexorable present; and the prophecy of the inevitable future strangely blended again.

He went into the village church again, on returning. There was a deeper twilight here than without. He knelt to make his evening visit, and say his Rosary. Here and there were scattered some of the pious villagers. You heard only their whispered prayers, and the rattle of their beads. At the altar rails, bowed in reverential love, was the old pastor, his head slightly inclined to one side. Luke envied him.

"I wish I were old," he said, "and done with these life's enigmas. These old men seem to cast untroubled glances into eternity."

He stopped a moment at his cottage gate, before retiring for the night, and looked down upon the street, the neat cottages, outlined against the dark, deep bank of the thick foliage behind. It was very peaceful.

"A wise man would make up his mind to be happy here," he said. "But will it last? And what can I do to preserve and extend it?" The problem and puzzle again.

"Anything that man can do, I'll do," he said vehemently, "to solve this dread enigma, and save this devoted people."

The following morning two letters lay on his breakfast-table. One was from Amiel Lefevril. It was one of many. And it was the old cant.

"Humanity is incarnate in all great men in a supreme degree; the true *Shechinah,* says Chrysostom, is man. Every child of Humanity is a transfigured type of Humanity. We are immortal in the immortality of the Race. Seek the Divine in Man, and help its development."

"There is a hidden element of truth in the jargon," said Luke. "Wonder we were never told it."

And Luke forgot that he had taken *First of First* in Maynooth, in Dogmatic Theology; and that he had held with vigor and success that "the revelation of God in Man, through the lowly figure of Jesus of Nazareth, had a far-reaching object, apart from the immediate purpose of the Incarnation; and that was, to confound the pride of mortals in the perfectibility of the race."

"If we could only teach these poor people," he said, "that their lofty ambition: Seek ye the God in man, was once, and only once, realized, all would be well. But, then, they should become little children again; and Nicodemus said that was impossible."

The other letter was from Margery, asking for light and advice on a critical question, about which Father Tracey, who said he had no idea of theology or mysticism, was much concerned. It would appear that one of their penitents, Sister

Mary of Magdala, who had been a great sinner, was now developing extraordinary sanctity; and Father Tracey craved light on one or two knotty points.

"DEAR LUKE" [the letter ran], "don't throw this aside in petulance or disgust. I know, and if I didn't, Father Tracey would convince me, that you are a profound theologian. But somehow I feel, too, that these things are revealed to little children. Luke dear, be a little child, as well as profound thinker; and let me know all you think on this most important matter. You have no idea of the peace of mind it will give us all, especially dear Father Tracey.

"Mother is not too well. Won't you go see her?"

"Well, well," said Luke, "is there any use in talking to nuns, at all?"

He wrote his little sister to say, that the veriest tyro in theology knew that these poor penitent girls were either subject very frequently to delusions, especially in the way of superior sanctity; or, were unfortunately prone to simulation of virtue for the purposes of deception. He had no doubt, whatever, that the case submitted to him came under one of these two heads; and he would advise his sister not to get involved in any way in what would probably prove an imposture, which might also eventuate in a grave scandal. Father Tracey, he understood, was an excellent man; but rather prone to take unwise views about spiritual manifestations, on which the Church always looked with doubt and suspicion.

Clearly, Luke had become very practical. A good many years had gone by since he vowed his pilgrimage to the city to kiss this old man's feet.

He took up his sister's letter again: and read it in a puzzled manner.

"It is downright positivism," he declared. "Margery, too, sees the Divine in Man—this time, in a wretched penitent. Imagine—Amiel Lefevril and Sister Eulalie arriving at the same conclusion from opposite poles of thought."

CHAPTER XXX

Cross Currents

HE CONGRATULATED Mary warmly on the success of her dinner. He had seen nothing like it, since he had left England. Mary blushed with pleasure.

"I did not think it was possible to procure such fowl at this time of the year," said Luke.

"Oh, the neighbors were good, your reverence," said Mary.

"The neighbors?"

"Yes," she said. "Mrs. Mahony sint the chickens; and the ducks came from Mrs. Cleary's yard; and—"

"You surprise me," said Luke. "How did these people send them? You purchased them, of course?"

"Indeed'n I didn't," said Mary. "The laste they may do is to help their priests, who are workin' night an' day for thim."

"But, my good girl, it was highly improper to solicit from these poor people—"

"I didn't solicit," said Mary, whose temper was rising.

"Then how could they know that I had a dinner in contemplation?" asked the bewildered Luke.

"Know?" said Mary, with a toss of her head. "They know more'n that. They know what's inside'n you."

Luke was silent for a few seconds.

"Was there much glass broken?"

"There was, thin," said Mary. "But it wasn't ours."

"Oh, the parish priest's? That makes it all the more necessary that we should restore it."

"Ah! he won't miss it," said Mary. "Sure, he has double your jues."

"Oh, no, no, no," cried Luke, amazed at this liberal theology. "He has been very kind; and we must return every article he has lent us."

"There'll be a nice hole in your quarter's wages," said Mary

342

to John in the kitchen. "You'll have to pay for all the glass you broke."

"How could I help it?" said John. "Sure, every one knows that things *must* be broke."

"You'll pay for it," said Mary. "And they were the parish priest's; and worth half-a-crown a glass."

"Begor, thin, if I do, I'll have it out of him," said John.

"Not while I'm here," said Mary. "If you put a wet finger on anything while I'm here, you'll suffer for it."

Luke visited his pastor.

"I must congratulate you," said the kind old man, "on that beautiful dinner last evening. It was a rare pleasure."

"Only for that unhappy discussion," said Luke. "I really must forego everything of that kind in future. It disturbs me too much."

"Much better than foolish talking about each other," said the old man. "Youth is the age for problems; old age is for the one great certainty."

"You must give me a few days' indulgence," said Luke, "to replace that glass which was broken. I hope to have it all from the city in a week."

"Now, never mind, my dear boy! I'm disposed to make the little sacrifice cheerfully, you have made such a convert of that poor boy. You must lend him to me in future, when I give our little parties here."

Luke was not quite so enthusiastic about his convert. Complaints were coming in from the people; and little bills appeared on his breakfast table every second morning.

To wan pare of chickens, kilt by the mare—5/—
MAIRY HAIGERTY.

To five bags of otes for the mare, £2—7—6.
JOHN RAFFERTY.

To wan dashboard, kicked to pieces by the mare—15/—
DANIEL REGAN, *Carpenter.*

To wan sheep, run over by your car, with one leg broke, comin' home from the fare at Kildinan—£1—10—0.
JAMES DALY.

"This won't do," said Luke. "It means bankruptcy. Come here," he said to John; "read these. What does it mean?"

"Mane?" said John. "It manes that they're the graytest liards and rogues unhung. I admit the oats; but all the others are chayting."

"These people would hardly send in bills without reason," said Luke.

"They wouldn't only they think you're innocent-like," said John.

"Well, it must be stopped," said Luke. "You're giving the mare too much oats. She's getting restive."

"Annythin' you plaze, yer reverence," said John. "But don't blame me if she breaks down on the road."

"You seem to have taken whiskey this morning? I thought you had the pledge?"

"Me—whiskey?" said the startled John in horror. "Devil—ahem—not a drop since I took the pledge from the parish priest, so help—"

"Sh—sh," said Luke, horrified. "I may be mistaken. Our senses deceive us. But there's an unmistakable odor of spirits around the room."

"Maybe the decanther is broke," said John, looking with great anxiety towards the sideboard.

"Hardly," said Luke. "Now, be a man and confess decently that you have broken the pledge."

"Would it break the pledge," said John, with the tone of a casuist propounding a difficult problem, "to *smell* sperrits, or to draw them in wid your bret?"

"Well, hardly, I think," said Luke. "But I can scarcely conceive how such remote contact could leave behind such permanent results."

"Well, yer reverence," said John, with the air of a man unjustly accused, and who is playing the trump card for acquittal, "this is what happened, and you'll see I'm innicent. I wint down this mornin' to Mrs. Dennehy's wid a message for Mary—that's the housekeeper—"

Luke nodded.

"And just as I intered the dure, what wor they doin', d'ye think?"

Luke declined to conjecture.

"Watherin' the whiskey," said John; "watherin' the whiskey." He spoke as of a sacrilege.

" 'What the d—— are ye up to?' sez I. 'Thry is it wake enough,' sez Mrs. Dennehy. 'I won't,' sez I; 'I've my pledge an' I'll keep it, wid God's blessin'.' 'Thry it,' sez she agin. 'Sure, you needn't swalley it; and ye have betther taste,' sez she, 'than whin you wor drinkin'.' She was fillin' up a glass, as she was spakin'. 'Stop that!' sez I, 'stop that!' ' 'Tis only a sample,' sez she. 'Sure, ye needn't take but as much as ye like.' So I smelled the glass. ' 'Tis strong still,' sez I. 'So I thought,' sez she. 'It wants more wathering.' ' 'Twould spile it,' sez I. 'Taste and see how wake it is,' sez she. 'I tell you, 'oman,' sez I, 'I can't.' 'Did you iver see such a fool?' sez she. 'Sure, I'm not axin' ye to dhrink it, but to taste it.' Wid that I tuk a sup in my mout', when the young blagard began to laugh at me. And begor, I got mad, and was goin' to say somethin', whin I forgot all about the whiskey, and down it wint the wrong passage. An' I coughed and coughed, as if I was in a decline. Thin, Dennehy had to slap me on the back; but begor, 'twas no use. I was coughin' and coughin', till I was black in the face. 'Begor,' sez she, 'you'll have to swalley the dhrop now, whether you like it or no; or else we'll have a corp in the house.' So begor, I had to take the rest of it; but *'twas in wather.* That's all, yer reverence, the same as if I'd kissed the book."

"Well, you'd better go and renew the pledge," said Luke. "I won't keep you on other conditions."

"Sure I often hard yer reverence sayin' from the althar, that a thing is no harrum, if you can't help it!" said the bewildered John.

"That'll do," said Luke. "Get away, and bring me a note from the parish priest."

So Luke was not quite so enthusiastic as the good pastor; and he changed the subject.

"Some of these poor people," he said, "have been asking me to assume the presidency of the local branch of the League. Do you see any objection, sir, or do you deem it prudent?"

"There certainly is no objection," said the old man, "but it means trouble, and even disappointment to you."

"I shouldn't mind the trouble," said Luke, "but I fear the disappointment. I cannot make out why my good old pastor,

Canon Murray, is able to turn his parish into a little Paraguay, but all other efforts seem to be abortive."

"It's the dread of the superior powers, which are quite out of sympathy with the people, that paralyzes everything," said the old man.

"Well, if it does nothing else but to make them hold up their heads and assume an air of manly independence, it is worth trying."

"Quite so," said the old man, resignedly.

So the Rev. Luke Delmege became President of the local branch of the League. His first speech was sensational.

"I want you distinctly to understand," he said, "that if I am to remain your president, it must be on condition that your constitutions are strictly observed. I shall allow no backsliding. (*Hear, hear.*) Nor shall I have any distinction of persons. (*Hear, hear.*) If the rules are violated, you'll hear from me. Now, I understand that some gentleman has a resolution to propose. You will please mark its phraseology, so that no one can say afterwards that he did not understand its significance."

The resolution was:—

"*Resolved:* That we, the members of the Rossmore Branch of the Land League, hereby solemnly bind ourselves not to take off our hats to any man in future, except the priest."

There was a long and heated discussion. They all knew at whom it was directed—a local magnate, fierce and fiery, and military, with a great tawny mustache, that he tied behind his neck sometimes, like the mighty warriors of Jena and Austerlitz. He was by no means popular, but very much dreaded, and he loved salutations in the market-place. Indeed, it was whispered that sometimes, when he had English visitors at the Lodge, he used to dispense sundry sixpences to the gamins of the village to secure their fealty.

Sundry amendments were proposed, debated, and rejected. One demanded that the clause, "or when passing the chapel door," be inserted. Another insisted that the words "or our sweethearts" should be the final clause. Another thought that "cap" should be put in after "hat," "because," he said, "there were fellows mane enough to lave their hats at home in order to escape the pinalty." However, it was finally decided that the original resolution should stand. Then Luke arose.

"Now," he said, "that resolution is after my own heart. I am a thorough democrat in the sense that I hold every man is just what he is, in the sight of God, and nothing more. And I tell you, that until you conceive this lofty opinion of yourselves, and understand the necessity of the self-respect that accompanies it, there is no chance that our generation can work out the liberties of Ireland. We want men, not pieces of putty in the shape of men—" Much more he told them, as they wondered and were glad. And he read a page or two of Carlyle, and wound up with the declaration, "that the true *Shechinah*—the revelation of God to the world—is man!"

This evoked tremendous cheering, and Luke floated on the blissful tide of popularity.

"Yerra, that's the man we want."

"That's the way to talk to 'em. Begor, now we'll see who's who!"

"Afther all, 'tis these quiet min have the go in 'em. Faith, he'll make 'em quake!"

"The ould Gineral will be a sight on Sunday. He'll want a pound in sixpences to bribe the young blagards to shaloot him."

There were some other trifling matters, however, where Luke was not quite so completely in touch with his admirers. His proposal to bring down an organizer, or teacher, in the shape of a young lady from Dublin, who would instruct the farmers' wives how to prepare poultry for market, was met with a kind of playful scorn. It was unintelligible. Luke explained; and told them a good deal about the anatomy of fowls, the various chemical elements in food, and the carnal desires of the English, who wanted fat fowl for good money. It was no use. The idea of importing a city girl to teach farmers' wives how to raise chickens was too absurd. And when the good women heard it, there was great hilarity. And many and pungent were the jokes that echoed around the hearths in many a peasant's cabin during these days. Yet Luke persevered. He had a mission, and was determined to fulfil it. He returned to the subject again and again; showed how many thousand chickens were imported into England from Normandy and the Channel Islands year after year; counted up the millions of eggs that were used in one biscuit factory in England; and dilated on the certainty of opening up a market for fruit and vegetables in London, and the thousands of pounds that might be made from strawberries alone. They only shrugged their shoulders, laughed, and turned it into a joke. Then Luke saw there was no use in appealing to the cupidity of this people. Some other chord must be touched.

His sermons, too, for similar reasons were a failure. Luke disdained appealing to the passions or sentiments of the people. He had read somewhere that the Greek equivalent for preacher is an interpreter or expounder—thence a player, or actor. And, with his high ideas of humanity, and his reluctance to gain an unfair victory, he reasoned, argued, but disdained using the least word or gesture that might affect the feelings of the people at the expense of reason. His choice of subjects, too, was original. He spoke of justice, temperance, punctuality, foresight—the great natural virtues which must be the foundation of the supernatural superstructure. Alas! what could these poor people, thirsting for the waters of life, as plants thirst for the evening shower, what could they make of such reasoning and philosophy?

"Begor, he must be very fond of the money. He's always talkin' about it. Post offices and savings banks, an' intherest! Why doesn't he spake to us of the Sacred Heart, or our Holy Mother, or say somethin' to rise us, and help us over the week?"

"Wisha, indeed, Cauth, 'tis a change from ould times. The ould prieshts used to tell us: Never mind! God is good, and He said He would. Trust in Him. And look at the Blessed and Holy Family! Didn't know, whin they had their brekfus, where they'd get their supper; nor, whin they had their supper, where they'd get their brekfus. But now, 'tis all money, money, money."

"I suppose he has a lot of it, Maurya?"

"They say he have. But he's the quare man. He thinks nothin' of givin' a half-crown or a shillin' to a poor man, but begor, if you put your nose inside his gate to look at a flower or a head of cabbage, he'd ate you. Look at that poor anga-shore, Kate Mahoney. In the ould times, she'd always a sate in the priest's chimley-corner; and whin the dinner wos goin' on, she'd stock her fist in the pot, and take a pratie, and ate it; or perhaps, pick a bit of the chicken, or rub the pratie agin the bacon. Pillalu! whin this man hard it, he got into a tearin' passion. Poor Kit will niver see the inside of that kitchen agin. But he gives her a shillin' a week all the same."

"And sure, they say he was goin' to dismiss that poor boy he has—and a hard job it is—because he caught him takin' out a han'ful of oats in his two pockets to give the poor widda Maloney for her little chickens."

" 'Tis thrue, I believe. And sure, what have he but what the people give him; and sure, what they give him is their own."

"I suppose he belongs to a high-up family intirely?"

"Wisha, hard to say. Nobody knows who's who, nowadays. But, if he's anything to the Delmeges of Lisnalee, he's be a cousin of me own—"

"You wouldn't be afther tellin' me, Cauth?"

"I would, indeed. But I wouldn't purtend it to him for the wurruld. I don't want bit, bite, or sup of him, thank God. If we're poor, we can be dacent."

The eventful Sunday came at last, which was to witness the triumph of the democracy—the first assertion of manly independence which the people of Rossmore were called upon to make. There was great exultation in the minds of the strong and virile—the glamour of battle and victory; and corresponding depression in the hearts of the weak and the wavering. For the "Gineral" was a great power. A faultless disciplinarian, he had been cordially disliked in the army. He now brought into civil life the iron discipline of the profession. He, too, was a beautiful, polished, merciless machine. He sought to make all his subjects like himself. He took credit of having made Rossmore what it was—an English village planted in the midst of an Irish population. And he drove through the one street of the village with great pride, when he showed his English visitors what he had effected. And the people hated him. He was a callous, unfeeling autocrat, who evicted remorselessly, if everything was not pipe-clayed; and sent his alarmed subjects to hell, if a hen walked across the tiled and sanded floor. And what a doleful place an Irish village would be without the morning *reveillé* of a dozen chanticleers!

The proposer and seconder of the famous resolution had posted sentinels all along the road through which the "Gineral" had to pass to church. Now, he always timed that triumphant march, so as to meet the great bulk of the villagers as they returned from Mass; and he always drove in a very high trap, so that the eyes of his subjects should be upturned

towards him. He got a little start of surprise, when the first
batch of rebels passed by, and laughed, almost hysterically, at
some particularly good story. They were so engrossed, that
they never even saw the "Gineral." He turned to his daughter,
Dora, who was with him, and said significantly: —

"There's something up!"

Batch after batch came on, talking, laughing. They seemed
to scan the entire horizon, except the particular arc that was
cut by the "Gineral's" hat. He got furious, and although he
was going to church, probably to hear a gospel on peace, he
dashed, and dashed, and dashed between his teeth at these
rascally rebels. He saw the mighty fabric of his despotism toppling to its fall. The sentinels rejoiced. It was the great renascence of the new spirit that was just then stirring the dead
clods of Irish life. They could not forbear smiling, as group
passed after group, and drove their hands deep into their
pockets, and glued them there, lest the force of habit should
prove traitorous to the great principle at stake. The "Gineral"
raged and grew pale, lashed his horse until he threw him into
a gallop, then reined him suddenly and flung him on his hind
legs. He was a beaten and baffled man. Just then, woman's wit
came to the rescue. His daughter quickly divined the nature
of the conspiracy; and taking the reins quickly from her
father's hands, she drew the horse and trap over against the
furthest wall, so that all the people should pass on her side.
Then, bending down, and fixing her brown eyes on a little
group, she said, with her sweetest smile:—

"Good morning, Pat! Good morning, Darby! Glad to see
you so well, Jem!"

There was a moment of bewilderment and horror. Then
Irish chivalry, that is always losing Irish battles, conquered
Irish patriotism. They took their hands from their pockets,
lifted their hats, and said with shamed faces:—

"Good morning, Miss Dora!"

The "Gineral" lifted his hat courteously. It was the first
time he was ever guilty of that politeness to his serfs, whose
very bedrooms he always entered and examined with that hat
glued to his head. But the occasion was critical. The battle was
won. Every succeeding group now followed the example; and
Dora smiled and saluted and caressed them, while the sentinels

raged and thundered, and formed dire projects of summary justice and revenge.

A meeting of the League was promptly called at three o'clock. Luke was wild with anger. The one thing that galled him most painfully was this dread servility. He believed that the first step to Irish independence was the creation of a new manhood, self-respecting, self-reliant; reverent, yet independent. This day he broke utterly through the crust of quiet, polished English mannerism, and poured out a lava torrent of Celtic eloquence. His audience grew white and trembled under such a sudden and unexpected display. They thought they could laugh it off. It was growing serious. Something should be done.

"Is your reverence finished?" said one of the delinquents.

"Yes," said Luke; "for this occasion," he added significantly.

"Would the secretary be plazed to read that resolution agin?" The secretary did, with great solemnity.

"I submit, your reverence," said the chief culprit, "that none of us who have been arraigned before this tribunal is guilty. We saluted Miss Saybright, not the Gineral, and the resolution says nothin' about ladies."

"That's a contemptible and miserable subterfuge," said Luke, angrily. And there was a roar of indignation through the hall.

"You know right well," said Luke, "that this was a ruse; and, like your countrymen always, you were led into the trap."

"I don't know about that, yer reverence," said another criminal. "Would ye be plazed to tell us what ye'd do yourself in the circumstances?"

"What I'd do?" echoed Luke.

"Yes, yer reverence, what 'ud you do, if you were saluted by a lady in the public street?"

Luke flushed, grew pale, stammered.

"That's not the question," he said.

"Oh! but it is the question," said his tormentor. "If you wor goin' home from Mass on Sunday, and if Miss Saybright said 'Good mornin', Father Delmege,' what 'ud you do?"

"I certainly should return the salute," said Luke in dismay.

"That's all we did," said the victor, looking around triumphantly.

And Luke had to admit in his own mind, as the meeting

broke up, that this race must lose their chivalry and become brutalized before they shall ever attain freedom in these days of savage force. But then, is freedom worth the sacrifice? Here again is the enigma, the problem of the race.

During the following week the weather continued warm, and one sultry afternoon, when Luke was away on a sick-call, Mary escaped from the heat of her kitchen and sat near the open window in one of the upper rooms. It was very cool and pleasant, and the woodbine, with all the beautiful familiarity of Nature, was pushing its scented blossoms over the boxes of mignonette that filled the window-sill. Everything tempted to a reverie; and Mary began to dream, to dream of one of those little diamond-paned cottages down there in the village, with its roses and honeysuckle, and she dreamed it was her own, and there was a lovely fireplace, painted brick-color, and shining pots and pans, and a tiled floor, and—at noon a shadow flung across the sunshine, and—from a corner, out from a mass of pink embroidery, came a tiny voice, and she saw the blinking blue eyes and the tossed, helpless hands; and then she woke up to see the garden gate open and the "Gineral" coolly riding up the narrow, gravelled walk.

"Bad—to ye," said Mary, now thoroughly awake to see the evil genius of her dream.

The General rode up on his gray charger, and his head was on the level with the window where Mary was sitting, with folded arms and all the self-possession of a Vere de Vere.

"Good-day!" said the General, trying to control his horse.

"Good-day!" said Mary, without stirring.

"Is the Rev. Mr. Delmege at home?"

"He isn't," said Mary. "An' I'm thinkin' he won't be plazed to see his flower-beds trampled when he comes."

"Will he return soon?" asked the General.

"He might, and he mightn't," said Mary.

"Would you kindly tell him," said the General, "that General Sebright called?"

"Gineral what?" said Mary, struck with sudden deafness.

"General Sebright," echoed the visitor. "Stop, I think I'll leave a card."

"Oh, ye needn't take the throuble," said Mary, grandly. "He has plinty of thim, himself, in his dhrawing-room."

The General put back the rejected card, and stared hope-lessly at this apparition.

"Perhaps ye'd be afther tellin' me your business with the priest?" said Mary.

"Oh! it was merely a call of courtesy," said the General. "Good-day!"

"Good-bye, and good-luck," said Mary; and then, *sotto voce*, "and that's not what I mane, me ould exterminator!"

For Mary was a red-hot little rebel, like most of her coun-try-women. She too had her idols and ideals. Amongst the former were Robert Emmet and St. Anthony of Padua, whose pictures graced her little bedroom, just under the great hier-archy of the Incarnation. Amongst the latter, neither rank, nor title, nor Mammon had a place. True as the needle to the pole are the instincts of her class and race. May no doctrinaires or self-elected prophets ever succeed in making such as this poor girl swerve one inch from their simple principles, which are the highest philosophy of existence!

At dinner she told Luke of the visit.

" 'Tis a wondher he never called before," she added. "I'm thinkin' he got a lesson on Sunday, tho' the stageens renaged."

Now, Luke was in another dilemma. Should he return that call or not? He knew perfectly well that that visit was purely diplomatic. The General had allowed months to elapse, since Luke's advent to the parish, and he had never shown the court-esy before. Well, then? Meet diplomacy with diplomacy. Luke determined that he would return that visit. But what construc-tion would be put on his action by his parishioners? How would they view this alliance with their deadly enemy? He saw all the possible consequences: but he despised conse-quences. The question is, What is right, and what is wrong? Yes! he would visit at the Lodge.

He did, and was received with a certain kind of courteous homage. He lingered there more than an hour over the teacups. No wonder. It was Aylesburgh again! The beautiful drawing-room, hung with such dainty pictures; the soft heavy hangings and portières, that deadened all sound, and made a dusk of color in the room; the large vases, filled with early chrysanthe-mums of every size and hue; the grand piano, covered over with costly furs, the wood fire blazing merrily in the grate—

ah, yes! it was the grace, the light and beauty of civilization once more; and Luke, with all his fine tastes, seemed to be wrapped in a dream of sweetness and luxury again. And Luke theorized, and made sundry complaints and suggestions, which were very flattering. Why could not the Irish gentry do what their brethren were doing the wide world over? Why could they not come down to the level of the proletariat, and by a little zeal and self-denial, introduce the sweetness and light of the higher life? Here, to his mind, was the radical difference between England and Ireland—that in the former country there was a perfect link between the classes, the nobility and gentry being gently associated with the laboring classes through the medium of the clergyman and his family; whilst here, in Ireland, there was an unspanned gulf between them, to their common detriment and disadvantage. The General and his lady and Dora Sebright listened with sympathy, and even enthusiasm. It was a happy idea! The very interpretation of their own thoughts. And Mr. Delmege really wished that they should enter into the cordial and intimate relations with the people he had so admirably expressed? Unquestionably! Well, then, they were most grateful for the suggestion; and would promptly act upon it. And Luke, as he passed down the avenue that wound through thicket and shrubbery, felt that he had gone far towards settling forever the eternal and insoluble problem.

In less than a month he had to confess to an uneasy and undefinable feeling that something was wrong. His remarks at the League meetings were received coldly; and he was greeted with soured silence on the streets. The good old pastor, in the most gentle manner, hinted at attempts at proselytism, which he heard had been made. It had been reported to him that certain ladies, on their visitation at the cottages, and under pretence of introducing a finer æsthetical taste among the villagers, had tried to remove the time-honored portraits of patriots and saints, and replace them with good loyal pictures from the *Graphic*. At home, Mary had hushed her merry songs; and alas! did slam the door twice or thrice violently. Altogether, Luke felt between Scylla and Charybdis, the cross currents and pitiless vortices of daily life.

CHAPTER XXXI

Greek Meets Greek

MRS. DELMEGE lay upon her death-bed. The physicians had been called in, and had shaken their heads. "This is *Mors*," said one to another. And those around the poor patient understood. And she also understood.

"Than' God," she said. "He has given me a long and a happy life; and now He calls me to Himself. Welcome be His Holy Will! But, I'm sorry for Mike. He'll be lonesome. But I'm glad 'tisn't I am over his coffin."

Luke came over to Lisnalee. When he entered his mother's room, and asked, with a faltering voice, how she was, she only took his hand, his priestly hand, and kissed it passionately. Then she spoke of the King of Terrors with such disdain, that he hid his head, and was ashamed.

"What should I be afraid of?" she said. "Sure, 'tis as natheral to die as to live; and what is it but goin' to God? Sure, I have had all I wanted in this world. Me daughter in her convent; and me son," here she kissed Luke's hand again, "at the althar of God; what more would any poor woman want?"

"Ay, I mind the time," she continued, after a pause, "when you, Father Luke, wor only a weeshy baby in me arms; and sich a rogue as you wor, too. Father Dimpsey, that was here before Father Pat, God be good to him! and to all our good priests! used have the greatest fun wid you. And wan day, when you caught his big, bony finger in your little weeshy fingers, and wouldn't let him go, he said: 'Mrs. Delmege, we'll make a bishop of this fellow?' 'I'd be satisfied,' sez I, 'if the Lord would only make him a priest.' And sure, I got me wish, and what more could mother's heart desire?"

"You'll recover, Mother," said Luke, weeping, "and we'll have many a pleasant day again at Lisnalee."

"No," she said, "the Death is on me. And how many Masses now, Father Luke, will you say for me, whin I'm gone?"

"That depends on other obligations," said Luke; "but you may be sure, Mother, that up to the day of my own death, I shall never say a Mass, without remembering you."

"At the *Miminto of the Dead?*" she said.

"Yes," said Luke.

There was a long pause. The instinctive refinement of the Irish peasant, that deterred from touching on a delicate subject, and the deep, reverential fear of the priestly character, held the mother silent. Then her great love bore down the barrier.

"An' how are ye goin' on wid these new parishioners?" she asked.

"Oh, very well, indeed," said Luke, airily.

"The people are good," she said; "but they're jealous-like of their priests. They worship the ground ye walks on; but they want the little word, and the 'Good-morrow! Good luck!' they're used to. I hard some of them say, over there where ye had the little throuble some time ago, that they'd die for you. But they have their little ways, and they must be humored."

"Has the Canon called?" asked Luke, changing the subject abruptly.

"Over and over again, God bless him!" she replied. "It was only yesterday morning he said Mass there on that table; and you'd think he was a 'uman, he was so gintle and nice."

"And Father Cussen?"

"He's here every day, and sometimes twice a day, poor man—"

"And Father Meade and Father Martin come up often," said Lizzie, who was in and out of the sick-room with her baby in her arms.

"And sure poor Father Pat should come all the way from the other ind of the diocese to see his old friend. 'Good right I have,' sez he, as if I ever did annythin' for the good, holy priest."

"I'm very glad, indeed," said Luke, as Lizzie now stopped the colloquy by putting her little baby beside her mother in the bed. And there they lay, the one commencing its little pilgrimage through this weary world, the other ending hers; and both in the hands of the All-Father.

The Canon looked more aged than ever to Luke's eyes. His tall form was slightly stooped, although he strove to move erect as ever, and the pallor of age was deepening on a face fringed with hair that seemed whiter than ever. And, somehow, a gentle resignation seemed to take the place of the old affectation, as if he, too, having tried everything in an attractive world, had found all things evanescent and shadowy in the light of the one reality. He asked Luke at once, had he heard of Barbara? Her fate seemed to be the one thing that still made life interesting. Luke had heard nothing.

"It makes but little difference," said the Canon. "It is quite clear she is quite safe in the shelter of some convent; and by degrees, by degrees, she will reach her proper station—"

"It is really surprising that she has not written to you, sir," said Luke. "The black pall that is thrown over a young novice at her profession symbolizes death to the world. But, there is no order so rigid as to forbid absolutely correspondence with relatives."

"Quite so," said the Canon. "Perhaps the family honor—shall I say, pride—withholds her. When she has reached her legitimate station, she will write."

"I confess," said Luke, "I am become quite indifferent to this question of honorary preferments. They seem to be scattered over the heads of mortals, as if by chance."

"Quite true, my young friend," said the Canon. "And as an exemplification of what you say, I have just had a letter informing me, that that young clergyman who, you may remember, was placed in a seminary in a position which you should have rightly occupied, has actually been advanced to the Chapter of the Diocese, as if the honorary degree, lately conferred upon him, was not sufficient recognition of his services."

Luke was stunned. He had not heard of this.

"Why, he didn't get an *Atque*[1] even in college," he was about to say, when an interior voice shouted peremptorily: Silence! For silence alone is worthy of thee!

But the wound was made, and festered. And it was with a

[1] The lowest distinction.

troubled and abstracted mind he entered the library at Seaview, where Father Martin Hughes and Father Cussen were
before him. The latter was rolling a ball in and out under the
great library table, under which Tiny and Tony, now full
grown, were screaming and scrambling for the prize. When
Luke was announced the fun ceased, and the children rushed
from the room.

After the first greetings and sympathetic inquiries about his
mother, the conversation between Father Martin and Luke
turned on general topics. Father Cussen—one of those restless,
impatient spirits that must be forever moving—strode up and
down the long room, now clutching at a book and examining
the title, then putting it back impatiently, all the time tossing
and twisting his watch-chain, as if eager to break it into its
separate links. Was it George Eliot who spoke about the inevitable convergence of lives, apparently distant as the poles;
and of the lines of human thought, shifted and changed forever by influences that seemed to be far remote from each
other and from their objects? It is inevitable that two lines not
quite parallel must meet, if pushed far enough into space; it is
inevitable that the Russian Bear shall hug the British Lion
in the passes of the Himalayas; and it was inevitable that Luke
Delmege and Henry Cussen should meet and thresh out the
mighty problem for which each had his own solution. Father
Martin felt, too, that the inevitable had come, and he strove
by gentle words and kindly stratagems to make the shock of
the collision as harmless as possible.

"Mother couldn't forbear," said Luke, innocently, "a little
lecture about that unhappy business at ——. She cannot see,
poor soul, that we have duties towards our people less pleasant
than necessary."

"And so Father Pat came over," said Martin Hughes, trying
to throw Luke off the track. "He has given me up since poor
Father Tim went to his reward."

"Of course," said Luke, "any man can live a good, easy,
comfortable life by doing nothing. Then no one can find fault;
but a man cannot do his duty in Ireland and remain popular."

"These are not the ethics of Lisnalee," said Father Martin.
"Every priest is beloved there, because they know but one test
—does he love the people?"

"There is love and love," said Luke. "There is the maudlin love of a foolish mother; and the wise love of a prudent father. And the first has been ours from time immemorial. The world tells us it is time to change."

"The world! What world?" said Father Cussen, hastily turning around.

"The world of progress and civilization," said Luke, calmly.

"Pah!" said Henry Cussen. "The world that we are colonizing and civilizing dares to dictate to us."

"My dear Father," said Luke, "these are purely insular ideas. If we do not climb to the best seats in the chariot of modern progress, we shall be crushed under its wheels."

"Of what does your modern progress exactly consist?" said Father Cussen, now coming over and facing his antagonist. "We are forever hearing of it; but we don't see it."

"It is a strange thing," said Luke, in his old crushing style, "to ask a definition of what is so visible and palpable. Progress is the onward and invincible march of humanity to the ultimate goal of the race."

"And what might that be?"

"What might that be? Simply the perfect happiness of the individual in the perfection of the race."

"Then why do we interfere with the perfect happiness of the savage; and compel him with gunpowder and dynamite to be as miserable as ourselves?"

"Ay! But that's mere sensual happiness. We are educating the savage to the higher ideal."

"And succeeding?"

"To be sure we are."

"And you want to educate our Irish people to a higher ideal?"

"Certainly."

"Tell me, can you conceive, even with your experiences of the English aristocracy, a higher life than that of your good mother, now closing in a death that the highest philosopher might envy?"

"Hers is an exceptional case," said Luke, faintly. "Indeed, I'm always wondering how the Canon has been able to raise the standard of living here; and everywhere else our efforts seemed to be doomed to failure."

"The standard of living?" echoed Father Cussen, contemptuously. "That appears to be the one idea of your modern progress, the worship of the Body, called otherwise the religion of Humanity."

"It is the spirit of the Church in our century," said Luke, "that we should keep abreast of modern progress."

"Yes. But what is modern progress?" said Father Cussen. "Do you mean the circus chariot, daubed all over with the abominations of hell in red and gold figures, and the devil holding the reins; or do you mean the safer vehicle, if slower, that moves to eternity?"

"I don't understand your figurative language," said Luke, impatiently. "I say that humanity has a claim on the Church; that the Church admits it; and that, therefore, she is in perfect sympathy with every element that makes for the betterment of the people."

"Precisely. But what *is* the betterment of the people? If you mean an improvement in their social condition, accompanied by a corresponding improvement, morally and intellectually: *concedo;* if you merely mean the acquisition of wealth with its acompanying vices and vulgarity: *nego.*"

"But why should wealth mean vice and vulgarity?" said Luke, bewildered.

"Because Mammon is an essentially vulgar deity," said Father Cussen; "as vulgar as Bacchus, and as disreputable as Aphrodite, and as insatiable as Moloch. Because no wealthy nation was ever characterized by education and refinement, but by brutality and sensuality. Witness Babylon and Rome, not to speak of modern empires that are rushing onwards to similar destruction. And what is true of empires is true of individuals; and your modern wealth, ill-got, ill-placed, and ill-managed, is simply begetting on the one hand a generation of bloated revellers, and on the other a generation of blaspheming and homicidal starvelings. And if you think that the Church of Christ is going to be bundled in, as a second-class passenger, in this chariot of destruction, with the devil holding the ribbons, I think you are much mistaken."

"The Church can never be indifferent to the interests of humanity," said Luke, faintly. "Her rôle in the coming century will be essentially humanitarian and philanthropic."

"Quite so, as it always has been. But with her own leading lights to eternity, not as a blind bureau of the State."

"It seems to me you are both saying the same thing in different language," said Father Martin, meekly.

"Not by any means," replied Father Cussen. "We are as far asunder as the poles. Delmege argues for time; I, for eternity; he, for the body; I, for the soul; he, for the real only; I, for the real and the ideal. In object and methods we are essentially distinct. But there's no good in arguing in a circle. Take the concrete."

"Certainly. Select your types, and judge what is progressive, and what retrogressive."

"I thank thee for that word! I'll take my types, the lowest and the highest according to your estimates, the Neapolitan lazzarone and the great British workman. Will these do?"

"Precisely," said Luke. "You cannot find better specimens of inertia on the one hand, and push on the other. The gods have given thee into my hands, Cussen!"

"Now," continued Father Cussen, "let me see! My picturesque Southern goes out in the morning after a breakfast of dry bread and black coffee, and stretches himself luxuriously on the parapet of the quay-wall that circles the bay of enchantment. Mind! He *is* picturesque. He is a handsome gipsy, clad in rags, but with all the glory of color. He comes in to a humble dinner, and, after a siesta, he does some trifling work for a few bajocchi; plays with his semi-nude but always picturesque babies; strolls down to the quay again; indulges in some light, winged sarcasm on the British tourist; and after a supper of maccaroni and sour wine, he takes part in an improvised concert on the sands, and serenades the stars. Is the picture correct?"

"Quite so," said Luke. "I cannot imagine a more worthless being, a more soulless scamp."

"Not soulless! I didn't say that. This man worships God in his own way; and womanhood, through his loving and beloved Madonna. And Italia! Italia! his goddess and his queen! Now for the British workman."

"Go ahead!" said Luke. "You are sinking deeper in the mire."

"Well, my model of progress and enlightenment is very unpicturesque. He is clad in coal-dust, and—a pipe. He goes down to hell every Monday morning; and there, by a Davy's lamp he digs and delves in smoke and heat and darkness, if he is not summarily blown into atoms by an explosion of firedamp. He comes up into the sun, that is, what ought to be the sun; but the sun never shines on England; and takes his wages —three pounds. Then, he drinks all day on Saturday, and sleeps and drinks all day on Sunday. He has no God; and he goes down to hell again on Monday morning—"

"At least, he is a producer," said Luke, fast losing temper. "He understands the sacredness and nobility of work. He is no contemptible parasite living on the labor of others."

"The same may be said for the horse and the ass," said Father Cussen. "But will any man tell me, that my low-typed Neapolitan is not in every way a happier, better, nobler fellow than—"

"Happier? There's your fallacy. Men are not born for happiness, but for—"

"You are quite right; but you are contradicting yourself hopelessly, Delmege," said Father Cussen. "You are just after stating that the whole trend and object of his modern progress is the happiness of the greater number."

"Quite so. Wrought out by *Entsagung,* the *Selbsttödtung* of chosen souls."

"Oh, Lord!" said Father Martin, in an undertone, "I knew he'd give himself away."

"Now, look here, Delmege," said Father Cussen, "I don't want to hurt you; but that's all cant and rot, the cant and rubbish of those who are forever dictating to the world what the Church of God alone can perform. You know as well as I, that all this modern enthusiasm about humanity is simply a beggar's garb for the hideous idols of a godless world. You know there is no charity but in the Church of God. All the humanitarianism outside is simply political self-preservation, with the interest of the atom lost in the interests of the State. And if you want a proof, go to your prisons, go to your workhouses, or go down to your ports of landing, and see paupers and helpless maniacs dumped on your Irish shores, because after giving their best years to build up the Temple of Mammon in England and America, their wretched support, half-crown a week, would lessen the majesty of the mighty god! There is the huge fiction of Protestantism—the Godless abstraction—the State, humanity, the race, etc. Never a word about the majesty of the individual soul!"

"That's all fine rhetoric, Cussen," said Luke, "and fine rhetoric is the bane of our race. But whilst your theories are depopulating the villages and towns of Munster, Belfast is leaping with giant strides towards prosperity and affluence."

"One moment," said Father Cussen. "Our southern towns and villages are being depopulated. Why? Because the great god, Mammon, is sending his apostles and missionaries amongst us; because every letter from America is an appeal to the cupidity and lust for pleasure, which is displacing the Spartan simplicity and strength of our race. The gas-lit attractions of New York and Chicago are rivalling successfully the tender, chaste beauties of Irish life and Irish landscapes. It is because all the chaste simplicities of home life are despised for the meretricious splendors of city life, that our people are fleeing from their motherland. But you spoke of Belfast?"

"Yes," said Luke. "While all down here is a slough of despond and misery, there in the North you have a metropolis of splendor, and wealth, and progress."

"Progress, again! In heaven's name, man, are you a Christian and a Catholic?"

"It is because I am both the one and the other, that I see the inevitable absorption of our race in the stronger one, or its absolute depletion under the overwhelming influences of modern life. If we do not adopt modern methods, out we go."

"And do you consider what you lose by your modern methods? Is the game worth the candle? Listen: I cycled around the North of Ireland last year—"

"I'm surprised," said Luke.

"Surprised at what?"

"That you could be so modern as to cycle at all."

"Never mind. I called at Portrush; and put up at one of the big hotels there."

"No, no!" said Luke, sarcastically. "You put up at a wayside cabin; and you had potatoes and potheen for dinner."

"Well," continued Father Cussen, "we were a pretty happy

party for the week—a few very nice English and Scotch families, over for golfing—"

"Not at all. You're dreaming, man. How could they be English and nice?" asked Luke.

"Well, Pandemonium burst on us on Saturday afternoon. Train after train disgorged the Progressives of Belfast—a loud, blatant, red-faced, amorphous set, who paraded their vulgar wealth everywhere, and filled every corridor and room in the house with an atmosphere of stale liquor. Champagne, carefully diluted with brandy, was their beverage. They drank steadily all day on Saturday; spent Sunday, with opera glasses on the beach, and champagne glasses in the bar. The frightened Saxons locked themselves in their bedrooms. On Monday morning they cleared out at seven—"

"And every man was in his counting-house at ten," echoed Luke, triumphantly.

"Well, that's your progress. Now, look on the reverse side of the picture. Last month, I was down in Crosshaven, at the mouth of Cork Harbor. It was Sunday. Railway steamer after steamer flung out its quota of passengers—pale-faced mechanics from the city, with their young wives, and little children swinging baskets of provisions between them; a crowd of laughing students or commercial men; a number of mercantile or professional men, seeking a breath of sea-air and a few hours' rest; a bevy of gaily dressed, laughing girls, etc., etc."

"Oh, go on, go on!" said Luke. "You are doing well with your word-painting."

"I saw them, these mere Irish," continued Father Cussen, with some emotion, "going out the white road towards the sea; I saw them on the cliffs; I saw them on the beach—a happy, bright, cheerful crowd. I saw them taking out their modest dinners—a sandwich or two, a bottle of lemonade, a few cakes and oranges for the children. I passed through and through these happy groups, near enough to hear every word they said. I peered over the shoulders of a young mechanic. He was reading *Sesame and Lilies*. I saw them return in the evening—a happy, bright, courteous, refined crowd; no hustling or jostling; but Celtic politeness and Celtic wit and humor. And then I thought of Portrush; and of their fellow-countrymen festering in the fetid tenements of New York, or gasping for a moment's breath in the siroccos of the Western States; and I thought, that progress consists not in miles of gas-lit streets, or millions of bricks piled squarely against the sky; but in human souls, taught to know their dignity, and the vast universe of their inheritance."

"I do not at all dispute your reasoning, or your conclusions," said Luke, meekly; "but how does it solve the problem, that is threatening, not theories of life, but the very existence of the race itself? Here it is: can you find a *via media* between modern civilization and Irish purity and faith? If you do not adopt the methods of the former, your very existence, as a race, is at stake. If you adopt them, all the characteristic glories of your race and faith vanish. Here comes modern progress, like a huge soulless engine! There is but one way of escaping being trodden out of existence by it, and that is, to leap up and go with it, and then, what becomes of your tender faith and all the sweet sincerities of your Irish innocence and helplessness?"

"We can create our own civilization," said Father Cussen. "Here is our initial mistake, with, God knows, what consequences. We are imitators, instead of being creators."

"And, meanwhile, what is to save you? English omnipotence is pushing from behind: American attractions are dragging in front. What can save you?"

Father Cussen paused for a moment. Then, lifting his hand with some solemnity towards the ceiling, he said:—

"THE GOD OF ABRAHAM, AND OF ISAAC, AND OF JACOB! The same God that has pulled our race through seven centuries of fire and blood."

CHAPTER XXXII

Percussa Et Humiliata

WHEN SISTER Mary laid aside her Norman cap, at night, she also laid down her crown of thorns; and, with her blue mantella, she put aside the cross she was bearing so bravely and lovingly. For it was a mighty cross, assumed in a spirit of love and penance; and it bore down to the earth sometimes the frail figure that supported it. For Nature is ever in protest against the spirit; and is ever asking querulously, Why? why? when the soul seeks pain, and the body cries for rest. But sleep brought more than rest to this penitent spirit. It brought dreams; and dreams brought anguish to the daylight. But they were very beautiful. Were there no waking, they would have made Heaven. And now some of these dreams occurred again and again; and Sister Mary was obliged, so very beautiful they were in sleep, so dread in the consciousness of day, to ask prayers frequently against their recurrence.

"Pray, Sister," she would say to the nun in charge of the dormitory, "that I may not dream tonight!"

But the dream that used to dawn out of the shadows of sleep most frequently was this. She thought she walked in a great garden, beneath the umbrage of trees, and brushed by the great, beautiful flowers, that leaned towards her to touch her feet, her hands and her garments. And in the garden was a mighty palace, always lighted for a festival; and she saw a long procession of the white-robed immortals entering slowly, but with uplifted faces, on which the lights of the banqueting hall shone. And, when all had entered, and the doors were about to be shut, a Figure came to the portals, and, shading His eyes with His right hand, looked long and lingeringly into the darkness. And Mary knew that it was herself was the desired

366

one; but she dared not come out of the darkness into the light, because the robes of humiliation were around her; and the blue serge of sorrow was not a fitting garment for the splendors of the King's Hall. So she turned away from the questing eyes; and sought the shadows again. Then she was suddenly aware that a Voice, quite near, called her; and that she was sought out amongst the shadows. For she heard, ever and again, the whisper: *Veni, Sponsa! Veni, Immaculata! Veni, Sponsa mea!* and then a hand was laid gently upon her. She was found, and reproached. But she could only point to the blue garment of penitence, and weep. And then she found herself in the Hall of the King; and with His own wounded hands He put on the bridal robes—the soft, white habit, and the veil, and drew around her the blue cincture and let the scapulary fall; and He hung the Silver Heart on her breast, and tied the rosary to her girdle; and lo! she was a Sister of the Good Shepherd. And He led her trembling into the lighted Hall; and all her Sisters gathered around her, and kissed her— and then,—well, then, she would wake up on her narrow bed in the gloom of a winter's morning, with just a yellow gas-jet above her head; and, ah, yes! here was the blue serge mantella and skirt; and here the high, frilled, Norman cap—the badge of penitence and shame. No wonder that her heart sank like lead, and that a film crossed her eyes, as she went about her weary work for yet another day; until, perhaps at Mass, or afterwards in the hushed silence of the afternoon, she would study and watch the white figure of her crucifix; and, then, with one swift aërial flight, as a mother-bird swoops on her nest, she would fly on the wings of love, and fold herself and nestle in the big, gaping wounds of the torn side of Christ; and then all was peace again until another dream.

But there were other sorrows, too, awaiting her, deep humiliations, that plunged her into the abyss, until rescued by prayer and faith. There is no use in arguing against the inexorable law. The gold *must* be fire-tried.

There was one young penitent who was the special object of Sister Mary's solicitude. She had come into this sacred asylum again and again; and again and again she had gone out unto the dread attractions of the midnight streets. But always, when she knocked humbly at the Convent gate, she was admitted with a smile of welcome. The charity of this Order, like the charity of Christ, is inexhaustible. It would be a terrifying novelty, except to those accustomed to the supernatural, to witness the fierce fury of the temptations that used to assail this young girl—the paroxysms under which she strove to resist her own dread inclinations, and the wiles of the unseen. It was here that Sister Mary had been most successful. Because, although her efforts at reclamation of this sister-penitent were doomed to disappointment, and the bird was forever breaking from her hands, there was some tie between them, some bond of love, that might have been stretched and strained, but was never broken. And whenever the poor girl returned, clothed in her right senses, after the spell of midnight madness, it was always Sister Mary who was privileged to take off the soiled gewgaws of fashion, and put on the cleaner vestures of penitence and grace. There was therefore great love between them, the love of the rescued and the rescuer.

Well, one day, after the dream of the Espousals, the old fury seized on this young girl; and she announced her intention of leaving the asylum. And, as there was perfect freedom to come or to go, the permission was accorded. She had most carefully screened her intention from Sister Mary, lest the entreaties of the latter should compel her to forego her resolution; and it so happened, that Laura Desmond (this was the young girl's name) was passing down the long corridor, in which was the oratory and the niched statue of the Good Shepherd, when she heard rapid footsteps echoing on the tiled pavement behind her. She did not look around. She fled. There was a moment's delay in opening the gate that led into the outer world; and she felt a gentle hand laid on her shoulder, and a voice as from eternity said: "Laura!"

"Well?" said Laura, turning fiercely on her pursuer.

"You are not leaving us?" said Sister Mary.

"I beg yer pardin': I am though," said the poor girl.

"Turning your back on the Sister and on Father Tracey, and on—our Lord?" said the pleading voice.

"That's me own business," said the poor fugitive.

"And then, going out to the world—and the horrors—the awful horrors of the streets?" And Sister Mary's hand trembled on the shoulder of the poor girl.

"Ye seem to know a good deal about them," sneered the poor girl. "Come, Mary, yerself, and we'll have a good time. Sure, ye can come back agin!"

"What awful spirit possesses you?" said Sister Mary, starting back horror-stricken. "Oh, child, child! come back! come back to God! There's no harm done yet. Return! and all will be well!"

But the dark spirit was filling to repletion this doomed soul. And he spoke, "Is it you'll make me?" he said.

"Not I, but our Lord," said Sister Mary.

"Stand back and lem'me pass!" he shouted.

The gentle hand was still on the girl's shoulder. It now stole around her neck.

"Wance more, I say, stand back, and lem'me pass!"

The arm unconsciously tightened around her neck.

"There, thin, take that!" and Sister Mary felt a stinging blow on the face, and she reeled and fell. And, as she fell, the wretched girl tore off her own scapulars and beads, and flung them on the prostrate form. Then she tore her frantic way into the outer world.

But a greater Power pursued her. She had reached the outer gate that led into the road, when she thought the world was falling to pieces, and that the end of all things had come. The trees seemed to crash down on her path, and the great iron gate smote her as with steel gantlets. Earth rose up to overwhelm her, and the universe seemed rushing to ruin around her. There was a sound in her ears of mighty waters that had broken their bounds, and were heaving and plunging in illimitable ruin, and a great darkness came down out of the angry skies, and whelmed all things in a dread and fateful night. And then, as an end to the sudden and fearful cataclysm, all was still, and all was dead.

When, after three days of unconsciousness, but of dread convulsions, Laura Desmond woke up from her epileptic fit in the Convent infirmary, it was quite clear that she had been saved. The brand was snatched from the burning, and would never again feed the flames. Her beauty was gone. One side of her face was hopelessly paralyzed.

During these three days Sister Mary knocked furiously at the gates of Divine Mercy; but varied her supplications with loud and fervent hosannas for the redemption of that soul. And when she heard that the poor patient had recovered consciousness, but was a hopeless physical wreck, great were her jubilation and thanksgiving. "What!" exclaims our ardent humanitarian; "jubilation over a wrecked and shattered body? Where is humanity and fellow feeling? And the Divine Altruism, etc., etc.?" Even so, my good friend! Such are the ways of these strange people, called Catholics, and the still more strange elect amongst them, called Saints. For to them a shattered and broken frame, even though it was honeycombed with a thousand diseases and racked by a million nerves, is a better thing than an impure body, were it that of Aphrodite herself; and, beyond the body, though still its inhabitant, and immeasurably separated from it in importance, is the soul; and the soul, the soul, the soul, here is the one thing that takes the place of gold and consols, scrips and shares, in the divine economy of the Church. And hence, Sister Mary rejoiced and was exceeding glad, because her little client could never again go forth to snare the unwary with her eyes and mouth. And, as for the rest, here was peace and rest, and all that Divine Charity could effect for the solace of the stricken one, and her strengthening under her trial.

A few days after the patient had recovered consciousness, Sister Mary was admitted to see her. She was not prepared for her reception. For the moment the eyes of the poor girl, wandering around the infirmary, rested on the meek face of her rescuer, a look of awe and unspeakable dread crossed her face. She looked pleadingly at the Sister Infirmarian, who interpreted the look as one of aversion and pain, and who instantly said:—

"Sister Mary, your presence is painful to this poor child. I think you had better leave the infirmary. And, if you have hurt this poor girl's feelings, ask God to forgive you."

The patient seemed to make a feeble protest, which the Infirmarian interpreted as assent; and Sister Mary bowed her head, and left the room.

The following Saturday, the penitents around Father Tracey's confessional were quite sure they heard the sound of sobbing, when Sister Mary was at confession. And, on this occasion, she remained a very long and most unusual time on her knees. And they wondered, when they saw her emerge, with red swollen eyes—it was so unlike her, who was always so calm and composed. But their wonder was nothing to that of Father Tracey, who, commencing with his usual formula, "Yes, yes, my dear, to be sure!" was surprised to hear behind the screen the sound of a voice broken with sobs, and utterly unable to proceed with the usual weekly confession. Then a transformation took place. His great saint, whom he had feared to address, was but human after all. She, too, had come down from the mountains into the valley of desolation, and claimed comfort and strength at his priestly hands. And as nothing melts the heart of a priest so much as an appeal for help and pity, this holy servant threw aside all his reserve and fear; and drawing out gently the source of sorrow from this afflicted soul, he poured out of his great priestly heart a torrent of balm and consolation, until his very emotion choked him, and he wondered at himself, as he closed this first exhortation to that soul with the words: *"Thou didst call upon me in affliction, and I delivered thee; I heard thee in the secret place of tempest; I proved thee at the waters of contradiction."*

Some days elapsed; and Sister Mary was alone in the infirmary with Laura Desmond. The latter had recovered the use of speech; but her faculties seemed to be wandering. At least, she stared at Sister Mary as at an apparition; and, after a long time, and many kind things said by the latter, Laura drew her down gently, until her face almost touched the poor paralyzed cheek, and whispered:—

"Who are you?"

"Don't you know me, dear,—Sister Mary, your old friend?"

"You are *not* Sister Mary," said Laura; "nor Sister anything else! Who *are* you?"

"There now, dear," said her friend, thinking this was the delirium of illness. "Rest, and only talk in a whisper to God!"

"I will," said the poor patient. "But I'd like to know who you are."

"Dear God! restore her to her senses!" said Sister Mary. "I am one of the Magdalens, dear, a poor soul, like yourself, whom the love of the Sacred Heart has rescued."

Laura shook at her. "Don't tell me," she whispered. "You are nothing of the kind. *You* never sinned. Don't tell me!"

"We have all sinned, dear," said Sister Mary. "We are all unworthy children. It is but God's mercy that spares us."

"You are good," said Laura, "and you should not lie. You are *not* a Magdalen."

Then Sister Mary felt the hot blood mounting to face and forehead, as she drew back from the revelation.

"There," said Laura, pulling down the sweet face again, and touching the cheek with her finger, "there's where I struck you,—may God, in His mercy, forgive me! There is the print of my four fingers."

"Forget it, dear," said Sister Mary; "although it was a happy thing for me and you."

"An' you won't tell me who you are," said Laura. "Well, some day I'll find out—"

"No! no!" said Mary, frightened. "Leave me as I am. It's God's will."

"I suppose now," said the affectionate girl, "some mother is thinkin' of you, and wondherin' where you are; or your father is wishin' that he had you with him, and that he could sthroke down your beautiful hair, like this—"

"Don't, dear, don't," said Sister Mary. "We are all gathered here by God. Let us forget everything else."

"Well, whatever you like," said Laura. "But you're not wan of us. Don't tell me. You're not wan of us, whoever you are."

Sister Mary left it so, answering nothing. But the poor puzzled brain was busy solving the enigma. It was clear, clear as noonday to this poor girl's infallible instincts that her friend, though she wore the garb of penitence, was immaculate before God. How she arrived at the conclusion, it would be difficult to conjecture. It might have been some faculty, like that which the saints possessed, but struggling and obscure, and which recognized that here were none of the indelible marks of sin, which remain, even after years of repentance. But it was quite clear that she saw something quite unique, and different from ordinary experience in this girl, who had so often rescued her; and her poor brain began to trace causes and origins and reasons for the bewildering fact, that a sinless soul had chosen to assume a character from which every one, not imbued with the charity of Christ, turns away with loathing and abhorrence. It was inexplicable,—a deep, awful mystery for which there was no explanation. For days Laura Desmond dwelt and rested on the thought. Sometimes she would watch Sister Mary performing the ordinary offices of the infirmary, where she was assistant—watch her with curious speculation in her eyes. And when her good friend came over to perform some little kindly act around her bedside, or to ask a question, or to whisper a prayer, Laura would stare her all over with the unconsciousness of a child, and study her eyes and mouth, and touch her hair and her dress, and take up her hand to study it, like a palmist; and then would turn away to pursue the vast enigma which was thrown on the blurred canvas of her own life.

After many days of deep cogitation; and after patching and piecing together all that she had ever heard of, and all her own experiences of Sister Mary, she came to a dread conclusion, which plunged her back into despair. It was midnight when it seized her in her sleepless meditations; and starting up wildly, she rang her bell, and summoned the Sister Infirmarian. In a moment the latter was by her bedside, but was appalled to see the look of horror and dismay on the features of her poor patient.

"Call the priest," was the cry, "at once! at once!"

And so Father Tracey heard in his slumbers the familiar sound of the midnight bell, and woke up, confused, and put on in a dream his dingy clothes, praying and asking: "What poor soul wants me now?"

If there be on earth one reward greater than another for the sacrifice a priest is forever called upon to make for his flock, it is the dawn of hope and comfort that shines in the eyes and on the faces of the pain-stricken, or the sorrowful, or the despairing, when a priest approaches their bed of sickness or suffering, and all the phantoms that haunt poor humanity fly at his approach. The murmured "Thank God!" the little laugh, half-smothered, of triumph and peace; the very manner in which the sick and the wounded arrange themselves on their couches of sorrow, as if they said: "I have got a new lease of life now; for the Healer and Consoler is here!"—all this faith and confidence and hope, placed in his very presence, as apart from his ministrations, is a reward, so far beyond all earthly guerdons and triumphs that it can only be said to foreshadow the blisses of eternity. So, at least, Father Tracey felt; and so did he thank God every moment for the sublime vocation, which, in all humility and meekness, he was following.

When he entered the infirmary this night, every one gathered around Laura Desmond's sick-bed felt a kind of sensible relief. And she turned to him wistfully, and when he bent down to hear what she had to say, she locked one finger in the button-hole of his coat, as if to secure him beyond all doubt. Then, in a husky voice, she whispered her secret.

He drew back in amazement, and looked at her, as if her mind was astray. When she persisted, he only smiled, which seemed to reassure her; and then he laughed the idea to scorn. This seemed to compose the poor girl, but she held the buttonhole firmly.

"On your word of honor, as a priest, are ye tellin' me the truth?"

"Of course I am," he cried. "Compose yourself, child, and try to get some sleep."

"There's no more sleep for me," she said, "until I get God's assurance that it is not so."

"Take my assurance," he said. "What more can you have?"

"Very well, yer reverence. But I tell you this,—she's no more wan of us, than—than—than—"

"That may be, too," he said, although he felt he was venturing dangerously near the King's Secret. "God alone knows the secrets of hearts."

"Thin why is she here?" asked the bewildered girl. "Sure this is no place for her likes. Unless," she drifted back to the old idea, "she is what I say."

"Put that idea forever from your mind," he said, gently disengaging himself. "And pray, pray. There are more saints in the world than the world is aware of."

A few days afterwards he had a long conference with Sister Eulalie on the subject.

"Sometimes I begin to doubt, myself," he said. "The whole thing is so strange and wonderful and beautiful. It will be many a day before the idea leaves that poor girl's mind."

"It is strange and beautiful," said Sister Eulalie. "Sometimes, I am inclined to kneel down and kiss the ground where she walks. And fancy poor Luke's suspicions about imposture and hysteria."

"You're quite sure you know her?" Father Tracey said
meditatively. "That you have seen her; and there is no doubt?"

"There! you're nearly as bad as Laura," said Sister Eulalie.
"There is no mistake, except that, God forgive me, I thought
ill, too, of this sweet saint, and thought her stuck-up and
proud and disdainful."

"But you may be mistaken, my dear," said Father Tracey.
"One never knows. And fancy, if—"

"There now, you're off, too. There's no doubt, Father," she
said reassuringly. "It is she; and she does not dream that we
know of her and her awful vow."

And Sister Eulalie shuddered to think if such an oblation
were ever required of her.

Sister Mary began to be very much pained and very much bewildered. Just as her confessor began to regard her as human,
and therefore pitiable, her associates began to consider her
as something superhuman and celestial, and sent amongst them
through some secret and ineffable design of God. It was a long
time before Sister Mary's humility would permit her to recognize this fact. Nay, even, she regarded the reverence and timid
shrinking from her, the slipping aside from her path when she
appeared amongst a group of penitents, the sudden silence,
the quiet watchfulness that followed all her movements, as indications of aversions and suspicion. And, interpreting all this
by the remark of the Sister Infirmarian after Laura's recovery
of consciousness, she concluded that, in some way, she had
been guilty of undue harshness, apparently as the result of
self-conceit, and that she was, in consequence thereof, shunned
and disliked by those she loved so much. It was a subtle and
most painful delusion, and it caused her infinite anxiety. It was
the sharpest mortification she had yet received. The cross
was weighing heavily; the thorns were pressing sharply, and
she was about to faint. Then one day, to her intense amazement, she found, as she passed by a group with averted faces,
her mantella slightly touched, and turning around, she found
that one of the group had raised it reverently and kissed it.
And she trembled all over with the sudden revelation that she
was regarded with reverence, and not aversion, and then she
grew pale and trembled still more, for the dread that the
mighty secret of her life was about to be revealed.

The truth was, that Laura's whispered suspicions, though stilled by the voice of authority, had taken wing and flown from soul to soul of the community of penitents, and very wild surmises were afloat. "There are more saints in the world than the world is aware of," said their own dear saint, Father Tracey. Well, then, who knows? Doesn't every man, woman, and child in Ireland understand and believe that in one shape or another the Blessed Virgin, the great Mary of Ireland, the Mary of her ancient litanies and Masses, is always amongst the Irish people? Hasn't her sweet face been seen again and again? Hasn't she appeared to poor sinners on their death-beds, and haven't they pointed out her white, refulgent figure to the priest, as she hovered over their beds and beckoned them to Paradise? Hasn't she appeared to little girls over there in France? Why not, therefore, to her own Irish, who love her more than all the world beside? Well, we say nothing, but we think a good deal, even we, poor penitents. May not the all-sinless one have come down here, and put on our poor garments, even as her Son put on the flesh that had sinned? Oh, no, we daren't say anything; but—who knows?

And Laura's dread thought, that this might be the very Mother of God whom she struck with her open hand—the dread thought that rang the midnight bell, and summoned Father Tracey from his dreamless sleep, began to pursue its way, under a thousand modifications, through the minds and hearts of these poor, repentant ones; and although no one dared breathe such a whisper, and Sister Mary could only conjecture that there had come a great change over her associates, she only knew that her cross had been suddenly lifted by an Unseen Hand, and that He had verified His words: "I heard thee in the secret place of tempest; I proved thee at the waters of contradiction."

CHAPTER XXXIII

Dagon Dismembered

THE LAST words of Father Cussen in the library at Seaview Cottage may be said to have commenced Luke Delmege's Illumination. The world's catchwords seemed to have lost all meaning in the appeal to God. He began to understand how divine was the vocation of the Church in its mission to the individual, and how sublime was her carelessness under what form of government she worked, so long as she was not interfered with in her quest after human souls. Side by side with this conviction there grew up the perception that his own race were following out this divine apostolate in secret and hidden ways. Sometimes, when entering a city convent, he would meet a batch of nuns just returned from Benin, or a young Irish Sister just about to start for Java. And they thought no more of the journey and its hardships than if it were a picnic to some picturesque spot on the Shannon. And he found the entire burden of their conversation was concerning the souls of Negroes, whom modern imperialism would gladly blow into space with lyddite and dynamite, or corrupt and corrode into disease and death by the agencies of modern civilization. And when these young martyr apostles left, they left behind them the divine contagion; and little Irish children, who, perhaps, themselves were in want of bread, brought their halfpennies to the treasury of the convent, "to buy a black baby for God." And Luke's heart often wailed aloud, because he had turned his back once and forever on the same divine vocation; and his conscience murmured more than once, Idiota! Idiota! But he had gained two facts by experience: (1) That the individual soul was everything to the Church and God; and (2) that the feigned and fictitious watchwords of the new gospel of humanity were the unspoken but well-fulfilled vows of his own race. "The horse-leech hath two daughters which say, Give! give!" But "renunciation" is the motto of the apostles of his race.

So, too, there began to dawn upon him, stealthily and insensibly, the marvellous beauties even of the most commonplace landscapes of Ireland. The very solitude, which had oppressed him with such lonely and melancholy feelings, began to assume a strange and singular charm. There was a mysterious light over everything that gave an aspect of dreamland and enchantment, or of old, far-off times, even to the long, lonely fields, or the dark, sullen bogland. He could not well define it. There was some association haunting everything, inexpressibly sweet, but so vague, so elusive, he could not define what it was. The fields in the twilight had a curious color or cloudland hanging over them, that reminded him of something sweet and beautiful and far away; but this, memory or imagination could never seize and hold. And when, on one of these gray days, which are so lovely in Ireland, as the light falls somber and neutral on all things, a plover would shriek across the moorland, or a curlew would rise up and beat his lonely way, complaining and afraid, across the ashen sky, Luke would feel that he had seen it all before in some waking dream of childhood; but all associations had vanished. The magic of Nature alone remained. But the mountains, the mountains haunted him perpetually. He never rose in the morning without asking, How will my mountains look today? And whether the great Artist had drawn them far away in a beautiful mist of pencilled shadow, and they leaned, like a cloud, on the horizon; or brought them up close and defiant, their blue-black faces seamed and jagged, where the yellow torrents had torn off the soft peat covering and left the yellow loam and red pebbles distinctly visible, the same dim, haunting memories hung around them, and he asked himself a hundred times, Where have I seen all this before? And how does Nature, as she pushes forward her mountains or withdraws them, and paints them every day with a different brush—how does she draw on the background of memory some shadowy, elusive picture, and associate it so strongly with that marvellous coloring on mountain, and cloud, and sky?

The October of this year, too, was a marvel of beauty. The weather was so dry and frostless that Nature took a long time to disrobe herself, and she changed her garments in such beautiful, varied ways, that the landscape became a shifting mass of color. There was no sun, either, to make the gradual decay too palpable—only a hushed, gray color over all the land. And Luke watched the beautiful death from the moment the chestnut put out her pale, yellow leaf, and became a golden blot on the thick mass of foliage, which filled the entire hill behind the village, until all was over, and only the evergreens vaunted their immortality. Every day was a new pleasure; and he began to think, with some contempt, of long, dusty streets, and the stupid uniformity of houses, and the asphalt pavements, and the miserable patch of blue sky, which one is privileged to see in cities. And to think, also, that there is such a thing as the populous deserts of civilization, where man is but an exile and a waif; and the delightful, homelike feeling in Ireland, where you feel you are always sitting by your mother's hearth; and, come weal, come woe, this is home, and all around are friends and lovers.

And, as in a happy home, the very worries and vexations of life have their own charm, so Luke began to find, in everyday simple and very prosaic experiences, a relief from thought that was quite refreshing.

It is true, indeed, that the eternal squabbles of the kitchen hurt his nerves, until he began to find that they meant but little; and that the strong language sometimes used was only the hyperbole of a people who are used to express themselves picturesquely. When Mary described John as "the most outrageous fool that the Lord ever created. He don't know his right hand from his lef';" and when John averred that "Mary had the worst tongue the Lord ever put the bret' of life in;" and that her "looks would peel potatoes, and turn sugar into vinegar, and even sour the crame in the middle of winter," it disturbed Luke very much, until he heard a musical duet of laughter from the kitchen five minutes after, and an experienced friend assured him that it was a sound maxim of domestic economy that when the man and the maid fell out, the master's interests were safe. So, too, when approaching the stable in the morning he heard unmistakable sounds of dancing to the everlasting tune of "Welt the flure, Biddy McClure," and knew, by every law of sense and reason, that John was practicing a heel-and-toe for the dance at the cross-roads the following Sunday; and when he found the said John, sitting demurely on a soap-box and polishing the harness for all it was worth, he began to think he had a Valentine Vousden in disguise.

"I thought I heard the sounds of dancing," Luke would say, in a puzzled manner.

"Dancin'? yer reverence. Ye hard the little mare stampin' her feet."

"Stamping her feet? What for?"

" 'Tis a way she has whin she's hungry," John would reply. "She's not aisy in her mind since ye cut her aff her oats." And Luke would give up the riddle.

He found, too, that in the horticultural department, John's knowledge was strictly limited to the cultivation of potatoes, and his experience of flowers was equally circumscribed. In young ladies' "books of confessions," a favorite flower always has a place, the tastes varying from a daisy up to an amaranth. John had his favorite flower. It was the homely nasturtium; and he was so loyal to this love that he declined to have charge of the more aristocratic garden-belles which Luke affected.

"It costs no throuble," said John.

"It is only a weed," said Luke.

" 'Tis just as purty as thim that must be watched and tinded like a baby," said John.

"The very etymology of the flower condemns it," said Luke.

"Well, indeed, it hasn't much of a scint," said John.

"I didn't mean that. I meant it has a nasty name—"

"There's many a wan has a bad name as doesn't deserve it," said John.

It is not difficult to sympathize with John's tastes. It is impossible not to feel a kind of pitying love for Nature's homely creations. They are so generous, so prodigal of their beauties, that one cannot help being grateful; and, like gipsy-children, they thrive in all weathers without care; and Mother Nature loves them because they do credit to her handiwork without any help from the bungling and blundering hands of man. There is reason to fear that contempt is largely blended with our admiration of the Lady Rose. She is a petted and spoiled beauty. She must have attention and admiration. She must have her toilette carefully made every morning; and *eheu, infandum!* she must have those ugly green parasites brushed away from her lovely petals; and, more dreadful still, the dainty lady has to be fumigated and disinfected; and, with all, as she hangs her lovely and languishing head with rain or dew-pearls in her bosom, no bird or bee will come nigh her. And here, in the same bed, up springs a hardy tramp of a thistle, and careless of wind or rain, and untouched by para-sites, he shoves his yellow, unkempt head above the golden tresses of my rose; and the sparrows steal away his frowsy petals, and the bees find something sweet deep down in his scraggy breast. Or that insolent, lawless beggar, Robin-run-the-hedge, draws his ill-smelling coils around the dainty lady, and smothers her in his embraces, and mounts up, higher and higher, until he flaunts his white, clear bell flowers, a summer anemone, high above the regal rose-crests. Of course, the policeman, that is the gardener, comes and carries off these tramps to jail or death,—that's the way with the world—the hardy child of the people must give place to the perfumed and delicate aristocrat. Nevertheless, there are a few that sympa-thize with Mother Nature's children, and amongst them may be numbered John and—another.

It may be presumed, therefore, that Luke, with his passion for flowers, got little help, and a considerable amount of embarrassment from his gardener. His large ambition to re-duce the picturesque irregularities of Irish life to the dull, rectangular monotony of geometrical perfection, was here too, in large measure, doomed to disappointment. It was quite useless to try to persuade John that all this digging and manur-ing and clipping and watering and cutting was recompensed by the fleeting beauties of what he called "a few posies," which hung out their fragile loveliness and scented the air for a few days, and then peevishly threw down their pretty petals the moment a light breeze disturbed them or a shower of rain bowed them to the earth. Neither could he see the use of cut-ting flower-beds into diagrams of Euclid; and his heart smote him as he ran the razored edges of the lawn-mower across the grass, and all the pretty daisies lay decapitated beneath the ruthless guillotine.

"Begor," he said, "the masther was watchin' all the winther to see the first daisy put up her purty little head; and you'd think he'd go mad whin the first primrose looked out of the black earth. And here he's now with his: 'John, cut down thim

daisies;' 'John, that grass is dirty;' 'John, get away thim weeds.'
Did ye iver hear the likes of it?" And John was discontented,
and the "masther" was in despair.

"Bring out the bulbs that you took up last winter," said
Luke, late in the October of this year.

"What balls?" said John.

"The tulip and hyacinth bulbs which I gave you to put by
against the winter," said Luke.

John was bewildered. Mary heard the conversation and
giggled.

"Yer reverence giv me no hicense," said John, fairly puzzled.

"I gave you last May four dozen of tulips from this bed,
and two dozen hyacinths from these beds," said Luke, angrily
pointing to where the geraniums and begonias had just been
lifted.

John was still puzzled. Then a great light dawned, and he
looked at his master with all the compassion of superior
knowledge.

"Oh! thim inguns, your reverence! Yerra, sure the chickens
ate every wan of thim."

"What?" cried Luke, now thoroughly angry. "Do you mean
to say that you have thrown away those tulips that cost me
four shillings, and those hyacinths that cost six a dozen?"

"Yerra, not at all," said John smiling. "Sure ye can get any
amount of thim up at Miss Smiddy's. They're hanging in ropes
from the ceiling, and they're chape now. I'll get a dozen for
ye for tuppence."

Then Luke collapsed. He was genuinely angry; what florist
would not be? And he half made up his mind that John should
go. He was incorrigible and utterly incapable of being educated. After long and deep deliberation, in which the saying
of a friend, whom he had often consulted on John's retention
and dismissal, "If you hunt him, you'll only be gettin' a bigger
blagard!" came frequently uppermost, he at last decided that
he could not stand this worry. He told Mary that John should
go. Mary had been laughing at John all the morning, and had
told him several times that it was all up now. The master
would never forgive "thim chewlips." He should go. Luke was
surprised to find Mary bursting into an agony of tears, and
rushing wildly from the room. But he was inexorable. The
misery was going on too long and should be ended. He moved
out towards the stables with a certain amount of nervousness,

for he hated to do an unkind thing. Instead of the usual patter
of dancing, he heard the sound as of prayer. He listened. John
was preparing for confession, and making his examination of
conscience aloud. Luke walked away, but he was determined.
When he thought the examen was over, he returned. John was
making his act of contrition. There was no harm in listening
there. The voice came, broken with sobs—yea, the voice of
John! It said, amidst the weeping:—

> What was Thine of sorrow and pain, O Thou, who in heaven
>   dost reign,
>   O King, both good and great;
> It comes not into my mind, the amount to find,
>   Nor, if found, could my tongue relate
> The bitter anguish and smart of Thy Sacred Heart,
>   And the spear-cleft in Thy side,
> That moved with a holy awe of Thy Sacred Law
>   Even kings on their thrones of pride.
>
> O Father! O Jesus mine! who by Thy Death Divine
>   With life our souls dost warm,
> Thou, in creation's hour, whose plastic power
>   Made man to Thy own blessed form,
> Is it not, O Christ! O King! a cruel, cruel thing,
>   That naught has been loved by me
> Save sins that the soul defile, save all things base and vile,
>   That are loathsome unto Thee?

It was the beautiful old lay of the Sacred Heart, translated
from the ancient Irish,[1] and which John had picked up at the
church door and retained,—as it appealed strongly to his
fancy,—as an act of contrition. Everything in prayer and
proverb that rhymes or sings touches the heart of Ireland. And
Luke heard the sound of sobbing again as John went over
the line: —

> Is it not, O Christ! O King! a ca-ru-el, ca-ru-el thing?

Then he turned away, muttering, Poor fellow! and John was
saved.

A few days after, Luke was summoned to his mother's
funeral. She had lingered on through the summer; and though
Death had taken up permanent lodgings in the house, he was
afraid to ask his hostess to leave with him. But one night he
stole through the door and a soul was with him. The good old

[1] By D. F. McCarthy.

mother had passed away in her sleep whilst the household slumbered. She was spared the pain of weepers and watchers around her as she stole over the threshold and out into the night.

With all his intense dislike for noise, or demonstration, or too much ceremonial for the dead or for the living, Luke was hoping that his mother's obsequies would be celebrated as quietly as possible. The last wish of the deceased, "to have a dacent funeral," did not quite agree with his instinctive hatred of fuss and noise. But the matter was quietly taken out of his hands. To his intense amazement, nearly thirty priests had assembled on the morning of the funeral. They had come from all parts of the diocese. Some of them Luke had never seen before. The names of others were unfamiliar to him. No matter! This was a priest's mother. She shared in the Levitical consecration of her son. She should be equally honored. There was to be a full Office and Mass for the Dead.

The morning was wet. Some one said, "It rained ramrods." The little sacristy was full of priests, whose friezes and mackintoshes created little lakes of water everywhere. Some had come ten miles, some twelve, some even nineteen, straight away from the stations, that last through October and into the first week of November. Luke, touched to the heart, had great pity for them.

"We'll have but one Nocturn," he whispered to the master of ceremonies. The latter went over to the Canon, who was to preside. He brought back word that the entire Office should be sung. It was the wish of all the priests. And Father Daly, too, was one of the chanters; and very beautifully he intoned the noble antiphons of the sublime Office of the Dead. The church was packed to its farthest extremity by a silent, devout congregation. From their wet, sodden clothes steamed up a cloud of vapor that mingled with the incense smoke and filled the entire church with a heavy haze. They too had come from far distances to testify their reverence for the dead. And Luke remembered there, in the dawn of his great illumination, that all this was slightly different from the cold, mechanical heartlessness of England, where the dead were unprayed for and unremembered; and a few black mourning coaches were the only testimony of respect to the lump of clay which had to be hustled from the sight of the living as speedily as possible.

The long procession commenced. Larry, the old retainer, jealous for his family's honor, counted carefully every car.

"There wor wan hundred and thirty," he told old Mike Delmege afterwards, "and twinty horsemen. There should be wan hundred and thirty-six, if she had her rights, and if thim who ought to be there hadn't stopped away. But we'll remimber it for 'em."

Down came the weary, weary rain, as the long, slow procession defiled along the slushy roads. A group of beggars was assembled down near the house, who gave vent to their feelings in language that was only measured by gratitude. True for them! It was never known that neighbor's child was ever "broke" on that farm; or that a beggar was ever turned from that door. And many a piece of rusty bacon, hanging from the ceiling, and many a huge semicircle of griddle cake disappeared in the wallets of the indigent, to the consternation of Nancy, who crossed herself devoutly and prayed Heaven to guard the house against the depredations of the "good people."

Down still came the rain, when the lonely procession reached the Abbey grounds. But no one heeded, except to repeat the distich: —

> Happy is the bride the sun shines on!
> Happy are the dead the rain rains on!

When the coffin was lifted from the bier on to the shoulders of the men, among whom there was heated rivalry for the honor, the cortège, instead of moving directly to the Abbey across a smooth pathway, made a circular detour around the entire graveyard. This entailed much discomfort on priests and people, for the high grass was sodden with rain, and the nettles and hemlocks threw a spray of crystal drops on the passers-by. And down into hollows, and over the crests of graves, and stumbling against fallen tombstones, and falling into pits, the priests and bearers went on, whilst the mournful *Miserere* was carried out in strong current of wind and rain across the landscape, or echoed sadly over the graves of thirty generations of the dead. No matter. It was the custom of the land, and no power on earth could change the tradition of the most conservative people on earth. And for the hundredth time Luke Delmege concluded that there was but little use in attempting to transplant foreign civilizations here. This race must create or develop a civilization peculiarly its own.

When the circle of priests was completed around the open grave, the Canon resumed the funeral service. Luke stood near him and held his umbrella over the old man's bare head. Just before the *Benedictus,* as that glorious antiphon, *Ego sum Resurrectio et Vita,* was being chanted, Luke resigned his umbrella to a young priest standing near and went over and stood by his father, who, bowed and sorrow-stricken, was gazing mournfully into the open grave. And here a sight met his eyes which was a shock, and then—a revelation. The gloom which overhung the whole proceedings had deepened in his soul into a strange overpowering melancholy, which the leaden skies and the weeping landscape intensified. All through the Office in the church he had tried to close the eyes of his mind to its terrible significance. The mournful music of the Psalms, with their alternate cadences of grief and hope—now sinking almost into despair, and then soaring aloft into an exaltation that seemed almost to presume too much on the Eternal—did not affect him quite as deeply as the lessons from the Book of Job, which, read slowly and solemnly by dignified priests, seemed to sound as the death-bell of poor humanity. And all that he had ever read in the poetry of mankind blended and mingled with the inspired threnodies of the man in the land of Hus; and it was all, all about the nothingness of man and his momentary existence on this planet.

Remember, I beseech Thee, that Thou hast made me as the clay; and Thou wilt bring me into the dust again. Hast thou not milked me as milk, and curdled me as cheese? Against a leaf that is carried away by the wind, Thou showest Thy power; and Thou pursuest a dry straw. Who cometh forth like a flower, and is destroyed, and fleeth as a shadow, and never continueth in the same state. I should have been as if I had not been, carried from the womb to the grave.

And—

A little soul for a little holds up the corpse which is man.

And—

> They wrought with weeping and laughter,
>   And fashioned with loathing and love;
> With life before and after,
>   And death beneath and above;

> For a day and a night and a morrow,
>   That his strength might endure for a span,
> With travail and heavy sorrow,
>   The holy spirit of man.

Not a word about the "perfect man" that is to be, or his immortality on this his little theatre! Not a word about the "deity in embryo," or the "slumbering godhead." He shall pass! he shall pass! That is all!

The grave was dug close beneath the great northern window of the Abbey, which almost filled the entire gable, its slender shafts holding aloft, like the stems of candelabra, the beautiful tracery that spread itself into flame shapes, terminating in one sharp jet at the apex. The floor of the Abbey had been raised, in the course of centuries, six or seven feet, for only the curved arches of the sedilia were visible in the side walls; and Luke, staring into the open grave, saw that it was lined on all sides with human remains. Brown bare skulls filled every inch of its walls; and here, tossed also on the grass were fragments and shells that once held together the little pulp that makes man's body. Some one, pitying the people, had ordered the coffin to be lowered; and the rude laborer who acted as sexton had caught up a handful of earth-stained bones and flung them into the grave as carelessly as a woman flings a handful of twigs on her fire. Then he lightly kicked a large round skull after them. It fell with a heavy thud on the coffin, turned up its ghastly visage and grinned, rolled over in another somersault, and was finally jammed between the angle of the coffin and the brown walls of the grave. There it leered up hideously at the indifferent spectators. Luke felt sick. Here was the end of all his youthful dreams. There lay the little god of this planet. And his dream of Humanity was buried in that grave where Dagon lay dismembered before the face of the living God!

Luke had been quite unconscious of the singing of the *Benedictus*, so absorbed was he in his reverie. He now woke up to hear, in a kind of triumphant pæan, the words:—

Visitavit nos, Oriens ex Alto!

The words seemed to unlock the secrets of the grave, and to open up the far vistas that lay before the fallen race. *Oriens ex Alto! Oriens ex Alto!* The far visions of the prophets—the proximate revelation to the Father of the Precursor—the mighty apparition of the Sacred Humanity seemed to hover over that charnel-house of bones; and Luke saw, what long ago he had maintained as a theological thesis in the halls of Maynooth, that there is but one, and can be but one, perfected Humanity; and this it is that shall lift the whole race into Itself, drawing the certainties of eternity from the doubts of time, and out of the despair of earth, deriving the hope and the bliss of heaven. "Seek ye the man in God."

The aged father, stooped with years and sorrow, hung over the grave to the end. Then Luke gently raised him, and offering the feeble limbs the support of his strong arm, they moved towards the Abbey entrance. All else had gone; but there lingered a small group of peasants at the gate that led into the inclosure. They, too, were sodden with wet and damp, and tiny rivulets of rain ran down from their felt hats. Luke, with his head stooped in sorrow, was about to pass them without noticing them, when one stepped forward shyly and held out his rough hand.

"We kem to tell you, Father Luke," he said, "that we are sorry for your throuble."

Luke grasped his hand, but looked bewildered at the speaker.

"I'm James McLoughlin," the latter said; "you remimber, yer reverence, where we had the little dissinsion, you know?"

Then Luke remembered his former parishioners, who had given him all the trouble, and had procured his dismissal from their parish. The poor fellows, anxious to make up for past delinquency, had come across the country from a great distance to testify their respect. As Luke did not immediately respond, they thought he was resentful.

"We thought that bygones should be bygones, yer reverence," said James McLoughlin, "and we kem—"

"Don't speak of it, my dear fellow," said Luke. "I have long since forgotten and forgiven everything. And I'm infinitely obliged to you for your kindness in coming so far on such a day. Father, these are my former parishioners, who have come miles from home to attend mother's funeral."

And they had to go back to Lisnalee and were well entertained there. And there is some reason to fear that the statutes of the diocese were ruthlessly broken, and Luke made no protest.

BOOK V

CHAPTER XXXIV

Cremona and Calvary

IT WAS the wish of the good Canon that Luke should spend a few days at his rectory. But Luke preferred Seaview Cottage. The Canon was always courteous, kind, hospitable. Father Martin was always outspoken, sometimes even brusque. Yet Luke preferred the easy comfort of Seaview Cottage, even though it sometimes blew heavy guns, to the calm, untroubled dignity of the rectory. The best of men like an arm-chair and the luxury of crossed legs. Yet the atmosphere even of the sunny library was somber these dark days. It was only lighted by the eyes of Tiny and the laughter of Tony. Some time in the course of the evening, before they were dismissed to bed, the former, after a long and careful study of the grave, solemn stranger, drew a chair silently behind his, mounted on it, and flung her arms, and closed them, like a spring, around Luke's neck. He drew the child around and kissed her.

"There's somethin' hurtin' you dere," said the child, pointing to his breast pocket.

"True, Mignon," he said, drawing out a bundle of letters, which in all his hurry he had brought from home unopened. He had now leisure. The first was from his Bishop.

"A letter of condolence!" conjectured Luke. As he read it, his face fell. He handed the document to Father Martin. It was a gentle reprimand; but it was a reprimand, and a Bishop's words cut like an acid. Luke had been reported to his Bishop for not only permitting, but even encouraging, proselytism in his parish. The matter had been referred to his parish priest, who tried to extenuate it. Nevertheless, the facts remained; and the Bishop warned Luke to be more circumspect in future.

"I am hopelessly doomed," said Luke, "to desire what is good, and to accomplish the reverse."

"You look too much to principles—too little to men!" replied Father Martin.

"Could anything be better than to seek to reconcile and make mutually tolerant and helpful the two great classes in this country? Surely, it is the only solution of this apparently insoluble problem."

"Quite so. But did you ever consider that in this attempt you are seeking to reconcile not only interests which are hopelessly conflicting, but the very spirits of affirmation and negation?"

"I cannot see it," said the bewildered Luke.

"Don't you see the gist of this complaint?" said Father Martin. "The people object to the dethronement of their saints and heroes. These stand to them in the light of the embodiment of a great idea or principle. It is an affirmation that there have been, and therefore can be again, heroism, bravery, truth, in this weary world. Now, your fine ladies come, and with the best intentions introduce the spirit of denial. 'Who art thou? What is thy name?' said the student to the Spirit of Evil. 'I am the Spirit that denies,' was the answer. And the little poodle of Reformation heresy that has been running around in circles for the last three hundred years has now swollen into the big monster behind the stove. And out of the swollen monster, Materialism, and to the music of the spirits of Poetry and the Fine Arts, steps the urbane, cultured scholar, who makes his bow: 'I am the Spirit who denies!' "

Luke shuddered.

"And yet," he said, "there are the sweetest, beautifullest souls I ever met over there across the border. Oh, what a riddle, what a puzzle!"

"Well, don't puzzle!" said the matter-of-fact Father Martin. "Keep close to your own people—the people of eternity! Let alone the sons and daughters of men!"

"The people of eternity!" Yes, indeed! so they are, as Luke was every day more fully ascertaining. Time and the world were nothing to his race, who seemed to look at everything as if they themselves were already disembodied.

Luke sat in the dim sacristy of Rossmore on the evening of All Saints'—the eve of All Souls' Day. A long list lay before him—the names of the departed, who were to be prayed for on the morrow. The sacristy was filled with an eager crowd, and there was a murmur of voices outside. One by one they came to the table, laid down the little offering, and with scrupulous exactness had the names of the deceased registered. There were tears on many faces, and many broken voices repeated the names of the dead, and always with a note of gratitude and respect. And not only relatives, but even the mere passing acquaintances of life, were remembered.

"For me poor boy, yer reverence, that's lyin' out on the snows of the Himalees."

"For the good father that reared me, and brought me up clane and dacent."

"For the poor sowl, yer reverence, that's in the greatest howlt."

Luke put down his pen.

"Any relation of your own?" It was his first blunder. He was coming round.

"Faix, it might be, yer reverence. How do I know? But no matther who it is—if it wor the blackest stranger from Galway, so long as they want it."

Luke wrote down his own translation.

"For Mary Carmody, yer reverence," said a voice in a whisper, that was made still more gentle by the hood of the shawl wrapped around his face.

"Your sister?" said Luke.

"Yerra, not at all, yer reverence! But a poor crachure that we picked out of the sthreets. The old boy had his *glaum* upon her; but faix, we chated him in the ind."

"For me cummerade, Mike Mulcahy, yer reverence," said a stalwart pensioner, putting his hand to his forehead.

"Killed?" said Luke, who never wasted words.

"Begor, he was, yer reverence," said the pensioner, settling down for a long narrative, and utterly heedless of the fifty or sixty persons who were waiting behind him, and who had heard the story a hundred times. "It was in the Crimee, before Sebastopool, and we were lyin' in the trinches up to our nicks in mud; and the Rooshsian shells flyin' over our heads, like a flock of crows cummin' home of an evenin'. 'Look,' sez I, 'an' put up yer head.' 'There's'n room,' sez he. 'Niver min', so,' sez I; and shure I'm thankin' the good God every day since, that I didn't sind him to his death. 'They're quiet now,' sez he, 'and here goes!' 'What did ye see?' sez I. No answer. 'What did ye see?' sez I agin. No answer. 'What did ye see, ye —— of an omadhaun,' sez I. No answer. I looked round. His head was blown clane away. There was nothin' left but from his nick down, and—"

"Poor fellow!" said Luke, seeing the impatience of the crowd. "Well, I hope he was prepared."

"Prepared? Faix, he was. We all wint to confession a few days before to Father Walsh."

"I'll tell you what you'll do," said Luke. "I cannot afford to lose any of that story. Will you call at my house tomorrow night, and let me hear the whole thing from beginning to end?"

"Faix, I will, with pleasure," said the good pensioner; and he went away with his head in the air, six inches higher for the honor. He always spoke of Luke after the interview as "me friend, Father Luke," adding: "That's the kind of min they want as army chaplains. If the Juke knew him, he'd have him in Aldershot in a mont'."

"For me parents, and decased friends," said a strong, rough man, who spoke in a rather superior manner, as if he were offended by the want of tact shown by his predecessor. Luke wrote the names.

"Put down now, yer reverence," said the man, "the name of Martin Connolly, soldier of the Federal Army, who died from wounds received in the gallant charge of the Irish Brigade at Fredericksburg."

"That's hardly necessary," said Luke.

"Oh, but it is, yer reverence. I want me poor cummerade to get his rights in the next world, as he didn't get them in this."

"That was Meagher's Brigade," said Luke, in a moment of forgetfulness and enthusiasm.

The poor soldier smiled, drew himself up erect, and put out his right hand.

"Ah, you know it, yer reverence. God bless you! Put the hand there!"

Luke placed his hand in the big, broad palm. The old man raised it reverently, and kissed it.

"Put down the sowl of Thomas Francis Meagher, there, yer reverence," said he, sobbing. "Sure it isn't I should forget him. I was as near to him as to yer reverence this minit on that day.

'Boys,' sez he, 'remimber who ye are! Sure 'tis I'm the proud man to be lading to death or victory the bravest and best min in the Federal Army. Boys,' sez he, 'there's your flag, don't disgrace it! I wish to God, boys,' sez he, 'that I had ye on the slopes of Slievnamon. Wouldn't we make the redcoats fly?' He stopped thin, as if he wor thinkin' of ould times and cummerades. 'Dimpsey,' sez he to the bandmaster, 'play up Brian Boru's march. Slope arms, four deep—forward!' And on we wint to our death. Father Walsh, not this man's Father Walsh," he said, jerking his hand contemptuously at the last pensioner, "but our own Father Walsh—God be wid him, he was the fine man—sat on his horse, as we passed by. He was a big man, wid a big black beard, and he was risin' his hand over us, as we marched past. I put me hand on his knee, and sez I, 'Father,' sez I, 'gi' me a double blessin', for I'm a double blagard.' He laughed, poor man, 'twas the last we seen of him. For we weren't twinty minits in the field, thryin' to take that hill (sure we might as well be thryin' to take the gates of Heaven), whin down I wint, with a splinter of a shell in me calf; and down wint poor Martin, with a bullet in his left lung. We wor out on the field, all night in the cowld, watchin' the stars, widout a bit, bite, or sup, only the wounded moanin' and groanin' all around us. About twelve, we saw lights; and whin they kem near enough, we saw they wor the Confederate ginerals come out to see after their own. 'Here goes,' says Martin, shovin' in a cartridge; 'one shot at the rebelly rascals, and thin I die aisy.' 'Dang yer sowl, ye ruffian,' sez I, and 'twasn't that I said ayther, yer reverence,—'do ye want to go before God wid murder on your sowl?' 'They killed many a brave man today,' sez he, spittin' blood. 'Fair play is bonny play, sez I,' taking the rifle from the ruffian. An' shure, if he fired that shot, yer reverence, all the rebels in camp wud be among us in a minit, stabbin' and shootin' like the divil. But, I'm afeared I'm delayin' the nabours," he said, turning round, "that ould Crimean pinsioner kep ye sich a long time."

"This offering is too much for you," said Luke, pushing back a half-crown. "I'll keep just half."

"Not a bit of it, yer reverence," said the old man, pushing the coin back again. "We're not like these poor English *anga-shores*—on sixpence a day."

He passed out triumphant, though limping from that splintered shell. In a few minutes he returned, and pushed his way through the crowd of women to the table.

"I thought you might be forgettin', your reverence. Did you put down, Martin Connolly, soldier in the Federal Army, who died of gunshot wounds, received in action—"

"It's all right, it's all right!" said Luke.

"And Thomas Francis Meagher, Brigadier Gineral—"

" 'Tis all right, 'tis all right!" said Luke.

It was a gloomy night, starless and moonless, and with a heavy black-brown pall, as of faded velvet, hanging down over the world, as Luke passed out from the iron gate, and picked his steps carefully down the uneven ways of the village street. He had passed up through his little garden, and was placing his latch-key in the door, when he became aware of a stooped, humble figure, evidently waiting for him near the doorway. The figure, silently and uninvited, followed him into the lighted hall.

"I have made bould to call on yer reverence," said the voice, the voice of a wizened old woman, whose face and figure were hidden under a mass of clothes.

"Well, my poor woman, and what can I do for you?" said Luke.

"I had nothin' to offer you," she said, "and I didn't like to be seen in the vesthry; but if your reverence would remimber in the Mass the sowl of Father O'Donnell—"

"Father O'Donnell? Father O'Donnell?" said Luke. "I never heard of the name."

"Av coorse you didn't, yer reverence," she said. "You're too young, God bless you! He's dead these forty years. 'Twas I nursed him in his last sickness, and he used to say, 'Nellie, don't you forget me in your Masses and prayers! The people think that we have no purgatory; but they don't know what a hard judgment we have for all the graces we get!' I remimber the words well. An' sure, if anny wan ever desarved Heaven, it was you, me poor dear priest! But I have never forgotten thim words: an' I never left an All Sowls' Night pass without gettin' him mintioned in the Blessed Mass."

"It shall be done, my poor woman," said Luke affectionately.

"God bless yer reverence!" she said, humbly passing out into the night.

And Luke sat down near his parlor fire. He didn't read. He had many things to think of. Thought, after a little while, became unbearable. He put on his biretta, and stepped out on his little garden walk. The night was extremely dark, and here and there a light shone in the village.[1] And, far above the village, out of the black breast of darkness, there gleamed the lights of the Lodge. The wind was moaning dismally; but it was a warm wind; and if one could believe that spirits in pain seek their places on earth to do penance for their transgressions, and to ask the alms of prayers for atonement, it would not be hard to realize that the heavens and the earth were haunted on this eerie night, and that the pitiful prayer, *Miseremini mei! miseremini mei!* was the burden of the wailing wind. But it was not this, but the pathetic remembrance of the dead by these poor people that affected Luke deeply. He thought of his sister's words: "Luke dear, love the poor, and life will be all sunshine." And he did love them: loved them deeply, earnestly; but in that hard, mechanical way, that never touches their hearts. He wanted to lift them up; and lo! there they were on the summits of the eternal hills far above him. He desired to show them all the sweetness and light of life; and behold, they were already walking in the gardens of eternity! He was preaching the thrift of money to the misers of grace. Where was the use of talking about economizing to a people whose daily fancies swept them abroad to regions where Time was never counted? And the value of money to a race, who, if parsimonious and frugal, became so through a contempt of physical comfort, and who regarded the death of the rich man as the culmination of all earthly misfortune? Then it began to dawn upon Luke's reason that it was moral, not altogether economic, causes that were driving the people from their motherland. They were bitten by the dogs of Mammon here and there, and the unrest, that sought peace and pleasure in the saloon, and the electric-lighted streets, and the music-hall, and the theatre. And he began to understand what was meant when his confrères spoke of the creation of a new civilization, founded on Spartan simplicity of life, and Christian elevation of morals, and the uplifting to the higher life, to which all the aspirations of his race tended, instead of the steady downward

[1] In Ireland, lights are kept burning all night on All Souls' Eve, as on Christmas Eve.

degradation that was certain to ensue, if the new dogmas of mere materialism, founded on the purely natural virtues, were allowed to supplant the larger lights of the Gospel, and the sacred doctrines that set at utter naught all the ordinary dictates of selfish prudence and purely temporal ambitions. And if for a moment his old ideas returned of a race self-seeking, prudential, hard-hearted, and endowed with all the virtues of the fox and the squirrel, and his reason cried, Utopia, Utopia! to the creation of a spiritual Kingdom—well, here were the voices of the night, *Miseremini mei! miseremini mei!* the children of eternity crying to the children of time for the alms of prayer and sacrifice.

Luke was extremely busy this week. He had no time to prepare a sermon for Sunday. He had exhausted all his political economy; and he was beginning to tire of it. Saturday evening came. He had returned from his confessional; and he was depressed. Here, too, he was shunned by the people. Nothing used pain him so deeply as when entering the church on Saturdays or the eves of holidays, he saw his own confessional deserted, and a great crowd around the old pastor's "box"; and the little children, even, whom he loved so much, would hold down their heads, half afraid to be seen, or would look up with a shy, furtive glance at the grave, solemn curate. He could not understand it. He was always kind, gentle, merciful to penitents. Why was he shunned? He had lost the key of the supernatural; and he didn't know it. One word about grace and eternity; about the Sacred Heart or the Precious Blood; about the Virgin Mother or St. Joseph, would have opened floodgates of sorrow and love. Nay, if he had scolded them, and abused them, for their soul's sake, they would have loved him. But goodness for prudence' sake—virtue, because it was a paying transaction in the long run, they could not well grasp; and all his exhortations fell, dry and withered, on hearts that thirsted for higher things.

He took up a newspaper this evening. There was a brief account of a certain battle that had been fought some centuries ago, in far Cremona. The details amused him—they were so characteristic. He laid down the paper.

"By Jove!" he said. "I will. I'll preach on Cremona and Calvary."

He did; but it cost him a tremendous effort. He had trained

himself so perfectly to self-restraint, particularly in his language, that his measured words fell, at first, on a cold and unsympathetic audience. He introduced the subject in connection with the great All Souls' Feast, which had just passed. He wished to prove that love for the dead was always a characteristic of the race; that soldiers prayed for dead comrades— ay, even for the enemy they had destroyed. Then he spoke of Cremona; of the two regiments, Dillon's (the old Mountcashel Brigade) and Burke's, that were quartered in the city. He drew a picture of the great French army, asleep in the famous Italian city—the stealthy approach of the enemy—their successful entry—their bivouac on the square while the garrison slept. The congregation woke up at the old familiar names— Dillon, Burke, Mountcashel. The U. S. pensioner and the Crimean veteran rose in their seats. And as Luke went on to describe the reveille at midnight, the sleepers aroused from dreams to the terrible cry: "The enemy is upon us!" the sudden rush for arms, and then the mighty valor with which the two Irish regiments, in very pronounced undress, flung themselves unaided on the foe, and drove them beyond the walls, and then drew up at the bridge-gate that commanded the town entrances, and drove back charge after charge of the cuirassiers, —and all this, whilst their marshal was in the hands of the enemy,—he let himself go, the first time for many years, and painted with all the emphasis of Celtic imagination the valor of this remnant of the Irish Brigade. There was a broad smile on the faces of the people as he spoke of the *deshabille* and unfinished toilettes of these Irish exiles; but when he went on to describe how, after the battle, the victors went out to bury the dead, and found some hundreds of their fellow-countrymen amongst the Austrians, who had fallen under their own fire, and how they knelt and prayed over the dead, and then built a mighty cross over their remains, Celtic fire yielded to Celtic sorrow; and for the first time in his life, Luke saw tears on the faces of his audience. He went on to speak of the Calvaries that were everywhere erected in Catholic countries on the Continent—by the wayside, on mountain summits, at the corners of streets; and he expressed great surprise that in a Catholic country like Ireland, such manifestations of faith and piety were almost unknown. He closed his discourse by a homily on death—his own recent bereavement adding pathos to his words—and turned to the altar, with a full heart.

The first fruit of his sermon was visible in an excellent dinner. Mary's temper was variable; and her moods affected her cuisine. This day, she did not know whether to laugh or to cry. The picture of these Irish fellows rushing straight from their beds at the foe, and driving, half armed and unarmored, four thousand Germans from the city, tickled her fancy. Then, the thought of Luke's mother (to whose death he had delicately alluded) subdued her; but she walked on air all day; and Luke saw delicacies whose very names were unknown to him. And Mary told John confidentially:—

"I knew the masther was always right; but priests can't talk out their minds, like common people."

There was a vast and sudden change, too, in the attitude of the great bulk of the parishioners. Instead of the shy, furtive looks—half-frightened, half-respectful—men walked up to him with a certain gay freedom, and accosted him. Some ventured so far as to say, with a cheery smile, "A fine day, Father Luke!" And the women courtesied, and whispered: "God bless your reverence every day you live!"

The village butcher, who held very strong National principles, and who was usually taciturn, if not surly, towards Luke, grew suddenly familiar. And sweetbreads, and liver, and kidneys began to pour into Luke's larder. And from afar, poor women brought in their early turkeys, for which they could get ten shillings a pair, and the yard became melodious with the cackling. And now, when he passed the young men on their Sunday walks, or going to work, instead of the silent, cold reverence of old with which they doffed their hats as they passed by, there was assumed a certain jaunty air of familiarity; and with it, a sort of confidential smile, as if they would say: "Well, your reverence, it *was* a good joke—that of those Irish *sans-culottes,* tearing like mad through the streets and squares of Cremona."

About a fortnight after, as Luke was going out to say last Mass, he thought he saw something unusual in the landscape. He rubbed his eyes, and scrutinized carefully every minute feature, now so well known to him. At last he discovered the novelty. Beyond the red tiles of the village roofs stretched the precipitous slope of woodland and forest in which the Lodge nestled. The Lodge was hardly visible in summer, so thick was the foliage of beeches, and oaks, and elms. But there was always visible a white pencil of a flagstaff, crossed by a yardarm, and netted with white ropes. The gilt ball on its summit glittered whenever the sun shone; and, when the General was at home, the red flag of England gleamed like a flame of fire against the black foliage. Sometimes it was the Union Jack, sometimes the flag of an admiral of the high seas, sometimes one symbol, sometimes another; but always the flag of England. And some of the villagers passed it by unnoticed, and some stared at it curiously; and some, especially on days when the staff was garlanded by all the flag signals in the British Navy, cursed low and deep at the symbol of their subjection. This day, it was a gleam of red, against the deep umbers and ochres of the autumn woods; and right behind it, and cresting the summit of the hill, and clearly outlined against the gray sky, was an immense black cross. Luke rubbed his eyes again, and called Mary.

"Do you see anything strange there right over the Lodge?" he asked.

"Where, your reverence?" said Mary, smiling, and looking everywhere but in the right direction. She had been in the secret for the last fortnight.

"There," said Luke, pointing. "There seems to be something unusual against the horizon-line."

"Oh! so there is," said Mary, slowly making the discovery. "There's something like a cross."

Then Luke saw that Mary was smiling.

After Mass, Luke strolled around the road that swept through the village and ran behind the General's demesne even to the summit. On the highest point of the hill the road cut off the demesne from the farms that were in the vicinity. And inside a hawthorn hedge and beyond the General's jurisdiction was a mighty cairn of stones, moss-grown, and lichen-covered, and dating from Druid times. It was visible for miles around, and was still known as *Knockane-na-Coppaleen,* the Little Hill of the Little Horses. No one dared touch it, though it was well known that gold was piled beneath; for didn't Farmer Mahony, a hard unbeliever, once remove a few stones from the cairn to repair a ditch, and wasn't he struck dead on the spot? and weren't the stones brought back to the cairn by invisible hands? Yet it could hurt no one to place the all-conquering Sign there—and there it was, cresting the cairn, an immense cross, with the spear and sponge, and a crown of real thorns hanging in the center. Luke gazed long at the mighty symbol; then, turning round, he noticed that the turf or grass surface had been removed in regular patches on the face of the high slope. He moved down, far down, and then looked upward. Yes! unmistakably, in clear-cut letters on the grassy swards, and so large that they might be read from the far hills of Clare, that today looked near and threatening, were cut the words—

PRAISED BE JESUS CHRIST, FOREVER!

CHAPTER XXXV

A Lecture on Biology

IT WAS fortunate for Luke Delmege that this momentary contact with the best side of human nature had softened his feelings towards men. Because he was just now face to face with that most deadly temptation—to despise and shrink from his kind, and to live in such solitariness of thought as would barely allow a margin of time for the discharge of sacred duties. The mighty abstraction, Humanity, which he had worshipped in the high atmosphere of thought, had been rudely dispelled, and had left only the sordid precipitate of a few wrecked fragments of bones and dust. And in the awful revelations of the grave he read the utter insignificance of human life. He began to perceive, too, in his close observation of Nature, that the same law was everywhere—life springing from the bosom of death, and then chased back into death again by the operations of some inexorable law. It was with infinite pity he saw how, in the springtime of the year, the buds had scarcely unfolded themselves in tender, silky leaves, when frost, or canker, or blight withered and dried up their infantine beauty; and, on the other hand, the leaves were hardly changed in color under October frosts, when tiny buds shot forth only to be paralyzed and shrunk under the icy breath of winter. So, too, in the fairest child, death and decay made themselves manifest. Scarcely had life begun, when death stood by the cradle, his thousand-winged messenger of disease hovering around that infant form to arrest its growth and destroy it. The carious teeth and the anæmic lips of young boys and girls affected him strangely. A chemist's shop, with all its sights and smells—its iodoform, and creosote, and carbolic, the ill-smelling wardens against decomposition and dissolution—made him sick. Death and

403

decay haunted all Nature like a hideous specter. So, too, in his reading, Luke gave up everything that was merely ephemeral. History he could not bear. What was it but the record of human passion and folly—the amateur theatricals of a race that must cheat time and ennui with its battles and diplomacy, and whose stage mimicry would be a tragedy, if its unimportance did not make it ludicrous? No. There was nothing lasting but the Idea and the Soul; and Luke turned away with loathing from his race and sought earth's only blessing of peace in solitude and thought. He was driven farther inward on himself by the attitude of his brethren towards him. They were kind, but critical. Their swift, impetuous ways, always seeking action, action— their emphatic principles, their intolerance of abstractions, and their insistence on facts; and all this, coupled with idealism that seemed to him utterly visionary and impractical, alienated his sympathies from them. He was always unhappy in society, except, indeed, the society of his beloved pastor, whose suave gentleness subdued all riotous questioning on his part. And he haunted the mountains and the streams and the pine-woods, and came home happy from his association with the peace of Nature. A day on the lonely mountains sitting over the rough bridge which spanned the yellow torrent, with the furze and the bracken waving around him, and a hare leaping out to wonder at him, and the whir of the partridge over his head, and the fresh, clean air wrapping him around like a cool garment on a fever patient, and the long, lone vistas stretching away to the hazy hills that crowned the pathway of the lordly Shannon, was an unspeakable pleasure. But it was morbid. Not in action alone, or in thought alone, but in the interplay of thought and action, true life consists. And Luke was saved from this morbidity for a time by the opening up of men's hearts towards him. And when again he was driven back upon himself, this generous expansion of his people's affections always protected him from the temptation of contempt.

Immediately after the events narrated in the last chapter, he made two gallant attempts to get into touch with the outer world. He was stung into making the attempts by some unkind things he had heard. They were but two simple phrases, but they meant so much. "Sub nube!" He only heard it in a whisper; but oh! how much it signified! And that cruel and unjust

saying of Lactantius: "Literati non habent fidem!" so untrue,
yet so easily applicable on the lips of the uncharitable, cut him
to the quick, as it magnified the episcopal warning into a
grave censure, which might be removed by Mother Church,
but never by the world. He determined to assert himself—to
come out into the arena, as he had so often stepped into the
palæstrum of his college, and show himself for all he was worth.
There were two ways open to him, literature and the pulpit;
two weapons, the voice and the pen.

He took down his books—some, alas! mildewed and damp
from want of use—and set to work steadily. He gave himself
full time for careful elaboration; and in six weeks he had a
paper ready for the press. They were the happiest six weeks he
had spent since his return to Ireland. Blessed is work! Blessed,
the sentence: "In the sweat of thy brow shalt thou labour
all the days of thy life!" He got his essay carefully type-written,
though typing was a costly novelty at the time, and sent it on to
the Editor of a great *Quarterly* that was just then setting out
boldly on its career as the organ of Science, Literature, Polem-
ics, and Art, for all that was cultured in the country. In a few
weeks, alas! the little roll was returned, with this letter:—

"OFFICE OF THE INDICATOR, April 6, 188—.
"MY DEAR LUKE:—In compliance with your modest request,
and the dictates of the editorial conscience, I read your paper from
Alpha to Omega. Like the famous critic, who opened 'The Ring
and the Book' for the first time, the dreadful suspicion crossed my
mind: Have I become suddenly demented? On the suggestion of
my sub, we read the paper backwards; and then a great light
dawned. Nothing could give me greater pleasure than to oblige
an old schoolmate; but if I published your paper, there would be
an immediate demand for auxiliary asylums all over the country;
and the doctors would at last have a tangible cause for the increase
in insanity, instead of tracing it to that harmless drug, called Tea.
Accepting your theory, however, about the *Identity of Contradic-
tories,* I accept your paper; and, in the same sense, you will hereby
find enclosed a check for £20.
"I am, dear Luke, Yours etc., THE EDITOR.

"P.S.—You will pardon an editorial joke, for *auld lang syne's*
sake. But, my dear Luke, you are a hundred years behind or a
hundred years in advance of your age. Don't you know we are

just now passing through the 'bread-and-butter' cycle? that we
have hung up *Erin-go-Bragh;* and are taking Sidney Smith's advice about Erin-go-bread-and-butter—Erin-go-boots-without-holes-
in-them, etc., etc.? Write me something practical, thou agricultural
curate—the quantity of nitrogen in a cubic foot of solid guano, how
to get sulphur out of turnips, and sugar of phosphorus out of apples,
or anything that will help on the material prosperity of the country; but abandon your idealism, and not only for a time, but forever. How I envy you!

> O, fortunatos nimium, sua si bona norint!

My only chance of exercise is on a piano-stool, which is my tripod;
and on which I make conscientiously three thousand gyrations
every day. And you, on your gallant steed, spurning the earth, and
climbing the Heavens! Ah me!!!"

Luke read the letter three or four times. He was disappointed; but he could not be angry. The good-humor of his
old classmate disarmed him. And certainly it was a good joke,
that Luke Delmege, the methodical, the practical, the realist,
should be warned off from the dangers of a too exuberant
imagination.

"There is no end to the human enigma," he said, as he tied
the roll and flung it into the recesses of his bookcase.

Some months after, he was invited to lecture at a great literary club in the city. The letter of invitation implied that
Luke's estrangement from the active life of the Church around
him was extremely unlike all that they had read about his
career in England, and gently hinted that a persistence in these
solitary habits would infallibly lead to his being considered
peculiar and strange. The subject of the lecture was left to his
own selection, with one proviso—it should be up-to-date.

With all his morbid shrinking from publicity, partly the
result of the secret contempt of men of which we have spoken,
and partly arising from a dread of being misunderstood, Luke
would have declined the invitation; but that word "peculiar"
stung him; and he determined to go, and show the world what
he was, and what he might have been. He ransacked his brains
and his library for an up-to-date subject; and, at last, decided
that biology—the latest of the sciences—was exactly suitable
to his own tastes and the capacities of his audience. He wrought

laboriously at his lecture, determined it should be his last cast of the dice.

There was a full house; and a brilliant gathering of priests and laymen on the platform. The president happily and generously spoke of Luke's splendid career in college, and his after-successes on the mission; and he spoke so warmly and so sympathetically, that Luke felt all his anger against mankind oozing away; and all the bitter things that had come back to his ears, all the more bitter for the translation, began to fade away in happy feelings of trust and love and gratitude. When will the world understand the mighty magic of kind words? Luke rebuked himself. "It is self-knowledge," he said, "that has made me uncharitable." Surely the heart enshrines mysteries and secrets beyond the power of its own divination!

His young spirits bounded back at this generous introduction; and he spoke under the intoxication of stimulated genius. His reception by the audience, too, was cordial, almost enthusiastic. His fine figure, a face animated with the glow of talent and the excitement of a novel experiment, his clear, well-modulated, ringing voice that sounded quite musical even after the splendid chorus of the Orchestral Union of the society, seemed to awaken all present to the fact that this lecture was to be something quite unique in their experiences. Nor were they disappointed. It was a clear, well-knit lecture, full of facts, as well as arguments; and when Luke completed a peroration in which he welcomed every fact, and scorned every conclusion of modern science, and declared that the cry of the Church in every age, most of all in our own, is for "Light! more light! that all knowledge may finally expand and be lost in the Light Supernal,"—the audience, mostly young men, arose, and gave him an ovation that seemed to console him for all his years of enforced seclusion. One member after another stood up to express his gratification; and then—well, then—there was the "little rift within the lute," that was tingling so musically in his ears. For one member made a comic speech about the "blastoderms" and "gemmules" and "amœba" which Luke had introduced into his lecture; and another hinted the suspicion that it was fine, but was it sound? It was eloquent; but was it orthodox? Luke flushed angrily. The president intervened. He took Luke's part nobly; and, being a man of vast erudition and unimpeachable honor, his words were regarded as final. But the sting remained. And for many months did Luke puzzle himself with the enigma that the more closely he studied, and the more accurately he expressed himself, the more was he misunderstood. He spoke angrily on the subject once to a lively confrère.

"I'd advise you, Luke," said the latter, "to keep to Grattan and O'Connell, or that venerable subject—The relative merits of a monarchy and a republic, or—Was Napoleon a greater warrior than Wellington? You can't trip there."

"But I didn't trip," protested poor Luke.

"Of course not! of course not!" said the confrère.

But there was one member of the audience that famous evening who was utterly disgusted and disedified. Matthew O'Shaughnessy was a retired merchant, who had accumulated a pretty fortune in the bacon and butter line; and, having provided well for his family, he wisely determined to retire from business, and, with his excellent wife, to spend the twilight of their lives in peace. He was a very pious man; kind, and good, and charitable, almost to a fault. But he had one imperfection —only one; and that, very venial. He was critical, especially about matters affecting religion or the Church. He always raised his silk hat—for he was a dreadful formalist and belonged to the old school—when passing a priest in the street: kindly, if he met an acquaintance, ostentatiously, if he met a stranger. But he would not salute a priest who was cycling. He thought it undignified and unbecoming.

He sat, on Sundays, a little distance from the pulpit; so near, that, being somewhat deaf, especially in the left ear, he might hear the preacher; so far, that he might see him, and watch his expression and gestures. When the Gospel of the day had been read, which Matthew followed word by word from his prayer-book to see was it correctly rendered, he sat with the audience, but slightly turned towards the wall, and with his right hand folded over and pressing down his ear. If the remarks of the preacher pleased him, he punctuated them with several nods of the head and half-audible remarks: "That's good!" "Bravo!" "I wouldn't doubt you!" If the preacher was weak or irrelevant, Matthew turned around, wiped his spectacles, and read his prayer book. He objected strenuously to "priests in politics";

and often asked: "What in the world are the bishops doing?"

On the evening of Luke's lecture, Matthew, as an honorary member of the committee, should have been on the platform with the priests and distinguished laymen, and grievous was the disappointment of many who had been anticipating a great treat from Matthew's remarks on biology. But he came in late —they said, purposely so—and was accommodated with a seat at the furthest end of the hall. He took it graciously, bowed all around to the young men, took out his red silk handkerchief and folded it on his knee, leaned slightly forward, folding his right hand over his ear, and listened. Luke was just saying that scientists had not yet fully determined whether man was a regenerate and fully-evolved anthropoid ape, or whether the anthropoid ape was a degenerate man; and he instanced experiments that had lately been made in London on a certain simian, called Sally, who was made to count numerals up to ten by placing straws in her mouth. Matthew's face lengthened, as he listened with open mouth. He couldn't believe his ears. He looked around cautiously to see what effect these extraordinary statements were producing on the faces of the young men around him. They were preternaturally solemn. He listened again. This time Luke was using manifestly profane language. Matthew looked around. The boys shook their heads mournfully and nudged each other. They then looked to Matthew for a clew. "I thought so," he said, drawing in his breath sharply. "I knew my sinses didn't deceive me. Did any mortal man ever hear the like from a priest before?" But, then, here was a chorus of congratulation from president, vice-president, and committee.

"I wouldn't stand it, if I was you," whispered a young man, who read Matthew's mind as if it were a book. " 'Tis a burning shame, and you're one of the committee."

But just then the one critic was opening his batteries on the lecture and expressing grave doubts about the lecturer's orthodoxy. Matthew was delighted.

"Good man!" he whispered. "Go on! Pitch into him! Right you are! Send it home!"

He then folded his silk handkerchief with a sigh, took up his silk hat, and turned around. He saw the expectant faces.

"Well," said he, "if that doesn't bang Banagher, I'm—a—

I'm—a—street-preacher. What the—— is comin' over the counthry at all, at all?"

He went out into the night. It was a moonlit night, very bright, and soft and balmy. The streets were deserted. The audience had remained for the final chorus. Matthew was puzzled, angry, shocked. He had to relieve his feelings. He addressed Diana, as there was no one else around.

"Egor! 'tis a quare business altogether! We don't know whether 'tis on our heads or heels we're standin' with these young men! Did anny wan ever hear the like before from the lips of a Roman Catholic clergyman? Egor! Jim the mule, and Mike the rogue, an' Sally the ape! Wasn't the poor 'uman as good as God made her? An' if He didn't make her as handsome as me young bucko, wasn't that His business? An' why should any poor 'uman be called an ape?"

Diana looked solemnly down, conscious of her own beauty, on these microbes of earth, but did not reply. Matthew went further towards home. Then his feelings overpowered him again, and striking the reverberating flags with his heavy stick, he again addressed Diana.

"That was bad enough; but whin he comminced cursin' and blasphemin', I thought he'd rise the roof aff. 'Blast ho! Jane Ettick,' he says; 'blast ho! Jer Minahal!' Egor! the ind of the world is comin'! What will Mary say, I wondher!"

Mary had been taking a gentle snooze over the parlor fire, while the cat slept at her feet and the kettle sang on the hob. She woke up on Matthew's entrance, rubbed her eyes, and said dreamily:—

" 'Pon my word, Matcha, I believe I was akchally asleep. How did ye like the leckshure?"

Mary looked well in her black silk dress, and the thin gold chain around her neck; but Matthew was too indignant to heed such things just then.

"Lave me alone, 'uman," he said. "Where are the matayriels?"

Mary said nothing, but touched the bell. She was accustomed to these moods. The "matayriels" were brought in, and Matthew, with sundry grunting soliloquies, brewed his tumbler. He then bent forward, and placing the tips of his fingers together between his knees, he said:—

"Mary O'Shaughnessy, you and me are a long time in this wurruld, and maybe we'll be longer, plase God; but of all the demonsthrations and exhibitions you ever hard of, tonight bate thim all."

He moistened his lips. Mary woke up.

"If it was a Methody, or a Prosbyterian, or wan of these new acrostics, that I hear 'em talk of sometimes below there, I wouldn't be surprised. But a Roman Catholic clergyman, an ordained minister of God, who'll be standing at the althar to-morrow mornin'—"

Here Matthew's feelings overpowered him. He threw out his hands in an attitude of horror and unspeakable disgust, and then moistened his lips.

"What was it about, at all?" said Mary, to help out her husband's inability to explain.

"About? I'll tell you, thin. It appears that this young gintle-man was in England; and there, like here, thc blagards will call names. But what was the manin' of telling a respectable congregation about Jim the mule, and Mike the rogue? But that wasn't all. There was a poor half-deminted crachure over there, called Sally, and what did they do wid her, d'ye think? Brought the poor 'uman up upon a stage, and asked her to count tin. And whin she couldn't, they put sthraws in her mout', and made her take 'em out, wan by wan, to count 'em. But," continued Matthew, as he laid down his wine glass, "that wasn't the worst of the business. Mary O'Shaughnessy, did you ever hear a priest curse?"

"Yerra, what's comin' over you, Matcha?" said Mary, peering at her husband intently. "Curse? a priest curse? Niver, nor you ayther!"

"Didn't I?" said Matthew. "Faix, an' I did. Not wance or twice nayther; but every second word from his mout'."

"If I didn't know you, Matcha O'Shaughnessy," said Mary, with some anger, "I'd say you wor dhramin'."

"Faix, I wasn't, nor more nor you this minit," said Matthew. "Egor, I thought he'd rise the roof av me head. 'Blast yah, Jane Ettick,' he says; not 'you,' at all, but 'yah,' wid his grand English accent: 'Blast yah, Jer Minahal! Blast yah, Der-mody'—"

Mrs. O'Shaughnessy was tapping the brass fender with her

slipper in an ominous manner; and her eyes were glinting, like the sparks in the grate; but Matthew, with all the unconsciousness of a fated mortal, went on, twisting poor Luke's scientific terminology into horrible profanity. Then the storm broke suddenly.

"D'ye know what I'm thinkin', Mr. O'Shaughnessy?" she said, in an accent of forced calmness.

"Somethin' good, Mary, I'm sure," said Matthew, a little frightened and surprised.

"I'm thinkin', Matcha O'Shaughnessy," said Mary, beating time with her slipper, "that you lifted yer little finger wance too often since yer dinner."

"If you mane, Mary," said Matthew, apologetically, yet sure of his defense, "that I took dhrink, ye were never more mistaken in yer life. Since the day I took the teetotal pledge for life from Father Matcha, me friend, down there in the bowlin' green, exactly forty-five years ago come this Christmas, on two dhrinks a day, and whatever the Doctor would ordher as medicine, I never tasted a dhrop since."

"Thin can't you let yer priests alone?" cried Mary, angrily turning around.

"Yerra, is't me, 'uman?" cried Matthew. "Yerra, I'd die for me priests!"

"Thin why are you always nagging at 'em, an' placin' 'em and faultfindin' with 'em? Begor, the poor gintlemin can't please ye, at all, at all. If they wear a high bayver, they're too grand; an' if they wear a Jurry-hat, they're demanin' thimselves. If they're goin' about their juty in the sthreets, they ought to be at home; and if they stay at home, why aren't they walking the sthreets? If they go to Kilkee or Lisdoonvarna for a bret' of fresh air, they're spindin' the money of the poor; an' if they stop at home, they're savin' and miserly. If they take their masheens an' go out for a whiff of fresh air, afther bein' cooped up all day in their boxes, pious craw-thumpers an' althar-scrapers won't take aff their hat to God's ministers—"

"Yerra, 'uman, take yer tongue aff me," cried Matthew, in agony. "Sure, I'd lie down in the mud of the sthreets and lave me priests walk over me body—"

"Begor," continued Mary, now thoroughly roused, "wid yere Parnellites, an' yere Indepindints, an' yere Faynians, there's

no respect for God nor man. Ye'll be soon tellin' the Pope of
Rome what he ought to do. But 'tis only sarvin' 'em right.
Manny and manny's the time I tould 'em: 'Do as the ould
priests did—give 'em the stick acrass the small of their back,
an' they'll respect ye.' But, begor now, the priests of the Church
must take aff their Caroline hats to ivery little whipster of a
girl that comes home from her convent school wid her rowl
of music under her arrum—"

"Go on!" said Matthew, resignedly, turning round to his
only consolation. "What the Scripture says is true: There's no
stoppin' a burnin' house, nor a scouldin' 'uman."

"An' what'd ye be, widout yere priests?" continued Mary,
unheeding. "Who looks after the poor and the sick? Who goes
out into the house where there's sickness and faver, and brown-
cheeties, and mazles? Who gets up yere Young Min's Societies
for ye? An' yere concerts? Who's at the top, bottom, and
middle of iverything that's good or gracious—in the counthry—"

"Yerra, 'uman, shure I'm not denying that our priests are
good!" pleaded Matthew, in despair.

"An' there ye are, like a parcel of unwaned childre wid yere
mouths open to be fed. 'Tis the priest here; an' the priest there!
An' very little thanks they get for their throuble afther all. But,
believe you me, Matcha O'Shaughnessy," continued Mary, in a
tone of great solemnity, "an' believe you me agin, there's a day
of reck'nin' comin'; and manny a poor crachure, who hasn't
as long a bade as you or your aiquals, may inter the Kingdom
of Heaven afore ye. But take me advice—let the priests alone!
They belong to God; an' if they go astray let Him dale wid
them!"

There was a deep, solemn hush of ten minutes' duration
after this tornado. Matthew was struck dumb. What can a poor
fellow do but bite the dust after a cyclone? "Tic-tac," solemnly
went the clock on the mantelpiece. "Tick, tick, tick, tick, tick,
tick," went Mary's gold watch in her belt. At last Matthew
raised himself with a deep sigh; and commenced to compose
an *Eirenicon*. When this was ready, he said, in a gentle and
deferential whisper:—

"Mary!"

There was no reply.

"Mary!" he said, more loudly.

"Well?" said Mary, without looking around.

"Mary, I'm makin' a little sup for you."

"You won't," said Mary, crossly.

"But I say I will," said Matthew. "Mary, I've been noticin' for a long time that you're not lookin' quite yerself. You're only pickin' and pickin' at your males like a young chicken. Why, you ate no more for your brekfus thin a child of four. You must see the docthor, and take somethin' every day for nourishment. Here, take this!"

" 'Tis too sthrong," said Mary, making a grimace over the steaming wine-glass.

" 'Tis *not* too sthrong," said Matthew, in a tone of righteous indignation. " 'Twill rouse you up."

"Put a little hot wather in it," said Mary, pleadingly.

"I will *not* put hot wather in it," said Matthew. "Is it to make you sick, I'd be?"

"Well, I'll lave it up there to cool," said Mary, placing the wine-glass on the mantelpiece.

After a long pause, during which the temperature settled down to normal, Mary said:—

"That young priest is a cousin of mine!"

"What young priest?" said Matthew, with affected indignation.

"The young pracher," said Mary.

"Is't Father Delmege you mane?" said Matthew.

"Yis," answered Mary. "He's me second and third cousin be me mother's side."

"An' why didn't ye tell me that before?" said Matthew. "Did I iver see such people as women are? They draw you out, an' out, an' out, like a talliscope, until you make a fool of yerself, and thin they shut you up with a snap. But, faix, an' 'tisn't because I'm sayin' it to yer face, ye have raison to be proud of him."

"I'm tould he's a fine-lookin' man," said Mary.

"Fine? Fine is no name for him. He's wan of the grandest min ye ever saw in a day's walk."

"I suppose he'll be coming to see me," said Mary, "if only on account of his poor mother."

"D'ye think will he come tonight?" said Matthew, in alarm.

"Faix, he might. He might dhrop over afther his supper."

"I'm better be puttin' these things out of the way," said Matthew, hastily removing the glasses. "I'm tould he hates this, as the divil hates holy wather."

Just then, a tremendous knock was heard at the hall-door.

"Here he is!" said Mary, straightening herself up, and arranging her toilette. "Do I look all right, Matcha?"

"Never better in yer life," said Matthew. "He'll be the proud man whin he sees you."

There was a colloquy in the hall; then a heavy foot on the stairs. In answer to a rather timid knock, Matthew shouted "Come in!" The door opened just a little, the servant-maid put in her tousled head, and said:—

"The milkman, ma'am, sez he wants that tuppence for the mornin's milk!"

"Bad luck to you and the milkman together," said Mary, fumbling in her pockets. "Here!"

But Luke did call the following day; and he was very grand, but gracious and even affectionate. He had been learning that in this old land, and amongst its simple, faithful people, there were mighty treasures of warmth and love, for which the cold, steely polish of other lands was but a poor exchange. And Matthew and Mary lived on the honor for days afterwards, and cut out the paragraph in the paper about "The Lecture on Biology," and Matthew went around, and asked every one "Did they ever hear the like before?" and "Why the mischief doesn't the Bishop bring that grand young man into the city?" And Mary placed on her mantelpiece, side by side with the portrait of the Bishop himself, Luke's photograph, gorgeously framed; and in answer to all inquiries, she said modestly:—

"Me cousin, Father Luke!"

CHAPTER XXXVI

A Boast and Its Consequences

IN THE cool, gray dusk of his little parlor Luke saw things in a light somewhat different from their gaudy coloring under the gas-jets. The clapping of hands, and the eager faces, and the flattery had passed away; and there remained but the stinging remembrance that for the third or fourth time in his life he had been accused of coquetting with heresy. With his clear-cut ideas on theological matters, he knew right well that this suspicion could not be sustained for a moment; and he was so conscious of his own deep attachment to every jot and tittle of the Church's teachings that he grew by degrees very indignant at the shameful assumption. All the applause and enthusiasm were forgotten. Of the handsome bouquet of praise and adulation offered him a few nights before, alas! there only remained a few withered leaves and the wires that cut his fingers.

"I don't think the game is worth the candle," said Luke to himself. "Let me calculate the matter nicely."

And he wrote down this calculation neatly and in the most approved form of bookkeeping, thus:—

Dr.	Cr.
1. A good deal of anxiety and deliberation about lecture, subject, etc.	1. A little flattery.
2. Six weeks' hard work on encyclopædias, books, magazines, etc.	2. A little applause.
3. Three weeks' hard work at writing, correcting, revising thirty pages of manuscript.	3. A good deal of criticism, mostly unjust and unintelligent.
4. Expense of typing same.	4. Accusation of heresy.
5. Expense and inconvenience of journey, hotels, bills, etc.	5. One tiny paragraph in a local newspaper.
6. The nervous fever of lecturing.	6. Oblivion.

Luke totted up, and then proposed, seconded, and passed unanimously the resolution: "The game is *not* worth the candle."

And Luke said to his soul, "Sleep now, and take thy rest!"

Beaten back, then, and baffled once more, it was a happy thing for him that just now all the flowers of human respect and affection were opening up their beautiful chalices in the warmth and sunshine of his own smile. And the next few years, —the years of perfect manhood and strength, and alas! also of decay, for now his hair began to be streaked with silver and the lines deepened about his mouth,—were very happy, and the mighty enigmas of life became no longer too personal, but only the puzzles of the academy and the porch. His illumination was not perfect, and once again his mighty Master woke him up with the sharp edge of the sword of trial. But these years of middle life were very smooth and peaceful, and the prophecy of Father Martin was well fulfilled. Luke had found his America in Rossmore.

He was helped on in great measure by a new experience. He had noticed, with mixed feelings of pleasure and surprise, that the village children were totally unlike in demeanor and conduct and methods of expression to any children of whom he had hitherto had experience. And it shows how abstracted and wrapped up in his own thoughts he must have been when it was some months before he was aware of the contrast and the originating cause. Then it was suddenly revealed to him that the respectful, subdued attitude of the children, their reverence in church, their brisk politeness and attention to the aged and infirm, were very unlike the rampant and reckless boisterousness of youth. For some time further Luke was either indifferent to, or unconscious of, the cause. Then, one day he came into school at an unexpected time and was surprised to see the children ranged around the wall and holding their arms and heads in different degrees of attention and reverence. The silence was so deep and the absorption of the children so great that Luke's entrance was not noticed, and he heard the master, a grave man of middle years, saying:—

"Reverence is the secret of all religion and happiness. Without reverence, there is no faith, nor hope, nor love. Reverence is the motive of each of the Commandments of Sinai—reverence of God, reverence of our neighbor, reverence of ourselves. Humility is founded on it; piety is conserved by it; purity finds in it its shield and buckler. Reverence for God, and all that is associated with Him, His ministers, His temple, His services—that is religion. Reverence for our neighbor, his goods, his person, his chattels—that is honesty. Reverence for ourselves—clean bodies and pure souls—that is chastity. Satan is Satan because he is irreverent. There never yet was an infidel but he was irreverent and a mocker. The jester, and the mime, the loud laugher and the scorner, have no part in the Kingdom. These very attitudes you now assume betoken reverence. They are the symbols of something deeper and higher—"

Here he saw Luke, though the children's eyes did not direct him; and he said, without changing his voice:—

"Children, the priest is here!"

The children raised their heads gently, their arms still crossed on their breasts, and bowed towards Luke.

"Now," said the teacher, "you will pass into your desks, and sing

'In the sunshine; in the shadow.' "

The children moved to their places, singing the part song, not loudly, but sweetly; and the master turned towards Luke. A grave, silent man; his attitude, too, betokened reverence. He was a man of middle age; for his pointed beard was streaked with white hairs. He was tall and angular in appearance; but his whole manner was subdued, not with the instinct of fear and watchfulness, but with the gentleness of an urbane and thoughtful spirit. And he was a mystery, which was another attraction to Luke. He had an only daughter, a girl of twenty years or thereabouts, living with him; but his antecedents were known only to Dr. Keatinge, the pastor, who had found him out somewhere, and brought him to Rossmore to take charge of his little school. So much Luke had heard; and then dismissed the subject. It was trivial and commonplace. In his former visits, too, he had seen nothing remarkable, probably because he was too much engrossed with his own reflections. Today, he was surprised and pleased.

"Where did you find material for that excellent discourse!" said Luke.

"In my own experience, sir," said Mr. Hennessy.

"How have you trained the children so beautifully in the limited time at your disposal?" asked Luke, who knew well the red-tape regulations of the National Board.

"It would be impossible, sir," answered the teacher. "But I supplement the day's teaching at night."

"At night?" said Luke, wonderingly. "I thought night-schools were things of the past."

"We don't call it *school*," said the teacher. "But, perhaps, sir, you would come up some evening to see what we are doing. It may interest you."

"I shall be delighted," said Luke. "But, do you often speak to the children in the way I have just heard?"

"Yes," said the teacher, though this was supposed to be an assumption of a higher privilege. "I think the moral training of children the most necessary part of education. The National Board provides for the intellectual department; there is the mid-day hour for doctrinal and catechetical instruction. But the training of youth in moral culture must be left to the teacher; and in my humble way, I try to discharge this duty."

"With your permission I shall come up this evening," said Luke. "At what hour?"

"We hold our little *soirées,* sir," said the teacher, smiling, "we dignify them by that name, from seven to nine o'clock."

"I shall be there," said Luke. "By the way, how many children on the rolls?"

"Fifty-six," said the teacher.

"How many in attendance?"

"Fifty-six," said the teacher.

In the evening Luke went to the school. It was well lighted; and it looked bright and cheerful to eyes that had just brought in with them the gloom of the night. The desks were unmoved; but the school harmonium was open; and here and there around the room full-blown chrysanthemums threw out their colored blossoms of light fragrance and great loveliness. All the village children were there; the country children alone were absent. The master touched a gong when Luke entered; the children stood up respectfully; and, the master's daughter presiding at the harmonium, they sang a pretty glee in part time—a composition of the master's. When they were seated, the master read for them a poem called *The House of Hate.* The children then took up their lessons for the following day, the master's daughter moving gently through the desks, and guiding their young hands and minds. Meanwhile Luke and the master were in close conference. The whole system appealed strongly to Luke's sympathies and ideas. Here, at least, was positive, practical work. No note of criticism, or complaint; no theorizing about great political possibilities; no flinging of charges; and above all, and this touched Luke more closely, for it was his own great weakness, no fretting with enigmas; but the quiet positivism of work, ennobled only by the motive, and the great possibilities it awakened. And it was quiet, unpretentious work, unacknowledged by the world and unseen—the work of great principle and a pure, lofty mind.

"Why do you insist so strongly on reverence?" said Luke. "It seems to be the burden of all your teaching."

"Because I think, sir," replied the master, "that it is the secret of all religion; and therefore of all nobleness."

"And you think it necessary?"

"I think it the first necessity for our race and for our time."

"Our race?" questioned Luke, with opened eyes.

"Yes, sir. We are always alternating between reverence and irreverence in Ireland. Our literature and language are quite full of sarcasms, as well as of great ideas. And sarcasms about the most sacred things. Great wit and madness are nearly allied. So, too, are great wit and irreligion."

"But now," said Luke, "with all our splendid idealism there can be but little danger?"

"No," said the master, "except that one ideal may supplant and destroy another. All ideals are opposed. At least," he said modestly, "so I have read. Would you kindly say a word to the children, sir?" he said, as the gong sounded.

"Certainly," said Luke. And he did, generously, warmly, emphatically. It was work, work, with an object. And Luke realized that there was something in life beyond

The little soul for the little that holds the corpse, which is man.

At eight o'clock all work was suspended. And the remaining hour was devoted to the practice of singing, particularly the preparation of Church hymns, etc., varied with the little glees and part songs. Just before nine o'clock the master read a

chapter from the Gospel of St. John, recited one decade of
the Rosary, and the children rose up to depart. The master
and his daughter stood near the door. As the children passed
the latter, they bowed respectfully. The master took each child
by the hand as they passed into the night. There was not the
slightest trace of the familiarity that annihilates all reverence.

"I have read something like it somewhere," soliloquized
Luke, as he went homewards. " 'Moral culture,' 'reverence,'
'attitudes,' where?"

But this school was a perpetual wonder and attraction to
him during these years, until at last came the great cross, and
behind the cross—the great illumination.

The aged Canon having cast aside all the other subordinate
anxieties and interests of life retained but his love for his niece,
Barbara Wilson, and his intense and beautiful pride in the
prosperity of his parish. This, indeed, was more than justified
by the happiness of his people; and the Canon's parish became
the great object-lesson to his diocese and country. And eminent
political economists came from afar to see the great Sphinx-
problem of Irish contentment solved, once and forever. Only
one held out against the general enthusiasm—one sceptic,
Father Cussen.

"You're a horrible Cassandra," said one of his confrères,
"if I may apply the term. You are forever croaking of ruin
in the midst of success."

"Time will tell," said Father Cussen.

The Canon's recreation, in his old age, when he rode no
longer, and cared little for driving, was to stroll down in the
evening to the village post-office, and there watch, with intense
gratification, the vast piles of Irish agricultural produce that
were about to be sent by parcel post to England. It was a rare
and delightful exhibition. Huge canvas bags containing poultry; square boxes full of rich, yellow butter; cans of cream;
larger boxes yet, filled with consignments of eggs, each egg
nestling in its own dry fresh moss; and even small tin boxes of
amber honey—these were the exports that filled the little office
to the ceiling, and made Miss Carey, the postmistress, declare,
again and again, to the infinite delight of the good Canon, that
the Government should, by sheer force of such gentle circum-

stances, build a new post-office. One such evening, as the Canon entered the office, he saw a young man, leaning against the counter and chatting with Miss Carey. The conversation clearly was about the vast resources of the parish, for the young man, whom the Canon took to be a groom, for he was dressed in riding suit and flicked his boot with a short whip, was just saying:—

"And you calculate the net profits from this admirable plan should be about—how much a year did you say?"

"The Canon knows better than I," said the postmistress. "He has created the industry." She looked significantly and warningly at the Canon; but the latter took no heed.

"I have carefully—ha—gone into details, sir," he said grandly, "and I have found that, season with season, the net profits of these agricultural—ha—exports average from fifty to eighty pounds a week."

"You quite astonish me," said the groom. "I did not believe that such things were possible outside of Belgium or Normandy."

This might have shown the Canon that this stranger was not a groom; and Miss Carey hummed significantly as she stamped the parcels, and looked at the Canon in a way that would have paralyzed or petrified any one else. But the Canon went on:—

"I assure you, sir," he said, "I depreciate rather than—ha—exaggerate our net income from these industries. My parish has been called 'a happy Arcadia' in the midst of the—ha—howling deserts around."

"I'm sure I congratulate you, sir," said the stranger, flicking his boot impatiently with his whip. " 'A noble peasantry their country's pride'—is it not so?"

"You have quoted correctly, sir," said the Canon. "The peasantry are the backbone of the country."

"It is really so interesting," said the stranger, taking out a notebook, "and I am so often asked in my—well—travels about the prosperity of the Irish people, that I should be glad to have it, in black and white, from your lips that such an account can be authenticated. I think you said the net income from these industries varies from fifty to eighty pounds a week; that is, from three to four thousand per annum?"

"Precisely so, sir," said the Canon. "And, as I have said already, this is rather under than over the real estimate."

"It is really most interesting," said the stranger. "I'm sure I'm extremely obliged for the information. One favor more. Whom have I the honor of addressing?"

"The pastor of this parish, sir," said the Canon, with great dignity. "Canon Maurice Murray."

"Oh, I should have known," said the stranger with great courtesy. "But I have been absent on my travels for some years, and I am quite unacquainted with this interesting place. I have the honor to wish you good evening."

"Good evening, sir!" said the Canon, bowing the stranger out.

"An extremely interesting gentleman," said he, turning to the postmistress. "What a powerful educational—ha—factor has travelling become!"

Miss Carey did not reply.

"No letter from Austria or Hungary for me?" he asked.

"No, sir!" she replied. It was the hundredth time she had to say no! She almost wept for her aged pastor.

A few days later there was a scene in a certain agent's office in Dublin. The clerks saw an interchange of courtesies between a stranger and their master; heard themselves peremptorily ordered from the office; thought they heard heated language and even profane; and one said he heard the swish of a riding-whip and a heavy scuffle and a fall. But, no, they were mistaken. For Captain Vermont and his agent were, like Mr. Kipling's canonized saints—"gentlemen, every one."

But, when the clerks were ordered back to the office, the agent was gone; and there only remained the stranger, who was dressed very like a groom. And he was very pale, and trembling with excitement.

"Which of you is head-clerk here?" he said, turning round.

"I," said a young Scotchman. "Henry Simpson."

"Well, Simpson, you take charge here, until I appoint another agent. I am Captain Vermont. And when you are sending out notices for rent on my estates in Limerick and Kerry— when is next rent due?"

"The twenty-ninth of September," said Simpson.

"Well, stop that reduction of twenty-five per cent, and call in all arrears. And, mark you, all of you, no more—nonsense. By G——, I won't stand it." And Captain Vermont departed.

And so, over happy Arcady, the model parish of Lough and Ardavine, the shadow fell—the shadow long threatened, but never feared. For had they not their mighty Samson, patriarch and king? and was it not a tradition in the parish, that landlords and agents scurried about and looked for rat-holes to hide them from the terrors of his face? He was indignant. The old leonine spirit woke within him, when he found his people in danger. At first he laughed the threats of the agent's office to scorn. Call in arrears! Nonsense! They dare not do it. But, when the rumble of the smooth mechanism of British law began to be heard afar off, and writs came to be served on two or three of the principal parishioners, the Canon saw that business was meant. He called his people together, and told them he was going to Dublin to settle the matter without further ado. They gave a mighty cheer; and felt the battle was won. Father Cussen was silent. He called his league together; and bound them solemnly to stand firmly shoulder to shoulder. He then demanded their receipts from the rent office. They brought the grimy bundles—yellow, stained, rumpled, torn. He examined them closely. Quite so! The very thing he expected.

"Did you pay your March rent?" he said to one of the farmers.

"To be sure I did, yer reverence," he replied.

"Did you get a receipt in full?" he asked.

"To be sure I did," the farmer replied. "There 'tis in your hand, yer reverence."

"This can't be the receipt," said Father Cussen. "It is dated five years back."

" 'Tis the last resate I got," said the farmer, thoroughly frightened.

"Quite so. And you see there are due five years' arrears, amounting to over £260."

Father Cussen examined all the other receipts. One by one was antedated, thus certifying to arrears due.

The fire that burned so hotly in the aged Canon's breast on his journey to Dublin, burned up also his little physical strength. And it was a bowed and weary man that tottered down the steps of the Shelbourne Hotel next morning. The waiter helped him to the pavement.

"Shall I call a cab, sir?"

"Oh! no," said the Canon. "I feel quite strong—ha—quite vigorous!"

The excitement of entering the agent's office, and making a mighty stand for his poor people, gave him a little unnatural vigor, as he asked, in his own grand way, the group of clerks that were writing behind the screen:—

"Can I see Mr. Noble this morning?"

"No," said Simpson, shortly, "you cannot."

"Then when might I have the—ha—honor of an interview with Mr. Noble?" said the Canon.

"I suppose," said Simpson, "whenever you have the honor of meeting him."

"I regard that reply as an impertinence, sir," said the Canon.

"Now, look here, old gentleman," said Simpson, coolly, "if you have missed your way, and strayed in here, the porter will direct you back to your hotel, or place of residence."

"I'm really—ha—surprised," gasped the Canon. "This is utterly unexpected. Perhaps you do not—ha—know who I am."

"I have not that honor," said Simpson, "and to be very candid, I don't much care."

"I pass by that gross discourtesy, sir," said the Canon, "as I'm here on business. My name is Maurice Canon Murray, parish priest of Lough and Ardavine."

"Well, Maurice Canon Murray, parish priest of Lough and Ardavine, would you now state your business as briefly as possible, for our time is precious?"

"I came, sir," said the Canon, "to inquire the meaning or object of this gross outrage on my parishioners."

"What outrage do you speak of?" queried Simpson.

"This serving of writs, and demand for a wholly unreasonable rent," said the Canon.

"You call yourself a Christian clergyman," said Simpson, "and represent a legitimate demand for moneys due, and which, under proper management, would have been paid at any time for the last five years,—an outrage?"

"I see," said the Canon, who felt his strength rapidly ebbing away, "that it is—ha—useless—to discuss matters with a subordinate. Please let me know Captain Vermont's Dublin address."

"He has no City address," said Simpson. "His country address you should know better than I."

"I regret to say—ha—I have not—the honor—of Captain Vermont's acquaintance," said the Canon, as the room began to swim around.

"Oh! dear; yes, you have," said Simpson. "At least it was you that gave Captain Vermont the happy information that he was steadily robbed of three or four thousand a year by your excellent parishioners."

"Me, sir? How dare you, sir? That is an un—sertion—rantable—wa—please, might—chair—have?"

One of the clerks rushed out and placed the falling Canon in a chair.

"Yes," said Simpson, bitterly and mercilessly; "and they would have met their demands were it not for the interference of disloyal and turbulent priests like you—"

"Stop that, Simpson," said the clerk, who held the fainting Canon upright in his chair. "Don't you see the gentleman is fainting?"

"Me, sir—distur—loyal—turb—"

"What is your hotel, sir, please? and I shall fetch a cab."

"Shel—tel," murmured the broken voice, as the lips fell twisted by paralysis, and the right hand lay helpless at the side.

"The Shelbourne!" cried one of the clerks. "Quick, Harris, or we shall have an inquest here!"

And so the poor Canon, on his mission of mercy, met the first forerunner of dissolution in an agent's office. His limp, heavy form was pushed into a cab, and, in an unconscious condition, he was carried to the *Mater* Hospital, where he remained many a weary month. And despair settled down on Lough and Ardavine. They had the bonfires built that were to celebrate the Canon's triumphal return, and the League Band that had serenaded him so many years ago, and tried to infuse some patriotism into him, was practicing, "See the Conquering Hero Comes!" Then the news arrived. Their king, their patriarch, their mighty champion, was stricken down in the fight. And what hope remained?

CHAPTER XXXVII

Disillusion

WEARILY and anxiously the months passed by in the parish of Lough and Ardavine. All work was at a standstill. The people were paralyzed. No one knew, from day to day, when the dread messengers of the law would swoop down and commence the work of destruction. The post-office was now empty. The postmistress was idle. The great export trade of the parish was a thing of the past. Worst of all, the great father and friend was lying on his bed of sickness in a Dublin hospital. They had not heard from him for some time; and then his message was fairly hopeful. He assured them that the landlord would not proceed to extremities. He was partly right. The case had got into the English press; for the buyers at Manchester were losing heavily by the enforced inactivity of their clients in Ireland; and the Canon had written from his sickbed a strong letter to the Dublin and London press on this new instance of injustice and rapacity. And so the office hesitated to enforce instructions, repeatedly received from the landlord in Paris; and all was wrapped in surmise and uncertainty.

Father Cussen was savagely exultant. His prophecy was fulfilled to the letter. He had foreseen the evil day and was prepared for it. It was sure to come, he said. Better now than later on. One sharp tussle; and their tenure was secure forever. Only let them stand shoulder to shoulder, and all the might of England could not dislodge them.

Luke went over to Lisnalee. The good old father was grievously troubled. Lizzie and her husband were anxious, but determined. Was there no chance of a settlement, asked Luke.

"None whatever. The landlord was demanding an impossibility. That margin of twenty-five per cent reduction just kept them afloat, and gave them heart to carry on their industries. If they paid that, all the profits of their skill and labor were

427

sacrificed. And then, to demand arrears, due over thirty years
—the thing was monstrous!"

Father Cussen said the same, adding: "You see, Luke, it's
all your beautiful law and order! The man is doing a strictly
legal thing; and a strictly brutal thing. He wants this three
or four thousand a year, which your sister here and the rest
are making, not out of the improved condition of his property,
but from their own industry. He wants it to stake it on the red
at Monte Carlo; and he must have it, or ruin! And the law
says, Yes! It is brutal, but strictly legal! And it will be carried
out at the point of the bayonet."

Luke returned to Rossmore with a heavy heart, full of
forebodings.

There was a great mission given in the parish of Rossmore
during the month of May in that year. Like all missions in
Ireland it was well attended. People flocked from near and far
to hear the sermons, and go to confession. The good Fathers
had a busy time, and Luke was kept in the church from early
morn till late at night. This distracted his thoughts, and made
him happy. The closing demonstration—that most touching
ceremony of the renewal of baptismal vows—was a wonderful
sight. There were over fifteen hundred persons in the large
church. The heat was stifling; but they did not heed it. Mothers
brought their babies from their cradles, lest they should lose
the glory and benediction of that night; and they held the tiny
fingers around the wax candles, and spoke their vows even for
the little ones, who had no need of renewal. All felt regener-
ated after a good confession and communion; all were happy,
with that strange, beautiful sense of lightness and peace that
one feels after a good sincere confession; all were prepared to
live for God, and to die rather than fall into the hands of His
enemy. Luke was more than happy; he was buoyant, even enthusiastic. He had had a glorious week's work, and he felt
sustained by the mighty tonic. And he knew his good pastor
was pleased and gratified; and this, too, was a great pleasure.
But there will be always some little accident to mar great
events; and it occurred this evening. One poor fellow forgot
himself; but, notwithstanding his condition, he had insisted on
coming to the closing of the mission. He kept fairly quiet during the sermon; but just before the candles were lighted for
the concluding ceremony, he became troublesome. Luke saw

the commotion, and, gliding down by the side aisle, he ordered the delinquent to rise up and follow him. The poor fellow obeyed, and came out into the yard. Luke ordered him home. But this was resisted. The young man stood, with legs wide apart, and swaying to and fro. His candle, bent with the heat, was twisted around his hand, and he was weeping and blubbering like a child.

"Come now, like a good fellow," said Luke; "go home, and no one will miss you."

"I wo'not go home," was the reply. "I wants the bilifit of the bission; I do—a."

"How can you gain any spiritual benefit in your present state?" protested Luke. "Go home, and go to bed."

"I wo'not go home," the poor fellow protested. "Oh! oh! to be turned out ov the House of God, and the last night of the bission! Oh! oh!"

"'Twas your own fault," said Luke. "You have disgraced us all tonight. Go home now, like a good fellow!"

"I wo'not go home," he replied, weeping. "I wants to go back to the House of God, an' to get the bilifit of the bission. Oh! I do—a."

"You shall not return to the church," said Luke, determinedly. "I cannot have the congregation disturbed this evening. There, I'll get some one to take you home. You can sleep it off, and come tomorrow for the pledge. There, your candle is gone and 'tis all over."

That extinguished candle was decisive. The poor fellow turned away, ashamed and sorrowful, and went towards his home in misery.

Luke was very angry. He quite ignored the vast, pious congregation inside, and the glorious work that had been wrought during the week. He saw only the one blot, and that saying, "the bilifit of the bission," haunted him during the week. He had worked himself into the fine fury of those who are angry and sin not, by Sunday morning; and at last Mass on that day he delivered a fierce invective on the abuse of divine grace, on the folly of mistaking the means for the end, on the superstition of supposing that the mission was a light coat of armor, that would save them from relapsing during the year, without any corresponding effort on their part to coöperate with grace, etc.

On Monday morning he set out on his annual holiday. It was now ten years since he had left England, and although repeatedly invited by his old confrères to cross the Channel, he had always declined. He dreaded the return of his first experience of the contrasts between the countries. He was now fairly happy; and he did not care to plunge again into the fearful despondency that haunted him during his first years on the home mission. But now he had cast the past so thoroughly behind him that he no longer dreaded the experience; and he had a secret longing to see once more the place where he had spent the first years of his priesthood, and the faces of old friends. He called at the Cathedral. All was changed here. The old staff had passed away, removed by promotion or death; and new faces were all around him. There were the old dining-room and library; there was the table where he was drawing his map when suddenly ordered to Aylesburgh; there his bed-room. But the Bishop? Dead. The good, kind old Vicar? Dead. Sheldon? Gone to Aylesburgh. Oh, yes! he knew that. That faithful friend had never forgotten his Irish comrade; in fact, it was Father Sheldon's querulous invitation that had con-quered Luke's repugnance to visit England again. Was his name remembered? Oh, yes. The story of his struggle with the Bishop for the *Cappa magna* had come down by tradition; for, whenever a young priest tried to put that splendid vestment on the Bishop, he was warned, *Remember Delmege!* Oh, yes! And it was also remembered that he it was who had brought around the lamentable apostasy of Halleck.

"It's an utter and calumnious falsehood," said Luke.

They lifted their eyebrows and looked at one another. Luke was glad to get away.

Father Sheldon, really delighted to see his old friend, re-ceived him in English fashion, with cool, courteous welcome.

"Good heavens!" thought Luke; "they're all stricken into stone."

By-and-bye Father Sheldon thawed out, and the old spirit of *camaraderie* revived.

"The years are telling on us all, Delmege," he said. "I'm as bald as Julius Cæsar, and you have more silver than silk in your locks."

"Everything seems changed here," said Luke. "I'm just wondering how I ever liked this place."

He looked around and contrasted this place with his own little home in Rossmore. He thought of his garden, his flowers, his books, his pictures, his horse, his freedom, the total absence of anxiety about debts, his sense of freedom from responsibility, the patient gentleness of his people, their reverence, their love.

"How is John Godfrey?" he asked.

"Dead."

"And Mrs. Bluett?"

"Dead."

"And the Lefevrils?"

"Clotilde is married to your friend Halleck. The others are in the South of Europe, Cap St. Martin, or some other English hive."

"But Halleck is not here?" said Luke, somewhat nervously.

"Oh, no. He gives lectures occasionally at the Royal Society; picks up stray apostates from France or Italy, lionizes them, and then drops them."

"Then he has never returned to the Church?"

"Never. You put a bad hand on him."

"If I didn't know you were joking, Sheldon, I would resent that remark. They flung it at me at the Cathedral also. It appears to be the one unfragrant memory I have left. And Olivette?"

"Remains an artist, and haunts South Kensington."

"But her religion?"

"Oh, she's an 'eclectic.' So she says. Which, as you know, is another and a prettier name for heretic."

"And poor old Drysdale! Gone too, to his reward. He was a good man. He never knew how much I reverenced him; and how grateful I am for his example."

"So he was," said Father Sheldon, rising. "Now, you'll spend all your holidays here, Delmege; and get up one or two of your fine sermons. No heresy, though, mind."

Luke was going to protest again. But Father Sheldon continued blandly: "Ah, what a pity, Delmege, you didn't let me draw that tooth that day by the Serpentine. You would be here with us today."

"Thank God for that, whatever," said Luke. "I'll stroll around, and see if I can recognize any old faces."

He passed along the High Street, and recalled to memory the

names over the shop doors. He visited one Catholic house. It was a large commercial establishment. The shop girls stared at him. Was Mrs. Atkins at home? No; but Miss Atkins could be seen. Miss Atkins tripped downstairs, and stared. Oh, yes! she had heard mother speak of Father Delmege, who had ministered there many years ago. Perhaps he would call again, when mother might be at home.

"How did I ever come to love these strange people?" asked Luke of himself, as he passed down the street. "I must have been mesmerized."

He turned from a side street and found himself in Primrose Lane. It was abominably paved with huge rough stones, and an open gutter ran down the center of the lane to the river. But it was dear to him. He had visited it in the broiling days of midsummer. He had slipped over these horrid stones in frosty January. He had always been welcome.

"Dead and forgotten here, too, I suppose," he said. He became aware of loud whispering behind him from the open doors.

" 'Tis him!" " 'Tisn't!" "I tell you 'tis him! Wouldn't I know his grand walk annywhere!" "Yerra, not at all. Sure, he's away in the ould counthry!" "But I say it is, 'uman! I'd know him if he was biled!"

In an instant every door was blocked. There was a hurried consultation, some doubtings and fears; and then Mrs. Moriarty, rubbing her hands fiercely in her check apron, burst from her door, flung herself on her knees on the rough stones; and sobbing, laughing, weeping, smiling, she grasped Luke's hands, covered them with passionate kisses, whilst her great love tumbled out word after word, jostling one another in their fury of affection.

"Oh! wisha! wisha! did I ever think I'd see this day? Oh! asthore machree! pulse of my heart! Oh! a hundred thousand welcomes this blessed day! Oh! praise be to You, sweet Lord an' Your Holy Mother! Oh! Father, sure we thought we'd never see you again! Yerra, come here, Mary McCarthy! Yerra, what's come over ye all? Don't ye know yere own priest? Yerra, yer reverence, manny and manny's the time we spoke of you! Oh! wisha! wisha! wisha! and here he is agin! Yerra, and I forgot to ask ye, how are ye? An' I suppose ye're a parish priest now in the ould counthry!" And *da capo*.

"Wisha, yer reverence," said another, "sure 'tis we're glad to see you. An' here's little Mary, yer reverence; sure you ought to know her! 'Twas you baptized her!"

"And this is Jamesy, yer reverence! Don't you remimber, how you said he was winkin' at you all the time of the christenin', because he had wan eye open all the time?"

"Oh, Lor', sure the min will never forgive theirselves for being away this blessed day. Mike will murdher us all. That's all about it."

"But, perhaps yer reverence won't be goin' away so soon? Maybe the min would have a chance of seein' ye?"

"I shall remain for a few days with Father Sheldon," said Luke. "He has kindly asked me to remain over Sunday, and to say a few words to my old congregation."

"Is't to prache, yer reverence? Oh, glory, did ye hear that, Mary? Did ye hear that, Kate? His reverence is goin' to prache on Sunday. Every Prodestan' in the city will be there!"

"Wisha, yer reverence, not makin' little of the priests here, we niver hard a right sarmon since ye left."

"That's thrue for ye, thin. Sure they mane well, poor min, but they haven't the flow."

"Look here," said Luke, deeply touched by this ovation, "ye must all come back with me to Ireland. That's all about it. Ireland is your motherland, and she wants ye all."

"We wish we could, yer reverence, a thousand times over. But where's the use? We've a little livin' here, which the bailiffs and the landlords wouldn't give us at home."

"That's true, too, Kate," said Luke, remembering his own impending troubles.

"An' sure they're sayin' the people are all lavin' the ould counthry, yer reverence, an' flying to Americky."

"The fools are," said Luke. "They could live at home if they liked. But what's become of all my little Italians?"

"Oh, they're here yet, your reverence," said Mrs. Moriarty, with a little pitying smile of racial superiority. Then, going over to the foot of a staircase, she shouted: "Come down at wance, Jo Kimo. Are ye there, Carrotty? Come down at wance, I say, an' see yere own priest.

"Don't spake about the monkey," she warned Luke. "Sure, he's dead; an' the poor man feels it, as if it wor his child."

And Gioacchimo and Carità and Stefano came down, and

smiled and wept, and kissed the priest's hand; and he caressed
them with words of their own beautiful language; and went
away, feeling in his heart for the hundredth time the truth of
his sister's words: "Love the poor, Luke, and 'twill make life
all sunshiny."

And he wondered how he ever came to love this gray, ashen
city; with its lamps and asphalt; and icy formalities, except in
that one spot, brightened by the aliens. And he thought with
what joy he would get back to Rossmore, and its mountains,
and plantations, and its pretty cottages, and the dear love of his
people. And he resolved to buy a new set of breviaries for his
dear old pastor, with good large print to suit the old man's
eyes; and a workbox for Mary, that would make her big eyes
twice as large with wonder; and a grand chibouque for John,
that would be the talk and admiration of the countryside.

"Come over; come over," he said, when bidding good-bye
to Father Sheldon. "Come over, all you Saxons, and we'll
show you our green fields, and our glorious mountains, and
our seas; and we'll put some of the love of God into your cold
hearts."

But Father Sheldon only laughed.

"No, thank you! I haven't many years to live; but I don't
care for a sudden and unprovided death."

And so the friends parted.

"To put the thought of England out of my head forever,"
thought Luke, as he passed through London, "lest the idea
should revive again, I'll see it at its worst."

And he went down to the Bank and the Exchange. Before
he realized it, he was wedged in by a huge bank of humanity—
a swirling, tossing mass, moved hither and thither by some
common impulse, that seemed to make them utterly oblivious
of each other. Pale-faced men, all dressed in morning costume,
silk hat, morning dress-coat, gloves, glided along singly or in
twos or threes; but every face wore an expression of intense
anxiety, as men questioned each other, or frantically dragged
note-books from their pockets and jotted down something with
trembling hands. He passed through into the Exchange. Here
again was a swirling, well-dressed crowd. Groups here and
there discussed some mighty problems; clerks, with bent heads,
jotted down names and investments; you heard everywhere:
"Santa Fés," "Orientals," "Kimberleys," "Tanaga Mines,"

"Great Westerns," "Durnley Tyres." It was a horrid Babel; and it was made worse by the accents of calm despair with which one man announced his failure and his ruin, and the tone of calm triumph with which another boasted the successful issue of some perilous investment. The air was hot and thick with the breath of many mouths and the dust of many feet. But they heeded not. They worshipped at the shrine of the great god Mammon. Luke stared around for the idol. There were white marble statues erected here and there to successful worshippers of the past. But there was no idol, no image of the great god himself. No need. He was enshrined in every heart; and lo! here was a victim. A young man leaned heavily, as if drunk, against the wall, his feet wide apart, his hat far back on his head. He was the very picture of despair. Luke saw one gentleman nodding to another, and winking over his shoulder at the ruined man:—

"Better see Angland safe to his own door!"

Luke fled from the Mart of Mammon.

The next evening Luke was in Dublin at seven o'clock. He went out after dinner to finish his Office, say his Rosary, and make his visit. He strolled into Gardiner Street Church. The twilight outside was deepened into gloom within the walls; yet he could see that the church was pretty full with devout worshippers here and there. He passed up along the central aisle, and got into a quiet nook under the Lady Altar. He was bent down for a few minutes in prayer. When he raised his head, he found he was wedged in a dense crowd that filled the benches on every side, and left no possibility of escape. They were of all classes, ages, and conditions of life, as Luke saw, when in a moment the whole church was brilliantly lighted, and the great organ pealed forth with a sweet hymn to our Blessed Lady. He noticed beads in all hands—fifteen decade beads in the hands of the young girls.

"What's going on?" he whispered to a venerable old man by his side.

"A novena for Pentecost," he whispered.

The Rosary was then recited the moment the red-robed acolytes had taken their places in a corona around the high altar. After the Rosary a sermon was preached on the first gift of the Holy Ghost—wisdom.

"Who's the preacher?" whispered Luke to his neighbor.

"Father——," was the reply. "A grand man, your reverence!"

"I'm in Ireland for a surety," thought Luke.

He was dying for a cup of tea; but there was no escape until
Benediction was over, at nine o'clock.

Next morning he presented himself at the same church to
say Mass. As he passed up the corridor to the left of the
church, he saw a number of men awaiting confession. They,
too, were young and well-dressed, in morning costume. Their
silk hats and gloves lay quietly on their knees. They sat quietly,
meditatively, with gentle, grave faces. Luke thought of Mr.
Hennessy and the village boys. Here was the practical result
of habitual training in reverence. He entered the sacristy, and,
after some delay, received permission to say Mass. The sacristy
door was opened by his acolyte, and a gush of hot air blew in
his face. He expected to see a few worshippers, here and there.
He stood in presence of a vast multitude. Some were kneeling,
but most were erect and moving as in an endless eddy, circling
around some common center. It was the altar rails. They who
moved towards the altar rails looked up, with hands clasped
around their prayer books or wreathed in their beads. They
stared before them, as at some entrancing object that riveted
eye and soul in one absorbing glance. They who returned bent
their faces reverently over clasped fingers. They had received
all that they had dreamed of and expected. And, as all moved
backward and forward in apparently endless circles, Luke
heard the only sound that broke the reverent stillness: *Corpus
Domini nostri Jesu Christi custodiat animam tuam in vitam
aeternam. Amen.* With the greatest difficulty, and following
his acolyte closely, he at length reached a side altar and deposited his chalice. In an instant there was a rush to the place.
Women snatched up their children as they knelt, and hurried
forward. Young girls quickly took their places around the
balustrade. Young men knelt stiffly erect, with reverent faces,
and in an attitude of mute attention. Old men threw down their
handkerchiefs and bent heavily over the rails. Then there was
the hush of mute expectation of the mighty mystery wrought
at the altar, and the graces that were to pour like torrents on
their souls. Luke trembled all over at the unusual surroundings
—he thought there was a panic in the church; then he trembled
under the very dread of great delight. The moment he had

said the last prayer, the crowd rose swiftly and hurried away to another altar where another Mass was being said. No time for idle curiosity here. The gold must be stamped as minted. Time is precious, for the heavens are opened this thrice blessed morning, and the mighty treasury of the Church lies here with uncovered lids, revealing all its wealth of grace, and all its opulence of merits; and swiftly the souls that covet must dip their hands and depart. And so, unfevered, but restless as the fur-clad gold-seeker who treads his painful way over snowy mountains that his eyes may rest on the valley of riches and rivers that are thick with the yellow dust, do these speculators in the banks of God claim vast returns from His thrice generous hands of the only wealth they care for or covet. And here was neither bankrupt nor suicide. They might dip as deeply as they pleased without peril or the danger of exhaustion. For are not His mercies without limit? And who shall plumb the vast seas of omnipotent generosity?

"Yesterday I stood in the Mart of Mammon," said Luke. "Today I have seen the Mart of Christ. Is this quite unique? or are there other Exchanges in the city?"

He tried. He entered another church in a deep narrow lane off Grafton Street—a great vast, gloomy church, with all kinds of niches and nooks, where a modest soul might commune freely with God, and never be seen of men. He would have been even more interested, had he known that this was the church where Barbara worshipped in the far-off days. And this was the porch through which Mrs. Wenham fled in terror; and that old woman might be Norry, who was always rattling her beads. Here too were vast speculators on the treasury of Heaven. To and fro, to and fro they moved, praying, weeping, watching. All but one! A young man, also well dressed in faultless morning coat, his silk hat and gloves lying on the seat near him, gazed upwards, as he leaned heavily on the bench rail, at the Face of the gentle Christ. He seemed like one who had just awoke from a trance of horrid dreams, and had just begun to realize that he still lived, and that there were great solemn realities about him. He seemed to be asking still, Is it all true? or, Is it all still a dream? But the gentle, vivid faith of all around him, the quiet realization of the supernatural, the reverent familiarity with which these young girls placed the ruby candle in the sockets of the great candelabra, then looked up into the Face of Christ, and bowed, as if the eyes were wide open and watching—all reassured him; and, after a long interval, he sighed deeply, then knelt, and buried his face in his hands, and prayed.

"God send another Philip Neri," said Luke, "if he is not already here."

He should see the Canon, of course. He drove to the "Mater," and was ushered into the Canon's private room. He apologized at once. There was a great mistake. That venerable old man, his long hair floating on his shoulders, white with the yellow gleam of an Alp in the sunlight, and the long white beard flowing in two forked plaits on his breast, was not the Canon. It was Elias come back from heaven.

"I beg pardon," said Luke; "I have been misdirected."

"Ha, my dear young friend, you fail—ha—to recognize your old friend?"

"A thousand pardons, sir," said Luke. "I really did. I took you for one of the greater prophets, come back to life."

"Ha, indeed? And is my—ha—personal appearance so greatly changed? I have scarcely thought of it here. There were other things—other things!" said the Canon, wearily drawing his hand across his brow.

"I've just returned from England," said Luke, "where I had a brief holiday—"

"Ha—have you any tidings of my niece—of Barbara?"

"I regret to say, no, sir," said Luke sadly. "I questioned Father Sheldon, who had been so kind to Miss Wilson and her brother in England; but he never heard from or saw Miss Wilson since the interment of her brother."

"It is strange, and mysterious," said the Canon. "I fear we must give her up as dead."

Luke was silent for a long time.

"I must congratulate you, sir," he said at length, "on your rapid recovery. I hardly expected to find you so well."

"Yes, indeed, I feel remarkably well," said the Canon, raising with some difficulty the arm that had been paralyzed. "Thanks to careful nursing, and the—ha—skill of the medical practitioners here, I hope soon to be able to return home."

"You may expect a warm, and even an enthusiastic welcome," said Luke. "It will revive the spirits of the poor people to see you; and they need some comfort now."

"Oh! it will be all right! it will be all right!" said the Canon, with his old confidence. "In the face of public opinion, our—ha—adversaries cannot proceed further. The English press has taken the—ha—matter up; and English public opinion cannot be despised."

"Perhaps so," said Luke, despondently. "Somehow, things over there look so different to me under the light of experience. I have begun to feel a strange, passionate attachment to my country and people."

"There's a good deal to be said on both sides," said the Canon.

"I shall warn the people to look out for your coming, sir," said Luke, rising. "You may be prepared for a great ovation."

"I think you may—ha—say, that I shall be home in a month or six weeks," replied the Canon.

He stood up to say good-bye, but he fell back wearily.

Luke's last visit was to his beloved sanctuary—the University College Chapel. This time he did not reach the altar rails or the side chapel. He was arrested by the noble bust of Newman that had been just erected in the side wall. He went over and sat beneath it, looking up into the fine face, with the expression of sadness and resignation that was so characteristic of the great Cardinal in later life. And, as Luke watched the white marble, there came into his mind that tragic exclamation when the letter of his elevation to the Sacred College was placed in the trembling hands of the great convert: *"Thank God! the cloud is lifted at last!"* The most mournful and pitiful of all the dim echoes of *Eloï, Eloï, lamma sabacthani!* that have been torn from bleeding breasts since that cry startled the darkness of Calvary. And Luke began to question and inquire.

"Why should a cloud ever have rested on that sacred brow? Why are the great and the holy dishonored in life; only honored in death? Why are men so cruel and vindictive towards each other? What is the dread secret of man's inhumanity to man?"

Poor Luke! he can never leave these turbulent questions alone. Why, and why, and why? As if there were any key to the mighty riddle, except that which is hidden away somewhere in the folds of God's garments, and which He never shows until after He has unlocked the secrets of the grave.

CHAPTER XXXVIII

Logwood Day

SISTER MARY of Magdala—let us give her the full title, for she will not bear it much longer—had now spent ten years of penitence, subjection, mortification; but, oh! ten years of such supreme happiness within the sanctuary of the Good Shepherd; and, as the undetermined period of fulfilment of her mighty vow was approaching its end, her cross became more heavy, her anxiety more acute. True, she was surrounded, encompassed, followed by reverence and love, such as even a great saint might envy, could he feel such an unworthy emotion. Her sister penitents adored her, though she never understood the reason; the nuns loved her; Father Tracey was infinitely kind; Sister Eulalie treated her as one of the community; and Laura, her little patient, followed her with eyes of speechless devotion and affection. But that dream! that dream!

It had now become a waking dream, and was especially insistent in the Convent Chapel. For when Sister Mary sat down there in the little sanctuary to the left, where her sister penitents were gathered together at Mass or Benediction, she would feel herself carried out in spirit into the choir-stalls, where the sixty white-robed Sisters were singing Vespers or mutely hearing Mass. And, sometimes, when the mighty organ rumbled, and the great seraphic voices arose in some glorious *Tantum ergo* or *O Salutaris!* she distinctly heard her own voice carried out and above all the others as it struck the gilded ceiling and the decorated walls, and then fell down in a whispered echo, and hovered around the monstrance, where the Divine Lover of her and of all was hidden. Then with a violent start she would wake up and look around, and behold with a little shudder her own dread abjection. And then again she would rebuke herself sternly amidst her tears for her involuntary treason to her mighty vow. Had not the Eternal kept His

440

contract, and why should she repudiate hers? Had not the All-Merciful snatched her brother from the pains of hell and the deep pit, and why should she repine for a few years of such sweet penance? If God had sent Louis—poor dear Louis—to hell—oh! the thought was too dreadful; and she would go out on the wings of resignation and clasp, like her great patroness, the nail-pierced feet, and cry, *"Elegi! elegi!* I have chosen to be a despised one in the house of my God rather than dwell in the tents of sinners!" And then there would be peace. But the waking dream of the white, spotless robes and the veil of honored espousals and the organ and the choir, and herself amidst it all, would recur again and again; and the very respect and love, of which she now found herself an object, only intensified the vision.

One such day Sister Mary was in the Infirmary, tending on Laura Desmond, now a hopeless and helpless invalid. She had done some trifling little service to her patient, and the latter drew her down with her arm and whispered:—

"Won't you ever tell me who you are?"

"What difference, dear, does it make, so long as we love one another?"

"No; but I should love you more, only that sometimes I am afraid of you."

"Why should you be afraid, dear? I am but one like yourself, only perhaps more sinful before God."

"You are not," said the patient, quietly.

Then taking up her prayer book, she opened it, Sister Mary helping, and took out a little picture.

"Do you know what it is?" said Laura.

"Yes, dear—a Sister of the Good Shepherd."

"I shall not die easy till I see you in that dress," said Laura; "that is, if you do not put on something even better."

Sister Mary shook her head, and, after a little while, when Laura slept, she went over to the farthest southern window and took up her book to read. The Holy Mountain now seemed very near. She did not know that she had to pass through the deepest and darkest valley of humiliation before she reached the shining summit.

On this same day Luke Delmege was in the city, in obedi-

ence to a peremptory summons from the Bishop. Before he
left Dublin for home, he satisfied a long-felt desire to see his
Alma Mater once more. He went down to Maynooth by an
early train, hoping to be able to pass through some of its best-
remembered spots, the Chapel, his own old room, the circular
walk, etc., unnoticed. When he entered the gate, beneath the
old Geraldine Keep, it struck him for the first time that
sphinxes were placed to guard the portals of the greatest
Catholic college in the world.

"Strange that I never noticed such an anomalous or, perhaps, significant circumstance, during all my college years!"
he said.

All around was still as death. For, if academic peace is to
be found on earth, it is within the hallowed precincts of Maynooth.

"They have all gone to breakfast," he cried, looking at his
watch. "I shall have the Senior Chapel all to myself. I shall
see the place where I lay prostrate the morning of my ordination. I shall recall my vows, my emotions, my resolutions. I
have seen so much lately to cast me into the past again, and
to compel me to retrace my steps, that is, my ideas and principles, back to the fresh inspirations of the most hallowed and
peaceful days of my life."

He entered the narrow porch at the northern side, touched
his forehead with holy water, and again, for the third time these
last few days, felt a breath of hot air fanning him, and found
himself in the presence of a great multitude. He had forgotten
that it was Whitsuntide. The church was full; the very drama
of his own ordination, that most sublime of the Church's ceremonies, was being reënacted before his eyes. Quietly and un-
observed he stole up the short aisle, the students courteously
yielding place, and saw the broad floor of the choir between
the stalls carpeted with prostrate human forms, over which
the white and red and gold of the chasubles gleamed. There
was an awful stillness as the Pontiff stretched his hands over
the prostrate Levites. Then there burst on the stupefied senses
of Luke that glorious hymn, the *Veni Creator Spiritus,* that
mighty *epithalamium* of the priesthood, which, in some peculiar sense, too, seems to be the royal anthem of this college;
for, heard for the first time by the young, raw student, as it is

rendered by six hundred voices at the opening of Retreat, it haunts him all through his college course; and, heard for the last time at his ordination, it accompanies him, the rhythm of supreme, melodious sanctity, during all his priestly life. And Luke, enchanted, intoxicated by all the sweet associations of the past and all the tender environments of the present, could only watch and study the air of rapt recollection and happiness that suffused the faces of the young priests with the oil of gladness, and compelled him to pray, deep down in his heart, not for himself, but for them, that the Holy Spirit might keep fresh forever in their hearts all the sacred inspirations of that day, and never allow them to be uprooted by the false maxims of the world, or withered and faded under the deadly breath of custom or compromise.

He slipped out quietly from amongst the students, the young cadets of the great army of Christ; took a rapid run around the ball-courts and the great circular walk that stretches far up amongst the mighty elms and sweeps around by the Grand Canal; lingered for a moment by the little cemetery, where slept many of his old professors, and, entering the corridor once more, found himself at once on the scene of his old triumphs—the Fourth Year's Divinity Hall. Ah, yes! there was the very desk at which he sat; there the pulpit, beneath which he pulled his soutane over his knees so often, and annihilated his antagonist with a *Sic argumentaris, doctissime Domine!* He sat down, and burying his face in his hands, he tried to recall old faces and associations. Alas! the old faces had faded away in the far mists of memory; but the old associations came up, looming dark and threatening from the past, to upbraid him with his treason.

"My reason tells me," he cried, "that my life has been flawless and immaculate. My conscience, some higher power, declares my life to have been a failure. Where, and in what measure?"

And the ghosts of the past said:—

"In this, that you have mistaken, as you have been already told, the blue and green fireworks of the world for the calm, eternal stars. You have groped for light, and beheld darkness; brightness, and you have walked in the dark. You have groped for the wall, and like the blind you have groped, as if you had no eyes; you have stumbled at noonday as in darkness; you have been in dark places, like dead men."

And Luke answered and said:—

"Yes; but wherefore, and how?"

And the answer came:—

"In that you measured your college and your country, ay, even your Church, by the measure of a false civilization. You judged your motherhood, as all your fellow-countrymen do who go abroad, by the false standard of modern progress; you found her wanting and despised her. Now, what has the world profited you? She hath given you little for your apostasy. And for your own people you have been a crackling of thorns under a pot."

Luke was glad to hear the noise and laughter of the students in the corridor. Anything to escape that reverie, that synod of accusing ghosts. He opened the door and rushed out. Groups of students in threes and fours were wheeling along, file after file, each group clustered around a newly ordained comrade, who trod on air and spurned the sandy flags. Group after group stared at Luke and passed by. Then, a young Levite detached himself from his batch, and coming over deferentially, he asked:—

"I beg your pardon, sir; but are you Father Luke Delmege?"

"Yes," said Luke.

"Luke Delmege, that was *First of First?*"

"Yes," said Luke, blushing at the old honor and at its remembrance.

"The diocese was speaking of you only yesterday and re-calling all your triumphs, and one of us from Limerick thought he recognized you. Won't you come see them?"

"By all means," said Luke. And he did. And they made him the center of an admiring circle, and told him, half shyly, half familiarly, how well he was remembered in his own college; and round and round they swept, linked arm-in-arm, until a professor, rushing down the library stairs near the refectory, caught sight of Luke's face, hesitated, advanced. The students doffed their caps and retired; and the professor, linking his arm in Luke's, drew him on to the superiors' corridor, murmuring all the way:—

"Luke Delmege, Luke Delmege, whom we gave up as lost! Why? why? how many years since you left us?"

"Seventeen," said Luke, very happy.

"Seventeen?" murmured the professor, unlinking his arm and looking at Luke. "Seventeen years away from us, and never condescended to visit us? You deserve to be turned out, neck and crop, from your Alma Mater!"

He was brought into the refectory, where he met some old comrades and some of his old professors. He was surprised at the familiarity with which these latter were treated; surprised that they accosted him familiarly; surprised that they ate and drank like mortals. They were the *Dii Majores* of his youthful worship—the gods that moved in a different and loftier sphere. It is the awful reverence of youth for its superiors —an instinct that no good man ever wholly lays aside.

Luke was overwhelmed with kindness. He said he was returning home tomorrow, Wednesday.

"Nonsense! No vacation ever terminated on Wednesday. He was expected home on Saturday at midnight; and there in Maynooth he should remain until the last train started!"

And he did remain; and drew up the entire past with all its happy reminiscences, met old classmates and talked of old times; challenged disputations here, where at last he felt he was on congenial soil and would not be misunderstood; recalled old debates and theses, and formulated any number of new plans for the social and intellectual regeneration of Ireland.

It was a happy man that passed out on Saturday morning between the sphinxes on the gates.

"They did well who placed ye there," he said. "Life is a mighty riddle. And I have been a fool in trying to solve it—a fool in more ways than one; but most of all in my silly imitation of that old dyspeptic cynic who ridiculed the controversy about ὁμοιούσιος and ὁμοούσιος all his life, and admitted in his old age that on that one letter depended the whole fabric of Christianity."

But Luke was happy and strong. He needed it. Greater revelations of the possibilities of sanctity in the Church, and greater personal trials were yet before him.

He found a cold, stern letter from the Bishop awaiting him when he returned home—a summons, officially worded, to repair at once to the city and present himself at the episcopal palace. Wondering what new accusation was laid against him, and searching his conscience in vain for a delinquency, he presented himself before his Bishop. The Bishop was cold and stern as his letter.

"Sit down," he said. Luke sat, wondering.

"Now, Father Delmege," said the Bishop, "I have tolerated a good deal from you, but my patience is nearly exhausted. I passed by that imprudence on your first mission, because you acted consistently with the statutes, although you might have acted more prudently; I also contented myself with a gentle reprimand when you, I dare say innocently, introduced a system of proselytism into your parish. I have also not noticed your singular habit of introducing into your sermons rather painful contrasts between the customs of our Irish Church and those which obtain, under happier circumstances, in other more favored countries. Even your very perilous observations at your lecture in the city some months ago I left unnoticed, because I knew you could do no harm there. But now I hold in my hand a melancholy report of a sermon delivered by you, immediately after the last mission in your parish, and in which, if I am rightly informed, you denied the sacramental system and denounced the use of the ordinary means sanctioned by the Church for the sanctification of the faithful, and insisted on the individual power of self-sanctification, apart from the ordinary channels of divine grace—"

"Might I ask the name of my accuser?" said Luke, faintly.

"I cannot give it, unless the matter proceeds to an official investigation and trial. Your parish priest writes to say that he is quite sure you have a satisfactory defense; but then, Dr. Keatinge is always inclined to take an easy and optimistic view of things."

"My only defense, my Lord," said Luke, "is to deny the allegation *in toto*. I see clearly what originated the report. A poor fellow, intoxicated, came to the closing ceremony of the mission. I took him from the church and bade him go home, for that he could derive no benefit from the renewal of vows in his then state. I made the incident the text of my discourse the following Sunday. I warned the people not to confound the means of sanctification with the end—not to repose in external observances, but to look within; and to use the Sacraments and sacramentals with a view to their own sanctification, and not as finalities that would operate miracles without co-operation on their part—"

"That puts a rather different complexion on the matter," said the Bishop, softening. "I should be surprised that one who obtained such distinctions in his college course should fall into such a lamentable blunder. Have you any further observations to make?"

"None, my Lord," said Luke, in despair. "My college distinctions have availed me but little. I am a weary and perplexed man."

He bent down his head on his hands in an attitude of hopelessness. The little gesture touched the Bishop. He gazed down for a long time at the stooped figure and the head where the snows of life's winter were now fast gathering. Then he gently touched Luke.

"You'll spend the day here, and dine with me at five o'clock. No! no!" he continued, as Luke strove to excuse himself, "I shall take no excuse. I want to see you more closely."

"I have been nearly a month from home, my Lord," said Luke, anxious to get away, "and—"

"Now, now, I make it a matter of obedience," said the Bishop. "You won't find me so crusty and disagreeable as you think. You'll have a few hours in the city; but be here punctually at five. By the way, I want you to take a letter from me to Father Tracey. Do you know him?"

"I regret to say I do not," said Luke. "Years ago, when I was wiser than I am now, I had determined to make his acquaintance, but unfortunately I missed the opportunity. I shall be very glad to get the chance now."

"You shall have it," said the Bishop. "I wish I could break through his humility, and hold him up as a model to the diocese. But his example is telling in a quiet way."

Luke took the letter, and made his way to the hospital where Father Tracey served. He found he did not reside there, but in a side street. He passed down through a shabby lane, eagerly scanning the houses to detect some indication of a decent residence. He narrowly escaped a deluge of purple, dirty water, which an old woman was flinging from a doorway, right across the footpath, into a dirty channel close by.

great suspense; and then Will McNamara, a splendid, stalwart young farmer, came forth, the cradle of the youngest child in his arms. He was bleeding from the forehead; and the people, divining what had taken place, raised a shout of anger and defiance, and rushed toward the house. The police moved up hastily, and Father Cussen beat back the people. But they surged to and fro on the outer line of the cordon; and the young English officer threw away his cigarette, and drew in the long thin line of the soldiers. In a few moments Lizzie came forth, holding one child in her arms, and a younger at her breast. Following her was her husband again, still bleeding from the forehead, and with two frightened children clinging to him. Lastly, Mike Delmege appeared. The sight of the old man, so loved and respected in the parish, as he came forth from the dark framework of the cottage door, his white hair tossed wildly down on his face, and streaming on his neck, and his once stalwart frame bent and broken with sorrow, roused the people to absolute fury. They cursed deeply between their teeth, the women weeping hysterically; and a deep low moan echoed far down the thick masses that stretched along the road and filled the ditches on either hand. For over two hundred years the Delmeges had owned Lisnalee—a grand race, with grand traditions of an unstained escutcheon and an unspotted name. And, now, as the last member of the honored family came forth, an outcast from his father's home, and stood on the threshold he should never cross again, it seemed as if the dread Angel of Ireland, the Fate, that is ever pursuing her children, stood by him; and, in his person, drove out his kindred and his race. The old man stood for a moment hesitating. He then lifted his hands to God; and kneeling down, he kissed reverentially the sacred threshold, over which generations of his dead had been taken, over which he had passed to his baptism, over which he had led his young trembling bride, over which he had followed her hallowed remains. It was worn and polished with the friction of the centuries; but so bitter a tear had never fallen on it before. Then, raising himself up to his full height, he kissed the lintel of the door, and then the two doorposts. He lingered still; he seemed loath to leave. And the bailiffs, growing impatient, pushed him rudely forward. Weak and exhausted, the old man stumbled and

"I beg your reverence's pardon a thousand times," she said. "I hope a drop didn't tetch your reverence."

She examined with some anxiety Luke's fine broadcloth.

"Not a drop, my poor woman," he said. "But it was a close shave. Can you tell me where Father Tracey lives?"

"Here, yer reverence," she said, piloting Luke into the kitchen. "But I'm afraid he'll hardly see you today. This is Logwood Day."

"What is Logwood Day?" asked Luke, with curiosity.

"Wance in the six months," she replied, "we have to steep his ould clothes in logwood to make thim someway dacent. That's the first bile I threw out. We're now giving 'em the second." She pointed to the huge pot; and Luke, bending over, saw a grimy black mass swimming in some dark red liquid.

"And has he but one coat!" he asked.

"Only wan, yer reverence. He won't dress himself dacently like iverybody else. 'I'm more comfortable,' he says 'in me ould duds.' And faith, I've enough to do to keep him from givin' away thim same to every poor man that calls. That is," she added, "if they'd take 'em."

"Well, take him up this letter from the Bishop," said Luke, "and say a priest would like to see him."

After a long interval she reappeared at the top of the stairs and called down: "Ye may come up, yer reverence; but mind thim steps, and don't lane too heavy agen the banister."

The ante-room into which Luke was ushered was miserable enough. It served as a bedroom; and, though clean, it was denuded of every stick of furniture, except the wooden chair, the wash-stand, and the simple pallet where the old man sought his often-broken repose. He passed into the inner room. The old man, dressed in a green soutane, stood up, and, without asking his name, greeted him warmly, and asked him to be seated, while he broke the seal on the Bishop's letter. The contents must have been pleasant, for the old man smiled.

"I have for a long time cherished the idea," said Luke, "that I should wish to make your acquaintance. My sister at the Good Shepherd Convent has again and again asked me to call, but one circumstance after another prevented me."

"Then you have a sister at the convent?" said the old man,

nervously, fussing about and showing not a little trepidation.

"Yes, Father—Sister Eulalie—you know her?"

"God bless me, you don't say so," said the old man, rising up and greeting Luke again warmly. "And you are Luke Delmege, the great theologian and lecturer!"

"My name is Luke Delmege," he said meekly.

"Well, I heard of you long before I saw you," said the old man. "God bless me! And you are Luke Delmege?"

"I have had a rather bitter trial today," said Luke. "I was summoned before the Bishop to repel a most calumnious accusation."

"God bless me, now! And what did you say?"

"Of course I defended myself," said Luke, "and I think I satisfied the Bishop that I had said or done nothing wrong. But the sting remains."

The old man remained silent, looking steadily at Luke. The latter grew embarrassed now.

"You seem to think I have been wrong," he broke out at last. "What can a man do but defend himself?"

"God bless me! quite true, quite true! But he could say nothing, you know, my dear."

"And remain silent and condemned under a frightful accusation? No theologian binds a man to that," said Luke.

"Of course not, of course not," said Father Tracey. "But I think, well—I'm not sure—but I think our Lord was silent before His accusers, my dear. And He was justified by His Father!"

"That's very true, Father," said Luke, twisting around on the hard chair; "but these things are written for our admiration, not for our imitation. At least," he continued, noticing the look of pain on the aged face, "I heard a distinguished man say so very many years ago."

And then the old man opened up to Luke's wondering eyes, out of the treasures of his own holy experiences, the riches of knowledge that come not to the learned, but to the simple—the wisdom of the child and the angel, of Bethlehem and Calvary. And just as a clever artist shifts his scenery so that light falls behind light, and scenes blend into scenes, yet are absolutely distinct, so did this old man show to the wondering Luke how the mighty empire of the Precious Blood permeates and leavens the entire world, and holds undisputed possession only where its laws and maxims are fully acknowledged. And that elsewhere, where that most agreeable and fascinating amusement of men—the neat mortising and fitting in of the world's maxims with the Church's precepts—is practiced, there the shadows are deeper and the lines that bound the empire fainter. And Luke also learned that the one central decree of the empire is: Lose thyself to find all; and that the old familiar watchword of self-renunciation and vicarious suffering was in reality the peculiar and exclusive possession of Christianity and the Church. And he looked back over his own life and saw that his soul was naked and ashamed. Then he flung aside the riddle.

"Let me see but one or two examples, and it is enough forever," he said.

There was one before him. The other, even more noble, more divine, he was about to see.

He bade the old man an affectionate farewell, and bent his steps towards the Good Shepherd Convent to see his sister. The lay-sister who answered the door told him that his sister would be engaged for some time in the Orphanage; but that, if he would kindly wait till Vespers were finished, he could see Reverend Mother. On second thoughts, she invited him into the outer sacristy, where he could assist at Vespers. He saw for the first time the beautiful choir; he saw the sixty professed Sisters, the white veils, the postulants standing in the choir-stalls; he heard the *Magnificat* chanted by these daughters of Jerusalem; the poetry, the beauty, sank into his soul.

"Ah!" he said, "if this were all religion, what a poem Christianity would be!"

He quite forgot the pause that is essential to melody—the chords in the minor keys that are the essentials of all harmony.

The choir broke up, and the Sisters passed swiftly to their duties. He heard a rustling behind him, and a voice:—

"Sister Eulalie will be engaged for about half an hour, Father. Perhaps you would like to see the institution in the interval?"

"I shall be very pleased," said Luke.

She led him into the corridor, full of flowers and fragrance;

thence by a rapid transition into the first workroom. He was face to face with the Magdalens. The shudder that touches every pure and fastidious soul at the very name crept over him as he saw the realities. The awful dread that the sight of soiled womanhood creates in the Catholic mind, so used to that sweet symbol of all womanly perfection—our Blessed Lady—made him tremble. It was only for a moment. There was nothing repulsive or alarming here. Seven or eight long tables, running parallel to each other, filled the room; and at each table, eight or ten women, ranging from the young girl of fifteen to the woman of sixty, were silently occupied in laundry work. All modern appliances to save human labor were there. The workers were neatly dressed, and happy, if one could judge by their smiles. No human imagination, however powerful, could associate these eager workers with the midnight streets, the padded cell, the dock, the jail, or the river. It was a happy sisterhood, working in perfect silence and discipline. And over all there presided a young novice, in her white veil, who stood calmly working, like her poor sisters, taking up now a white cuff, now a collar, and giving her gentle instructions.

"It is the old mechanism and perfection I once desired," thought Luke; "but the motive power is love, not fear."

They passed into an inner room. Here was miracle number two. The Cistercian silence no longer reigned; but over the boom and buzz of vast machinery came a Babel of voices as the workers fled to and fro.

"Yer blessin', Feyther," cried one; and in a moment all were on their knees for Luke's benediction. And then, with easy familiarity, these poor girls took Luke around, and showed with intense pride the mighty secrets of the machinery; how steam was let on and shut off; how the slides worked on the rails in the drying-room, etc. And, moving hither and thither amongst them, in an attitude of absolute equality, were the white-robed Sisters, their spotless habits carefully tucked, for the floor was wet, and they labored and toiled like the rest.

" 'Tis the commonwealth of Jesus Christ," said Luke.

And dear old Sister Peter came forward, an octogenarian, and showed him all her treasures and her pretty little oratory, with all its dainty pictures.

"How long have you been here?" he asked.

"Fifty years, yer reverence, come Michaelmas."

"Then your purgatory is over," said Luke.

"I don't want purgathory, nor heaven ayther," she said, "as long as God laves me with the Sisthers."

The Sister and Luke passed out of the steamy atmosphere and the rumble of the machinery into a narrow corridor, which led to the boiler-room and engine-house.

"I should like you to see our new boiler," she said; "I'll run on and tell the engineer to have all ready. This is our Infirmary. Perhaps you would like to see it. There's but one patient here."

She opened the door, and pointed to the bed where Laura was lying. He went over at once, and, leaning over the sick girl, said a few kind words. Then looking around, he saw another figure over near the southern window, her face bent down over the book she was reading. He thought it would be unkind to pass her by, so he went over and said cheerily:—

"Convalescent, I suppose?"

She rose up, trembling all over. Then a blush of untold horror and shame flushed her face and forehead as their eyes met; but only to give place to a pallor deeper than that on the faces of the dead. He started back as if stung, and cried:—

"Great God! Barbara! Miss Wilson!"

"Hush!" she said softly, placing her trembling finger on her lips. "That poor child is watching."

"But what? what? what?" he stammered. "What in God's name is this mystery? Why are you here?"

"God's will, Father," she said simply.

"Of course," he said, in an excited manner; "but in what, in what capacity? Are you infirmarian?"

"No," she said, casting down her eyes.

"And how long have you been here?" he cried, his eyes wandering vaguely over her blue penitent's dress, and searching the calm depths of her face.

"Ten years," she said, in a low tone. "Ever since Louis died."

"Ten years! And your uncle and father searching all Europe for you! What is this horrible mystery? How long are you professed?"

"I am not a professed Sister, Father," she said bravely.

"Then you are a nursing Sister attached to the city and coming in here—"

She shook her head. Her heart was breaking with shame and sorrow, as she plunged deeper and deeper in the valley of humiliation. He drew back, as the horrible thought flashed across his mind, and he recalled the dress of the Magdalens. She saw the little gesture and flushed again.

"I am afraid to ask further," he said coldly, and with reserve; "but do you belong to the community?"

"No, Father," she said bravely—it was the "Consummatum est" of her agony of ten years—"I am a penitent."

She was looking out over the trees and shrubs, looking with eyes dilated, like a consumptive's, her temples still flushed, and her face drawn and strained in agony. He, too, looked steadily through the window. He scarcely concealed the loathing with which that reluctant confession filled him for this young girl, standing there, apparently so calm. The shudder that he felt on entering the laundry where the Magdalens worked, and which gave way instantly before the sublime spectacle of their resurrection, now filled him with tenfold horror. Here, he thought, there was no excuse. Neither ignorance, nor poverty, nor heredity to palliate the shame. He was side by side, not with a sinful woman, but with a lost angel. The transformation was perfect. He thought he read it in her face. There was— there could be—no resurrection here. He paused for a moment to consider what he would do. As he did so, the vision that he had once seen in the garden of the Schweizerhof came up before him, the vision of the wrecked soul and its guardian angel. The thought was too terrible. His memory of that one night tempted him to stretch out his hand and say a kind farewell to one he should never see again. But one side glance at that ill-made, coarse, bulky dress of penitence deterred him. He bowed stiffly and said "Good-day!" with a frown. Barbara continued staring blindly through the window. Then slowly, as her heart broke under the agony, her hot tears fell, burned her hand, and blistered the book which she held.

As Luke passed Laura's bed, she beckoned to him.

"Would yer reverence tell me," she said, "on yer word of honor as a priest, do ye know that girl?"

"Yes," he said sharply; "I know something of her."

"Would ye tell me, yer reverence, once and for all, is she the Blessed Virgin Mary?"

"No," he said shortly; "she is not!"

LUKE DELMEGE

"Than' God an' you," the poor girl cried. "I struck her wance with them five fingers. I saw the print of 'em this minit on her face whin she blushed. Than' God, I now die aisy."

The Sister, who was awaiting him in the corridor, was surprised at the change in his manner and appearance.

"Can I see the Reverend Mother, Sister," he said impatiently, "and at once?"

"By all means, Father," she replied; "come this way to the parlor."

What occurred at that momentous interview we are not privileged to know. But Luke Delmege came forth a changed and a shamed man. He knew then that all the sublime supernaturalism, with which he had been brought face to face for the last few days, had touched the summit in that heart which he had left torn and bleeding in the Infirmary. He had seen what he wanted to see—the supreme example of self-abandonment; and he knew then that heroic sanctity, as taught by the Church and the Saints, was no myth.

He had gone far down towards the entrance lodge before he thought of his sister. She had seen him pass her by, but was afraid to accost him. She felt that he knew all; that the secret of the King, so faithfully kept for ten years, was no longer a secret. She called out "Luke," just as he thought of her. He came back, dazed and blinded. She had a hundred things to say to him; but now her lips were closed, as she stood, niched in a clump of laurels, and looked at his wild eyes and his drawn face. He stood before his little sister for a moment, and the thought came back of her warning the evening he dined at the Canon's; and Margery's rash judgments then, and his own rash judgments an hour ago, clashed together. He placed his hands on his dear little sister's shoulders, beneath her black veil. He would have given all the world to kiss her. But he felt he dared not. The glamour of the unseen world was round about him, and he was afraid. Margery said faintly:—

"Oh! Luke! what's the matter? What has happened?"

He stooped down, and, snatching up hastily the white ivory cross that hung from her rosary, he kissed it passionately, and, without a word, strode out into the city.

CHAPTER XXXIX

Martyrdom

AS LUKE Delmege returned home the following day, he was
a prey to anguish and remorse such as rarely visits souls, except those who are called to the high planes of thought and
trial. The sudden contrast between his own life, flawless and
immaculate, but commonplace and unheroic, with the life
of that humble priest, stripped of all things for Christ's sake;
and the sharper contrast with the sublime heroism of this
young girl, filled him with that poignant self-contempt, which
fine souls feel when they contemplate the lives of the saints
of God.

"I have been troubled with problems," he said. "Here is the
great solution—Lose all to find all."

Even the great kindness of the Bishop, which augured great
things for his future, could not dissipate the thought. Nay, it
intensified it.

"I have been in touch with great souls," he said. "Now, let
me see, can I be worthy of them. Can I see that great old man
again without compunction; and that young saint without
shame? Surely, heroism and heaven are for me, as for them!"

He commenced at once. Bit by bit, every superfluous article
of furniture was secretly disposed of, until his bedroom became as bare as that old bedroom on his first mission, where
he had sat and meditated in despair. And, except one or two
articles, souvenirs of old friends, he denuded in like manner
his little parlor, saving only his books. Then he begged for a
cross. "Cut, burn, and destroy." He placed no limit to God's
judgment. He asked for the unknown; and shut his eyes. And
the cross came.

One morning he had a letter from Father Cussen saying

that all preliminaries had been arranged, notices had been served on the Board of Guardians; and it was almost certain that the evictions in Lough and Ardavine would commence during the ensuing week. Furthermore, it was suspected that an example would be made of the leading Nationalists; and that, probably, Lisnalee would be visited first. A few days after, a second letter told him that the evil day had come. A company of soldiers had been drafted into the village, and the police were concentrating in a neighboring town. He made up his mind to leave that day, and go to Seaview Cottage to await events. Whilst he was reading these letters, he noticed that Mary was lingering in the room, under one pretext or another. She poked the grate assiduously, arranged and rearranged the two vases several times, until at last Luke said:—

"Well, Mary, what's up?"

Mary, trembling very much, faltered out:—

"I was thinkin' to be afther asking your reverence to get another housekeeper."

"Oh, you are anxious to leave me? I thought you were fairly happy here, Mary."

"And so I was, your reverence," said Mary, biting the lace edging of her apron, and studying the pictures carefully.

"Then why are you leaving? Do you want higher wages?"

"Ah, 'tisn't that at all, your reverence," said Mary, with a frown.

"Well, surely you're not going to America with the rest?"

"Yerra, no! your reverence," said Mary, biting her apron more furiously.

"Well, I mustn't try to discover your secrets," said Luke. "You have your own ideas—"

"Yerra, 'tis the way I'm goin' to be married," blurted out Mary.

"Married?" cried Luke, aghast.

"Yes, your reverence! Why not a poor girl get married if she gets the chance?" said Mary, with a pout.

"Oh, to be sure, to be sure," said Luke. "But I hope, my good girl, you are making a good choice. You deserve a good husband."

"Indeed'n he is a dacent boy enough," said Mary.

"He doesn't drink, I hope?" asked Luke, anxiously.

"Ah, not much, your reverence. No more than anybody else."

"Because you know, Mary," said Luke, kindly, "that the worst thing a young girl ever did is to marry a drunkard in the hope of reforming him."

"Ah, he's not as bad as that at all, your reverence," said Mary.

"Do I know him?" asked Luke.

"Yerra, you do, of course," said Mary, blushing furiously.

"Does he belong to our parish?"

"Yerra, of course, he does, your reverence," said Mary, with a little giggle.

"I won't ask further—" said Luke, turning away.

"Yerra, 'tis John, your reverence," said Mary, now scarlet with confusion.

"John? what John?" said Luke.

"Yerra, *your* John, your reverence," said the poor girl.

"What! that ruffian!" cried Luke, in dismay.

"Ah, he's not," said Mary, pouting. "He's a dacent poor boy enough."

"Well, marriages are made in heaven, I suppose," said Luke, resignedly. "But I thought you and John were always quarrelling."

"Ah, we used make it up agin," said Mary.

"Of course, you please yourself, Mary," said her master at length. "But it would be very embarrassing and awkward for me, if you were to leave just now. I expect within the next few days that my father and sister will be thrown upon the world; and they have no shelter but here!"

"Don't say another word, your reverence," said Mary. "If it was for seven years, John must wait."

But John didn't see the force of this unnecessary procrastination. And there was another big row in the kitchen.

"An' you won't?" said John, as an ultimatum.

"I won't," said Mary, determinedly.

"Well, there's as good fish in the say as ever was caught," said John.

"Go, an' ketch 'em," said Mary.

But John relented after some hours' meditation.

"An' 'tisn't for your sake," he said, "but for the masther's.

It would be a quare thing if we wor to lave him in his throuble."

So Luke went down to Seaview Cottage to await events.

He had not long to wait. The following morning, as they sat at breakfast in the neat little parlor fronting the sea, there came to their ears a low wailing sound, that appeared to be caught up and echoed by similar sounds here and there across the country.

"Some steamer going up the river!" said Father Martin. "That's the foghorn, and the echoes along the shore. Run out, Tony, and tell us what she's like."

Tony soon returned.

"There's no steamer in the channel," said Tony; "but the people are all running here and there up towards Ardavine."

" 'Tis the signal of the eviction," said Luke, rising. "Let us go!"

"Sit down, man, and eat your breakfast," said Father Martin. "You have a long fast before you."

But Luke did not sit down again. The home of his childhood and manhood, the dream of the London streets, the vision that hovered ever before his eyes, even in his moments of unfaithfulness, was about to vanish in flame, and smoke, and red ruin. How could he sit down calmly and eat? He gulped down a cup of tea, and waited impatiently for Father Martin.

They drove up rapidly, to find that the terrible proceedings had already commenced. As they passed with difficulty through the vast, surging crowd, that swayed to and fro with excitement, they saw the red dotted line of soldiers, who formed the cordon around the house; and within the cordon was the black square of police, who were to guard the bailiffs from violence. The soldiers, standing at ease, gazed sullenly into the mouths of their rifles, never lifting their heads. It was dirty, unsoldierlike work, and they were ashamed. Their young officer turned his back on the whole dismal proceeding; and lighting a cigarette, stared out over the landscape. The priests briefly saluted Father Cussen, who was trying by main strength of arm to keep back the infuriated people. He had barely time to whisper to Luke:—

"I wish we had all your coolness today. There will be bad work; and we'll want it."

He struck the hand of a peasant lightly, as he spoke, and a large jagged stone dropped on the ground.

Luke and Father Martin begged leave of the Resident Magistrate to approach the house, and give such consolation, as they might, to the poor inmates. It was refused courteously. No one could pass inside the cordon. They stood on the outskirts, therefore, and watched the eviction—Father Martin, anxious and sympathetic; Luke, pale with excitement, his eyes straining from their sockets, his face drawn tight as parchment. In dramas of this kind—alas! so frequent in Ireland—the evicted as a rule make a show of hostility and opposition to the law. Sometimes, the bailiffs are furiously attacked, and their lives imperilled. When the keen, cruel hand of the mighty monster is laid upon them, the people cannot help striking back in terror and anger—it is so omnipotent and remorseless. But, in this case, the beautiful faith and resignation to God's inscrutable will, which had characterized the life of old Mike Delmege hitherto, and the gentle decency of his daughter and her husband, forbade such display. And so, when the bailiffs entered the cottage at Lisnalee to commence their dread work, they were met silently, and without the least show of opposition.

It was heartrending to witness it—this same cold, callous precision of the law. The quiet disruption of the little household; the removal, bit by bit, of the furniture; the indifference with which the bailiffs flung out objects consecrated by the memories of generations, and broke them and mutilated them, made this sensitive and impressionable people wild with anger. In every Irish farmer's house, the appointments are as exactly identical as if all had been ordered, in some far-off time, from the same emporium, and under one invoice. And when the people saw the rough deal chairs, the settle, the ware, the little pious pictures, the beds with their hangings, flung out in the field, each felt that his own turn had come, and that he suffered a personal and immediate injury. And Father Cussen had the greatest difficulty in restraining their angry passions from flaming up into riot, that would bring them into immediate and deadly conflict with the forces of the Crown. As yet, however, the inmates had not appeared. There was an interval of

fell. An angry scream broke from the people, and a few stones were flung. And Luke, who had been watching the whole melancholy drama with a bursting heart, broke away from Father Martin, and forcing his way beyond the cordon of soldiers, he rushed toward the house, crying in a voice broken with sobs and emotion, "Father! Father!"

As a river burst through its dam, sweeping all before it, the crowd surged after him, breaking through every obstacle. The police, taken by surprise, fell away; but a young sub-inspector rode swiftly after Luke, and getting in front, he wheeled around, and rudely striking the young priest across the breast with the broad flat of his naked sword, he shouted:—

"Get back, sir! get back! We must maintain law and order here!"

For a moment Luke hesitated, his habitual self-restraint calculating all the consequences. Then, a whirlwind of Celtic rage, all the greater for having been pent up so long, swept away every consideration of prudence; and with his strong hand tearing the weapon from the hands of the young officer, he smashed it into fragments across his knees, and flung them, blood-stained from his own fingers, into the officer's face. At the same moment a young girlish form burst from the crowd, and leaping lightly on the horse, she tore the young officer to the ground. It was Mona, the fisherman's sunny-haired child, now grown a young Amazon, from her practice with the oar and helm, and the strong, kind buffeting from winds and waves. The horse reared and pranced wildly. This saved the young officer's life. For the infuriated crowd were kept back for a moment. Then the soldiers and police charged up; and with baton and bayonet drove back the people to the shelter of the ditch. Here, safely intrenched, the latter sent a volley of stones flying over their assailants' heads, that drove them back to safe shelter. In the pause in the conflict, the Resident Magistrate rode up and read the Riot Act.

"Now," he said, folding the paper coolly, and placing it in his pocket, "the first stone that is thrown I shall order my men to fire!"

It is quite possible, however, that the people would have disregarded the threat, so infuriated were they; but their attention was just then diverted by a tiny spurt of smoke, that broke from the thatch of Lisnalee Cottage. For a moment they thought it was an accident; but the smell of burning petroleum and the swift way in which the flames caught the whole roof and enveloped it in a sheet of fire undeceived them. It was the irrevocable decree of the landlord. It was the sowing with salt; the fiat that never again should bread be broken or eyelid closed on that hallowed spot. The solemnity of the tragedy hushed people, police, and soldiers into silence. Silently they watched the greedy flame eat up thatch and timber, and cast its refuse into a black, thick volume of smoke, that rolled across the sea, which darkened and shuddered beneath it. Then, there was a mighty crash as the heavy rafters fell in, a burst of smoke, and flame, and sparks; and the three gables, smoke-blackened, flame-scorched, stood gaping to the sky. Father Cussen took advantage of the momentary lull in the fierce passions of the people to induce them to disperse; but they doggedly stood their ground, and sent shout after shout of execration and hate after the departing bailiffs and their escort. And as they watched the latter moving in steady, military formation down the white road, a strange apparition burst on their sight. Across the valley, where the road wound round by copse and plantation, a carriage was seen furiously driven toward them. The coachman drove the victoria from a back seat. In the front was a strange and imposing figure, that swayed to and fro with the motion of the carriage, yet kept himself erect in an attitude of dignity, and even majesty. His long white hair, yellowed and almost golden, was swept back upon his shoulders by the land breeze; and a white beard, forked and parted, floated and fell to the waist. He held his hand aloft with a gesture of warning. With the other he clutched the carriage rail. The priests and people were bewildered, as they stared at the apparition. Some said it was the landlord, for they had never seen that gentleman; and with the eternal hope of the Irish, they thought he might have relented, and was coming to stop the eviction, and reinstate the tenants. Some thought it was supernatural, and that the great God had intervened at the last moment, and sent them a Moses. But they were not disappointed, nay, a great light shone upon their faces, when, on cresting the hill, the Canon's coachman was recognized, and, by degrees, the old familiar face of

power and dignity beamed on them. There was a mighty shout
of welcome, that made the soldiers pause and turn backward.
The people, mad with delight and a new sense of hope and
protection from the presence of their mighty patriarch,
crowded around the carriage, kissed his hands, knelt for his
blessing, told him that if he had been in time, Lisnalee would
have been saved, etc., etc. Slowly the carriage forced its way
through the thick masses that surged around it. The old man
saw nothing. His eyes were straining out to where the peaked
burnt gables cut the sky. Then, when he came in full view of
the horror and desolation—the broken household furniture
the smoking ruin, the evicted family, lingering in misery
around their wrecked habitation, saw the old man bending
over his grandchild in the cradle, and the wound on the forehead of its father, he groaned aloud, and with a despairing cry,
"My people! oh! my people!" he fell back helpless in his carriage, and covered his face with his hands.

A few days after Luke Delmege received a summons to
appear before a special court that was to sit in the Petty Sessions room at Ardavine, to answer to a charge of obstructing
the police in the discharge of their duty, assaulting a police
officer, etc.

In the afternoon of that day of trial, Barbara Wilson was
summoned to the parlor of the Good Shepherd Convent. The
Sister who summoned her took her young charge gaily by the
hand, and led her, wondering and trembling, along the nuns'
corridor to the large reception room in front of the Convent.
With a bright, cheery word, she ushered Barbara into the
parlor, and closed the door. There were two in the room—
the Bishop and the Mother Provincial. The former, advancing,
placed a chair for Barbara, and bade her be seated. Barbara
sat, her hands meekly folded in her lap, not daring to lift her
eyes, but filled with a sweet emotion of mingled apprehension
and hope. She knew that the crisis of her life had come. The
Bishop looked at her keenly and said:—

"Miss Wilson, the secret of your sojourn here, in the character of a penitent is known. You cannot remain here any
longer!"

"My Lord!" she said, trembling, "I have been very happy
here. Could you not let me remain?"

"Quite impossible," said the Bishop. "In fact, I'm not quite sure that the whole thing has not been irregular from the beginning. You must now resume your proper station in life."

"I am very helpless, and quite unfit for the world, my Lord," said Barbara. The dream and its realization seemed now totally dispelled. "What can I turn to now, especially as my past is known?"

"Oh, you can easily assume your proper place in society," said the Bishop. "You are young; life is before you, and you may be very happy yet."

"My Lord," said Barbara, weeping, "if it is happiness I seek, I shall never know such happiness again as I have experienced here. But I know all now. I was murmuring against my cross, and dreaming of other things; and now God has taken away my cross and my happiness forever. O Mother, dear Mother, plead for me, and let me go back again!"

"Impossible, child," said Mother Provincial, but with a tone that brought Barbara to her knees in a moment. She buried her face in the Mother's lap, crying passionately.

"Oh, Mother, you can, you can. Keep me here! I'll do anything, anything you like; but don't send me out into the world, the dreadful world, again. Oh my Lord," she cried, "I saw things once, that I never care to see again—one dreadful night when I lost poor Louis in London, and sought him, up and down, for hours. And, oh! I found heaven here, and I didn't know it. And God is punishing me dreadfully. O Lord, dear Lord, give me back my cross, and I promise never, never again to repine, or revolt against it!"

The thought of facing the great, hard, bitter world had never occurred to her before, until now, when the door of her happy home was opened, and she was bade to depart. All the nervous fear of an inexperienced soul, and all the horror of one which has been *in* the world, but not *of* it, combined to fill her with a strange dread, which became almost hysterical. In her great agony her white cap fell, releasing the long, rich tresses that now flowed down, tossed and dishevelled, and swept the ground. And the Bishop thought, that if the picture could be transferred to canvas, it would make a "Magdalen" such as no painter had ever dreamed before. But he remonstrated, reasoned, argued, pleaded. What would the world say? what would even good Catholics think? what reflections would be cast upon the Church, her discipline, her teaching, etc.? But the silent, prostrate figure made no reply. And the Bishop went over to study carefully a picture of the Good Shepherd, which he had seen a hundred times.

After an interval, Mother Provincial said, looking down on Barbara, and smoothing with her hand her long, fine hair:—

"My Lord, I think there is one condition on which we could keep Miss Wilson here."

Barbara lifted her face. The Bishop turned round rapidly.

"What is it?" he said, without a trace of dignity, and with very red eyes.

"If Miss Wilson could care to change this dress," said Mother Provincial, touching the blue mantella, "for the habit of the Good Shepherd—"

"Oh, Mother, Mother! there's my dream, my dream!" cried Barbara, in a paroxysm of surprise and delight. "O Lord, dearest, sweetest Lord, how good art Thou! and how wicked and unbelieving have I been! Oh, my Lord!" she cried, turning to the Bishop, with clasped hands, "there was hardly a night in which I did not dream I was a Sister of the Good Shepherd; and I thought our dear Lord Himself clothed me with His wounded hands; and I used even touch the gaping wounds with my fingers, as He said: 'Arise, and come: the winter is past!' But oh! the agony of waking and finding it was all a dream. And then, I used reproach myself with being unfaithful to my vow; and I used pray; but oh! with such faltering heart, 'I have chosen, I *have* chosen, to be an abject in the house of my Lord!' And now, here is my dream realized. Oh, Mother, I shall never, never distrust my dear God again!"

"Very well, Mother," said the Bishop, trying to steady his voice. "There's one clear sign of a vocation whatever, that this young lady has been thinking of your white habit so long. Now, can she make her novitiate here?"

"I think not, my Lord," said the Mother Provincial. "I shall send her to Cork, for many reasons."

"Well, then, the sooner the better, I presume," said the Bishop. "There's a train at 5:20. Will the young lady have time to change her dress in that time? Very well. My carriage will be at the Convent door at a quarter to five o'clock. And, as I have some business to transact in Cork, I shall have the honor of escorting Miss Wilson to her new home."

"Mother," said Barbara, "I'm stupid with delight. Can I say good-bye to my—to the penitents?"

"No!" said the Mother, "you must enter on your obedience at once!"

"Not even to poor Laura, Mother?"

"Well, yes, when you have changed your dress," said Mother Provincial, with some hesitation.

It was a happy parting, that between Barbara and the soul she had saved; for it was only for a time. And it was a happy little soul, that moved down amongst the lilies and azaleas of the nuns' corridor, escorted by Sister Eulalie, who whispered:—

"If only Luke were here now, how happy he would be!"

And out from behind doors and recesses and flower pedestals, rushed ever and again some white-robed figure, who flung her arms silently around the young postulant, silently kissed her on the face and mouth, and silently vanished. And as she rolled along in the Bishop's carriage she thought: "To see uncle and father now would be heaven. But no! not till I am clothed. Then they'll see me, and rejoice. Oh! how good is God!"

As they entered the Cork train, there emerged from a train that had just run in on the opposite platform a strange procession. First came a detachment of police, with rifles and full equipments; then a batch of poor peasants and laborers, evidently prisoners; then a young girl, with a plaid shawl around her head; then a priest, with his arm in a sling. Barbara caught her breath, and could not forbear saying aloud:—

"That's Father Delmege, my Lord!"

"So it is!" said the Bishop, who had been watching intently. "Take your seat, whilst I go to see him!"

And so, as Barbara passed from her martyrdom rejoicing, Luke entered on his.

He had been duly arraigned before the constituted tribunals of the land, and had taken his place in court. He would gladly have gone into the dock with his fellow-prisoners; but the law, always polite and courteous and inexorable, would not allow it. It was a wonder that he was not invited on the Bench to try himself. When the magistrates entered, all present uncovered their heads but the prisoners. They wished to protest against law, and legislators, and executive alike.

"Take off your hats!" shouted the police angrily.

The prisoners refused; and one of the constables, roughly seizing one of the young men, dashed his hat furiously on the ground.

"Remove your hat, boys," said Luke, from the place he occupied near the Bench. "Respect yourselves, if you cannot respect the Court."

The young men doffed their hats immediately. It was almost pitiful, this little protest of defiance; pitiful, by reason of its very impotence.

The Court proceeded to try the cases, with calm, equable formality, each case being individually handled to show complete impartiality. Every one in court understood that the conviction was a foregone conclusion. But everything should be done regularly and in form; though every prisoner felt the merciless grasp of the law upon him. And so the proceedings moved steadily on to their conclusion, like well-oiled machinery, smooth, harmonious, regular, irresistible. The magistrates consulted for a few minutes and then announced their decisions. The poor peasants and laborers were sentenced to terms of imprisonment, varying from three to six months, but always accompanied with hard labor. When Mona's turn came, she was sentenced to six months' imprisonment without hard labor. She stood in front of the dock, looking calmly and defiantly at the Bench. Her eyes alone blazed contempt and determination.

"I want no favors from ye," she cried, as her sentence was announced. "Ye are inimies of me creed and country."

"In consideration of your sex and youth, we dispense you from hard labor," said the presiding magistrate, "although your offence was a most serious one, and might have imperilled the life of the officer—"

"He struck a coward's blow," said Mona, "an' it was right that a woman's hand should chastise him."

The magistrates were passing on to the next prisoner, when she again interrupted:—

"Will ye gi' me the hard labor?" she said. "No wan shall ever say that I showed the white feather."

"Then we change your sentence to three months, and hard labor," said the magistrate.

"Thank ye," she said, pulling the shawl again over her face.

"We have taken into account, Mr. Delmege," continued the magistrate, courteously, "your position, and the excellent character you have hitherto maintained. We also took into account that in one sense, the grave assault of which you were guilty, and which might have led to lamentable consequences, was possibly owing to the great excitement that unhappily accompanies the operations of the law in this country. We, therefore, are of opinion that the requirements of the law and justice shall be satisfied by asking you to enter into your own recognizances to observe the peace for twelve months."

Luke arose, pale and weak. His right hand was badly swollen, and he still was in danger of blood-poisoning.

"I am sure, gentlemen," he said, "you do not intend it; but I can hardly regard your decision as other than an insult. There has been nothing alleged in my favor to extenuate the offense, or mitigate the severity of the law. I am more guilty than these poor fellows and that poor girl. If there be any reason for clemency, let it be extended to her. She has an aged father, and a sick sister at home——"

"No, Father Luke," said Mona, "I want no mercy from the government of England. I'll go to jail, with more joy than I'd go to me weddin'; an' God and His Blessed Mother will look afther Moira and father."

Then she broke into hysterical weeping.

"It is an extremely painful duty, but we are unwilling to proceed to extremities in such a case. If you can see your way, Mr. Delmege, to accept our decision, I assure you it will give us great pleasure," said the magistrate.

"Once more, gentlemen, I appeal to your clemency on behalf of this poor girl," said Luke. "Prison life is not suitable for the young."

"Don't demane yerself and me, yer reverence, by askin' pity from him," said Mona, with flashing eyes. "Sure we're only goin' where all the hayroes of our race wint before us."

"Once more, Mr. Delmege," said the magistrate, "will you enter on your own recognizances——"

"Impossible, gentlemen," said Luke, sitting down.

"Then it is our painful duty to direct that you be imprisoned for three calendar months from this date, and without hard labor."

"And so you're a prisoner?" said the Bishop, after he had blessed the crowd of kneeling prisoners, and given his ring to little Mona to be kissed. "I expected it. Take care of that nasty wound in your hand. I hope the doctor will send you straight to the infirmary."

"Don't fill my vacancy, my Lord," said Luke, "at least till I return. My father has no other shelter now."

"Never fear," said the Bishop. "I'll send a temporary substitute, with special instructions to Dr. Keatinge."

"Thank you, my Lord!" said Luke.

"Well, good-bye! We'll see you sometimes in your hermitage. By the way, do you know who's accompanying me to Cork?"

"No, my Lord!" said Luke, wonderingly.

"You might have heard of Miss Wilson, the niece of Canon Murray?"

"To be sure, I know her well," said Luke, eagerly.

"She has had a strange history; but I'll tell you some other time. These fellows are growing impatient. She's about to commence her novitiate as a postulant of the Good Shepherds in Cork."

"Oh, thank God!" said Luke, so fervently that the Bishop wondered exceedingly.

CHAPTER XL

Reunion

"SORROW GIVES the accolade!" Yes. The blow is sharp; but the quickening is very great. It was just what Luke wanted. All great souls covet pain; and Luke's was a great soul, though he was unconscious of it; and though he had been striving to stifle during all his life his sublime aspirations, and to sacrifice them on the modern altar of mere commonplace and respectability. Circumstances, or rather the Supreme Mind that guides circumstances, had now brought him face to face with suffering and even shame, and he exulted. For, if there is a glory in the prison, and a sunlight on the scaffold, nevertheless, the very thought of personal restraint, and the sense of loss of man's highest prerogative, liberty, bring with them a deep humiliation; and the sharp knighthood of the sword is forgotten for a moment in the vulgar grasp of the jailer. Then comes the reaction; and the sense of exultation; and the keen embrace of pain has a quickening and vivifying power over soul and nerves not yet strained and unstrung by selfishness.

Then again, Luke found he was an object of respectful solicitude to all around him. The doctor instantly placed him in the infirmary. His right hand was swollen to an alarming extent; and it was only after the lapse of some weeks that the dangerous symptoms subsided.

"If that hand shall ever get hurt again," said the doctor, "I won't answer for his life."

These days were days of depression for Luke—or moments of depression in hours of deep thought. Left completely to himself, his mind ran over the events of his life in detail. There

470

was little with which he could reproach himself. Yet, he was unsatisfied. Then, from time to time, odd phrases that had fastened on his memory would come up at most unexpected times, and plague him with their persistency. His verdict on Barbara Wilson ten years ago in the Schweizerhof: "She's not mortal; she's a spirit and a symbol—the symbol of the suffering and heroism of my race"—came up, again and again, doubly emphasized now by all he had heard and seen of her years of renunciation and suffering. And his thoughts passed over from the symbol to the symbolized; and the strange expressions used by so many priests about Ireland surged back upon his memory.

"We have to create our own civilization; we cannot borrow that of other countries."

"We are the teachers of the world; not the pupils of its vulgarity and selfishness."

One night, in the early weeks of his imprisonment, he lay awake in pain, tossing from side to side in great agony. His mind was unusually active; and the sudden thought seized him to sketch a visionary future for his country, founded on this ideal of simplicity and self-renunciation. As his thoughts worked onwards, and built up this airy commonwealth of Christ, the pain was completely forgotten; and he fell asleep early in the morning. The doctor found his temperature much higher on his morning call; yet he declared him somewhat better.

"Doctor, I want something badly," said Luke. "Can I have it?"

"By all means," said the doctor. "What is it?"

"Pen, ink, and plenty of foolscap paper," said Luke.

"Not yet," said the doctor. "I presume you have not yet learned to write with your toes."

It was so much the better, because Luke had time to think and develop his ideas more fully, before he committed them to paper.

Then the pain and sacrifice met with their immediate reward. There was no demonstration on his release from prison. He was an unknown factor in politics. Even in Rossmore there was no ovation. It was felt that he was above such things. But, during his imprisonment, every kindness and attention was lavished on his father and sister and her children, who had to become his guests in his little home. And the same silent, gentle sympathy flowed around him when he returned. Mary wept hysterically, and kissed his hands passionately; and wept still more when she saw his face drawn and pale from much suffering. John said:—

"Bad luck to the government and the landlords! Wondher they let him out alive!"

Every kind of shy, pathetic question was put to him by this sympathetic people; every kind of gentle, unobtrusive benevolence was shown him. They could not presume too far upon this grave, silent man; but they spoke their mute love and admiration in a hundred ways. Yet things were a little tightened in economical matters sometimes. Will McNamara had gone to America; but the father and Lizzie and the children were there. And children must have bread, and meat, and clothes, too. Nature says so, and must not be denied.

One day Luke was walking down the village street in his silent, abstracted way, when he heard a voice challenging him and rather defiantly:—

"What's the matther wid me mate, yer reverence?"

He turned round, and came face to face with the village butcher, Joe Morrissey. Joe seemed to be angry. There had been for a long time a certain want of sympathy between Joe and the "Cojutor." For Joe was a Nationalist, and an extreme one. He had been out in '67; had cut the telegraph wires between the Junction and Limerick; and had been one of the last to part from the young Irishman who gave up his life gallantly for his country in the woods near Shraharla. And he had taken it as granted that this polished, well-dressed young priest, who was always preaching the virtues of the Anglo-Saxon,— their thrift, punctuality, etc., and consequently emphasizing the defects of his own countrymen,—could not be a Nationalist or a patriot. His opinions changed a little after the sermon on Cremona; and had now completely veered round after the scene at the eviction and the subsequent knighthood of the jail.

"I beg your pardon, Mr. Morrissey," said Luke, humbly, for life's events had made him very humble.

"I want to know, yer reverence," said Joe, clapping his

broad knife across the palm of his hand, "what's the matther wid *my* mate that you're reflectin' on it?"

"I'm sure I'm quite unconscious, Mr. Morrissey," said Luke, quite puzzled, "of having said anything derogatory—"

"Look at that for mate," said Joe, unheeding, and slapping with the knife the joints that hung in the open window. "Is there the likes of that in the County Limbrick? Look at that for lane, red and juicy; and that fat, rich and cramey; and what's a poor man to do whin his clergy and the heads of his Church—"

"Don't mind him, yer reverence," said Mrs. Morrissey, coming out, and wiping away with her check apron the tears that were streaming down her face; "he doesn't mane what he says, yer reverence—"

"Will ye hold yer tongue, 'uman?" said Joe, angrily; "can't you let me talk whin a gintleman comes into the shop? I say, yer reverence, 'tis a shame that our clergy should be turnin' their backs on their dacent parishioners, and sindin' for their mate to Limbrick and elsewhere, whilst—"

"Never mind him agin, yer reverence," interposed Mrs. Morrissey, still weeping. "What he manes is, that every Saturday, wid God's blessin', for the future, a leg and a line (loin) will go down to you; and, sure, some time or other, you can pay us. And sure if you never did, God is good."

Joe had gone out in his indignation; and was looking up and down the street, in a very determined manner. Luke came out, and was about to express his gratitude when Joe stopped him.

"There's jest wan favor I want to ask yer reverence," he said.

"To be sure, Mr. Morrissey, if I can possibly grant it," said Luke, in wonder.

"Oh, begor, you can," said Joe, cheerfully. "Since I wos the height of that," he said, stooping down and putting his open palm within six inches of the ground, "no one ever called me anything but Joe. Me father called me Joe; me mother called me Joe; me brothers and sisters called me Joe; the schoolmaster called me Joe, whin he didn't call me, 'You d—d ruffian!' Whin I grew up, and got married, me wife called me Joe; and whin God sint the childre, wan be wan, begor! they never called me anything but Joe. The youngster inside in the cradle

knows me as well as yer reverence; and faix! he never calls me
'daddy,' but Joe. And to tell you the truth, yer reverence, whin
you call me Misther Morrissey, I don't know who you're
talking to. Would it make any difference to yer reverence to
call me Joe, like all the nabours?"

"Certainly not, Mr. —Joe," said Luke, deeply touched, and
stretching out his hand. "God bless you!"

" 'Tis dirty," said Joe, hastily rubbing his hand on his
breeches, "but 'tis the hand of an honest man."

And Joe had the reward of his generosity. It came quickly,
and in its most attractive form. That is, the little incident gave
him the opportunity—the dearest that can fall to the lot of an
Irishman in this world—of making a good joke. And so, when
he sat that evening on the leaden ledge of his open window,
and lit his pipe, he was a happy man.

"Begor," he said to the group that always surrounded his
establishment, " 'tis the best thing that occurred for manny a
long day. 'Mind the pennies,' sez he, 'an' the pound's will take
care of theirselves.' Ha! ha! ha! 'Look out for a rainy day,' sez
he, 'an' make hay while the sun shines.' Ha! ha! ha! ha! Begor!
the poor man wint to a bad schoolmaster whin he began to
tache himself. For, faix, he hasn't even a butcher's pinny to
bless himself wid."

"How could he have it?" said a bystander, "whin he gives
it to this, that, and the other wan. Begor, the Bank of England
wouldn't sthand it."

"Look here, hones' man," said Joe Morrissey, taking the
pipe out of his mouth, "that's all right; and 'tisn't me as is goin'
to find fault with him. But, what did he want talkin' to us
about savin' money, whin he wasn't savin' it himself; and all
about English ways, whin the man has an Irish heart, no matter how he consales it? That's what kills me. Sure, the ould
sayin' is thrue—Do what the priests tell ye; but don't do what
the priests do theirselves."

So public opinion surged around Luke in these days of trial.
For now, Lizzie and her little children had to go away. The
strong, brave young farmer had got a job in the docks of New
York; and had paid their passage. And, with breaking hearts
on both sides, they parted with all they held dear on earth,
and exchanged the free, pure air, the sweet waters, the rushing

winds, the rustling trees, the murmuring seas, and freedom and happiness, for a flat in the tenement house in the great city, and the fever and the fret of a new life. Ah, me! will it ever cease—this dread transformation in lives that were never created but for the sweetness and purity, the silence and the holiness of simple rural environments? And one day, old Mike Delmege, "heart-broke afther the little childhre," bowed his head, and was gathered unto his fathers.

Then there came a great void in Luke's life. He shrank ever more and more into himself; and without being in the least degree moody or reserved, he detached himself from all human things; and wrought in simple earnest love towards the Divine. But the few ties which circumstances had created for him,— spiritual ties that grew all the stronger by reason of their unworldliness—drew him from time to time from his hermitage, and maintained for him that perfect poise between the world and God, which would otherwise have been broken by a morose asceticism or a too great leaning over to the creature. And so he kept up a constant and mutually edifying correspondence and intercourse with Father Tracey and Father Martin; and sometimes he found himself in a closer and more intimate friendship with his Bishop than he had ever dreamed of.

And one day, he found himself the happy intermediary in a little scene in the Canon's drawing-room, which seemed to him a beautiful and divinely appointed *denouement* in the little drama in which he had been not always a successful actor.

The good Canon had had a relapse after the exciting scene at the eviction, and had sunk into a condition of extreme helplessness. One side was hopelessly paralyzed; and he had to be wheeled from room to room in a bath-chair. The tolerant legislation of the Irish Church reflects strongly the charitable bias of the people's minds; and allows an aged pastor, "who has borne the burden of the day and the heat," and who is disqualified for further work, to retain his parish and presbytery to the end, in sturdy independence. And it was very beautiful and edifying to see the broken and enfeebled giant, rolled in and out to his little church, where he spent the greater part of his declining days. The little children used fight for the honor of rolling back across the gravelled walk their aged pastor. They had lost all fear of him now, even of the great snowy beard that swept down on his breast. And still the people came to consult him in their troubles, and to talk to the golden age that had been. And so calmly and peacefully his days glided on to the great sea, over which he looked without fear, or terror, or misgiving. One thing only troubled this calm evening of life—the mystery that hung around his beloved niece. Her strange history had been carefully concealed from him, until all should be ripe for revelation.

He was dozing calmly one summer afternoon, when Luke was announced. The latter had often called to exchange ideas with his old pastor, and to relieve the monotony of his illness. The Canon was not surprised, therefore, only deeply pleased at the announcement.

"Ha, my dear young friend," he said, "you caught me—ha —napping. Take a chair, and sit down with me for a while. Somehow, old times seem to have come back most vividly this —a—afternoon."

He was silent for a time, his mind busily gathering up the broken threads of the past. Luke sought to divert his attention by telling of his own experiences.

"My sister and her husband are doing well in New York," he said. "I have had a letter lately, asking had any one taken Lisnalee."

"That is not very likely," said the Canon. "Lisnalee remains a monument, and forever—well, we must not be resentful. But—the events of that—ha—miserable day had one good effect. The horror has not—ha—been repeated; but the people are anxious, frightened, dispirited. They know not when the evil spirit will come again."

"Yes," said Luke, mournfully; "the golden age of my poor parish is passed forever.

"Yet," he said, brightening up, "the world is not all a hopeless and helpless place; nor life altogether an insoluble problem."

"You have heard—ha—something that might excite your hopes, and—ha—sympathies?"

"Yes, sir," said Luke. "I have heard something that deeply concerns me, and—"

"I hope my conjecture is correct," said the Canon, listlessly;

"and that his Lordship has yielded to my repeated—ha—solicitations; and, consulting for your unique circumstances, advanced you to a—ha—benefice?"

"It is not quite that, sir," said Luke, feeling his way nervously. For now the drawing-room was opened as gently as if only the summer breeze had stolen in and touched it with a light finger. "It is a something that also, if you will pardon me, may also concern you."

Luke was never so nervous before; not even on his first student visit to that dread presbytery. He thought the great clock on the mantelpiece quite impertinent in its noisy ticking.

"Alas!" said the old man, feebly, "very little concerns me now except that one great event. I did think, indeed,—perhaps you will esteem it—ha—a harmless vanity—that the Bishop might have—well—offered me the Archdiaconate, before I died. But that was not to be! That was not to be!"

"The diocese thought he would have done so," said Luke, watching the door, intently; "but the Bishop looks mostly to the young. He would, however, have given any honor to our old friend, Father Tracey, I believe; but that great saint will have none of these things."

"I haven't always agreed with that excellent but—ha—rather eccentric clergyman," said the Canon; "but I dare say he is right—quite right!"

"What I am referring to, however, sir," said Luke, now in a state of desperation, "is something that concerns you even more deeply—something that has been the thought and dream of your life."

The old man seemed sunk in a kind of stupor; but something in Luke's words seemed to wake him up to a new life; for he started, and asked in an excited whisper:—

"Barbara!"

It was the question he had been asking for twelve weary years. He now dreaded to hear again the eternal answer—No! And his face pleaded eloquently against it.

"You know something?" he said. And Luke said, "Yes!"

"It is a strange coincidence," said the Canon, his face lighted up with a new emotion, "that just as you were announced, this afternoon, I was dreaming of Barbara. I suppose it is senile weakness, or the mental debility arising from my condition;

but in a half-doze I thought I—ah—saw my dear niece entering just as long ago she used—ha—sweep into this drawing-
room with such easy grace and dignity. Ah me! those were
happy days, did we but know it. But you were about to say—
ha—my dear young friend, that you had some news from
Barbara. There is that—ha—singular delusion again. I fear,
my young friend, that my intellect is becoming weak. It's a
singular delusion, but now I think, of course, it is only an
hallucination, that there in that doorway—ha—what—my
God!—"

Ah, yes! dear old soul, this time there was no delusion; for a
figure of light did stand in the dark framework of the door,
clothed all in white, save a tiny thread of blue; and that figure
of light did tremble all over under the sweet, tremulous dread
of shocking with too sudden bliss the frail old man. But now
there was no time for further concealment; and with a little
glad cry of delight and pain, Barbara, clothed now in the white,
beautiful habit of the Good Shepherd Nuns, was at her uncle's
feet, and was kissing his two withered hands passionately amid
her tears. Luke had done his part well; and had quietly gone
out, leaving uncle and niece together.

He went down to the old hut by the sea-shore to visit his old
friends, to say a kind word to poor Moira, who was wasting
away slowly in consumption, and to exchange the account of
his prison experiences with Mona, his fellow-martyr. When
he returned to the drawing-room, Barbara still sat at her
uncle's feet; the old man, with a look of rapture on his face,
was toying with her white scapulary, and murmuring something that sounded like, *Sans tache!*

Ah, yes! spotless and immaculate, and with all the purity
of a fire-tried soul, she had passed under the mighty yoke of
Christ, who had put his own stole of suffering around her. But,
strange to say, though now enrolled in the glorious band of
Virgins, who follow the Lamb, whithersoever He goeth, and
sing the canticle none other can sing, there were hours and
days when the thought haunted her with a sense of pain and
fear, that perhaps after all the day of trial was sweeter than
that of victory; and that, like Alexis of old, it would have been
better, or more glorious, to have died a reputed Magdalen.
For saintly souls, like this, are ambitious. They want the high-

est and the noblest. The martyrdom must continue to the last
breath; nor do they care to yield up their souls but in a sigh
of pain and the agony of dereliction. But then, here too, the
Supreme Law, God's Will, was manifested; and beneath it she
sheltered herself when regrets for the lost nobility of perpetual
pain reproached her. And hence when, in the ecstasy of this
reunion, which was the one thing that nature demanded, the
thought recurred: Would it have been better otherwise; or if
this meeting with the beloved one had only taken place on the
far, eternal shore? she brushed aside the thought as a temptation, and gambolled around the dear old presbytery as a child.
And she showed her companion-sister all the wonders of the
place—the dairy, where she had—indeed she had—made butter; and the poultry—the same identical Orpingtons and Dork-
ings which had won so many prizes for dear uncle; the flower-
beds, alas! now not so neat and perfect as when her gentle
hands had tended them. And "here," she said, "Father Delmege stood, leaning on that mantelpiece, the evening he sang
that fierce, rebel song; and I, a giddy young girl, raced down
after him along that footpath that runs to the gate, and begged
him to look after Louis in England! Ah! poor Louis! if he were
only here now!"

And the happy Barbara wiped away a tear with her plain
cotton handkerchief. And then, after tea, these birds should
shake out all too prematurely their wings in the great clock;
and the deep gong tolls out, like a bell of doom, the hour of
six—and then—the parting, as of all things else on earth, for
Luke had to drive the nuns to the evening train for Limerick,
where they would get one night's lodging before going back to
the novitiate.

CHAPTER XLI

A Profession Sermon

THEN, AFTER another brief interval, the great day arrived, the day that was to witness the consummation of great hopes, a far foreshadowing of the final *Veni, sponsa mea!* It is doubtful whether there is any moment in the life of mortals so full of pure and perfect bliss as that which marks the taking of the final vows of profession. Around the marriage feast there hangs some shadow of fear and anxiety for a future, which at best is problematical; and the eyes that watch the happy couple, stepping out, hand in hand, from their fellows, to walk the ways of life in a new partnership so exclusive and so responsible, are filled with a vague anxiety and foreboding; and the sunlight is broken in the prism of tears. But at a profession ceremony there is neither parting, nor sorrow, nor fretful fear; only the calm intoxication of a too great joy, for the spouse is given into the arms, not of man, but of God. And hence the profession morning of Barbara Wilson broke with a promise of a glorious day; and the very atmosphere seemed to hum with Halleluiahs—the glad echoes of all the music that filled the hearts of sisters, priests, and penitents. For the latter knew now all the pathetic heroism of their former sister; and if they regretfully parted with the assumption that the great Mother of God had been amongst them, they comforted themselves in the assurance that at least one of her saints had been their gentle companion during ten eventful years. And it mitigated their shame and remorse to think that a pure soul had shared their lot. Her heroism had been a second absolution.

The little chapel, then, to the left of the high altar, was filled that morning with a curious, happy, loving, eager throng of penitents; and the very idea that one of their number was about to be raised to the glory of the white habit, and a place

480

of honor in the choir stalls, filled all with a kind of personal pride and exultation. And so they whispered and watched and pointed and conjectured, until the great organ rolled out its mighty volumes of sound, and the opening hymn announced the advent of the Bishop and his assistants. Then, after the preliminary ceremonies, Mass commenced; and, after the Gospel, Luke Delmege knelt for the episcopal blessing, and ascended the predella of the altar.

Luke was by no means nervous. He had long since acquired so thorough and perfect a command of thought and utterance, that he knew a breakdown to be impossible. Yet, he felt all the solemnity of the occasion; and he was about to depart from the usual style of pulpit utterances, and pass from abstractions to the concrete facts of his own life and the workings of his own conscience. For, although that life was immaculate, and that conscience unrebuking, he felt that an *amende* was due to God and his own soul for the one fault—that he had failed to grasp his vocation to soar unto the highest; and as a penalty of that infidelity that his life had been dragged "along on a broken wing." Now, such an unveiling is at all times embarrassing; and, especially, as it now broke through the thick folds of a reserve that was almost haughty, and showed the world, who only deemed him an unapproachable and coldly perfect character, an estimate of self that shrunk into the smallest dimensions under the light of great humility and sublime contrasts. He felt, also, that he had to enunciate principles that would seem so large for human effort as to appear affected and extreme by their very difficulty; and he had to synthesize and compare religion and philosophy in a manner that would seem to ordinary understandings the outcome of pedantry and vanity.

He took for his text:—

"At that time, Jesus said to His disciples, 'If any man will come after me, let him deny himself, take up his cross, and follow me. Whosoever shall save his life, shall lose it; and he that shall lose his life for my sake, shall find it.' "

"The divine peremptoriness and the seeming contradiction in these words," continued Luke, "would yield another proof, if proof were needed, of Christ's divinity. 'Never man spake like this man.' An earthly philosopher, a Grecian sophist, would either promise vast things to his followers, as the adversary tempted the hungry and weary One in the desert; or, if he affected truth, he would teach it in abstractions, and leave nature to cut its easiest path toward happiness. But the great Divine Teacher laid down the minimum condition of being His disciple in that stern command, Deny thyself; and He appended the vague, and apparently contradictory promise, that 'whosoever shall lose his life, shall find it.' It is strange, that men not only were not scandalized at His words, but readily accepted them as doctrinal truth and infallible promise; and the half-educated publican and the totally illiterate fisherman rose up hastily to follow a Teacher who demanded so great a sacrifice for so problematical a reward. And stranger still it is that, generation after generation, souls are to be found who, fascinated by the very arbitrariness of this command, rise swiftly to the high levels of sanctity which it connotes; and, passing beyond the dictates of a protesting self-love, or the still more dangerous platitudes of a compromising world, find themselves suddenly in that desert where the Hand of their Master is as a shelter of a rock, and the sound of His voice as the murmur of running waters. Such a sacrifice we are witnessing today, such relinquishment of youthful desires and ambitions, such a calm severing of ties that bind as closely as the silver cord of life, such a renunciation and self-abandonment, such sacrificial vows written and sealed on parchment in the presence of the King, yet more truly written and sealed with the heart's blood, as if to meet the theological condition of destruction and consumption. But there is a peculiar and individual feature in the circumstances of today's immolation that lends to it a special significance, and from which I shall be pardoned if I deduce a special meaning, and perhaps a wider and far-reaching application. You will have noticed that my text implies, not only the idea of Renunciation, but also the idea of Sacrifice. 'Deny thyself!' 'Lose thyself!' This is the command. In the great generality of religious professions, the first precept alone is insisted upon; the latter idea of sacrifice, particularly vicarious sacrifice, seldom enters. The Church deems the absoluteness of the former as embracing and containing the latter.

But, in the present instance, it is at least a peculiar feature, that the life of vicarious sacrifice should be terminated by vows of renunciation; and that the latter, which generally denote the incipience of a life of self-denial, should, in this case, mark a termination of a sacrifice so great, that, like the command to the patriarch of old, only the Supreme Will could impose it on one of its best-beloved creatures. It happened thus. The good Sister will pardon the details, because they show how steadily and invisibly God's hand is ever moving through His creation."

Here Luke narrated all the details of Louis' errors, and his sister's devotion, and continued:—

"Then the soul of the beloved one was in great peril. His life was doomed. The danger of eternal damnation, from being remote, became proximate. Nothing but Omnipotence was between that soul and hell. In the mighty agony of a sister's soul, which alone seemed to yearn after the lost one, a sudden inspiration dawned. That soul had just shuddered, in the involuntary shrinking of pure minds, from the very name that, if symbolical of love, is also suggestive of forgiven sin. And the Most High, in His secret and ineffable designs, decided that this should be the sacrifice. The price of the brother's soul was to be the sinless shame of the sister; he was to be saved through the voluntary ignominy of an immaculate and spotless victim. It is the reflection in miniature of that mighty oblation made by our great Brother, Christ; just as this latter was foreshadowed, almost in the words I am using, by the greatest of the Hebrew prophets. There was, of course, the dread, the human trembling before the altar; but then the soul spoke through the firm will; the sacrifice was accepted, the brother's soul miraculously snatched from the flames; and the sister, unknown to all but God, passed from the bright world into the hiddenness of this asylum; and here lived, to all outer appearance, a Magdalen, with all the outer marks of humiliation, her sinlessness only known to God and the good priest who represented Him.

"Whilst all this was in progress, another life ran on in parallel lines; but alas! with what a chaos between them! A young priest had rejected a similar inspiration to a life of absolute sacrifice communicated at the moment of his ordination, had descended from the heroic to the commonplace; and

there, his instincts, still active and alive, were fascinated by
the very watch-words on the lips of the world, which were the
daily maxims, reduced to daily practice, of the saints. 'Renunciation,' 'sacrifice,' 'abandonment of self,' 'the interests of
the race,' 'the sacred calls of Humanity,' here were words forever ringing in his ears, and calling, calling to some high,
mystic life, far removed from selfish ease or the cravings of
ambition. Alas! it took many years to teach him how hollow
was it all—that there was no God in Humanity, except the God
who embraced Humanity to raise it almost to the Godhead;
nor were the sublime doctrines of renunciation and sacrifice
practiced except by the lowly followers of the one Divine
Man. Yet, this was the eternal craving of the human soul; and
as the young priest moved along in the painful path of wisdom,
he saw how human philosophy, with a dark lantern in its hand,
went painfully groping along the tortuous mazes of the human
mind, to emerge in the full light of the Gospel, yet with darkened eyes; for the sublime word 'Renunciation' he found in
the last note in the music of the greatest of modern poets; and
the divine contradiction, 'He that will lose his life shall save
it,' he found to be the ultimate of one of the greatest of modern
philosophers. But what have ideas, however sublime, to do with
the conduct of modern life? Action, and men of action, rule
the modern world. Ideas ruled the vast worlds of Oriental mysticism, until they culminated in the sublime realities of the
Christian religion; but the Occidental bias is toward materialism, and its one great dogma—the ETERNAL I. But that which
was so familiar to the sages of old, which is found in labor and
much pain by the great moderns, who agonize in the birth-
throes of monsters, is easily grasped by the little ones who
seek wisdom in simplicity; and are fain to follow as guides
those who, divinely ordained, teach, not in the persuasive
words of human wisdom, but in the direct interpretation of
plain language, more than philosophy can discern, or learning
fathom, or fancy conceive.

"And so the young priest, coming back to his native land,
dreamed he had a message to his race. He would inaugurate a
new era; he would bring his generation into touch with all
modern ideas of progress; he would introduce a new civilization in place of an old and effete system. The idea was a gener-

ous one—only it rested on a wrong principle. Or rather it sought to build without principle—the great underlying principle of man's dualism—ideas and action, matter and form, soul and body; each with its interests, each with its destiny. He had heard it said, and said with some show of authority: 'Seek men's souls through their bodies! Make a happy people; and you make them holy! Sanctity follows earthly prosperity; and in riches are to be found the secrets of great grace!' He hardly believed it. Yet he would make the experiment. He was warned: This people must create their own civilization. There is no use in appealing to purely material and mercenary principles. If the spiritual air-ship of Irish aspirations must be anchored in a kind of mild materialism, remember always that the latter is but an adjunct. And so the people rejected at once his suggestion to move on to happiness in the lines of modern progress. To his plea for prudence they answered, Providence; for human foresight, they placed divine omniscience; for thrift, charity; for advancement, humility; for selfishness, generosity; until he began to feel he was clipping the wings of spirits, and bringing down to the gross earth souls destined for the empyrean. He then found himself face to face with the problem, How to conserve his race, and their old-fashioned ideals at the same time?

"In searching for this, he stumbled into an error, and found a solution. He thought it was a first principle that nations work out their own destinies, and that character forces its way to conquest. He made no allowance for a nation's environments, for dread surroundings, through which no purely human energy can cut a path to long-deferred, ever-vanishing, yet still realizable, ideals. He saw the confirmation of this idea, he thought, under his own eyes, in his own native place—the Ireland which poets have dreamed of, and for which patriots have died. Under the vivifying power of a great personality, the people rose up to seize the possibilities within their reach; and moving on to great spirituality, they seized at the same time every opportunity of advancing themselves materially. And they succeeded. Whilst all around was a desert, here was a land flowing with milk and honey; and the dwellers on the barren mountains looked down with envy on the smiling plains of Arcady. Alas! the element of permanency, the element of security, was absent; and one day, under a touch of evil, all the beauty and happiness vanished in smoke and flame and ruin. And, as the two illusions disappeared—that of Ireland, built from its ruins on purely material and selfish principles; and that of an Ireland, built without the foundation of security and independence, the young priest woke up suddenly to the vision of his country, developing under new and stable conditions her traditional ideas; and becoming in the face of a spurious and unstable civilization rocked to its foundation by revolution, a new commonwealth of Christ. The possibility of such an event had been vaguely hinted at by priests, who evidently were struggling to evolve coherent ideas from a mass of sensations and instincts, righteous and just, but yet unformed. It was foreshadowed by the manner in which the people, untrained and illiterate, groped after and grasped the highest principles of Christian civilization; it was foretold by the energy with which men contemned the mere acquisition of wealth, and felt ashamed of possessing it; it was outlined in the simple, human lives, with all their Spartan severity toward themselves, and all their divine beneficence toward others. It took shape in the sharp and violent contrasts presented by the fierce rivalry for wealth that animates the citizens of the world's great metropolis, and the milder, yet not less energetic, emulation for grace that was witnessed in our own capital—a contrast as great as that which distinguished the bandit of the Apennines, surrounded with barbaric pomp, from 'the poor man of Assisi.' And finally, it was personified in the example of a humble and hidden priest, who long ago had denuded himself of all things for Christ's sake, and chosen all that was lowly and hard to human nature, before all that was pleasant and attractive; and the still more picturesque example of a young girl who voluntarily embraced humility and suffering, and found in her cross the satisfaction of all earthly desire, the perfection of all earthly happiness. It was the old story, which we read so often, of days far distanced from ours by time and change—of souls who brushed with the tip of their wings the fire of Hell, and then soared aloft even unto Paradise.

"There can be no question," continued Luke, "but that such a life of heroism and self-sacrifice is closely symbolical of our beloved country. It argues a disbelief in the divine economy to suppose that our martyrdom of seven hundred years was the accident of human events, uncontrolled except by their intrinsic possibilities and ultimate developments. That this long cycle of suffering is to close even now is as certain as that our young postulant has put off the robes of penance and humiliation, and put on the garments of gladness. Her future it is easy to forecast. She will move down the valleys of life with an eternal song of love and gratitude in her heart, passing from hour to hour, from thought to thought, from deed to deed, and gathering from each some sweetness that will be dropped in the bitterness of chalices which some have yet to drink. It is as easy to forecast the destiny of Ireland. She will never adopt the modern idea of placing all human happiness, and therefore all human effort, in the desire of purely natural splendor, and sink down into a nation of money-grubbers and pleasure seekers, becoming at last, not an island of strength and sorrow, but a Cyprus for voluptuousness, and a Lydia for effeminacy. But she will strike the happy mean, and evolve her own civilization by conserving her ideals, whilst seeking after the practical. For it is certain that the traditions, the thoughts, the instincts, the desires, the very passions, of this people tend towards the supernatural. And this must be the germinal idea—the primary and palmary principle in her future development—the cornerstone of the mighty building which the hands of her children are tingling to raise, the keystone in that Arch of Triumph, beneath which her crowned and garlanded heroes will pass unto the jubilee of her resurrection.

"Sister Barbara, I make no apology for having made your life a symbol of your country's destiny, and not merely a subject of a barren discourse. I make bold to continue the parallel to the end. I interpret your thoughts very faintly, if I do not perceive that now and again, whilst accepting the decision of the Supreme Will, your thoughts revert to, and linger lovingly upon, the hours you spent with your crucifixion. I never doubted that, even on the sunlit morning of the Resurrection, such generous souls as John and Magdalen did revert with some tender longing to the darkness and gloom and sorrow of Calvary, and the love that went forth to the agonized One, and flowed back in a stream of sanctity to their own hearts. Perhaps, indeed, you have sometimes dreamed that it might have

been greater and more noble, if you had borne your shame
even unto the eternal gates, and allowed the hands of Christ
alone to take from your head the crown of thorns, and place
thereon the golden fillet of His love. Such ideas are the heritage
of your race. I, too, shared them once. But, led by purely utili-
tarian ideas, I flung aside the call to heroism, and descended to
the commonplace. Let wise teachers beware of bringing down
the mind of the entire nation to a common level of purely
natural ambition and purely materialistic success. However
necessary for the masses such efforts may be to save the race
from extinction, it is not the specific genius of our people. That
soars higher: and material prosperity must not be the ultimate
goal of our race; but only the basis of the higher life. The world
was never so much in need of thinkers and saints as at present.
It never needed so much to see the embodiment of the positive
teaching of Christ, not the nebulous reflection of that teaching
in the wisdom of latter-day philosophy, as now. One such
example as that which we have before us today would be a
powerful lever in lifting up the ideas of the world from the
rut into which they have fallen; and you might have a thousand
such examples amongst so generous a people if the higher life,
with its struggles and glories, were placed before them. Nor
have I the least doubt, that, like the gentle regrets after her
cross that mingle with happier feelings in the heart of the professed Sister of today, when the Resurrection day shall have
dawned for Ireland, when her valleys are ringing with music,
and her exiled children have come back, bearing the many
and beautiful sheaves garnered in the harvests of the world,
many of her chosen souls will look back with regretful eyes on
the days of her gloom and martyrdom; and, escaping from the
Hosannas and the palms, will ascend her lofty mountains and
create there once more Golgothas of vicarious suffering for
the entire race. For unto the end of time there will be sin, and
sins demand retribution and atonement, and it is not the
sinner but the saint that makes it. And men, to the end of
time, will be consumed with selfish desires; and selfishness
must find its constant corrective in Renunciation. And where,
in all the wide earth, can this sublime philosophy of Christ be
practiced, if not here? And where shall the divine contradiction, Lose, that you may gain; Give, that you may get; Die,

that all may live;—be verified, if not amongst the people that has held its hands to heaven in an agony of supplication for twice three hundred years? Where shall the fatal sin of self be extinguished, if not amongst the race which has given to the world in its apostles and martyrs the highest examples of divine altruism? And where shall the final law of love be established, if not where all that is holy and most pure stoops to all that is sordid and stained; and blends, in the alchemy of charity, sin and purity, shame and pity, so perfectly, that, as in the example before us today, men fail to discern beneath the outward shows of life the sinner and the saint, the fallen and the unfallen, the lambs that never wandered from the fold, and the sheep that strayed in the forlorn and unlighted deserts of Sin and Death?"

When the ceremony was over Luke sought the solitude of the convent grounds, to calm the emotion under which he had labored. He cared little what verdict would be passed on that sermon. He only knew that he wished to reveal himself—to make a clear, noble confession of his own shortcomings; and he felt he had only half succeeded. He knew he dared not have spoken more plainly, lest he should shock sensibilities too delicate and tender not to be respected; yet he also felt that he had wrapped up his thoughts so well in a cloud of words that his feelings were but half revealed.

And this was really the case. For at the *déjeuner,* very various were the opinions expressed about the sermon. One said it was all "rhetoric," a word that has come to mean unutterable things in Ireland. Father Tracey, who looked quite spruce in the newly dyed coat, called over Sister Eulalie, whose eyes were red from weeping, and asked her in a whisper:—

"That was a grand sermon, my dear. But my poor brains could not follow it. What was it all about? Why, my child, you have been crying! God bless my soul, crying, and on such a day!"

Sister Eulalie answered not; but went away weeping all the more.

Matthew O'Shaughnessy, who, as a great benefactor to the convent, had always the privilege of an invitation to these ceremonies, said to a priest across the table:—

"That was the grandest discoorse I ever hard, by me friend, Father Luke."

"What was it all about?" said the priest, without a smile.

"Eh? About?" said Matthew, bewildered. "Tell him what 'twas about, Mary. I'm a little hard of hearing."

But Mary, with her woman's quick intuition, divined how matters stood; and said, with a good deal of dignity:—

"What would it be about, but the young lady's profession?"

"Of course," said Matthew, who, as the Bishop entered, stood up in an attitude of adoration, and sought, in a most humble, deprecatory manner, to catch the Bishop's eye.

Then Barbara came in, led by the Mistress of Novices, and passed up along the ranks of visitors to kiss the episcopal ring, and get once more the episcopal blessing. Then, turning swiftly around, she saw, for the first time in twelve long years, her father's face. It was now framed in white, and deeply furrowed by care and the labors that are needed for ambition. It was stern, too; for all the explanations made by the Mother Provincial and the priests failed to convince the man of the world that there was not a terrible cruelty and injustice inflicted upon his child. But something—the swish of her white habit, the rattle of her beads, the swift grace of her movements, or the radiance that shone from her features, unnerved him; and, with a little sob of pleasure, he clasped his child to his heart, and kissed her face before all the people. Lady Wilson was more conventional and reserved. She felt she had been ill-used; but, in a spirit of Christian meekness, she was willing to forgive. Each priest stood up, as Barbara approached, and touched her hand reverently. She sat for a long time near Father Tracey, who was much embarrassed at the honor, and said, "God bless me!" several times.

When the guests were dispersing in the great hall outside, the Bishop said aloud: —

"Where is Father Delmege? I missed Father Delmege!"

Luke was found with some difficulty, and came forward.

"That was a fine sermon, Luke," said the Bishop.

"Thank you, my Lord," said Luke. Then, with a little malice:—

"I hope there was no latent heresy in it?"

"No. But don't print it; or some fellow will ferret out something heterodox by the aid of a dictionary. By the way, here's a letter for you. You needn't read it till you return home. Good-day! Come see me, whenever you are in the city."

"He'll be in St. John's in a week," said Matthew, winking at Mary. "That's his appintment."

"And St. John's isn't half good enough for him," said Mary.

But Matthew for once was wrong. It was not to a curacy, but to a benefice that Luke was now appointed—to the neat, compact little parish where he spent the few remaining years of his life. Here, divesting himself of all things, he lived the life of an anchorite—a grave, gentle, loving man; and happy in having nothing and possessing all things. Revered and beloved by his own people, it is not surprising that he acquired the character of being somewhat eccentric among his brethren. But this he did not mind. He had found peace by abstracting himself from passing and fading things, and fixing his thoughts on the unfading and eternal. One little luxury, as we have seen, he allowed himself—that of looking out, as a disinterested, if perplexed, spectator, over "the beautiful madhouse of the earth" and

> Musing the woes of men,
> The ways of fate, the doctrines of the books,
> The lessons of the creatures of the brake,
> The secrets of the silence whence all come,
> The secrets of the gloom whereto all go,
> The life which lies between, like that arch flung
> From cloud to cloud across the sky, which hath
> Mists for its masonry and vapory piers,
> Melting to void again which was so fair
> With sapphire hues, garnet, and chrysoprase.

CHAPTER XLII

Aftermath

HERE WE bid farewell to Luke. But some readers of life's history may yet feel a kindly interest in the souls with whom he was brought into most frequent contact, or who exercised, consciously or unconsciously, some influence upon him. With most of these the author was obliged, in the course of his work, to enter upon terms of friendly intimacy, in order to glean the particulars that he has ventured to offer to the public. All, without exception, had a kindly word for poor Luke; most gave his memory the more eloquent tribute of a tear.

Father Martin, at first very crusty and rather abrupt, probably from great sorrow, developed into a most kindly, and, needless to say, most intelligent adviser and editor. That little parlor at Seaview Cottage became quite familiar to the author; for here they discussed, argued, reasoned, planned the scope and argument of the book. Tiny and Tony, too, now pretty grown, became intelligent and decidedly interesting guides. It was they who led the narrator to the sloping ledge of rock where Father Meade had heard the cry of Allua! across the waters; and there, yes, indeed! there was the identical curl upon the placid bosom of the great estuary, where the jealous sea challenges its mighty invader.

"I can swim to the current," said Tony, with a triumphant glance at his sister.

"You got cramps, and you'd be drowned only for me," said Tiny.

"I can ride a cycle, standing on the saddle," said Tony, unabashed.

"An' I can ride side-saddle with one pedal," said Tiny.

"I'll tell you what it is," I interposed; "I shall strongly recommend your guardian to apprentice the two of you to the next third-class circus that honors Ardavine with a visit." I meant to be sarcastic; but the project was warmly taken up.

"Oh! the very thing," said Tiny.

"I shall ride bareback," said Tony.

"I can jump through a paper hoop," said Tiny.

"You tried, and fell, and broke your nose, and cried, like a girl," said Tony.

"Tony," I said, "this is unchivalric and unfraternal. Let us return."

I did not visit the Canon. I shared Luke's nervousness; but, unlike Luke I failed to conquer it. But I saw Father Cussen. He is now quite enthusiastic about his parish priest. We visited the ruined cottage of Lisnalee together. It is not a very unusual sight in Ireland—that gaping ruin, the pointed gables, the nettles, the fire-scorched hearth, alas! which will never shed a ruddy glow upon happy faces again. Far down on the rocky shore is the fisherman's cabin, where Mona still lives; and, amidst all changes of death and ruin, there is the eternal sea! Calmly it sleeps under the eye of God. It is one of the many things that make you detest the doctrine of evolution, and fly back to a direct Creation: "God also said: Let the waters that are under the heaven be gathered together in one place. And it was so done. And the gathering together of the waters He called Seas. And God saw that it was good."

"Will the McNamaras ever come back, do you think?" I asked.

"They certainly will," Father Cussen replied. "And what is more—we'll have the old state of things back again, as sure as God is just, when landlordism is dead and—"

"Hush!" I said, "I should have to put that down to be loyal to my readers; and it would sound badly. However, you made the evil thing abstract and impersonal."

"They say the ghost of old Mike Delmege haunts this place," he continued. "He has been seen wandering around here on moonlight nights, his gray hair tossed wildly on his shoulders, as on that awful day. I'd wish he'd go to Paris, and haunt the silken curtains of that—"

"Is Mona married?" I interrupted charitably.

"Not yet. She has had a hundred offers, since she proved such a little heroine; but she says she'll never marry until 'the ould stock' come back to their rightful inheritance."

"A faithful little soul," I said.

"Yes. But she thought poor Luke was entirely too polite to

the magistrates at that trial. They were all expecting a tremendous philippic from him."

"That was hardly his way," I replied.

"Of course not. I think he was right; though I am not quite sure if I would have taken it so tamely," said Father Cussen.

I had a most delightful interview with Dr. Keatinge. He was one of those beautiful old priests who see good in everything and every one—a perfect optimist, as if he had been transported hither from one of those delightful planets on which sister suns are ever shining. There was no Night for him, nor blackness, nor sin. All was Day, and light, and grace. He was enthusiastic about Luke.

"A perfect character, my dear young friend—a noble character, with eternal aspirations after what is True and Right and Just."

"But a little perplexed?" I said.

"All good men are perplexed," he replied, "until they make up their minds to one fact—the necessary imperfection of all human things, until complemented by the perfection of the divine. Then all is right. It was the impatience at imperfection that annoyed him. But he was tolerant, exceedingly tolerant, for example, with that eccentric youth."

"John?" I exclaimed.

"Yes," said the Doctor, a little disturbed.

"What has become of that hopeful?" I cried.

"I have him," said the Doctor; and I thought his face fell.

I was silent. After a little while, the good old priest, looking shyly at me, said in a rather embarrassed way, "Perhaps you would like to see him?"

"By all manner of means," I replied. "Is he married?"

"He is," said the Doctor.

John came in reluctantly from the garden, when told he was wanted. He never liked to be "wanted." It foreboded trouble or anxiety. His face wore that furtive, frightened, suspicious look, that used to make Luke wild; but it cleared off into the sunshine of a smile when he found it was not a policeman, but only an old acquaintance that desired to see him. Nevertheless, he did not lay aside his habitual caution.

"How are you, John? I'm glad to see you so well," I said, holding out my hand.

John touched my hand with the tips of his fingers.

"I'm very well, yer reverence," said John.

"And so you're married?" I said.

"I dun know, yer reverence," said John.

"What, you scoundrel," I said, "you don't know whether you're married or not?"

"Begor, I believe I am, yer reverence," he said, smiling sheepishly, and scratching his head.

"Mary, of course?" I said.

"Begor, I believe it is, yer reverence," he said, with a grin.

"I hope you're steady now with these responsibilities," I conjectured.

"Oh, I am, yer reverence," he replied. "She'll tell you herself."

"You know how anxious Father Luke was about you," I said; "and how glad he'd be to know you were doing well."

"Ah, thin, manny's the good advice the poor masther giv me," said John, with just a little emotion, "if only I tuk it," he added.

"How am I to find out Mary's house?" I inquired. "I must see her."

"Oh, 'tis aisy enough," said John with a broad grin; "you'll know it among all the nabours' by the flowers."

"Your favorite flowers?" I conjectured.

"Begor, yes, yer reverence," said John.

He seemed to linger as if he wished to say something.

"You wouldn't mind doin' me a little favor, yer reverence?" he said.

"Certainly not," I replied.

"Would you mind sayin', yer reverence, that the baby is the dead image of herself? It puts her in wondherful good humor!"

"But is it?" I asked.

"Well, some say it is; and some say it isn't," said John, with a puzzled look. "But sure that makes no matther."

"An' you won't be offended?" I said.

"Oh, begor, I won't," said John, "if it pleases herself."

It was not difficult to find John's house. Afar off, it blazed in colors against the more modest drab appointments of its neighbors; and when I came quite close to it, I was blinded with the splendors of the much despised, but gaily painted favorite of this great gardener. Nasturtiums of every color, orange, red, deep maroon, purple; and striped and spotted in every imaginable hue, flaunted their glories all around garden, window, and door. Two beds of dwarf nasturtiums filled the little plots in front of the house; and from their centers, two rose trees, in full bloom, but looking very much ashamed of themselves, were propped by little canes, and languished and faded in the midst of their more picturesque and hardier brethren. But these latter plebeians forced their strong tendrils everywhere, and threw out in splendid profusion their beautiful bells. What music they would make, if God had given them tongues, that would swing in the breath of the breezes!

Mary was bending over her fire-place, when I drew the bolt of the half-door. She came forward, with a hot blush on her face from the fire and the surprise.

"I was up at the Doctor's, Mary," I said, "and met John. Do you know what the fellow told me?"

"I don't know, yer reverence," she said.

"He told me he didn't know whether he was married or not."

"He's the biggest *omadhaun* from here to Cork," said Mary, with a frown. "I do' know what to think of him; or how the Docthor has patience wid him."

"However," I continued, "he told me I should find the house by the flowers; and there was no mistake there. You have the neatest cottage in Rossmore, within and without."

I looked around; and it was pretty. The tiled floor was spotless; the brass candlesticks and pewter vessels shone brightly; a canary sang out its little welcome in the window, and tried to drown our voices with its shrill piercing notes; the kettle sang merrily on the range. The whole was a picture of comfort.

"The General," I said, "could find no fault here."

"I wouldn't lave him," said Mary. "He kem wance to the dure; but no farther."

"Boiling water?" I suggested.

"Not as bad as that, yer reverence," said Mary, laughing. "But he kem, and looked in, and said: 'I am very much plased to see your cottage kep' so nate,' sez he. 'I'm thankful for yer opinion,' sez I. 'I shall tell the missis and Miss Dora,' sez he, 'that this is a moral (model) cottage, an' I'll have 'em put down yer name for the next distribution of prizes for nateness and claneness,' sez he. 'Ye needn't,' sez I. 'It isn't for prizes I'm workin' day and night, but because it is the right thing to do;

and 'twas what the nuns and the priests taught us.' He looked cross at this. 'I hope ye keep no fowl here,' sez he. 'That's me own business,' sez I. 'Did ye get yer rint on Saturday night?' sez I. 'I did,' sez he, shamefaced like. 'Thin,' sez I, 'what brings ye thrapezing around here, instid of mindin' yer own business?' With that aff he wint, an' he never kem near since."

"Do you mean to say that you talked up to a landlord like that?" I asked.

"An' why not?" asked Mary. "Didn't the masther tell us, a hunder' times that we wor as good as they, ivery bit, that we wor all the same flesh and blood—"

"He would be glad to see you so happy now," I said; "and all his lessons so carefully carried out."

"So he would, yer reverence," said Mary, with a little sob.

As I looked around, my eye caught some pink embroidery in a corner. There were little bits of lace and edging on a deep background of pink calico. I looked at Mary.

"It isn't?" I said inquiringly.

"It is, yer reverence," said Mary, with a smile and a blush. "Won't you give her your blessing?"

I went over and gazed admiringly at the little bit of humanity, that was blinking its black eyes, and groping with its soft, tiny fingers, for the mystery of the world on which it was embarked. Dear God! it was turned out perfectly from Thy adorable hands, even down to the little pink finger nails.

"I don't want to flatter you, Mary," I said, "but it's the dead image of you."

"Oh, law, yer reverence," said Mary, with a smile of pleasure, "sure every wan says she's as like John as two pays."

"Like John?" I exclaimed indignantly. "Nonsense! She's no more like John, than—than"—the metaphorical faculty failed me, until my eye caught a tendril that was pushing a yellow blossom over the half-door—"than a rose is like a nasturtium. Not that I'm disparaging the latter," I interjected. "So it is a young lady?"

"It is, yer reverence," she said.

"Might I ask her name?" I said.

"Well, thin, 'tis a quare wan enough. At laste, we niver had it in our family," said Mary. "I wanted to have her called Mary after the Blessed Virgin; but the Docthor said, 'No! call her afther yer late masther's pattern saint,' sez he, 'and call her

Barbara.' And sure it sounds quare, yer reverence, like them haythens and blacks we hear about in the *Annals*."

"Barbara Glavin!" I repeated. "It sounds well; and I may tell you, Mary, the Doctor was right. It is the name of one of the sweetest saints in the calendar, who died some centuries ago; and another dear saint, who is still living. May your baby take after both; and she will be happy!"

This appeared to satisfy Mary; so I had less reluctance in asking was John fond of the baby.

"Fond?" said Mary. "He's dying about her. He thinks of nothing, morning, noon, or night, but the baby. And when she has a little fit, you'd think he'd gone clane out o' his mind."

"And he's keeping all right?" I asked.

"He is, your reverence; but 'tis the baby agin. Whin John has the fit on him, he's moody and sullen like for days. 'Tis the thirst, you know, comin' upon him. Thin I gets wan of the boys to come in, be the way of no harm, and say, 'John, that baby is a like you as two pins.' John says nothin', till they go out. Thin, he ups and takes the baby out of her cradle, and dangles her, and kisses her; an' I know the fit is over him."

"God bless that baby," I cried. "She's doing a hard thing, playing a double part, and doing it successfully."

"Would your reverence like to see our little parlor?" said Mary.

"To be sure," I exclaimed. And it was worth seeing. I recognized some of Luke's little belongings which he left to his faithful servant; and over near the window, looking to the north, which I believe is the right location for neutral light, Mary, with true artistic taste, had placed an easel, and on that easel was a picture. I took it up. It was the oil painting of Olivette Lefevril—the scene of the skeleton ship from "The Ancient Mariner." And over the mantelpiece were Mary's two heroes, Robert Emmet and St. Antony; and between them, in the place of honor, was a gorgeous photograph of Luke Delmege. I went over. " 'Tis the masther," said Mary.

"So it is," I said. "You have put him in good company, Mary."

"Not too good for him, yer reverence. He was aiqual to them all."

I don't know what that "all "comprised; but I said as I parted from Mary:—

"At least," I said, "he has a noble immortality. Mary, you are a good girl. God bless you!"

"An' God bless you, too, sir!" said Mary.

I should call on Father Tracey. When I entered his humble lodgings, and saw them stripped of everything but the barest necessaries, the old spirit of joking came over me, and I was going to say:—

"I hope you have complied with the statutes, and made your will, Father! There will be serious litigation about your assets—"

But the holiness of the old man stopped me. And it was not that holiness that brings its burning-glass to bear on the naked, quivering nerves of your soul, and lights up all its multiform diseases; but that humble sanctity that places itself at your feet, and gently proclaims its superiority by the abasement.

He too, was enthusiastic about Luke.

"He was not known, my dear, he wasn't known, except to the Bishop and myself. Ah, my dear, the world is full of saints, if we could only find them out."

"I am writing Luke's life," I said, "and I thought you could give me some lights."

"Is't me? God bless me, what do I know? But say, he was everything great and good; and would have been a Bishop, if he lived."

I stole the old man's beads. I couldn't help it. The axle of this weary world would not creak so loudly, if the oil of gladness, poured from such humble hearts, were lavished more freely.

Lastly, I visited the well-known scene of Luke's latest ministrations. This was easy enough, for it was quite close to me. It was a lovely summer evening as I drove into the village. The present incumbent was not at home; but I put up my horse and trap at his house, and strolled leisurely up to the church where Luke is buried. As I entered, there was a whispering in the gallery overhead; and the little village choir, seeing a priest, thought they should manifest some piety and good works. They sang, *Nearer, my God, to Thee!* I listened; and it sounded very sweetly and very appropriately there in that calm, summer twilight.

Though, like the wanderer,
The sun gone down,
Darkness comes over me,
My rest a stone;
Yet in my dreams I'd be
Nearer, my God, to Thee,
Nearer to Thee.

I went up quietly to say a prayer over where he slept. A poor woman, her frayed shawl drawn over her head, was leaning on the Communion rails, right over Luke's grave. Her hands were clasped around her little child, who sat on the broad ledge of the rails, and kicked and crowed, and tried to take the beads from her mother's hands. The woman was praying aloud. I gently said:—

"Where is Father Delmege buried?"

"There," she said, pointing to the floor. "May the heavens be his bed tonight!"

"You knew him?" I asked.

"Good right I had to know him," she replied. "Look at thim, yer reverence," holding up the child's chubby leg, "thim's the last he give me and mine—God be good to him, me darlin' priest!"

Sister Eulalie may rest easy now. The poor did love him indeed.

I passed into the sanctuary, and copied for my readers, there in the summer twilight, the Latin inscription on the marble slab in the wall. It runs thus:—

HIC · JACENT
OSSA
ADM · REV · LUCAE · DELMEGE
OLIM · IN · SUO · COLLEGIO · LAUREATI
NUPER · HUIUS · ECCLESIAE · RECTORIS
NATUS · OCT · 12 · 1854
OBIIT · NOV · 20 · 1898
AMAVIT · LABORAVIT : VIXIT
REQUIESCIT

It is Father Martin's composition. I should have liked to add another word, but I couldn't find the Latin for it; and in any case Father Martin wouldn't allow it; for he would never admit that Luke was perplexed about anything. Poor Luke! It's all the same now! He has long since found in the vast mirrors of the Infinite the solution of the Great Enigma.

A THOMAS MORE BOOK TO LIVE

THOMAS MORE BOOKS TO LIVE

Weeping Cross

a novel by Henry Longan Stuart

RICHARD FITZSIMON, Irish Cavalier, is condemned to ten years penal servitude in the New England colonies. He arrives in Boston in 1652, to find himself the victim of the hard-shelled, Bible thumping pioneer community, where everybody hates him blindly and instinctively—because he is a Catholic, because he is Irish, and because he is a gentleman through and through.

The story, told in autobiographical form by the hero who later became a priest, describes his life in the Puritan community and his disastrous love for Agnes Bartlett, the daughter of his master.

Cain

a novel by Rogier van Aerde

A POWERFUL and deeply imaginative tale of Cain, the Rebel and begetter of the Children of Man. From an episode scarcely more than touched upon in Genesis, Rogier van Aerde has created a dramatic and vivid story. The tragedy of Adam and Eve becomes the reader's personal tragedy. With a sense that in that far yesterday lies the story of today, the reader watches the human race recede from God. This book is indeed a "mighty cord, an impressive song of prose," interpreting the profound meaning of Cain's life.

The Path to Rome
by Hilaire Belloc

IT IS NEARLY half a century since this book was written, but its high place among English books of travel was never more secure. Described long ago as "quite the most sumptuous embodiment of universal gaiety and erratic wisdom that has been written," there is now scarcely a prose anthology that does not contain some passage from its fascinating pages. This is a story of a pilgrimage on foot from Toul in Lorraine to the Eternal City, by the straightest possible line. It is rich in every page with wisdom and the joy of living, a book of which you never tire and to which you will return again and again.

Superstition Corner
by Sheila Kaye-Smith

ELIZABETHAN ENGLAND in the year 1588 was a nation beset by fear—the threat of Spanish invasion and seething religious controversies had created a turbulent atmosphere in the normally peaceful English countryside. This is the setting for the story of the Alards, one of the few remaining prominent Catholic families. In particular, it is the story of Kate Alard, a headstrong, quick-witted tomboy fervently devoted to her Catholic faith.

Letters from Baron Friedrich Von Hügel to a Niece

WHEN Baron Friedrich von Hügel began this correspondence with his niece toward the latter part of his life, he had become one of the outstanding scholars and Gwendolen Greene was a married woman. These *Letters,* however, are written with the kindly wisdom of an old uncle dealing with a young niece, guiding her by word of mouth and by letter. He explains to her why she needs the Catholic faith. It is a superb apologetic in operation, a presentation in the simplest and easiest terms of the Catholic case to non-Catholics.